Paramour Promise

also by Chelsey Blue Spicer

Requited Rival
Optimistic Oath

Paramour Promise

Chelsey Blue Spicer

To the 40% who have faced closed doors yet continue to embrace their authentic selves.

May these pages be a sanctuary for your stories, a celebration of your existence, and a testament to the undeniable power of love and the unwavering spirit that refuses to be confined by closed minds.

1

The lone scarlet stocking sadly did not catch fire from the flickering fake flames on the electric fireplace. Dilynn's name had been sewn across the fuzzy fold two years ago when she thought having a stocking would mean Christmas meant something to her new family. Her stocking was as pointless this year as it was last year though. And she knew next year wouldn't be any different, so she created a new plan to avoid being forgotten in 364 days.

A Christmas with no stupid coordinated socks for some creepy trespasser to sneak in and fill would draw questions from the two people who didn't seem to notice Dilynn's dancing deer covered stocking this year. There would have to be oversized socks to avoid any questions from her fiancé and her daughter. So, she would hang them: one for Brandon and one for Evie. Neither would notice Dilynn's was missing.

Since it was after midnight, Dilynn reached behind the tree and yanked the cord from the outlet. The colorful lights stopped blinking their slow rhythm immediately, bringing a villainous smile to her face. She'd been dying to pull the plug on Christmas since the fiancé and the daughter had begun competing for who was worse, Brandon Scrooge or Evie Grinch.

This hadn't been the life Dilynn imagined when buying cheesy Christmas decorations for their first family holiday. However, Dilynn looked forward to the decorations coming down after the 28 straight days of nightmares. She'd take Evie to the mall tomorrow morning like she'd promised. Just a quick trip to Sephora before everything would get packed in black plastic bins and shoved into the garage with everything else Dilynn didn't deal with.

The garage was pretty full of the past, and the catastrophe of Christmas would only take her one step closer to becoming a hoarder. She looked around at things that didn't matter. None of the tinsel or gifts had mattered to them the first year. It was stupid to think it was going to happen this time around.

Momentarily, she decided she would trash it all. She imagined their faces as she constructed a scene where she slapped a twig to the wall and taped up a star atop it after Brandon and Evie screamed at each other over their Thanksgiving dinner plates next year. She shook her head slowly and cast away all thoughts of holidays.

No more massive holidays. No more extravagant events.

Except the over-the-top wedding being directed by her mother.

Her head fell back against the couch. She needed to get the wedding invitations out tomorrow, too, or her mother would call her and yell at her again. Mall and post office on the day after Christmas felt like cruel and unusual punishment.

Dilynn grabbed the laptop from the kitchen table. The new MacBook Pro was a gift she'd gotten herself. Along with the microphone and sound buffer so she could record her novel into an audiobook.

That could be her reward tomorrow. After the mall and the post office, she could take her new toys to the guest house and play with them without interruption. The space could be a real office since there weren't any guests even though she and her mother were now speaking. She cast away the thought of her mother ever caring enough to come and pretend to be a grandmother to her granddaughter. It was a dream that had been proven wrong twice now— so it was stupid to keep the structure out back prepared for the woman.

She could paint the space, she decided. Put up a giant whiteboard. Create a detective's murder board as she charted out the second novel. The proposal for the sequel would need to be submitted while the hype from book one was still strong. It could be a fun project to occupy her mind while she was on winter break.

The sound of Brandon snoring dragged her focus from decorating her new office to their bedroom door. He sounded like he might be choking, but she didn't move because a part of her was still pissed at him. She scrunched down letting her sweater cover her ears some. At least in an office there would be quiet. Something she couldn't find in the house. Brandon's monstrous snores were enough to keep her on the couch most nights he was home. She didn't want to sleep with him right now anyway. Not when he'd walked past her without saying goodnight or Merry Christmas.

She glanced over at the destroyed kitchen. Dinner was more of a disaster than the kitchen, but she'd tried. Sucking back the tears, she decided her New Year's Resolution would be to learn how to cook something besides pizza. Then, she could avoid the fight at the table next year, which is where the final battle of the day began. Brandon and Evie couldn't get through one meal without throwing sharp words at each other even though Dilynn had reminded them it was fucking Christmas. No, she wouldn't cook next year, just like she wouldn't put up her stocking. She added ordering Chinese food to her 'Next Christmas' list.

At least she'd had the sense to get herself something to open this year. She wasn't disappointed by the pack of men's socks from Brandon or the Starbucks gift card from Evie. Not when she had the new computer to open. She'd waited patiently all day for the computer to update. Typed a new story in a Google doc on her phone while the biscuits turned into stones in the oven.

She waited for the fanfiction website to load, then scrolled through the plethora of Christmas fics written by fans of her novel. Dilynn had found a haven on the website during her early days of motherhood when Evie would scream at Dilynn for pretending to be her mother. Now a published author, Dilynn used the same username to hide as a fan. She used the fandom for her debut novel *Atlas Stands* to fight against the imposter syndrome. After months of reading stories the young writers created about her teenage protagonists, she found an entire fandom focused on two of her supporting characters. Two adults, who were pieces of Dilynn's past she wasn't ready to fully process.

She'd never considered there could be more between Morgan, the stone-hearted general, and Priya, Morgan's daughter's nanny. However, 2,563 of the nearly 8,000 stories on the fanfiction website were focused on the duo.

Dilynn found herself intrigued enough to explore "what if" scenarios with several of her own spin-offs between the characters. Her stories were inappropriate for her young adult audience. Ones where she imagined what it would feel like to be brought to the edge of ecstasy next to a crackling fire or stifle moans of pleasure while she was fucked atop the war planning table with a firm hand over her throat. The universe she'd constructed was her own escape from the mundane existence in the heterosexual world she'd never imagined herself in.

Tales from her kinky imagination became somewhat popular in the fandom. And Dilynn enjoyed waking up to a litany of comments. Measured her success in the number of hits. She'd even managed to hook an online troll, at least that was what Evie had called the person who left Dilynn daily comments about her writing being trash. Story after story, the troll on the other side of the screen tried to tear her down.

Dilynn licked her teeth and imagined RunnerAT89 in the flesh. Made them short like her because tall people probably didn't feel small enough to squish under a boot. She gave them a wart on their chin because Disney made warts and meanness synonymous. The details came together until she was sure she had all the necessary things to create the person she would mutilate in the sequel. It was a justifiable punishment because no troll was going to stop her from dreaming of a different reality, especially with a muse like her coworker, Alex Trikru. Morgan originally was modeled off the person Dilynn wished she could be: tall and strong like Xena; smooth and powerful like Lara Croft; and badass like Wonder Woman. All women she'd idolized growing up with traits she couldn't physically or emotionally possess, yet a few months after the novel hit the best seller's list Dilynn's eyes landed on the corporeal action figure of her stoic general. Alex Trikru had stood by as Dilynn was pulled on the court with the football team to make a fool of herself at the Welcome Back Cactus

High School pep rally.

She closed her eyes and put herself in the small hillside house with Alex. Imagined Alex's soft smile and silent nods. She wasn't able to capture Alex's voice well because she'd only heard a few mumbled words accompanied by a kick to the copy machine in the teacher's breakroom.

Her fingers broke in the new keyboard as she brought the scene to life. Told a story about a night that wasn't Christmas, because there was no fucking Christmas or goddamn stockings in the Aurorian world. She wrote the stoic general pulling covers up over her daughter asleep in the ornately carved bed. She told of Morgan kissing the young girl atop the head before leaving the room. A detail RunnerAT89 would deeply despise because it made Morgan sensitive when, according to the troll, she was logical and devoid of any nurturing.

They didn't know how right they were. Morgan's stoic edge was modeled off a wealthy woman, who sent gifts the day after Christmas and never called them a Christmas present because living in a closet meant never celebrating holidays together. Those were things people in a relationship did, and Dilynn's not-ex-girlfriend, Sylvia, would never publicly be in a relationship with a woman.

Just a situationship. A sexuationship.

Morgan wasn't her ex though. Just like Morgan wasn't Alex Trikru. Morgan was just another piece of Dilynn's past twisted and tangled up trauma she hadn't resolved. Morgan was her anger at the world blended with Sylvia's indifferent words. The fact Morgan looked like Alex Trikru had just been a coincidence. Alex couldn't be Morgan like Dilynn couldn't be Morgan, which is why Morgan lived on the page. Morgan ran her sword through people like trolls on the page so Dilynn could take care of people in real life.

Her fingers paused to read over Morgan tucking in the daughter she gave to Priya to raise in the book. It made Dilynn think about the baby she'd only met once before handing her over to the adoption worker.

She looked through the sliding glass door towards the guest house her mother never came to visit. Twelve years later, and Dr. Leigh Greyson was as interested in her second granddaughter as she had been her first. Dilynn's mind raced like a rollercoaster through the conversations she'd had with her mother since calling to announce she was adopting Evie.

Her mind screeched to a halt as the coaster track suddenly stopped beside the nineteen-year-old brunette living in Brandon's homeless shelter. She'd pulled the girl's and her daughter's paper Christmas Angel from the tree she'd set up in the teacher breakroom for other teachers to help. A young woman whose story had broken Dilynn's heart as the college student clung to her three-month-old baby girl in the small shelter four days before Christmas.

Dilynn made a mental note to reach out to the young mother, Sarah, on the number she'd provided. She'd follow up to see if public housing came through yet. She glanced back at the guest house. She could make it a space for the small family instead of an office for herself. Give them a chance she didn't get. Especially since she had enough when they had nothing.

Evie's bedroom door creaked open, so Dilynn scrunched down to blend in with the couch. She hoped the teen was just going to the bathroom. Unfortunately, there was no quiet in the house, and Evie padded out of the dark hallway without washing her hands. The hall light was still out, so Dilynn added 'fix light bulb' to her list of things to do.

Evie quietly moved to the kitchen and pulled a tub of cream cheese from the refrigerator. Dipping her finger into the shared tub, Dilynn's need to be invisible vanished.

"You have got to be kidding me," Dilynn hissed. Her hand gestured to the cabinets. "At least get a fucking spoon."

Evie looked down at the container, then stuffed another cream coated finger into her mouth. She smiled guiltily towards Dilynn, and whispered, "Guess this one's mine now."

"Why are you up?" Dilynn asked, in order to move past the terrifying question of how long she'd been eating contaminated cream cheese.

"Christmas sucks," Evie whispered. She tucked into Dilynn's side and pulled the throw blanket over both of them.

No amount of pine scented candles could cover the girl's overripe odor. Dilynn breathed through her mouth so she could hold on to Evie. She'd never gotten a hug from the kid before. A snuggle like this was maybe a Christmas miracle.

"I wish I could, like, go into the therapist's office and she could wipe it away." Evie held her hand in the air and pretended to click a pen. "Like the men in black had that little flashy light. Just flash me and make those two years just disappear."

Dilynn didn't tell the girl she was wrong for wanting two years of traumatic memories to disappear. She just pulled the kid in closer and pressed her lips to the oily hair.

"When was the last time you showered?" Dilynn asked while trying to wipe the grease from her lips on the sweater from her Secret Santa. She stopped when she remembered this was the only real gift she received. One she really liked.

The girl chuckled and lifted her arm. She shouldn't have needed to, but her face said she understood how rancid she smelled.

"Is it because Brandon's home?" Dilynn probed.

Evie didn't answer. She just stared at the fireplace.

"It's Christmas... and... I just don't want to take any chances," Evie whispered.

Dilynn understood without needing more. She held the kid closer and decided to talk to Brandon again about making an effort to fix his relationship with Evie. He wasn't a monster, and Evie should feel safe here, especially on Christmas.

"Landon's coming over tomorrow to take down the Christmas lights." Evie ran her finger over the track pad, scanning over Dilynn's story. "I'll shower before he comes."

"We don't need your boyfriend to climb up that ladder. If he breaks something, his mother will beat me up." Dilynn turned the ring on her finger. "Brandon said he would do it."

Evie let out an exasperated huff. "He never does anything he says, and I heard him on the phone. He's not going to be here tomorrow."

Dilynn's nose crinkled at the information. He hadn't mentioned he had anywhere to be tomorrow when she'd asked him to take down the decorations.

"Landon's coming and he's going to take down the lights, so you don't fall and break your ankle again," Evie stated. "You and ladders are not friends."

Dilynn tried to roll her foot. The stiffness still made her nose crinkle. Maybe she would take up jogging. It would possibly help loosen up the ligaments.

"We don't need him," Evie whispered. Her head shot up. "Also, you have to tell the ogre he can't walk around in his boxers. It may turn me gay."

Dilynn's head fell back to the chair.

"I know we covered you can't turn gay, especially since you aren't straight."

"Yeah, well I wish you would so you would dump that dipshit," Evie said as Brandon choked on his own snore. "Maybe, call up your ex, Sonia... Sympathy... umm... Saphron."

With a snort, Dilynn said, "Sylvia."

"Yeah, her," Evie bounced up. "I saw her on Instagram. Bitch is like one of the top fifty richest people in the world now, plus she's hot like Morgan in your book."

"Morgan has brown hair," Dilynn reminded the girl. "Sylvia is blonde, like me. Well, blonder. Also, she doesn't want kids."

"Cool, we can *Flowers in the Attic* it, only like put me on the beach somewhere," Evie offered.

Dilynn's head dropped to the side. "You never finished the book, did you?"

"I heard the brother and sister kissed so I was out," Evie said falling back against Dilynn's chest. Her fingers played with the blue cotton of the sweater. "This is new."

Dilynn smiled at the sweater. "My Secret Santa got it for me. Also, the mother tries to poison the kids in the book because she is getting remarried."

"Cause it's so different with him," Evie grumbled. She pushed up from the couch while Dilynn twirled the ring around her finger.

"Just think about the whole gay thing. Girls at least wash their ass."

Dilynn's eyebrows tried to touch in the middle. Her chin ducked down and she could still smell Evie's stink on her clothes.

"Says the girl who hasn't showered," Dilynn stated.

"My therapist says it's a defensive mechanism." Evie shrugged. "Simple and effective and after a day or two, I don't really notice anymore."

Evie left Dilynn to her new computer. She'd written about Evie's defensive tactics before. She'd have to do it again, however, not tonight.

Safe from prying eyes and interruptions, she detailed Priya watching Morgan gaze at the child in the bed adoringly. She romanticized the moment, having Morgan glance sweetly back at Priya, who'd given up her rank and her position by Morgan's side to keep the woman's daughter safe. Then, they kissed because Dilynn needed a kiss.

She'd been engaged for over a year, and the kisses had slowed to the point of non-existence. So, she took her time imagining kissing someone like Morgan. Someone who commanded the room with just a look. Whose taught muscles stretched the linen of shirts and could hold her. Someone like the stoic social studies teacher on the opposite side of the Humanities floor.

Morgan had always reminded Dilynn of Sylvia. The character was built in her contrast at the same point. Built with the same demi-goddess structure of the AP Government teacher, Alex Trikru.

Her fingers told tales of hidden depths within each of the women that caused lips to part and gasp so gracefully it was impossible not to miss being touched. They brought each other to the edge of a moonlit cliff, but never pushed the other off. They leapt in each other's arms, drawing out the pleasure so their minds were still foggy and their limbs still shaky the next morning when the child crawled between them asking for breakfast.

Flushed and frustrated, Dilynn composed her own anticlimactic event under the throw blanket on the couch. She had moved past feeling guilty for getting aroused at the thought of the government teacher months ago. Now she held on to the calm gaze of Alex Trikru's green eyes. Imagined the slow cadence of words telling her how much she was wanted.

A loud snore tore her mind from Alex's hand on her thigh. A stark reminder, she was engaged. Engaged even on the nights he didn't want to touch her, which seemed like every night since Halloween. At least in Dilynn's naughty musings, Alex always wanted to touch her.

She hummed slightly as she washed her hands. She could still see Alex's eyes in her head, and she decided to describe them as Morgan's in the next fanfic. Write a realistic universe where Morgan was a history teacher and Priya an English teacher.

With clean hands, Dilynn casually edited the eight thousand words she'd written before getting herself off. Made minor corrections to anything underlined in blue and red. Then she posted it.

The internet troll would probably strike by morning. She prepared herself for their cruelty and reminded herself there would be others who didn't tell her she was worthless.

Making her way to bed, she looked over the stocky man taking up a majority of the mattress. She hated how hairy his man boobs were, and wondered how she went from Sylvia to him. She shook her head trying to force Evie's words out. Evie was the one that was disgusted with Brandon. She was the one that didn't like him. Dilynn loved him. Loved that he was home. It was rare he was home since the homeless shelter she helped open for him was so short staffed.

She was lucky and she knew it. Luckier than RunnerAT89, who was probably alone on Christmas.

2

Saturdays shouldn't suck, but Alex's did. It wasn't specifically Saturdays that Alex didn't like. They hated the days that ended with y, in the months that ended in r, y, h, and e. Also, they despised the ones that ended in t and l.

On weekends and holiday breaks, Alex tried to reconcile being alone. Justified that engaging with other humans eventually meant talking pronouns. Conversations where Alex explained they and them pronouns as acceptable and correct to describe one person when that person was non-binary. Types of conversations people didn't understand. The kind of conversation where everyone had an answer to a non-question about Alex's identity, and that they were always wrong. Who they were was wrong.

Being alone was better than always being wrong, even on Christmas. Christmas Day was the loneliest. Even their Secret Santa at work hadn't bothered to show up so there was nothing.

Then just be normal.

Christmas was just another day. The day after Christmas was another that ended in y in a month ending in r. Just a normal day for stuff to go wrong, like the sole of their running shoe splitting from the shoe part two miles from their apartment. Their last pair of running shoes.

Alex tried to psych themself up about a new pair of shoes.

"A late Christmas present," they told themself. "Maybe some new sweats, too."

They considered getting a punching dummy. One with a face that Alex could hit every time the voice in their head called them a freak.

The 'if they were on sale' part went unspoken.

'It'll be okay,' they told themself. 'It might not even be crowded since it's early.'

Alex felt the tension creep up their neck while looking for parking. Everyone seemed to be at the mall trying to spend their Christmas gift cards, which forced Alex to park at the very end of the lot so no one would accidentally ding their Audi SUV; the one splurge they made in celebration of landing the job they wanted.

People walked in wonky chains that didn't curve well enough to avoid touching Alex. They'd barely made it past three stores, and they felt like they'd unknowingly joined a human petting zoo.

They stopped outside of Express. The new line of slim fit, button up shirts caught their attention. They could use new work shirts. Plus, forty percent off was the type of deal Alex couldn't just pass up.

The cotton felt crisp, promising the pressed look they preferred. With multiple prints and colors, Alex measured which would be the most androgenous. With forest green, cranberry red, and deep purple hanging over one arm, they added two black ones to the pile. The black ones would end up being the only ones they wore. They might wear the color ones if they don't do laundry, but it was not like there was much to interfere with Wednesday laundry day.

When they regained cell service for a moment, a parade of emails caused the device to dance in their pocket. Alex scrolled through the emails once more to keep from second guessing what people would think if they showed up in something that wasn't monochromatic while they stood in line.

Still holding all five shirts, they scrolled until they saw an alert for another post from GreyAltEgo. The username caused them to suck their teeth in disapproval. They hated GreyAltEgo's unrealistic sappy stories almost as much as they hated the voice in their head telling them loving women made them a freak.

With the line at least twenty people long and purple maybe too much of a feminine color, Alex opened the story to avoid analyzing the gender of colors and thinking about the purse that just tapped them in the rear.

Strangers grazing, rubbing, or pressing against Alex was on par with how they knew they would feel about GreyAltEgo's newest sugar-coated crap. The sappy smut dipped in glue and rolled in glitter nauseated Alex. It was sweet and loving, and just the type of sex that Alex found too vanilla.

Someone had to tell GreyAltEgo she'd managed to pollute the fandom space with nonsense again. It was too important to Alex that the original universe was protected in fics claiming to be canon like GreyAltEgo had tagged it. It was even more important that the characters were still who they were written to be. And there were too many typos. Too many typos when there were people breathing in Alex's space. GreyAltEgo deserved a headache from trying to sort through the messy compilation of elementary writing like she offered readers.

Alex read through their comment once it was posted at the bottom of the story.

> RunnerAT89 on Chapter 1:
> this is worse than the others. complete trash stop, polluting the fandom with your dry sex life. to do any of the things you described they would have to have four hands and seven-inch fingers. seriously worse than the shower sex

> scenes in the last one where you apparently forgot water isn't lube or arousal. just give it up and get a day job.

They looked through their inbox to see if GreyAltEgo had responded to their comment from a couple days ago. Not all of their comments received any acknowledgement. When they did though, it was always honey-coated apologies for errors and a brief message relaying her hope they would like the next one.

Outside the store, a teenage girl was screaming profanities. Several of the people around Alex had turned to the scene playing out, while Alex ignored what other people began flocking to.

"It's Evie Greyson, Mom. The girl from school that I told you about." A girl standing in front of Alex tugged her mother from the line. "She's the one that punched that senior in the nose because he undid that girl's bra."

Alex's gaze was instantly pulled from their phone to the dark-haired girl standing outside the entrance to Express. They knew about Evie Greyson. Their best friend Simone's varsity softball catcher, who was going to be the first kid to get a scholarship for softball for Cactus High School. At least that's what Simone told Alex when she wasn't huffing and puffing over the girl's mother being an annoying Barbie.

"Dilynn Greyson," Alex whispered to themself.

Alex loved the way their coworker's name melted in their mouth. It tasted sweet like the dessert-based perfume Dilynn brought with her into the breakroom. A sacred space for just the two of them to silently occupy during their morning shared prep period.

Stalking Dilynn Greyson was their favorite part of going to work. They'd even gone to a few football games that fall because Simone complained Dilynn was always there with the screaming kid.

She would rather choke than be with you.

"I told her you were a piece of shit!" Dilynn's kid cussed at a hairy man.

His hand was intertwined with a lean girl by his side. She was too young to be with the guy getting chewed out.

"I fucking told her, and she still gave you a goddamn chance."

On their toes, Alex searched for Evie's mother. They slid around a group of teens practically sewn together. If Alex couldn't find Dilynn, they would keep Evie from getting in trouble. Keep her from ruining a scholarship opportunity, since teacher salaries didn't pay enough for college funds.

A few people bounced on their toes to see what was going on. Bodies bumped into Alex, leaving less space for them to get through.

"You never fucking deserved her!" Evie continued to yell.

They found Dilynn Greyson. She ran out of Sephora, sidestepping through the crowd that didn't seem to notice her. She reached for Evie just as the teen's fist cracked against the man's face.

It was a hard punch, but not a good one. Evie was off balance with her lunge too far into the man. The lack of any sort of form made her core weak and she stumbled.

A shove from the man sent Evie stumbling backwards. The back of her head smacked into Dilynn's face. A hit hard enough to pull out a choked cry from the woman, her hands coming up to hold her nose.

Alex grabbed the shoulder of the teen filming in front of them. Then, they began to push the looky-loos when the man's fist raised to hit Evie back.

The girl, who'd been clinging to Dilynn's fiancé, locked her hands around his bicep and pulled back. Her bulky work boots slid over the floor as he tried to move. She kept pulling, succeeding in keeping him from hitting anyone.

Alex was still trying to get through the herd of humans when Dilynn stepped into the line of danger. Her arms held Evie behind her.

Blonde hair hung around Dilynn's face. With her chin up, she stared at the man and prepared to take the punch for Evie, who was still casting curses from behind her.

They kept barreling forward like a bull towards the man in the red shirt that barely covered his beer belly. They had to get there in case he went after Dilynn or her kid again.

The girl at his side was barely bigger than a sapling, but she yanked on him until he turned around. Alex didn't reach the inner circle before the too young girl won the jerk's attention.

He snatched his arm away from her, then barked something unintelligible at her. Dark eyes fell to the floor when he pushed past her. In a moment of quiet, the two females studied each other. Alex locked eyes with the mystery kid when they made it to the space just behind Dilynn.

Up close, there was no question she was a teenager. No older than the seniors in their AP Government class.

Alex silently begged her not to follow him. They even shook their head. Her brow furrowed for a moment, then her gaze fell on Dilynn once more.

She didn't say anything before she turned her back on Dilynn to follow the man. Her boots squeaked with each drag of her feet, until she reached him. He grabbed her by the arm and led her to the nearest exit like a kicked puppy.

They opened their mouth to call out to the girl but shut it as Dilynn's blue gaze turned to them. The crystal stare was wet with unshed tears.

"If you could... not tell anyone," Dilynn whispered. She had never spoken to them before.

With a solemn nod, they promised to keep her secret. Alex tried to think of something to say. Even as Dilynn cast them one more desperate look, before she ushered her daughter away from the scene.

"I fucking told you he was a dick," Evie growled.

The aggression Simone loved about the kid still hadn't dissipated. She shifted her flushed face to her mother and found a new target for her anger. The hand, still an angry red from her punch, shot towards the exit the man had left through with the girl.

"Did you see that girl? That could have been me. And you just brought him home."

She picks losers, but still wouldn't want you.

They stood frozen in the same spot, watching as Dilynn led the way to the escalator. After working so hard to get to that place, their slides seemed to melt into the waxed flooring.

An alert drew Alex's attention from watching the Greysons walk away. They sighed, reading the text from the chemistry teacher they'd sat through an AP seminar with over summer.

Jason Jordan couldn't get the message. Alex blamed his lack of observational skills on his awkwardly shaped head; however, looking like a half alien didn't excuse that they'd made themselves abundantly clear they were not interested in going on a date with him.

'Hey, this is Jason Jordan. Simone gave me your number in exchange for three reams of copy paper. I wanted to see if you were busy Wednesday.'

A moment later another text came through.

'Greyson makes pizza every Wednesday night and you should come. It's good food and other teachers come, too. Plus, D is good people no matter what you've heard.'

Leaning against the upper floor railing, they spotted Dilynn now following her daughter through the food court towards one of the many exits. Dinner at Dilynn's house could possibly move them from stalker to friend. She'd talk to them if they were in her house.

They wanted more than talking. Yearned for her to fantasize about them between her thighs. Wanted her to do that thing they read in the spicier fanfictions. Ones where eyes would dilate as they stared at lips, needing to be kissed.

Far too often, Alex imagined pulling the woman's shirt off. Pictured her topless on the break room table with her hands held over her head. They would work their tongue over her nipples. Each stroke within her would have her saying their name over and over and over again until she saw the stars GreyAltEgo liked to talk about. Only they'd leave her covered in their marks. She might be into it.

You're not her type.

The sporting goods store was across the walkway. Alex shoved off the railing to get what they came for. Then they could leave the human zoo.

Running a hand over the back of their neck, Alex played with a few stray curls. Maybe they would defy Simone's protest over getting that undercut. It would be different, but maybe it was time for different.

The walls of shoes distracted them from other big changes like cutting their hair or going to Dilynn's for pizza. They checked the treads, the flex, and the support of a black and white pair of Nikes. It was dense enough to not fall apart. The only issue was the width of the toe.

Women's shoes were always too narrow, so they walked to the men's section. It would make too much sense to just put all the shoes on the wall and have a universal sizing system. No, gendered shoes were a social importance in a world where feet were feet, no matter the biological sex of the individual walking on them.

When the sales boy brought Alex the box of black and whites they'd settled on, he didn't leave. Alex wiggled their toes some before they began to lace them up. Once tied, they tried to walk away from the boy. He must be related to Jason Jordan though, because he followed them to the mirror. Hovered near them as they decided these shoes wouldn't have inhibited their ability to get to Dilynn's ex. At least, they hoped he's an ex now. If they'd been wearing these, instead of slides, they could have shown Evie how to knock him on his ass with one strike.

"Yes, they are what I was looking for," Alex said, again hoping the kid would take a hint.

They took another look in the mirror. Their eyes wandered back to the wall. Two pairs of shoes weren't necessary. They would probably only wear the black and white ones. However, Alex made a decision before the voice in their head could talk them out of it.

"Can I actually get another pair in the same size, but in purple?"

Glancing back at the mirror, Alex wondered what the dress code for pizza was at the Greyson house. They didn't really have normal clothes. Even now the sweatpants and T-shirt looked like they belonged at the gym instead of the mall.

Simone would know more. She knew all things Dilynn Greyson and guarded the information like nuclear war codes.

Alex twirled the phone once, then twice. It would be painful, but they had to try to find out if there was a chance Simone would be their wingman for one night. Afterall, they'd gone out with her and played designated driver while Simone picked up a girl to take home to her girlfriend.

The box of shoes waved above Alex's phone. The boy looked more annoyed than they felt. They checked the box, and the colorful shoes made them second guess the decision.

Choosing to distract themselves from putting them down like the dress shirts, Alex called Simone. At least with back-up, maybe they wouldn't be so scared.

> *You should just go out with Jason.*
> *He is the natural choice.*

"*Alex, this better be important,*" Simone barked after a few rings.

Alex couldn't help but groan. Simone's breathing told them she wasn't sleeping. The sudden chuckle from Marissa said Simone answered the phone in the middle of sex, again.

"Why do you have to answer when you're—"

"*You're always interrupting,*" Simone snapped, but she didn't sound like she was still humping her barely legal girlfriend. "*What the hell do you want? I'm on my honeymoon.*"

"You got married?" Alex choked out.

They had just made it to the punching dummies. The scrunched face called for a punch that they landed with ease. Alex sighed at the price tag. They would not be buying a dummy for only a 10% discount. That was not a real sale.

"*Don't get your boxers in a twist. It was just at the courthouse. We didn't want anyone to feel left out so we did it quick and quiet.*"

"So, you're actually married?"

"*Fuck! Just like that!*"

Alex's head fell back as they gagged. This was worse than GreyAltEgo's vanilla smut.

"*Yes, fucker. I'm married. Now, what do you want? I'm trying to set a record to see how many times I can cum before I have to stop for food.*"

Thousands of things that needed thoughts. Simone and orgasming did not belong together in a sentence in Alex's head. Those thoughts were there now, and they couldn't shake them.

It wasn't that Simone wasn't attractive, she just wasn't Dilynn. Comparing the two women was like trying to decide between snuggling a pillow or a cement block. Simone also didn't smell like home. Her musky woods deodorant was powerful and sturdy and too much like their own. And they weren't attracted to themself.

"*I'm hangin' up.*"

"Wait!" Alex practically shouted as they set the two boxes of shoes onto the checkout counter.

The young man across the counter jumped. They mouthed him a quick, "Sorry."

"*What!?*" Simone growled. "*Just like that. Yes!*"

Alex spat the words out before Simone climaxed. "Have you everbeen toa Greysonpizzanight?"

The line went quiet. They pulled the phone away from their ear to check if their best friend did, in fact, hang up.

"*You called me to ask about Dilynn fucking Greyson. You fucking traitor.*" Simone barked. "*You're trying to go to that Barbie bitch's house for one of those stupid pizza nights.*"

Nodding to the kid, Alex took the receipt and the large bag of shoe boxes, just as a sadistic cackle came through the line.

"*She's getting married, you idiot. To a man. A fugly man at that. A short, fat, hairy man. Dirty fingernails and probably wears socks when he fucks her. I don't care that she's bi, you're just setting yourself up.*"

Simone's continued laughter was like an acid bath. Hearing that shit in their head was one thing, but from their only friend was worse.

"*Born to be a bimbo Barbie with a douchy dick husband.*"

Alex could agree that the man was a dick, and he was sleezy. But Dilynn wasn't his anymore. At least hopefully she wasn't going to take him back. She couldn't after he put his hands on her kid, right?

"I am under good information to believe that she is, in fact, no longer engaged," Alex stated. They swallowed the lump that immediately rose as they did the only thing Dilynn had ever asked of them.

They moved through the mall more quickly than when they'd arrived. Ignored the sales and the humans living around them.

"*So what? Engaged or not engaged, there's no pansexual Barbie, Alex. Not that she's even really Barbie. She may have the tits, but she's more like a chubby Skipper doll.*"

"*Not okay, Simone,*" they heard Marissa say in the background. Followed by what may have been Simone being shoved away. "*Dilynn isn't chubby and she's nice.*"

"*The fuck she is. She's a drunk ass whore, and I don't want to hear about you spending time with her when she comes in to get plastered since she's single again,*" Simone barked.

Simone was a liar, and they knew why Marissa was upset by what her new wife had said. Marissa was a large framed masc, so Simone's attack had nothing to do with Dilynn not being attractive. It was a story Simone had refused to share though, something to do with the feud that started three years ago.

They thought of Dilynn against them. Imagined how she would feel in their arms. She was the perfect size to hold; the kind of little that could be enveloped into a tight hug. Her head would tuck under their chin, and they were strong enough to protect her from all the mean in the world. Even Simone's mean.

"Hey!" Simone called out. *"How did you end up getting an invite? I have never even heard her speak to you."*

The sun warmed Alex some even though the air pecked at their cheeks. They waited for a car trying to get through the herd of teenagers entering and a parent quacking orders at three young duckling-like children as they tried to leave.

"He asked you out again. Jordan." Simone laughed once more. *"I shoulda known that's why he wanted your number. One day he's going to need to wake up and realize he's gay. That's the only excuse he has for hitting on you."*

Their eyes roll back into their head. "Rude, Wyatt. Just Rude."

"Look, ignore him. And don't fucking go to that bitch's house. You'll just end up getting your feelings hurt when she's already fascinated with some new nasty looking boy. She doesn't want the gay life, so at most you may get laid and then dumped."

Alex ran their hand over the back of their neck. It was the answer they were expecting, but it didn't suck any less.

"Yeah. Okay," they relented.

They scanned the parking lot for their SUV, then looked back at the mall. The shirts were still 40% off and there was a whole stack of black ones.

"I'm gonna go," they said, turning back into the mall to go to Express.

"Bye, asshole."

While they waited in line for the second time, Alex scrolled through the email of subscriber notifications. Various notices that other authors updated a chapter, but no response from GreyAltEgo. The harshness of the last message felt too mean now. After all, the writer was probably a kid that didn't need an adult making her feel like shit.

They went to delete the comment, hopefully before GreyAltEgo saw it. They searched for the story, only to find it gone. All of the writer's stories were gone.

Their lower lip slid between their teeth. They had been mean like the man who'd shoved Dilynn's kid, only it was worse because they had been cruel to someone they didn't even know. Someone that wasn't doing anything but sharing a story. A sweet story that probably made normal people smile.

Maybe GreyAltEgo was right. Morgan needed to be softer. Afterall, if she remained indifferent and cold, she'd probably be killed in the sequel Alex was hoping would come. And if GreyAltEgo stopped writing, then the writer would stop responding to their comments.

Then no one would be talking to them.

3

The nearly empty vodka bottle was to blame for the whole sentence swaying on the computer screen. Dilynn pressed her fists against her eyes before putting them back on the keyboard. The burn from the booze broke her filter, and she began spilling his indifference and her desperation onto the page. Stripped away the happiness like RunnerAT89 had demanded on the last story.

She could hear their voice in her head, and it sounded like Brandon, so she'd deleted everything she'd created in a matter of minutes. Thousands of words, comments, and kudos gone.

The troll was right. Aurora was created in the depths of Dilynn's despair, therefore, anything not dropped in toxic waste first was romanticized bullshit. Each character began with a trauma. She studied the trauma responses for losing a parent and compared them to her experiences, and then Evie's. She examined the role that her mother's unmeetable expectations had on her and poisoned her protagonist with a longing for acceptance that could never be satisfied.

She would do the same with Brandon. He'd wrapped around her like a snake, and she was naïve enough to think it a hug. Suffocated the sense out of her and left her foggy headed while he stuck his prick in someone younger.

Someone thinner.

Someone quieter.

Starting a new piece that didn't fit the fandom she was writing for, she began with rough and dark smut. One of the more toxic scenes filled with degrading remarks and bruising. The type of relationship she'd had with her ex, Sylvia, but she left out the aftercare Sylvia was always careful to provide. Left Priya broken on the bed as she prayed to be good enough to be loved when she knew Morgan was incapable of such affection towards her. There was no way for Morgan and Priya to end up together. However, it was a story to prove RunnerAT89 wrong.

Responsibility and duty, that was the core of Morgan's character; the character Dilynn hadn't based on herself. She leapt with her heart open at every person interested in her. Daddy issues Sylvia had called it when she came to pick up the pieces of Dilynn's heart when Brandon had thrown it on the floor. She'd been wrong though. Timothy Greyson hadn't been absent. He'd died, and the hugs had stopped when he was gone. The concern for her existence had vanished when one Wednesday night his car had crashed on the way home to make pizza for her. She was wrong because Dilynn had mommy issues, but she was right, too.

Dilynn searched for hugs from anyone willing to give them. And Evie didn't want to be touched. So, Dilynn made it safe for Evie to not be hugged by taking hugs from a man that pretended to want her.

"So stupid."

With words as her weapons, she sliced through characters' hopes and dreams. Used the keyboard to give them wounds that festered until their own blood poisoned them.

She twisted blades when she yanked them out of innocents so their screaming would be more chilling. Bashed the ones still living over the head until their semi-lifeless bodies lay in witness to their loved ones choked on their own blood. She left the lost on the battlefield with pieces of herself. The pieces she couldn't carry anymore. She poured her disillusionment and betrayal into Priya as she watched Morgan walk away, knowing she probably wouldn't come back. Not for the fantasy romance Priya wanted.

Dilynn's body tapped into a fresh well to drown any memory of her wanting him. Deft fingers moved over the keys. Anyone spared from physical assault was left to try and sew the lost back together. Those smart enough to hide from Dilynn's pain, like Evie had when she'd gone to her best friend's house for the rest of the weekend, crawled back to the scene. But they weren't equipped to help.

Her eyes were so tired from crying it weakened her resolve to even finish the story. She swallowed more of the bottle. Felt the fire catch again, then pushed forward. There was no stopping, just a single need for something to go right. For someone to tell her that everything she did wasn't garbage.

No, that wouldn't be enough. She also needed RunnerAT89 to stop telling her she sucked at the only thing she did for herself. Just one bully to change their mind about her. Tell Dilynn that she, even a red-faced blubber fish choking on land, was not trash.

She read through the pain. This wasn't why she started writing in the fandom. With all the other stories removed, her 783 subscribers would know her world was falling apart. RunnerAT89 would know she was broken.

No matter what RunnerAT89 said, it wouldn't matter. They didn't even know how to use the fucking shift key. Or where a comma should be placed. RunnerAT89 could go fuck themselves off the top of Fuck Off Mountain if they thought they could bully her into silence. She already had a real-life bully in Simone Wyatt. She wasn't going to take that shit from some wart covered cyber troll.

While leather clad teenage warriors cleared away the wreckage from what was once their home, Dilynn found herself gazing around the room. The decorations had been torn from the contact strip hooks. Several of the hooks had come off with each yank, chipping the paint. She'd calmed down enough to save the three ornaments that mattered before she dragged the tree out the front door, lights and all. Christmas was gone; however, Brandon was still everywhere she looked.

Bloodshot eyes paused on the entryway where the mistletoe had hung. She'd stood there not knowing he was going to see the girl with the hair so dark and long and straight.

Her fingers wrapped around the black liter bottle of White Gold Black Diamond Vodka. It was a stupid name for a stupid drink that reminded her she was stupid so might as well fill herself up with more stupid since her stupid life was basically over.

The picture from last Christmas still hung on the wall. She was smiling in the picture. She'd been in the middle of Brandon and Evie's war for so long that she refused to acknowledge that it wasn't working because it would mean she'd failed as a mother and a lover.

Dilynn turned back to the computer. She'd written her fair share of creeps. Brandon's character would be no different, so she put him in the blast zone. It was messy work, but Dilynn didn't shy away from a single gory detail. She made him live so she could torture him. Detailed how he watched the stump of oozing flesh between his legs being cauterized by Priya's pulsing red sword. Had him associate the smell of his seared crotch with the burnt pork roast while the pig he'd tormented earlier that morning devoured the tiny head of his manhood. Only then, did she allow him to pass out. She wouldn't kill him; he needed to live in a tortured new form.

With three chapters completed, Dilynn logged back into the fanfiction website. The red and white banner made the tears thicker, and the mucus in her throat denser. She stuttered in the posting menu, unsure if this was the best plan. A part of her knew she was just seeking attention. Specifically, RunnerAT89's attention, just like with her mother and Sylvia.

Neither of those women gave a damn about her. Especially her mother, who'd called to tell her Brandon cheating on her was a failure on her part. That she'd seen the photos from Christmas morning and could understand why Brandon had sought the company of another. Dilynn had listened like the dutiful daughter she'd tried to be since getting engaged, but when the call ended, the anger had turned to guilt. And she tried to drown in the booze to keep herself from calling Sylvia to hear the woman laugh at her for taking him back after last time.

There were a lot of choices she could make that would fix all the things wrong with her. She could eat less. Exercising was another one of those things. It wouldn't change that he cheated on her or that he'd raised his fist to Evie. Nothing could change that Brandon and she were done.

The others though. If she could just get any of them to change their mind about her, then maybe she wasn't a waste of space.

Getting up from the table was harder than the first time she tried. The room doesn't move like it had two, or was it three, hours ago. And her knees were not ready to withstand her weight. They were shaking too much.

Everything was shaking. Her hands. Her vision. Her will to live.

It's not like she would ever do something like *that*. She couldn't. Especially over an ogre whose teeth were probably caked in buttery plaque because she wasn't there to remind him to brush every day.

No, not over him.

Evie had already lost her real mother. Dilynn couldn't let her think she was going to lose Dilynn, too. Not when she'd finally hugged her on Christmas. Maybe more hugs were coming after two years of watching the girl hug friends. Years of hugs from only the ogre that was hugging other girls. Kissing other girls. Fucking other girls.

Her nails dug into the entry table. The wax from the polish came off easily. But it wasn't enough. She ripped the picture from the wall. The metal triangle snapped off the back and dangled off the nail head.

Under the picture laid the wedding invitations; their golden wax seals were pressed with a singular star. Her finger grazed over the little extra she'd done by herself, like all the other plans. She could still feel the burn. Remembered picking the wax from her fingertips.

She scanned the room. Located the little things left behind when he had thought he could come back. The stained red flannel smelled like burnt hopes and dead dreams. His dirty socks stuck out from under the couch.

"It all has to go."

She'd wallowed within the silent house for long enough. Brandon had been nothing more than a long-lived mistake. At least she'd been smart enough not to let Brandon get her pregnant. Made sure her birth control shot was taken regularly to not make the same mistake twice.

No, she was done with men. Done pretending to be straight so Evie didn't fear her. Evie had sanctioned Dilynn's queerness just days ago, and it was time to rebuild Dilynn Greyson. She'd start making things right in the next chapter of her biography. A chapter focused on being a mother, instead of a lover.

Lovers sucked anyways. Just like sex sucked with Brandon over the last year.

Brandon hadn't noticed that she couldn't get off with him on top of her. No, her orgasms only came when she'd clenched her eyes shut. At first, she'd imagine Sylvia was with her. But since seeing Alex, she would think of the woman after she faked it so Brandon would roll over and go to sleep. Then she would take matters into her own hands after he began to snore as she imagined Alex holding her down on her desk or taking her against the door of her classroom. It was always the social studies teacher who had been there to see her life fall apart.

Sex with a woman was different. And RunnerAT89 must not have much experience with women, if they didn't know how deep the g-spot was. She couldn't touch her own, but Sylvia always hit it. Sylvia's fingers were longer than Brandon's dick. Sylvia had known what she needed and how to take her time.

That's what she needed. She needed to get fucked instead of fucked up.

Drunk Dilynn knew the answer was to call Sylvia and see if she was in town. It wouldn't be complicated with Sylvia like it would be if Dilynn waited until winter break ended to try to talk to Alex Trikru. She'd never slept with a co-worker, and flirting wasn't her forte. Calling Sylvia wasn't complicated because it was what Sylvia wanted. She wanted one-night stands or non-relationships, and if Dilynn was going to kick the habit of jumping into relationships it would be best done while being sore in all the right places.

She picked up her phone and pulled up a blank message. Messages to Sylvia were always blank because they were immediately deleted shortly after being sent or received. A habit from the closet at least Dilynn was out of now.

'He fucking cheated on me,' she sent first. Then she began to rapid fire messages to the woman she'd loved but had never been loved back by.

'She was younger.'

'I hate her.'

'I need you to fuck me.'

'Like you used to.'

'He couldn't do it right.'

'And I can't ask the hot social studies teacher.'

'I won't try to make you stay.'

'Just need to feel something.'

'Whatever you want to do, I don't care. Just please come.'

Dilynn waited for Sylvia to respond. Stared at the messages as they turned from delivered to read. She glanced down at the tank top hanging off of herself. She couldn't see her toes, but it would be okay. She could just turn out the lights when Sylvia got there.

She thought of the last time she'd felt the white heat spreading through her body. She hadn't felt even the slightest burn or seen fireworks since Thanksgiving, and that was just sparklers she'd caused herself because Alex had told her she was such a good girl while spreading her cunt open with two fingers in her imagination.

Alex could probably give Sylvia a run for her money. There was no way Alex's cold demeanor wouldn't translate to cool calculated control in the bedroom. Fuck the bedroom, she'd let Alex have her in any room and any position if the sturdy woman would tell her she was a good girl.

Dilynn's phone vibrated on the table pulling her dirty mind from the scene playing out in her head. She dropped the stuff she'd gathered in the middle of the floor before retrieving the device.

If Sylvia was in town, she could be on the doorstep in an hour. She'd done it once before, when Evie was at a sleepover and Brandon had called her a selfish cunt for not wanting to invest in his shelter. Sylvia had come to make the hurt he'd caused disappear. Then she vanished and he reappeared, and Dilynn wondered why everyone else got to come and go as they pleased while she was standing still.

Sylvia didn't respond. She probably could tell Dilynn was drunk, and that was against the rules. A drunk blonde tied to a bed was not the type of fantasy Sylvia had. No, Sylvia preferred a bratty sub that would talk shit to justify the pain Sylvia would cause.

Instead on Dilynn's screen was a warning text from her kid to get her shit together: 'I'm on my way home.'

She skipped posting the story and clearing away Brandon's belongings to make herself look like a mom instead of a drunk. And that started with a shower.

Steam filled the space while the three-day old sweats and rank tank top dropped to the floor. Each article of clothing removed reminded Dilynn of why Sylvia wouldn't be interested anymore.

She wouldn't date herself either, and she definitely couldn't let Sylvia see her now that she felt like a stack of marshmallows held together with toothpicks.

The tears mixed with water settled around her ankles due to the clogged drain that refused to function as needed, because he'd never fixed it like he promised. He'd never kept a promise, now that she thought about it. He wasn't needed; she could clean a drain herself. Or hire someone to do it for her. Either way, she could get it done.

Dilynn pulled on a clean pair of yoga pants and the frayed 'Fight Censorship' t-shirt.

When she looked in the mirror this time, she found a different person staring back. She wasn't sure why, but she felt ready to face anything. Even Evie. Which was a good thing because the girl was sitting on the couch with a smorgasbord laid out on the coffee table.

Evie held out the plastic cup with the perfect starting solution to Dilynn's sorrows. Chai tea lattes fixed tears. The first sip felt better than chicken soup at the end of a weeklong flu. It coated her still raw throat and sweetened her outlook on life.

"Thanks, E," Dilynn whispered as she dropped to the couch. She looked at the food. "Why is there so much?"

Evie didn't have to answer, because Landon walked through the door with Evie's best friend, Casey on his heels.

"Lights are down," Landon stated, then he moved towards the hall bathroom. "I need to wash off because it was really dirty up there."

"And I dumped all the shit that was on the floor and anything that I found in the laundry room into a box in the garage," Casey proudly stated. "I was gonna just put it in the trash but—"

"Let's google how to hex someone," Evie interjected. Her face spread into a wicked smile.

Casey's eyes rolled, then she finished her sentence, "We should burn it."

With arms folded over her chest, Evie pouted some. "Fine, we can burn it, but I still want to try and hex him."

Landon's shower was quick, and Dilynn realized he probably had no hot water. She didn't have much time to contemplate it as she took in the very tight Cactus High softball shirt that rode up his chest like a crop top. His manhood wasn't concealed at all from where he'd squeezed himself into a pair of basketball shorts that on Evie were very loose.

"What the fuck, babe?" Evie cried out. "You're ruining my shirt!"

Casey tossed a throw pillow at him, then covered her eyes. "Bruh, I can totally see your whole dick, like nothing left to imagine and it's definitely safe to say that I am a bonified lesbian."

Landon caught the pillow before it hit him. He held it in front of himself and mouthed a "sorry" towards Dilynn.

Evie made room for Landon beside her, and a blanket was wrapped over the two of them. Dilynn curled up into the corner of the couch cradling her cup as she searched for any hint as to what Evie was about to play on the television.

Casey ripped a piece of packing tape from the roll with her teeth before Dilynn could protest. Why teenagers had to put everything in their mouths like toddlers was beyond Dilynn, but that roll of tape was now Casey's.

A poster board was slapped to the wall, and Evie proclaimed, "I do declare the annual hunger games in session."

It wasn't the actual Hunger Games. It was quite the opposite. And to make it even more confusing, they weren't even watching Katniss. They were watching Harry Potter.

"If the scar hurts, you eat a blue Dorito," Evie began. "Nasty ass jellybeans for every time Hagrid says, 'I shouldn't have said that.'"

"A shot of butterbeer for each time Snape yells, 'Potter!'" Casey added.

The rules were rambled off until the kids accounted for each of the items on the table.

"And we will be marathoning this!" Evie declared. "So, strap in. First one to puke loses."

They were bloated by movie three. Dilynn's buzz was gone, and she had surprisingly not puked. In fact, Landon looked the worst. He blamed it on the slugs being vomited, but Dilynn assumed it was probably the inability to breathe in Evie's clothes.

By movie four, the house wasn't any different from a week ago. Well, besides the decorations; they'd be back next year though. They would come back out of the box and there would be another Christmas.

Nothing would really change without Brandon.

He was never around anyways.

4

The knock on the door startled Alex. The wide tooth comb they'd just finished pulling through their thick curls was now a shield held over their chest. After an attempt to ignore whoever was standing outside, their phone pinged. They rolled their eyes at Simone's text.

Simone leaned against the wall, staring down at the small park just on the other side of the street.

"What are you doing here?" Alex asked, scrunching the curling cream into their long curls with an old t-shirt.

"Making sure you don't do something stupid. You know, like go on a date with Jason Jordan to Greyson's house."

Alex's hand dropped from their hair. They had been thinking about pizza and Dilynn before the doorbell rang. Thinking over the cost of betraying Simone to spend just one night in the blonde's presence.

"Why would it be so bad to go to Dilynn's?" Alex asked.

Simone pushed off the wall only to lean against the banister. Her hair fell over her face, blocking Alex from reading her facial expressions.

"You're mine, not hers." Simone pulled her hair into a ponytail "Get your shoes. We're going for a run."

Alex's arms crossed their chest. It was almost eleven, and their daily run had taken place at seven. They were not scheduled to run again until before dinner. That was supposed to be the distraction from going to Greyson's.

"I already ran today," they stated.

Simone glanced back, then pulled her foot up to her butt. "So run again."

Whatever was going on with Simone, standing on the porch and arguing with the woman was decidedly a waste of Alex's time. Plus, if they ran now, then they could technically go to Dilynn's if they got the courage tonight and a second run wouldn't be an excuse.

"Lemme change," they said.

They left the door open for Simone to follow if she wanted. Most people would be anxious about their landlord showing up unexpectedly. Alex didn't have to worry about that with Simone. It's not like they had bothered to hang anything on the walls, and painting something was out of the question.

Simone tossed the purple shoes at them when they came back dressed to run.

"Those new shoes?" Simone asked.

Alex looked down at the Nikes. With a slight hum, they nodded.

"Never seen you wear color before," Simone stated.

Alex rolled their eyes. "Black is a color."

"Black is a shade," Simone corrected. "Like a shadow or your soul."

"My soul?" Alex pressed their hand to their chest feigning hurt. "Please provide your evidence for such a shameful claim."

Simone plopped down on the single chair with the mismatched kitchen table. Then she pointed to the other side of the table.

"Only serial killers have one chair," she stated.

Alex held up a single finger. "Or someone who lives alone and never has any company."

"What the fuck am I?"

"Company entails being with a person that provides you entertainment or enjoyment," Alex explained.

Simone's hands shot out in the air and waved around herself. "Am I not entertaining?"

Alex began to count off on their fingers.

"One, you showed up with no food just before lunch time. Two, you came demanding I go for a run after I just showered. Three, you basically insinuated that I am your personal property. Four, you let some kid move in below me and now I spend my evenings with a contact high. And five, you didn't come to hang out with me, you came to just run interference, which is the opposite of a wing-woman."

Simone's lips pursed as she scanned the vacant space around her. It was clear she was unimpressed with Alex's decorating skills. Only after the five items in the room had been carefully examined, did Simone say, "So, you were going to go."

Alex fell back against the couch. It was a mistake because the black-like-their-soul Ikea couch had no give. Just a hard surface to bounce off.

"No, I wasn't going to go," Alex grumbled. They turned to Simone as they said, "But I wanted to. I really wanted to go because... someone actually invited me to go somewhere."

"I invite you to go places," Simone stated.

"To lesbian bars," Alex reminded her.

"Yeah, so?"

Alex waved over themselves. "Simone, I'm queer, not a lesbian. And I don't drink."

Simone squinted at them suspiciously. "You don't drink?"

When Alex nodded in affirmation of Simone's statement, she rolled her eyes at them. "What type of person doesn't drink? You can't be serious."

They sucked their teeth. An explanation shouldn't have been needed. They should be able to say they don't drink just like they should be able to say they don't like avocados. Both seemed to be as acceptable as being a they instead of a she though.

"My mother is a raging alcoholic, so no, I don't drink. I don't drink and I don't find drunk people amusing, and bars... they just make my skin crawl. So yeah, I was excited to be invited to Greyson's house because there would be food and it wasn't a bar, and no one," they took a deep breath, "has invited me over to do anything since college. Not even you. I am just this permanent loner that spends every weekend alone."

No one cares about freaks.

"Every weekend?"

"Yeah."

Simone scanned the room again. "What do you do?"

Staring at the probably cheapest carpet Simone could purchase, they listed the things they'd done over the last week. "I read a lot. I leave comments on stuff other people write. And I run. I run a lot."

"Why don't you have a TV?" Simone asked, after cataloging the room once more.

"That's your question?" Alex asked.

Simone shrugged and waved her hand in Alex's direction. "You have a lot of feelings right now and I'm... I'm not a feelings person. I'm just the wrong friend for this."

"You're my only friend," Alex whispered.

A smile spread over Simone's face at that factoid. She leaned back in the chair, then glanced at the kitchen. "So, I guess you don't have any beer. Beer would make the feelings easier."

"What is your beef with her?" Alex spat out. "Like, what happened that makes it so you are so determined to make sure I don't talk to her? Even though you know I am attracted to her."

They knew the rumors. Had heard some students recalling when Simone and Dilynn had possibly broken up and turned the older woman into a mean bitch. They hadn't given it much thought, but maybe the kids hadn't been that far off.

"She's a fake," Simone snapped. Her arms folded over her chest. "She's always pretending to be happy, but she isn't. And she just plays games with people. Like, the kids all think she's perfect and she's nice, but she isn't, and... and... look around, there ain't shit to be happy about."

Alex had spent a great deal of time watching Dilynn. Studied the way she engaged with her co-workers and the students. The kids loved her. Even seniors who never had her as a teacher talked about Dilynn. But her heartbreak hadn't been fake. They'd seen it in her eyes. The pain of her relationship falling apart, while Simone...

"Didn't you just get married?" Alex asked.

Simone moved her head in a slow circle until her neck popped. Then she looked at them blankly as she said, "Yeah, so?"

"So, you're a newlywed. Shouldn't you be happy about marrying someone you love?"

The eye roll was unnecessary, and the scoff was overkill. Simone's hands rubbed up and down her face as she said, "Do you just read romance novels?"

Alex licked their teeth and confessed, "Mostly YA dystopia and fanfiction on my favorite book."

Simone's eyebrows rose and she chuckled lightly. "That is oddly believable."

Alex shrugged. "It's free."

"So is a library card." With a shake of her head, Simone lifted her gaze to them. She licked her lips and looked away again. "Well, all that melodrama has apparently warped your mind about this unbelievable type of love."

She looked down, then tugged at the bottom of her tank top. "Love is just lust. It hits hard in the beginning, but then that shit fades."

> *Don't worry.*
> *No one lusts after you.*

Alex tried to sort through their feelings about Simone's confession.

"So, you don't love Marissa?" they tried to clarify.

Simone's sigh was more of a growl that connected to her answer. "We didn't get married for love or any of that bullshit."

Alex leaned back against the couch. This wasn't the seventeenth century. Marrying someone just to marry them felt oddly out of place. Unless Marissa wasn't a US citizen. They glanced back at Simone. No, she wouldn't be kind enough to marry someone to help them get a green card.

"Then why'd you marry her?"

"Insurance," Simone stated frankly. "She didn't have any, and the bar she works at doesn't have benefits."

Alex ran their hand over their neck. Questions about Marissa's health ran through their head. They tried to find answers to them through the conversations they'd had with Simone. There were no hints buried that Alex could recall.

"She's nineteen, Alex," Simone reminded them. "She's not going to stay with me forever, she just needs to get her shit together and I don't give a fuck about the insurance. Plus, she has, like, no income, so it helps me with taxes on the properties. Financially, it was the best option for me."

Taxes were still somewhat of a mystery to Alex. They came out of their check, and they filled out the TurboTax Easy form every year, but they didn't have anything to claim so it wasn't something they really thought about.

"Look, you've met Marissa," Simone stated.

"She's a good person," Alex verified. "Does she know you don't believe in love or happily ever afters?"

"More of your romantic crap," Simone huffed. "She doesn't know about my properties. Doesn't know shit about finances. She just doesn't care about stuff like that. Look, she's been through some shit. She needed to talk to someone that does the feelings, because Marissa might be this big bull but she's got so many feelings and she needed some meds because she has these nightmares that are pretty intense, so it was the least I can do."

Alex chewed on their lower lip. The whole situation made them feel queasy, because Marissa was a good person and Simone was Simone. It didn't feel right how things were going, but they'd never been in a real relationship. Just a short adventure in college, but they still wanted a happy ending. One preferably with Dilynn.

Freaks don't get happily ever after.

"Look, Alex, it was financial, simple as that," Simone said again, like it would make the ants crawling under their skin any less itchy.

"Well, I know the apartment complex is going well since I am paying almost double what I used to be paying," Alex stated. They pointed to the kitchen, "You know for $750 a month, it would be nice to have a stove that isn't mustard yellow."

"Hey, it's market value," Simone reminded them, but she looked over at the stove. "Fine, I'll replace the stove."

They sat in silence, the run clearly no longer something that was happening.

"Why do you hate her?" Alex pressed once more. "It really can't be just because you think she's fake. There's tons of fake people around you, and none of them anger you the way she does."

Simone's eyebrows squeezed together. She stood up from the chair and moved to the window. Staring at the park across the street, she shifted her weight from side to side.

"We're never talking about this again." Simone turned to them. "After I tell you, it's done.

Alex's cheeks puffed outward. They pushed the breath out with a simple, "Okaayyy."

"Never again after I tell you," Simone repeated. Her hands balled into fists and shook at her sides. "I need your word."

Alex raised their hands in surrender. "Yeah, okay, I promise."

Simone took her time chewing on every sentence. Her jaw moved slower than a cow working through cud. A few times, they thought she was going to speak. She just shut her mouth and continued breaking down the story, which meant it wasn't going to be the truth. Not the whole truth at least.

"District used to have this teacher mentor program where first year teachers were assigned to a veteran and the first semester meant planning with them, helping them with classroom management, fuck wiping their tears and—"

"This sounds like a job you definitely shouldn't have been given," Alex stated.

"Fuck you." Simone's hand hit her chest hard as she said, "I'm a great mentor. Dilynn Greyson is the teacher she is today because of me."

Alex's lips curled over their teeth. Quietly, they reminded her, "You just told me that I had feelings, and you didn't do feelings. And you like me, which means I can imagine you being very, very mean to Greyson."

"Well, I didn't used to be," Simone countered and turned away again. "I was so fucking nice to her, and the fact that you think I would be mean to her when she first started just shows how much she fucked me up. God, I just... I spent so much time with her."

Alex fiddled with their Fitbit. A run may have been a better plan than sitting on the couch while their rump went numb.

"So, you mentored Greyson." they grumbled. "She cried a lot, and you don't do tears. That's a pretty lame reason to hate someone."

"No," Simone declared sharply. "She did *everything* I wanted her to do."

Alex's head tilted slightly. Searching Simone's face for the meaning of everything, they found nothing, so they asked, "Wait are you saying... you and her..."

Simone made her hand into a shield, and blocked Alex's words as she said, "No. Not like that. But—"

"Wait..." Alex leaned forward once more. They tried to put together Simone's words with what hadn't been said. They couldn't make it make sense though, so they said, "I don't understand."

Simone pulled the neck of her tank top up. She continued to stare down at her chest, like if she couldn't see them, then they weren't there.

"We were spending a lot of time together."

The strap of her shirt needed to be adjusted next.

"She wanted to run all her lesson plans by me, and she changed them every fucking day. So, we would spend every day after school together. I got her a job tutoring the volleyball team so she got paid extra, and we would go out to happy hour with other teachers because she was always inviting everyone. She has to be the center of attention. And she was. She was the center of attention. Even mine.”

Simone walked back towards the kitchen and pulled open the fridge. There wasn't much in there, but Simone found a bottle of water to draw the story out even longer.

Alex's head fell back. If this was part of Simone's interference, it was getting old quickly. They sucked in their breath and tried to wait Simone out.

Simone apparently needed to undress the bottle and make a projectile with the wrapper. Then she needed to drink half the bottle. Then play with the cap, screwing it on. Then off. Then on.

“You know this would be much easier if you spit it out,” Alex stated. “Just tell me what happened in chronological order.”

Simone took a long drink. Water even dribbled down her chin to her shirt. When the bottle came back to rest on the counter, she stared at it.

“I tried to kiss her,” she whispered. “I took her home after happy hour and she was drunk and stumbling everywhere and... I thought she wanted... me. It was just a game though. She just played games and she flirted and...”

The brown eyes returned to Alex as she begged them to understand, “You're not blind, she's very attractive and she did that innocent eyes thing and I tried to kiss her and she...”

Alex felt like their spine had been screwed into a 2x4. Slowly, they asked, “She what?”

Simone closed her eyes. Her voice was barely audible over the screeching of passing car's brakes as she confessed, “She reported me to HR.”

“Because you *tried* to kiss her?” The question tasted like two-day old milk. Not right but not bad.

“Yeah. She just stood there like a mannequin and...” Simone rubbed her face again. “She just stood there staring at me until I left. And that was it.”

Alex narrowed their eyes at their friend. “If it was just a misunderstanding, why would she go to HR?”

Simone's head hung. The water bottle crunched in her hand but thankfully did not spill everywhere.

“She said that I... that I crossed an ethical boundary and that she felt like I was abusing my power over her.” Simone looked at Alex with that pleading look again. “She made it into a whole fucking thing, and I just thought... just thought she liked me.”

“Woah.” Alex couldn't think of anything else to say, but not for lack of trying.

See, she definitely wouldn't want you.

They looked back at Simone expecting to see the weight lifted from her shoulders, but she was still closer to the ground than normal.

"I feel like there's more," they said. Then they clarified, "To the story, I mean."

Simone licked her lips. Then she took another drink. Only when the bottle was empty did she continue.

"Nothing really happened after the whole HR thing." Simone's shoulders rolled back slightly. "She was assigned a new mentor, and I was told to leave her alone. So, I did. I did... but then everything happened with Everliegh."

"Greyson's daughter?" Alex asked, putting a name to the girl with the off-balanced punch.

Simone nodded and pulled at the back of her neck.

"Okaayyy," Alex said slowly. "What happened with the kid?"

A siren pulled Simone and Alex's attention away from the question. They followed the cop car from their vantage point as its lights flashed behind a poorly aged car. The officer was a hefty bulk of a man. He touched the rear fender before making his way to the window. The close-cropped hair reminded Alex of their brother. He'd always kept his hair short and talked about being a cop when he grew up. They wondered if he made it. If he got his happily ever after running his mouth to their parents about Alex kissing a girl in the park.

Simone cleared her throat. She'd finished the first water, so she got another from the fridge. After another long drink, words began to spill from Simone in one long strand that wrapped around them like a lasso.

"Everliegh was being abused, like, bad bad, and she basically lost it in the middle of the season because her mom had died a few years earlier and she was living with her stepdad and he... he really hurt her, so she took a bat to his car after DCS didn't pull her from the house, which only happened because Greyson had called in the report and they just... they just left her, and—"

Alex held up their hand, "Wait... DCS just left her there? With her stepfather who was abusing her?"

Simone nodded. Then summarized, "Yeah, and she got angry, and she just lost it."

The plot points of Simone's story didn't connect for Alex. She seemed to be adding side stories and Alex couldn't see how they got from unreciprocated kiss to kid being arrested. The woman needed an editor as badly as GreyAltEgo.

"Okay, that's terrible; however, what does that have to do with Greyson?" Alex asked, trying to get back to the point.

Simone tapped her chest as she explained, "I tried to foster Everliegh, but... Greyson, she just... she just swooped in and when I tried to.... I just wanted to.... I told Dilynn I wanted to be in her life."

"And she said...?" Alex probed, not wanting to have to wait for Simone to drink another bottle of water before getting to the point.

"She told me I would see the kid at school, and she would still be on my team, but that was it." Simone took a deep breath and held it. It didn't seem to calm her down though, because the volume was cranked up to her voice box. "She won't even let me train with her. She hired this fancy coach and put her on a club team, and she just cut me out of Everleigh's life when she was... she was just as much mine as she was hers that year."

Alex stood there for a minute. They hadn't really built any relationships with the students in their class. Their class was only a semester though, so they didn't have the time the others did. They could see, though, how that would hurt Simone.

"Look, you work with her, too," Simone stated. "And you're new. I had spent years building relationships with people, so when she went to HR, I just didn't have to defend myself because people knew me. So, just stay away from her because you don't know people."

"I—"

"Alex, just trust me."

They inhaled deeply, then breathed out, "Okay."

The agreement didn't feel right. All the things they'd thought about both women twisted into a knot that they just couldn't work out.

They didn't know Dilynn, so they couldn't just ask her. Even if they did, she may not give them an honest answer. Just another version of a story that was a little bit the same and a little bit different.

"I mean it, Alex. She... she flirted with me, and then just blindsided me."

Alex nodded, then justified that they hadn't responded to the text anyways, so it wasn't like they were going to go tonight. Even though Simone bailed after the story was out.

5

There was a point that Dilynn prepared to be homeless. She'd woken up after withdrawing from her first semester of college classes and realized she would lose her dorm room. There hadn't been a plan when she'd tried to drown in a bottle of booze on a day she didn't want to remember, but midterms had come and gone during that week that she remained inebriated. She was failing out of college and her campus housing was going to be canceled.

She hadn't ended up on the streets because she'd met Sylvia. That was why she put up the money for the homeless shelter after Sylvia had left last time. She'd watched Sylvia walk away once more and realized most women wouldn't be as lucky as she was. Probably like the young woman that had been holding Brandon's hand. She'd known he was taken, but she was too young. In the pit of her stomach, Dilynn knew they'd met at the shelter. A part of her had even felt guilty for the possibility that she'd given him the idea.

Whoever the girl was had gotten Brandon. She couldn't change that. What she could do though was make sure the nineteen-year-old mother still at his shelter didn't end up under him. Another woman that was slim and sweet, and needed to be as far away from that asshole as Dilynn could get her.

The guest house renovation had taken a full week of Winter Break to accomplish. A week of Dilynn using her post break-up rage to smash drywall and hammer nails so Dilynn could turn the space into a one-bedroom apartment for the girl that was in Brandon's homeless shelter with a kid.

Dilynn stood near the entrance with her gaze focused intently on the young woman, Sarah, and her infant daughter; she watched as they moved through the one-bedroom space. She leaned against the door frame; her arms crossed lightly over her chest. Her eyes, sharp and discerning, took in every detail of Sarah's reactions as they explored the main living space before the tired mother disappeared into the bedroom with her daughter cradled against her chest.

When Sarah stepped into the living room, Dilynn watched for signs of interest, noting the slight widening of the girl's hazel eyes as Dilynn told her the furniture came with the place. Throughout the tour, Dilynn tried to retain a composed yet attentive demeanor, ready to answer any questions or address any concerns Sarah might have.

Sarah walked through the living space with the tiny infant in one arm as her fingertips ran over each surface, almost testing if the structures within were real. Three weeks of sleepless nights in the shelter were etched into the college student's face. Sarah opened the doors to the short kitchen counter, then to the compact refrigerator that still had all the stickers on the outside.

It had been two days since that counter was installed. Just looking at it made Dilynn's thumb hurt, A residual pain from when it had been smashed under the countertop during installation. An installation that happened because the guy that was helping her at Lowe's spoke to her in that tone Brandon would use to insinuate that she was too blonde and too dumb to do it herself. The installation of that counter was a big challenge, and she did end up getting an x-ray to see if her thumb was in fact broken. After that she got it in with minimal help from the kids, who were watching her like vultures. Plus, she'd become reacquainted with the tools her father had taught her to use so long ago.

"I'm sorry it isn't bigger," Dilynn offered quietly to keep from waking up the infant. She moved to the couch and tugged on the handle. "If you pull on this, the couch pulls out."

She moved to the table that managed to survive after Evie and Landon had a wrestling match over the instructions, followed by another one over who would use the drill. She picked up the flyers she'd retrieved from Marcus.

"My friend, Marcus, he's a social worker at our school. He gave me these and said they each offer something that will kinda get you the stuff that is not already here."

Sarah glanced up, then pointed to the cabinets. "You bought all this, didn't you?"

Dilynn chewed on her lower lip for a moment, and decided to pretend Sarah made a statement instead of asked a question. She sorted through the pamphlets until she found the one that would help get food in Sarah's grumbling stomach.

"Special Supplemental Nutrition Program for Women, Infants, and Children... um... it goes by WIC. You probably heard of it in class, but if you call this number, they will help you get set up with an EBT card for formula and food benefits. They will supplement formula so don't make them force you into breast feeding, just be nice because they get to make decisions about what types of food you can buy. They can also direct you to getting childcare set up for while you're in school."

Dilynn shuffled through the pamphlets once more, until she found the one that she'd already called. She waved that one in the air slightly as she explained, "And if you call St. Vincents. They have beds. They'll give you a mattress and frame and a crib. And I called already and checked that they have some available, so you're good."

Sarah looked down at the small head covered in thick dark curls. She swayed side to side when the infant's eyes scrunched up.

"You have to go and, like, show your ID, but one of us can stay behind with the baby. Evie and her friends offered to help you move it in. And Evie's boyfriend has a truck, and he is available every day until we go back to school."

"That's very kind," Sarah whispered. "Too kind."

Dilynn noticed Evie coming through the yard with Landon behind her. "So, I know they will give you a crib, but we wanted to do a little something for Trisaya for, like, a late Christmas present."

Landon set a large box of diapers on the table. The box of bottles and a box of wipes tumbled off the top of the diapers and slapped against the wood. Landon looked up apologetically for the noise as Evie followed it with a laundry basket. The basket was filled with enough baby clothes for Trisaya to not have to ever wear the same outfit twice.

Evie tucked her hair behind her ear and began to hold up baby clothes. With a simple onesie held up, Evie explained, "We went a little crazy because it was just a lot of fun. We kinda chose a lot of different things and not a lot of pink because we weren't sure how you felt about the whole pink for girls thing, so we figured all the colors were better than just pink."

Sarah picked up the large pack of Dr. Brown's bottles. She shook her head, and whispered, "This is too much."

The infant in her arms squirmed and mouth opened wide. A heart-breaking cry came from the girl that caused the young mother's eyebrows to cinch together.

"Look, Sarah... I know, okay. I... I know there's a lot weighing on you." Dilynn waved to the basket. "This is just one less thing for you to stress about. And we... we have a shopping problem. Like, for like, other people."

"She just broke up with her boyfriend," Evie said, pointing at Dilynn. "She basically bought all new furniture for her bedroom and the living room, so we just got stuff that would fit in here. I told her that she couldn't give you the bed she slept on with him. That would be gross."

"I wouldn't have done that," Dilynn said, rolling her eyes.

Evie peeked at the baby who'd settled with the figure eight sway Sarah had begun. Dilynn could tell her daughter was dying to hold that baby. She hoped having a baby around wouldn't give Evie any ideas. The girl wanted kids, that much she'd shared with Dilynn, but Dilynn wanted Evie to live before parenthood. She wanted her daughter to have a different life than she and Sarah faced. She made a mental note to get a box of condoms and put it in the girl's bathroom.

"I can babysit, too." Evie offered. "If you wanted, I mean."

Sarah looked them over quietly. "You're sure you can take the public housing voucher. Because we can't just.... I mean, we, like, have to give you something."

"I would prefer not to take anything," Dilynn answered honestly. "But yes, I gave the worker a tour yesterday. It is approved for public housing assistance. And it's all yours for as long as you want to stay. We won't bother you; I promise." Dilynn nudged her daughter. "Right, Evie?"

Evie nodded as she verified, "Yeah, no bothering. But I really like babies and I could watch her when you want to go out with your friends or if you need to do your homework."

"It's still too much." Sarah looked over the small apartment, then out the window towards the main house. "I... uh... in high school I used to work part time as a maid. I can clean for you. Or I could—"

"Sarah, you don't have to do anything besides take care of your daughter," Dilynn stated. She pointed back at the house. "The laundry is in the main house, and if you have a day that works best for you for laundry then we can make a schedule, but really if you don't mind just moving things into the dryer when you want to do a load that's cool, too. We aren't home much because of work and Evie's sports schedule. Also, if you ever need to, like, use the kitchen then have at it."

Sarah's eyes fell to the infant. "She's not..."

A putrid smell filled the space faster than anyone could run for cover or Sarah could finish her sentence. Sarah's face turned bright red, and she held the child away from her body. She glanced down at the basket, clearly looking for something she must not have.

"Is there baby wash?" she asked.

Evie held out her hands, and offered, "I can take her and change her. Maybe put her in a new outfit."

Sarah's lip popped from between her teeth. "I think, she's going to need a bath. There isn't... the shelter doesn't have baby baths in—"

Evie's eyes grew wide with excitement. She pointed to the bathroom. "We got one. We put it in the bathroom. I can get it ready."

Sarah nodded but didn't hand over the baby. "Uh... I'll just hold on to her while you... uh... just make sure it's not too hot.

"Check it with your elbow," Dilynn said, remembering the nurse's instructions when Dilynn thought she might just run away with the baby that was never hers before her mother came back.

Evie nodded eagerly and disappeared into the back bathroom.

Landon pointed to the main house, "I'm gonna head to the store for sodas. Is there anything else we need for tonight?"

Dilynn patted her jean pockets. "Umm... we need some sausage and pepperonis. My wallet is on the table by the door. There's cash in it."

He left Dilynn and Sarah still standing in the middle of the room. Trisaya squirmed in the new mother's arms, while Sarah stared at her. There was something familiar about the look etched into the girl's face.

"Why are you doing this?" Sarah asked, shifting her gaze to Dilynn.

Sadly, Dilynn had heard the question before from Evie. Every time there was a breakdown. It had been a topic of conversation over and over again; a conversation where Dilynn never told the girl the whole truth. She was too afraid of what Evie would think of her, or how she would use it against her.

It was clear to Dilynn that Sarah had seen more bad in life than good by the way she studied her benefactor. Dilynn hadn't been as experienced in life when she'd met Sylvia at seventeen. Maybe if she had been, she wouldn't have trusted the barely older girl who took her home and kept her in a less than decent fashion like Sarah was thinking was about to happen.

"Sit," Dilynn said gesturing to the table.

Sarah followed the instruction, while Dilynn busied herself with selecting an outfit for baby Trisaya. The child was still smaller than the average infant, so she sorted through the premature options.

"So, I don't really talk about this," she began with.

The purple footie pajamas brought a pained smile to Dilynn's face.

"I was younger than you. Much younger than you, still in high school and... I slept with a boy because... well, it doesn't matter why I did it. Just that we did it and I was in a situation similar to yours. Faced with choices. Hard choices."

Dilynn tucked her hair behind her ear and glanced at Sarah to see if she had to speak more plainly. Luckily Sarah nodded to her, a signal she took as not having to give more details.

"I was fifteen." Dilynn sat down in the second chair.

"Evie?" Sarah asked.

Dilynn shook her head, and let the words come out, "No, I... adopted Evie two years ago, but my other daughter was placed for private adoption. A closed, private adoption." Dilynn fought back the tears. "My mom... she arranged everything, so when I had the baby, she had a family before she was even born. I just know her name was Charlotte before she was adopted, and that the family was from Arizona."

Dilynn's shoulders dropped back. She took a few deep breaths and reminded herself that this was a reality she had accepted a long time ago.

"She would be twelve now," Dilynn admitted. "And I will never know anything because I let my mom convince me that I had no other choice. I didn't know a lot of things. I didn't know that I could have... It's pointless thinking about any of that."

The water running in the bathroom shut off, and time was running out.

Dilynn glanced at the laundry basket as Evie came out.

"E, we forgot washcloths and towels. Can you go grab some from the house?"

The teen didn't have to be told twice. She ran to the main house, which Dilynn knew gave her maybe five more minutes.

"Do you regret it?" Sarah asked. She looked down at the baby. "Like if you could do it again, you wouldn't have... given her up?"

Dilynn bit her lip. She'd asked herself that question many times, but always accepted the answer had to be no. She would do it again.

"I wouldn't have Evie. Like, the world would be different. Everything different. That's what I tell myself, but I have a garage filled with boxes of presents for each birthday. I still look at every kid that walks by me and search their face wondering if she could be... if maybe in this place, our paths would cross."

Dilynn looked at the baby. Even with skin the color of chocolate, Dilynn could see Sarah in the girl's face. The same pursed lips, and a single dimple pressed into the side of her cheek.

"Are you... thinking about adoption?"

A single tear slid down Sarah's cheek.

"I don't... I don't want to be... a parent. I never wanted..." Sarah sucked back the snot that was cutting her sentences in two. "It doesn't matter. I made a promise, and I have to keep it."

"Being a mom is hard," Dilynn admitted. She reached out and placed a hand on the girl's thin arm. "I don't want you to think that all this is me telling you you have to be a parent. Just give yourself time to think about it. Don't walk away because you feel backed in a corner."

"Would you... ever...?" Sarah held the baby out to Dilynn.

Dilynn bit her lip. She knew she would take Trisaya and raise her in a heartbeat. It had been a consideration before Brandon had shut down the idea of any more adoptions. She couldn't tell Sarah that. Not right now. She ran a finger down Trisaya's cheek and left her in her real mother's arms.

"Sarah, let's not talk about anything like that until you decide if that is something you want to do." Dilynn let the infant wrap her delicate digits around her finger. "Just... please, don't think you have to do this all alone. Literally any time of the day. I'm here."

"Thank you," Sarah whispered. "For everything. One day, I'm going to—"

"Help someone else," Dilynn stated before Sarah could finish. "I don't need anything, so one day you are going to help someone else."

Sarah looked down at the baby.

"How about I make the phone calls to St. Vincents and pretend to be you, and I can run to the grocery store. Actually, I can call Landon and have him pick things up. He'll be back quickly because it's Wednesday."

Sarah's eyebrows rose slightly as she asked, "Is Wednesday grocery shopping day?"

Dilynn chuckled. "Sort of. Wednesday is pizza night. Evie's friends come over. Some of my co-workers. It's never the same really, and we just... hang out."

"Oh, okay."

"Six," Dilynn offered. "You can give your arms a break and—"

"Got them!" Evie proclaimed like a victor returning from a lengthy quest. She was out of breath, but the items were held in the air.

Dilynn nodded towards the bathroom. "Go do bath time. I'll call St. Vincents."

Sarah looked at the couch. "We just need a crib," she whispered. "I want... I want to make the room a nursery. I'll sleep on the couch."

Dilynn didn't argue. She knew she needed to let the young woman make choices for herself. Her phone going off was an excuse to walk away.

"I have to take this," she said waving the phone in the air.

Sarah offered her a half smile as Dilynn accepted the call. She stepped outside before she said, "Hey, Sylvia. Yeah, Evie is home... Yeah, now is not a good time. Sorry, about the texts.... Maybe in a few weeks, when my head is a little clearer."

6

The fact Simone promised to replace the stove should have meant Alex wouldn't still be staring at it. Or that one burner now refused to work, and it was still in their kitchen.

Alex didn't complain about stuff often. Only themself and that was internal and in a voice from their past that had used the same words. But they had complained about the stove to Simone, and she agreed to replace it.

Over a week later, Alex still stood over the ugly yellow stove. The only color in the apartment besides the purple shoes, which were now back in the box after being discussed by the woman.

Their life went back to shades of the shadows they lived in, well except the yellow stove. The stove they couldn't avoid because eating out was a luxury for people with companionship and expendable income.

They spooned the bubbling butter over the Manager's Special NY Strip. They clipped a sprig of rosemary from their small hydroponic garden. An expense justified by not having to purchase herbs for $3 a pack that would only last for a week. The microwaved potato was ready and waiting for the last two minutes they needed for the steak to be the proper temperature within.

Alex looked over the lettuce covering the edge of the garden container. They would have salads this upcoming week for lunch so the lettuce wouldn't go to waste.

Green could be a neutral color. They could avoid throw pillows. Maybe add a blanket. A jade blanket for the couch wouldn't cost too much and could swing either way. Or they could just add more plants to the space. Like on the end table by the couch. Another on the coffee table.

'Not like anyone would see it anyways,' they reminded themself.

If you were just normal,
then people would like you.

The rosemary gave off just enough scent to make the space feel less like a spaceship and more like camping. Green would be a good color for a them. They could get some green candles. Less darkness, more life.

Winter break made them miss life. Miss even half-asleep seniors, who Alex determined were better company than the fictional characters they read about at this point. The new stories they'd consumed all read basically the same: two teenagers that hate each other, then fall in love; two adults that hate each other, then fall in love; and love at first sight, but their families hate each other.

Without anything new, Alex found themself considering taking Simone's advice about a television. A television, some plants, and a blanket for the couch. Maybe a second chair for the kitchen area so they could ask Dilynn over for dinner. They could do that, especially since Simone hadn't told them the whole truth.

The single chair at the table waited for them. It hadn't felt weird only purchasing one chair from Ikea at the time. Chairs were $45 a piece, and they didn't see the point of buying a second chair to just add further insult to their singular life. Now, there was a glimmer of possibility.

Dilynn cooked dinner for people. They could cook for her. Cooking was something they could do well.

The notification came while Alex was plating their meal. They stared at GreyAltEgo's name, then at their own username. After a week of digital silence, the writer had composed something new. And dedicated it to them.

With their laptop retrieved, Alex cut the steak into bite sized pieces while they waited for the story to load. Choking to death was not on the agenda for the night. They'd fought too hard to be themself to give anyone the satisfaction of being notified they died alone.

Alone wasn't the forever plan, so they needed a second chair. The world was changing around them, and Dilynn was single. They just needed a little more time for society to catch up. Then maybe people wouldn't always tell Alex they were wrong. Maybe Dilynn wouldn't.

GreyAltEgo was not one of those people though. She was back and she had left them a message. A decently long message at the start of chapter one. Chapter one of three, with more to come. A message that made their face flush at being publicly called out.

> RunnerAT89, this is dedicated in spite of you rather than to you. I wrote two whole stories where Morgan murdered the person I imagined you to be for a being a jerk. However, I decided I wasn't going to give you the satisfaction of being immortalized in fiction. Also, since you hate that I write about a place that you can't find on the map inside the cover of the book, I went ahead and wrote something in a real city. The place is called Phoenix, Arizona, and it really exists, which means you're going to have to find something else to whine about, but whatever, you're not going to win. The only pollution in this fandom is you, so I hope you don't enjoy this. In fact, I hope you hate it so much you puke. For everyone else, I decided to

write something a little different, hope you enjoy. But not you Runner. Don't enjoy.

The laughter ripped through the apartment, shocking even Alex. It shouldn't be funny, but this was the most fight they'd seen from the author who'd always ended replies with a promise to do better. Then a sobering realization hit them.

They were in Phoenix. Technically, they lived in Glendale not far from the new football stadium, but to anyone outside the state it was basically all Phoenix. And that meant GreyAltEgo may also be in Phoenix.

They took their first bite of steak as they started to read. In every paragraph, Alex searched for landmarks hinting to where GreyAltEgo may be in the city. She didn't use names of streets, and the high school was named after the village GreyAltEgo claimed was on the map.

Alex devoured the story with a fresh plot line of two seemingly hopeless teachers that equally pined after each other. It was disturbingly raw and the detailed intricacies involved in educational politics made Alex wonder where GreyAltEgo taught.

They chewed on each metaphor that complemented the steak so pleasantly. By the end of chapter one, Alex was fully invested in the well-choreographed dance between an English teacher and social studies teacher. They were transfixed by the way each character pulled back to protect themselves whenever there was a chance of something resembling an actual conversation. It left Alex with a lingering desire to have the courage to speak to their own enigmatic English teacher.

By chapter three, they needed to know what happened in the break room. Their food was left half eaten on their plate while they read.

Priya didn't know if she should run back to her room when the coffee pot was blocked by no one else than the stoic Social Studies teacher, Morgan Emir. It would of course be strange to just walk out when she was holding an empty mug in her hand. However, Emir would have to look in her direction for it to even be noticed.

The green eyes did look at her though. Looked up from the phone the woman spent so much time staring at. She nodded and stepped aside from the still gurgling machine. At least the scent of dark roast would cover her sweating through her cardigan.

As Priya reached for the pot, Morgan closed the

distance. The soft smell of fresh rain made the blonde wet, and she ducked her head down to hide the arousal painted on her cheeks.

Morgan retrieved a community cup from the counter. She examined the inside before setting it alongside Priya's own mug. Clearly Morgan had brewed the pot herself, so Priya filled the other woman's cup first.

She went to slide the cup to her coworker, but it was stopped by Morgan's warm, calloused hands. Of course, they were rough, the woman was built like a goddess and that surely required working out.

Morgan's warm breath cascaded over Priya when she reached for the creamer, which had ended up on the other side of the smaller woman. It ignited a desire in Priya she tried to keep hidden.

She glanced up at the woman's lips. Plump kissable lips that are smiling.

"You okay?" Morgan asked, still so close.

She wasn't okay, though. She was a dripping mess of need standing so close to the woman. And it wasn't like she could tell the social studies teacher that she got herself off each night thinking about Morgan's lips and hands on her. That she would do anything the bossy woman told her to if it meant she would get to say the woman's name.

She could just trip. If she fell even an inch, her nose would press against the firm perky bust of her coworker.

She looked up though. The woman was waiting for her to answer not to be assaulted before first period ended.

"Goo... good," she stuttered. "I just... it's early. Need caffeine."

Morgan smiled but didn't step back. She placed a finger under Priya's chin, applying pressure until Priya was perfectly positioned to be kissed.

And goddamn it, she needed to be kissed by the green-eyed goddess with her pillowy lips. Kissed and put on the counter where her coworker could have her way with Priya.

"You look like you're having dirty thoughts," Morgan said, a devilish grin spreading over her face.

Priya's mouth went dry at being called out. Her whole face felt hot.

"I bet you're thinking about the fact that no one has vacuumed your room all year," Morgan said.

Morgan's hand dropped away, and she laughed. Her laughter was so full of life. Life Priya had been missing when she'd locked herself away pretending to want someone else. She wished she could bottle it so when the nights were dark and the house was quiet, she could let a little out and feel like Morgan was with her.

The other teacher walked away, like winding Priya up like a sexually frustrated top was just part of her daily routine.

"It's homecoming," Priya said to Morgan before she could leave. "Are you doing anything tonight? There's the—"

"You" Morgan stated, then opened the door to the break room.

Priya's eyes grew wide as she bit her lip. She searched Morgan's face for the joke, but found nothing.

Morgan took a glance down the hallway, then back at Priya.

"I'll see you after school, Ms. Killian," Morgan stated.

A group of students passed behind Morgan.

"After school in my room. There's more room to work on my desk."

The door closed before Priya could react. She just stared at the door to the room and wondered if she'd made the whole thing up. She had to have. There was no way she couldn't have.

Alex went to click the next chapter button, but there wasn't one. That brat, GreyAltEgo had left them on a goddamned cliff hanger. Didn't even bother to provide any internal monologue hinting as to where Priya stood on the offer.

There wasn't another chapter but there were comments from other authors expressing similar feelings to GreyAltEgo's dedication. Many championed the woman for her petty note.

They considered not responding just out of spite. It would make all of the comments right though. Provide some proof to the notes from others that Alex only commented when they had something mean to say, which wasn't true. They'd left some nice comments. Or ones that weren't necessarily mean.

Staring at the sliver of steak on their plate, they decided not to respond.

They'd wait to see if the sex scene was as vanilla as all the previous ones. That was typically the issue with GreyAltEgo's stories. The mental gymnastics Alex would have to do to figure out where hands and arms were. If that scene didn't mess up the story, they would comment then.

For now, they would finish their meal without puking.

No, they wouldn't. Waiting had done nothing for them. Responding now was a requirement.

They needed the woman to know they'd seen her pettygram. That they were there, and they were down to play her little game. Not like there was much else to do.

RunnerAT89 on Chapter 3:
didn't puke yet

7

The benefits of having first period prep were insurmountable. Most favorable of those was Dilynn's ability to avoid Simone Wyatt for the entirety of the day. She waited in her classroom until the bell rang before making her morning break room run, and the first day back to school following Winter Break was no exception. She'd killed her venti Chai on the drive to school, so break room coffee was a must.

She almost dropped her mug when she stepped into the office and her pre-break failure slapped her in the face. When Alex Trikru stood behind her in the mall, Dilynn had forgotten her Secret Santa catastrophe. Now, she remembered.

Alex silently glanced up from the copy machine as part of their daily routine. Normally, Dilynn would retrieve her coffee and run away before she could embarrass herself since her dirty mind couldn't behave.

"Don't move," she practically shouted at Alex before she slammed her cup on the table and bolted from the space.

The breakroom was on the other side of the building, in the heart of enemy territory. An enemy who was scowling at a tardy student. Dilynn didn't run, she sprinted passed Simone.

"Great example, Greyson!" Simone yelled after her.

The words chased her to her classroom at the far end of the hall. She let them smash against the wall as she slid to a stop. Her classroom key fought her, but after a jiggle left and a yank to the handle, the door let her in.

Alex's gifts were still on her desk where she'd left them. She held up the smaller box, still struggling with the question of whether or not Alex would like it. Too late now. She couldn't give it to Jason or Marcus because whenever she'd see it, she'd still think about Alex.

Her lungs were too weak and energy level too depleted from the first flight to sprint back to the breakroom. By the time she walk-jogged into the space, she was panting and sweating and couldn't help but feel like she'd already written this scene over break.

Alex had moved while she was gone. Dilynn's cup was full, and the creamer that never managed to run out was being poured into the World's Best Teacher mug.

"I was your Secret Santa," Dilynn declared with the presents held out to Alex. "I'm so sorry I missed you. I was... I lost track of time and by the time...

"

She looked up into the green eyes that had made it into her latest fanfic.

"I shouldn't have been late," she said. "My mother always said I would be late to my own funeral, which means they'll probably lose my body or the GPS will fail on the hearse, however, I don't think that could really be my fault. She'd make it my fault though."

Alex reached out but didn't take the gifts. Instead, two fingers rubbed over the cuff of the Secret Santa cardigan. A shade of blue that rivaled the mid-day Arizona sky.

"I wasn't sure if you would like it," Alex whispered. "You always wear the green or maroon ones, so I went with the blue. I thought it would match your eyes."

It did match Dilynn's eyes. She'd noticed when she put it on the first time. Appreciated the softness of the material and the fact that it didn't itch like so many sweaters did.

"You were my secret Santa?" Dilynn asked.

Delicate blossoms bloomed on Alex's cheeks. "I may have traded one of the math teachers."

"Well, I love it," Dilynn stated. "I wore it most of break because it's kinda heavy and it feels like a hug. I mean, I needed a hug after this break."

She thrust her own gifts forward. "Here, I hope you like them."

Alex took the presents in exchange for the coffee. The tape was torn slowly, and the wrapping paper pulled apart without a tear. It was so slow, Dilynn almost ripped the paper from the package herself.

At least the mug kept her hands busy. She looked down briefly to find the liquid within the perfect shade for her morning cup. The needy part of her brain determined it meant Alex noticed how she liked her coffee.

"This one doesn't really count as a present because I had it already," Dilynn shared when the hardback copy of her novel came into view.

Alex stared at the cover. A single finger ran over the embossed title, before those eyes were staring at Dilynn once more.

She pushed her damp hair behind her ear and toed the ground softly. "I... uh... I saw you carrying a pretty beat up copy, so I thought maybe you'd like one that's autographed."

Alex's lips parted just enough that words should be coming out. They weren't though.

"I'm sorry," Dilynn whispered, realizing the disappointment her co-worker must be feeling. Afterall, the sweater she was wearing had to be expensive and she'd just pulled a copy of her own book from her shelf. "There wasn't really anything written on your sheet, and I saw you with the book and I took a chance.

I probably should have snooped through your classroom to find something you really—"

Alex held it up to Dilynn. "This is my favorite book. I think I have read it ten times in the last year, and every time I read it there's something else there. Something I missed."

Dilynn swallowed the confession. She'd never been one to read a book more than once. Never assumed her novel would mean enough to anyone to give it a second look.

"How did you...?" The cover of the book was opened, and the inscription was examined. "He doesn't have a website. One of the most elusive writers. No public appearances. You know him?"

Dilynn bit her lip. She'd been told to switch her name. Told it would help her stay below the radar, since YA fiction with a bisexual protagonist was something that could have some parents aiming for her head.

"Yeah, I know her," Dilynn chuckled lightly. "Known her for, like, ever."

"Thank you," Alex said. "This... thank you so much."

"It really was no problem," Dilynn said to her coffee cup. She looked at the second present waiting on the table.

As Alex set the book down, Dilynn felt the need to explain what was in the box before it was unwrapped.

"So... I just want you to know that I put the gift receipt within the box. I know.... Actually, I didn't know anything, however, you always look so... dapper in your dress shirt and your slacks, and.... I don't know if you like...."

The paper came loose, almost falling to the floor before Alex snatched it up. It was set atop the other sheet as Dilynn continued to ramble.

"I just saw it and I guess it was like the sweater. It was just the perfect shade of green. And since you only wear black and white, I thought it would pop."

Alex stared at the thin necktie within the box.

"I don't know if you even like ties, so like I said, the receipt is in the box. But I just walked around and around the mall and I kept coming back to it because I just couldn't get it out of my head. And if you hate it, I am so sorry. I just—"

"I've never had a tie before." Alex pulled the tie from the box. "I was always afraid that... when I looked at them, I wasn't sure how other people would feel."

"Fuck other people." Dilynn's hand slapped over her mouth. She felt the blood rushing her face, but she parted her fingers and offered another apology. "I'm so sorry. I have a mouth that belongs on a sub, not a teacher."

Alex's gaze rose to meet hers. Teeth bit into that lip Dilynn had tried to write the night before and couldn't find anything else to say other than kissable. So damn kissable. And her brain caught up to her dirty mind and realized what she'd just said.

Sub had two meanings, and the way Alex was looking at her, Dilynn wondered if there was an understanding of both.

The lip popped free just as Alex said, "Do you think I could pull it off?"

Dilynn felt her eyes roll. She couldn't stop it. Nor could she stop her mouth from making an ass of herself.

"You could wear a burlap sack and I would still be drooling over you."

This was why she left the break room without speaking. Saying something stupid the first time she managed any semblance of an actual conversation was inevitable. At least it was more material for her story.

"So, I'm going to go and wait for HR to call me," Dilynn whispered, thumbing towards the door.

She couldn't leave. Not because her feet had grown roots or anything indicative of her body telling her to stay. It was definitely screaming at her, but not because she tried and failed to run away on her own. It screamed because Alex caught her by the hand.

"Please don't go," Alex whispered. A finger ran over the ring still on her finger. The ring she'd put back on that morning to keep the questions at bay. To keep her students from asking questions, which could possibly make her cry in front of the kids, who'd convinced themselves they would all be invited to her wedding.

"That was so inappropriate," Dilynn said to the door, because she hadn't turned around. She couldn't face the rejection she knew she'd find if she did.

"I'm flattered," Alex stated. "More than flattered, because it came from you."

It sounded genuine, but Dilynn waited for the other shoe to drop. For the 'but' or 'however' that was going to follow. Another sentence, which would require her to avoid the breakroom altogether.

She turned to face her crush when Alex didn't say anything else.

They shared the electrified silence. A normal for them, only different now that confessions were bouncing off the walls. Alex's gaze dropped to the ring, held between them. Dilynn remembered Alex knew, and what wearing the ring must look like.

"I didn't let him come back," she said quickly. She looked at the tiny bland stone. "I just didn't want the students to.... I didn't want to answer the questions. There will be questions when it comes off, but... I need time to make sure when I answer them that I can be... calm."

Alex shifted the ring slightly on her finger. They licked their lips, before they said, "He was an idiot."

"He was a jackass," Dilynn corrected. Her chin dropped to her chest since there wasn't any sand to bury her face in. "There were so many signs, and I just didn't want to see it. I just thought if I was better... looked better. I mean, you saw the girl he was with."

"You deserve better," Alex stated like it was a fact. "I would.... There are many who would... I'm not good at this type of thing."

Dilynn tried to sort through the myriad of questions she had for Alex Trikru. She didn't have a chance to come up with one when the door to the breakroom swung open and smashed into the back of her. Her mug flew from her hand and smacked Alex in the chest. The coffee immediately covered the white button down while the cup shattered on the floor.

"What the fuck, Greyson?!" Simone yelled at her.

Dilynn couldn't find words as Alex stared down at the shirt which was quickly becoming transparent. She pulled off her sweater and held it out to Alex, but Simone pushed her out of the way. The sweater barely made it to the table instead of in the pool of coffee and glass surrounding Alex's boots.

"Are you burned?" Simone asked, grabbing a roll of paper towels and trying to soak up the coffee off Alex's chest.

"I'm fine," Alex growled. They yanked the towels from Simone and blotted the shirt. "At least I have a spare in my room."

"You're so weird," Simone snarked.

Simone didn't seem to notice the way Alex flinched at the comment, but Dilynn did. She saw the grimace and slight shift away from Simone.

"You're amazing," Dilynn whispered so low, she didn't think anyone could hear her.

Alex's blotting paused just for a moment. Green eyes looked up at her, so Dilynn moved to get more paper towels.

Simone held up the empty coffee pot. With eyes locked on Dilynn, she snapped, "So, you just drank all the coffee and didn't even bother to brew another pot?"

Dilynn had made it two and a half years without playing into Simone's attempts to bait her into talking. She would survive this one as well. Dropping to her knees, Dilynn gathered the largest pieces of her mug.

"Why aren't you in class?" Alex asked, pulling their shirt from their pants.

Pausing, Dilynn glanced up just in time to catch the smooth lines of Alex's abs. It was enough of a glimpse to distract her from what she was doing. She squeezed the glass in her hand just hard enough for the pain to remind her that ogling Alex was wrong, even though Alex was now looking at her and still holding the shirt out so Dilynn could see more.

"I have a student teacher this semester," Simone said. "She said she would watch my class so I could get a pick me up, which apparently isn't going to happen since someone decided to be inconsiderate."

"I took the last of the coffee, so stop being a jerk," Alex snapped, letting the shirt go.

Dilynn dropped the pieces of the mug into the garbage. It was where the mug belonged since Simone was the one that gave it to her on her first day of teaching.

"You don't even drink coffee," Simone said, leaning against the counter while Dilynn did her best to soak up the coffee from the floor.

At least the breakroom had real paper towels instead of the brown roll of unabsorbant crap found in the bathrooms. Alex crouched down to assist. Their hands paused just over Dilynn's, like touching her may cause some form of electrocution.

"You should go change before the bell rings," she whispered. "I'll... umm... replace your shirt."

"Like you should for being so clumsy," Simone said while the coffee maker gurgled beside her.

Dilynn eyes rose to the cause of the whole situation. She catalogued all the ways to murder Simone in the next book. Technically, she'd already killed Simone in the first one, but she could kill her again in the second. This time more slowly, definitely involving third degree liquid burns.

"You don't need to," Alex offered, taking Dilynn's hand. "To get coffee stains out you just have to presoak in a quart of warm water with half a teaspoon of dishwashing detergent and a tablespoon of white vinegar. Takes about fifteen minutes before washing."

Dilynn studied the human who didn't drink coffee but knew a precise formula to get coffee stains out.

"I worked in a coffee shop when I was in college," Alex followed up with.

"I think I drank my weight in coffee, like, every day when I worked at Starbucks," Dilynn said. "Free coffee was probably my favorite part of that job."

"Was that when they started closing stores to recoup costs?" Simone interjected. She drained the contents of the fresh brew into her own mug. "I mean, that had to be, what, 200lbs a day? No, 160. You used to be smaller."

Blue eyes fell to the coffee-soaked paper towels. She fought the urge to clench her hands together and went to the sink to wash away any glass that may be stuck in the sugary coffee covering her fingers.

"You were probably their most expensive employee unless you're just lying."

Dilynn put her sweater back on. Tugged it tightly around herself to hide away Simone's cruel truth.

"You missed a spot," Simone's unpolished finger jabbed at the floor. "At least have the decency to clean up your own mess instead of leaving it for someone else, like you usually do."

"You clean it up," Dilynn snapped. She willed away the tears and reminded herself it wasn't a big deal. It was just Simone Wyatt being a bully.

The same bully who'd told her the best way to get a contract for the upcoming year was through a stellar evaluation provided by her mentor. The same lie she'd used when she hovered over Dilynn in her townhouse after Dilynn had told her she wasn't Sylvia's prostitute. The only time she claimed to be Sylvia's girlfriend to get the woman out of their home.

Simone Wyatt didn't care though. She'd never cared about anything but making Dilynn feel small and powerless. She didn't win then though, and she wouldn't win now.

Without another word, Dilynn left the breakroom and vowed never to go back. It would be a long day without caffeine, but it wasn't that big of a deal.

At least Alex liked the gifts. And there was actual conversation for the first time. She thought it would be a first time of many, but Alex was Simone Wyatt's best friend. Which meant conversations with Alex would go back to Simone.

8

The World's Best Teacher mug sat on the table, unfilled for the third day in a row. Three days of only the copy machine running double sided dittos. The fresh pot Alex brewed sat on the warmer while they scrolled through GreyAltEgo's latest chapter.

The smutty scene they'd anticipated to come in chapter four was derailed by an argument with another teacher. They were now at chapter 8, and the distance between Priya and Morgan had grown. Chapter after chapter of Priya's desires and deprecation, while Morgan walked through chapters without saying anything to the other woman.

Alex yearned for a glimpse into Morgan's head space. Wanted to know how Morgan could be so bold about wanting Priya, then simply ignore her. Was it a move to get Priya to come to her. Because waiting on a girl clearly was working for Morgan as much as it was working for Alex.

They checked the time, then the door. With thirty minutes left of first period, Dilynn could come in. She'd avoided the breakroom since Monday though. Left Alex to fill their mornings with practically begging GreyAltEgo to give them Morgan's POV.

They read through the author's latest response to their plea.

> GreyAltEgo on Chapter 8:
> At this point, shifting POV to Morgan would be a poor writing choice. If I wanted to include her voice, it should have happened earlier. I don't want to, so I'm not going to.

Alex tapped the table. It was a valid argument; they just didn't like it. This was supposed to be a story about both characters, but the last four-chapters was too much Priya. Just like mornings were too much Alex's own thoughts, and not enough Dilynn.

> RunnerAT89 on Chapter 8:
> it would be something new instead of the same thing since it seems like you are just dragging this out. do you even care that readers are getting bored.

The copier finished but they sat at the table while the coffee was burning. Maybe Dilynn snuck in between periods. No, Simone came in during breaks.

This sucked. Simone wasn't supposed to be in the breakroom with them in the morning. It was their time to occupy the same space as Dilynn and they'd finally made it to talking. And it was their fault. They'd ruined it by calling Simone over break. She'd come in because they'd put their interest on her radar, and now it was ruined.

Their phone vibrated on the table, and they went back to their distraction.

> GreyAltEgo on Chapter 8:
> The point of a longer work is to develop the character. I just ran a search. There are 638 fics where Morgan and Priya have sex in the first three chapters. Go get yourself off to one of those and leave me alone.

Alex's diaphragm collapsed. Dilynn was already MIA; they couldn't piss off GreyAltEgo when she was the only person talking to them. Technically Simone was talking to them, she just hadn't noticed they didn't have anything to say back.

> RunnerAT89 on Chapter 8:
> i don't need to get myself off. and i don't want to read some other fic. i want to read yours. and I want to know why Morgan is being so cold.

They waited for GreyAltEgo's response. Refreshed the page at least six times before they got their answer.

> GreyAltEgo on Chapter 8:
> You must be desperate since you actually capitalized a letter, which means you do know how the shift key works. I'll make you a deal. You leave me a comment that doesn't look like you're illiterate and I will give you an entire conversation between Priya and Morgan.

Alex chewed on the offer. It was obviously a trick. A power play they were about to lose, and they hated losing. They weighed if giving GreyAltEgo what she wanted was going to be worth it.

Their phone buzzed again.

> GreyAltEgo on Chapter 8:
> Or type something that makes you seem uneducated and I
> can hold out. I mean, you still haven't puked yet but I'm
> sure I could write Morgan having feelings and that would
> do the trick.

They sucked in a deep breath of concession. Losing on all fronts was in their cards for the day.

> RunnerAT89 on Chapter 8:
> If I don't do what you ask, the conversation could already
> be written and it is not an actual reward. If I do what you
> ask, then I probably still won't get a chapter until tonight.
> Sounds like I'm giving and you're taking, which feels rude.

As they sent the message, Alex decided there really wasn't a way to lose at this point because they weren't just invested in the story. The real loss would be the story getting pulled down and they would never get the spicy scene.

There were twenty minutes left in first period. They looked at the door again, thinking if they hoped hard enough Dilynn would appear. She didn't though, and neither had another message from GreyAltEgo in the five times they refreshed the page.

Dilynn was avoiding the breakroom, but they hadn't done anything wrong. They shouldn't be punished because Simone was a jerk. It just wasn't fair, and they had to do something about it. They'd even worn the replacement shirt they'd found neatly folded in the box yesterday morning on their desk. That was when they were certain she wasn't coming back to the break room, but they'd sat there all morning still thinking maybe she'd know they were wearing the tie she'd given them, too.

They filled the replacement cup and counted to four as the creamer filled the remaining space. It was the average length of time the blonde poured so it was mostly correct. The copies were left on the machine as they went in search of the woman. They had to do what Morgan hadn't. Go to the woman, maybe even do the chin thing.

Just as the breakroom door closed behind them, Dilynn was trying to push her way through the door to the school with a large box and a bag so filled it looked prepared to topple her.

"Greyson," Alex called out.

Dilynn didn't turn. She struggled through the door weighed down by the box. Then, she headed towards her classroom. The breath in their lungs caught when their fears were confirmed. The heavy box in her arms was a silver Keurig machine. They realized her struggle wasn't due to the box but from the several liter bottles of water stuffed into her bag at her side.

"Hey, Greyson," Alex said again, trailing just a few feet behind her.

Coffee spilled from the cup, splashing over their hand and to the floor.

She paused and turned slowly. Blue eyes didn't crinkle in the corners, instead a crease folded over her forehead. She scanned the hallway behind them, before her eyes found the coffee spilled on the ground.

"Please let me," Alex offered, holding the cup out for her.

"It's okay, I can--" Dilynn started, but Alex took the box from her arms and handed her the coffee cup without a word. Then they lifted the strap of the bag from her shoulder, holding it up until she gave in and let it be pulled over her head.

She didn't look up at them, simply shifted side to side. The mug was held in both her hands as she clutched the cup close to her body.

"Okay, then," she whispered.

She walked alongside Alex, with her head hung slightly. She looked over only once before they made it past Simone's classroom. The woman's guard dropped when they were safely in the English department territory.

"Did I... get the size right?" Dilynn asked. "For the shirt?"

Alex nodded, not trusting their voice. She didn't look up though, so they had to find words.

"I think so," they whispered. They paused for a moment and held the box off to the side. "What do you think?"

Dilynn glanced up to where they gestured at the replacement on their frame. She stared at the tie hanging over the buttons. Her lips curled upwards only in the corners, but it was a smile. They were sure it was a smile.

"Green looks good on you," she said.

Alex's shoulders fell back some and they stood a little straighter. The box and the waters on one side were heavy though, so they had to adjust it, setting them a few paces behind her.

The trip down the remainder of the hall was done in silence. Only an occasional squeak from their boot against the waxed floor even hinted they were walking instead of floating.

Dilynn fought with her door before Alex was engulfed by a rainbow of colors from the room. Repurposed pallets lined two walls with hundreds of novel covers begging to be read under student made posters.

"I love your room," they said after setting the box on a desk.

Dilynn tucked her hair behind her ear, then fought with the golden mane until it lay in a messy bun atop her head. She offered a soft, "Thanks," before setting the cup of coffee on her desk.

Alex rubbed their neck. Silence had been the status quo for so long, but it had ended when she'd yelled at them to freeze Monday morning. They couldn't go back to silence.

"Uhm... where do you want it?" they asked, scanning the already filled space.

"You don't have to," Dilynn said again. "I can--"

"It's not a problem," Alex promised, cutting her off. They couldn't let her dismiss them. Even if it meant an HR call and no contract like Simone had said would come.

They pulled the box open and searched for a place to put the machine that would be replacing them. If they dropped it, maybe they could keep their morning routine.

"Just over there, where the last one was," Dilynn said. She pointed to a table at the back of the room next to a full-fledged snack bar. "Just next to the fruit baskets."

"You like oranges, huh?" Alex asked while they dropped down to plug the machine into the surge protector under the table.

"They're for the kids," Dilynn answered. "The buses are usually late, and they don't get breakfast, so I keep fruit, granola bars, some bread, and almond butter back there so no one has to go hungry."

Alex studied the table. They wouldn't have had the courage in high school to take something from the basket. It may have set off a teacher's radar of their homeless status.

"Do they... like they are not worried about what the other kids will think?" they asked.

When they turned, Dilynn was busy tapping into her phone. Her eyes rolled dramatically, before she glanced up. It took her a moment to process what they'd said apparently.

"Sorry." Dilynn shook her head. "Uh... just distracted by someone being needy and whiny at the same time. Anyways, you said... uh... worried? I mean, I can't really say. It's kinda like at Pizza Night. People come if they want and don't if they don't want to. We don't make it a big deal. It's just there, and my freshmen see the juniors swing by to grab snacks, too."

She retrieved the cup of coffee from her desk and examined the mug. It wasn't perfect; however, they'd tried their best to find one as close to the one that had shattered on Monday.

"You don't drink coffee," she said to the cup. Blue eyes rose to them once more. "I've seen you make coffee several times, but you don't drink it."

Alex rubbed their neck roughly before remembering. They pressed their hand into their pocket to keep from disheveling themself anymore. They felt their phone vibrate but ignored it.

"I just... you came in once and there wasn't any left and you... you left, so I make a fresh pot each morning," Alex admitted. "I just wanted to make sure you had coffee."

"Well, I guess you have one less thing to do in the morning now."

Alex watched as Dilynn studied the mug in her hand again. They couldn't just watch her anymore without saying something stupid. She already knew they were a stalker. No need to make it weirder.

> ***Nothing is weirder than you.***
> ***Freak.***

"About Simone," they started.

"She's your friend," Dilynn interjected. "I get it. You don't have to apologize for her."

"I—"

"Really, it's not that big of a deal," Dilynn stated. "It's just better this way. I just have to make it through one more year, and then..."

"What happens in a year?" Alex asked.

Dilynn poured the coffee into a cup on her desk, then held out the mug to Alex.

"Evie graduates," Dilynn stated. "Then, I'll find a place where if there is a Simone Wyatt, I won't get on her bad side."

Alex looked around the room. It didn't take a stalker to know the school would be worse off without Dilynn Greyson around.

"You would just leave?" they asked.

Dilynn nodded just as the bell rang.

"But you can't leave," Alex stated. "You are Queen Greyson. Every kid on campus knows you. Everyone loves you."

Dilynn twisted the ring around her finger. "I was going to leave that first year, but Evie... it was better to keep some semblance of normal for her. And I thought... I thought if I gave Wyatt space, she'd back off. I'm just tired of looking over my shoulder or hearing her talk shit about me whenever she thinks I can hear her."

Alex tapped their chest. "I can... I'll make it stop."

Dilynn shook her head. "I shouldn't have said anything. I just didn't want you to think you had to... it doesn't matter. I replaced my busted Keurig, and it's just better this way. You don't have to get in the middle, and it's just better this way. Yeah, just... better so that... so that there's less drama."

The bell rang before they could muster a response. Dilynn pushed the cup into their hand. "Wyatt got me one, too, when I first started."

The door to Dilynn's classroom slammed open with a ferocity that had Alex jumping at the thought that Simone was launching a second attack on Dilynn. They held their chest as three freshmen boys walked straight to Dilynn, each taking a turn to perform a complicated handshake with the woman.

"I will see you later," Alex said.

Dilynn didn't acknowledge them. She moved to the door and began greeting her students like nothing in her life was wrong. Her smile wasn't real even though it crinkled the corners of her eyes.

Slipping through the stream of freshmen, they walked down the hall. They fished their phone out of their pocket. The vibration wasn't GreyAltEgo's response to their complete sentence. It was an email that the latest chapter had been updated.

The warning bell rang while they stood at the midpoint of the hallway. They read through the author's note that was written to them.

> RunnerAT89, you were right about it already being written. Keep up the good grammar and maybe they'll kiss in chapter 10. Leave me a comment that reads like you're a kindergartener again and that kiss will be with someone else.

Their brain sorted through all the characters they'd been introduced to. There were two that would make them want to clean their eyes with bleach if Priya or Morgan kissed them. Kind of like the idea of Simone and Dilynn kissing. And that sort of happened.

No, they couldn't let their fictional world be ruined. They also couldn't just let Dilynn leave. Not when they still had so much they wanted to say to her.

They would have to get her to understand they are not just Simone's friend. It would start with stopping the bullying. It should have happened Monday, when they witnessed it.

They could change her mind, just like they'd changed GreyAltEgo's.

Glancing back to Dilynn's room, they watched her finish the last of her intricate handshakes. Her eyes met theirs as the last student entered. She chewed on her lip, then her gaze shifted to the hallway behind them. Her half smile fell, and they knew the hallway bully was still standing behind them.

Turning to Simone standing in her doorway, Alex narrowed their gaze at her. It earned them an eyeroll.

"Your funeral," Simone said before she let the heavy door close behind her.

The final bell rang while Alex's seniors gathered in small groups outside their room. With a glance back at the nearly empty hall, they thought of the woman who'd mastered fake happiness. It might have been for show, but the kids entering all engaged with Dilynn. Something the seniors seemed uninterested in doing in their class.

They would try something new today. Something that defied their normal. Normal was overrated anyways.

"Listen up," they called to the students.

Alex waited until eyes were on them, eyes they'd previously worried were judging them. Those eyes should be learning from them more than the facts they needed to vomit onto the AP Government exam.

"Today we are going to work on handshakes," they explained. "I understand that physical contact may be unnerving for some of you, however, it is the first thing many potential employers are going to offer, so it's important to do it right. So, we are going to work on it every day until it becomes natural."

With the door unlocked, Alex looked the first senior straight in the eye. "Good morning, Jarome."

Jarome blinked twice. He pointed to himself. "You know my name?"

"Yes, Jarome." They held out their hand, waiting for the gumby like wrestler.

Jarome's arm wiggled like a noodle when Alex shook it. A few students watched the interaction.

"Grasp firmly," they stated, and squeezed the boy's hand, not tightly enough to be threatening but to signal the young man. He matched their grip, and a smile spread over his face. "Good. Always look the person in the eye and shake twice with arm slightly bent."

He followed instructions surprisingly well, and offered Alex a simple, "Morning."

The students lined up to shake Alex's hand, and by the fourth student, there were only minor corrections to be made. The others picked up on the first students' mistakes. It was the first contact any of them had with Alex, and they felt good about the chance to start over with a new group of students. And it was all because of Dilynn Greyson.

They glanced down the hall again. She may not come to the breakroom anymore, but they could visit her in the morning. Ask her questions on how to get kids to like them. Maybe she would like them, too.

9

Saturday afternoon, Dilynn blushed profusely as she read over chapter 12. Since her desire to have Runner puke went unfulfilled, she'd drawn out the impending sex scene. The time had come though. Her other readers were hungry for it, and she couldn't punish them just because Runner was a brute.

"Mom," Evie whined. "Please, can we go to that Cajun place? I need to try crawfish."

Dilynn's nose scrunched up. Her daughter needed to try seafood like she needed another ear piercing. She checked the time to see if there was a way out of this newest obsession.

"I thought you were going to the basketball sleepover tonight?"

Evie's whole body leaned over the table.

"That's tonight and it's barely noon. I need to eat, and you said I can't just eat chicken nuggets and pizza." Evie pressed her chin to the top of Dilynn's computer. "Feed me, mother."

Dilynn glanced down at the fourteen pages of smut she'd composed since RunnerAT89 had continued to use capital letters at the start of sentences.

"Let me just post this real fast."

Evie got off the table. "I thought you quit after that troll was so rude."

The teen didn't wait for a response. She left to get ready to leave the house, which gave Dilynn enough time to copy, paste, and post.

The aroma of spicy seasonings and boiled crustaceans filled the air, causing Dilynn to have a momentary sensory seizure when the doors of the Cajun restaurant closed behind her. The din of chatter and laughter from nearby tables added to the lively ambiance, but Dilynn already regretted letting Evie rope her into engaging with this new, needed experience.

Evie's face spread into the type of smile Dilynn expected on Christmas morning when they were finally led to their table after a thirty-minute wait. Dilynn returned the smile with a mixture of excitement for her daughter and dread for herself. In the time they'd spent waiting for a table, Dilynn's insides had informed her she would not be enjoying this meal.

As the Greysons perused the menu of Hot n' Juicy, Dilynn offered Evie minimal guidance, pointing out things she'd heard other people describe as their favorite dishes. Evie didn't care about anything on the menu besides crawfish; the girl's newest fascination for a reason Dilynn would never understand.

As they waited for their drinks, Dilynn took in the newest chain of the Westgate Entertainment District. The walls were filled with warning signs for crocodiles and crawfish, buoys, lifesavers, dingy license plates, and paddles, while nets that looked to be dragged along the bottom of a swamp hung from the ceiling. She'd avoided places like this for all of her adult life, but the girl sitting across from her was bouncing in her chair.

Dilynn stopped scanning when she noticed the single occupant at the table behind them. She considered herself lucky that Alex hadn't seemed to notice their entrance as the woman was engrossed reading something on her phone that had her face flushed. Alex hadn't even touched the food yet, but Dilynn knew the eating part of the meal took the least amount of time. She would breathe a little easier though when Alex left, and she was able to avoid another conversation where she had to measure every word she said in fear it would just get back to Simone.

When the server arrived to take their order, Dilynn and Evie engaged in a silent standoff that ended in Evie ordering her own food. It was something the girl hated to do. An act of betrayal by Evie's standards so Dilynn engaged in a one-sided conversation as Evie stole the kids' menu Dilynn had requested to amuse herself.

Dilynn's phone vibrated with the comment alert as she was explaining to Evie that talking to people of different ages was a skill she would need when she was an adult. The sentence Dilynn was halfway through didn't seem to matter anyway; Evie was focused on coloring the crustaceans. Occasionally, the kid's eyes shot up over Dilynn's shoulder to the human Dilynn knew was sitting behind her.

Annoyed that Evie dragged her out only to ignore her, Dilynn turned her attention to the person who actually wanted her attention.

> RunnerAT89 on Chapter 12: You still haven't edited much but at least there's smut finally. This time you wrote it spicy and not the same boring fingers saw through her vagina nonsense. Made it real, not like a horror story.

Tin buckets were dropped off on the table before them. Dilynn looked over the edge at the plastic bag tied in a knot. She'd never had to pull her food out of a bag before, and now the plastic bib she'd been issued made more sense.

Dilynn peeked into Evie's bucket and noticed that the girl's bag was much redder than her own. By the look on the kid's face, Dilynn could tell Evie hadn't meant to order anything spicy, but she wouldn't complain. It was food, and even though Dilynn had spent the better part of two years trying to teach the kid she didn't have to eat food she didn't like, old conditioning from before she was adopted still took its toll.

Dilynn twisted open the top of the bag her crab legs came in. Humming quietly to herself, Dilynn studied the inside of the bucket before picking up the plastic bib that Evie had stated would not be worn by either of them. Clothes could be replaced; humiliation was something that wouldn't just go away, according to the teen. Evie's need to please people differed from Dilynn's though, and Alex had a bib on which meant Dilynn would definitely be needing it, so she didn't walk out with food on her shirt like a toddler.

"So did the troll find your story again?" Evie asked as she stared into her bag.

"I don't think they're a troll," Dilynn answered with a long crab leg in her hand.

She snapped the shell in two. The butter sauce the legs had been doused in squirted back at her, hitting her in the chin and the bib. She laughed at herself while she wiped away the mess.

"I just...." Her sentence dissolved when she considered what it was she was looking for. She couldn't exactly tell the girl that the troll was the only person she talked to each day besides kids. "Look, I just want to prove them wrong and screw with them for being a jerk face earlier."

"So, what are you going to say to the troll this time?"

Evie picked up a crawfish between her thumb and forefingers. Neither of them had eaten crawfish before. Dilynn thought they would come like lobster, not with eyes to stare at the kid.

"Are you supposed to eat the head?" Dilynn asked, making Evie lose the staring contest.

Evie looked up at her mother and swallowed. Dilynn followed her daughter's gaze and noticed Alex still sitting at the table alone. She watched as Alex snapped a crawfish in two with a twist of the wrist. The head was raised to the teacher's lips and... nope.

Dilynn turned back around before she puked. Those lips that she was so fascinated with trying to describe were now tainted. How anyone could do that to the head of something was... nope.

"I'm sorry," Evie apologized to the remains of her own lobster wannabe before snapping it in half. She stared at the now decapitated head, and Dilynn closed her eyes in case her daughter wanted to actually try crawfish in the manner in which Alex demonstrated.

She heard Evie gag, and it was enough to send Dilynn's stomach into somersaults. The mother pushed her bucket of crab legs towards the girl, but

Evie shoved it back.

"I can't do that thing, but I figured it out," she stated. Her eyes were still watching behind Dilynn, but the mother didn't have the courage to turn to her co-worker again.

Evie picked the lobster looking part from the tail, and said, "I can't do the head part. It's just... I don't know how Landon does this. He said last summer when we went to New Orleans to see his Nana that they had a crawfish boil, but he didn't say they suck out the brains."

Dilynn shrugged and picked the phone up from the table, ignoring the food that she couldn't eat without puking at the thought of eating something's brain. She focused on responding to the comment. She typed. Deleted. Retyped. Deleted. Twisted her mouth around a little, then started the whole comment over again.

'Ha! Aww, there you are! I thought I lost my harshest critic. Welcome back. BTW, I still despise your sentence fragments and run-on sentences. You write like one of my freshmen now.'

The message was sent before the phone was handed to the girl for approval. Evie tried not to roll her eyes while she read. She failed, but it was less dramatic than usual. An effort Dilynn felt was growth for them.

Enough time had passed for Dilynn to at least be somewhat hungry, and crab wasn't the worst type of seafood Sylvia had forced her to at least try. Crab legs turned out to be as much work as the crawfish. At least it was a distraction from the person still behind her. The person who'd shown up with a lesson plan Friday morning and claimed to need an orange.

Evie nudged Dilynn's hand. Nodding in Alex's direction, Evie asked, "Doesn't she work at school?"

"Yes," Dilynn whispered. She glanced back at Alex, taking in the distinctive difference between work Alex and Saturday Alex.

"Ask her to sit with us," Evie prodded. "She's going to be my teacher next year."

This was a new version of Alex for Dilynn to fantasize about. In a well-fitted t-shirt, the tall brunette's biceps seemed constantly flexed. The thin dri-fit joggers also left little for Dilynn to imagine as they clung to well chiseled thighs.

'Could probably lift my body weight,' Dilynn thought. She made a mental note to have Morgan throw Priya over her shoulder in the next chapter.

When Alex turned just enough to look back at them both, Dilynn practically fell out of her seat when her coworker locked eyes. Dilynn waved just enough to be polite and pointed at the license plate just over the loose head of dark curls.

"There's a V!" she declared. "We're just... playing the alphabet game."

Alex nodded with just a set of sharp green eyes. It was possibly the most impressive power move, and Dilynn added it to her list of new ways to describe Morgan.

"Uhm... so yeah, good to see you," Dilynn said in an overly cheerful voice.

Dilynn's work smile fell off her face when she turned back to her food. Silently, she signaled to her daughter 'nope' with a shake of her head; they were not asking Alex to come over. Lunch would not be another opportunity for Alex to learn new things to tell Simone that would be used to humiliate her. It was bad enough Alex had shown up yesterday morning, only to brew Dilynn a cup of coffee from her own coffee machine and ask a bunch of mentee-like teaching questions, just waiting for her to do something stupid.

"Wyatt's friend," Dilynn whispered so only her daughter would hear her.

"Are you two ever going to get over your little feud?"

Dilynn was breaking open another leg. There was no answer, just her already short body shrinking deeper into her seat.

Evie's lip slipped between her teeth, and she just gawked at Dilynn for a whole minute. A whole minute of people chewing, banging, and sucking the heads of crawfish loudly enough to make Dilynn's skin crawl.

Then words fell out of Evie's mouth too loudly. "You have the hots for my coach, don't you?"

Evie wasn't just teen girl loud. She was so loud Dilynn knew Alex had to hear the nonsense. And the worst thing was seeing the gleam in Evie's eyes. She would try to play match maker. Probably believed she wouldn't have to worry about her coach crawling into her bed in the middle of the night. But Dilynn knew better. Knew Simone wasn't just intimidating, but aggressive and determined to get what she wanted.

"I... crush no...." Dilynn shook her head violently and rubbed her hands over her face. "Not Simone. She's intimidating and she... she hates me."

Dilynn turned again, but Alex was walking away. Her eyes locked on the toned ass, and she imagined what it would be like to have someone like Alex actually interested in her, like that brief moment of hope she'd had before the break room door knocked some sense into her. Like scraping gravel out of a fresh cut, Alex was just playing another one of Simone's games with her already fragile heart.

She turned back to the table where the food she didn't want still sat. Getting through the food would be similar to getting through Simone's new game. She'd just make sure not to fall for it again. Like the mug Alex had tried to replace, knowing Simone had given it to her as a present when Dilynn had been stupid enough to think the other woman gave a damn about her.

Her forehead rested against the tin bucket. A small red line marked her pale skin when she sat up. She covered her face, then peeked through her fingers.

"Your coach and I... never going to be a thing." She checked the door again, then confessed, "Trikru. I have a crush on Trikru, but she's Wyatt's best friend so, it's not going to happen. And I just don't want to say anything that your coach can use to make life more hard. I'm just going to stay in my classroom for another year. Then I'm going to look for AP jobs at another school and I am going to get the experience I need so Sylvia will see I have the leadership skills I need to open my own school."

Evie tilted her head again. Fighting the smile back, she bit into her lip. The girl leaned against her hand and glanced down at her food.

"You know, we should go shopping, and a pedicure and food we actually want to eat," Evie stated. "I still need new cleats and you need new everything."

"Why would I go buy new everything?" Dilynn asked, genuinely concerned there was something wrong with her clothes.

Evie's finger played over the baggy cuff of Dilynn's bulky sweater.

"Is this sweater collecting unemployment? Because it's doing nothing for you," Evie's smile spread slowly over her face.

It was meant to be a joke, but Dilynn's sweaters had gotten so large they looked to be trying to swallow her whole. Except the one Alex had gotten her for Secret Santa. It had fit and she'd loved it until Monday morning when she'd realized Simone just had a new player in the game to fuck with her. A player that knew she was single.

Alex had probably called Simone and told her immediately about Dilynn getting dumped in the mall. Laughed together about her getting humiliated.

Evie reached out and took Dilynn's hand in her own. She ran her thumb over Dilynn's fingers.

"What are you scared of?" she asked. "Trikru looked back at you at least a hundred times. She probably likes you too. Like, you have no idea how many teachers at school are always looking at you."

Dilynn couldn't tell Evie that her coworkers looked at her because they thought she was a prostitute. She couldn't share with Evie that Simone's and her feud wasn't just something dumb. Telling Evie that Simone had spread rumors to force her to leave would only make the kid go on a tirade to dispute the rumors, which would only make them the talk of the faculty again.

"Alex Trikru is just... beautiful. I mean, I know you have eyes. And I couldn't sit with her because every time I speak to her, I say something stupid, and I turn into a tomato because she is out of my league. Like way, way out of my league."

Dilynn picked at the skin on her lower lip. Her eyes flicked back to the door that Alex had left through. Cheeks were still flushed when she admitted, "Plus, it's too soon. No one even knows... you know that... I'm single besides you and Trikru, and she only knows because she was there at the mall. And... the only person I have had a crush on is that human, who is built like a demi-god. Like Sylvia is beautiful, but Alex... and I shouldn't. I can't crush on Wyatt's best friend."

Evie's eyes scanned over Dilynn. She chewed on an invisible bite of food with her planning face on. Slowly, she asked, "And you're sure you don't have a thing for Coach?"

"I'm sure," Dilynn promised, because she didn't. She wanted to get as far away from the other woman as possible. "I never did, and I never will."

10

The giant box fought Alex all the way down the stairs. It was actually more difficult to get it down than it had been up when it was filled with the smooshed face punching dummy. A dummy they'd named Simone for hurting the woman now doing her best not to look at them.

They dragged the box down a flight of stairs, then chucked it over the landing. The haul to the dumpster was almost as bad, but nothing compared to trying to get it into the recycling container. The job needed two people. One to hold the lid and the other to pick up the box. There were never two people though, so Alex used their anger to push the box up under the lip of the lid. Forced it open with a grunt and a few Spanish curses. Once the box slid within, they carried themself back upstairs.

Blinds clicked against one another. The front door caused the slightest disturbance in the air, just enough to bring the suggestion of life to the room. Closing their eyes, Alex tried not to focus on the emptiness.

With nothing pressing to do they grabbed their phone. The email app had a small red bubble with the number four. Four new messages. The second was the important one though. The subscription notification that GreyAltEgo had updated her fic.

They were about to click the link right there on the phone and read it while standing at the counter. They reconsidered though.

When they were out and the update came through, then yes, the only sensible thing to do was to drop everything to read it. However, at home they were able to fully absorb the story. They could take their time preparing for a potentially feisty conversation with the author, who always seemed to be up late.

Opening the laptop, Alex brushed away the few particles of dust on the desk. They avoided disheveling the stacks of meticulously graded writing samples and took a glance at the calendar.

Tomorrow was Sunday, which would be just another lonely day. Monday, though, they would go see Dilynn in her classroom again. They'd get to talk to her about what they would say to Simone, and she would let them say it this time. Let them tell her that they wouldn't be friends with the woman if she didn't stop hurting Dilynn. Then maybe they'd get invited to a Greyson Pizza Night.

'She'd said hi at Hot n' Juicy,' Alex reminded themself.

If Simone hadn't hurt Dilynn, maybe she would have asked them to join her and her kid for lunch. Evie hadn't known what to do with the food. They snuck a peek back and saw her staring at the crawfish. They showed her so she could do it without making a big deal out of it. But Evie had brought up Simone. They'd heard her say Dilynn had a crush on Simone.

Evie had to be wrong though. She had to be, because Dilynn did everything possible to avoid looking at Simone. Dilynn also avoided them now, and she'd admitted to drooling over them. But she said she was going to leave because of Simone.

'Dilynn couldn't like Simone.'

Alex's shoulders relaxed. They practiced smiling at the computer. Imagined the woman's oceanic eyes lighting up as she looked at them like she actually saw them. Not just another coworker in the crowd when she helped the pep rally team keep the kids in line. She would look at them like when she'd given them the tie.

Imagining her looking at them again made Alex want to be stronger. If she was crushing on Simone, then Alex could show her they were stronger and not mean.

Alex could make her laugh. She probably needed someone to make her laugh. They tried to think of a joke to practice. Nothing came to mind besides 'knock, knock.' Even then, they had nothing to follow with but, 'Go out with me'. They kicked the part of themself that threw out halfheartedly, 'and then have babies with me'.

Their brain malfunctioned briefly as they concluded that if Dilynn wanted babies and they looked like her, Alex would be in love with them. They could be a parent. Better than theirs, at least. Love a kid for who they are, not who society wanted them to be.

Love.

They'd read hundreds of stories about love at first sight. They never believed one of them, but the Secret Santa smile on Dilynn's face was one they immediately loved. Just like they knew they would take a punch from the ex or give up ties with Simone if she didn't stop hurting the blonde.

So many things were running through their head that Alex had to catch themself. They had to remind themself that gorgeous women like Dilynn Greyson don't want anything to do with people who are too far outside of normal. She just wanted to hide in her classroom.

The computer logged in, and they were opening the link to GreyAltEgo's story. Alex lost the nervous energy two paragraphs in. Found themself lost in the scene. The follow up to the smut was filled with dreaded angst, like happiness was constantly out of reach.

Each sentence from Priya was a little more betrayed, and they wondered if maybe GreyAltEgo was alone, too. If she saw herself in Priya, then it would make sense why she would write stories where Morgan saw her. In the book Morgan never gave Priya the time of day she deserved. Alex could understand that. They found Morgan's need to be seen as stoic and strong in the novel relatable.

Whoever GreyAltEgo was, it was clear she understood what it meant to fall head over heels for a woman out of her grasp. How if felt to pine after someone, and never be able to say the right thing.

Slowly, they read through the scene again.

> Priya left Morgan's classroom when the sun had long since set. Her legs were still weak from holding her position through her climax. She hated the way she felt empty now.
>
> It had been everything Priya had dreamed of. The other woman's cool command pressing Priya's face to the desk as they worked her panties to the side. Stuffed her dripping core with her fingers and set a rough pace she'd continue to feel for hours later.
>
> She could still hear Morgan telling her how much of a good girl she was. A part of her felt ashamed of giving herself up to Morgan so easily. No date. Not even dinner. Just letting the other woman spank her ass for a snarky remark she'd made and then fuck her with all her clothes still on.
>
> Walking passed the social studies classroom would never be the same. Her scalp still ached from where Morgan had twisted her hair into a fist so Priya couldn't hide her moans. It had been amazing, and Morgan had kissed her afterwards.
>
> Then it was done.
>
> Priya left without the woman's phone number. Realized she'd fallen for a woman who'd never love her, just wanted her compliantly bent over the desk. Didn't want her naked since she was built like marshmallows stuck together with toothpick limbs. The type of girl Morgan wouldn't want to see naked. Morgan hadn't even wanted Priya to touch her.
>
> She stepped into her own classroom. What once was a place she used to escape, now felt like a cage. A cage she'd have to come to everyday knowing just a few doors away Morgan would remember her ass up like the proper slut she'd reminded Priya she was.

> It was hot for a moment until it settled on the surface of
> who Priya had become. Just another stupid girl giving
> herself over to the first person that feigned interest in her.
>
> She was just a slut, wasn't she. Needy enough who let her
> coworker use her as a fuck toy and send her back to her
> cage until the woman would want more. If she wanted
> more.
>
> What if she was so lousy Morgan wouldn't want more?
>
> Priya wiped the smeared eyeliner from under her eyes.
> She'd wanted too badly for someone like Morgan to want
> her. Someone to want her.
>
> No one would love her though. She was just the girl
> Morgan wanted to fuck when no one was around. Would
> never want to be seen with her in public. Never want to hold
> her and press kisses to her head as she promised that
> tomorrow she'd still want her.

Alex was grateful for once that they lived alone. At least no one could see the first tear escape as they felt the cage closing in on them. No explanation could have better described their every day.

Still sobbing and just trying to catch their breath, Alex looked over the house. Took a moment to measure their own creation. Their own self-imposed solitary confinement with sharp lines and hard surfaces.

Alex hadn't meant to end up in a cage when they ran away from home. They'd never wanted isolation, and they tried to figure out at what point they chose this life. The running began as a way to escape the closet they were locked in, but they put themselves back in because of money. Convinced themself safety came from hiding. Hiding while telling themself they were valid wasn't validating.

They looked for a way out.

The chair tipped backwards when Alex stood. It was time to stop being someone they didn't like. Time to break out of the cage. Break out of the closet by redefining their wardrobe so they could live in the light instead of the shadow.

Time was changing. Marriage was legal now no matter what gender a person was. People were talking about gender.

Grabbing a baggy shirt, they made their way to the front closet and pulled on the colorful shoes. The shoes they'd regretted buying because they'd convinced themself it was a label.

They got them on, and they were out the door. They had to go back to the mall for the second time. Or maybe Kohl's. Any clothing store really.

Towards the stores to spend money that they never thought they should spend to create a new version of them. A version of Alex that on Monday they could be proud to present to the English teacher. The woman who'd said they could pull off a burlap sack.

Dialing the phone, they called Simone. She may be an asshole, but she was the only person who'd made it a point to somewhat care. She'd have to be there if they asked.

Simone's voice was just as annoyed as last time, and they wondered if there was ever a time that she and Marissa were not humping.

"I need your help," they told Simone.

"What now?" she grunted.

They hadn't stopped screwing even for a second. Alex felt like maybe they should be disturbed that the couple answered the phone and proceeded to have sex while they were a third-party witness. The couple liked a third person though, which is why Alex had stopped going out with Simone. She was always taking someone else home to Marissa, and Alex decided they didn't want it to be them.

"And I swear to God, if this is about fucking Dilynn Greyson, I will evict you."

"I need new clothes," they tell her. "I need to stop living like my body is a cage. I'm headed to the mall... but you know... I can't just go into the sections because the guys look at me weird. The girls look at me weird. Just come with me, please."

There was a whispered, *"I got to go,"* and then movement. The phone was covered, and Simone and Marissa must be arguing because their voices were loud enough to be heard, but not clear enough to be understood.

Alex paused in the parking lot. Orion's Belt shone down at them. They thought of GreyAltEgo. Maybe she saw the same constellations as they did.

"Stop hating yourself," Simone yelled through the speaker. *"I'm coming. Just promise me, no more black. Something with color."*

"I want her to like me." The confession was quiet, and Alex felt like they were losing all the control they'd worked so meticulously to hold onto.

Simone didn't answer right away. They only heard her breathing for several moments. After a heavy exhale, Simone had apparently worked through her thoughts.

"I hate her," Simone reminded them. *"You know that."*

There was another sigh, followed with a plea, *"Anyone else, Alex. I'm begging you to choose anyone besides the blonde Barbie with her plastic crown and cardboard fucking castle."*

There was no one else though. No changing their mind. Even as they stood in the yellow lit lot, they could see her hips swaying while she lip-synced in front of the entire student body. She made them smile that day, even though they'd vowed not to smile for the first month of school. Dilynn cracked Alex with her sparkly shirt wrapped so perfectly over her chest, hair bouncing around in a messy knot atop her head, and laughter dancing when she moved left and the football team right.

"I can't help it if I met my queen," Alex said.

There were several choked gags, and then they heard, "*Your queen?!*"

Alex rubbed their hand over their face. It was a terrible line. Worse than their knock-knock joke.

"I swear to everything holy, I am disowning you."

"You wouldn't," Alex stated. They remembered then what they had to do. "And you're going to stop being mean to her. Completely and totally stop being mean to her because I love her and if you don't stop being mean to her, she's going to leave. She told me she is leaving after Evie graduates because of how cruel you are to her. And I know you are a good person, so stop being mean to her."

Simone's car beeped. The line went dead for a moment before Simone was talking like she was in a tunnel.

"She's planning on leaving?"

"Yes, she doesn't feel safe because of you. You... you made fun of her weight, Simone. There is so much more that you have said about her, but that one.... Did you even see how much that hurt her?" Alex rubbed their face. "I'm pretty sure you could have punched her in the face, and it would have hurt less."

"I was... I just..."

"It needs to stop," Alex stated. "You have to stop trying to punish her for not wanting to kiss you. Because if you don't, then you really are a bad person. Because she should be able to say no to you and you respect it."

Simone was quiet for a moment. Long enough for Alex to need to check that the phone hadn't disconnected.

"I'll be civil, but I can't promise it will be easy. She... she tried to get me fired."

"You should apologize to her," Alex stated.

"Fuck right to the top of Fuck Off Mountain and yeet your ass off of it." Simone snapped. *"I'm on my way, but you can forget that apology. It's not happening. I will be civil. That's it because you are important to me."*

They made their way back up the stairs trying to figure out where they had heard that phrase before. Simone's house was twenty minutes away. Alex had twenty minutes to comment on GreyAltEgo's new chapter.

11

Dilynn's keys fell to the entry table. The bags of her Evie-approved wardrobe were set on the ground. She hadn't even set her purse down before Evie retreated down the dark hallway to her room to prepare to go to her friend's party.

The mother paused at the entrance to the hallway. Flipping the light switch, she realized the bulb was still out. With a sigh, she added a lightbulb to her mental list of things to get at Target again. There were other things she needed, but she couldn't remember them at the moment.

Retreating to her own room, she stripped away the clothes reserved for strangers. Yoga pants and a loose tank were much more appropriate for staying home and pretending not to exist. No one was there to notice her tits hung lower than they should at 27 years old.

She went through the parental pre-party checklist in her head. As she turned the corner though, she felt the need to reiterate the agreement Evie and she had forged after the first party war.

"No drugs!" Dilynn called out.

There was a loud groan, and Dilynn could picture the eye roll she seemed to always get from the kid. Drugs didn't seem to be an issue, but it was an extreme and Evie typically tolerated extreme reminders better than the others.

Evie echoed her mother after the drawers of the girl's dresser slapped closed. "Don't do drugs!"

"Call if drunk," Dilynn added the more sensitive item. She couldn't expect her daughter not to drink when all her friends were drinking. Dilynn would have jumped at the opportunity to drink in high school if she had any friends. Possibly her greatest overcompensation as a parent was embracing her daughter's popularity and not pretending to be a mother that would interfere with it.

Dilynn gathered the things she would need to enter hyperfocus while Evie was out. When getting ice for her coffee, she noticed the bottle of vodka in the freezer. She tried to remember the last time the girl smelled like booze.

Evie had been to at least a dozen parties since the start of junior year. Dilynn scanned over each memory of the next day. She never seemed hungover the next morning. In fact, there had only been once. At the beginning of the basketball season, but she'd sworn she wasn't drunk. Promised she'd just tried to talk some sense into someone, and they didn't take her seriously, which ended in the other person wearing a beer that splashed back at Evie.

Evie's head peeked around the wall separating her space and the living room. She was parting her hair to damage it some more with the curling iron.

Dilynn added 'check that curling iron is unplugged so I don't burn to death in a house fire,' to her list of things to do. Then she added, 'go to Target,' after it. She wouldn't get drunk if she had to go to the store.

With hair parted, Evie said, "Call if I need a ride because I drank."

Settling at the table with the laptop open, Dilynn tried to picture her main character sitting across from her. The conversation would happen in Dilynn's head, of course. She couldn't have Evie thinking she had completely lost her mind, especially after Brandon had told her talking to fictional characters was crazy.

The writer chewed on the inside of her cheek when she manifested the sixteen-year-old warrior queen. The last time they'd chatted, her character had been unmarked by war. Now, her cheeks were sunk in, and the once shiny face was coated in ash and anger. Dilynn catalogued the gruesome scene where she castrated Brandon. It would go into the next novel.

Dilynn wanted to start at the big moment. She needed her main character, Atlas to tell her what the climax of the story was. So, she asked her. Well, she tried to until the girl disappeared from Dilynn's mind. The warrior teen left her with a blank document. The flashing line was painfully irritating.

Just as she saw a short mental clip of the wreckage it vanished. The front door closed like a director's clapboard, and Dilynn looked up from the still blank document to Landon walking through the house. He didn't look up from his phone when he navigated into the kitchen and opened the refrigerator. Finding a Tupperware of mystery food within, he held it up.

"This taken?"

Dilynn's lips pursed, and she shook her head. "I don't even know what that is or how long it's been in there."

Tupperware in the refrigerator of the Greyson house was like a jellybean on the Hogwarts's Express. It could be something Evie made, which at least meant at one point it was probably edible. It could be something Dilynn cooked, so it probably wasn't good. Either way, there was still a chance it was a science experiment at this point.

Landon's nose crinkled up, and the 14-year-old she'd known from her third period freshmen English class stood in her kitchen. She could never thank him enough for coming to her when he'd worried about the mean girl who tried to cover the bruises. The girl he took home to his mother because she was too drunk to consent to the senior with his hand up her shirt. He'd come to Dilynn for help, not knowing it would change all of their lives.

When she got a daughter after that conversation, she didn't realize she would be getting a son as well. One that she would share custody of with his military mother. His mother loved Dilynn's daughter just as fiercely though, and the arrangement was beneficial for both women. Imara and Dilynn weren't friends, but they'd made an agreement that neither kid would face the uncertainty of what happens if they lost their parent again.

Dilynn blinked twice as Landon's face twisted in disgust. Whatever was in the container must not meet muster. The whole thing was tossed in the trash before Landon opted for a safer route by pulling a party sized bag of chips from the pantry.

Evie's footsteps drew Dilynn's gaze from Landon. The mother tried to fix her grimace, but she couldn't. Her upper lip curled over her teeth. With a shake of her head, Dilynn pointed back to the hallway.

"At least a shirt that meets the shorts, please."

Evie looked down at her outfit. Her hand rested against her generous abdominal muscles.

"But..." Evie began to argue, then stopped. She must have noticed the 'no' in Dilynn's eyes. Grunting in displeasure, Evie stomped back to her room.

Landon took a seat at the head of the table. Not wanting to be rude, Dilynn closed the laptop and gave him her full attention.

"How's life?" she asked. "Last we talked your mom wanted you to go to an ROTC camp this summer."

Landon's head fell back while his shoulders drooped under the weight of his thick arms.

"She arranged some meeting with her Colonel so he will write me letters of rec for West Point." He licked his lips. "I don't know how to tell her that I have no interest in enlisting. My dad died in a war. She's gone every year or two for another. And it's just... it's not for me. I want to be a lawyer and I told her that, but she just said that I should join so they will put me through law school."

His fingers fisted the legs of his jeans. He clenched tightly, with forearms flexing. Dilynn couldn't hear him. The subtle movement of his lips was a clear conversation being had with himself before he exhaled very slowly.

"It's just... just the same shit, different day," he whispered. As the words left his mouth, he looked up wide-eyed. "Sorry, I meant same stuff, different day."

Dilynn couldn't help but laugh at him.

"You know fuck is my favorite word, right?" Dilynn offered. "It's just a word. They are all just words, and some hurt. However, shit, fuck, ass... dick... umm... fartknocker."

She was still trying to think of others, but fartknocker had broken through. His mouth spread into a wide smile, and he rubbed the stress from his face.

"My mom would..." his words faded away before they reached Dilynn, and he changed subjects. "Just, why won't she listen?"

Dilynn reached over and laid her hand on his forearm. Imara was Dilynn's coparent. They didn't have to be in a relationship for Dilynn to know she couldn't undermine her. She had to support Imara, even though Dilynn felt sending Landon to basic training felt like a disservice to the boy and the world. Imara believed military service was the best route for her son. She'd explained to Dilynn the importance of her son going through the ROTC program because she saw it as an opportunity for him. Their family were all soldiers, and she saw her son as a commander one day. Dilynn didn't have to agree with it, she just needed to support Imara because Imara had come at times when Evie was at her worst to talk sense into the girl.

Before Dilynn could think of something to reassure Landon that his mother was listening to him, Evie reemerged in a thin floral printed top that covered her stomach and bust. Dilynn sighed, one spilled drink and it would be for naught.

If this was one of Evie's tests to see if Dilynn would break, Dilynn was not going to fail it. Not today, not ever. She claimed the change of attire as a win and waved the young couple away.

Evie kissed Dilynn's head before taking Landon's hand. With his arm pulled out in front of him like a leash, he offered Dilynn a lazy wave before loyally following his girlfriend.

The kiss was something new. A new form of contact from the kid that always kept an arms distance away. That was a real win for Dilynn.

Reopening the computer, Dilynn tried to manifest the warrior queen again. When the royal pain in the ass refused the call, Dilynn distracted herself on the fanfiction site. Opening the site turned in to reading through canonical stories by other authors. She stayed away from any of the explicit tales of sixteen-year-old Atlas and any of the other characters. She really avoided any stories that weren't focused on Priya and Morgan. Especially the ones labeled as ABO fics. The last thing she needed was to imagine her kid growing a dog shaped dong and chasing after anyone that smelled like flowers or forest. She noticed the fandom was currently focused on werewolf stories, so she tucked that into her back pocket. If she couldn't think of anything else to write, she would play in a different universe to appeal to more readers.

After reading what felt like the same stories with song titles, Dilynn decided the time had come to write a chapter for her own alternative story. She'd left Priya in her classroom beating herself up for letting Morgan have her way with her. What should have been a huge win had turned painful, so she needed Morgan to make a move. Show the interest was greater than just a need to get off.

It was a dangerous game to play, because she knew where the hope was rooted. The part of her that wanted Alex to have come to see her not for a game had been gagged and tied up in a corner. To write this scene, Dilynn would have to let that part of herself free. Have to listen to what her mind said Alex might be thinking, and it would hurt when it turned out the rest of her had been right. When Alex proved what Dilynn already knew.

She did it anyway though. Began with an event that had happened because the setting would be easy, and she could still remember the way her body had come to life when Alex had been standing outside her door on Friday morning.

Dilynn placed the new chapter the next morning with Morgan coming to Priya's classroom. Like Alex had visited her, Morgan came with a simple request for planning help. A moment of fluffy happiness RunnerAT89 would despise, which was well worth it. She provided Priya a flicker of hope, like Dilynn felt when Alex came in before she remembered it was just a move in a game of chess that she'd managed to wear time down on.

Tapping the keys, Dilynn wrote Morgan kinder than the commanding domme from the day before. She gave the character a gentleness not focused on forcing Priya into a constant state of submission. Dilynn charted out questions that gave Priya a moment to shine. Dilynn's lips formed an evil smile at her cruel witchery. She'd cast a spell so annoyingly gentle and kind it was bound to get another rise out of RunnerAT89. At least then her night wouldn't be boring.

The chapter took about twenty minutes to write out the dialogue. She went back and added the body language to show the reader how the characters were really feeling when they lied through their teeth that everything was okay. Then she added critical setting details between the other two components to allow the reader to pause and, at times, lose track of the conversation briefly like one would while listening to people talk.

By hour two, she had a little more than 2000 words covered in milk chocolate RunnerAT89 would surely call shit. Dilynn was okay with that though. She wrote of what she'd wish would come from her own parallel tale. One where Alex stopped being Simone's knight.

She posted the new chapter without previewing it, knowing it would taunt the troll into engaging her. Her finger pulled back with satisfaction settling over her lips. A short-lived satisfaction due to the knock coming from the door.

Checking the phone, Dilynn realized whoever was at the door wasn't going to be asking her to sign a petition. Nor was the person a friend, because a friend would've just walked in.

She couldn't help but construct a litany of ways this could be the beginning of a horrible murder plot. Dilynn got up quietly and moved into the kitchen. She pulled a knife from the wooden block on the counter. Decided she'd written enough battle scenes to know what to do. Justified she could use it if someone attacked her.

As Dilynn approached the door cautiously, the bell rang. Whoever was there wasn't going away. Her hand hovered over the handle. She could just snap the lock in place. It would be that simple.

Looking through the peephole, she was immediately grateful the porch light outside did, in fact, work when the hallway light was still out because she never went to Target. She was not grateful for the girl, who'd locked lips with Brandon several weeks prior, standing on her porch. Dilynn took a deep breath, then threw open the door like a crazed psycho.

The girl's dark eyes were wide, and her lips spread into a streetwise smile until she saw the knife. Tension bubbled up in a wall between them. It was just clear enough for each to take their time judging each other. The silence broke when the girl spoke with a playful cadence that tickled Dilynn like a stranger poking her in the side.

"Promise, I'm not here to start shit." The girl's hands rose, showing Dilynn she was unarmed. "Let's not be those girls that hate each other. Let's blame the asshole."

Blue eyes attempted to kill the woman telepathically but failed. Irritation and inadequacy blanketed the few growing embers of success she'd had with finishing her chapter. This girl was what Evie had said, probably the same age as she was.

Dilynn breathed out the deadly carbon dioxide with the question, "What the fuck are you doing on my porch?"

"I am sorry," the girl began with. "I just... there was... I was—"

The girl was still talking, even though Dilynn wasn't listening. She watched the ochre arms sway at her sides and hickory eyes rise to the spider witnessing the event. The spit and fire erupting from Dilynn only minutes prior evaporated in the hazy yellow glow on the porch of the house, replaced with a distinct need to vomit.

The war drum raging in her ears got louder as Dilynn processed Evie's justified fear of Brandon. She'd told Dilynn he was a pervert, and Dilynn wondered if Evie had known more than she'd ever shared. He'd worked at the group home she was at. It was how they had met, and her heart broke at the thought of how many girls had been at his mercy.

"I came to make peace with you," the girl said breaking through.

Dilynn ran her eyes up and down the kid again. When faced with a shitty situation, teenage girls lied. Evie taught Dilynn that to its fullest, but Dilynn had her own secrets. She'd told her own fair share of lies and the look in the kid's eyes was enough to tell Dilynn, this girl was no different.

'She's too thin,' Dilynn assessed. She looked over the girl's clothes and hair. 'She hasn't showered in a while. Toes of the boots are curled. They're too big.'

Her eyes wandered to the street where a beat-up truck sat in front of the racist neighbor's house. Dilynn memorized the plate number in case the girl decided to rob her while she was at work.

"What's your name?" Dilynn swallowed the follow up question where she wanted to know how old the girl was.

The thin hand pressed against the same shirt the girl had been wearing a few weeks ago. "I'm Lyra. Lyra Reyes."

Dilynn briefly wondered if this was her first lie, and how many more she would have to listen to before the kid left. But Dilynn suddenly reconciled the reality that when the kid left, she probably had no place to go.

"I didn't know about you," Lyra told her.

The look on Lyra's face at the mall told Dilynn she'd known. She'd known he was taken. This was for sure a lie.

"He told me I was his one."

Brandon didn't talk like that. He didn't believe in the concept of one love. She counted that as lie 2.

Lying Lyra's eyes fell back to the knife in the woman's left hand. The girl took a step back, causing the porch board to creak under a tattered boot that was obviously too big.

"We met a few years ago," Lyra continued. She opened her mouth to keep going, but snapped it shut. Her eyes searched the ground, making Dilynn feel like that actually might be the truth. That was when she'd purchased the building for him after he found out she had money. Shelters were open at night, so he was supposed to be there. At least, that's what he said. He was a liar like the kid though.

"He had an apartment, and I moved in with him."

He had lied about being at the shelter then. The apartment was supposed to be gone. He'd claimed it had flooded when a broken pipe caused the tub in the unit above him to fall through the ceiling. She'd only seen the place once. Couldn't even remember where it was because two weeks later it was destroyed. She'd let him move in when he'd worried about paying for a hotel that the apartment complex would only reimburse him for.

She briefly considered paying the kid for the address. Lyra could clearly use the money for food or rent, and Dilynn could buy the apartment complex, then light it on fire with him still inside. She shook her head slowly. Apartments had lots of people and burning other people's homes wouldn't fix her rage.

"I thought he was working at the shelter when he wasn't home." Without a doubt, this was Lyra Lie #3, and it caused Dilynn's eyes to roll.

"I thought he was getting ready to propose."

Dilynn's body felt like Lyra cranked the furnace dial to the hottest setting. Maybe he had told Lyra she was his one true love. Maybe the plan was to leave her and stay with the girl.

She retreated within the house and set the knife on the entry table. With shaking hands, she twisted the engagement ring from her short finger. Tears fell as the skin on her hand brightened.

Holding it in two fingers, she examined it. Dilynn had dozens of rings in her jewelry box from the woman that never proposed to her. Sylvia had paraded her through enough jewelry stores to spoil her once upon a time, so Dilynn knew the stone wasn't worth more than a hundred bucks.

She never should have put it back on after he called her a selfish cunt. He'd shown her who he was in that moment. Showed her he would do anything to get her money, and she'd refused to accept it. Needed to be more than just a wallet.

With breath caught in her throat, she stopped hearing the clock on the wall ticking. Time froze to give her a moment. Just a single stolen moment that snapped back into motion before the drums of war ceased their pounding. An immeasurable expansion from isolation to shared fragile existence. Speeding up only when the dead air seemed to come back to life.

"Well, he is all yours!"

The dust lifted into the air as though Dilynn's bellow was the very source that all wind came from, whipping Lyra's ponytail around her ears and face.

With a flick of her wrist, the ring twirled through the air in Lyra's direction. The girl snatched it in her fist.

Lyra sized up the ring, then shook her head. Holding it back out for Dilynn, she said, "He was never going to marry me. I know that now. I... I wouldn't have married him either. I just came to apologize."

More excuses exited Lyra's mouth without much thought until she was blubbering. She snapped her lips closed. Then, Lyra took a deep breath so the words would come out slowly, "Look, I need you to know—"

Evie's ringtone started playing within the safety of the walls. The annoying overplayed radio song blaring in the kitchen dragged Dilynn's attention from the unwanted visitor to her phone.

Without saying a word, Dilynn turned from the door, and left Lyra on the porch. She didn't shut the door. Didn't have it in her to close a door in a kid's face. Especially one who'd been used by someone she trusted.

"Hey, E. What's up?" Dilynn said, trying to school her tone.

"How young is too young to have sex?" Evie asked on the other end of the line.

Dilynn turned just enough to see Lyra standing in her house and taking inventory of the table. Maybe she should have shut the door.

"I can't just give you a number," Dilynn stated. "I trust you to know your body and your mind so just... use a condom, okay?"

"Ewww, no. Not me. Casey is with this girl. She's a freshman, and I just... I'm not okay." She could hear Evie trying to count her breaths, before she added, *"I know when I was with Casey, I was too young, but it's different. We're juniors and the girl.... She's just a freshman."*

Lyra's finger grazed over the empty nail head protruding from the wall over the table. Dilynn's eyes fell back to the knife. The huge ass knife that she could have used to gut Lyra and simply called it trespassing.

"E," Dilynn said, as she continued to watch the girl. *"Tell Casey to stop. If she refuses, then you have my permission to hit her."*

Lyra's whole body froze. For a second, she looked back at the door, and Dilynn was satisfied the girl remembered Evie could throw a punch.

"She's my best friend," Evie whispered.

Dilynn understood why Evie was worried. High school was a tough place without a friend but being friends with someone who takes advantage of younger girls wasn't someone Evie needed to be friends with.

"I trust you to do what needs to be done to protect the girl," Dilynn stated. "Stay with the kid, too. Don't storm off. You two can drive her home or stay there with her, just let me know which way you decide."

"Kay."

Evie hung up without saying goodbye. She never said goodbye, and Dilynn loved that. It meant she was planning on coming home.

Lyra was looking at herself in the mirror hanging over the table. She fixed her ponytail. The drooping bags under her eyes gave away the last few days of no sleep. The purple shirt had a grease stain on it like she'd crawled out from under a car after stealing a catalytic converter. Dilynn's eyes dropped back to the kid's boots. She wanted to know why Lyra was wearing work boots. They looked like they were steel toed, which felt a little extreme. Maybe a protective measure if she's back on the street.

The phone clattered against the table. Dilynn's molars disintegrated the questions she wanted to ask. She chose to focus on a problem she could address with a kid that didn't lie to her. She'd need to have a one-on-one with Casey. The girl knew what Evie had been through. Knew that girls that young were off limits. Like Lyra should have been off limits.

"She's a beautiful girl," Lyra said. She pointed towards the picture.

Dilynn would deal with Casey at school if she showed her face in Dilynn's classroom. Right now, there was a different kid that had walked through the door. One scared enough to lie over and over again, but desperate enough to stand on a porch she knew she wasn't welcome on.

"Dilynn," she said.

"That's a good name," Lyra answered, glancing back at the photo of the mother and daughter. "She'll get interviews with that name because people will think she's a white boy."

"No, not her." Dilynn's hand tapped her chest. "I'm Dilynn. You're Lyra."

"Oh, right. She's Evie," Lyra answered.

If there was any lingering question of Lyra knowing before, she'd just provided the proof she'd known. Dilynn hadn't said Evie's name, but Lyra knew it. Which meant Lyra didn't just know that Brandon was with someone. She'd known who both Dilynn and Evie were.

Dilynn looked around and wondered how many times Brandon had brought Lyra here. Brought the girl into her home. Probably slept with Lyra in her bed. It was the only way Lyra would have known where to come to.

Lyra extended her hand out for a proper greeting. "Nice to meet you, Dilynn."

Dilynn looked at it for so long it started to shake. Instead of the hand, the blonde shook her head. Slowly she caught her breath after choking on a half-hearted laugh.

"There is nothing nice about this meeting, Lyra."

Dilynn left Lyra standing in the self-imposed quicksand to pull an almost empty bottle of vodka from the freezer. "Evie's not here so I'm going to take a minute to forget that him and you were.... I just need to forget."

She poured a shot, then looked at the cabinet. Lyra wasn't old enough to drink, but Dilynn also knew she wasn't going to get any information from her if the kid knew Dilynn was counting her lies.

"You are old enough to drink, aren't you?" Dilynn asked, pulling another glass from the cabinet and holding it out.

Lyra moved to the granite topped breakfast counter. She looked at the shot glass for a moment, then said, "I don't think I can handle just vodka."

Dilynn sucked her teeth. It was a well-played move on the girl's part. She walked back to the table and scooped up her phone. The Thai food place down the road delivered, and she had the number saved for nights without Evie.

"My kid made me eat seafood today and I still feel like the crab is trying to crawl its way back up my throat," she told Lyra. "Fried rice and pad Thai, okay?
"

"Yeah, sure," Lyra stated with a hesitancy that made Dilynn think she probably should have ordered pizza.

After a few more taps, she declared, "Food should be here in like thirty minutes."

Her phone clattered against the counter, then her shot of vodka was in her hand and the other was held out to Lyra.

"I'm a teacher, so I'm going with the story that you showed me an ID saying you are at least 21."

Dilynn watched the girl look at the shot. Even though the bird-like frame didn't shake nervously, there was a bubbling of impatience in the room. When Lyra took the shot from her, their fingers barely touched. It was just enough contact to cause the guilt to rise in her chest at backing the kid into a corner.

She released the glass quickly and threw back her shot to sterilize her insides. The bottle was at the shot glass rim instantly, and Dilynn poured another. She could handle at least a fourth of the bottle. Years of practice had her on the verge of being an alcoholic. The edge she would walk away from tomorrow.

Dilynn picked up her phone again. Checked it to see if RunnerAT89 had responded and give Lyra time to make some decisions. She'd gotten in the door, which seemed to be the girl's goal. Whatever she wanted was still unclear though.

With no message from her troll yet, she turned her attention back to Lyra. The shot was still in the girl's hand, and Dilynn took note of the fact the girl didn't want to drink. Maybe it was the type of booze, or maybe she didn't like booze. Or she had crafted the next steps of her plan.

It was the latter, Dilynn noted when Lyra leaned over the counter. Dropped her chin just a little and looked up at Dilynn. She'd written the action probably a hundred times in different fics. A façade of flirtation that the kid doubled down on when she angled so the top of her shirt was open. There was just enough space that if Dilynn looked, she could see down.

Holding the glass up, Lyra offered a toast. "To freedom... and new possibilities."

Dilynn didn't echo her call. Short fingers just tipped the third shot into her mouth. Her head fell back, and she groaned.

Lyra choked for air to ease the burn of the shot she took. A liar that doesn't drink were two truths Dilynn could count on.

Dilynn poured the kid another shot. Then held it out to Lyra. When she took the shot glass from Dilynn, Lyra touched her a little more deliberately. A graze that couldn't be accidental. Lyra smiled softer, dropped her chin again so her eyes would be bigger. Played innocent in a way that probably got her what she wanted.

She could see another fragment of the young soul fracturing as she prepared to be whatever Dilynn wanted—however Dilynn wanted. She knew the look. Gave the look to Sylvia in a club at seventeen, but Sylvia was nineteen and just as desperate as Dilynn.

'She needs a place to stay and doesn't know how to ask,' Dilynn told herself.

Lyra reached over and took Dilynn's hand. The girl's fingers felt like ice, and Dilynn pulled out of her reach.

She grabbed the phone when the alert came through. She was hoping for food, but instead she got the message from the troll she'd been waiting for.

> RunnerAT89 on Chapter 9:
> Not sure what to say since I didn't dislike the chapter. There seems to be issues when I like something though so let's just call it a draw. I'm just going to have to stretch the suspension of disbelief.

Dilynn moved from the table to the couch. The alcohol was hitting her harder than she'd planned. She slid over the suede arm and sank into the corner seat.

Lyra followed her. Her calloused hands rubbed over beige suede hugging her back and rear. Her whole body seemed to relax in the cushions, another clue for Dilynn to add comfortable couch to her list of things the kid was clearly unfamiliar with.

The girl's eyes seemed to flutter closed like Lyra could fall asleep right then. Dilynn briefly considered just letting it happen. Let the kid pass out and give her a chance to explain herself in the morning. If she needed a bed, there was one more in the house. One more room in the house because Sylvia had known Dilynn wanted more than one kid when the woman bought it for her.

Her eyes snapped open when Dilynn's phone went off again. She glanced around, then leaned against Dilynn. Her head rolled side to side, and Dilynn could tell Lyra was pretending to be drunk. Two shots weren't enough to make the kid tipsy that fast, but Lyra clearly didn't know that.

Dilynn watched Lyra out of the corner of her eye, but she didn't say anything. Her chest stuttered though. Lyra seemed only to breathe when the blue eyes focused back on the screen.

She typed out: 'I do appreciate your critique, but would appreciate it if you would continue to leave out the more cruel remarks that you used to use. Calling people's creative works trash can hurt someone deeply. That being said, when you feel like you have to suspend disbelief in a reality-based story that means there are issues with the realism, and that is something that would improve my craft.'

The message was sent, while Lyra continued to play drunk. Dilynn felt the vodka trying to make its way back up as she thought of Lyra doing similar things to stay with Brandon. She knew she did it to Sylvia, but they were both young. Brandon wasn't young. He was older than her, and he wasn't pretty enough for Lyra to have wanted to seduce him for any means other than survival.

Her phone chimed again, and she appreciated Runner's distraction. That was, until she read the clear copy-paste definition of what suspension of disbelief meant. As an English teacher, Dilynn should have known what Runner was talking about.

> RunnerAT89 on Chapter 9:
> Suspension of disbelief is the avoidance—often described as willing—of critical thinking and logic in understanding something that is unreal or impossible in reality, such as something in a work of speculative fiction, in order to believe it for the sake of enjoying its narrative.
>
> The story is fiction. Most of what you write is not real even if the accuracy of the Arizonan education system is accurate. I would argue Morgan's overly generalized language suggests she doesn't understand her own content. Since you are basing her off the original character, you should make her a government teacher instead of a world history teacher. She was a governmental figure, so her focusing on the different types of government would allow for less need of that suspension of disbelief and you could reference more of her characterization from the novel.

Dilynn couldn't tell Runner she had chosen World History as Morgan's focus because she was already partially ashamed of all the naughty things she'd written about Alex Trikru. It was, in a sense, her own way of suspending her disbelief that this wasn't just an alternate reality of her own imaginary school romance.

Lyra scooted closer to Dilynn, clearly reading her words as she typed them.

> GreyAltEgo on Chapter 9:
> That was a very appreciated analysis. Maybe at some point in a future chapter, I will explain why Morgan is a World History teacher instead of a Government teacher. I would suggest you use that same type of curtesy when you

comment on any fic, since you clearly have a greater understanding of creative writing than your normal comments suggest.

"Damns gurl, yous goods at them words," Lyra slurred, settling the debate in Dilynn's mind that the girl had no idea what drunk even sounded like.

It didn't matter though. Someone was there and complimenting her. Dilynn turned to high five Lyra, but she missed. Her palm collided with the thin face.

Lyra's cheek took the brunt of the blow. The dark eyes narrowed as she jumped back. She was clearly ready to fight, which fit the boots more than the slurring and the swaying. Dilynn was a slurring and swaying drunk more often than she wanted to be, and she'd taken more shots. She tried to calm Lyra some by rubbing the girl's cheek and repeating apologies.

Her motion paused, and she held the kid's face. Dilynn grazed her thumb over the almost completely faded bruise under her eye. Lyra didn't get protection, she needed it. She looked into the eyes no longer pretending to be faded. They were a dark hickory with spires of amber, and so new, yet so old. Those eyes had seen more darkness than Dilynn had experienced in her parents' plush home and Sylvia's sleek townhouse. Lyra didn't get lucky with the person that plucked her off the street.

They were so close that Dilynn almost missed what was happening. Almost missed Lyra leaning forward to catch Dilynn's lips in a kiss.

"Stop," Dilynn said, pushing up from the couch and moving to the armchair.

Lyra let a few apologies tumble out, "I'm sorry. I didn't mean to... you know. I don't even know what got into me."

Glancing up at the ceiling, Dilynn reached for a random half full bottle of water from the end table.

"Look..." Dilynn licked her lip. "I know... okay, I know, I drank with you tonight. However, even drunk me is not an idiot."

Dilynn's gaze was clearer when she looked up from the coffee table.

"I'm not going there with you," she stated. "I mean, you're clearly pretending to be an adult, but I can tell you're barely older than my kid."

Lyra's chest shook slightly with her laugh. Her knees fell open, and it was a new tactic. That street experience came to the surface of Lyra's gaze.

Dilynn took a deep breath, and worked over all the things she could tell the girl. All the experiences that she'd had that would show her Dilynn understood the plan. She didn't think shared experience would matter to the kid. Not when she was safe, and the girl had come to her. Come to her because there was nowhere else to go. Which meant she knew she could come. She knew Dilynn wouldn't close the door.

"I'm not going to ask why you are here because I don't think you'd probably tell me." That was Dilynn's truth, and she wanted Lyra to hear the truth. Hear that even hard things could be said. "You're just like my kid, which means you probably don't have any place to go so... just be here, okay?"

Lyra folded her arms over her chest. The big dick energy she was trying to exude pulled back as she held herself. Held herself like no one had hugged her in a long, long time. Dilynn wanted to fix that, but she needed the girl to know she couldn't try to seduce her. Not her or Evie.

"Look. My kid has a past. A complicated story that if she saw you throwing yourself at me would make her scared. She'd be scared of you and of me, because she knows, like you know, that everyone can be a predator. But I'm not one. I'm not him. So, please, don't put yourself or me in a position that would hurt my kid or ruin my life more than has already happened. You can stay. Just... don't do that again."

"Okay," Lyra whispered.

Lyra wasn't okay though. Dilynn knew Lyra needed more than just the ability to stay. It would take time to get out of the girl what she really needed. To learn what she'd actually been through. What landed her in Brandon's apartment.

A tear slid down Dilynn's face. She'd almost married a monster. Brought one home to her bed.

"Can I give you a hug?" Lyra asked quietly. She licked her lips. "I promise, no moves. You're crying and I know I'm the reason and I came to apologize... so can I hug you and just say I'm sorry."

Dilynn got up from the chair. She didn't fall into Lyra's arms, instead she pulled Lyra against her. Tucked the girl's head to her chest and held her like a child. Her lips pressed against Lyra's oily hair while the tears dripped off her chin.

Dilynn's crying was contagious. They leaned into each other so the lonely shadows couldn't pull them into the darkness while they waited for the food to arrive.

12

Running away wasn't the same as giving up because if Alex took enough left turns, they would always end up back where they started. Four weeks and two days prior, Alex had left the mall wanting nothing more than to take left turns on whatever path they were traveling on to find a way back to Dilynn in a moment that she was smiling.

With a new Simone approved wardrobe, Alex made it a point to cross paths with Dilynn every chance they got over the last three weeks. They'd started Monday morning after their shopping trip. That was two weeks ago but Dilynn was no closer to looking at Alex than she had been before the late Secret Santa gift. The first Monday was more of a flop than after setting up the woman's coffee machine the Thursday before. And the first Friday morning was worse than Dilynn actively trying to ignore them on Saturday.

Tuesday morning was different. It started out differently at least. Dilynn opened her classroom door without confusion painted on her face. They hadn't caught her in a moment to pull a smile from her, but she let them in. Wednesday was a little bit of the same, but she'd rolled her eyes. Thursday, she'd smacked the handle of the door, demonstrating it was unlocked from the outside. A silent cue to them to stop making her get up from her desk each morning.

Two weeks in, Alex's daily visit became a new routine for both of them. They'd begun last week by bringing a bag of oranges to contribute to Dilynn's crusade, which had earned them an eyeroll. But she stopped making herself coffee each morning. Waited for them to arrive and make it for her. Almost three days into a new normal.

She'd smiled into the cup for the first time that Tuesday, when they'd set it on her desk that morning. They'd added an extra second when pouring the creamer, and she seemed to like it sweeter. They decided to pour five instead of four from now on.

While Alex sat in a student desk peeling an orange, Dilynn would smile occasionally at her computer screen from behind her cardboard castle. She'd glance in their direction only when prompted with a question, so Alex came with questions. Today they had prepared lots of questions because they were starting a new unit next week.

"How could I get them to practice for an interview without losing time for the Government content?" Alex asked from their seat across the room.

Dilynn's furiously typing fingers paused. She didn't stop reading over her own personal project when she posed her own question.

"What types of questions are you asked in an interview?"

This was something Alex had to get used to at first. The woman never just gave them an answer. She asked questions and expected Alex to answer the questions to their questions. It was a significant difference from working with Simone, who always had an answer. It was a tactic that they'd begun to use in their own class, and it was working so far.

"Strengths and weaknesses are always covered," Alex stated first. They pondered for a moment, then added, "Experience with the job duties."

"What content do you start with in Unit 2?" Dilynn probed, her hands back to completing her own task.

They bit their lip. She'd remembered they mentioned starting a new unit. Little things were a way Dilynn communicated. Like how she added Earl Grey tea bags to the coffee area after once asking them what they drank, since coffee wasn't their thing. She didn't make them tea, but once they caught her watching them as Alex made it themself.

"Maybe pull up the curriculum if you forgot," she said, glancing up just for a moment to show Alex those eyes they wanted to swim in.

They ran their hand over the back of their neck, wishing they'd hadn't asked Simone again about potentially cutting off their hair. They needed to answer Dilynn's question though, not wonder if she would want to run her hand over their head if it was shaved.

"Uh... we compare different types of governments. I was thinking about doing a project where the students study a government and present to the rest of the class."

They watched Dilynn's eyes move from left to right as she read over what she'd just typed. It was clearly long, like she was composing her own essay, possibly a report to HR for Alex annoying her since the second week of school.

"What challenge would you have with combining answering strengths and weaknesses in a project like that?" Dilynn asked.

Alex looked at the lesson plan already sketched out for the next week with the project.

"They could address the strengths and weaknesses of the country's government," they said.

"They could." Dilynn's gaze rose to her own board for a moment. "But I asked what the challenge would be."

Alex tapped against the desk and looked at the plan again. It was student led, like Dilynn had led them to believe was important three days ago. The kids would do the work instead of Alex giving them the information like would normally take place.

"What skills are you trying to build?" Dilynn asked, even though Alex hadn't answered the last question.

"Interview skills," Alex stated.

"Is the presentation building those skills?'

Dilynn closed her laptop. She moved out from behind her castle and sat on the weathered couch in the center of her room.

"They would be speaking, but not answering questions."

Dilynn hummed in approval. She leaned her head back and pulled her legs up. They wanted to drop down on the floor in front of her. Be the reason her head had fallen back against the seat. Their name would fall from her lips as they wrapped their arms around her thighs and pulled her closer to them. They would hear her asking for more instead of asking, "So, what could you do to get them to answer the questions?"

Alex bit their lower lip and tried to shift their mind away from their lusty imaginings. Unfortunately, all they could see were images of Dilynn in various states of undress around the room. On the desk behind the castle, like they'd read in GreyAltEgo's fic. Her face pressed against the laptop all focus on them delivering her to the stars from the two fingers they'd twist with each pull back.

A more recent chapter had the two teachers fucking against the white board. Dilynn would have her leg wrapped around them as they kissed her and told her they would still be there when she came back from her space travels.

"Earth to Trikru," Dilynn called out. They blinked, only to refocus on the very confused blue eyes staring at them.

They'd been staring at her when they were thinking. Worries rose if they had said anything aloud. Whispered any dirty thought that had passed through their mind.

"A gallery walk," Alex whispered. They licked their lips and took a drink of their water. "Instead of presenting, I could... uh... have them do a gallery walk. Maybe split them into two groups. One group presents their country's governmental strengths and describes the weaknesses that have caused... uh... civil discomfort."

Dilynn turned back to her board.

"And what is important when disclosing weaknesses in an interview?" she asked. She couldn't just tell them if they did a good job or not.

"How they could improve?"

Dilynn's head tilted to the side, then she slowly shifted her gaze to them. It wasn't like she was looking at them before. Just in their direction, but it was enough to make them sit up straighter.

"Are you asking me or are you telling me?"

Alex ran their hand over the back of their neck again. Their voice dipped midsentence as they answered with a question-like statement again. "Telling you?"

Dilynn licked her teeth. "Your friend, Ms. Wyatt, once taught me a very important lesson. Probably the only thing she taught me that I didn't toss out the window the first chance I got."

She moved to the board, popped the top of an Expo marker, and scribbled against the white surface. It was dead.

"She said, even if you're unsure, make it sound like you are." Dilynn tried the next marker. "She followed it with some shit about being much more attractive, which is true, there is something very alluring about someone who has that command in their voice."

Alex had a commanding voice. They scared a number of students with their directness. And they could be commanding for Dilynn, if she wanted that.

"So..." Dilynn popped the top of another marker. The passionately pink marker worked, but Dilynn did not approve of it and chucked it towards her desk.

She glanced back at them, and Alex realized she was waiting on them. Waiting for them to tell her what they were going to do.

"I'm going to have them discuss ways the country's government could improve their weaknesses. And the students can use a rubric, like you suggested Friday, to judge their peers' answers."

Dilynn nodded with her gaze still focused on the scribbles she'd created. They were beginning to look like a flower garden.

"You sounded strong, just now," she whispered. "That voice with your power attire is something for the kids to look up to. Especially our kids that don't maybe fit into the gender stereotypes that society tries to push on them."

Gender stereotypes were the bane of their existence. It made shades their life, because colors were part of the problem. Something to tell people who they were supposed to be.

Alex adjusted the new tie Simone had helped them pick out. It was blue like the sweater the woman was wearing. Not the sweater they had given her, but it was something tighter than the normal bulky ones she wore.

She looked lighter than normal. The bags of her grief were still somewhat heavy, but she didn't seem to be trying to shrink away. And her ring was gone.

"Did you always want to be a teacher?" they found themself asking Dilynn while she attempted to write her objective on the board with the green marker she'd used to sketch out leaves and grass for her scribbled flowers.

Dilynn hummed slightly, before she snapped the lid back on the marker. She tried a black one, but it had died, so she chucked it at the trash can on

Alex's left. It hit the wall but bounced back at Alex instead of into the can.

"No," Dilynn stated. She worked her way through the markers on her tray, missing each shot at the trash can and pelting Alex unknowingly. They breathed a little easier when she finally found one that worked. An ugly brown that streaked with every stroke, but it got the job done.

"What did you want to be?" Alex probed.

They crossed their fingers under the desk that she would answer instead of asking them a question like 'what do you think I wanted to be?'

Dilynn glanced back in their direction, but she didn't look at them. If this was how the woman had been with Simone, then she was right to call HR. There was nothing flirtatious about Dilynn's behavior. Even the compliment on their attire was professional.

Stop looking for what isn't there.

"I studied genetic engineering," Dilynn stated. "My mother is a doctor, and I spent a lot of time at the hospital. Her boyfriend studied genetic disorders and he was kind to me even though I hated him. I liked the idea of how genes mutated under specific conditions. Thought I could find a new way to help someone like the kids I had met in his trial study. This one boy. He had a rare mutation. It causes Hemochromatosis. Basically, if the gene is passed down it can cause liver failure."

Dilynn's lip tucked between her teeth. She stared at the board.

"I went to school because I thought, I could.... I could find a way to make a screening for the gene before it caused damage."

Alex's head dropped back as their jaw fell open. "You went from genetic engineering to English teacher? That's... uh... quite the major change."

"My friend. A boy I knew from the study. He died when I was a junior in college. His liver failed because he didn't have insurance after he aged out of the foster care system, and I just... I told one of my professors to go fuck himself when he was angered by my questions," Dilynn stated. "Had to have the class to graduate, but he was the only one to teach it so... yep. I changed my major."

"Do you regret it?" Alex asked. "I mean, you'd make way more."

"Don't care about money," Dilynn provided. "I have plenty of money."

"Oh." Alex briefly wondered how that was possible since they had to count every dollar on their budget. Then they remembered Dilynn say her mother was a doctor and it made a little more sense. "So, why English and not science?"

"I like books. I like listening to people talk about books. I like writing stories so I can deal with my feelings. I like teaching kids how to write stories. Kinda a no brainer."

Dilynn finished writing her objective on the board and then added the phrase, 'I need to learn this stuff so one day I will...'

She capped the marker and returned to her desk. Without looking up, she asked, "Is there anything else, or do you have your lessons planned out?"

Alex felt the temperature of the room drop. Whatever wall Dilynn was building behind her castle was made of ice.

"Why are things different now?" Alex asked before they could stop themself.

She didn't look up. Instead, she logged back into her computer. While it booted, she said, "I'm going to need more context to answer your question."

Alex got up from their chair and moved towards the desk. They needed her to look at them. Needed to know why she'd told her daughter no, when the girl had asked to invite them to lunch. Why the smiles she'd shared every morning were replaced with a mask of indifference. Why she'd gone from bubbly and bouncy to an ice queen.

"You... used to smile at me," they said quietly. "And we finally spoke and... now... we were starting to.... Did I do something to upset you? Is coming here... Am I bothering you."

She shut the computer. A pile of essays on her desk toppled. Dilynn didn't look up from the papers she began putting back into a pile.

"You're Wyatt's best friend," she said as though that was all the answer they would need.

Guilt by association would make sense, but Alex couldn't let the woman think they approved of Simone's behavior. That they would ever treat her like that.

"I want to be your friend, too," Alex offered. "If you wanted."

Dilynn didn't say anything. The papers were stacked. Her computer was shut again. And her cup was empty.

"Why are you here?" Dilynn raised her gaze to meet theirs. "Like you said, we didn't talk. You never asked me for advice. Never spoke to me until your friend got a good laugh at my expense. Now, you are here every day with questions you know the answer to, and no one that likes oranges that much doesn't just buy their own. In fact, you do buy your own. So, why the sudden interest in how I teach when you could go to your friend that you had no problem talking to since you got here and get the same answers to the same questions?"

Alex tried to swallow the lump in their throat. They could argue that Simone didn't have the good answers. She only had the easy answers. Could tell the still hurt woman before them that they'd learned more from her in three weeks than they had in all their years at school and working with Simone.

They go with a truth. One that had nothing to do with their lessons that they'd initially lied about to get in the door. Because before engaging with

Dilynn, they'd believed themselves a great instructor. They'd taught like they were taught in college, but Dilynn made them realize they'd become just another pompous lecturer.

"I'm someone that likes routines." Alex gestured between themself and Dilynn. "You and I, we had a routine and it got messed up. And I just... I like starting my day out with being with you in the same room. I went to the breakroom every morning because it was when I got to see you. The only time I could see you."

Dilynn wrapped the sweater tightly over her chest. She looked down as though to check she was now fully covered.

"We never spoke," she reiterated. "You just made your copies and ignored me, then Wyatt...." She looked up at them again and searched their face. "Is this just a game?"

Alex waited for Dilynn's eyes to stop scanning over their face, but they didn't. They were being studied like the mutation they were under the scientist's gaze.

"Like, is this all just a game to you?" she asked again. "You saw me get dumped the day after Christmas. And then I made a fool of myself in the breakroom when I admitted.... And so, what? You and she made a new plan to torture me because I stopped coming to the breakroom? You didn't get to see me and tell her I cussed out the creamer or spilled coffee all over the counter, so you had to come here instead?"

Alex shook their head. "I would never--"

"You had no interest in knowing anything about me until that day," Dilynn stated. "Now, you are here every morning. I just feel like...."

She looked down at her chest again. Pulled the sweater even closer.

"I'm tired of being made to look stupid," she whispered. "I... I liked you, okay? Like, it's stupid, I know. But I had a crush on you, and now... look, I get it. Girls like me... that look like me... they don't end up with people like you. And I can't do this with you. I can't when you are... and I just.... I'm not mad at you. You are just here. Here in the only space that's mine. Only place that is Simone-free, but you and her.... You can't just be here for me like you say because that doesn't make sense because people like you don't see people like me."

She gestured to the machine that replaced Alex. "I got my own coffee maker, so you and she couldn't.... So, I wouldn't get made fun of again. I'm tired of being the butt of Simone Wyatt's jokes. I know I get roped into doing every stupid little activity for the pep rallies but those are supposed to be fun, not ammunition for social studies faculty members. And I didn't need you to know... you didn't know me when I first started, and you were nice, and you were looking at me that morning and then she... I used to be pretty. I know I was and I just.... I didn't need her to remind me. I didn't need her to laugh at me and call me fat because I own a fucking mirror and I already know, and I just.... I'm tired of being humiliated."

Alex felt the weight of the world crushing in on them. She'd liked them. She'd seen them and thought of them and had a crush on them.

"You're beautiful," they whispered. "I know you probably don't believe me since you think—"

Dilynn closed her eyes and shook her head. She didn't believe them. She whispered, "You don't have to."

They rubbed the back of their neck.

"I'm not some pawn in her game," they promised her. "I didn't realize that me being here would make you feel... unsafe." They hated the way the words tasted. But they kept going. "I'll go. You should feel safe. But you should know, I want to be around you. Me. Just me. And I didn't say anything for months because.... I want to know you. I...."

They looked at the door to the cage Dilynn had created herself. A space to lock herself within so no one would see her. But they didn't have the key yet to get her out and coming in wasn't helping. It had made everything worse.

"I'm going to go," they repeated. "But I want you to know that I didn't tell anyone about what I saw at the mall. I didn't say anything to Simone about it. And she showed up that morning because... because I told her I liked you. I like you. And I couldn't speak because... I'm not good at this whole talking stuff. But I did tell her that her cruelty would not be tolerated. I just thought...."

Dilynn gaze didn't raise to them with the affirmation of their mutual attraction. She couldn't believe them here, they realized.

"It doesn't matter," they whispered.

Nothing they said would matter when she didn't feel safe. They couldn't make her feel safe enough to melt the walls around her, so they left like they said they would.

When the door closed behind them, the click of the lock sounded like a bad prison movie. This wasn't the pipeline to prison the media warned about, but maybe they didn't understand the way some teachers hid within their classrooms like cells.

Dilynn was too wonderful to feel like she should have to hide. She was too amazing of a teacher and a mentor to not feel safe to leave her room.

They fished their phone from their pocket. They opened the message from practically a month ago. Then typed out a response to the man they'd ignored.

'Is the invite to Greyson's Pizza Night still open?'

Jason Jordan didn't hesitate in providing them an affirmative answer even though he should be teaching his class. He was still interested in taking them to Dilynn's.

'I can pick you up and we can go together,' he offered in the next text.

Alex smiled at the phone. Why he was chasing them instead of Dilynn, who'd finally taken off her ring was beyond them, but it didn't matter. They were going to prove to Dilynn they wanted her. Show the woman her interest in them wasn't unreciprocated.

They thought of GreyAltEgo. Remembered the chapter where Priya had walked away from Morgan feeling like a slut. Morgan had fixed it by showing up at Priya's classroom. Apparently, they had suspended their disbelief too far, and taken it as a sign to get to Dilynn.

Dilynn wasn't a character in a fanfic, but she seemed to be so similar to Priya. Seemed to be stuck in the same mindset. One they hoped they could break.

They'd do it right, too. They'd go to the pizza night and bring the woman flowers. Make it clear that she was worth wooing. Ask her out not once or twice before trying to even kiss her. They would do everything Morgan hadn't to boost her confidence in their desire for her as a whole person and not an object.

They closed the message and found a new alert from GreyAltEgo. She'd posted a new chapter that morning. A new chapter not safe for work. One that had the two teachers screwing on Priya's classroom couch during first period. Alex let out a heavy breath, wishing GreyAltEgo's fiction could be their reality.

13

Dilynn could see the bird framed girl standing on her porch as she pulled into the driveway. Her neck tightened as she gripped the steering wheel. The morning routine she'd reestablished with Alex was broken after her blow up yesterday. A routine she'd depended on to write. Between her anger with herself and her writer's block, she honestly didn't want to deal with whatever trauma Lyra was about to bring into her home. Not to mention that now Dilynn would have to keep Evie from losing her crap on the girl who was still in the same clothes as the last time she'd shown up. She gathered up all her courage before getting out of the car.

The dark eyes didn't move from the ground even as Dilynn walked up the steps. Lyra waited silently for Dilynn to open the door to the house the kid had walked out of before the sun rose the last time she'd shown up unexpectedly.

Standing before the door, Dilynn silently waited for Lyra to raise her gaze. Just like she'd shown Alex a few weeks earlier, Dilynn clicked the handle to the door and let it open wide.

"Did you forget your keys?" Lyra asked. She tightly clutched the single strap to a faded purple backpack covered in skulls.

Dilynn sighed and pointed to the door. "It's open. Always open. So, don't wait on the porch or someone will call the cops. Especially the racist assholes next door. They called the cops on Evie's boyfriend once for sitting in his car outside. You understand, right?"

She didn't want to have to have *the* talk with a girl she barely knew. It was bad enough when Landon's mom had shown up to give Dilynn *the* talk. A talk she'd never heard and would never forget as the woman relayed the possibility of her gentle giant of a son with his espresso toned skin getting shot like young Treyvon, who was just walking home.

Lyra looked at the threshold, then back at Dilynn. One eyebrow rose, before the girl said, "Do you, like, want to get robbed?"

"Do you, like, want to take a shower?" Dilynn waved her hand around Lyra's space. "Because you look like you woke up in a parking lot."

"Rude," Lyra whispered as she followed Dilynn into the house. She held the bag tighter.

As Dilynn dropped her bag by the entry table, she pointed to Evie's hallway. "You know where the bathroom is. Do you need clothes?"

Lyra pulled the bag to the front of her. Dilynn noticed it was missing a strap and the bottom had been stitched back together. The zipper tag was missing, and Lyra had replaced it with a key chain ring that she used to open the large compartment. She held it out to Dilynn, revealing a few shirts and pants buried under a couple packs of ramen and some crushed granola bars. They weren't exactly clean.

"We have people coming over, so I'm going to get started making pizza dough," Dilynn said. "Evie will be home in about an hour and a half. She will need to shower too, so please don't use all the hot water. Also, drop all your dirty clothes in the laundry room when you're done, and I'll throw them into the wash tonight."

Lyra tried to squish something under the same tattered work boots she'd worn last time. Dilynn noted that the bag hadn't contained shoes, so the boots were more than just a precaution.

Dilynn tried to not appear obvious as she looked the kid over to ascertain what size shirt and pants she would need to pick up. The girl was definitely a size small and no bigger than a three in jeans. The shoes would be the hardest thing to get the girl because Dilynn had no idea what size feet the kid was hiding.

She decided to start with what she had. She gestured to Lyra to follow her to the garage. Lyra grumbled something about Dilynn being a hoarder, but that stopped when Dilynn pulled back the lid to a plastic container. Evie had been a size small last year, but she'd grown into her frame over the last year. Dilynn pulled out a few plain t-shirts, then a pair of slide-on Vans and a pair of low-top Nike's that Evie had outgrown.

"I know they're not brand new," Dilynn said. She waved at the shoes. "But Evie wore them only, like, three times before her feet grew outta them, so try them on and if they fit, then they're yours."

Lyra studied Dilynn's face carefully, then dropped her gaze to the shoes. She waved at the bucket. "Isn't your kid gonna be pissed you're giving her shit away?"

Dilynn shook her head. "Nothing in here fits her."

The teen didn't stop staring at Dilynn as she slid her foot out of the boot, revealing she didn't have any socks on. Dilynn did her best to remain unphased by the verification of Lyra's homeless status, remembering how Brandon had told her that deodorant was a secondary need to socks when she'd asked how to help. People on the street apparently went through a single of pair socks because they weren't in a position to change or wash them, which is probably why Lyra didn't have any on. But the stare Lyra was still giving her, told Dilynn not to speak about it.

After scrunching her toes in the Vans, Lyra pointed at the bucket of clothes. "Could I...?"

Dilynn nodded and helped Lyra sort through the bin silently. Everything in the container would fit Lyra, but the girl only selected a few plain shirts and one with the Cactus High logo on it. She stared at that one for a minute, then she added it to her pile of keeps. She took two pairs of jeans and a pair of sweatpants that were thick, before she stood up and shoved the stuff into her backpack.

With the new clothes tucked away, Lyra followed Dilynn back into the house.

"You not even going to ask?" Lyra asked, still wiggling her toes in the Vans after they returned inside.

Dilynn pulled out her scratched KitchenAid mixer. As she dropped six cups of flour within, she said, "At some point I hope you will tell me what's going on. Until then, go shower and put your shit in the spare bedroom. No more sleeping in parking lots or wherever you're staying. Just sleep in that room. It has a lock on the inside and no keyhole on the outside, so you can lock it, so you can feel, like, safe. I know Evie's going to lock hers."

"Do you lock yours?" Lyra asked as her eyes glanced around the house. "You don't lock the front door, so you, like, lock yours when you sleep, right?"

"I don't lock doors."

The kid didn't argue with her. She raised a single eyebrow and muttered under her breath, but she didn't argue about putting her stuff in the room. She didn't share the story weighing on her shoulders like Dilynn had hoped either.

With the bathroom door closed, Dilynn took the quiet time to mentally prepare for the night. She ran through her pizza night check list. Drinks and ice were taken care of because she'd given cash to Landon after the last class period to pick drinks up after he dropped Evie off. Casey had volunteered to grab ice.

She checked her phone for the time. Two hours before guests would arrive. Two hours wasn't a lot of time to get the dough to rise with the end of January chill. She started the oven, turned up the heat, and flipped on the electric fireplace to warm up the room. The dough would need the heat, and she could just crack some windows when it got closer to the time everyone else would begin showing up.

Once the ingredients were added, Dilynn turned the mixer on and slowly added water to the bowl. It went from powdery to sloshy to lumpy quickly. She kneaded it for a full five minutes into a circular lump before putting it in a larger bowl and leaving it to rest on the coffee table right in front of the electric fireplace.

As she waited for the dough to rise, Dilynn ran the vacuum over the tile and living room rug. With the white noise calming her mind, she considered Evie's request for a dog. Dilynn had always wanted a dog. Sylvia had said no dogs, which Dilynn respected because Sylvia was the boss of her house that Dilynn lived at for free. Brandon was adamant about no dogs, however, there was no more Brandon, and she was the damn boss. Always had been.

She could get a dog. A big dog with floppy ears and happy, doggy smile. A rescue naturally, and one that wasn't a puppy. Maybe a teenager dog. She was good with teenagers.

A dog would need to be walked, socialized, and house trained. Things she'd barely managed with Evie. The more Dilynn thought about it, the more she felt like it wouldn't be so bad to have a giant mutt around, especially since Evie was leaving in a year. The kid couldn't take a dog to college, which really meant Dilynn would have a dog. Maybe a dog would be good to have when she was alone. A big dog though. Not one of those little ones.

Dilynn's phone buzzed in an almost continuous rhythm in her pocket. Each message would tell her who was coming, but she ignored them to sort through the different types of dog breeds in her head. She wanted a mutt, not one of those pure-bred beasts like Sylvia had once suggested in a moment of weakness that passed faster than a lightening streak flashing across the summer sky.

Once the floor was clean, Dilynn set aside her potential doggy adoption to plan for how many pizzas she needed to make. Evie, Landon, and Casey would be there, and Evie had said three of Landon's friends would be joining, along with a few girls from the basketball team. That was probably seven pizzas.

Dilynn's occasional lunch companions, Parker and Christiana, were coming, which would be nice because she hadn't eaten lunch with them since Simone had made the breakroom part of her territory. She checked her phone again and realized Christiana had messaged that she and her husband would be late, but they would be bringing their baby. She also had a message from Jordan that he would be bringing a guest. Emilie, the school resource officer would be late, but she was bringing her wife. Adults were probably another three pizzas.

She looked at the dough that wouldn't be enough. The kids came earlier than the adults, so she'd at least be able to tackle it in waves. She made another batch of dough and set the second bowl alongside the first that had already begun to rise.

Her phone buzzed with another text when she started the sauce. Marcus Thompson, the school social worker, would be there with his son, Kyle. Dilynn was glad he was coming because he hadn't been out of the house a lot since his wife kicked him out for wanting to leave their church.

Dilynn looked around the space. She didn't have a lot to do for an eleven-year-old. The older kids would have to be reminded to include him and to keep their talks a little more reserved. Her eyes rose to the bathroom door opening.

Lyra was out of the shower, looking a little less worn down, and smiling. A smile that appeared genuine.

"Thank you for letting me shower," she said. Her hand dug into her pocket and pulled out Dilynn's engagement ring. "I actually stopped by to return this."

Dilynn glanced at the ring, then at the backpack that was back on Lyra's shoulder looking no less full. So much for not arguing.

"Did you put your clothes in the laundry room?" Dilynn asked.

Lyra glanced at the strap, then shook her head. "You got people coming over, so I'm gonna dip before your kid punches me in the face."

Dilynn struggled with the lid to the marinara as she said, "You don't... have to... leave."

The lid didn't move, so Dilynn stared at it and tried to find a superpower within herself to force it open. She wasn't a superhero though. She wasn't a hero at all. Just a woman with a jar being watched by another young female, who found her predicament amusing.

"Give it here," Lyra said, too happy to take over.

Lyra exchanged the sauce for the ring and popped the top with minimal effort before handing it back to Dilynn. With a soft shrug, she added, "You loosened it for me."

"I'm not a man," Dilynn growled. "You don't need to stroke my ego."

The jar was dumped into the large pot. Dilynn yearned to learn how to make real sauce, however, cooking wasn't her forte. She could doctor a jar up decently enough to fill her house on Wednesday night though. She sprinkled onion powder, oregano, and garlic salt within the pot until some entity told her to stop. Then, she began gathering other ingredients for the pizzas and laying them on the island where she'd work while the others ate.

"Before you go, grab the bowl by the fireplace," Dilynn requested.

The bowl wouldn't take long, so Dilynn started making a list of other things she could ask Lyra for to keep the kid from walking back out into street where the storm clouds had already gathered.

She grabbed the flour covered Starbucks apron and put it on while Lyra did as she asked. Stirring sauce wasn't really a job, but Lyra the Liar wouldn't know that. The ice chest needed to be brought in from the backyard also. She really needed to just invest in a beverage refrigerator, but that didn't matter right now.

Through the back door, Dilynn caught sight of her renter juggling an infant car seat and her bookbag.

'Remind Sarah about dinner,' that was something Lyra could do. It would take time, also.

Lyra set the bowl on the counter. Her mouth opened, but Dilynn cut her goodbye off with, "It's going to rain."

Dilynn nodded her head towards the front window where the dark clouds could be seen rolling in. "It's going to rain and your truck isn't outside."

"I don't have a truck," Lyra said. "I borrowed my boss's truck, but I had to give it back."

The blonde pushed a spoon into Lyra's hand. "Stir the sauce while I get the dough rolled out."

Once more Lyra did as instructed. Stood over the pot staring at the red sauce like it was a potion preparing to blow up any minute.

"So, no truck. And there's no bus," Dilynn started rattling off. "No apartments for at least two miles away."

"So, you are going to ask," Lyra grumbled.

Dilynn poked the fluffy dough, then pulled it out of the bowl. She smacked it against the counter, talking as she kneaded it. "I'm just making observations. Like that you should stay for dinner instead of eating ramen again tonight. Or that it's going to rain so wherever you were planning on sleeping tonight is going to flood. And Brandon told me when storms are coming the shelters fill up by noon. Not the most reliable source, but I think there is some truth to that. Plus, we are too far from any shelters out here."

Lyra met Dilynn's gaze only for a moment. She didn't say anything, just stirred slower.

The aroma rising from the pot wrapped around Dilynn like a childhood blanket. One she needed after scaring Alex away from coming to visit her and coming home to find Lyra on the doorstep. She couldn't apologize to Alex without walking through Simone's territory. She could help Lyra though. She was someone who also kept showing up. And Lyra clearly needed a blanket and a bed, which was something Dilynn had extra of.

"I won't ask questions," Dilynn stated. "But I am going to go off my observations. And right now, I don't think there is a place to stay. And I don't think you want to eat ramen again or granola bars. And I think sleeping in the rain outside is worse than letting me handle my kid, so you don't get punched in the face."

She looked out the window to where Sarah was carrying a diaper out in front of her, and holding her hand over her mouth like she was going to puke any second. Hopefully, the girl would come to pizza night instead of hiding in the guest house like she had since moving in.

"Do me a favor," Dilynn said. "Okay, two favors. First, go put your backpack in the spare bedroom like I already asked you to do and your clothes in the laundry room. Then, go out back and knock on the door to the guest house. Remind Sarah that pizza night starts at six and we would love to see her and the baby."

Dilynn glanced back at the girl staring at the pot still.

"You mean it?" Lyra asked quietly. "That I can sleep here tonight?"

"Yes, Lyra. You can sleep here tonight, and you don't have to leave before the sun comes up."

The girl's feet still hadn't moved. She just looked at the pot. "And I... I don't have to sleep... with you? Like ever."

Dilynn dropped the dough and turned to the kid. She shouldn't but she did. She wrapped her arms around Lyra and pulled her in close like the first night the girl arrived. Held her tightly and told her, "You never should have had to sleep with someone. You're safe here."

Lyra didn't hug her back this time. She just held her breath and leaned against the older woman.

"I'm sorry," Lyra whispered. "I'm sorry I hurt you."

"I'm sorry he made you think help came with a price tag," Dilynn answered.

When Dilynn released Lyra, the girl set the spoon down and did as she was told. Her ability to follow instructions was nice. Evie would have never just done what Dilynn told her to do, and a part of Dilynn ached for Lyra to push back. If Lyra pushed some, it would give Dilynn hope that someone hadn't broken her will to fight.

While Dilynn worked the dough on the pad, she thought about her dad. He'd taught Dilynn not to let anyone break her. The lessons came when they made pizza together. A skill from his high school days making pies in Seattle that he passed down to Dilynn.

Pizza had been the one thing they did together. The only thing since it was the one night he was home while her mother was at the hospital. His job as an engineer kept him away in different states, but he came home from California or Las Vegas every Wednesday for her.

She looked back to see his translucent body fan a hand over the pot of sauce. He looked over her shoulder, towards the back door where Lyra was returning from.

Dilynn heard her father's voice whisper, 'Open doors, right?' She didn't answer him because he wasn't really there.

There wasn't a chance to thank the girl before the front door smacked against the wall and rattled the frames.

"Mom, this is Sadie," Evie announced as she dropped her sports bag on the floor. "She's a freshman and she—"

Dilynn watched Evie's mouth clench shut. She rose to full height, which made her taller than Lyra the Liar. Before Excessive Evie could attack with words or fists, Dilynn's finger pointed to the chalkboard sign hanging on the wall. The sign the mother and daughter had made together.

"No hitting," Dilynn stated. "Or yelling, or kicking, or biting."

Evie's narrowed glare shifted from Lyra to her mother. Lips pulled back over her teeth, the girl growled, "What the fuck is she doing here?"

Dilynn looked at Lyra, then back to her daughter. "Ask her without yelling, hitting, kicking, or biting her."

"Or spitting," Lyra added. She pointed at the board. "It says no spitting, too."

Evie didn't ask Lyra though. She just stared at her, and Lyra stared back. Only, Lyra smiled when she stared, probably because she didn't know pissing Evie off was a bad idea. That a pissed off Evie was why they had to have a chalkboard sign of house rules that Evie had on multiple occasions broken. Even the biting one. Why the kid thought play wrestling included biting was beyond Dilynn's comprehension, but she wasn't about to pay for another trip to urgent care so Lyra could have a human bite wound cleaned.

"Sadie, get your shit," Evie snapped at the younger girl still standing in the entry of the house with her bags on her shoulders.

"Sadie, sweetie," Dilynn said to the girl who wasn't one of her students.

The younger girl turned towards Dilynn. Her shoulders hunched forward under the two heavy bags she carried. Looking up from under her hoodie, she whispered, "Yes, Ms. Greyson."

"Do your adults know you are staying for pizza night?" Dilynn asked.

Her eyes flicked to Evie standing in the hallway and back to Dilynn. Then she nodded. She followed Evie like a shadow before Dilynn could ask the girl anything else. And Dilynn remembered the late-night phone call a few weeks ago about the freshman and Evie's best friend.

"What exactly is pizza night?" Lyra asked, pulling Dilynn's mind away from the kid who was having sex way too young. The older teen walked around the large farmhouse table that still needed the eaves added to accommodate the growing list of attendees until she made it to the counter where Dilynn worked.

"Basically, it's an open house with food," Dilynn explained.

Lyra glanced around the space, looking for something. She licked her lips when her gaze fell on the open bag of pepperonis.

"Lemme see your hands." Dilynn commanded.

The thin fingers extended towards Dilynn, who shook her head. "Go to my bathroom. There's a little brush on the sink. Use it to scrub the dirt out from under your nails with soap. Then you can have a pepperoni."

Lyra didn't question her. She reached the bedroom door where she stopped at the threshold and turned back to Dilynn.

"I'm not a thief," she stated. "That's why I had to give you back the ring."

Dilynn met the hickory orbs. She tried to wash the venom from her words before she said, "Says the girl who slept with my fiancé."

Lyra bit her lip. Her nose scrunched slightly, and it was evident she was trying to come up with something to say.

"He was really bad in bed," she offered.

Dilynn couldn't stop the laughter that erupted from her. Nodding her head in agreement, she said, "He really was terrible."

Once they both finished laughing, Dilynn said, "I don't think you will find anything worth stealing in my bedroom. Except maybe my clothes."

The brunette gave Dilynn a once over and shook her head. "I don't think I can pull off the soccer mom look."

Dilynn didn't have time to come up with a retort before Lyra disappeared. She looked down at her sweater and apron. She did look like a soccer mom even though her kid didn't play soccer. Even her new wardrobe said mom, but maybe that wasn't the worst thing.

With the air thick with Italian seasoning and too much heat, Dilynn went back to her task of sectioning out the dough. She heard the shower in Evie's bathroom turn on. At least she had a few minutes before having to potentially break up another fight.

She was so preoccupied with getting things ready, she didn't hear Evie come around the corner from her dark hallway still sweaty from practice. Her whole body jumped when the quiet was broken by Evie's gravelly voice.

"We need to talk," she demanded.

Dilynn squeezed the dough between her fingers like a lifeline. She'd have to reshape it, but that would take less time than deescalating her daughter.

"E, I—"

"Not you," Evie growled at her mother.

Dilynn's eyes shot up to Lyra coming out of her bedroom.

"You," Evie said. She pointed to Lyra, then herself. "You and I need to talk."

Lyra's head tilted. With a twisted smile, she asked, "Is that code for step outside so I can punch you in the face? Do the rules only work in the house?"

Dilynn didn't give Evie a chance to give that question a thought. She couldn't when she knew Evie would punch Lyra. So, she called out, "No hitting!"

She held the mangled dough up towards the sign again. "No hitting! It's on the list!"

"Talk," Evie repeated. Then she added a little louder, "Since NO YELLING is also on the list."

Evie took a breath before she spoke directly to Lyra, "Plus, if I was gonna hit you, I would've already done it. I would have done it at the mall when I caught you kissing that fucking asshole."

"What if I don't want to talk to you?" Lyra said, folding her arms over her chest. "Last time you and I talked it didn't go so well."

"You two know each other?" Dilynn asked her daughter. She'd promised Lyra not to ask questions. She hadn't made the same promise to Evie.

"Yeah," Evie growled. "She was in my history class freshmen year. I didn't realize it when we were at the mall. But I remember you."

Lyra ran her tongue over her front teeth. "So, you remember being a giant bitch and harassing me every day when I never did anything to you?"

Dilynn watched some of Evie's anger fizzle. The boiling within her veins seemed to be at the same state of simmer as the sauce behind Dilynn.

"What I did..." Evie's fight evaporated. "It was mean. I was mean and—"

"You kicked my ass and called me a nasty dyke because I told you you could get an infection for cutting open your hip with that rusty ass razor blade," Lyra stated. Her hand hit her chest. "I was trying to be your friend and you pushed me in the shower and doused me in cold water when it was fucking winter. Then you kicked me until I couldn't breathe. Does she know that? Does she know how to you used to beat the shit out of me?"

"I was—"

"You were what? You were angry at the world because your perfect life wasn't going the way you wanted?" Lyra snapped. She held her hand out to the house. "Yeah, you had it real bad when you came home to this, while I slept in the park and almost froze because it was too cold for my clothes to dry."

"I didn't know," Evie said. "I wasn't... I wasn't here then. I was living my own nightmare, and what I did was wrong. I'm sorry, okay? I'm sorry, but I was trying to... I just had to make the pain real and when that wasn't enough... I had to share it and I gave it to you. So, I'm sorry. I'm sorry that I hurt you because I was hurting, okay?"

"No, it's not okay," Lyra said. "And I don't forgive you."

Evie folded her arms over her chest. She wasn't accustomed to not being forgiven. It was something Dilynn gave her. Forgiveness for the meanness. Understanding when she shared her pain.

"Why are you here?" Evie snarled. "I mean, you knew she's my mom. Did you come here to get revenge? To tell her I'm a shitty person, because, trust me, she already knows. She knows better than anyone how fucking awful I am."

"You're not a shitty person," Dilynn stated. "And Lyra can choose not to forgive you. You apologized and sometimes that is all you can do."

Dilynn faced Lyra. "Whatever happened in the past between you two, it clearly hurt a lot. The whole 'your kid is going to punch me' thing makes way more sense now, and maybe give a little more detail so I can prepare more effectively. Sorry, rerouting back to what I was saying."

Dilynn took a deep breath. "You don't have to forgive her, but—"

"Mom! Whose side are you on?" Evie snapped.

"No sides, E," Dilynn stated. "This isn't something to take sides on. You can't force someone to forgive you. You both should just know that holding anger is heavy. It's like adding bricks to your backpack to carry around with you."

Evie's eyes rolled, then fell back on Lyra. She pointed to the backyard. "Please can we just go outside and talk? It's the only place she won't interrupt us with some weird old person analogy."

"I'm ten years older than you!" Dilynn shouted. She picked up a handful of pepperonis and chucked them at the girl. "Like, I should be your sister, not your fucking mother."

The meat saucers didn't reach the girls. They slapped against the tiles and Dilynn decided she needed a dog. A dog would love her and clean up the evidence of her non-athleticism.

"You're really only ten years older than us?" Lyra asked. Her eyes ran over Dilynn once more. "But you look like... I dunno one of those moms who, like, tries to be their kid's best friend."

Dilynn blew out a heavy breath. First Simone and now the girls. Did anyone not have something to say about the way she looked?

"Let's go before she blows," Evie said. "See how her face is pretty red, it can turn purple when you talk about her clothes."

Lyra licked her teeth once more. Her gaze ran over Dilynn before she said, "Fine. But Dilynn, you're a hot mom if it makes any difference."

Evie gagged when Lyra winked in Dilynn's direction. It didn't make the blonde feel better, but it had stopped her from turning purple.

She beat the dough as she watched the girls, wishing she could be a little more Evie and a little less herself. She wanted to get to hit something. Wanted the anger and the hurt she felt when Alex hadn't shown up that morning to just go somewhere else. Or when Brandon just stood there with Lyra.

Evie got to hit Brandon. She wasn't afraid or ashamed. She just hit him. Dilynn would have loved to hit him. She still wanted to hit him with more than words in a story.

A smile rose up her face when she thought about hitting Simone. Three years of cruelty packed into a punch. It was her fault Alex wouldn't come anymore. She showed up after break and made Dilynn think Alex could be visiting her just to make fun of her. A worm that had burrowed so deep in Dilynn's head, she couldn't see the social studies teacher had come to see her. Just like she'd always wanted.

She squeezed and strangled a portion of dough off the large lump. Pulling and stretching until it was too lumpy, then she got to slam it against the counter. Then smash it with the rolling pin. When she looked down, she realized her mistake. It lacked any semblance to a circle, instead lay in a sort of wonky triangle. She balled it back up and started over again.

The talk felt like it lasted forever. Evie spoke with her hands while Lyra sat curled into a ball. The girl's sweatshirt was too thin, and Dilynn made a note to find one of Evie's that she'd grown out of.

The shower had turned off, but Sadie hadn't come out from Evie's bedroom. Dilynn considered going to get her, but she had to get the first two pizzas in the oven before time ran out.

She'd barely finished when Landon arrived with Casey on his heels. Landon's arms were loaded with cases of soda while Casey struggled with two bags of ice.

Dilynn smiled at the boy and wrapped him in a hug. Everyone was getting hugs today, she decided. Even if they didn't hug her back, they were getting hugs.

Landon did hug her back. When he released her, Dilynn remembered an item on her list.

"Landon, Mr. Thompson is bringing his son with him and he's still in middle school. So can you, maybe—"

"I'll keep him involved," Landon promised. He glanced up to where Sadie had finally reappeared from Evie's hallway. Her hair hung in damp spirals around her face, and Dilynn couldn't be certain, but the girl looked to be swimming in one of Evie's sweatshirts and the leggings were just a little too loose. Like the girl had raided Evie's closet.

"What's she doing here?" Casey asked, moving to get her hug from Dilynn.

Dilynn looked between Sadie and Casey. The younger of the two stepped back into the hallway with her chin pressed against her chest, while the older looked around in search of something or someone.

"Where's Evie?" Casey asked.

Dilynn nodded to the back of the house, then gave the kid a brief embrace. She pressed her hands to the larger girl's cheeks and looked up at her.

"She is talking to Lyra out back," Dilynn told her. "You and I are going to be having a chat before you leave. Understand me?"

Casey gave the barely teen a side-eyed glance, then looked back at Dilynn. "Yes, Momma G."

"Go get the ice chest from the backyard and tell Evie she needs to shower before dinner."

"Yes, ma'am."

Landon worked on pulling the table apart while Casey dragged the ice chest in from the back.

"Sadie, honey," Dilynn called over to the girl still standing as though the hallway would collapse without her back to hold it up. "Come here and get your hug."

Sadie couldn't be older than fourteen, and her limbs were still awkwardly lanky. She wrapped her arms around Dilynn though. Let the mother hold her for longer than anyone else would have. Dilynn didn't let go until the girl did.

"You give great hugs," Dilynn praised.

The girl's smile told Dilynn more. In a time where teens with braces were the standard, Sadie's teeth were still crooked. Without a question, this kid was in foster care. Those were the only kids who didn't get braces in high school or already had them on in middle school.

"I have a bin of Evie's clothes in the garage," Dilynn offered. "She was smaller last year. Before you go home, let's get you that bag so you can grab some things that won't fall off you, okay?"

Sadie bit her lip and glanced at the backyard. "She won't be mad?"

Dilynn shook her head. "No, honey. They were going to be donated anyways. She would definitely rather you have them."

"Thank you," Sadie whispered.

Dilynn hugged the kid again. She made a mental note to get in at least two more before the kid left because a kid already having sex at her age probably wasn't getting any healthy contact in her placement. She'd talk to Marcus about that tomorrow.

The ice chest's wheels scratched against the floor. Tomorrow, she'd talk to Marcus and order the mini refrigerator. Two things for tomorrow, along with a light bulb.

"Sadie, can you please check the bathroom you were just in for toilet paper?" Dilynn requested. "Also, pull out a couple of rolls from under the sink and put it on the counter."

Once Sadie was out of view, Dilynn returned to her post at the counter and chucked a pepperoni at Casey's thick skull. The mousey blonde turned to Dilynn, and her hands rose in the air.

"Evie already hit me," the older girl whined. She wrapped her hair up in a messy knot atop her head.

"Also, are you the reason there are pepperonis all over the floor?" She pulled a smashed meat saucer from the bottom of her shoe. "Like, that can't be sanitary."

"Why did she have to hit you?" Dilynn asked, hitting the girl in the face with another pepperoni. She hit Casey with another pepperoni. Then another, until the girl raised her hands in surrender.

"I know. Okay." Casey whined. "I know. But she hit on me. She came up and I was just talking to Evie, and she did that thing that pretty girls do when they look up at you with their big eyes and... and she had already... you know... with Tania and Gizel and —"

"I don't want to know that." Dilynn swatted Casey's words away. "I don't care if she wanted you or not. She is too young."

"I know. But I like her. Like, she's funny and she's pretty. And she's gay. Not like a little gay. Like me gay." Casey rubbed her jaw. Dilynn noticed the yellowish tint to the faded bruise. "It's just... not a lot of girls are out and I just... she liked me, and no one ever really likes me. Not since Evie, and she cheated on me with Landon."

"Well," Dilynn hissed. "Evie was the same age as that kid, and what was going on, Casey?"

Casey's eyes fell to the table, while Landon made himself scarce.

"I know," she whispered. Dilynn was sure Casey did know. She knew Casey knew now, when she hadn't known then.

"Then leave the kid alone. I will handle her, and you just worry about school and basketball. Plus, softball is just around the corner, so you won't have time for a girlfriend."

"Evie does all the things I do, and she has time for a boyfriend," Casey's hand jutted out to Landon, who was studying the writing books on Dilynn's desk.

Landon pointed to the front door. "I think I forgot some of the sodas in my truck."

"Yeah, well," Dilynn didn't know what to say. "Look, you will meet someone someday. Someone who is ready to be in a relationship with you." She pointed her rolling pin at the hallway. "But that kid is not ready. Evie was not ready. You weren't even ready."

Casey made her way over to the counter and stole a pepperoni. "Okay, Momma G, you have got to call my parents. They are talking about Bible camp. Like, all summer sending me to camp so I can pray the gay away. And the last one was terrible. You know the last one was terrible. They made us sit through hour after hour of lectures about hetero bullshit. I promise to stay away from Sadie, but like, what if they send me to one of those places that is worse. You know, the ones that they send the bad kids to. The last one was bad enough."

The girl's head hung. She tapped her finger to her hair line, then shook away whatever thought had popped in. Casey had been doing her best to fake being straight since coming back after last summer, but the kid had her own brick filled backpack pulling her down.

"Why can't they just leave me alone?" Casey asked. She held her hands out, staring at her. "Like, is there something so wrong with me that they can't just... like they don't even care about me, so why can't they just leave me alone."

Before Dilynn could answer Evie and Lyra returned from outside. Instead of scowling, they're laughing and play-fighting as though Lyra was just another school friend.

Landon had returned from the front with more sodas. He almost dropped them when he saw Lyra. He fumbled with the boxes, then let them land hard against the table.

"You're backpack girl from Walmart." He pointed to his chest. "Do you remember me? My mom, she was talking about you just the other day."

Lyra looked everywhere but at Landon. She nodded, then said, "Yeah. I remember. How is she?"

"She's good. She would really love to see you again," he said. He walked to the girl with his hands out. He was about to wrap them around her but paused. "Can I hug you?"

Lyra nodded. She didn't reciprocate the hug, which was a good thing because Evie was watching Lyra closely. Whatever relationship Lyra and Landon had once had would potentially only complicate things more. Especially since Lyra was already a potential cheater.

A thought popped into Dilynn's head. She could call Imara. Imara maybe knew more about Lyra's situation and could help her figure out if she needed to make a DCS call or if the girl was actually an adult.

"We brought cookies!" Marcus Thompson announced when he walked through the door with a plastic platter. His son trailed him, and Dilynn hugged them both together.

She sent them into the house and returned to her one job of the night. Feeding everyone. Two pizzas came out of the oven when Landon's friends walked in. They each gave Dilynn a hug and carried the pizzas to the table where the trays were emptied. Evie's teammates arrived in time for the second pizzas to come out.

Marcus took up position on a couch in the living room while the kids spread out around the table. Christiana and her husband arrived shortly after, and Dilynn set a pizza on the coffee table for them with some plates. The baby in the car seat held up her stuffed giraffe for Dilynn to see.

Dilynn took a moment to snuggle with the baby, then introduced her to little Trisaya in Sarah's arms as the other woman came in from the guest house. Dilynn inhaled the soft scent of infancy. She'd never be this type of mother, but that would be okay.

Her eyes wandered to the teenagers in the middle of the table, sandwiched between the kid now staying in the guest room and the one shadowing Evie. They were each so different, but seemingly attached to one another in less than an hour.

When Evie sat in her classroom with tears streaming down her face three years ago, Dilynn was no more ready to be a mom than she'd been in high school. She still wasn't ready today, but she knew now what she knew then. She wouldn't be perfect, but she wouldn't hurt them. Love would come later. They needed first to know she wouldn't hurt them. And that's why she couldn't punch Brandon or Simone.

She handed the baby off to the real mother. Then squatted next to Marcus. Quietly, she asked, "You know the curly headed freshman next to Evie?"

Marcus looked over at the table. He whispered, "Sunrise Homes."

Dilynn's eyebrows crinkled together. "If she's in a group home, how'd she get permission to be here? Or the party last week?"

Marcus turned away from the group and spoke towards the back of the house. "She's a runner. Runs away from every placement. If she's here and was there, she's probably on the run again. Which means..."

Dilynn's eyes widened. "They'll send her to the detention center."

Marcus nodded.

"Is she staying here?"

Dilynn shook her head. But she knew now why the kid had thrown herself at Casey. She was two years early for Lyra's path.

"Don't let her stay here," Marcus warned. "I know what you're thinking, and we can work on it tomorrow, but you know they won't let her be here if they find out she was staying here."

Dilynn bit her lip. She hated the long game. The long game had taken a year to get Evie home permanently.

She got up and made her way back to the kitchen. Two more pizzas came out of the oven. One she set on the table, and other in front of the adults.

Without time to waste, Dilynn focused on getting more pizza dough rolled out, sauce and mozzarella spread, and pepperonis tossed in heaps atop. Two at a time go in the oven for twelve minutes and less time for the empty trays to be returned.

Jason Jordan was the last to arrive. He walked into the house as Dilynn wiped her flour covered hands on her Starbucks apron. She wrapped her arms around the skinny man who'd been the one to support her when Simone had told everyone she was a hooker years before.

"Hey, Jace," she said. "Where's your...."

Alex Trikru stepped through the front door still dressed for work with a bouquet of lilacs.

"For you," Alex said, holding out the flowers.

14

The first scent of the pizza hit Alex like a gentle breeze. The rich undertones of melted mozzarella and Parmesan cheeses had their stomach making its arrival known. There was still time to leave before she saw them. They could make it to their car and go back to their life.

Alex lingered close to the door in case she told them to leave. She hadn't ever asked them to leave her presence, nevertheless, this was her home. It would be less embarrassing that way, even with the flowers held out before them.

The room pulsed with conversation while a fake fireplace crackled in the background. Whatever playlist Dilynn had running provided a melody fit for a fantasy realm as a backdrop to the symphony of voices while the rain pouring outside provided the beat.

The occasional chuckle and the gentle hum of appreciation for the food cast a spell over Alex. The warmth and joy floating in the air chased away the cold from Alex's bones as they stood behind the lanky chemistry teacher. Dilynn, being the tiny human she was, disappeared when she embraced him.

The flowers, disguised as a peace offering, acted like a shield for when the woman's sentence fell short, and her eyes landed on Alex. There was no running away now. Not as she stared at them.

Jordan left Alex standing before Dilynn. He'd grumbled when they'd arrived late that they should have just told him they were gay. They couldn't explain why labels didn't work because they were a gray area in a psychology book who had fallen for a woman now staring at them like they'd grown two heads.

"For you," they said.

Dilynn's hair fell alongside her face. Her own shield from the others while she whispered, "I usually hug everyone that comes in. I just... after I said that I am... I don't want you to feel uncomfortable because I told you I was... attracted to you. But... if you wanted one... a hug... from me. I would... like that."

The air seemed to hum with unspoken understanding when Alex took a tentative step forward. Alex extended their arms, a silent acceptance of Dilynn's invitation. The first contact was a cautious brush, a whisper of connection sending ripples through their being as the chaotic energy of Dilynn's bubbly persona transferred to them. Her arms didn't wrap around them in a familiar sense like they had around Jordan. They collapsed around Alex's back, and her head found rest against their chest.

The pizza didn't smell nearly half as good as Dilynn's rich perfume. They leaned their cheek against the golden hair they'd yearned to touch each time it fell to block her precious face.

"About yesterday," Dilynn whispered while still pressed against their chest. "I'm just jaded of, like, everything right now, and I... I'm just sorry."

The simple confession caused their arms to envelop the woman tighter. Alex clung protectively around her. They would be her shield, even against Simone.

Whispering against her hair, they said, "I didn't come today to give you space."

Dilynn's head leaned back. Her amused gaze was crinkled in corners, but they couldn't focus on anything beyond her lips. How they were raised at a perfect angle for Alex to steal a kiss. It could get them fired if they were wrong. It could make everything very, very bad, but what if it wasn't.

She doesn't know you're a freak.

They didn't believe the voice. Not with the way the blue eyes were crystal blue on the outside and darker on the inside. A whirlpool of emotion as she said, "But you showed up at my house with flowers."

The lips they didn't kiss spread into a full smile. Dilynn leaned back some, stealing away her warmth. The hug was done, her hands now just resting against Alex's back.

They didn't want to let her go, even though they would have to. Dilynn's guests, scattered around the room, lowered their voices. The only sounds were the muffled rustle of fabric and the quiet sighs that whispered through the air. People were watching them, and she'd said she didn't want people talking about her anymore.

Dilynn pulled away but immediately came back for a second embrace. The first hug turned into a second. Two hugs in five minutes. More physical contact than they'd had in years. Not since their girlfriend in college had called them an 'it' before walking away.

"Can we do this whole hug thing more often?" Alex asked quietly, when Dilynn leaned back in and rested her face against their chest once more. "I read this article that humans need four hugs a day for survival, eight for maintenance, and twelve to feel alive."

They took a deep breath, and added, "I don't know about you, but according to that statistic, I'm not going to make it much longer without your arms around me."

Dilynn's laughter danced around them. Her hands pushed on their chest as she shook her head. "That was so cheesy. Did you work on that the whole way over here?"

Alex shrugged slightly. They'd worked on many lines during their drive over, but not that one. It had never even occurred to them Dilynn would hug them.

"No, I just looked up information about flowers," Alex confessed.

When they separated, Dilynn took the bouquet from them. She inhaled, and a smile softly curled up her lips. "They smell amazing."

"Jordan said lilies are your favorite, but it turns out lilies mean fertility." They rubbed the back of their neck, "And that felt weird, you know?"

Dilynn looked at the flowers, then up at them. Her teeth pulled her lower lip back. It popped out when she asked, "And these are?"

"Lilacs."

"And you're not going to tell me what they mean," Dilynn stated. Her gaze moved to her phone on the counter, then back to Alex. Dilynn smelled the flowers again and her eyebrows rose. "You want me to look up what they mean. That's why you told me the meaning of lilies."

Alex didn't acknowledge Dilynn's statement because their eyes had been drawn to a roar of laughter from the table. The girl from the mall sat alongside Dilynn's daughter. They were each trying to shove an entire piece of pizza into their mouths. It was a race, and mall girl was about to lose simply because her narrow face had less space than the girl who didn't know how to throw a proper punch.

"Jesus, I hope you know CPR," Dilynn stated. "One of them is going to choke."

They didn't correct Dilynn, even though the kid would need the Heimlich, not CPR. Just the fact that she said CPR, made them pray they never choked around her.

"You know her?" Alex asked, looking back at Dilynn. They turned the volume of their voice on low before they clarified, "The girl from the mall?"

Dilynn played with the strings of her apron tied around her waist. She tugged on one a little too harshly and the sloppy bow came loose. She stared at her hands as she explained, "Not at our initial introduction. She showed up about a month ago, but... uh... no, I don't know her."

She turned away then. Made her way to the stove while Alex watched her stand on her toes that were covered in dino socks. Her fingertips barely grazed the cabinet over the microwave before she managed to get the cabinet open.

The large pot of simmering sauce was too close to her chest for Alex. They could tell there was no way she'd be able to reach the vase within. It was tucked so far back, clearly not used often. Something they would rectify.

"Let me help you with that," Alex said, coming up behind her as she leaned dangerously close to the hot pot. They placed a hand on her hip, pulling her back from the stove and against them while they reached over her.

"Thanks," she whispered. "I usually have to climb on the counter, so I basically don't use the top shelves for anything."

It wasn't often they appreciated being almost six feet, but with the woman barely over five foot tall pressed against them, they knew it would always mean they would have a job in her life.

"Glad I could be of use," they offered, then reluctantly released her.

She placed the flowers in water and spread them out to fill the space. With a glance back at them, she promised, "I'll look up the meaning of lilacs when everyone is fed."

Dilynn checked Alex with her hip after she placed the flowers away from where she was cooking. They stepped aside, so she could pull two pizzas from the oven.

Alex looked around the open floor plan as the woman transferred pizzas to wooden serving trays and sliced them. There was a clear divide between the teens and the teachers. The teachers were far enough away that their conversations were barely audible. Their glances back at them made it clear Alex wasn't necessarily welcome in their group. Dilynn must not have been either since she was in the kitchen, and the teens had chosen to occupy all the space nearest to her.

"Things are pretty informal around here," Dilynn explained. She gestured to the space. "Everyone you probably want to hang out with are over there. But I would like to at least introduce you to the kids because a lot of them will have you next year. At least, if I have anything to say about it."

She ran her eyes down them, then reached out and stroked the green tie she'd gotten them for Christmas. "Would you prefer to go by your last name or first? And do you want a title?"

Alex's head tilted slightly. "A title. Like The Great and Powerful Trikru?"

Dilynn's eyes rolled dramatically, and she yanked on their tie slightly. "No, goober. I mean like Miss. I tell my students to just call me Greyson. I have never liked the Miss. Hate that people are supposed to know my gender before my name." She shook her head and gestured to the kids. "But these kids mostly call me Momma G. Even at school. Your friend was all up in arms about it a while back, but she doesn't have them anymore, so... you know."

They looked down at the tie still in Dilynn's hand. They pressed it flat, and raised their shoulders so the gendered word would roll off them. She didn't know, and she was being polite.

"Just... uh... Trikru with the students here, por favor," Alex requested.

The dark-haired girl from the mall's head popped up and she shouted out over the kid's conversation, "Hablas Español real o la basura que enseñan en la escuela?"

Alex couldn't help but smile at the girl. By the looks on the other kids' faces, no one else understood what the girl had said, so they said, "El Español de la escuela no es Español real, solo es mas propaganda colonizadora."

They turned back to the woman standing with the pizzas in her hands. Her blue eyes were comically wide, and Alex felt like they'd tapped into a superpower they hadn't realized they had. They took one pizza from her and gestured to Lyra with their free hand.

"She asked if I learned Spanish in school, and I told her no."

Dilynn closed her mouth, but the flush of her cheeks remained. She nodded to follow her.

"Hey, guys," Dilynn said as she took the pizza from Alex's hand and placed it on the table. "This is Trikru. Since you all will be in AP Gov next year introduce yourselves."

A giant boy-man at the end of the table got up and made his way around the table. "Hello, ma'am, I'm Landon. Landon Woods. I already signed up for your class. My friend Jarome said he loves your class. He just got his first job and said it all happened because you taught him how to shake hands."

Alex took the boy's hand and swallowed the need to correct him for calling them ma'am. "You have a fine handshake, Landon."

"Thanks," he smiled back. "Jarome was giving lessons at lunch the other day. Said it was the first useful thing he learned all year."

When he released their hand. The kids around the table sounded off. Alex didn't recognize any of them, but they all were wearing various versions of the school's logos with one team or another. Even mall girl was in a Cactus High shirt. The girls seemed to all play basketball, and the boys were split between wrestling and football. They tried to keep the names straight, but they were grateful the two girls sitting on either side of Evie were last to go. They seemed to be the two kids closest to Dilynn's kid. Theirs were names they would need to remember.

"Soy Lyra. Te vi en el centro comercial," Lyra from the mall offered. She'd been more made up when she hung on Dilynn's ex. At the table, she was clearly within the same age bracket.

"Sí, te recuerdo," Alex affirmed. "No pareces lo suficientemente mayor para estar con él. ¿Estás a salvo ahora?"

Lyra looked around at everyone at the table watching them. She licked her teeth, then answered, "Ella me está permitiendo quedarme aquí esta noche. Ahora deja de actuar como si me conocieras, o podría echarme."

Alex didn't blame Lyra for not wanting them to acknowledge her anymore. The others were watching, and it was clear she was still trying to keep her head down. They didn't have to respond to the girl though. Dilynn's kid was impatient for her introduction, and they remembered her telling Dilynn to invite them to lunch so she could get in their good graces.

"I'm Evie," Dilynn's kid stated. "And I'll learn Spanish if it will help me get an A in your class."

Alex offered her a smile. A real smile because they needed to make a good impression on her. She would be the one in Dilynn's ear when the night was done.

"If you want to learn Spanish, I am sure Lyra and I could help you be able to at least speak so you don't get laughed at," Alex offered.

They didn't mention fixing her punch. They could do that another time. Build a relationship as they beat the crud out of their new dummy together. Maybe the kid would want to join a Dojo with them. They would never be her parent, but they could be someone that was there. Someone the girl could vent to. They were a good listener. Such a good listener that they missed half of what the kid said.

"... so close. If I can just pull up my grade in AP Chem, I may have a shot at valedictorian next year."

Dilynn rested her hand on Alex's arm. "Evie has big goals after graduation. Some Ivy league school visits are scheduled this summer."

"What do you want to be when you're an adult?" Alex inquired.

Evie looked at her hands, then up at them. "Some days I think I'm going to be a lawyer, but they're all pretty sketch. Never met one that wasn't secretly a vampire, and I don't know if I could live off blood."

Casey, the burly girl at the end of Evie's bench, snorted. They remembered her name only because she was constantly in Simone's class after school. While Evie was Simone's star, Casey was Simone's special interest project. When the kid wasn't at practice, she was with Simone on the weekend. It was pretty intense. Simone had once told them if Evie was going to get a scholarship, then Casey would need her pitching to be top form.

"Dude, what the fuck is your problem tonight," Evie snapped at the other girl.

Casey waved her pizza slice in the air. "Just you pretending like you don't like blood."

Evie's face went pale, but Casey was silenced when Landon scolded her. "Not cool, Casey. You don't want people puttin' your business out when you're trying to make a good impression."

Unsure what to do, Alex looked at the youngest kid at the table. When she looked up, Alex felt like they were staring in a mirror. Her almond shaped eyes were still years younger than the others, and she pointed to herself, as though they hadn't been going in a circle and she wasn't last.

"I'm Sadie," the girl quietly offered.

"Do you have a last name, Sadie?" Alex asked.

"A couple of them." She smiled at them with a mouth full of crooked teeth. "If you could choose a last name like they did when people checked into Ellis Island, what would you choose?'

Alex's head fell to the side. It was such a random question, but the kids at the table began to rattle off answers. Several of them chose names that reflected ancestral roots to continents across the sea. Lyra said she'd choose something that would make her sound white and change her first name to something that would look good on a job application.

Sadie didn't answer her own question, but Evie leaned back and looked at her mom. Quietly, she said, "I'm good with my last name."

Dilynn stood up straight and dropped her hand on Evie's shoulder. She gave the girl a tight squeeze, and said, "Yeah, I'm good with Greyson, also." Then she looked at the rest of the kids. "Well, all of you have now met Trikru, so there's no reason any of you shouldn't be signing up for AP Gov next year."

Sadie looked up at Dilynn with a furrowed brow. She raised her hand slightly, like she was in class instead of at dinner. Alex studied the kid. She looked so much like their brother; it shook them enough to start working out the math to see if they should be running out the door.

"Sadie, sweetie," Dilynn said softly. "We're not at school. You don't have to raise your hand."

The child's hand dropped, and her voice was so low Alex could barely hear her. "I think... I... I'm supposed to take World History next year. That's what I take when I'm a sophomore, right?"

The kid was a freshman, so she'd be about fourteen. Ryder was two years older than them, and they were twenty-five. Math was never Alex's favorite subject; nevertheless, they were confident in the reality that the kid couldn't possibly be related to them. Ryder would have had to be 13, but he didn't lose his virginity until junior year. They knew this for a fact, because he'd done it with the girl they'd liked. Done it and then outed them when the girl left his bed for theirs.

Dilynn placed her hand on the girl's shoulder. She gave it a softer squeeze than she gave Evie, and told her, "Yeah, we'll get you enrolled in AP World next year, so you'll be ready for Trikru's class when you're a senior. Plus, the AP World teacher is great."

The kid shook her tangled curls. No one had taught her how to manage hair that wasn't straight, and Alex felt like they could do that. They could teach the girl how to take care of her hair and the other kid how to throw a punch.

"I'm not... they don't let people like me take advanced classes," Sadie told Dilynn. "I'm not smart like Evie."

"You don't wanna take Wyatt's class anyways," Casey announced. "She may be the softball coach, but her class is boring as hell. It's like all memorization and she's not going to help you, so I wouldn't do it. Plus, you're already going to end up spending all your time with her like I have to. She said you have to come to practice with me on Saturdays now. Said she wants you to be ready when Evie graduates and trust me, you don't want to spend more time with her than you have to."

Evie threw a slice of pizza at Casey, "Shut the fuck up. Coach's class may be boring, that doesn't mean it will be too hard for her. Stop being a bitch."

"I'm not being a bitch." Casey's hand shot out towards Alex. "You're just being a kiss ass because Coach's friend is here and you're her favorite."

Evie rolled her eyes. "Why are you so psychotic lately? You're the one she practices with every weekend, not me. She doesn't even want me to come catch for you because she said she doesn't want any distractions while you two are working together."

Dilynn cleared her throat, and all the kids turned to look at her. "Whatever your personal feelings are about a teacher, or their class, are your opinions. We have rules in this house, Casey. And you know them. We don't talk shit."

Alex internally ran over Dilynn's words twice. They felt uncomfortable having witnessed this interaction. Dilynn defending Simone, the very person who'd made her feel so unwelcome that she was planning on leaving, didn't fit with any of the narratives.

They'd never chosen a team. Even with Simone sitting in their living room, they'd known their friend's words were at most half the truth. And Dilynn had fought harder for Alex's friendship with Simone than they had. Had respected that they were friends with the person who mocked her. Now, Dilynn stood before a group of students in solidarity with her tormentor. And it pained Alex to watch.

Their insides felt like the barriers between their organs had dissolved, and everything within them was now just acidic mush. They hadn't chosen a side because Dilynn made it possible for them not to. It felt like they had to choose now. Choose the woman that didn't talk shit, because that was who they wanted to be around. Be with a person that respected them and their choices, not gaslighted them to do what she wanted.

Casey grumbled something under her breath, but Sadie shifted the conversation quickly with another random question. "What is the best type of cheese?"

The cheese debate became a focal point, drawing curious glances from the other side of the living room where Alex had followed Dilynn towards. They survived the brief greetings from the other adults and hung around the fireplace until the heat pumping from it had them looking like Marcus, the social worker who also had a sheen of sweat across his brow. Not wanting their deodorant to fail them, they tried to find another place to occupy near the teachers Dilynn had left them to socialize with.

These were Dilynn's people, but they were honestly boring. The two mothers were talking about baby stuff with the school resource officer's wife. Marcus, Jordan, and a younger boy were going through the intricacies of some game called Minecraft. Neither conversation Alex could contribute to, so they watched Dilynn moving around her kitchen, occasionally talking to herself.

The rectangular table became the epicenter of a large debate amongst the teens. Crumpled napkins were projectiles for unlikable declarations, and the remnants of half-finished pizza slices were left on the table with the votes being cast that mozzarella was not on the short list for cheese of the year.

Alex lasted alongside the adults for all of ten minutes, before migrating back to the debate. Gesturing to the chair at the head of the table, Alex asked, "Is this seat taken?"

"All yours," Evie said. She picked up a cookie from the tray and studied it.

The girl cast them a few glances, before she looked at Dilynn, then back at them once more. Maybe two hugs had set off the girl's radar and she was assessing whether she approved of them.

"You sure you want to sit over here?" Dilynn probed from her post at the counter.

Alex nodded. They picked up a slice of pizza and set it on a paper plate. It was still too hot to eat, so they listened to the kids talk in a language mostly foreign to them. The slang had significantly changed since they'd been in school, and they realized seven years was a long time.

As they worked through their first slice of pizza, Sadie was asked for another topic of conversation. Sadie tugged on the back of her neck for a moment. Her eyes wandered up to the ceiling, before she settled on, "Can a person be happy alone or do we have to have, like, a girlfriend or a boyfriend to be happy?"

"This is easy," Casey stated. "Only person you have to depend on is yourself. No one is going to ever actually be there for you."

Landon shook his head, "No way. I am a better person for having Evie in my life. Without her, it would be different. It would be dull and everything black and white."

The rest of the group were weighing in on Sadie's question, while Alex watched Casey read through a text from an unsaved number. A demand to come over now.

Alex bit into the corner of a second piece of pizza, while the kid fisted the phone and dropped it in her pocket. Whatever was going on, Casey was struggling with something the others didn't seem to notice. Or knew about and didn't care since she was clearly frustrating everyone.

"So, the wedding is just off?" one of the girls asked. Several sets of eyes rose to Dilynn as they leaned in closer.

Dilynn was engrossed in something on her phone and didn't appear to notice the kids were now focused on her new status as Cactus High's most eligible bachelorette. They smiled at the thought of her learning lilacs meant adoration.

"Yeah, no more wedding. Thank God," Evie whispered. She pulled at the neck of her shirt. "Right, Lyra?"

Lyra didn't look up as she said, "Yeah."

"She looks so normal," another kid said. "It's like she just doesn't care she just got cheated on."

Evie grabbed another cookie from the tray. Her fingers picked at it as she explained, quietly, "She's just been spending all her time writing."

"Did she get an offer for a second book?" Casey asked, glancing up from the phone that had come back out of her pocket. There were a half dozen messages from the same number.

Alex glanced up at Dilynn. She was quietly humming as she made another pizza. Alex tried to make sense of why they'd not known Dilynn had written a book.

"Not yet," Evie whispered. "She's mainly been writing for that fanfiction site. Casey, you know it. You read shit from there all the time. I think she is, like, working out different ideas for the next book. That's how she wrote the first one, actually. She used to write fanfiction all the time for that lame ass show, *The 100*."

"That show was only lame because they killed off the lesbian." Casey's shoulders fell inward as she tapped out a message to the person rapid firing demands at her. "Like every show ever. No happy endings for the queers."

"We should try to set her up," one of the girls said. "There's, like, at least a dozen single teachers on campus. Like, Jordan has had a crush on her forever. Or Talon, the PE teacher."

Landon's face cinched up. "Dude's a wrestling coach and always has ring worm. That's a big no."

Alex tried to become one with the chair. They made no movements in order to avoid any of the kids from noticing they were still at the table. Evie noticed them though. She would periodically glance in their direction; however, she stared at them when she spoke next.

"She won't do it," Evie whispered. "I tried to get her to call this girl she used to date. Like, the woman is dripping in money, but she was like, I just need time. I told her she could have all the time in the world while she lays on a beach, but she still said no. She's apparently crushing on—"

"Hold up." The boy in a football t-shirt looked back at Dilynn, who still seemed to be occupied in her own world as she tapped against her phone. She was glaring at the device while the boy asked, "Momma G's gay?"

Alex's phone vibrated in their pocket. They pulled it out to see they'd finally gotten a response from GreyAltEgo. The writer had given them the silent treatment all day, but that made sense. They'd told her Priya was acting like a MarySue and they'd secretly wished she'd just run her car off the road and get a TBI that would change her personality. It was mean, but they'd spent the day worrying about Dilynn kicking them out.

"She's bi," Evie supplied. "She always says it doesn't matter what the anatomy is. It's all about the person, but clearly her picker is broken. After all, she spent two years with the asshole. And I know the girl she dated is, like, super rich, but I don't think they really had a relationship. It was more of a secret thing because the girl wasn't, like, out yet. And the person she has a crush on... well, she just doesn't think she is pretty enough to be noticed by her."

Landon leaned in towards Evie but waited to speak until Dilynn had turned her back on them. When Dilynn was engrossed in her phone, he whispered, "I thought you said she's seeing someone online?"

Evie rolled her eyes. "She's not dating the troll, but there's definitely flirting. Which is gross because whoever she's talking to is, like, so mean to her." The cookie in Evie's hand broke in half as she looked Alex dead in the eyes. "I told you. Her picker is broken."

Alex's fingers absently traced patterns on the tabletop. A faint furrow etched itself between their brows. The cautious whispers became distant echoes, overshadowed by the rumbling of their internal contemplations. Occasionally, their gaze would refocus for a moment, as if glimpsing some distant revelation, only to retreat once more into the recesses of the reality that Dilynn was seeing someone else.

"Hey Mom, have you heard from the troll today?" Evie called out.

Alex's head turned slowly to the woman. The sauce covered spoon hovered over the pizza before Dilynn. Her eyes fixed on the girl, who'd clearly just announced a secret she wasn't supposed to share.

"What did you tell them?" Dilynn asked so slowly.

Evie shrugged. "Just that you write fanfiction and are having a flirty battle with an asshole online.

Dilynn licked her lips and returned her gaze to the pizza. She spread the sauce around in a circle.

"What do you write about?" Casey asked. "Is it still about *The 100?*"

Dilynn grabbed the bag of cheese and started piling it on the pizza. She seemed to barely be breathing, and Alex wanted to save her, but also needed to know what she was writing about.

"Uh... I was working on some ideas for a book. Dystopian stuff, but lately I have been playing with more realistic fiction," Dilynn explained. "You know, just working through the feelings from the break-up and all."

"So...." Evie waited until everyone was listening. "Has the troll said anything lately?"

Pepperonis flopped atop the cheese.

"You all need better shit to talk about," Dilynn stated.

"Come on, Momma G," Casey whined. "Are you in a flirty online romance?"

"Or do I need to kick someone's ass?" Landon offered.

Dilynn ran her hands over her face. She must have realized her mistake because she stared at her flour covered palms too late.

"Landon, no one needs their ass kicked," Dilynn said. She grabbed a paper towel and wiped her face off. "Except maybe you all."

Dilynn's eyes fell on Alex. There was a plea buried in her gaze, and she didn't have to ask them. She'd already asked them. Don't tell Simone this. Don't tell her this or anything else.

"So, what's the latest from the troll?" Casey pressed. "I read fanfiction on *Atlas Stands* all the time. Got to love it when the lesbian gets the girl instead of the brute."

When Dilynn didn't divulge what she wrote about, the girl continued.

"There's this one troll. Such a fucking douche. Like, the troll leaves comments on every damn story and is so rude. I just want to hack her comp and trojan horse her ass. RunnerAT89. Everyone knows--"

"That's the one!" Evie's hand hit the table. "Runner89 or whatever. That's Mom's troll."

Alex couldn't breathe. They were RunnerAT89. They were the troll harassing Dilynn. GreyAltEgo had even called them a troll. But there was no way that Dilynn was...

"I don't think Runner is a troll," Dilynn said. "I think they just... like probably have a really lonely life. And they don't really know how to give constructive criticism. I mean, when you all are mad, you try to hurt other people."

GreyAltEgo.

Greyson Alter Ego.

Greyson wrote stories about her friend's novel. She was Priya, maybe she really was who Priya was based off. It would make sense. The mother of the kids. The one the teens all listened to. The one who defended Morgan.

The pieces were all falling into place, but the table seemed to be tilting, making the pieces fall away as Alex tried to put them together.

"I didn't think that troll read anything besides *Atlas Stands*," Casey stated. She logged into the account and pulled up her history.

Alex saw it when it came up. The kid had been following Dilynn's story and didn't know it. They crossed their fingers under the table that the girl didn't pull up their comments.

"I mean, the only thing I have seen them be somewhat nice about is this one AU," Casey looked at Dilynn. "Funny thing is when I read that one I kept thinking it was so weird. Like it was you and Wyatt because it's like this English teacher and History teacher."

They were choking on pizza as a rainbow of irises turned to them. They smacked their hand to their chest because Dilynn thought CPR was the same as the Heimlich and they didn't want to die yet. They cleared the pizza lodged in their throat and looked at the blue eyes staring at them.

"May I..." they tried to take a breath. "... glass of water?"

"Yeah, of course," Dilynn said. She turned from the counter and rushed towards a cabinet on the other side of the kitchen.

Alex followed her as Dilynn rambled, "Can't have you dying at my table, it would... uh... kill my reviews."

Dilynn pressed the glass to the refrigerator and filled it with water. They were too close when she turned. Luckily, they'd learned not to trust the woman with any type of beverage after wearing a cup of coffee and watching the woman spill at least two more in the last week.

"Thank you, Greyson," Alex said too formally.

Dilynn looked up at them. She tucked her hair behind her ear once more.

"It's embarrassing," she whispered. "The whole fanfiction thing."

Alex took a long drink from the glass, only to find Dilynn's eyes still locked on their face. She was studying them carefully.

"You came with Jordan," she whispered. "But you haven't spent any time with him. And you brought me flowers."

Alex let out a huff of amusement. They wiped away the flour from Dilynn's chin. Then, they ran their thumb down the front of her neck.

"I prefer my dates without an Adam's Apple."

Alex could give her more. They could be her Morgan, only better. They wouldn't let her walk down the hallway wondering if she mattered to them.

"Do you have a preference regarding apples?" Alex asked, though the kids had already told them what they needed to know.

Dilynn's eyes shifted from Alex's lips to their gaze. Her throat bobbed slightly under their touch.

"No preference," she whispered. "And I don't have a flirty online romance. I just want.... Just no games. No secrets and no games."

Alex had a secret. Technically two. But they could manage at least one of them easily. They would just stop being RunnerAT89. They could just be Dilynn's. And Dilynn could be theirs.

"No games," they promised. They let their hand drop. "About yesterday."

"I was acting crazy."

"No, you had every reason to be concerned. I would have been, too. I just wanted you to know that you weren't alone in your crush."

Dilynn's face said she didn't believe them. They hated that she didn't seem to know she was pretty.

"Since August," they supplied. "I have been thinking about you and me since I first met you in August."

"You didn't say anything." Dilynn's eyes narrowed at them. "Like, anything at all."

Alex took her hand. They ran their finger over the tan line from where the ring used to sit. She nodded her understanding.

They didn't kiss her. It was too soon for that, especially when they'd looked up to find a set of very angry bluish-green eyes staring across the room at them. Evie's hands had crumbled the cookie she'd been picking apart.

Luckily, a subtle shift began to ripple through the house. Conversations, once animated and laughter-filled, tapered off as the adults exchanged light embraces and the kids tapped out goodbyes with their fists. The hum of communal warmth was replaced by the rustle of coats retrieved from the back of the couch and the jingle of car keys.

Dilynn walked Alex to the porch shortly after the last adults had left. Evie and the girls still at the table with Landon clearly weren't leaving anytime soon, but the heavy yawn that tore from Dilynn's mouth was Alex's cue to leave.

Outside, the night sky bore witness to the scattering of car lights. Alex ran their hands over Dilynn's arms until they gathered the confidence to pull the woman into an embrace on their own.

"I think this makes three," Dilynn whispered. She leaned back and pressed forward once more. "And that's four."

Alex chuckled softly. "You have saved me, Ms. Greyson."

"Ugh!" Dilynn croaked. "Absolutely not. I have been called an old soccer mom too many times this week. Now you called me by my teacher name. Something else. Anything else, please."

Alex licked their lips. 'Speak directly,' Dilynn had told them. Don't make it sound like a question or an option. She'd said it would be sexy.

"One day, I'll call you mine," they promised. Then a smile pulled up their face as they ruined the moment for her. "For now, we can go with cupcake."

Dilynn's jaw dropped open at the same time her nose scrunched up.

"No?" Alex said innocently. "What about pumpkin?"

Dilynn pushed at Alex playfully as she groaned. "Absolutely not. Fucking Pumpkin! Like seriously?!"

She twisted out of Alex's hold, but they pulled her back against their front. They held their arms around her and whispered just over her ear, "Eres la estrella más brillante en el cielo. Eres mi reina, mi amor, y te llamaré la reina de las estrellas. Aunque no tienes idea de lo que estoy diciendo en este momento, ¿verdad?"

"What did you say?" Dilynn asked, now completely compliant in their arms.

"My queen."

Dilynn turned her head back, gazing at them from the corner of her eye. "There was more. More words."

"I know many more words," Alex said.

"Say more words," Dilynn requested. Her head leaned back against them as the rain began to fall once more just past their protected position under the porch.

"In English or Espanol?"

"Whichever you want." Dilynn held Alex's arms against her. "I waited all year for you to talk to me."

Alex smiled at the knowledge of Dilynn thinking about them. They only get to smile though. There are no more words because the yelling started within the house.

"I fucking told you to stay the fuck away from her!" Dilynn's daughter shouted.

"What is your problem?!" Casey yelled back.

"Everyone stop yelling," Lyra announced.

"Sadie, stop fucking talking to her," Evie growled, and the table legs clawed at the tile floor.

Alex looked at Dilynn, who pointed at the door. "I have to go before Casey gets a black eye."

"Your kid needs to learn to keep her weight balanced. She lunges too much when she punches," Alex stated.

"Thanks, but I will not be telling her that," Dilynn said. She tapped Alex's collarbone, then dragged her feet back to the house. "Last thing she needs is to have an easier time punching people in the face."

Dilynn was already headed inside when Sadie bolted through the front door. She was carrying two heavy bags that she hoisted into the back of a large truck.

Her chin pressed against her chest as she leaned against the vehicle, clearly waiting for whoever was supposed to take her home.

"Guys, hitting each other isn't how we solve this," they heard Landon say. "Stop trying to punch-- FUCK!"

"What the fuck, Evie?" Casey shouted. "You plannin' on cheating on Landon with her now. After you punched me for fucking her when she literally put my hand in her pants and told me to--"

"Shut the fuck up," Evie yelled. "Don't you fucking talk about her like that. She's a fucking freshman, you fucking pervert!"

"I'm not a fucking pervert!" Casey snapped back. "She did it. I just didn't stop her. If anyone is sick, it's her. She's the little girl out here fucking the whole damn team. Like, what do you think she's doing here. You're just the next one on her list so she doesn't have to go—"

"ENOUGH!" Dilynn shouted.

Alex waited on the porch, not wanting to leave Sadie outside by herself. They weren't in a position to drive her home, so staying until someone came out was what they could offer the kid.

They were about to go stand with her when they heard Dilynn command, "Casey go home. And Lyra, go get Sadie. She can't stand out there in the rain. Shit. Landon your face. Evie, get some fucking ice before Imara comes for my goddamn head."

Lyra muttered her whole way out to get Sadie. "¿Por qué siempre tiene que ser una pinche psicópata? ¿Qué diablos estoy haciendo aquí?"

Alex's hand shot up to cover the snort that came from them.

Lyra looked over her shoulder at them but didn't stop going after the girl who was now walking down the street. Shaking her head, she pointed at the house. "Crees que estoy bromeando, pero en serio deberías correr."

The front door clicked shut, and Casey huffed past them. She didn't acknowledge Alex like Lyra had. Her phone was back in her hand though, and she was typing out a message before she growled at the phone, "They say I'm the fucking pervert. You're the one that is supposed to give a damn."

Casey got in her car, kicking up gravel as she sped away. She was driving too fast for the weather but there was no stopping her. Alex waited not wanting to be the person Casey might actually crash into in her rage.

The house had grown temporarily quiet, while Lyra and Sadie had an animated conversation that ended in the younger girl pressed to the elder's chest. Lyra wiped the tears from the kid's face with her thumbs. She nodded to the house.

Alex figured it was probably time to go, and knew it was so when they heard Dilynn through the windowpanes.

"Look at the goddamn sign. No. Hitting. No. Kicking. No. Biting. No. Spitting. And NO FUCKING YELLING!"

15

With everyone gone for the night, Dilynn sat down to take a chance she'd been afraid to even think about. Her resume was ready. Her cover letter detailed her ideas on responsible discipline. Ways to improve academic achievement. All things that would make an ideal candidate for an Assistant Principal. A posting that had gone up that morning on the school portal. A position that would give her a sense of power to not have to worry about Simone.

She submitted the application, still trying to shake the guilt she'd felt for sending Evie and Landon to take Sadie to a home she didn't have. Where she was going, Dilynn wouldn't know. Couldn't know. She had to focus on the fact that Evie and Lyra were both tucked safe into their rooms.

It was a little after ten when Dilynn snuck out of her room to get her computer. The mess from pizza night still covered the tables and counters, but she'd leave it for tomorrow when she got home from work. No one else was going to touch it, after all.

Her head shot up when she heard Evie talking. Lyra's door was closed, and Dilynn reminded herself that the kid routinely fell asleep on the phone with Landon. A part of Dilynn wanted to check in on Evie since she'd left to take Sadie, still angry at getting yelled at for trying to hit Casey.

Dilynn scooped up a cold slice of pizza and studied the hallway. When Evie returned, she was still stompy and had gone straight to bed without a word. Giving the girl space was probably the best choice, so Dilynn went back to bed. After the first bite of pizza, she regretted not snagging more. It wasn't unusual for her to forget to eat when she had that many people come for pizza night, but tonight had been much more eventful with Alex there.

She'd thought she'd just imagined Alex at first. It wasn't until Alex blinked twice that Dilynn accepted that those green eyes were real. The heart she'd laid her chest against had beat faster. And Alex looked like kissing her was something desired. She'd been so distracted by Alex's presence she didn't notice the comment from Runner until she was looking up the meaning of the lilacs.

The comment almost didn't matter. Almost.

She should have ignored it. At least if she'd ignored it, she would have been better prepared for Evie's betrayal. If she'd been focused on the conversation instead of defending Priya and herself, she'd have prepared something to say when Evie drove a double decker bus in her direction.

RunnerAT89's comment was waiting for her when she crawled into bed. She read through it again even though she'd already responded.

> RunnerAT89 on Chapter 10:
> Morgan pissed me off, but she does that in the book too so I guess she's in character? Priya is basically a Mary Sue in this though. She's so self-deprecating, it's no wonder Morgan doesn't actually talk to her. I don't understand why you keep writing her like she doesn't know she'd awesome because that is off character again. If you have to make her that way, then she should probably just drive her car off the road in the next chapter. Maybe she'll get a TBI and it will make her less annoying. I'm not saying kill her off, just make her less annoying.

This comment hurt more than the others. She'd thought she was finally making progress with Runner, and it was like being back to square one. Well, maybe square two since this time Runner hadn't told her to off herself.

She reread the last few chapters. Priya had become more conscious of her looks. The whole scene where she was staring in the mirror was probably over kill. It had just been on Dilynn's mind, and she'd used her own thoughts to remind herself that no woman should talk about herself like that. Had specifically written it to show how cruel Priya could be to herself and remind the reader not to talk to themself like that.

It was fiction, with only some of it real. The feelings of herself were real. Priya's self-doubt was hers. The rest, though, were fantasies she had about Alex fucking her senseless. Morgan didn't make love to Priya because Dilynn never imagined Alex would look at her like that, only the confession made it real. Made Alex's interest in her more than just a fantasy.

The story was the fantasy now, and reality was similar but different. She wanted that stoic and commanding version of Alex. Wanted to be bent and twisted to Alex's desires, but it lay in the realm of what she expected fantasy Alex would want from her because it was all she'd ever known.

Dilynn had never made love to anyone. There was the time she played make-a-wish in high school, but it wasn't love. It was fast and strange and confusing. Then she was with Sylvia. The woman did power and control, not love though. Never making love, or even vanilla sex; that wasn't why Sylvia kept her. And Brandon, well that always ended quickly and with her mind somewhere else. Once upon a time it had gnawed at Dilynn. She'd felt like a cheater each time her mind wandered to Sylvia while she lay under him. She didn't get into the daydreams until she'd met Alex. That was the moment she stopped lying in wait for something to happen. It was the point she had started chasing after Brandon for the attention, so she didn't have to feel guilty about thinking of Alex while she was alone.

Alex's smile had brought Dilynn back to the fanfiction site. Morning break room visits offered the blonde a muse, because Alex had looked exactly like Dilynn had imagined Morgan when writing her. She wrote of making love to Alex, at first, because it was a fantasy. The new story was too real though. She'd written the version of Alex she held in her mind before last month. Composed a narrative based in Alex not wanting her heart, just her cunt wet and spent.

Her eyes followed the ceiling fan's oscillations as she tried to figure out when she'd started hating herself. Middle school had been rough, but that was because when the other girls grew legs, she grew breasts. That hadn't been horrible really, but she hated the attention that came with them. Hid in oversized shirts she'd stolen from her dad until everyone else had boobs and legs. By the time she was ready to come out of hiding, no one cared she had boobs because she was still the size of a sixth grader, with a weird interest in reading romance novels written for horny housewives.

Going back to the comment, Dilynn read through it again. She'd had to look up what a Mary Sue was, but once she read the Wikipedia description, she could understand why RunnerAT89 would call Priya one. She smiled through everything. She was overly nice. It was an act though. Priya was her, not Evie. Evie's character was the one that got to punch people, while Priya had to keep her shit together. It wasn't fair, but it was real.

She'd already responded to Runner. Responded the moment she'd read the message. Even burned a pizza because she had been too focused on tapping out her response. It didn't matter though.

Runner hadn't responded. It had been hours, and they never waited hours to respond. They were waiting for the next chapter. The one that should have been happy because Morgan would show up. She would come to Priya's house, and it would feel real. Not like a game. Not like Priya didn't matter.

Priya wasn't a MarySue. So, Dilynn tore apart the draft she'd written during lunch. Stripped away the happiness she'd felt when she'd imagined Alex showing up.

The truth was Alex coming over was happiness because it was real. This was fiction. And Dilynn used fiction to manage the pain and the guilt still gnawing away at her gut.

Morgan had shown up, but it wasn't to fuck her on the kitchen table like she'd originally written. It didn't make sense anyways. Even Alex would look at her differently when she stripped away her clothes. Maybe she could just keep the lights off if they got to that point. Alex would be able to tell her sides squished, but it would be too dark to see it.

She paused as she felt like her skin was too tight. If her girls thought about themselves the way she was thinking about herself, she would be trying to convince them they were wrong. She needed to be wrong, but she poked her stomach. It was hard to love herself when she couldn't see herself as someone she would want to sleep with.

She didn't bother rereading the chapter before she posted it. It probably didn't make much sense, but her mind was too tangled up to make it make sense. She shouldn't have let Landon leave with Sadie. Even if he took her home to his mom, she shouldn't have had to leave.

Dilynn flipped on the television. She held the phone to her chest as the show began to play. The phone vibrated just as Dilynn's lids began to droop.

She was exhausted, but she checked her emails anyways. The first vibration was, in fact, not RunnerAT89. It was another one of her commentors. One she rarely responded to because the comment was typically the same. She was about to put the phone on the charger when it buzzed once more.

At this point she knew it was an addiction. In place of the vodka, she'd turned pathetically to reading comments as soon as they came in specifically searching for the troll.

Evie was right to make fun of her, though Dilynn was right to think there was more to her most determined critic. She opened the email from Runner.

> RunnerAT89 on Chapter 10:
> Had a bad morning. I don't actually want Priya to crash her car. I can't be more mean than this going forward cause you've grown on me more than I would ever care to admit. I bet you have that effect on most people you meet. I've started to think that your stories may be more real than fiction. Whoever Morgan was to you, they screwed up. Priya isn't a MarySue. It's easy to read her that way because she's kind. Even when she doesn't want to be. That says a lot about her as a character. Most people, like me, would not do or say the kind thing when we don't mean it. The fact that Priya does just that makes her a very precious and lovely human. The type of person I would want to know. A real-life princess. I bet you were the homecoming queen because people liked you. Not because people feared you. Sleep well, my storytelling princess.

Whatever image RunnerAT89 had of her was clearly romanticized bullshit. She wasn't homecoming anything. She'd made it through high school being known as the girl who'd gotten pregnant at fifteen. It made leaving Seattle so easy. She'd crossed the stage with a diploma her mother had said would be impossible to do with a kid on her hip, then loaded up the car, and moved to Arizona.

A place where no one knew her, even the baby that had been sent there two days after she was born. A few months later, she'd met Sylvia at a club in Scottsdale and learned she was not as straight as she had always thought. Sylvia had a way of making Dilynn feel safe, even when her hand was wrapped around Dilynn's throat. Treated her to a different type of life in the shadows but provided her luxurious accommodations to keep her willfully quiet and available as Sylvia tried to live up to her wealthy father's expectations.

It wasn't love and never gentle. However, Dilynn had woken up on birthdays to presents and very hot sex. She looked around the house the other woman had purchased for her when she'd told Sylvia she had to do something about Evie. Sylvia had smiled and told her she'd make a great mom. Left her the deed to the house in both their names two days later after clearing out their townhouse like they hadn't spent the last seven years living together. The deed came with a letter telling Dilynn to bring the kid home. This home, because the townhouse wasn't her home. Never had been. So, she did. Brought Evie to the house where Sylvia had put all her things in the garage. Then she brought Brandon home when a pipe had fictionally burst.

She hadn't realized Brandon was a rebound for a relationship she'd never actually had with Sylvia. She'd never trusted Brandon with her desires. He was the rebound, which is why she never really wanted him. After meeting Lyra, the feeling in her gut she'd felt guilty for had been right and wrong. She'd hated herself for thinking she wasn't enough for him. It wasn't about him though. He'd not wanted her because he was a loser, like Alex had said.

Alex.

Everything about Alex reminded Dilynn of her time when Sylvia would walk through the front door.

Alex wanted her though. Unless it was a game, but Alex said no games. Held her close and tight. Even Sylvia hadn't done that. Alex and Sylvia side-by-side were a testament to Dilynn's type: tall and stoically composed. Sylvia looked at her like a steak, which definitely made her feel desirable, but Sylvia would do what anyone appreciative of a steak would do. She consumed as much as she wanted, then threw away the rest. Alex looked at her differently, she just didn't know what it was yet.

The phone fell out of Dilynn's hand and smacked her square in the nose. "Damn it."

Rubbing her nose was a feeble attempt to fight back the tears as the still very real pain pulsed in her face. Once they started to fall, Dilynn couldn't stop them. Remnants of the still very raw emotions she couldn't squash resurfaced at the word princess. Sylvia had used it to degrade her. She hated the name, because she knew it was just a way to make her feel weak. Princesses weren't powerful. They were damsels in distress, locked in towers or put to sleep while the rest of the world moved on without them.

She sucked back the snot and wiped away the tears. The world wasn't moving on without her. It couldn't. There were too many people counting on her to keep her shit together. Being called cupcake or pumpkin wasn't better, but at least it wasn't calling her weak.

Getting her breathing under control, she typed out: "And the score is: Runner 1 GreyAltEgo 2. Success is mine!!!!"

She probably should have explained where the points came from. Establish some rules for the game she'd created in her head where she gets points if they say something nice to her or writes in grammatically correct sentences. Even praised them for writing grammatically correct sentences, which is why she'd given them a point.

The response came almost immediately.

RunnerAT89 of Chapter 10:
Glad to make your day.

'It's night :),' Dilynn sent back.

She looked at the message again. RunnerAT89 hadn't made her night. The commentor was fun to talk to, but she wanted more. She wanted hugs from Alex. Wanted to know if she could trust the person, who maybe wasn't as much like Sylvia as Dilynn had thought.

The phone vibrated again, pulling Dilynn from the Venn diagram she'd made in her mind.

RunnerAT89 on Chapter 10:
A day is a unit of time. in common usage, it is an interval equal to 24 hours. It also can mean the consecutive period of time during which the sun is above the horizon of a location, also known as daytime.

Her eyes rolled. The troll truly was a master of copy and paste.

> GreyAltEgo on Chapter 10:
> Dearest Dictionary.com or Wikipedia (I shall let you decide which is more appropriate OC Morgan), I am familiar with the various meanings of the term. I opted to read your statement in reference to the connotation of day as being a time when the sun is showing on the particular geographical region I was residing when I read your original comment. Obviously, this response was to elicit a defensive reaction on your part, therefore, would cause you to create an automated dictionary recitation. Either way, I was correct in both accounts: my analysis of your response coming during the evening, as well as your desire to correct me by regurgitating the dictionary to me. Bringing the score to: Runner: 1 GreyAltEgo: 4

Within minutes, two emails came almost simultaneously. Runner must be online and refreshing the page because there was no way with the normal lag time that they were waiting for emails.

> RunnerAT89 on Chapter 10:
> You're wonderful. You can win some now, but I still have some points. And I don't like to lose.

> RunnerAT89 on Chapter 10: It was wiki.

Even though it's stupid. Even though Evie would make fun of her if she knew Dilynn was up late talking to the troll, she couldn't stop her fingers from responding.

'Hmmm. Curiouser and curiouser. You don't even know the rules of the game we're playing yet you feel like you can win. I know nothing about you though. No gender. No age. No race. No nationality. You claim to know me from my story. But what about you? Are you in love with Morgan or just as broody and clueless as she is?'

There was movement in the kitchen that pulled Dilynn's attention from her phone. A grunt followed a bang. Evie was still up because it was her voice bouncing off the walls and floor saying, "Fucking cabinet."

"You, okay?" Dilynn asked, unsure why she was letting the kid know she was still awake after Evie gave her the silent treatment when she'd stomped back into the house.

Evie didn't answer her, which didn't surprise Dilynn.

What did surprise her was the sound of the kid's feet coming towards her room. She didn't say anything when Evie walked into the room and crawled into Dilynn's bed.

Evie wrapped the covers up to her nose and looked at Dilynn with tired eyes. It took everything in Dilynn not to panic. The kid had never breached her doorway before. An unspoken rule that Evie would not enter the space because she was afraid of Dilynn. A rule Evie broke.

"What's up?" Dilynn asked.

Evie's lip disappeared between her teeth. Chewing on her words and her flesh, she looked Dilynn over. Honesty was still a new development between them, so Dilynn waited patiently.

"She wouldn't answer most of my questions, but I knew her. I used to be really mean to her like she said, and I think I made her drop out of school."

Lyra.

"She said she came here. Said she spent the night with you when I was at the sleep over. Said she's going to be my new mommy, and I think she was joking, but..."

Dilynn's throat burned with the bile rising. She warned Lyra not to make Evie feel unsafe. She couldn't feel that unsafe though, not when Evie was in Dilynn's bed.

"Did you sleep with her?" Evie asked.

Dilynn shook her head violently. Then she said, "No. Absolutely not. But she did try. She thought it would make it possible for her to stay."

Evie's gaze flitted to the TV, then back at Dilynn.

"When I first came here..." Evie swallowed thickly. "After juvie, I thought the same thing. I thought I would have to... to stay. I didn't before but there was a guard in juvie, and she did things to other girls, and I didn't think girls would do that. But she tried... she tried to take me into the closet and another girl helped me. She shouldn't have helped me because I hit her like I hit Lyra. I hit her more afterwards. And then they sent me here. I came here and I just didn't know. I didn't know so I was mean."

This was a part of Evie's story Dilynn had never known. The kid's release from detention had happened so quickly, but she'd never said why.

"It's going to take some time for me to help Lyra feel like she is safe enough to not think she has to sleep with me," Dilynn told her daughter. "Kinda like Sadie and your teammates."

"She tries to be like me," Evie said, making herself comfortable. "I think she slept with the team to get my attention. I told her to stop that shit though."

Dilynn reached over the top of the covers and squeezed Evie's hand. "You did good with her. But remember if she is like you, she won't just stop."

Evie nodded, then punched a line in the covers between them. It was boundary line that signaled where Dilynn was allowed to sleep in her own bed. She didn't question it, instead Dilynn changed the show on the TV to *Friends*. Even with the background noise, the silence was unsettling.

"What if it was me?" Evie whispered.

Gravity shifted as Dilynn closed her eyes and thanked every deity she could name in the moment with the affirmation that it hadn't been her kid. That Brandon had never hurt her like her bio mom's husband.

"I would've killed him," Dilynn whispered.

Evie curled closer into Dilynn, breaking the barrier between them. The mother absorbed the heat radiating from the kid. The kid elbowed her softly though. Just enough to be playful as she poked holes in Dilynn's promise.

"You don't even kill spiders."

The phone vibrated on the nightstand, but this was more important than Dilynn's desire to know more about Runner the Troll. Evie was putting trust in Dilynn to protect her from monsters with nice faces.

Evie moved to be the big spoon. After all these years, she still couldn't turn her back to Dilynn. However, she trusted Dilynn enough to crawl into bed for the first time.

"I have a lot of money," Dilynn reminded the girl. "And I think of clever ways to mutilate and murder people in my stories. I promise, I would kill him or pay someone to do it for me. Plus, Sylvia is an heiress. She surely has some pull. A contact of some sort."

Dilynn expected a laugh, but she didn't get one. Instead, she felt the kid's breath on the back of her head.

"Are we going to kill him for Lyra?"

Heart pounding, Dilynn found it difficult to see straight, hear anything, or really think. She was thinking though. She was thinking so much she couldn't answer Evie. Thinking about calling Sylvia back in the morning. There'd been silence since Sylvia responded to her texts to come fuck her senseless on a Wednesday. She couldn't cancel pizza night to get laid though, so she'd called it off. She could call Sylvia though. Tell the woman what Brandon did to the kid on the other side of the house.

"In the morning, we should talk about keeping her and Sadie," Evie said. "I don't think Lyra has a place to go and Sadie... she's in a group home. We need to talk about keeping Sadie too."

Dilynn licked her lips.

"Is Lyra eighteen?" Dilynn asked, hoping Evie would know.

Evie's yawn was loud and long. She rolled away from Dilynn as she answered. "I think so, maybe. We had history together, but she was a sophomore when I was a freshman."

The phone continued to vibrate, but Dilynn ignored it. She had bigger things to worry about than Runner's age and gender.

"Someone's going to have to share a room," Dilynn reminded the kid.

Evie stole more of Dilynn's blankets. Her half-asleep grumble was enough to keep Dilynn up most of the night.

"I'll share with Sadie. I promised to keep her safe."

Dilynn looked over at Evie. Listened to the deep breaths shift into lawnmower like snores. Evie wasn't in her bed because she needed Dilynn. No, the girl promised to keep Sadie safe when Dilynn sent her out into the storm.

Her ears weren't superpowered, but Dilynn thought she could hear two others in the house instead of just one. Two girls hiding in her home, and she would have to pretend like she didn't know if she was going to play the game Marcus told her was necessary.

So, she didn't wake Evie to ask.

She waited until the episode had ended and Evie had stopped moving. Only then did she slip from the room to play ninja. The door to Evie's room needed some WD-40 but the kid in Evie's bed had apparently needed as much sleep as her daughter.

When she turned, Lyra practically gave Dilynn a heart attack.

"She made me promise not to tell you," Lyra said.

Dilynn nodded. She kept her hand pressed to her heart, as she told it to chill the fuck out.

"Keep her secret," Dilynn whispered. She looked at the girl. "Why are you still awake?"

Lyra looked at the door, then back at Dilynn. "I'm a light sleeper, and you walk like your feet are made of lead."

Dilynn shook her head and shrugged. She nodded to the room she'd promised Lyra. "Get to bed. It's late."

Lyra's eyes rolled. "I'm an adult, you don't have to mom me." But she turned back into the room. The lock on the door clicked into place, and Dilynn felt her heart sink. So much pain under one roof.

She ran her fingers over the walls of the hallway, and sent a simple prayer that Sylvia had the foundation checked for cracks before purchasing the house. It would need to be solid to survive what was to come next.

16

The pile of graded papers almost toppled when Alex gathered them from the passenger seat of their Audi Thursday morning. Swearing at them in Spanish didn't work, so Alex tried cussing them out in English. That didn't work either, it just pissed the pages off worse. They bit Alex's finger, drawing blood.

Alex sucked on their battle wound when a Prius pulled into the spot next to them. The same Prius that was parked next to them every day. The parking job was as crooked as always, but whoever the driver was had never dinged their car. Alex had never been there late enough to see who drove the vehicle but smiled broadly when they realized it was Dilynn. There were a litany of swear words coming from the white car where Dilynn sat behind foggy windows with not one but two kids.

The warning bell rang while Evie tried to pull a tri-fold presentation board from the backseat. She smacked it a few times on the car trying to get it through the space since Dilynn left her minimal room on that side of the car.

Sadie slipped out from behind Dilynn's seat. The top half of her hair was drenched, but the moisture did nothing for the knots at the back. She pulled a rubber band from her wrist and wrapped her hair up in a worse knot before she noticed Alex standing at the back of their SUV watching her.

"Hi," Sadie offered quietly.

Evie growled something at her mother before she yanked the board from the car. The rain paused for the girl with the project at least.

"Good morning, Sadie," Alex offered. "Did you have a fun sleep over last night?"

Sadie looked over at Dilynn, "I... uh..."

"I found Sadie walking to school this morning in the rain," Dilynn stated. She wrapped the kid in a hug, and told her, "Go, before you're late. And stop by between periods. I'll make you a sandwich."

"Thanks for the ride, Ms. Greyson," Sadie called as she chased after Evie.

She stayed a step behind the older girl who'd met up with a group of kids Alex had seen the night before. Landon took Evie's poster board and her sports bag on one arm, then Sadie's with the other. Alex decided the boy-man was possibly the most decent human they'd ever met.

They unfortunately had no hands to take Dilynn's stuff, but they realized she didn't have any of her belongings on her. Dilynn's arm waved frantically, as she called out, "Bye, baby. Make good choices!"

Evie didn't turn. She froze for a moment as a few of her friends teased the girl. Alex wanted to join in on their laughter, but Dilynn's voice pulled their eyes to her tiny bundled up body.

"Is this *your* car?" she asked. Her eyes were wide as she moved to the passenger side. She cupped her hands to the glass and leaned forward to peer within. "This is a really nice car."

Alex tried to think of something not stupid to say. Nothing came before Dilynn snapped out of her fan girl moment.

"Sorry, I've always loved Audis, just can't bring myself to buy one." She shrugged her shoulders, then added, "Maybe when the sequel comes out."

Sequel. The kids said she'd written a book. They needed to ask about it because when they'd searched her name the night before, nothing came up.

The start bell rang, but they still couldn't think of how to ask her for the title of her book. Feeling like a teenager being noticed by the popular girl for the first time, Alex was stuck in freeze mode.

Dilynn didn't seem to have anything to say either. Her eyes were locked on Alex's crotch, so they checked to see if their zipper was down. Thank goodness it wasn't.

Alex tried to smooth out the wrinkles from their slacks, but the papers shifted under their arm in another stealth attack. They tried futilely to stabilize them. However, their revolt was successful, and many escaped to the asphalt.

"Malditas putas. Todas ustedes son basura y deberían haber sido utilizadas como leña en lugar de documentar las primera etapas de la grandeza."

Alex dropped the pile, freeing them all.

"Las maldigo a ustedes y a sus primos para que acaben en la basura en vez de en el reciclaje."

Dilynn's hands came to aid them so quickly. She clearly had more practice as she moved the packets to and fro, arranging the staples to alternating sides of the pile. The pile was much flatter when she was done.

"I hate it when the papers just don't want to return to their owners," she said with a chuckle. "I always think of them as abused and neglected children not wanting to return to their parents."

She handed the last stack of papers to Alex. "Can't blame them, really, when I read the same mistakes all year."

"I don't even know why I bother writing on them," Alex confessed.

Dilynn bit her lip and looked back at the school. "Because if you don't, there will be one kid that goes home and whines that her teacher doesn't care enough to give her feedback on her work."

For some reason, Alex could picture the scene in their head. Evie bursting through Dilynn's front door and whining about their feedback on her essay.

"You sound familiar with this scenario."

"Bitter," she corrected them. "I have a few this year that are upset about how much feedback I give. One lady hates me and says I am overly critical because I expect her son to capitalize words. Then I have a freshman that thinks she's curing cancer with her definition essay on the word pontificate."

She ran her hands over her face. Then she peeked out between her fingers. "I'm just going to apologize in advance for my perfectionist daughter. Please let her do rewrites because if you give her a 98, she's going to want those two missing points."

Alex shrugged. "I'll keep that in mind just in case I decide to give her less than a 100. I feel like she probably knows how to write a decent essay though. I mean, she's your kid."

When they stand up, they are so close to Dilynn. Close, like they had been the night before. When they were allowed to pull her against them. This was work, though. Work wasn't a place either of them could stand in the parking lot and hug each other.

"So, I was thinking..." Dilynn started.

Her shirt caught Alex's attention, or maybe it was the way her breasts stretched it so perfectly that a part of the wording disappeared under her bust. Alex was trying to read the words, when Dilynn's hand waved in front of her tits. "Earth to Trikru? Hello?"

"Sorry, I—" Alex started, but there were no excuses. They could say they were trying to read the shirt, but they weren't even listening because there were boobs with nipples peeking out from the material because it was a rainy day. Plus, she'd worn the blue cardigan they'd gotten her.

"Alex," they tell her. Dilynn's head slightly tilted to the side. "Please, call me Alex."

"You mean, you don't want to go by muffin or snickerdoodle?" Dilynn teased them. A smile crawled up her face, revealing two rows of very well cared for teeth and dimples. "You know, I love that name, actually. There's a neutrality about it, while I always get confused with a dude. My dad liked it that way though. He never called me by my real name."

"Dilynn is your fake name?" Alex asked, realizing the woman was filled with secrets.

She nodded and sighed. "I was named after both my grandmothers. Diana-Lynn. My dad hated my mom's mom though, so he called me Dilynn, which pissed her the fuck off since my mom had put her name first."

Alex tried it out and had to agree with Dilynn's dad. It tasted weird.

They ran their hand over the back of their neck. "Well, I could never consider you of the masculine persuasion."

With a shrug, Dilynn said, "Yeah, well my publisher said it would be hard for people to find me with my name spelled weird, but it does keep people from stalking me, so that's nice."

They were about to ask what pen name she used, but Dilynn had other plans.

"So, picking up Sadie from the side of the road made us almost late for school and I didn't get to stop at Starbucks. I was going to head there now, if you wanna come. With me. I mean, you don't have to, but it would be, like, off campus so Simone wouldn't see you, like, talking to me. No one would see you."

Alex stood quiet for so long they sent the wrong message. Her smile fell slightly. She searched them and they knew what she was looking for. Had read it in the chapter she'd written the night before. Where Morgan had seen her outside of work and walked away from her.

"Yeah, I know stupid. You don't even drink coffee," she whispered to herself. Thumbing towards her car, she said, "I'm going to go before my foot ends up any farther in my mouth."

The car door was open, and she was about to get in while they were still looking for words. Looking for a way to tell Dilynn they don't ever want her to think they would keep her secret.

"You said no games," Dilynn said just loud enough to be heard. She looked back at them. "You said no games and you asked for more hugs and it's tomorrow instead of yesterday and I'm just really confused. Like, do you like me? Do you not like me?"

They opened their mouth but shut it as she kept talking.

"It's okay to say you're not interested. But if you're not, then I need you just to say it. Because last night you said you... Look, if you just wanted... something else. If that was what you came for. Just something easy... I can't. No matter what Simone told you."

She took a deep breath.

"I'm a mom. I can't be the bad mom in the movies who goes around fucking her coworkers. I wasn't that person when Simone tried to sleep with me, and I won't be that person with you. So, just stop pretending if you're not actually interested."

Alex wanted to fist the air at the verification there was no sex with Simone.

"I am sorry for holding you up. I'm sure you have stuff to do."

Her eyes were fixed on the damp concrete, and her hands tugged at her shirt. Pulled the material away from her curves like she was uncomfortable in her skin. Like Priya did when she'd stood before Morgan, and Morgan had walked away.

"I'll drive," Alex choked out. "I..."

The winter storm that had raged throughout the night had nothing on the storm in Dilynn's eyes. Dilynn was more scared of their rejection than they were of hers.

"Dilynn," they said, dipping their chin down. "I'm not sure what the boundaries are at work, but I'm not scared to be seen with you. Even in front of Simone. She knows. She knows how I feel about you."

They reached out and took her hand in theirs. There was a single freckle on the back, and they traced a finger over it.

"Being seen with you... that's like... like getting to hold hands with the homecoming queen when you're the history nerd." They pointed towards their car. "I mean, I have glasses in the car. I can show you how much of a nerd I really am."

Dilynn's arms wrapped around their middle. She'd moved so fast, they almost dropped the essays again. But she was hugging them. Hugging them in the parking lot, and it made five hugs in less than twenty-four hours.

"You smell like rain," she whispered. "It makes me think of home."

Their cheek rested on the top of Dilynn's head. They inhaled the sweet dessert-like perfume, and told her, "You smell like a cupcake."

Her tiny hand slapped them in the chest, so they added, "A violent cupcake. Like Devil's food. Eating you would probably be addictive."

As soon as the words were out, they sucked in a breath. Tried to inhale them back into their mouth before she heard, but she heard. Damn it, she heard them, and she had a quip faster than they could apologize.

"I've heard whipped cream adds to the enjoyment." She leaned back but didn't release them. "And you're right about one thing. I am not fucking vanilla. No matter how fluorescent my ass is at night."

Their hand moved up her back. Fingers carded through her hair at the base of her neck, tightening just slightly.

Her lower lip disappeared between her teeth as she looked up at them.

"Are you a good girl, Dilynn Greyson?" Alex asked, taking a line from Dilynn's own story.

"Not so much without my coffee," Dilynn whispered. "I can be an outright demon."

Alex's grip tightened on the woman's hair. The things they could do to her if she wanted them to.

"Let's get you your fix then," they said. They released her and opened the door to their car.

Alex fought the urge to sprint to the other side once Dilynn was in the passenger's seat. They settled with overly large steps to get themself back to her.

The papers were dropped in the backseat.

"I won't lie, Alex, if I was seventeen, I would date you just for this car," Dilynn announced once they were in the driver's seat.

Dilynn's hands roamed along the leather seats and the dashboard in front of her. She looked at the backseat and laughed. "Let's be real, if this was high school, we'd be fucking in the backseat, not going for coffee."

Resting their arm on the center console, Alex tried to look calm and collected, instead of horny and seriously contemplating how to get her into the backseat. They could call out. They'd tell her to do the same.

"You, okay?" she asked. "You look a little red."

Alex put the key in the ignition and started the car.

"I was just thinking about how much more I love this car now," they confessed.

They turned onto the main street, still thinking about what she would look like in the back seat as they ran their tongue around her—

"God, it's so smooth," she said. "It's like riding on air."

If they weren't red before, they were now.

"Would you like... uh... some music?"

Dilynn nodded, still running her hands across the interior as though she was caressing a lover. They plugged in their iPhone to the auxiliary cord and hit the shuffle button to stop another dirty fantasy about Dilynn caressing their abs as she sat on their lap. She was small enough to do that without even hitting her head on the roof.

Their phone was apparently sympathetic to the warring essays. It launched its own sneak attack. The first song to burst through the speakers was a female voice begging to be fucked.

Alex smacked at the power knob to the radio so hard it hurt their hand. 'Just watch the road,' they told themself.

Dilynn turned to face them, but they kept their eyes locked on the road. She pushed the power button back on and let the song play out until the chorus. That was when Dilynn changed the song. Changed the song to one that may be worse than the first. Another smutty song. All about vaginas and wetness, making Alex feel like a sex addict.

They hit the pause button and looked at Dilynn. She was staring straight ahead with a cheeky grin plastered across her face.

"Let's play a game," she said so casually.

They can tell she's plotting something devious, and they speed up. Coffee was like holy water. It would chase away the demons from the woman until they were better equipped to satisfy them.

"What kind of game?" Alex asked, narrowing their gaze at her.

"The kind that I get to know you through your music," she said simply.

Her chin was lowered, and she was doing that thing with her eyes. The thing she used in her stories when Priya was playing innocent to get Morgan's attention. It annoyed them in the story, but they understood the allure now. She looked so innocent, yet so needy.

'Trap,' their brain told them.

'But I want to be in her trap,' they reminded it.

"How do we play?" they asked

She wiggled a little in her seat.

Alex wasn't sure who was winning at this point. They hadn't figured out how she was keeping score the night before when they had ended up in a fight with another commentor on the story. They felt they deserved points though.

One for driving. One for pulling her hair. One for telling her they wanted her. Those were all things that made her happy, and they deserved points. Points in a game where she didn't know they were the other player.

"Simple rules," Dilynn stated. "I get to hit the next button three more times and then I provide you an analysis of what I learned about you." she explained.

"One more song," they negotiated stupidly.

'Wait,' their brain said. 'No,' it followed with.

"Ohhhkay," Dilynn said.

Before Alex can argue. Before they can make her go back to the initially proposed three songs, she hit next, and the metallic beat began. They tried to ride out the uncomfortableness knowing the words were only going to make it worse. The trifecta of smutty, inappropriate, and just fucking ironic music for Dilynn to judge them by.

She began to hum as "I Get Off" played. Her eyes were fixed on them, and she belted out the chorus. She knew every word and sang it at the proper pitch. Only Dilynn didn't know what Alex knew, and it made the guilt of knowing rise in the back of their throat.

They hit pause. They needed to talk about it. She'd said no games, and they'd agreed. She needed to know that they hadn't intentionally invaded her house and pretended to be someone else.

"Hey! I was serenading you!" Dilynn cried out a little too loudly for the silent car. She crossed her arms over her chest and stared forward with a pouty lower lip jutting out.

"So..." they started with. They were still chewing on the rest of the sentence when she clapped her hands. The clapping caused their mouth to shut and the prepared explanation to dissolve on their tongue.

Dilynn seemed to construct her analysis faster than most people could process the command 'run.'

"The first two songs suggest you are a very sensual person and are not ashamed of being sexual, maybe even a little... kinky."

Alex tried not to sound like a prepubescent boy when they asked, "And the... last. You said the first two. You separated... you must have separated them for... a reason."

Dilynn smiled with eyes fixed on her fingers. She glanced over just for a second.

"Are you sure you want to know?"

They weren't sure. So, they lied.

"Yeah. Of course, I want to know."

"The last one... it's dark and, like, manipulative. Like, it's about secrets and it kinda reminds me of that *Friends* episode where they pretend they don't know that I know that they know, and it just keeps getting bigger and bigger and bigger. Because no one really talks about anything."

The car next to them had its windows down. The mariachi music was so loud Alex's window rattled. They couldn't hear half of what she was saying over their own thoughts and the music.

"It's like you have secrets that you are trying to decide who knows and guess their reaction..."

The trumpets blared, drowning out part of her sentence.

"...don't seem to really like talking. Which is fine. I don't want you to think that you have to talk to me..."

They try to focus on her words, but the passionate vocals called to them. A longing song of missed opportunities and a need for second chances.

"And at first, I was like, 'okay, just not interested, Dilynn. Like, take a hint.'" She took a deep breath, robbing the car of oxygen. Then, she let it all out at once.

'Why doesn't she think I'm interested?' they ask themself. They couldn't understand that when they'd told her they were interested.

"And I said the vanilla thing... but that might also not matter because..."

They needed the light to change. Needed to get away from the car so they could hear her.

"And I get the whole fanfiction thing... like it's just a lot so... yeah."

They take a deep breath when Dilynn ran out of air. The song in the car next to them changed and it waged less of an attack, so maybe they wouldn't miss anything else she had to say.

She'd not moved on with her analysis. She sat beside them silently, and they realized she was probably waiting for them to say something. To respond to her ramblings.

She picked at the nail polish on her ring finger. When it was gone, she scraped off the purple from the thumb nail on the other hand.

"How'd I do?" she whispered.

Her chin dropped when they couldn't make words come out of their mouth. Words.

She'd compiled three thousand words in a night. Each sentence had torn the seams of their tattered being, then sewed them back together with stitching so sturdy, yet delicate, they felt less like a rag and more like a quilt ready to hold her. And they couldn't piece together three words to explain to her she was perfect.

The road had no answers, but Alex looked down it. It might be up or straight. Dilynn would be able to describe it to them, but they can't tell her they know she was faking a smile once more and they wanted to be the cause of something real. They didn't want her to have to wear a mask.

Maybe the creator of worlds, where warriors wore graveyards on their flesh, understood what it took to survive and would not turn away from them if she knew the truth. Maybe she knew what it was like to pull it off and see the scars of the others that were supposed to care etched into her skin.

"I know—"

They cut the sentence off and turned back to the road because the car behind them honked. The light was green, and first period was only so long. Alex drove instead of completing their sentence and Dilynn was looking out the window with no more nail polish on her fingernails.

Shifting in their seat, Alex pointed at the entrance to Starbucks. "We're... we're here."

They are unable to respond to the quiet chuckle of the woman beside them. The waves of her laughter hovered in the air instead of beating them in the chest. It wasn't real. Just like the smile Dilynn wore when she ordered her chai tea latte. It was fixed in place when she asked them to order something they wanted, which they did to make her happy. A $4 hot chocolate.

Dilynn's arm brushed against them while they waited. They needed to break the tension, so they bumped into her with a little more force. She swung like a pendulum and struck back. Her hip bone hit Alex just in the right spot on their thigh. A hit hard enough that their leg gave out slightly.

Alex caught themself on her shoulders. Pulled her against themself as they waited for their knee to work again. All the knots tied within them unraveled, and they can't do anything but drape themself around her.

"You're the first person to hug me in a long time," Dilynn whispered. "Like the hugs at pizza night... the others just do the back pat thing."

They rested their chin on her head and pulled her closer.

"The music was so loud. From the car next to us. I didn't hear a lot of what you said," they admitted.

Dilynn leaned back slightly and looked up at them.

"I don't actually know what your analysis of me is. But you said I have secrets. I don't really have secrets. I just don't talk to people."

They placed their finger under her chin to keep her from looking away.

"I don't even talk to Simone. She talks. I listen. That's it. So, if that is something... something you're still worried about, you don't have to be."

The barista called out their drinks. They needed to get them and get back to the school before they were late. But they couldn't wait any longer.

"I'm going to kiss you now, Dilynn Greyson," they said. "I'm telling you so you can tell me to stop if you don't want me to kiss you, but I have dreamed about kissing you for so long."

She didn't say anything. Her eyes closed as they held her in the perfect position to place a chaste kiss against her lips.

Her lips were soft, and she kissed them back. Their hand moved to the back of her neck, and they pulled her in closer. Noses nudged together, then her tongue traced over their lower lip.

Heat spread like a fire through them as the small flicker of fantasized need ignited. Her soft moan was gasoline for their desire.

Their lungs burned in need of oxygen, but Alex didn't want to leave the moment. Everything they ever wanted was in this moment with this beautiful woman that liked them. Wanted them.

"Go out with me," they commanded. "Tomorrow. Let me take you out."

"Yes... Tomorrow," was her only response before their lips met again, sealing the agreement.

Her lips pressed against theirs softly and slowly. The desperation of the previous kiss turned subtle and gentle. This kiss was shorter. They didn't have time because they still had to get their drinks and get back to the school. But they drove with their fingers intertwined over the console.

They had ten minutes to spare before the bell rang. Ten minutes to steal another kiss ending in Dilynn crawling over the console and into their lap when they bit lightly on her lower lip. Their mind spun as she made the sweetest sounds to the dragging of their teeth over her skin.

Using every clue to her desires that she buried in her stories, they worked their lips and teeth over the areas they could remember that caused Priya to fall apart. She ground her core against them. It didn't feel like a cold morning, but humid and hot. The motion of Dilynn's hips had them wishing Dilynn would have worn a skirt. With a skirt they would have had her come apart with their finger inside her as they left a mark on the side of her neck.

The parking lot wasn't the place to get her off for the first time, they knew this. Knew it was the type of thing that she would walk away from. Something she would chew away the skin on her lip in worry over. They prayed to any entity for strength to slow down, but their body had found the rhythm to the beat of her heart, and they couldn't stop themself from pulling her down against them to give her more friction.

"If you don't stop that, I'm going to ruin your shirt," Dilynn warned as they licked up the valley between her breasts.

"Don't care about the shirt," Alex said, running their teeth over her clavicle. Their fingers dug into her ass cheeks trying to get her closer, to show her how serious they were.

"Can't give it all away before dinner," Dilynn said playfully. But her mouth hung open when they nipped at the top of her breast. "What would you think of me then?"

"Coffee was breakfast. We had a meal," Alex promised into her chest. They needed her naked twenty minutes ago, and they started considering how quickly they both could call out of work.

She pushed back against them. Pulled her core down to their lap where they couldn't feel her heat anymore. Her finger traced their jaw line. "After the dinner date you can fuck me anywhere in this car. But I have to at least pretend to be a respectable lady."

Alex's nose scrunched up, but they knew she was right about not letting this be the first time. "Fine. But I'm holding you to that any way that I want."

"I said anywhere." Dilynn twirled a curl on the back of their neck. "But any way can be arranged. I'll wear something more conducive to be at your mercy after dinner."

Alex shut their eyes. They tried to imagine what she would look like with something car fucking conducive on. It did nothing to make them want to stop. Their hips chased her as she tried to navigate back to her side of the car.

Alex was barely out of the vehicle with the pile of papers once more in their arms when the first bell rang. Dilynn stood between the two cars with kiss swollen lips and a hickey hidden by her waves. They'd have to be more careful in the future about where they claimed her.

"God, today is going to suck," she grumbled as she fought her key in the gate.

"Why?" they asked, suddenly worried they'd ruined it by being a bad kisser.

She got the gate open and looked up at them. The warning bell rang, but Dilynn stood there for a moment studying them.

"You ruined my panties," she stated flatly. "I'm very wet and it's not like they are going to dry when I can still feel your lips on me."

A smile rose up Alex's face. With a slight shrug, they said, "I'm not sorry."

Dilynn's eyes rolled dramatically. She didn't hold the gate open for them. Let the metal smack against them as she moved on to the door to the building.

"Are you coming?" she yelled back at them.

"Yes, mi reina," Alex said, realizing they would probably spend the rest of their life chasing after the caffeine-fueled gremlin who moved faster than her little legs should be able to.

She finished her latte as they pushed through the door. The students were already moving in small packs through the hallway.

"Would you come to the game with me?" she asked, but her eyes were staring down the hallway. "Sadie plays first, then Evie. If you wanted, you could come to dinner with us afterwards."

Alex followed her gaze to the social studies side of the building. Found Simone leaning against the door studying their every move.

"Yes," Alex said. "I would love that."

Dilynn chucked her coffee cup into the trash. "I'll be in my room. After school. We can walk over to the gym together."

As she walked away, Alex heard a gravelly growl from beside them.

"It's awkward watching you ogle my mom's ass in front of my friends and her students." Evie looked them up and down. "I have to go to school here, and I'm already weird, so maybe chill out a little."

Alex shifted the papers under their arm and met the girl's stare.

"You were the homecoming princess," they reminded her. "That makes you popular, not weird."

Evie watched Dilynn slip into her classroom. She gestured to the people in the hallway. "They only like me because I'm a bitch, and movies tell them that the mean one is the top of the social pyramid."

Alex turned to the girl. The kid who'd wanted them to like her seemed to have vanished.

"I saw you at the mall. You saw what he did to her. And what I did to him," Evie reminded them. "It's my job to protect her because she's not a bitch like me."

Alex swallowed the critique of the kid's attack. They would tell her later. Tell her when they proved to her that they wouldn't hurt her mom.

The tardy bell rang, and they watched Simone yelling at kids to get to class. Evie reached out and took the papers from their hands.

"I never liked him, and I'm not sure if I should like you, but I'm willing to give you a chance. I just need you to tell Coach to get off her ass."

Alex licked their lips. They nodded towards their classroom. "Come with me so I can write you a pass."

Evie followed alongside them as they explained, "I already spoke with Coach

Wyatt. She promised to be civil."

"Don't bring Coach to the house." Evie commanded. She glanced back down the hallway. "I don't know what happened between them. I just know something went down freshman year and it was a big deal with the teachers and my mom had to basically hide in her classroom. This year is the first time she stopped hiding. Probably because her coffee maker broke, but she bought a new one so she's hiding again."

Alex held the door for their students. They shook each kid's hand and greeted them by name. Only when they were all inside, did Alex ask Evie, "Who was here when that happened? What teachers?"

Evie bit her lip and looked up at the ceiling. Slowly, she said, "Mr. Jordan was here. I know he asked her out a few times. Mr. Thompson was here too, and they have always been friends. She had us help him move when he got a divorce last semester. One of them might know what really happened. They won't tell me, but maybe they will tell you."

Alex gave the girl a half smile. "I can't make you any promises that I can tell if they tell me."

"Then I can't promise to like you," Evie warned.

Alex pointed to their desk. "Let's get you a pass."

17

When the final bell rang, Dilynn sighed out a breath of relief with the rest of the students. Teaching had taken a back seat in her head, so by the time the students finished getting settled, she'd rewritten the objective on the board to focus on defending their claims with evidence in oral discussion. A task she didn't have to participate in, gratefully, since her mind was trapped switching gears continuously between how to handle Runner's response to her question the night before and Alex's hands and mouth on her body.

Evie's bag hit the ground not even two minutes after the final bell. It was abnormal for Evie to come visit Dilynn after school, so the mother should have expected the words tearing through the quiet around her.

"So, what's up with Trikru and you?" Evie asked.

The words were out of Evie's mouth before Landon and Sadie made it fully into the room. Mixed emotions seemed to be the challenge of the day for Dilynn. At first, her brain focused on Evie's proclamation when the halls were still filled with kids who loved a good story.

"Evie, you can't just..." but her words tapered off.

Dilynn felt the guilt crawl up her spine at the sight of Sadie. Her lanky limbs were swimming in the baggy clothes her daughter kept in the back of her dresser but never wore.

She'd forgotten to get clothes from the bin in the garage for the kid like she'd done for Lyra. Forgotten to go see Marcus. Forgotten about Sadie because Alex had pulled her hair and she'd melted into a puddle of arousal.

Her finger ran over the hickey just below the snowflake tattoo on her neck. She must have been out of her mind, crawling over the center console to sit in Alex's lap because a kiss hadn't been enough. She needed Alex's lips and hands everywhere.

Dilynn made a mental note to call Marcus as soon as the kids left. He would help her. She could start the process tomorrow since she'd kept her foster license up to date. Tomorrow, when she was not straddling her coworker in her dream car during first period, she'd talk to Sadie's worker and order the kid a bed.

Lyra. The girl popped into Dilynn's head. Another distraction from Evie, still waiting on an answer to her question.

She abandoned the quizzes on her desk. Even though she hadn't done much of anything, she was still tired from getting the crap kicked out of her while Evie slept. Sitting in the ancient, orange Lazy Boy didn't help how tired she was, but tonight was going to be late, so she might as well rest while she can.

"What do you mean?" she asked finally. Her head fell back against the upholstery, and she closed her eyes. She couldn't sleep though. Alex would be there soon.

"I saw you totally flirting this morning after you tried to embarrass me and I watched you two leave together," Evie stated. Her lip curled up over her teeth. "Casey said she saw a hickey on your neck, and I told her that was bullshit, but your hair is down, and it's never down by the end of the day."

Dilynn reached up immediately to where Alex had marked her. Ran her finger over the bruise once more. She could feel her face turning red.

"Gross, Mom. You barely know Trikru," Evie growled. "Like, you're old. Old people don't walk around with hickeys."

Dilynn's eyes rolled. "I'm not that old. I'm not even thirty."

"What happened? Did Trikru offer to let you drive her car if you fucked her in the parking lot?" Evie snapped.

When Dilynn didn't answer, Evie's snapping turned to growling. "Like, gross. You just got rid of Brandon. Like, chill out. That's what you tell everyone else. Don't jump from one relationship to the next, but no, you're fucking your co-workers in their cars. Giant hypocrite."

The mother could hear her own words buried between the insults. She did tell the kids the gist of Evie's lecture. Told Casey the same thing not even a day ago.

"I bet that's what happened with Coach. That is what happened, huh? Wealthy Winters broke up with you so you did the dirty all over campus and then realized you shouldn't date people you work with, so you broke her heart and you're going to do the same thing with Trikru, and she's supposed to be my teacher next year. You're just going to fuck up my life even more because you know I need—"

Evie's rant stopped when Landon cleared his throat.

Both Greysons followed his eyes to the door where Alex leaned. There was no hint of how Alex felt about walking into the conversation. Just a steady gaze locked on Dilynn.

"Dude, it's creepy to just stand there listening in on a private mother-daughter conversation," Evie stated, clearly not caring after she was just worried about Alex giving her a good grade.

Alex's head tilted to the side as their gaze shifted from Dilynn to Evie. With a single finger held up, Alex said, "One, Landon and Sadie are here so this is not a private conversation."

"They're family," Evie grumbled just loud enough for Dilynn to hear.

Alex raised a second finger. "Two, you told me earlier when you caught me staring at your mother that you would give me a chance."

The third finger caused Evie's eyes to roll so hard there was no doubt in Dilynn's mind the girl would need corrective surgery for the permanent damage she just caused. She added eye doctor appointment for all three girls to her list of things to do.

"And three, no one but me drives my car." Alex's eyes shifted back to Dilynn. "That passenger's seat is all yours, but driving is out of the question. Especially since I have seen the way you park."

Dilynn's jaw dropped open. She patted her chest, "I'm a good driver."

Landon snorted, dragging Dilynn's glare from Alex to him. He didn't even try to hide his smile like any decent human would. Not an ounce of decency to even pretend like his betrayal hadn't taken place.

"Do you have something to say?" Dilynn asked him. She raised her shoulders like it would make him cave. Make him fix his damn face.

"I have changed three tires on your car in the last year from you hitting curbs alone," he stated. "And the one time I let you drive my truck, you hit a mattress on the freeway."

Forget worrying about her face turning red. Dilynn's entire body flushed and she decided Atlas cutting off the kid's hand in the sequel would be the least of his problems.

"You're going to regret that," Dilynn promised him. "Just wait. I will get my revenge and it will feel like walking on glass."

Landon apparently had a death wish for his character because he simply shrugged off her warning.

"Can't be any worse than having my keys taken away by my mom for letting you drive my truck."

Alex's lips tucked back, and Dilynn would make that frustratingly beautiful human pay for this defamation as well. She tried to find a way to punish Alex without punishing herself but came up with nothing before Landon added, "Momma G, you are good at so many things. Driving is about on level with your cooking though."

"Can we get back to the real issue?" Evie groaned. She looked over at Alex. "When I said I could maybe like you... well, that was before I found out you decided to act like a Dyson on her neck. Now everyone is asking me who she hooked up with, and..."

Her head fell to the side like the bones in her neck turned to jelly. She waved at Alex, and said, "I know that Trikru has the hots for you. That shit be obvious."

She rolled her eyes again before looking back at Dilynn. Her lips curled devilishly, and she was going to seek vengeance.

"The question is, does she make you need to change your—?"

Dilynn lunged towards Evie. The younger girl squealed before her mother smashed her into the back of the couch. Dilynn's hand covered the kid's mouth, cutting off the last word of her sentence. She tried to keep the loudmouth covered, but Evie's arms came around Dilynn, and pushed her into the crack between the top fixed cushions and the sagging seat.

She was stuck, but she still had a firm grip around Evie's middle with one hand and the other found a way back to her mouth. That was until the teen's teeth sunk into her mother's flesh.

"NO BITING!" Dilynn cried out. It hurt bad enough that Dilynn pushed Evie. Pushed her so hard, the girl rolled from the couch.

Landon chuckled when Evie hit with a thump against the concrete floor while Dilynn struggled to get out of the crack.

A lost pencil between the cushions threatened to impale her in the ass. It gave her a warning poke and Dilynn tried to pull up but there was nothing to grip. After clawing at the cushions for possibly a whole minute, she accepted her fate as a new addition of disposable items. Her arms flapped while she slowly sank into the abyss.

She was saved at the last moment, thanks to a mostly bald man-boy leaning over the stained material. Landon grabbed the woman's uninjured hand, then shifted his weight back to tug her free from the couch's portal to the unknown.

Once she was seated, his mahogany eyes examined the teeth impressions left on the side of Dilynn's hand.

"Good thing she didn't break the skin," he offered. He winked at her when he added, "Did you finally get her vaccinated, because I'm pretty sure she has rabies?"

Before Dilynn could explain that vaccines could only prevent diseases, not cure them, Landon fell face first into the couch. His knees hit the floor, and Evie was laying atop his back, holding him down.

"You're supposed to be defending me. You're my boyfriend," she hollered.

Sadie had her hands over her mouth. She'd managed to get off the couch and meld in with the whiteboard in her white basketball jersey while Evie smacked Landon on the back.

He rolled his body to the side. Dilynn knew football would take him to college, but wrestling gave him an advantage in his routine battles against Evie. He was more flexible than his dense frame made him out to be, able to bend and shift his weight around.

Being tossed and turned, forced Evie to hold on tighter or fall. She couldn't hit him when she was holding on to him like he was a mechanical bull, so she chose to fall back on the couch and kick at him instead.

"You traitor," Evie growled at the boy who'd managed to get out of her reach.

Landon turned to Evie with his hands up in surrender. He understood her daughter's need to control the things in her life. Had been there when she'd spiraled.

"Bae, it's Momma G. I have to protect her. You made me promise a long time ago to protect her." He waved his hand in a circle over Dilynn's personal bubble. "You said I had to protect her from even you because she is an angel. Your word. Angel."

Dilynn bounced on the couch, thrusting her fists in the air. She pointed her thumbs toward her shaking body and mouthed the word "angel."

"Fallen angel," Evie grumbled, folding her arms over her chest.

Dilynn continued making a fool of herself, dancing in the seat. Her legs kicked out and shoulders moved to the music in her head. Not for a second did she stop to remember it wasn't just her and the kids.

Stopping came with the sound of Alex laughing at her. Freezing came when she saw Alex standing farther in the room. Dilynn made a note of Alex's tell. A hand at the back of the neck every time things were a little weird. She was a little weird.

Adjusting her t-shirt that was close to showing a very un-flat portion of skin, Dilynn asked, "So... how was your day?"

"Fine."

Alex's eyes wandered the space like something might have changed in two days. It wasn't like she hadn't noticed Alex cataloging the room before; however, this time she felt the spiders crawl up her back when Alex's gaze settled on the cardboard castle around Dilynn's desk. It had been different when Dilynn was sitting behind the cardboard. She hadn't felt like Alex was watching her then.

"I swear, I didn't build it myself," Dilynn anxiously explained. "The kids in Landon's class, they brought in the boxes, and they had spray painted them to look like a castle. We were reading a book."

Landon interjected, "*Waiting for the Barbarians.* It's about these people that live life hidden in a castle because they think the barbarians are coming. But there are no barbarians. Just fear. My freshmen class did it because Momma G stopped leaving her room."

Dilynn's eyes dropped to the floor. She hadn't realized that was why they'd built her a castle. She'd imagined it differently, but it made sense why they wouldn't just tell her. She'd have come out to make them feel better, not because it was safe.

He leaned back in the chair he had originally been in. He looked over at Dilynn. "It didn't work, though. I know the rules are not to talk—"

"No," Dilynn whispered. "The rules are the rules for a reason. Trikru and Wyatt are friends. You would feel the need to protect your friend if someone was speaking ill of them, so we are not going to put Trikru in a position to feel uncomfortable. But I am going to clarify something for everyone here. I did not fuck anyone on campus. I did not fuck anyone in their car on campus. And I never slept with Wyatt. I never went on a date with Wyatt. I never made any advances towards Wyatt. I did not reciprocate her interest, just like I did not reciprocate Jordan's advances. I have only had sex with three people in my entire life, so I would appreciate just a little respect."

She turned her attention to Evie. "Kid, we both know I don't ask for much in respect, and I am going to ask you for this again. Please let the stuff with Wyatt go. She is your coach, and you care about her, and I don't want the past to tarnish your opinion of her or of me, so please, just let it go. You wanna talk shit about Brandon and tell me I'm a fucking idiot, have at it. You want to make fun of me for Sylvia, whatever. You want to tease me about acting like a foolish freshman and making out with Trikru, fine. But no more Simone Wyatt."

Evie wouldn't look at her. She picked at her nail bed, until her eyes rose to Alex.

"Does it make you uncomfortable?" Evie asked. "To know your friend made it so my mom didn't come out of her classroom?"

Dilynn opened her mouth to correct Evie, but she shut it. She shut it because she needed Evie to know it was okay to ask hard questions. She also wanted to know if Alex had an answer to that particular question. Because Alex promised no games, but everyone in her life had lied to her at some point or another.

"Yes," Alex said. "It does. I feel like I only have part of the story, and I know that part isn't the whole truth."

Leaning against a desk, Alex's jaw worked over the unspoken words. There was a question there, maybe even a confession.

"No one ever knows the whole story," Dilynn offered. "And sometimes it's better not to know."

"Is it though?" Evie countered. "Not knowing means you could end up on the wrong side of the fight."

"Wrong is just something someone doesn't like," Sadie said from the side of the room. She was staring at the floor, as though she hadn't realized she'd even spoken. She raised her gaze to the group. "Ms. Greyson doesn't want anyone not to like someone else, so she doesn't let people say things that make someone seem wrong. Do you think the world would be a better place if people just said nice things and no one ever said something mean?"

Dilynn licked her lips. She knew Simone was wrong for what she did, nevertheless, HR had told her it would be unprofessional of her to answer any questions regarding what happened. So, she'd swallowed the emotions of the event, and tried to be the better person.

"I'd rather know how someone truly feels than be lied to," Alex stated. "That being said, Sadie, I think maybe it would be a better place if people spoke kindly because if we said nice things enough, maybe we would believe them. Like if you tell yourself that you are smart, then maybe you would feel more confident about taking classes you fear are too hard."

Dilynn looked over at the girl. She, too, tugged on the back of her neck, and Dilynn had to look back at Alex. She hadn't noticed the resemblance between the two before now. It was strangely comforting to the blonde. Like, maybe they were meant to walk into her life at the same time.

"Do you know why Coach is so mean to my mom?" Evie pressed.

Alex took a deep breath before answering. "Honestly, even if I did know, it's not my story to share. If your mom or your coach wanted you to know, they would tell you. And your mom just asked you to drop the subject, which is maybe something you should do."

"So, you just keep secrets," Evie snapped back. "That makes you sound hella shady."

"I think, I'm going to take a page from your mom's book," Alex stated. "I'm just going to treat everyone the way I want to be treated. So, if my friend says something mean, then I will call her out on it. It does mean that I will probably never get my copy paper or my Expo markers back, but I will still stand up to her."

Dilynn added Alex's answer to her list of interesting things she could put in a book. She could easily use the copy paper and Expo markers in the next chapter of the teacher story.

"We did not get a chance to discuss plans for this evening," Alex said to Dilynn. "You mentioned dinner with the girls after the game. Should I make us a reservation some place?"

"You should ask them," Dilynn said. Her nose scrunched up. "Just please, not that seafood place again."

"Olive Garden," Evie announced. "I could eat my weight in breadsticks. And we should see if Lyra can come."

Dilynn looked at her kid. "Do you have a way to reach Lyra?"

Evie shook her head. "She was gone before I got up this morning. Maybe if we swing by the house, she'll be there."

Lyra had vanished that morning, but she'd probably left with Sadie. Dilynn searched the road, hoping to find both girls walking, but Sadie was the only one trekking down the sidewalk towards the school.

"You should call Sarah," Landon offered. "Or I can go to the house and see if she's there. I can bring her to the game and you all can go together."

"You're not coming?" Evie pouted. She looked at Alex. "He gets to come, doesn't he?"

Alex shrugged. "I'm not in charge. Your mother invited me to dinner with you all after the game."

"Oh, then see, you get to come," Evie declared.

It wasn't a rule that Landon was invited to everything, but it was the way things were. Dilynn could never say she secretly hoped her daughter had found her fairytale happily ever after in high school. She would hope for it though.

"Of course, you're invited," Dilynn added. "And I will call Sarah and see if she will go check if Lyra is home."

Dilynn turned back to Sadie, "You're coming too, so let your adults know that you will be going to dinner and that it will be late so you can just sleep at our house tonight. If they are okay with it, then I can bring you to school in the morning again."

Evie shot up from her seat and tugged Sadie by the arm. "She can call while we go to the gym. Come on, you have warmups."

The kids' shoes dragged against the floor on their way out. Landon carried both girls' gear, and Alex pointed to the boy as the door shut behind him.

"I like him," Alex stated.

"He is a great human," Dilynn provided. "I just hope my kid doesn't break his heart."

Alex looked at the door once more, then back at Dilynn.

"So... you're never going to tell me what happened with Simone and you."

"No."

Alex tugged on the tie some. "Is it because you don't trust me not to run to her and tell her what you said?"

Dilynn chewed on her lip. She considered if that was why. The more she let the idea settle in her mind, the more she knew that wasn't why.

"I never see you with anyone else," Dilynn stated. She pulled her knees to her chest. "Maybe you have friends outside of work, but I don't. You're, like, the only person that talks to me besides my kids and the troll on my story. So, if she is your only friend, then I don't want to take that from you."

Alex ran a finger over a minion water bottle, sitting in the watch tower of the cardboard castle.

"If you won't tell me, it means whatever happened was bad enough to potentially threaten my friendship with her. Which suggests maybe I shouldn't be friends with her."

Dilynn rested her chin on her knees. She couldn't get any smaller, but she wished she could sink into the couch.

"You said you have part of the story," Dilynn whispered. "I'm not stupid to believe my version of things is the only truth. I mean, I think about if I wrote a story from more than one person's perspective, then there are two truths. Neither are fun. Both sides were angry and hurt. And both sides are going to remember details that make them feel like they were not in the wrong. I have thought about what happened a lot. I have looked for reasons why what happened happened. At the end of the day, other people knowing... it just won't change anything. Just add more hurt."

Alex looked around the room again, before they finally approached Dilynn. Sat alongside her and took one of her hands in their own.

"You asked me for no secrets." Alex took a deep breath, before adding, "This feels like a big secret. A secret only you are keeping, because Simone did tell me her side."

Dilynn took her hand back. Wrapped herself up tighter in the corner.

"What did she say happened?"

"That doesn't seem fair," Alex said. "As a historian, I should look at two primary sources and form my own conclusions. If I tell you what she said, then it may impact what you decide to tell me."

Dilynn didn't want to have this conversation. She'd made it a point to state over and over again. Telling Alex about what happened would mean sharing details about her relationship with Sylvia. Details that would make Alex look at her differently.

"We should get to the game," she said to change the conversation. "Sadie plays first, and I want to be there for tip off."

Alex's head fell to the side. It was clear the conversation would continue to come up, but Alex was apparently going to let it go for now. Maybe after some time, when Alex got to know her better, she could say something. Maybe Alex would be able to see that she wasn't a prostitute like Simone claimed she was.

"So, question." Alex's smile rose. "Does making out only count as one hug?"

Dilynn unwrapped herself from her tiny ball. She moved to the couch and straddled Alex's lap once more. Making out with Alex was a distraction she thoroughly enjoyed.

"I think we should count it as one," she said as she stole a kiss from the plush lips. "After all it was only one embrace."

They took the time to properly greet one another. Steady hands pulled Dilynn down over hard abs once more as lips worked their way down her neck. Alex's hair came loose again while Dilynn held on. She was so close with just the friction of riding Alex still fully clothed.

"We should stop before you ruin your panties," Alex said.

"You did that this morning," Dilynn hissed when teeth grazed over her breast.

She wasn't having any of the stopping nonsense this time, even though she knew she would feel bad about it later. She took Alex's hand and placed it on her breast, too worked up to walk away this time. The emotions about it would be a future Dilynn problem.

"I have thought about this too many times," she confessed. "Please, don't stop."

Alex did stop this time though. She was pushed on to the couch so Alex could get up. Once the door was locked, Alex's body pressed her into the couch. Alex's lip sucked only lightly enough to not leave a mark on the top of her breast as hands kneaded the cotton covered flesh.

"I have wanted to do this to you every morning." Alex's confession tasted so sweet on her kiss swollen lips. A hand slid up her shirt and squeezed her breast. "Do you want this?"

Dilynn nodded, rolling her hips against them. She was breaking her rule. No sex in her classroom. She didn't care though. Not with Alex's weight pushing her into the cushion and her heels locked around the toned torso.

"What time is tip off?" Alex asked.

"4:45," she breathed out as Alex pulled her shirt up and stared at the bra she'd worn not thinking Alex would ever see it.

"If you want to cum it will be with me inside of you. That's the rule for the first time. I want to feel you and see you come undone." The button of Dilynn's slacks was tugged slightly. Hungry eyes stared at her, as Alex said, "May I?"

Dilynn swallowed thickly. She wanted Alex's long digits diving within her drenched core. She wanted to feel the hot touch on her clit that she's imagined so many times. She wanted to unwind so badly, but future Dilynn had entered the conversation, and she knew it was wrong.

"You're right," Alex whispered. They pressed a kiss to her lips, then said, "Not like this."

"Not like this," Dilynn echoed. She looked up at the lights. "I mean, the lighting here is terrible. Somewhere... with less buzzing beams and not in my laundry day bra."

Alex hovered over her. Her chin was raised, and a soft kiss was placed on her lips. It was gentle and brief.

"I want to," Dilynn whispered. "To do that with you."

"Me, too," Alex promised. "But I want more. And I think before we do that, I need to get the kid to like me."

"All of them," Dilynn said, hoping Alex wouldn't run away.

The dark eyebrows creased in the middle. "You have more kids?"

Dilynn pressed her hands to Alex's chest. She knew Alex deserved to know, especially before anything else happened. Give Alex an early out. She couldn't tell the whole truth, but she didn't feel like that would matter. The fourth child wouldn't yell at Alex. Alex would never meet her. The other three would be there though.

"Lyra and Sadie," Dilynn said. "Lyra moved in last night, and Sadie is in the group home. I'm going to foster Sadie. I was supposed to start the process with Marcus this morning but—"

Alex's eyes grew. "I'm sorry. I wouldn't have—"

Dilynn pressed her fingers over the kiss swollen lips. "I wanted to be with you this morning. I want to go to dinner with you tonight. But you should know that I'm a mom."

Alex gave her space to move by sitting on the other end of the couch. She sat up, not able to explain this with her stomach still in full view under the unflattering glare of the classroom lights.

"I'm a single mom," Dilynn reminded Alex. She knew Alex knew that, but she needed it to be said. "I'm a single mom and you should think about that. Like really think about it before we go out. Think about if you want to be with a single mom. They are going to come first. There will be rules and boundaries and... and they come first."

Alex leaned forward and pulled Dilynn's hair out from behind her ear, covering the mark left earlier.

"I wouldn't have it any other way. Plus, they're going to love me."

Dilynn's eyes rolled, and she shoved Alex slightly. "They don't even like me. What makes you think they will love you?"

With a shrug, Alex offered simply, "I'm basically a giant teenager. I like karate and I don't own a TV, but I am pretty good at video games. Evie will love that I can teach her how to punch people, and I already started looking up weird questions to ask Sadie, and Lyra and I have a secret language. So, yep. They'll love me. Plus, I will be good to you, and they will like that."

The phone in Dilynn's pocket vibrated. She pulled it out, then sent Landon a text.

"Everything okay?" Alex asked.

Dilynn's eyebrows rose as she messaged Sarah back that Landon said he would come get Lyra. She shoved the phone back in her pocket.

"I need to get Lyra a cellphone." Shaking her head, she realized she needed to explain. "Sarah spoke to Lyra. She was at the house and Landon went to get her. Don't worry about dinner. I will pay because I have the three girls, and Evie wasn't lying about Landon always being invited. His mother and I, we aren't in a relationship, but she's a single mom, too, so we kinda co-parent the kids together."

"He already likes me." Alex's hands rubbed together deviously. "All the pieces are coming together. Win over the kids with breadsticks tonight, sweep mommy dearest off her feet tomorrow. Promised christening of my car."

Dilynn shoved Alex again, but her hand was caught in Alex's grasp. Her body was turned around swiftly until her back pressed flush to Alex's chest.

"You know, when you're mine," Alex whispered just past Dilynn's ear. "All this shoving, is going to end in your ass being tied to the bed frame as I take my revenge."

Alex sucked in a breath. The hold on Dilynn's hands loosened. "If that is something you would enjoy. The tying up. The edging. If you don't, then I wouldn't. I wouldn't do anything to make you feel unsafe. We would talk about it beforehand. Talk about limits so that you... you always need to feel safe, and I... I am aggressive sometimes."

Dilynn's head fell back and looked up at the dilated pupil's promising her nothing short of some of her darkest fantasies. Something she would write about tonight and give Runner the Troll something new to complain about.

"I love marks," Dilynn said. "When we get there, you should know... I enjoy being marked. Bite marks. Hickeys I can hide. Fingerprints. Handprints. Occasionally a crop shaped welt."

Alex's hold tightened and lips curled upwards. "I enjoy marking what is mine."

"What is yours?"

"Yes, what is mine. And you will be mine." One hand wrapped lightly around her neck. Pressed just enough to show her who was in control in that moment.

A finger on the other hand grazed over her perked nipple. "These will be mine." It ran down to her navel. "This will be mine." Then the finger continued on its naughty path to her clit. "And this," her cunt was cupped, as Alex promised, "will be mine."

"You sound so sure of yourself," Dilynn whispered.

She gasped when the palm of Alex's hand pressed against her. Her eyes rolled back as they continued to rotate the amount of pressure they provided her, until her hips were grinding against their hand.

"Mine," Alex whispered. "It will be mine when I want it. How I want it. And I'll treat it so well, that just being in the same room with me will have you slick with need."

"It already does that," Dilynn confessed.

"Just wait until it meets my tongue and my fingers and my strap." The hand covering her squeezed her tightly, before it came back up to hold her. "But not today."

"You're mean," Dilynn whined.

"Maybe you should stop shoving me then," Alex said playfully. "Because I can be very vindictive."

Alex stole one more kiss before the door was unlocked. They were still sneaking glances at one another when their path unfortunately crossed Simone's just as they exited the building. Dilynn braced herself for whatever low blow would be slung in her direction.

Simone matched Alex and Dilynn's stride, walking with them to the gym. For the first time in almost three years, Simone spoke to her like a human, "Everliegh's three-point shot is getting better. I didn't approve of her playing basketball at first, but all the running has kept her in shape for softball season."

"I was surprised they put her on varsity since she'd never played before." Dilynn licked her lips, and added, "She has been working with the State U coach on her pitch framing. I take her to see her twice a week, and she's playing club on weekends."

"Good. We need to send out film of her playing this season." Dilynn hated the way Simone claimed Evie. It was worse than that fight that ensued when Dilynn told the woman that Evie would not be attending private training sessions with her. That she would not be permitted to spend time with Evie when she wasn't at school.

"Do you have videos from her tournaments? I could put together the reel." Simone stopped outside the gym. "If you are okay with that."

"It's how the scouts will come," Alex offered. "I did the same thing my junior year. Sent films to school."

"You played sports in college?" Dilynn asked.

"Track. 400 and 800 meters."

"They run a lot," Simone stated, but grunted when Alex elbowed her.

"What the fuck did I do?" Simone snapped. "I was literally civil like you said to be."

The two didn't say anything verbally, but Dilynn watched a whole conversation take place between them. Simone understood something. It was clear by the way her eyes rolled. And Dilynn knew in that moment that she wasn't the only one with a secret.

18

Waiting in the stands for a basketball game to begin was a familiar experience that left Alex with a warm nostalgia. They held their hands together, filled with a mixture of anticipation and excitement. The stands weren't jam-packed by any means, but Dilynn was a teenager magnet.

The benches around Dilynn filled before other sections. The sound of chatter filled the space as the teenage court surrounded the junior class princess pressed into Queen Greyson's side. One of the louder boys from pizza night even bowed to Greyson, earning a grunt of displeasure from Simone. The kids discussed the freshmen players that would possibly move up to varsity next year, the upcoming game, and predictions for the outcome. There was a sense of unity among the crowd, one that joined together with a bitter resentment for division rivals.

By the time Sadie's game began, Alex's seat next to Dilynn had been stolen. Simone and Alex were pushed down the bench with Landon and Lyra's arrival. The lithe framed girl squeezed between them and Dilynn when Evie refused to leave her mother's side. Landon, the group's prince, was given the space alongside his girlfriend, causing all the other kids to shuffle their seats to create a protective ring around Cactus High School's royal family.

Simone leaned into their space. With her gaze focused on the kid by Alex, she asked, "Who is that?"

"Dilynn's oldest," Alex answered so quietly, they couldn't be certain Simone understood them.

"Eighteen?" Simone asked.

Alex cast the woman a glare that they hoped said, 'shut-up'. They couldn't be sure how old the girl was. What they did know was Simone married a nineteen-year-old that she didn't love, and it had become clear her interests lay too close to the gray area of legal for their taste.

"No," Alex said, staring at the floor. "No more questions like that."

Sadie had the ball. Her movement up the court was chaotic at best. She dribbled in a swoop around the defender, repeatedly getting caught up by the other girl's long arms trying to smack the ball away. Alex had to give Sadie credit for her grit. She didn't give up, and she didn't get flustered no matter how many times she got shoved to the side.

In her fourth attempt to get past the other guard, Sadie's speed caught the other kid off balance. The guard's arm shot outward, karate chopping Sadie across the chest and sending her to the ground.

The home crowd booed while Dilynn was on her feet screaming at the referee. Cheering loudly wasn't something Alex typically partook in, but they found themself clapping and calling out to the future Greyson when she got up from the ground.

Sadie was fouled three times in the first two minutes of play and had made six of the eleven points on the board. The other team had come to play dirty, but the freshman team was taking the hits and putting up points.

Sadie pushed her hair out of her face and took the inbound pass. Her body was shoved from one defender to another, but she managed to split the defense down the middle and make another shot. She was at the foul line, once again wrestling with her hair.

Every time she ran down the court it came loose from the knot she kept trying to twist it in. When the other team was at the foul line, Sadie walked over to her bench and held up the busted rubber band.

"Jesus, the kid looks like she doesn't own a brush," Simone stated.

"She just needs someone to teach her how to manage it," Alex hissed. "She's in a group home. No one cares there."

Simone's head tilted. "I didn't know that."

She leaned back and spoke as she watched the game. "Casey said she would bring her to practice so someone would catch her." Carding her fingers through her hair, Simone added, "I need her and Everleigh to bury that shit before season. Like, I get Everleigh cheated on her with Landon, but that was over a year ago. And I know Casey is getting some, so just let it go."

The coach pulled Sadie from the game to deal with the busted rubber band that the kid was trying to tie in knot so she could reuse it. Alex felt their skin itch as they watched the kid struggle with trying to figure out how to fix things for herself, since no one had ever been there to help her.

"I don't want to know about any of that," Alex stated flatly. They shook their head. "They are kids. No one should be talking about them and that stuff. It's just not okay. Just let them be kids."

Alex pushed up from the bleachers. They ensured their faculty badge was visible before walking around the court to where Sadie sat on the bench. They pulled the extra-large hair band from their own low bun already coming apart thanks to Dilynn's hands. Their curls came loose in long spirals down their back still secured into a ponytail as they crouched behind the home team's bench.

"May I fix your hair?" Alex asked Sadie whose eyes were staring at the rubber band now in multiple pieces in her hand.

Sadie looked up at Alex, then down at the thick elastic band in their hands. She nodded silently, turning back to the game. They raked their fingers through the knots at the top, noting how dry and brittle the strands were.

"No more rubber bands," they told her. "Come to my classroom in the morning and I will have a pack of these for you. They are made for hair like ours."

"Yes, ma'am," Sadie said, not moving. "What kind of hair is ours?"

Alex smiled at the thought of a smaller human having something of theirs to make it ours. They ran their fingers over the girl's scalp. The flakes were thick, and Alex could tell she wasn't getting to the roots when she was washing.

"Well, it's a mix. You have strong roots from Africa. Possibly some Islander in you as well. My father's family is from Puerto Rico, and we have some Western European in there, too." Alex studied the lighter shade of brown. "You probably have more European than me because yours is a lighter shade. But hair like ours, it has to be cared for differently than Evie and Lyra do. And definitely different than Dilynn does hers."

Sadie quietly listed off the places Alex had said. "Puerto Rico. Africa. Europe. So many places and we're right here at the same time."

"You need to keep it oiled and there's creams that will help," Alex stated, focusing on getting the job done so the girl could check back into the game. "I'll just bring you a whole kit tomorrow and walk you through the steps. Right now, focus on the game."

They pulled Sadie's hair into a high ponytail, then completed a basic two strand twist until the crunchy ends met at the bottom.

"I know your instinct is to dribble around the defender, but you have to drive through them," Alex told her.

The twist was wrapped back around the ponytail holder into a bun and Alex pulled the second hair tie from their hair and secured it. With the kid's hair in check, Alex knelt down beside the girl.

Alex patted their shoulder, then jabbed it forward. "Use your shoulder, not your arm. Dribble with your right hand and move with your left shoulder forward, towards the basket. Their guard is bigger than you, but she's sitting on her heels. Use your shoulder. It will either draw in the foul or she'll stumble backwards."

"Trikru, you ready?" the coach called. Alex offered the math teacher by day, basketball coach by night, a nod to say the kid was ready.

"Yes, coach," Sadie said, hopping to her feet. Her hand ran over her head to the bun, and she gave Alex a crooked toothed smile. "Thanks. No one's ever done my hair before."

Alex's heart snapped like a glow stick. They felt the initial break, then stood up taller at knowing they'd made a difference for the girl.

Sadie didn't wait for Alex's response. She slid to a stop in front of the score table and checked in. She made it in time to enter play as the ball was slapped out of bounds.

Alex took their time on the way back to the bench, pausing to call out to the kid with the ball in her hands, "Drive through!"

They tore their eyes from the play where Sadie was still trying to go around the defender to find Lyra had moved up a bleacher, leaving Alex enough space to sit next to Dilynn. They didn't really have a lot to go on when it came to making Lyra like them. Lyra appeared to operate in unspoken silence a lot of the time. She may be just as green as they were though in the world of Greysons, so maybe her expectations were just lower. Fixing Sadie's hair had given them some points on Lyra's score card. Enough points to earn them the seat beside Dilynn.

Alex glanced back to make sure they were giving Lyra enough room, only to see the girl's mouth very close to them.

"Se merece felicidad, así que mejor no arruines esto," Lyra whispered, like anyone around them would know she was talking about Dilynn. "La otra está loca. Viste lo que le hizo a él."

Alex glanced over at Evie arguing with Dilynn over a call. They licked their lips. "Sí, vi."

"No es ni la mitad de loca que yo." Lyra pat Alex's shoulder. "Te va a golpear. Convertiré ese coche que aparentemente amas en un adorno de jardín si le haces daño."

"Come on, baby!" Dilynn called out. She reached over Evie and smacked Landon's leg. "We need to remember to make Sadie a sign."

Alex listened to the conversation as they contemplated Lyra's threat. Would they be in the car when Lyra turned it into a lawn ornament, or would they be forced to watch as the car died? The first thing they'd purchased for themself. Something too expensive but made them feel important. Even more so now that they knew it made them more attractive in Dilynn's mind.

Evie snorted and rolled her eyes. "We only have two games left."

"So," Dilynn hissed. "You said she plays softball. She's going to need a sign for softball."

"How you going to hold up a sign for her when you're at my game?" Evie growled. The blue-green eyes bore into Dilynn with nothing less than a warning pulsing in her irises. "She's a freshman. When Varsity plays home, she's going to be away."

Dilynn didn't answer, but Alex understood the problem. Understood the new challenge Dilynn would face as a single parent of more than one kid. She couldn't be in two places at once. She'd have to choose one kid or the other, and risk hurting Sadie or being murdered by Evie.

"I'll hold the sign for Sadie," Alex whispered to Dilynn. The blue eyes turned to them. "You have never missed one of Evie's games, and she only has a year left. I'll go to Sadie's until graduation... then, we can go to Sadie's together."

"How did you...?" Dilynn didn't finish her sentence. Her gaze flicked to Alex's shoulder. "Oh. She told you."

Alex snorted, and said, "I have heard that you are exceptionally loud behind home plate."

Simone leaned back and rested her elbows on the bench. "Last year, she got kicked out of a game by an umpire because she was screaming at him to get new glasses."

Dilynn stood up, without acknowledging Simone. Instead, she verified the tales of her fierce mama bear behavior as she screamed at the ref.

"Did you swallow your whistle?!" Dilynn hollered. "They're literally jumping on my kid's back."

The mother was pulled down in her seat by Evie. The girl's arms folded over her chest as she growled, "Stop pissing off the ref before I even play. I swear this is why I never get a foul call. Also, you can't call her your kid when she's not your kid."

"Not yet," Dilynn said. "I'm going to make it happen."

"Maybe that's not a good idea," Evie mumbled, her arms wrapped around herself. "How are you going to be her mom if you can't even go to her games? Maybe you should just slow all this shit down."

Dilynn licked her lips and kept her gaze on the game. "We talked about this, E. You were the one that asked me to foster her to begin with. Even offered to share a room, so she's going to come home, but she's not going to take your place."

Alex learned two things while sitting with the mother and daughter at the game. The first was that Dilynn knew a lot about basketball. She'd apparently never played but she understood the inner workings of the game that made Alex want to know why she wasn't coaching. The second thing Alex learned was that Evie was motivated solely by what benefited herself, and she was growly and grunty over everything that even slightly threatened Dilynn's attention on her.

With ears perked for any more conversation between Dilynn and Evie, Alex sat less quietly alongside Dilynn. They cheered with the future mother, like they were a future something, also. What that would be had their mind going through what being non-binary and a parent would look like. Had them asking questions like: what would they be called? Would their gender identification make the kids' lives more difficult, or would they have to pretend to be a girl, so the kids didn't feel out of place? Could they pretend to be a girl and just let everyone call them she or her without it hurting?

Their mind went through so many questions they didn't realize the game was coming to an end. They had no answers by the last buzzer, other than pretending wouldn't be okay. They had played pretend before, and it had hurt. Hurt too much, so they wouldn't do it again.

By the end of the game, Sadie was coated in sweat. Alex pulled the kid into an after-game hug once Dilynn got hers. They scraped their tongue over their teeth and prayed Sadie was not the last thing they ever smelled. It didn't matter when Sadie looked up at them with huge green eyes and whispered, "Thank you for coming to my game. I always wanted to have my family at my games."

Alex didn't say they'd always wanted a family. Didn't explain how much they wanted to be at every game, even if she smelled like a three-day old rotten corpse. They added deodorant to the list of things they needed to get for the girl's kit. They would just make it a hygiene kit.

"Let's get some snacks from my classroom," Dilynn offered. She looked at Simone. "I can brew you a cup of coffee, too."

There was an hour and twenty-minute break between games. Forty of those minutes were meant to be spent back in Dilynn's classroom as the kids raided her snacks. Alex shook their head at Simone when she started to enter Dilynn's safe space. The only place Dilynn had that was Simone free.

They nodded to the hallway and told Simone no with just their eyes.

Dilynn was of course confused, so they pulled her against their chest in a tight hug. Quietly, they explained, "We'll hang out here. You go in and spend time with the kids."

The blonde looked up at Alex. Her eyes searched them for something they wished they could just give her. They didn't know if she found it or not, but she went into her classroom.

Alex heard the teens arguing within the room, and then listened to Dilynn holler, "Stop trying to touch Evie with your pit stink!"

Simone stared at the door, then out towards the courtyard. She kicked the wall slightly before she cast them a glance. With a slight snicker, Simone said, "You look like a poodle on the side of the road."

"Rude," they said. Yet, they caught the dim reflection in the glass.

Where their hair had been flat and held tight, it was beginning to puff up into the ugliest brown football helmet. Alex scraped their fingers through their hair until they were able to work it into a messy French braid.

"Why are you even here?"

"Casey and Everliegh play next. I don't miss their games, even if it is basketball."

"Thank you," Alex said quietly. "For being nice. For staying out here and not throwing a fit."

Simone grunted in response. She rolled her head around until her neck popped. "I hope she does bring me coffee out. This late-night shit is getting old. I guess, if I get the AP job though, this will just be my life."

"So, you did apply?" Alex probed.

Simone nodded, then looked back at the door. "Your Skipper doll applied, too."

Alex's eyebrows tried to touch in the middle. Dilynn had talked about leaving, not moving into administration. It didn't make sense that she would have applied for an Assistant Principal position if she was planning on going someplace else.

"You know, if she gets the job, you can't date her right?" Simone stated. She smiled at them. "That means you should probably pray to whatever god you believe in that I get it over her."

Alex tugged on the back of their neck. They wouldn't be able to date Dilynn if she was their boss. However, if Simone was promoted, Dilynn would for sure leave.

"Did anyone else apply?" Alex asked.

"Why haven't you told her your pronouns?" Simone asked, changing the subject. "Worried she's going to prove to be exactly who I warned you about."

Alex stared out the window at the dark campus. They'd never been in the building this late, and the courtyard was barely lit. Shadows leaned over the walkways threatening to swallow anyone moving around outside the gym.

"You've spent practically every day with her. You can't tell me you haven't had the chance," Simone added.

Alex pulled at the back of their neck again. They hadn't brought it up because it hadn't really been a thing yet. The kids were the only ones who referred to Alex as she or ma'am, and they weren't in a position to talk pronouns with students. Not if they wanted to keep their job, no matter who was their boss next year.

"You know, if you don't tell her, she's going to fuck it up and you're going to get your feelings hurt," she reminded them.

"Yeah, I know," Alex grumbled. They pushed off the wall and glanced at the door. "You know, it's not easy."

They looked at Simone and gestured to themself. "No matter how much I try to appear androgynous, I still have tits."

Simone's gaze dropped to their chest. With a slight smirk, she said, "Barely. You were probably the national president of the IBTC."

"I don't like you," Alex said. They folded their arms over their chest.

Simone bumped them slightly. "Yes, you do. I'm your best friend. And you're mine. That's why I can say that."

Alex licked the front of their teeth. "I don't know how to just say, I'm non-binary. I don't have a gender."

"You just said it," Simone stated. "You know how to say it. You don't want to say it, because if you do, then there's a chance that I'm right, and she's going to hurt you."

"It's not about hurting me. That's not why I don't want to tell her," Alex confessed.

Simone's head fell to the side. "Then what are you worried about?"

"She fights for everyone," Alex stated. "She won't just let people refer to me by the wrong pronouns."

They stood there for a moment. Swallowed the real fear of not just Dilynn knowing, but everyone knowing. That was the part they were afraid of. Of everyone else knowing they were on the wrong side of normal.

"If I tell her and she goes to HR--"

They don't get a chance to finish their sentence when the door to Dilynn's classroom flew open. They can't finish or suck back their words in as coffee spills from the edge of the cup Dilynn was carrying for Simone. The woman had tried to freeze mid-step. The momentum of her hurried pace continued to carry her forward though. She caught herself, but more coffee spilled on the floor.

Alex licked their lips trying to decide if Dilynn heard them. Knew how it would sound to the woman when they'd split the sentence in half.

They looked over to find Dilynn staring at them. She wasn't searching them like she usually did. She was just staring, like she finally found what she'd been looking for all this time. Her eyes fell to the cup that was shaking in her hand.

Dilynn slowly shook her head. The blonde waves fell to the sides of her face, covering the flush trying to burn its way through her flesh.

"If she goes to HR," Dilynn echoed so quietly they wouldn't have heard her if they weren't looking at her.

Alex opened their mouth, but they didn't get a chance to say anything before Dilynn's pained eyes narrowed at them. Shaking her head again slowly, Dilynn balled her hand into a tiny fist at her side that shook as well.

"I wanted so badly to believe it was real," she snapped at them. Spittle flew as her voice dropped an octave and her volume lowered, as well. "I thought... For fucks sake, I fucking knew it. I knew it and... and.... I fucking said it and you said... I'm just a new joke. An even better joke. A slut. A whore. That's what you get to say now. I mean, I threw myself at you because I thought... Fuck."

She turned to Simone. Her finger pointed at the other woman.

"I didn't fucking do anything wrong," she said barely over a whisper. "I went to HR and asked for a new mentor. I didn't want to tell them shit, but they wouldn't release me from your fucking servitude unless I told them the truth. And you know what? I didn't even do half the shit I should have done, and you just kept going. You had to, right? One of your admin buddies told you I applied for the AP job, so you sent Alex in to fuck with me. Get her to try and fuck me on campus so I couldn't get the job."

Coffee splashed on the floor and Dilynn's shoes.

"Well, fine. I'm fucking leaving. I am leaving next year. Fuck the job that I would have been better than you at because I actually give a fuck about these kids and all you care about is power. You just want the power to stand over someone and make them feel so fucking small that they will do whatever you say, and then if they don't, you can actually ruin them. Ruin them like you tried to do to me."

"I—" Simone's mouth slapped shut.

"No." Dilynn's voice didn't yell, but her single word bounced off Simone's stony frame and hit Alex square in the chest. "No, you couldn't just let me ride out my time until the kids graduated. You had to send your friend in to make me think someone actually gave a damn. Because I only fucking applied because Alex made me think... and then you... you know what, fuck you, Simone."

Dilynn's eyes shifted to Alex. "And fuck you, too. Fuck you for playing with my heart. For making me think that someone would actually be attracted to me."

Alex reached out for Dilynn, but Dilynn snatched her hand away.

"No, you don't get to fucking touch me. Just like she wasn't supposed to touch me. You got your kicks, and, no, I'm not going to run to HR because I made out with you. I'll just withdraw my application. I won't tell anyone shit, and you two can have your laugh and whatever."

Dilynn's chin fell to her chest. She wrapped the sweater tighter around her body. Covered every part of her.

Alex looked at the dark courtyard. "I should go."

"Of course," Dilynn whispered. She rubbed her face. "I'll tell the kids... I'll tell them you had an emergency. That you had to go so they won't know. They don't have to know. You two can make fun of me all you want, but just keep it to you. Because it will hurt them. It will piss Evie off and then she won't want to play softball."

Alex held their hands out, to Dilynn. "I didn't... that wasn't what I was—" they tried.

Simone pulled their arm back. Had them stepping closer to the boundary line between social studies and English.

"I told you she was a crazy bitch," Simone said. Her hand wrapped around their bicep. "Come on, Alex."

Alex shoved Simone away and tried to fix it. They had to fix it. Even if Dilynn didn't want them, she needed to know they did want her. They wanted her and was attracted to her, and she was worth more than they could give her. And that they would do anything for her.

Dilynn wasn't waiting for them though. She'd rubbed the anger from her face once more and went back into her classroom with the kids. She'd be making an excuse for them. Telling the kids they had to leave, and she wouldn't be doing it for her. No, the easy route would be to rally her teenage army against them. Alex could fight but they were no match for Evie and Landon. And Lyra. Lyra said she would ruin their car.

Sadie. She didn't have anyone, and she'd called them family. Evie didn't want them, but Sadie had called them family.

They took a step towards the door because Evie would be upset. They'd gone to Sadie's game but didn't go to hers. Showing up was her love language. They understood that now. And they weren't going to show up, and she would be hurt.

But if they stayed. If they went back in the room, it would make Dilynn into a liar. They knew the truth. She was lying. Dilynn was lying to save them face, not herself. She was making them okay for the kids, so Evie wouldn't hate them. So, Sadie wouldn't hate them. She was doing what she did for Simone.

"Let's go," Simone said, pulling them away again.

They had to leave, but they weren't leaving with Simone. Not when they knew more than before. Knew a part of the story that Simone had lied about when Simone didn't have a reason to lie. Simone lied because she was guilty, not to protect anyone. Anyone but herself.

Without thinking, they grabbed Simone by the collar of the shirt and held her close to their face.

"You fucking put your hands on her," they hissed. A finger pointed at the door. "You fucking put your hands on her, and she told you to stop. But you didn't stop. She said you want nothing but power. You look at young women barely legal and see someone to fuck, and you don't fucking stop."

The fabric of the school polo stretched around their fingers as they shook their only friend. Their former friend.

"You fucking didn't stop," Alex growled again. "She told you to stop and you didn't stop, and she reported your ass, but she didn't tell them everything because she didn't feel like she had any power. Protecting everyone, even you. She never lets the kids talk about you. Never lets anyone say anything mean about you, and you tortured her."

Simone's hand yanked Alex's grip off her shirt. She looked at the damaged material, then back up at Alex.

"She didn't say stop. She didn't say shit. She just stood there, and when she said slow down, I slowed down. And when I kissed her, she pushed me away, and I left."

"Bullshit," Alex spat at her. Their finger pointed at the room again. "That... that reaction didn't come from someone that got kissed and then had her boundaries respected. That's someone who was backed into a corner and then forced to fight her way out."

"I'm not a fucking monster," Simone stated. "I didn't try to rape her. Jesus, you have lost your goddamn mind, and you're blaming me because you didn't just tell her the fucking truth about you."

Simone turned from them. A single finger was held in the air, as she walked away, and Alex accepted Simone's truth.

Alex's one shot with Dilynn was lost because of their own choices. They'd tried to hide who they were from her. She'd said no secrets, and they kept the biggest one.

The door to the classroom opened. Alex had just enough time to duck into the alcove by the stairs. Laughter danced down the hallway as Alex hid in the shadows.

They looked down at their hands still shaking. If they could use them to kick their own ass, they would. But standing in the dark was more befitting than a beating. It hurt more. Hurt as much as the closet under the stairs of the camp for teen girls. They didn't belong there. They'd tried to tell their parents.

Their parents hadn't cared what the camp did to them as long as Alex came out a girl who would marry a boy and wear a dress for the family Christmas photo. Alex was sent to the camp where the voice in their head was programmed in a loop that had focused on their interest in girls. Alex had gotten out before anyone knew they weren't a girl. The voice knew now though. It reminded them they are a freak.

They had pretended to be fixed and gotten out of the closet, only to end up on the street six months later. Alex looked over at the dark stairwell. It only led up to another level of classrooms. There was no escape up. Only out into the dark courtyard. Down the path covered in shadows to the car that would take them back to the apartment where laughter didn't exist. Nothing was waiting for them. No one would know or care if they made it.

The phone vibrated in their pocket. Dilynn had answered them on the story, not knowing that she'd just told them to fuck off.

GreyAltEgo on Chapter 15:

I deleted the asshole's comments. I'm sorry I didn't respond sooner. My kids needed me last night and as a mom, they come first. I don't know much about non-binary people. I would love to learn more though. I would love even more to be able to write a character into existences where non-binary people could see themselves as a hero. Maybe you could help me with that.

Anyways. I hope to hear from you soon, and that your night is going better than mine. I don't know if I can finish this story. My Morgan turns out wasn't a hero. Just another mean social studies teacher trying to make fun of me. I guess that's what you want to do though too. So, you all should be friends.

The crunch of their bones came before the white pain radiated in their wrist. A single punch to the wall was enough to make it so they wouldn't go home to silence. They would take themself to the emergency room with a broken hand. The hand that had been wrapped in silky blonde locks and caused the woman to moan.

She would have accepted them if they told her. They had the evidence, and they'd ruined it. Ruined it like everything else. So, they did the one thing they knew how to do. They ran.

19

Friday morning came with no questions from the kids about Alex's emergency. Dilynn had taken them to Olive Garden to celebrate the girls' wins, then went home to write out a brutal battle scene for the sequel to *Atlas Stands.* She'd stayed up too late, crying as she let go of the stupid fantasy she'd had of her and Alex being together. She cried until the sun came up, and she got in the shower to let the water wash away the rest of who she used to be.

The drive to school was done on autopilot, and she moved in the same routine around her room. Made herself a cup of coffee and catalogued the things in her room to try and predict how many trips it would take to clean it all out. That made her want to cry again though, so she went to her computer.

The mouse hovered over the delete button for the Assistant Principal application. Dilynn had applied on a whim. Determined the progress she was relayed from the kids about Alex was a direct result of her coaching and indicated she was ready for something bigger.

She could still do that. Spend another year as the ELA Department Chair, then apply for other schools. Admin experience was needed if she was ever going to convince Sylvia to invest in a school. She had to prove she could lead adults, since Sylvia didn't have much interest in teenagers. The woman didn't even care that she was guardian of her younger sister whenever the preteen's father would drop her off on Sylvia's doorstep.

Dilynn looked up from her desk when her door creaked slowly open. It wasn't even first period, and Alex must be fucking high as a kite to think she would be going out on that date. Her lips set in a straight line prepared to remind Alex of the boundary now in place.

"I thought I made myself clear—"

Sadie slid into the room, then turned quickly to leave.

"Sadie, shit." Dilynn got up from her desk. "I thought... I thought you were someone else."

The girl stood against the door still cracked.

"Please, come in. You are always welcome in here."

Sadie's shoulders were hunched over, but she moved silently into the space. Her hood was cinched over her head.

"You good?" Dilynn probed.

The kid's eyes rose to peek out from under the over large sweatshirt she'd borrowed from Evie. Dilynn made a note to go this weekend to get Sadie clothes that would actually fit her. Hopefully it would result in Evie feeling less threatened by Sadie, who would probably be sneaking in the window all weekend since Marcus was out sick.

Sadie pulled on the drawstrings. "You said Trikru had an emergency. Is she okay?"

"Umm... I haven't heard from her."

"Oh." Sadie dropped into the armchair and snuck her hand into the hood.

"Did you go to her classroom?" Dilynn asked. "Sometimes teachers don't answer their door even if they are there before school."

Sadie pulled the draw strings of the hoodie tighter. "She said to come today before school, and she would... she said she would give me some stuff to help me do my hair."

Dilynn's eyes widened. She had seen the matted mess that was atop Sadie's head. She'd even watched a few YouTube videos on curly hair to try and figure out how to help, but she hadn't gotten far.

"And she wasn't there?" Dilynn asked again.

Sadie shook her head. She played with the ends of the string, then pulled the hood away from her head. The bun Alex had created the night before had come loose. It was clear the kid tried to fix it, but she failed.

She pulled at a tangled strand. "I can't make it go back in."

Without words Dilynn went to work on the kid. She didn't have a brush so the most she could do was get it wrapped back up into a bun. It would be even worse by the end of the day, but she'd have to figure out a way to help Sadie if she showed her face at the house.

Dilynn doubted Evie would let that happen. She'd pretended not to be willing to share a room with Sadie last night, so the girl slept on the couch in the living room. She would figure it out though.

Sadie left without her hood on when the bell rang. It wasn't what the kid had hoped for, and Dilynn understood why. Alex knew the ins and outs of keeping curls in check, while Dilynn relied on messy buns for survival.

She returned to her computer when the room was once again an isolation cell. Her email told her Alex was, in fact, out for the day along with four other teachers on campus. Alex hadn't missed a class all year, and Dilynn felt angry that her stomach twisted up in knots. Even if it was her fault, she was the one that got hurt.

No amount of anger made the guilt subside in Dilynn. She'd checked her email before she left the house Wednesday morning to find Alex out for the fourth day in a row. She put in for her own PTO day and called in a favor from Marcus to sneak a peek into Alex's file. With a promise of an eventual returned favor, he exchanged Alex's home address and promised to get in touch with Sadie's case manager.

It was completely unprofessional, Dilynn realized as she drove over. Alex could go to HR and actually get her fired for showing up at the small apartment complex. Dilynn didn't care. Something was wrong. She could feel it in her gut. She knew it on Friday, and the digital silence from Runner didn't provide anything to distract her from worrying. And she had a lot to worry about.

She hadn't seen Sadie or Lyra all weekend, both coming in through windows or after she'd gone to bed. The rooms were slept in though because Lyra's bed was unmade, and Evie had taken most of Dilynn's covers all weekend. Apparently sleeping in Dilynn's king bed was safer for her daughter than sleeping with the younger girl known for trying to seduce the older teens.

Tracking down Sadie at school had been easy, while Lyra had left some cash on the counter with a note that said she took some PB and J sandwiches to work. But it was Wednesday and Alex was still missing, so she parked alongside the Audi.

Her initial examination of Alex's vehicle ruled out a car accident, which only exacerbated the anxiousness within her. She climbed the rickety stairs to the apartment landing. The building had a fresh paint job, but the structure was still in desperate need of renovation.

Swallowing her pride, Dilynn knocked on the dented front door.

"I told you I don't want to see you," Alex yelled from inside. "You ruined it, Simone, and I don't care you're my landlord, just go away!"

Dilynn looked around and decided it made sense Simone owned this place. She was always pretending to be in a social status she didn't belong to.

She cleared her throat and knocked again.

"GO AWAY!"

"Alex," she said loud enough to be heard through the cracked kitchen window. "It's Dilynn. Dilynn Greyson... from work."

Dilynn knew just enough Spanish curse words to know Alex was panicking. She could hear them coming through the door followed by something banging into the wall. She jumped when the door opened wide to a nearly naked Alex Trikru.

With eyes wide, Dilynn couldn't help taking in the sports bra at her eye level. Her gaze ran down the abs that almost gave her enough friction to cum and settled on the very form fitting boxer briefs fixed around Alex's thighs.

"I wasn't talking about HR like you thought," Alex said so fast Dilynn's brain got whiplash from being slapped with their truth. "I was talking about me. Not about you. I mean, yes, I was talking about you going to HR, but not to complain about me. To protect me. Because you protect people, and I didn't want you...

I didn't want you going to HR to demand things for me that I don't want people to know."

Dilynn swallowed the rant, and her eyes fell on the thick cast covering Alex's right hand.

"What happened to your hand?"

Alex held up the cast and bared a perfect set of straight white teeth at it. Clearly, this was the reason for the missed days. The slimy guilt grew thicker in Dilynn as the anger was absorbed by the sticky green goo.

"If I say I broke it on Simone's face, would you let me take you on the date I promised you?" Alex asked.

Dilynn's eyes rolled dramatically, and she shook her head.

"Simone has been at work all week without a bruise, and the woman can't do her own make-up, so I would have to call bullshit," Dilynn answered.

Alex's huff held more unfiltered emotional context than Dilynn knew what to do with. She took the silent offer to go inside when Alex stepped out of the doorway.

The apartment was sparse and dimly lit, telling Dilynn so much and so little in a matter of moments. The single chair at the small dining room table said Alex lived as isolated as Dilynn pretended not to feel.

"I don't usually have company," Alex stated, moving around the space. There wasn't much to tidy, and Dilynn realized Alex wasn't lying about not owning a television.

"You really don't own a TV," she said aloud before she could catch herself.

Alex gestured to the work issued laptop open on the coffee table. An episode of the L-word played quietly.

"Netflix is cheaper than cable, and I save on electricity by using the battery until I have to charge it."

Dilynn hadn't realized how economically minded Alex was. Maybe the sparse quarters were strategic instead of an indication of depression.

"So, what really happened to your hand?" Dilynn asked.

Alex shrugged. "I had an emergency and I had to miss the game."

"You hurt yourself so that I wasn't lying to the kids?" Dilynn asked.

"No," Alex whispered. "I was mad, and I couldn't hit Simone, so I hit a wall, but it was a very, very strong wall."

Dilynn bit her lip. She'd sent them away without giving them a chance to explain.

"How bad is it?"

Alex pulled an X-ray from the large folder and held it up to the sliding glass door. After years spent in her mother's hospital, Dilynn was able to quickly count the fractures over Alex's metacarpals and a clean break of the hamate bone.

With a slow whistle, Dilynn said, "That is going to hurt like a bitch every time it rains or winter sets in. And by then, they'll stop giving you the good drugs."

Alex's gaze ran over Dilynn's body. She pulled up the pant leg to show Alex the scar where the plate was placed in her ankle last year.

"I fell off the ladder trying to take down Christmas lights last year," she explained. "Make sure you go to PT and lie a little at the end to get some extra. I should have done more, but I tried to be okay. I pay for it now."

Alex looked at the cast. Holding it up, Alex asked, "Wanna be the first to sign it?"

Dilynn grabbed the sharpie on the coffee table. She put the cap between her teeth and ripped it off. With her body positioned between Alex's chest and the cast, she went to work drawing a cuddly cartoon raccoon. Then she added a thought bubble off its head and wrote: "If you have a cookie and someone takes it away, what do you have left?"

She could hear the deep inhale just above her. Apparently losing her shit did not change Alex's interest in smelling her, which should have been weird. She let her head fall back against Alex's collar bone as she looked up at the unfiltered hunger staring down at her.

Alex's uninjured hand snaked around Dilynn, pulling her in closer. A gravelly voice told her, "You look like little red riding hood in this sweatshirt."

Dilynn glanced at the hoodie. It was red and she was short, that was where the similarities ended though.

"Well, you are not my grandmother, and I didn't come here to be eaten by a lone wolf," Dilynn heard it after the words left her lips. It was too late to take the sentence back, and there was no doubt with the way Alex's grip tightened around her that the sexual inuendo hadn't gone unnoticed.

"Why did you come, Dilynn Greyson?" Alex whispered just past her ear. "If it wasn't to be eaten."

Dilynn's mind tried to create sentences, but the words wouldn't form in proper chains to explain that she came because she had been worried. Angry but worried. Hurt but worried. The worry had fled along with the fear. Leaving her with arousal.

Just arousal Alex may be able to smell. Just her heart beating too fast. Just her brain malfunctioning.

"Dilynn," Alex practically sang her name. "Why. Did. You. Come?"

Dilynn's eyes closed when Alex's good hand covered the side of her ribs in a steady hold. It was one of those places few people knew could turn her into a compliant mess.

"To see you," she confessed.

"And did you like what you saw?" Alex asked.

Dilynn licked her lips.

"Yes."

Alex inhaled her scent once more. This time dipping closer to the fading mark on her neck.

"Are you still mad at me?" Alex asked. "Still want me to fuck off?"

There was a moment of just the sound of Dilynn's own pulse beating out a different kind of beat. The war drum had been put away. Replaced with a rhythm fit for one thing.

"Or are you back to wanting me to fuck you," Alex asked. The hand on her ribs, moved up her body. Fingers guided her face to the side, so their eyes met.

"Your eyes say they want me," Alex assessed. "But I need to hear you say it."

"I want you," Dilynn said quietly.

"You want me to... what?"

Dilynn wanted to say, 'fuck me.' She desperately wanted to play into the fractured fairytale where Little Red Riding Hood didn't go to see grandma. She went to see the werewolf in some fantasy story. To be at the beast's mercy. And Alex had told her that she was a beast behind closed doors.

"I can't do this," she whispered.

Alex released Dilynn immediately. The barely dressed form moved across the room where boundaries were respected.

Her body hated her. Her cunt pulsed violently for being denied what it felt was long overdue attention.

"I would leave," Alex stated with eyes fixed outside the window. "But this is my apartment."

Dilynn's gaze fell to her chest. She got what she came for, and nothing more. It was more than most interactions in her life yet felt equally disappointing.

She pulled the card Sadie had made for Alex out of her pocket. Nothing fancy, but the girl had taken time drawing the basketball player on the front of the copy paper card, and even more time on the message that promised Alex she had learned to drive into the other team.

"Sadie asked me to give this to you," Dilynn said. She set the card on the low coffee table. "She is hoping you are well enough to come to the last game of the season."

Alex nodded without turning towards her, and Dilynn took it as her cue to leave. She opened the door to the apartment but paused in the doorway.

"The thing," Alex said. "The thing I was telling Simone about HR. She was giving me shit for not telling you about my pronouns."

Alex turned to Dilynn. The casted arm ran up and down the fit torso.

"I don't go by she and her. I can't tell people at work that, or the kids," Alex confessed. "And at first, I was worried... I was worried you would reject me. So, I didn't say anything. But then... uhm.... After hearing you talk to the kids, I was worried you would fight for me to be out."

Dilynn had been learning about pronouns. She'd been reading about it since RunnerAT89 had mentioned it over a week ago.

"It's not safe for me to be out," they stated. "I mean, I am out. Simone knows. I just don't talk to anyone else, but I'm not living in the closet. I just let people think... I wasn't going to tell you. Simone was giving me shit. Said I should have just told you, but I was scared."

Dilynn bit her lip. Alex was right, she would have fought for them. She would have fought as hard for them as she would have fought for any of her students.

"Thank you for telling me, so that I can... respect your wishes," Dilynn said. She nodded to the door. "I'll go. Text me if you need anything."

Alex turned back to the window. They spoke again, stopping Dilynn from leaving once more.

"Sadie needs specific products to get her hair healthy. She was supposed to come see me Friday so I could give them to her, but I didn't make it to the store. The pain meds.... I am not allowed to drive when I take them," Alex explained. "If you can pick them up, I will pay you back."

Dilynn tucked her hair behind her ear and pulled her phone out. "Sure. I can go get them now."

Alex hummed and glanced back at Dilynn. "Get her the As I Am brand. They are less heavy. She needs the shampoo and conditioner, the leave-in conditioner, and get her the curling custard. She needs a satin bonnet too, to sleep in at night. A wide tooth comb and a boar's bristle brush."

Pale fingers typed as fast as she could, but Dilynn knew she was missing things. She wasn't going to get it right.

"Could you maybe go with me to Target?" she asked. "I can drive, and you can show me what to get. Maybe afterwards you can come back to my house. It's pizza night. I'll cook you dinner, and Sadie.... She would really like to see you."

Alex turned back to Dilynn. Their eyes studied her carefully, before they looked down at their near naked form.

"I can't get my shirt on," they confessed. They pointed to their hair. The curls surrounded their head in a large lion's mane. "I can't get my hair up and getting my shirt on.... Pants are hard too."

"I can help," Dilynn offered. She closed the door. "I mean, I, of course, prefer you in next to nothing, but you are probably cold."

A smile pulled up in just the corners of Alex's lips. A single eyebrow in Dilynn's direction as they offered, "We could skip Target, and we could pretend we were trying to survive winter in Alaska. My hand is broken, but my mouth still works just fine."

Dilynn shook her head.

"It's not that I don't want to have sex with you, Big Bad Wolf," Dilynn whispered. "I just... I want more than sex, and last time I was with someone like you, I fell in love with someone that just wanted sex. And it hurt... like it hurt a lot when the sex didn't turn into more after all the years I put into it."

Alex tugged on the back of their neck. They looked down at themself.

"But you're okay with... me. With me being different?"

Dilynn's eyebrows scrunched in the middle. Her head fell to the side slightly and she considered the question.

"You're still you," she stated. "Still the same stoic social studies teacher with a very commanding sexual energy. Still have terrible taste in friends, but great taste in cars. Still dress very dapper. But your decorating skills could use some training."

Alex's chest puffed up slightly, and their eyes narrowed at Dilynn.

"Not everyone can pull off rainbow," Alex stated dryly. "Some of us prefer the color black."

"True," Dilynn confirmed. "But black is a shade not a color."

Alex looked out the window again. Their lips twitched just slightly, before they delivered the low blow.

"You promise not to hit any curbs on the drive?"

Dilynn's hand clasped over her heart, and she stumbled backwards some. "Knife to the chest."

Alex held up their hand and waved it in the air. "I can't change a tire with a broken hand."

Dilynn slid down the door. Let her arms flop to the side as her tongue hung out her mouth.

"Are you always this dramatic?" Alex asked with a roll of their frustratingly beautiful eyes.

"Are you always this mean to someone that comes to check on you?" Dilynn asked, pushing herself up from the floor. She dusted off her stretchy pants.

"No one has ever come to check on me," Alex confessed.

Dilynn licked her lips, then met their gaze. "Me either."

20

The cool air conditioning in Target greeted Alex. Even after six years of living in Arizona, Alex hadn't gotten used to the air conditioning running in stores even in the winter. Dilynn ditched them immediately after they walked inside. The scent of freshly brewed coffee from the Starbucks kiosk was a potion that pulled Dilynn away like a summoning spell had been cast over the woman.

Alex took a moment to pause and glance around, marveling at the vastness of the store. Brightly colored signs and displays beckoned shoppers, promising unbeatable deals and discounts. They rarely shopped at megastores, choosing instead to order most of their stuff from Amazon to avoid running into people outside of work. They stood along the shelf at the entry. Red and pink hearts covered throw pillows, cups, and glasses. The announcement of Valentine's Day's rapid approach had Alex glancing toward Dilynn, who stood laughing with a woman covered in piercings as Dilynn waited on her drink.

They had never celebrated Valentine's Day before. Just sat at home bashing every romantic fic that got posted on the site. They wouldn't do that this year though. No, they would take Dilynn out. Scratch that. They would bring Dilynn home. Even come back to get some of these red and pink throw pillows for their couch and give her a romantic night that didn't involve all the people watching.

"Drink this," Dilynn said, handing them some concoction in a plastic cup.

"What is it?" Alex asked.

"Not happiness," Dilynn supplied as she sipped her own version of holy water.

The woman was right. The cup did not contain happiness, but it was sweet. More sweet than they typically liked their tea. They studied the chicken scratch on the cup, but even that was written in code.

"You gonna tell me what it is?" Alex asked.

Dilynn shook her head and picked up a throw pillow. With a roll of her eyes, she said, "This is tacky. You need color, but not holiday tacky. What's your favorite color?"

"Black," Alex reminded her, as they scratched the throw pillows off their list. They took another sip of the drink. It wasn't their usual, but they would drink it again with maybe one pump less of the sweetener. "It tastes like vanilla iced tea. But why did you add milk?"

"Iced London fog," Dilynn supplied. "I bought you a green tie because of your eyes. I saw purple shoes in your house though. I think your favorite color is purple, so we should find you some purple accents."

"We're here for Sadie's hair stuff," Alex said, trying to lift a handheld basket from the small stack with their busted hand. "Not to decorate my apartment."

Dilynn took the basket from them when they winced and put it back. She retrieved a cart and put their drink in the cup holder. "You came with me to get hair products, but we let Target tell us what we need."

They took over pushing the cart after Dilynn immediately abandoned it once they turned the corner. Target apparently told her that she needed a new jacket. They quickly realized what was happening when she came back with two jackets. Both were too small for Dilynn.

"The girls need coats," she said simply as she dropped them in the cart.

When she tried to take over the cart, they nudged her away with their hip. This was their job, they decided. She seemed to get the picture but didn't just walk away. She hooked her arm around theirs and walked alongside them. Guiding them down the main aisle.

Keeping their hands to themself was a challenge Alex had very little interest in. Dilynn seemed equally unable to keep her hands to herself. The touching started with soft grazes in the hair product section of Target. Fingers caressed each other when containers were transferred from one person to the other. Everything Dilynn did felt oddly familiar, and they realized Dilynn's need for bodily contact was how she described Priya. Then there was the fact that Dilynn was a leaner. Anytime the woman had to stand still for longer than thirty seconds, she'd lean into their side, against their shoulder, or back against their chest. Alex briefly wondered if Dilynn's desire for human contact was why Simone had thought she had a chance with the woman.

Alex pushed the cart dutifully as Dilynn mumbled off items from her mental list. Hair care products were not the only thing on Dilynn's list of things to get. She led them from the product aisle back to the clothing section. Perused one rack, then every other. Occasionally, she'd hold up an item for their assessment of what girl it would suit most. When she'd finished in the clothing section, she looked down the main walkway.

"Oh, we need a lightbulb," Dilynn said with her finger in the air like it was the most brilliant idea she'd ever had.

Alex didn't ask why *they* needed a light bulb. Instead, they thought about going back to Dilynn's house and there would be a light that needed to be changed, and they would change it, because it seemed like a they job instead of a she job.

There's only boy jobs and girl jobs.

They didn't make it to the lightbulb aisle before Dilynn became distracted by the kitchen wares. Her pace slowed after veering down the small appliance aisle. She searched for new kitchen toys, while Alex sorted through the questions that were prompted by the stupid voice. Questions less about household jobs and more about expectations.

With only one prior relationship, they didn't have the slightest idea of what Dilynn would expect from them. Alex hadn't met their ex's standards, which made them watch Dilynn just a little more carefully as her finger caressed a KitchenAid mixer that looked like the one in her kitchen. To Dilynn it was obviously different, but to them it seemed like the same machine.

"Is that one you want?" Alex asked, hoping to file it away for a future birthday gift. It would require them to add it to their budget to meet the $380 price tag. Maybe her birthday was at the end of the year. She might be a Sagittarius with her pointy words and fierce independence.

Dilynn rolled her eyes and gestured to it. "It's just bigger than mine. When I started pizza nights it was just Evie and Casey, so the smaller model worked fine. Still works fine, which is why I can't bring myself to buy the bigger one. But maybe one day."

She tucked her hair behind her ear and smooshed her lips together. "I try not to just buy buy buy because I can. I mean, if I bought a new one, then I would have two and I don't know anyone to give the original to, so then I would have to donate it. But, like, who do you donate it to?"

Alex rubbed the back of their head. With a shrug, they suggested, "Goodwill."

"Man, that guy was a genius," Dilynn stated, turning away from the mixer and heading to the next aisle.

Alex quickly fished out their phone and snapped a picture of the mixer. Now they just needed to find out when her birthday was. They couldn't ask Simone, or Jason Jordan after the flowers fiasco, but there was that social worker guy, Marcus. He would probably know.

"Who is a genius?" Alex asked as they caught up to Dilynn with the cart.

"Uh..." She blinked a couple times at them. "Oh, yeah. The guy who started Goodwill. Like, he is a millionaire, and he pays the employees basically nothing while claiming to help people who need job experience, but everything they get is free, so he pays minimal operating costs."

Alex stared at the cart of clothes. They estimated at least half the items would end up in a donation bin at one point or another, since Evie seemed to never wear the same item twice. Plus, Sadie hadn't even finished growing. They were adding things up, wondering why Dilynn didn't seem phased by the $400 sitting in the cart already.

"Can I ask you a question?"

"Just did," Dilynn said, running her finger over a pizza pan with holes covering the bottom of it.

"Ha! Ha! Smart ass," Alex mumbled back.

"I promise you would rather my ass be smart than dumb." Dilynn put the pizza pan into the cart. She smiled back at them, and it felt like a smile she'd practiced in the mirror to write a scene. "What's your real question?"

Alex tapped their fingers against the cart handle a few times. They tried to find a rhythm that was appropriate for the personal question they wanted to ask, but the pattern seemed as chaotic as their heartbeat.

"So, please know you don't have to answer."

"I don't answer questions I don't want to," Dilynn stated with her attention back on shopping.

They briefly considered if she wasn't interested in shopping. It was something she'd described once in a chapter. Priya moving around the scene, talking without looking at Morgan. She described it as a test. One they didn't want to fail. But they would have to participate in and carefully manage their expressions. Lucky for them, Alex had spent a better part of their life training for this type of side challenge.

"How can you afford all of this?" Alex gestured to the cart. "Are you, like, a master budgeter?"

Dilynn snorted and shook her head. "Budgets are maths, and I am an English teacher for a reason."

Alex mouthed the word 'maths,' then chose to swallow the comment about the woman not being too good at the English. Of course, they already knew that after reading her stories. Dilynn was the snarky one, they had to be the one in control, like Morgan was in Dilynn's imagination.

"Do you want the long story or the short story?" Dilynn asked.

Alex glanced down the kitchen aisle. There was at least a half a store to go through, and they wanted to walk every aisle learning the things that pulled at Dilynn's interests. Plus, that was how Priya shared stories, and Dilynn had been very frank about writing her story about her interest in them.

"Long story," Alex said, smiling to themself. "I rather like your stories."

Dilynn's lips rose, then her eyes crinkled. "That you do."

A flash of fear burned through them. They tried to figure out how Dilynn knew they were reading her story. Had telling her their pronouns given her the information she needed?

They didn't have time to contemplate it farther, because Dilynn began speaking in paragraphs instead of quippy retorts.

"So, when my dad died, fifty percent of his insurance policy went to me. My mom didn't know apparently before the accident, and it was one of the things that apparently pissed her off, but she didn't tell me about it. Just like she didn't tell me that my Granny Lynn left me a very large trust fund. I mean, if she had told me, my life would have gone very, very differently."

Dilynn tucked her hair behind her ear again as she half mumbled, "Definitely wouldn't have run from Seattle to Phoenix in search of the unfindable."

She didn't provide time between elongated breaths to grant Alex space to come up with questions or ask them before she was speaking again.

"I got my dad's insurance money when I was eighteen. I was already here though. I had graduated at seventeen, and my mom didn't have any interest in trying to stop me from leaving when I said I was going to college. I mean, I got in, but I ended up withdrawing my first semester and getting a job at Starbucks, and just spent my time working and going to clubs I was too young to be in."

Alex didn't share that they understood the draw to clubs. The freedom of the beat with girls pressed against them on the dance floor provided them the chance to feel connected to other people.

"I met Sylvia at a club she owned. I was too young, like Lyra, but the bed I fell into wasn't like my sleazy ex. She was young like me, just with a name and Scottsdale type money that didn't require her to sneak in. God, I was... enamored with her. Kinda like how I felt about you. She was just in a different place in her life. Young but trapped in her father's expectations. She needed someone willing to keep her activities... quiet."

Dilynn glanced back at Alex. Quietly, she told them, "You can change your mind, now that you know. I would... understand."

"I... I was," Alex swallowed their shame in themself and hoped it didn't cause Dilynn to think they were ashamed of her. "There are things we do when we are young and... I'm not changing my mind."

Dilynn sucked her teeth and turned her attention back to the shelves.

"She took care of everything. She had a townhouse, even though she lived at home still with her father. And when I wasn't poor anymore, she set me up with a financial advisor. I stayed with her, and I reenrolled in college, which took me longer than I initially planned because of the whole major change thing."

Dilynn's pace through the kitchen section was slow. She had practically ran through the clothing section, which told Alex she preferred kitchen items over clothing.

"The trust fund I didn't gain access to until I was twenty-four, but Sylvia... she did what Sylvia does. So, after the surprise insurance money came in, she dug up the information. So, I knew it was coming and that pretty much ruined what minimal relationship I had with Mom, because she'd lied to me. But the money came at the perfect time. I was in my first year of teaching. And it helped me get a lawyer for Evie. Get her out of juvenile detention. And I went from being Sylvia's secret lover to a mother without Sylvia basically overnight."

Dilynn picked up a kitchen towel that had a friendly looking pup on it. Her finger grazed over the dog. Alex wondered if Dilynn would want a dog. Maybe a puppy with a bow for Christmas next year.

"Sorry," Dilynn whispered as she set the towel back on its hook. "The house was bought outright, so to answer your original question as to how I can live the way I do: I just have regular bills and the payment for the Prius, which I bought used."

She added a new cutting board to the cart, and Alex noted the only things Dilynn added were things she used for others.

"Thanks to people that do the maths, I have whatever a diverse portfolio means. I own several properties, and I just live kinda simply."

"So, you are basically rich," Alex whispered. "Like rich, rich."

Dilynn bit down on her lower lip. She didn't turn to look at them, but they could see her eyeing them out of her periphery. It was part of the test, they reminded themself.

"I figured your friend told you," she stated, returning her gaze to the shelves. "Does that... change things?"

"Your financial status is your business," Alex stated. "I would never ask you."

Dilynn's head tilted to the side like the pizza cutter options were actually interesting. Slowly, she said, "But you just asked."

Alex sighed and looked at the cart again. Stuff for the kids and a few things for pizza night. Nothing for herself, but she probably used to spend money on the ex. And she was probably worried they would use her, too.

That was the test of this moment. The information about her past was a distraction from the real issue.

"Okay, that's not what I meant." Alex squeezed the cart handle until their knuckles turned white.

Dilynn had never trusted them. Her pull was so quickly followed by a push that they knew she was still trying to determine how much they would hurt her. And they realized they would be stupid to not consider it themself: how much would it hurt her to know they used her own writing to trick her into being interested in them.

"I know," Alex said, trying to come up with how to explain themself. "I know what I said... but I mean more, like, your money is your money. I don't see you differently because you pay into different tiers of taxes than me, and I would never.... I mean, I am not interested in your money."

Dilynn moved down the next aisle.

"Would it bother you? The economic difference?" Dilynn asked. "Hypothetically, I mean. If you and I were more than coworkers."

"I hope we are more than coworkers," Alex stated. They pulled at the back of their neck. "I have never kissed a coworker before."

It was the wrong thing to say. They knew it as soon as it came out, but life didn't come with a reverse, only drive. So, they drove the cart to the next aisle, trailing Dilynn slowly.

The next aisle held nothing Dilynn felt the need to touch, so they walked through it quicker. Even though they followed Dilynn, their shoulders felt heavier.

"You still don't trust me," Alex stated, hoping she would tell them they were wrong. That she would push the sandbags of her distrust off of them.

Dilynn paused at the end cap. She adjusted several of the mugs so they could be read while passing by, but she picked up none of them.

"You walk away, instead of telling me things." Dilynn held on to the side of the cart. "You don't just tell me I'm crazy when I'm upset. It's like you just need to get away from me. Like you see a piece of me, and it isn't part of this narrative you have of me, so you walk away."

Water bottles didn't interest Dilynn. She walked right past them, and Alex had to follow.

"I've come back," Alex defended. "I leave because you seem like you need space, but I come back."

Dilynn scanned the cart. She picked up the cutting boards and put them back on the shelf next to the plastic bins. Then she changed the subject.

"We should probably head out before I try to buy the whole store."

The cart stopped moving, even though Dilynn started walking in the direction of the registers. They looked within the cart once more.

"Dilynn," they called after her. "Hold on."

She stopped walking, but she didn't come back. Just waited for them to reach her position. They opened their mouth but closed it once Dilynn broke the silence.

"You didn't come back this time," she said, before she turned. "I had to come to you."

"You told me to fuck off."

Dilynn scanned their face, before countering with, "You told me no games."

"I haven't played any games," Alex stated.

"Then why do you always walk away? You don't explain. You just walked away. You leave me in this limbo, and then you tried to hurt yourself."

Alex held up their hand. "I did hurt myself."

"That's worse," Dilynn stated.

They scanned her face, searching for what caused the shift from storytelling to defending.

"You told me everything about your ex and your money to see if I would run away," Alex stated. "And it didn't work, so you are pulling at a different string."

They stepped around the cart and committed to the game Dilynn decided to play. With a single finger, they raised her eyes to them.

"You terrify me," Alex stated in the coldest tone they could muster. "Falling for you may be the most dangerous thing I have ever done, but it's still happening."

"You don't know me," Dilynn whispered. Her eyes fell to their lips, and they knew she was in just as deep as they were.

"Look at me," Alex said, calling her eyes back to them. "I can't promise you I won't leave, but I can promise you I will come back. That is the truth, not the game you are playing."

"I'm not playing a game, Alex." Dilynn shifted out of their touch. "Telling you the truth about my past isn't a game. It was telling you the truth. Giving you the information you need to know, so that you can make an educated decision about whether you should stay or go."

Alex cupped Dilynn's cheek. Pressed their front to her and gave her the physical contact she seemed to relax into. Then they promised again, "I'm staying."

The kiss was brief. Just enough to seal another promise, in hopes this time it wouldn't be broken.

By the time they walked out of the store, their hands were intertwined like they'd been in a relationship for the past several months instead of secretly pining for one another. The contact Dilynn wanted was only more intense when they got back to her house. She pushed them down on her couch and resumed her position on top of them from the week before.

The slowness Dilynn asked for that morning didn't seem to apply in her own home. They still had their clothes on, but it did not stop her fingers from ghosting under Alex's shirt to feel their abs. It also didn't stop the woman from pressing her chest against their face.

They were certain if the door hadn't hit the wall hard enough to shake the pictures, Dilynn would have fallen apart with their teeth biting her nipple through her shirt while she ground her soaked stretchy pants against them.

Dilynn's head popped up, and her hands smooshed Alex's face against her breasts. They didn't get to see her deer in the headlights look.

"NO!" Evie's gravelly voice screamed. She repeated the word over and over again.

There was a scuffle muffled by Dilynn's grasp on their head. Evie was still saying no, while Lyra's voice cut through the other girl's protests.

"Get it, Dilynn," Lyra called out like Dilynn's personal hype person. "Next time put a sock on the door though so we know you're gettin' some."

"NO!" Evie cried out again, even louder. "No sock. No sex. No sex in the living room. Or the kitchen. Or in the house. Or the car. Or the classroom."

Alex managed to free their face to see the middle Greyson covering her eyes and shaking her head. Sadie peeked through the two older girls.

"I sit on that couch," Evie cried out. "Other people are supposed to sit on that couch. Other people who should be here in an hour."

"Screw other people," Lyra stated.

Evie shoved the older girl. "No screwing."

The sharp eyes turned back to Dilynn and Alex. Her hand gestured in their direction.

"You two haven't even been on a date," Evie reminded them. "Fucking on the communal couch is not okay. No. No. No."

Sadie waved slightly from behind the girls. Her face spread in a wide smile, clearly the only person actually happy the two were showing some progress in their relationship.

"Enough, E," Dilynn stated with her head thrown back. "We are not having sex. We were just making out."

"I could hear you moaning from OUTSIDE!" Evie's arms folded over her chest. She huffed out in annoyance and shook her head again. "I thought we were done with Social Studies teachers when someone bailed on my game last week."

Dilynn grabbed Alex's casted hand and thrust it into the air. She clearly didn't understand how broken bones worked, or that a cast didn't stop jarring movements from being incredibly painful.

"I told you Alex had an emergency."

Evie narrowed her eyes at the cast, then shifted her gaze to Alex. Alex tried to school their features even though the pain was radiating through their fingers.

"You broke your arm standing in the hallway," Evie stated. "Sounds like bullshit to me."

Alex's head fell back. They didn't want to lie to the girl, so they told her the truth.

"I got in a fight with a wall, and I lost." Alex looked at Dilynn pleadingly, "Can I please have my broken hand back?"

"Shit. Fuck," Dilynn released the cast so suddenly, Alex barely recovered before it smacked against the couch.

Evie's attention shifted from the adults' awkward positioning, and she began to dig through a drawer in the entry table. Brandishing a thick marker like a sword, she declared, "Found it."

Dilynn almost fell off Alex's lap as they turned to follow the girl to the chalkboard sign. They grabbed hold of Dilynn just enough to keep from sending her to the floor.

"No hitting. No biting. NO YELLING. No kicking," Evie recited as she elegantly scripted a new rule on the board. "And No Sex on Communal Furniture."

Dilynn's eyes rolled dramatically, and she waved at the sign. "Everleigh Blake Greyson, you cannot—"

Evie flipped around so fast her hair whipped her in the face. She pushed it away, obviously annoyed with it ruining her dramatic move, but she still snapped at her mother.

"Don't you government name me, Diana-Lynn." The girl hit the sign. "You're the one doing the nasty with someone that didn't even feed you first."

Lyra walked down the hall muttering in Spanish about Evie's hypocrisy, while Sadie continued to stand in the threshold of the door.

"Evie, please stop trying to embarrass me," Dilynn said, pulling out of Alex's grasp.

The contact was missed immediately. When the chill of winter had settled into the house, Alex wasn't certain. Without Dilynn pressed against them, they felt the cold tickle their stomach where Dilynn's dampness still left them a memory of her desire for them.

For them as they are. Not someone else.

"Let's make a deal," Evie said. "I'll stop embarrassing me, when you stop embarrassing me."

Dilynn's head dropped to the side, as Alex tried to process the statement.

"Shut up," Evie hissed. "You know what I meant."

Dilynn ignored the broody older girl and focused her attention on the youngest. She pointed to the Target bags on the table and called Sadie to attention.

"Alex and I went and got the products for your hair," Dilynn said. "I also picked up some basics. If you are free this weekend, I already promised Evie a new bat, so we can head to the mall and pick up a few more things."

Sadie looked at the four large bags on the table, then back at Dilynn. "Are those all for me?"

Dilynn shook her head. "No, two are for you and two are for Lyra, but she—"

"Did I hear someone say my name?" Lyra's head poked out from the hallway that led to what Alex could only assume was the girls' bedrooms.

"Yeah," Dilynn said. "I picked you up some jeans, t-shirts, socks, and you each got a hoodie and a jacket. And don't make it weird but I got you both a pack of underwear."

Lyra's eyebrows cinched together in the middle. She held up a finger and disappeared back down the hallway.

Alex pushed up from the couch and made their way over to Sadie, who had begun pulling the products from the bag. They were about to explain the order to use them in, when Lyra came back with her tattered wallet.

Lyra flipped through one of the bags, then another. She looked at Dilynn. "Which ones are mine?"

Dilynn peeked over Lyra's shoulder and pointed out two of the bags. "You got the purple sweatshirt and the black jacket in that one. And there's the rest in the other bag."

Lyra rifled through the bags. She searched the items, pulling the tags out so she could see them. Clearly, the kid was good at mental math because she managed to add up a total and pulled out the bulk of bills from her wallet.

"Here's a hundred," she said to Dilynn. "I will get you the rest Friday when I get paid."

Dilynn scoffed at the exchange. "I'm not taking your money."

Lyra looked at the bags, then the cash in her hand. Her face fell, and Alex could see the struggle.

"Then you should take them back," Lyra stated.

Alex stepped closer to Dilynn, and lowered their voice to a whisper, "You have to take the money."

Dilynn searched Alex's face, then shifted to Lyra putting the cash back in her wallet.

"People don't give things for free," Alex added to try and help Dilynn understand something she clearly was refusing to acknowledge. "If you don't take the money, she'll have to pay you in... another way."

Dilynn's head fell back, but her hand extended. With a heavy sigh, she called out to Lyra, "Gimme the cash."

The mother and motherless girl didn't make eye contact when the exchange happened. Fortunately, the tension eased as Sadie and Lyra pulled their new clothes from the bag.

They compared the items and swapped two t-shirts. Lyra did not, in fact, prefer the shirt with the motorcycle on it, like Dilynn had declared she would. Sadie, on the other hand, was elated to have it in her possession and readily parted with the excessively floral print top. The kind Evie wore on the regular.

"I think, we mixed up the kids," Alex whispered in amusement.

Dilynn seemed to catalogue the girls' reactions to every item they pulled from the bags. "I guess so."

Evie stood at the end of the table with the chalkboard marker gripped in her hand. She looked over at Dilynn, and asked, "Did you get me anything?"

Alex hadn't expected the girl who had everything to expect something. Dilynn pointed to the armchair where Alex had dropped the last bag of purchases.

"You didn't need anything, but I picked you up a few things."

Evie licked her lips as she looked over the other girls' prizes. Being reminded of her privilege seemed to humble Evie momentarily, and she began to compliment the things the other girls received without moving towards her own bags.

Alex wrapped an arm over Dilynn's shoulder, and Dilynn met the gesture by placing a hand atop theirs. She looked up at them, and her eyebrows scrunched together.

"Are you going to try to pay me too, if I get you something?"

The question wasn't just a question. It was Dilynn seeking answers to other questions she wouldn't just ask.

"Probably," they confessed. "One day we can talk about it. Just not today, kay?"

Dilynn gave their hand a squeeze, and then called the room back to attention.

"We have two hours before Pizza Night starts, not the hour Evie said. E, please shower first. Lyra, you're next, and remember to wipe away any greasy fingerprints from the counter this time. Also, take your stuff and put it in your rooms. AWAY. Not just dropped on the floor."

Both girls nodded and set off to accomplish their tasks, while Sadie waited for her instructions.

"Sadie, Alex is going to give you a product tutorial and they—" she paused and looked at Alex apologetically. Clearing her throat, she made a self-correction. "And then you can go shower in my bathroom and when you're done. Then you need to help the girls get the house ready while I work on getting pizzas in the oven."

The youngest girl looked at the bags of clothes, then back at Dilynn. She tucked her chin to chest, and whispered, "I don't... I don't have any money to pay you, but I can—"

"Nope." Dilynn waved the cash in the air that Lyra gave her. "I don't want anything from any of you. I can't just make Lyra believe that, but I think you will actually listen to me."

Sadie looked from Dilynn to Alex, then back again.

"You shouldn't trust people," Dilynn stated frankly. "I think you know that. That being said, I am not people. I am me, and a gift from me is a gift. End of story."

Alex knew it couldn't be the end of the story. There was still a lot for Sadie to learn, and probably more to unlearn. They could only hope that Dilynn got to her in time.

"Grab your stuff, Sadie," Alex said. "I'll show you what to use and how."

They dropped a kiss on the top of Dilynn's head. Before they could walk away, Dilynn wrapped her arms around them. She didn't say anything, just held them tightly. So, they held her back and tried not to say something stupid. Like marry me.

21

Between basketball and softball, Dilynn's mom schedule was packed. Wednesdays were typically the only day Dilynn was actually home since the rest of the week was filled with practices or games. This week was particularly busy since Friday night was the last regular season basketball game. Dilynn and Evie would have to leave after the game to travel to Tucson for Evie to play in a club softball tournament. She knew she could solve the issue if she just bought the kid a car, but Evie hadn't shown any interest in driving herself anywhere, even though she had a license. Plus, she was a worse driver than Landon claimed Dilynn to be.

With Alex anxious to secure the already once canceled first date, Dilynn agreed to go out with them on Thursday after Evie's catching coach canceled their normal session.

She had less than two hours after school to get everyone home, which included picking Lyra up from a bus stop in one of the sketchier areas of Glendale. Bags were dropped unceremoniously in the entry way, and they followed Dilynn into the bathroom like she wasn't about to get into the shower. They searched Dilynn's closet not caring she was naked behind the shower curtain trying to psych herself up for the date she was terrified to go on.

They argued over the clothes in her closet, while she shaved every hair on her body, including her arms. She wasn't up to date on what women were expected to be doing with body hair these days. Figuring it was better to be smooth than prickly, she went all out, and prayed the girls selected something that would cover the new cut on her knee.

With thirty minutes to go, Evie worked her way around Dilynn's head with a curling iron. Dilynn had protested at first, since Evie had spent twenty minutes blow drying her hair straight, but the kid was right in the end.

She drew around her face with the contour stick, then added the highlights. Sadie watched every motion she made, until Lyra held up two pairs of heels for Sadie to weigh in on. Neither had won the battle of the date night outfit, that victory had gone to Evie.

She demanded the black dress that wrapped around Dilynn's curves and secured with a single tie. Dilynn wasn't sure showing off her calves was the best idea. Not to mention the flowing skirt didn't do anything to suck in her hips. She didn't say any of that though. She smiled and said it was a great choice, because the girls needed to see someone that didn't hate herself when she looked in the mirror.

Looking at the shoe options, Dilynn silently hoped they went with the ones that would not make her pinky toe scream at her at the end of the night. Her prayers were unanswered when the black strappy heels were set on the counter. She shifted gears and hoped for a night with minimal walking expectations.

The blending of make-up on her forehead and cheeks was finished when the doorbell rang. It pulled all their gazes in the direction of the front of the house.

"She's early," Evie groaned.

Dilynn felt her guts twist into a knot. She retied the single strap holding the dress closed and tried to close some of the gap that exaggerated her bust.

"I'll get the door," Sadie offered, pushing herself up from the floor.

Evie finished the last two curls while the younger girl's voice could be heard greeting Alex.

"She really likes Trikru," Evie stated as they heard the girl's laughter dancing through the doorway. "She told me the other day she wanted to run track instead of play softball because she heard Trikru went to college on a track scholarship."

"Leave her be," Dilynn warned. "It's good for her to have someone to look up to."

Evie scoffed. "Yeah, but she's a good catcher. She could be better than me, but she can't run track and play softball."

Lyra pushed off the wall and pretended to adjust her tie. "Well, I should go give Trikru *the* talk." She winked at Dilynn. "Can't have her thinking she can take advantage of you."

With the other two gone, Evie set the curling iron down and sat on the counter. Her phone flipped in her hand while Lyra rambled off whatever talk she was having in a language the mother and daughter couldn't understand at a rate they couldn't keep up with even if they had a basic vocabulary.

Dilynn blended the contour down her jaw, hoping it would hide any hit of the double chin she occasionally found. Hopefully, the restaurant would be dimly lit as well.

"She doesn't, like, give me creeper vibes," Evie said quietly. Her eyes rose while the rest of her still looked to be pulled downward.

"That's good then," Dilynn said, fighting the urge to tell her daughter to use the correct pronouns. "I want to know if that changes."

"Just don't, like, U-Haul with her, kay?" Evie asked. She dropped her eyes back to her device. "Like, if you want to stay at her place tonight and have sex on her communal furniture, like, I get it. Better there than here. Plus, we aren't little kids, and we didn't plan a party or anything, so you could... you know. If you wanted."

Dilynn's brush paused just under her chin. She looked over without turning and raised an eyebrow at the girl.

"I swear," Evie said with her hands up. "We are not having a party. We are just going to stay here and watch movies. Bonding time, you know?"

Dilynn resumed her task, knowing Alex was in the living room getting lectured by Lyra, of all people. The same person who whispered to her that the dress was perfect because it would easily come off with one pull of the tie.

"Does Sadie's adults know she will be here tonight?" Dilynn asked, watching her daughter from the corner of her eye.

Evie chewed on the inside of her lower lip, and Dilynn knew she was struggling to keep her secret. She immediately felt the guilt of calling Evie out when she knew the kid was trying to do a good thing.

"Don't answer that," Dilynn interjected when Evie's mouth opened. "I'm going to keep pretending that you are sleeping in my bed because Lyra makes you uncomfortable. It's better that I don't know so when I call DCS to get her placed here, I don't have to lie to them."

"How long have you...?" Evie paused in the middle of the sentence.

Dilynn set the blending brush down and turned to her daughter.

"Evie, you won't hug me. Christmas was the first time you touched me that wasn't forced because we were taking a photo." She waved to the bedroom just outside the bathroom door. "You have never walked into my bedroom before a month ago. And now you are sleeping in my bed."

Dilynn's eyes rolled and she picked up the brush to work at the line she noticed by her ear. "I knew the first night. At first, I was like, oh it's because Brandon was gone. Then, I knew. I just knew."

"You didn't say anything," Evie said quietly.

Dilynn forced a smile on her face, and reminded her daughter, "Because I don't know anything."

Evie looked at the door, then back to Dilynn. "Does she even want kids? Or is this a Flowers in the Attic situation?"

Shoving her daughter from the counter towards the door, Dilynn said, "You want me to ask them on the first date?"

Evie licked her teeth, and a wicked smile rose up her face. She moved faster than Dilynn could even though she hadn't put the heels on yet that the other girls had selected. Grabbing them from the counter, she chased after Evie, coming face to face with a very dapper Alex.

Their eyes ran down Dilynn's body while one of the shoes was held like a dagger ready to stab her daughter. She reflexively covered her middle with her arm as she waited for their assessment. An analysis she wouldn't hear because

Evie decided to ask Alex her own questions.

"Do you even want kids?" the girl practically shouted still mid run to the other side of the room. She froze out of Dilynn's reach, her body hidden partially behind Sadie.

Alex's eyes grew wide, and they glanced around the younger faces in the room before stopping at Dilynn. Opening and closing their mouth like a fish out of water, the household waited for Alex to crumple to the floor from a heart attack.

They ran their hand over the back of their neck, and the green eyes moved back to Sadie, who was standing closest to them.

"It's okay," Sadie said. She gestured to the three of them standing together. "No one wants teenagers. So, if you--"

"No, it's not," Evie declared. Her arms folded over her chest. "You want her; you get us. And I already did the thing with the one that didn't want kids but pretended to, and she already did the thing with the one who dumped her because she didn't want kids. So, it's a way more important question than Lyra telling you to have her home by 10 or she'd come after you with a wrench."

Lyra shrugged, then corrected Evie, "Technically, I said a blow torch."

"Who the fuck would let you have a blow torch?" Dilynn asked, suddenly very aware she knew nothing about the girl.

"I weld shit at work," Lyra stated. "No biggy. Unless you hurt her. Then... well, I can promise, it's way worse than a wrench."

Everyone stared at Lyra while Dilynn watched Alex still trying to make sense of what was happening. Sadie was the first to turn back to them, and the first to reach out to Alex. She didn't touch them though. Her hand hovered in the space before them like Alex was encased in a forcefield, keeping her away.

"You don't have to be my mom," Sadie said as though understood Alex better than anyone else. "Evie said Ms. Greyson was going to help me come live here. Said I'm going to have a real home, not just live in group homes anymore. But if you were just, like, here and, like, nice. Could you do that? Just be here and not be mean like Evie said the other guy was?"

"That wasn't my question," Evie huffed out.

Dilynn could tell Evie was placing new bricks to fortify her walls. The time Alex gave her would only make them taller and thicker. They would be harder to break through, and Dilynn wasn't sure if even teaching the kid how to fight better would be enough to get her to open a door or drop a draw bridge for them.

"I never thought about kids," Alex finally said. "I don't *not* want kids. When I think about stuff like that I think about babies. Like, having babies." Their eyes shifted to Dilynn, and they made themself very clear. "And I don't want to have babies from me. I know that and I hope that's okay because I didn't think that would be something we would talk about tonight. But if that is... if you wanted to talk about it tonight... we could. We can talk about anything. Anything you want."

Alex turned their gaze to Evie. They pulled a tulip from the bouquet and handed it to her. "But if you wanted me to be more than someone that loves your mom, then the answer is yes. I could be that. I could want you like that. Like a parental type of figure."

Evie's spun the tulip around by the stem between her fingers. She looked up at them, but the anger in her eyes had slowed to a simmer. "I don't know if I like you yet."

Nodding Alex showed they understood. "Yeah, I... uh... I get it. But maybe we could do some things together. And we could get to know each other so I wasn't just that person that was... uh... dating your mom. Like, I'll teach you how to throw a proper punch, which is something I noticed at the mall."

They raised their cast, but let it drop by their side. "I was... uh... saving that until I thought it wasn't a punch I would have to take. I could show you though and maybe teach you how to punch a pad... and not my face. I kinda like my face."

Dilynn's hand rested against her heart. She could hear how nervous they were, and she had no way to signal to them that they were doing great. She could only hope that they knew.

Alex moved from Evie to Sadie. Another tulip was pulled from the bunch. They handed it to the girl who held it to her nose.

"I... uh... I can't be your mom." Alex rubbed their neck once more, and Dilynn logged this as their nervous tick, not something they did because she was weird. "I think that Dilynn.... She's the mom. She would be the mom that you want. Not me. But I can be your something. I don't know what that is yet, but we don't have to decide tonight."

Lyra didn't wait for Alex to give her a flower, she plucked her own from the bunch, and waved it in the air. Dilynn had just enough time to switch on the translator app on her phone.

"Mi turno. Dime cómo no vas a ser mi papa."

Dilynn's mouth fell open as she read through the translation. "Did you just agree to call Alex daddy?"

"You're so fucking weird," Evie groaned.

"She didn't," Alex said, glancing back at Dilynn. "She said it was her turn and to tell her how she would not be calling me father."

Shaking her head, Dilynn said, "Padre is father. Papa is daddy."

Alex's eyebrow rose. They scanned her face, before saying, "I thought you didn't speak Espanol."

"I don't, but I'm not dumb," she said. She sat on the coffee table and went to work on getting her shoes on.

Lyra waved her flower again, and said in English, "Come on, Not the Daddy. Tell me how you're going to be in my life."

Alex's eyes rolled, and their face lost the intensity they had with the other girls. There was a clear understanding between Alex and Lyra. Something that bonded them together, almost like they had known each other for years instead of meeting only twice.

"Sé lo que es vivir en la calle. Ella no te va a hacer irte. Así que voy a decirte lo mismo que me dijiste." Alex glanced towards Dilynn, but then turned back to Lyra. "Trátala bien porque es especial. Yo haré lo mismo. Entonces tal vez ninguno de los dos tenga que irse."

Dilynn read the translation and hoped it was accurate: 'She's not going to make you leave. So, I'm going to tell you the same thing you told me. Treat her well because she's special. I'll do the same. Then maybe neither of us would have to go.'

Lyra looked down at the flower. "Yeah. I hear you."

"Ya sabes que un día ella va a aprender español y no te vas a salir con la tuya diciendo cosas así," Alex said, looking at Dilynn once more.

Dilynn rolled her eyes at Alex's assessment of her ability to learn Spanish. She barely survived her college ASL classes and that was still English.

Lyra gave them another shrug. She gestured towards Dilynn as she said, "Cállate y ve dile que es hermosa. No te creerá, pero me aseguré de darte un vestido de fácil acceso."

Alex's eyebrow rose, and they turned their gaze towards Dilynn. "¿Qué tan fácil?"

Lyra gave Alex a shove in Dilynn's direction. "Un tirón y se abre. Además, la loca iba a decirle que podía quedarse en tu casa esta noche, así que no la arruines."

Dilynn's eyes narrowed at Alex. She knew what they said. Knew they knew how easy her dress was apparently to get off her. Knew that Lyra was the provider of the information, and apparently had chosen a side that wasn't Dilynn's.

She pointed at Lyra, and asked Alex, "What did she say?"

A hand straightened the green tie she'd gifted them. They looked up with cheeks still blossoming while Lyra's face spread into a cheeky grin.

"She said we should go."

Licking her teeth Dilynn's gaze flicked between Lyra and Alex. "There were more words than that."

The three tulips left in the bunch were held out to Dilynn. With a shy smile, Alex said, "Lilies may have been more fitting for today, but I went with tulips."

Taking the flowers, Dilynn asked, "Are you going to make me look up the meaning again?"

They nodded shyly, stepping closer to her. Their fingers played with the bow tied at her waist. Quietly, Alex said, "I really like this dress on you."

Dilynn looked up at them. "I'm sure you do, since it's apparently so fácil to get off."

"Fácil," Alex corrected Dilynn's pronunciation. They cast Lyra a knowing grin. "I told you she was going to break the code."

Alex wrapped their arms around Dilynn, making it their third hug of the day. Not like Dilynn was counting.

"We should go," they cooly whispered, "Before we break any house rules."

With a soft shove, Alex's grip on Dilynn tightened. Their hand moved up her back and fingers carded through her hair. They pulled slightly at the roots. Just enough to excite her. They didn't need to repeat their warning from the day before. It was in their eyes looking daringly down at her.

"I made us reservations," they said. They didn't have to say, 'don't make me cancel them.'

"We should go," Dilynn repeated. She stepped out of their embrace and gathered her purse and jacket from the hall closet.

As Alex helped her into the lightweight pea coat, Dilynn reminded the girls. "It's a school night. No parties. No staying up late."

She tossed Lyra her key fob. "Take them to get dinner and straight back home."

Evie's eyes grew wide. Her hand shot out and tried to take the key from Lyra. "Why does she get to drive?"

"Obviously, because I'm the only adult here," Lyra stated with a smirk.

"Bullshit, you're an adult," Evie almost yelled. "You're literally half my size."

"So es tú mama." Lyra fished out a driver's license from her wallet and held it up to the girl. "I turned eighteen last week. I am 100% a legal adult."

Dilynn didn't yell at Lyra from not telling her. She wanted to, but she knew that was probably why Lyra had been coming in and out without saying anything to anyone. She was waiting to be there, so Dilynn wouldn't take that choice away from her.

"Make good choices," she called back to them as Alex and her left the house.

On her walk to the car, she tried to think of something the girl would like for her birthday. She didn't know Lyra well enough to know anything she might enjoy. Maybe a phone, but that wasn't really a gift.

"Did you do that on purpose?" Alex asked once they were in the car.

Dilynn's lips rose into a smile. She hadn't planned it, it just worked out in her favor. The truth was, she knew Lyra drove well enough that her boss lent her a truck, which meant she had more driving experience than Evie.

She realized Alex was waiting on her answer though, so she said, "I promised her not to ask questions. What she gives up on her own... well, that's just useful information. Kinda like I don't ask her to translate. I ask you, but you are a fibber is what I learned."

Alex's eyebrows crinkled in the middle. "Why do you think I am a fibber?"

Dilynn held up her phone. Showed Alex that she'd installed an app to perform live translations. She proudly shared, "She did say daddy."

They didn't ask Dilynn if she got the rest of the conversation. She didn't share that she had.

"We missed her birthday," Alex said, staring at the house.

"Just means, we'll celebrate it a little late," Dilynn offered. She turned off the translator. She didn't want to know what Alex said to her in Spanish. She preferred thinking it was only romantic. "Speaking of being late, where are we going?"

Alex's head rolled against the head rest, and they looked at her. "Not seafood that's for sure. Evie told me you apparently hate seafood, so I am confused how you two ended up at Hot n Juicy."

Dilynn watched Alex carefully as they pulled out of the driveway. "When did you talk to Evie?"

The drive was smooth, and Dilynn really did want to buy a new car. She considered if it be weird to get a car that matched Alex's though. She could probably find a different model. Well, it would have to be bigger. Something that could fit everyone.

She was grateful Alex decided to answer her as the word minivan echoed in her mind.

"The first date. Evie saw me staring at you in the hallway. I told her I asked you out and she informed me you do not eat seafood or apparently most things that are green." Alex chuckled lightly, then tapped the steering wheel. "That being said, one of your English teacher friends stopped by the breakroom this morning before school. Christian... Christmas?"

"Christiana."

"Yeah," Alex said. "She said you regularly have salads for lunch. So, I figured I was safe with a steak house. Salad will come but it's not the meal. Plus, it takes out that whole weird thing girls do when they order a salad because they don't want people to think they eat."

Dilynn corrected the front of her dress, pretending not to feel attacked. So much for Plan A. She smoothed out the top layer that had flipped open revealing the disconnect between the pieces.

"I do love steak," she admitted. She made a mental note to wait to see how Alex ordered theirs cooked; in case they were a well done type of person. She didn't want to order a medium-rare steak that would gross them out, after all.

She sat beside Alex with her hand intwined with theirs. Her mind ran through all the approved topics of conversation provided to her from Evie and the weird get-to-know- someone questions from Sadie.

"If you could live in a tree, what type of tree would it be?" Dilynn asked when they drove up the freeway ramp.

Alex pointed to themself. "Government teacher."

Considering it for herself, Dilynn realized she also didn't know shit about trees, so she googled it.

"Google says a European Beech tree."

22

The skyline of Phoenix at night was not breathtaking. It was a vast city, but it was short and stout. The only remarkable quality it possessed was how it glowed in the expansive desert valley.

Rustler's Rooste Steak House sat at the top of a hill. Alex selected it because it boasted the best view of the city. They preferred the top of South Mountain, but Evie said Dilynn didn't do physical activity with her two left feet and gruesomely described how the woman's face would bloat and leak in the presence of dust thanks to an air allergy.

Dilynn appeared delighted by the western type of fun with a live country band. She even let them lead her on to the dance floor while they waited for their food. They didn't force her to dance long when they noticed the woman's toes were a vibrant shade of red from the strappy heels that had raised her five inches in height.

Guiding her back to the table, they tried not to focus on their wrist since they had to forgo the strong pain meds to be allowed to drive. They listened as she talked about her favorite books. Alex tried to pay attention as she explained at length the Hero's Journey and how she'd written her master's thesis on the rise of villain's tales in modern literature and the connection they posed to dystopian literature. She animatedly described the teenage protagonists as villains, who were depicted as heroes because they were the ones telling the stories.

When the food came, the steaks were thankfully cooked correctly so nothing had to be sent back. Dilynn's lips released a slight moan as she appreciated the meal. Evie had said she would order a salad and nothing else whenever they went out with her ex. Apparently, Simone wasn't the first person to make Dilynn feel like her body wasn't perfect.

After a few quieter bites, Dilynn set her fork down and took a sip of her wine.

"Did you always want to be a teacher?" Dilynn asked. "You asked me. It's only fair that I get to ask you."

Alex finished chewing and set their fork down. Pressing the napkin to their lips, they sorted through their story.

"I actually wanted to work for the FBI," Alex confessed. They felt the heat creep up their face. "I have always been a bit of a sci-fi nerd, and the X-Files was kinda a turning point in my life."

Dilynn twirled her glass before she took another sip. She closed her eyes as she seemed to sort through the flavors, so Alex picked up their own glass. They didn't understand the allure of wine. To them it just tasted like rancid grape juice. Dilynn had ordered a glass, and they didn't want her to feel like it made them uncomfortable, so they ordered a bottle for them to share.

"Xena was probably my queer awakening. I didn't know it back then. I used to want to be Gabrielle though. Traveling with the warrior. Telling stories," Dilynn admitted. She raised a finger in the air, "But I did appreciate Dana Scully in her pant suits."

Alex ducked their head and scrunched their face together. "I had a huge crush on Gillian Anderson."

"I haven't heard that name in ages," Dilynn said. She plucked her phone from her purse. "I'm just going to make a note for myself for later. I think I'll use it in the next book."

Alex's fork froze on the way to their mouth. "What is the name of your book? I tried to find it, but you said you used a pen name, but never actually said what it is."

Dilynn's head fell to the side. She stared at them for several moments that made them feel like they had missed something.

"You really don't know." Her glass raised once more, and she smiled into it. "I kinda don't want to tell you at this point. See how long it takes you to figure it out."

Alex chewed on the steak as they chewed on their thoughts. They apparently knew her book, but how would she know that they knew it. They'd only ever talked about—

The steak lodged in their throat. Alex's hand hit their chest, trying to clear their own airway. Tears welled in their eyes, while the blue irises grew wide. She was staring across the table at them but didn't move. After enough time to kill some of their brain cells, they managed to clear the blockage with no aide from the woman.

They chugged the water they gratefully had requested with the wine. With an achy throat, they rasped out, "You were going to let me die."

Dilynn bit her lip and stared at them with guilty eyes. "I told you I don't know CPR."

"Wasn't your mother a doctor?" Alex whined slightly. They rubbed their neck in the front for a change.

Dilynn nodded, then stated what she apparently felt was obvious, "And I'm an English teacher."

"So?"

"Well, with that logic, you would think I knew how to perform surgery because she is a surgeon. You wouldn't want me to do that either though. I saw,

I don't slice."

She demonstrated the accuracy of her statement as she dragged the serrated edge of the knife back and forth through her steak. Before she took a bite, she smiled at them and waved it in their direction.

"I take it you figured it out."

Alex remembered then. Remembered why they had choked.

"You wrote *Atlas Stands*," they said. "You're Greyson Dillion."

Dilynn's head bobbed side to side. "I mean, yeah. However, I prefer to think that Greyson Dillion is me, not the other way around."

Alex wanted to kick themself. They tried to remember how much rambling they'd done when she gave them a copy of the book. Thought about her laughing when she'd said she'd known the author her whole life.

"Why don't you tell people?" Alex asked. They tried to school their face. The list of questions they'd always said they would ask couldn't be the focus of tonight. But there were so many questions.

"People know," Dilynn responded simply. "Like, the kids all know but that's because the characters were based on them."

Alex's eyebrows almost touched in the middle. The kids' faces flashed in their head. Slowly, they started to list off the characters with the kids.

"Atlas is Evie." That one was easy. A moody teenager with a knack for hitting people.

"Landon. Legend?"

Dilynn nodded, then swallowed. "Casey and Evie were together when I wrote it, so Casey is Kalia. A part of me still feels guilty because Evie basically cheated on Casey right after the book released, and a part of me thinks that Casey still believes they are meant to be together because of that."

Alex considered this, but it didn't fit their narrative. "I thought there was a fight about Casey and Sadie, which I just will say I don't approve of. Casey is too old for Sadie."

"Agreed," Dilynn stated. "Casey is... trying to figure out how to be gay still. And her first everything was with my daughter, who... well... Evie doesn't know what her sexuality is yet and I don't feel like labeling it is really that important because, I know it's stupid, but I hope she and Landon go to college and they get their careers and some day they marry each other."

She waved her knife in the air. "But not straight out of high school. I want them to do all the things before marriage."

Alex nodded in agreement. "Sadie is too young to be dating."

"Sadie is too young to do a lot of what she does, but she is definitely gay." She raised her gaze to them. "I know what I said about labeling, but it is very clear she knows what she is interested in, so all I can do at this point is normalize it for her."

They nodded.

"So, who else do you recognize?" Dilynn probed, clearly enjoying their correlations.

"Marcus is the advisor. Stalky man without a sword always sweating. And Jordan is the Plains clan leader."

She nodded with a smile.

Alex flipped through their mental yearbook. They stopped on a picture of Simone Wyatt. She dyed her hair blonde, but Alex knew she was a brunette.

"Simone is not Morgan," Dilynn stated as though she could read their mind.

"But you're Priya?" Alex asked, figuring they already knew the answer. The character was built like Dilynn and seemed to use a lot of the same questioning strategies the character used in the book.

Dilynn gaze rose to the ceiling. Her face contorted into a variety of expressions, not settling on one for any extended amount of time.

"So... I'm going to let you in on a little secret to my process," she said, dropping her gaze back to them. "The looks and the attitudes are all things that came from the kids. Priya is based a lot off of me, yes. But they are all me. I mean, Atlas is always tugging at the neck of her shirt because Evie does that, but Atlas's relationship with Morgan is the result of the fallout with my mother. Evie's mom didn't reject her, she passed away. My mom on the other hand... pretty sure the only thing she liked about me was that I got engaged to Brandon and I wasn't with a woman anymore."

Alex felt the fear creeping up the legs of their pants. Their leg began to bounce quickly. They'd been here before. A family didn't accept partners that were not normal. Last time, the woman walked away because of it.

"Anyways, Priya got, like, my pain of being a mother to a kid that wasn't biologically mine, while watching her own child being raised with someone else."

Alex's ears perked up, along with their chin. They weren't certain, but they thought they understood.

"You have..." they started, yet the rest of the words dissolved when they watched the woman lose interest in her food.

"Evie doesn't know, but on that long list of shit that ended up with me being here was coming to look for my kid." Dilynn drained the rest of her glass, and stared at it like it would magically refill. When it didn't, she set it down. "This was not on the list of approved topics for conversation Evie gave me."

Her laughter was pained, so they reached across the table and took her hand.

"I don't want you to feel like you ever have to hide anything from me," they promised. They needed to make sure she believed them though, so they shared some of their own story that they'd outlined as not first date conversation material.

"I ran away in high school. My junior year, to be specific," they started with. "They had sent me to a conversion camp the summer before to fix me. They were going to send me back though, so I left."

"Where did you go?" Dilynn asked.

Alex's thumb rubbed over the back of Dilynn's hand. They licked their lips and told her the truth.

"My dad was in the military, and he was pretty high up. Enough to afford things that normal service members can't, so we had a housekeeper. She lived a few towns away, so I went there. Figured no one would find me. But my brother, Ryder. He showed up one day, and I hid in the closet."

They sucked in their breath. "I had to leave after that. He would come back. He was determined like that. Always wanted to be a cop, and apparently was trying to hone his skills early. So, I left in the night again. I made my way to LA. LA has a lot of shelters. Ended up at one for LGBTQ youth, and they helped me enroll in high school without a guardian. And I had a coach that helped me put together tapes like Simone was talking about. Got a scholarship for track to State U and came here to start over."

Dilynn twisted her hand and intertwined their fingers. "You don't have to run away anymore," she whispered. "Not from me."

Alex's leg bounced so violently the table was shaking, and they realized she knew. Knew their feet were telling them to escape.

"It's like an instinct," they explained. "Like, leave before they can kick me out."

"I'm not going to kick you out," Dilynn promised, and there was an honesty in her voice that was just as scary.

Dilynn didn't kick people out. She let them stay. Let her ex stay when it was clear he'd treated her poorly and set Evie on edge. They would have to know when it was time to leave so she wouldn't stay despite it hurting her.

"Did you find them?" Alex asked. "Your...."

They didn't know the sex of Dilynn's child to make it any clearer, but Dilynn understood. She always seemed to understand when they couldn't find the right thing to say.

"No. I... uh... I was in high school, and my mom said adoption was the only way because she wouldn't support me and a baby." She tucked her hair behind her ear. "I didn't even know where to start. I just overheard a conversation between my mom and the adoption agency. I apparently had to sign over rights once more after she'd been here six months. They kept the first name I gave her because I named her like my parents had named me. Charlotte-Leigh.

Charlotte after her father's mom and Leigh after my mother. My mom told me that they were a 'nice Christian' family who lived in Phoenix, Arizona. I was seventeen when I left. I didn't know Phoenix was one of the most populated areas in the U.S. And Sylvia probably could have helped me find out, but I never told her. I never told anyone. I mean, besides you and Sarah."

Alex had heard the name before but couldn't place it. Dilynn knew though. Dilynn understood.

"She lives in my guest house. She and her daughter, Trisaya. I told her because she... she is like Lyra. Can't take, like, kindness without feeling like she owes you, but I could tell she was, like, struggling. So, I just.... I wanted her to know that I understand and that she didn't have to do it alone."

"I won't say anything," Alex promised. "To the kids. But if you want to talk about Charlotte—"

"I don't," Dilynn stated flatly. "I guess.... I just told you because it is just one of those things, like at Target yesterday. This is something you should know, because it's a part of me and I try really hard to, like, keep it together. I think I do a pretty good job but, like, in October when her birthday comes around, I always get a little sad and a lot of angry. And you should know that it doesn't mean you did anything. I just... I wish I could have known her."

"Me too," Alex said. They squeezed her hand once more. "For what it's worth coming from a non-parent, I think you're an amazing mother."

Dilynn's eyes fell to her plate. She took her hand back, and ran her thumbs under her eyes, trying to wipe away her emotions.

"I'm sorry, by the way," she said, her tone more even. "For letting Evie put you on the spot about the whole kid thing. I know we, like, talked about me being a single mom but... I think I let it happen because I was too scared to ask the question. In case, you know, if the answer was no."

Alex had gone through 700 different ways that could have gone while they drove, and they still weren't sure if they'd said the right thing to each kid. If Evie would ever want them around. Sadie did, and they could feel that in their core. Lyra, though, she seemed indifferent to them, more worried about herself to care if they were with Dilynn or not.

"I think I am just as afraid of rejection," Dilynn confessed.

That confession wasn't needed. Alex already knew she expected rejection from reading Priya's thoughts. They considered their window into Dilynn's world. Morgan didn't have a point of view, and they wondered if it was because Dilynn hadn't put herself in Morgan in that particular story.

They looked up. "Who was Morgan based off? In the stories?"

Dilynn laughed. "You say that like there is more than one Morgan."

Alex tried to fix their face as they realized their misstep. Luckily, Dilynn was pouring herself another glass of wine.

"I originally based Morgan off Sylvia," she admitted. She moved her glass towards them. "That's why Priya has a tattoo of Morgan's mark."

Dilynn gestured to the snowflake tattooed in an icy blue on her neck. She'd said she liked to be marked, and a part of them wanted to find this Sylvia woman and hit her for marking Dilynn for life and hurting her. Because it was clear Sylvia hurt Dilynn with the way the woman's name always exited her mouth covered in sadness.

"I was eighteen and dumb," she explained. Then she looked at them. "Sylvia and you... let's just say... it's pretty clear I have a type because when I first saw you, I was like holy shit that's Morgan. Like, I know it sounds dumb, but I felt, like, in that moment that I had just... I had, at some point, known I would meet you and I just saw you in my dreams."

She took another drink of wine, and her face flushed. "So, I will just be honest, I recognize now that Brandon was a rebound and he was never my type. I never... found him attractive in the sense of, like, I would fantasize about him or anything."

Her hand covered her eyes, but she peeked out between her fingers. "Okay, this definitely shouldn't be said but I'm just going to say it because I am laying all my cards on the table anyways."

Her fingers closed though. They couldn't see her eyes as she licked her lips. She kept her face covered when she said, "I used to... when him and I would... I would imagine it was you, which is probably why I can't keep my hands off of you."

Alex's mouth dropped open. They couldn't count the number of times pre-Christmas present exchange that they'd gotten off to the thought of Dilynn. It was definitely more since then. Especially with knowing that she smelled earthy and rich from the scent that lingered on their clothes after she sat atop them. They wouldn't tell her that they still hadn't washed that shirt from when she'd ground against them in the car.

It was a whole different world being told she'd done the same. She'd thought of them, only upped the game by doing it while with someone else.

Their hand shot up in the air. They waved the server down, and said, "Can we get the check, please?"

Dilynn's hand dropped. Her face was bright red, but she studied them carefully. "I'm... sorry. I shouldn't have... that was inappropriate."

Alex wiped their mouth with their napkin, then dropped it on their plate. They smiled and ducked their chin. Pulled a play from Dilynn's own book by giving her the same innocent eyes she used on them. Then they dropped the innocence for hungry as they said, "I need to take that dress off you."

Dilynn's napkin hit the plate. She dug through her purse. Two one-hundred-dollar bills dropped on the table and she got up.

"I got dinner," she said. "You can get dessert."

Alex's arm pulled Dilynn to their side as they made their way out of the restaurant. They hated that they hadn't thought to bring cash, but they weren't going to delay leaving to fight over who was going to pay the check.

"You are dessert," they whispered just past her ear.

They barely made it to the car before their body pressed her against the passenger side door. Her arms wrapped around their neck, keeping their lips on hers. Fingers pulled her by the ass closer to them. It was more daring than holding her by the hips. They needed to touch her though.

"I have to get you home," they said between kisses.

"First time..."

Her lips worked down their neck, and they tried to hold themselves up against the car as their knees felt weak.

"Not in the car..."

She held them by the tie and tugged their lips back to hers.

"Yes," she said. "Fuck me now. In the back of this car, because you know you want to. And you know I want you to."

The first time was in the back of the car. Alex's apartment was too far away, and Dilynn's moans too appealing. She scooted over the back seat and gave them room to crawl in after her.

Her dress opened easily. Just a single pull and the entire thing came undone. Her pale flesh glowed heavenly in the light as raindrops began to tap against the roof.

Dilynn released the front clasp of her bra and let her breasts come into view. Nearly naked before them, they ran their finger over the black lace of her thong.

They didn't have a chance to undress. Her hand wrapped around the tie and tugged them down atop her. She pulled their hair from their slicked back bun as their fingers pushed the lace aside.

A single digit slid within her soaked core, and they pressed their hips into her when she moaned. They added a second finger, setting a smooth but rough pace. She rocked with the rhythm of their thrusts, shaking the foggy windowed SUV.

They latched their lips around her nipple and drew figure eights over the bud with their tongue to match the ones they made against her pulsing bundle of nerves. When they felt her walls starting to contract, they released her nipple with a pop.

"Look at me," they growled almost ferally. They needed to make sure she was thinking of them when she came apart. Not the asshole who'd marked her and left.

Dilynn's eyes opened, and she met their gaze. She nodded as though she understood. Kept her eyes fixed on theirs.

"Say my name," they commanded. "Say it loud enough to let everyone know who's fucking you right now."

Alex's name rolled off Dilynn's lips in a tone sweeter than any song they'd imagined. Her body shook with the crescendo as she continued to stare at them until her head fell back and her body unraveled.

Chest heaving, they held Dilynn through the aftershocks. They whispered how beautiful she was the way she'd described wanting in her story. Made sure that even though she'd not even let them partially undress, she wouldn't feel like this was any less than if they'd taken her home first.

"I got you," Alex whispered just past her ear. "When you're ready, I'll take you home and we can have dessert."

Dilynn's hand shoved Alex's chest lightly. "I thought that was dessert."

"No, mi reina. Esto es solo el principio." Alex raised their soaked fingers to their lips and ran their tongue up to the tip. "También te advertí acerca de empujarme. Esta vez pagarás por eso."

Dilynn's smile was soft as she rested against their chest. The contractions in her torso had ceased.

"What did you say?" she hummed. "I don't have my translator."

"That I warned you about shoving me," Alex said calmly.

"There were more words."

Alex smiled and sucked a mark over the blasted tattoo. Only when they were satisfied that theirs was darker did they elaborate. "I'm going to take you home and tie those violent hands up."

They drew a circle around her sensitive clit that made her hips buck.

"I'm going to eat my dessert, then fuck you deeper than you thought possible."

Dilynn's hands held the arm wrapped around her as she pressed her ass back against them.

"Hard," she whispered. "Deep and hard, please."

With a slight chuckle, they promised, "Si, mi reina. It will be hard."

"And you'll leave your mark?" she asked.

Alex nipped at her ear as they stroked her clit up and down without gentleness.

"You'll still see my hands on your hips tomorrow," Alex promised. "My bite marks on your breasts."

Dilynn moaned.

"You're mine, Dilynn Greyson. And I plan on making that very, very clear."

Her body crested another peak, this one not as high and the tumble over not as violent. But she called out their name in praise.

They nuzzled their nose into her neck and inhaled the scent of her arousal. She was right to say they would be addicted to her.

"Let's go," they said. "This wolf is hungry."

Every aspect of their being was on fire as they mentally prepared themself to make sure she understood she would never have to imagine being fucked by another.

"Lyra is going to take the girls to school in the morning, and we have to stop and get them donuts as penance for me not coming home," Dilynn said as she stared at her phone. Her fingers twirled the curls at the back of their neck casually, as she answered her daughter's text.

Alex glanced from the road momentarily. "You're going to stay the night?"

The twirling stopped, and Dilynn's lip was pulled back between her teeth. They had to pull their eyes back to the road when a car cut across all the lanes of traffic.

Quietly, the woman beside them tucked herself back into her seat, and they realized what had happened.

"I didn't mean to assume," Dilynn whispered. The confidence in her voice was now gone. "You can just take me home... when you are done with me."

Alex squeezed the steering wheel just wanting for once to say the right thing.

"I didn't mean I don't want you to stay," Alex said through gritted teeth. They watched her shrink into her seat, and they sucked in a deep breath. "It was a surprised, 'you're going to stay with me'. Not a 'I don't want to sleep next to you'."

Dilynn sucked her teeth and looked out the window. Her body was less tense, but the doubt was still there. They could feel it coming off her.

"I have no intentions of sleeping," she whispered.

Their right foot pressed the gas pedal lower. The speedometer arm rose as they tried to shave minutes off the time GPS told them it would take to get them back to their apartment where they would take the dress off of her and teach her there will be no more shoving them away.

23

Sleep did happen. It happened after Dilynn passed out after a very intense orgasm with Alex still buried within her. She didn't know what time it was when she woke up. There was no alarm going off, just Alex's lips making their way down her body.

The promise to leave her covered in their marks was kept, she realized as she looked down at her breasts. She scraped her fingers against Alex's scalp and pushed them towards her core. Everything was sore, but the right kind of sore. The kind that told her she'd been fucked properly.

"I put in for a sub for us," they said, then licked through her slit. "Hope you're not mad, but you passed out before I was finished with you."

Dilynn wasn't having the talking. She pushed her cunt against their face. "Less words, more licking."

The vibration of their chuckle sent her head back to the pillow. She took some control of the situation for the first time. Using them like they had done to her the night before. When they used her thoughtful gift to bind her hands together, then straddled her face and took their pleasure for shoving them.

She decided there would definitely be more shoving. Much more shoving. Their fingers dug into her thighs. There would be marks there too, and she loved it.

She was getting close. So close and her voice was going hoarse from saying their name when her phone went off. They licked through her and said, "I'm not stopping, even if you answer that."

Dilynn reached for the phone to silence it but stopped when she saw Marcus's name on the screen.

"I mean it," Alex said between flicks of their tongue on her clit. They sucked her bud between their lips. She was close again.

Dilynn closed her eyes, but the phone kept ringing. She was trying to focus on what Alex was doing, but Marcus didn't call her unless something was wrong. Only once had he called her in the three years she'd known him, and it was when Evie was arrested.

Her eyes shot open.

"It's Marcus," she said, pushing their head away. "If he's calling, it's an emergency."

Alex didn't growl when they sat back on their heels. Their face said they understood, and they waited for her to answer.

"Hey," Dilynn said into the phone once the call connected. "You, okay? You've been out sick for, like, a week."

Marcus cleared his throat, and she could see him wiping sweat from his forehead. "*Uh... yeah. I'm... ummm feeling better.*" There was a pause, then he asked, "*Are you on campus yet?*"

"No. I'm... uh... I'm out for the day," Dilynn said, getting up from the bed.

After a moment, Marcus told her, "*You need to come in.*"

She looked at the floor and immediately realized her mistake as she took in the crumpled dress. She held her hand over the receiver, and told Alex, "I have no fucking clothes."

Alex licked their lips. "Because it's your naked day. I called us out."

"Fuck you," Dilynn hissed.

She turned back to the phone as Alex grumbled, "I already did. Eight times."

"Just find me something to wear," she told them.

They rummaged through their closet as Dilynn turned her attention back to the phone.

"*... get here quickly. And... if you have Alex's number. Maybe call her, too, and have her come.*"

Dilynn's feet froze. She stared at the back of Alex. She wondered if someone had said something. If Simone had gone to admin and told them she and Alex were dating to stop her from getting the AP job.

"*It's about Sadie,*" Marcus supplied. "*There's an officer here, and ... uhmhmm... You need to get here. Now.*"

That didn't ease Dilynn's anxiety. It only made it worse, and she searched the ground for her panties.

"*And bring Alex,*" he said again. "*There is something that Alex needs... just bring Alex.*"

Dilynn ran her hand over her face.

"Yeah," she whispered. "I'm... I'm with Alex. We'll be right there."

She hung up the phone and met Alex's questioning gaze. Gripping the device in one hand, she held her breasts with the other.

"Marcus needs us to come to the school. The police are there for Sadie." Her eyes narrowed at them. "He said you need to come. Specifically, that you need to come with me."

Alex's head fell to the side. They held out a shirt for her, but their face gave away nothing. It never did, and Dilynn felt like an idiot all over again.

"Look," Dilynn sucked in a deep breath. "I don't want to go in there and be completely blindsided, so whatever it is.... Just tell me. I would rather hear whatever is going on from you and not from someone else."

She watched their eyebrows try to touch in the middle. Their hands extended to Dilynn completely empty.

"I swear," they said. "I have no idea why I need to be there. I have only seen Sadie when I was with you... so why I need to be there? I don't know. I mean, I think I am the one that is about to be blindsided."

Dilynn took the T-shirt. She didn't pull it on right away. First, she had to find her bra. Luckily, Alex found that for her.

They got dressed in silence. Alex in their jeans and button up, while Dilynn had to squeeze into a pair of their joggers and the shirt that was too small for her chest. Shaking her head, she realized this was the equivalent to the walk of shame.

"I look ridiculous," she said.

"I think you look perfect," they said quietly. "I like you in my clothes."

"Then buy bigger clothes," she growled, tugging at the shirt as she descended the stairs.

The drive over was quiet. Dilynn's stomach was flipping over and upside down. She flipped down the visor realizing she didn't check her make up before she left. She rubbed at the eyeliner under her eyes, but something caught her attention.

"Seriously, Alex!" Dilynn hissed, pressing at the giant hickey covering her tattoo. "Like, how in the actual fuck am I supposed to hide this."

Alex didn't say anything. They just smiled broadly, and Dilynn learned Alex was apparently jealous. Jealous of the past.

"You know Evie's going to lose her shit," Dilynn reminded them.

That wiped the smug grin off their face. Their hand flexed around the steering wheel.

"You know the tattoo is permanent," Dilynn reminded them. She waved to their mark. "This shit is going to fade."

"I'll just put it back then," they declared.

"Do I need to tattoo your fucking name over it?" Dilynn asked, thinking they would see how ridiculous it was.

"I like swords," Alex stated. "Less subtle than my name. Maybe a sword through it. Like slicing it off."

"Not happening," Dilynn stated.

Alex's face scrunched up. "Does she have one too? A tattoo."

"No," Dilynn admitted. "It was different. She wasn't mine."

Alex took her hand. They didn't say anything else about it, which she was grateful for. She wasn't grateful that they didn't say anything at all, so her mind was able to travel back to that time. The time when she'd thought Sylvia would see the snowflake and the woman would know how much she meant to Dilynn. It didn't matter though. Sylvia had just laughed at her.

Alex pulled up to the front of the school. It was not the best message to send. Coming in together when they'd called out, but Sadie needed her. Needed them both.

When they got to Marcus's door, Alex gave Dilynn's hand a slight squeeze and knocked. She adjusted her hair the best she could to hide the hickey.

"Come in," Marcus said.

Alex held the door for her, and she stepped into the office where Sadie and an officer sat across from the sweaty social worker. Marcus wiped a handkerchief over his brow.

"Good... uh... you're here," he said. He held his hand out to the officer. "This is—"

"Ryder," Alex whispered.

The officer raised a set of overly familiar green eyes to Alex. Dilynn's head twisted on the swivel, then she looked at Sadie. Then back at the other two.

"It's actually you," the officer said. "I was just... I met Sadie."

Ryder ran his hand over the back of his neck. He looked Alex dead in the face, and asked, "Why didn't you tell me you had a kid?"

Dilynn felt like she'd been hit in the chest by a bus. She stepped back until the wall was the only thing keeping her up. She ran through all of Alex's and her conversations. All the confessions. She'd told Alex about Charlotte last night. It would have been the perfect time to tell her. They knew she would understand. But they hadn't told her.

Her eyes fell to Sadie looking up at Alex expectantly and Dilynn remembered. She remembered Alex telling Sadie that they couldn't be her mother. They must have known. Must have done what she did, but not regretted it like she had. Not cared their kid ended up in a group home and on the street.

"I don't have a kid," Alex said. Shaking their head violently, they met Sadie's stare. "I told you yesterday. I can't be your mom. I am... I'm not... Dilynn. She's the mom."

The officer was on his feet, and he stood just as tall as Alex. "Cut the shit, Alexis. I didn't know why Colonel and Mom sent you away that summer, but now I get it. You got pregnant and they sent you away to have the baby."

Alex's eyes narrowed at their brother. Their hand hit their chest, and they said, "I don't have any kids."

They raised their cast to the girl still staring at them, but her expression had changed. She hadn't had the years Alex had to learn how to wear the mask they were so accustomed to adorning.

"She is not my kid," they said again. Their voice was louder, like everyone would believe them because they were yelling.

Ryder held up a photocopy close to their face. "Then why does this kid have your damn name on her birth certificate?"

Alex grabbed the paper. They studied it carefully, before they handed it to Dilynn. Why it was given to her, she didn't know but she read it carefully. And in the area that listed Sadie Trikru-Smith's mother was Alexandra Trikru.

"Just stop lying, Alexis," the man said. "Just own it, and if you don't want her then... then I'll take her. I'll adopt her. She should be with her family."

Alex stepped closer to their brother, putting a barrier between him and Sadie.

"You are not her family," they growled. "She has a family. Dilynn is going to be her mom and I am going to be her something. And you... you are going to go away. Go back to wherever you came from and leave me and her alone."

Ryder's nose was just a hair higher than Alex's. He stared directly in their eyes as he told them, "You don't get to dump your daughter into foster care, and then say I can't have custody of her."

"You apparently still can't read and also can't do basic subtraction," they growled. "That says Alexandra. My name is Alexis. Or did you not know that, Alexander Ryder Trikru?"

"Don't call me that," Ryder said. "That's Colonel's name. Not mine."

"Yeah, well, my name is Alex. Not Alexis. And it sure as hell isn't Alexandra." They looked down at Sadie. "Look, Sadie, I'm sorry but I swear, I'm not your mother. I never had kids, and when you were born... I was eleven. I wasn't away for the summer when I was eleven, but my brother failed algebra, which is probably why he never got into college and had to be a cop."

Ryder's hand ran over his buzzed head. He was processing, while Marcus sat behind his desk perfuming the room with a very unfortunate scent.

"I don't understand," Ryder mumbled. "I got the call to come pick this kid up and I opened the file, and it was you."

He turned to Alex. All the burly bravado fell away from him as he looked at Sadie.

"She looks exactly like you when you were fourteen. And it was just... holy shit. I found your kid. After all these years, I thought I found you. Well, a piece of you, but I got here, and this guy said you were here. And he called her up and she said you are her mother. Said she found you and that you were going to take her home so I couldn't... I couldn't take her home."

Alex's head dipped. Their jaw shifted back and forth, molars grinding together. When they looked up, their gaze was nothing less than deadly.

"That summer. The one they sent me away. They sent me to be fixed because you told them I was gay." They used their cast to hit themself on the side of their head. "They sent me to get electroshock therapy and to have some asshole make me hate myself."

Alex's cast dropped to their side. Their chest puffed up, and the anger was still there.

"I got out." Spittle flew from their lips. "I pretended to be who they wanted me to be. And I got out and I came back, and I was hiding. I was hiding so I wouldn't have to go back."

They hit the bullet proof vest with their cast. Dilynn could see Alex wince with each strike, but they hit him in the chest anyways. "And you told them. You told them again. You told them you saw me kiss Katie in the park."

The officer's whole body stopped moving. Dilynn watched the straight-backed figure slowly lower himself to the chair. His huge hands covered his face, but Dilynn could see the subtle shakes begin to take over.

"I didn't know," he said barely more than a whisper. "I... I wouldn't have... I didn't."

He looked up at Alex. Years of pain painted his face.

"I looked everywhere for you."

Alex's arms folded over their chest. "I didn't want to be found. If they found me, they would have sent me back."

Ryder's gaze dropped to the girl now staring at Marcus.

"Then where did she come from."

Alex's head fell back. "I don't know. Does Colonel have another kid?'

"Had," Sadie whispered. She looked at Dilynn. "I thought that maybe I had been adopted like Evie. That she wasn't really my mom because I didn't know her name."

Dilynn dropped into a crouch beside Sadie. She wiped the tear from the girl's cheek.

"I thought... I thought Trikru was my mom," Sadie confessed. "You said her name was Alex Trikru and I knew that was my mom's name from court. But I guess it really was her."

"Who really was her?" Dilynn asked.

Sadie looked at Dilynn, then at Marcus.

"She told me to hide. He was drunk and she said to hide behind the couch when he came home." Sadie wiped at the tears, but they didn't stop falling. "And they were fighting, and he shot her. My dad... he shot her, and I couldn't hide anymore. I went out to help her. There wasn't... so much blood and her eyes were open. She was looking at me, but she didn't blink. She didn't move. And he was holding the gun and I thought... I thought he was going to shoot me, too."

Sadie's body was falling. Dilynn caught her, but the girl's momentum sent her to the ground on her bruised ass. The kid was just as big as she was. It didn't stop her from sitting in Dilynn's lap with her face pressed to the shirt that was too small. There wasn't spare material for her to cling to, but her fingers tried to find purchase, clawing at Dilynn's collar bone.

"He shot... himself," Sadie choked out between her sobs. "I don't... I don't have... she was my mom. She really was my mom."

Dilynn held the child as she rocked back and forth gently. Her eyes found Alex's stoic stare watching them. They blinked several times, the only indication that they were not made of stone.

"Call Colonel," Alex whispered when Sadie's sobs turned to quiet cries. "If he denies it, find out who Alexandra was. Find her. You're a cop. Find her. Pull her birth certificate. Her death certificate. His name will be there."

Ryder nodded and pulled his phone from his vest. He moved to exit the office but stopped in front of Alex. He didn't ask permission before he wrapped his arms around them.

"Don't run away," he told them. "Please. I just... I can't lose you again."

Alex didn't hug their brother back. They stood ram rod straight, staring out the window. And Dilynn knew they hadn't run yet. It would happen soon though.

Marcus cleared his throat. "I spoke to Sadie's case manager. She's on her way here and... she said she would do the home check today. It was for him, but I don't think she cares who it's with. The group home closed her out. So, she goes home with you or him, but know... if it's true. If she is related by blood. He can fight you, and he will win."

Dilynn nodded, and cradled Sadie's head closer.

"You hear that, Sadie?" she whispered. "You're coming home. Today. Don't worry about him. I'll take care of it, okay? I'll make it work out. Whatever it takes."

Dilynn shifted her gaze back to Alex. Waited for them to meet her eye now that Ryder was outside arguing on the phone.

"Can you call Landon out of class?" Dilynn asked Marcus while still looking at Alex. "We need his keys and Alex is going to have to drive because his mom said I can't drive his truck."

Marcus did as she requested. He typed into the computer, then picked up the receiver.

Alex still hadn't stopped staring out the window. Their gaze moved over the sparse courtyard like they were plotting an escape route from prison.

"Alex," Dilynn called to them. "Look at me."

Confused green orbs shifted to her.

"I need you to find your Morgan," she said. "I know a lot of shit is going on, but I need you to put that on a shelf because we have to convince your brother that he can't take her. He can't take her. She needs to come home, so we need to go get Sadie a bed and a dresser."

Alex didn't move.

"The case manager will not let her come home if we don't have it already set up before they do the check. So, I need you to drive Landon's truck and I need you to take me to the furniture store after we get him to back off."

Alex stared at her, just blinking.

"Nod so I know you understand me."

Their head rose and fell very slowly.

Dilynn pressed Sadie's hair down and gave her a kiss on her forehead. She added call Evie's counselor to her mom list.

"Sadie, sweetie," she said, drawing the girl's red rimmed eyes to her. "I have to go buy you a bed. You have to stay at school because I can't check you out, but you don't have to go to class. You can stay here with Marcus."

She looked at Marcus.

"She can stay with you, right?"

The older man nodded and set the receiver back down. "Yes, and... uhm... Landon is on his way up."

"Good."

"I have to go to class," Sadie whispered into Dilynn's shirt. "Coach won't let me play tonight if I miss class."

Dilynn kissed the kid's head again. "Okay, baby. You can go to class when you are ready. Alex and I will be there. Tonight, for the game. We'll be there."

"I'll be there too," Ryder said, reentering the room. He held up the phone. "I have to... I have to see my niece play in her game of..."

"Basketball," Dilynn supplied.

"I love basketball. I'll... uh... I'll bring your cousin. Alexis. She looks just like you. Younger. Only seven, but she... she'd love to meet you." Ryder looked over at Alex. "She'd like to meet you too. Meet the person she was named after. Have an aunt."

"I can't be her aunt," Alex said. "I'm... I'm not a girl."

They held their hand up toward Sadie. "You can't have her. She has a home. It was already in the works. She has a home with Dilynn and sisters. And Dilynn is with me. We're together. Her and me and the kids, so you can't take her. I don't care what homophobic bullshit you believe. You can't have her."

Ryder licked his lips. His gaze ran up and down Alex, then he shifted to Dilynn. She felt like she was being put on a scale, and she was definitely not wearing the correct outfit for judgement day.

"You promise that she's going home with you?" he asked. "You're going to take her home. A forever home."

Dilynn nodded vigorously. "Yes. Like Alex said, it was already in the works. We were just waiting for Marcus to get back. He was sick, but she... she has a home."

"I want to be part of her life," he said softer. His gaze turned back to Alex. "You can be whoever you want. Whatever title you want. You want to be Uncle Alex, that's fine. Just... be there. That's all I'm asking. Just be there. I mean, we've lost so much. I don't want... I can't be cut out of either of your lives."

The Trikru siblings shared a look. Their eyes fell to the ground at the same time, and Dilynn couldn't imagine what it must be like to find out their sister had been murdered when they never had a chance to meet her.

24

Nine years. Alex hadn't run far enough. Towns away. A state. They'd left the state to make sure.

The case manager met with Dilynn before they left the school. Alex was there. The lady was blonde like Dilynn but not blonde like Dilynn. She was also homophobic, or queerphobic. They weren't really sure what it was called to disapprove of them and Dilynn being in a relationship.

Ryder didn't fight for Sadie though. He told the case manager he supported Sadie's choice, and Sadie said she wanted to come home to Dilynn. To Dilynn and the girls.

Alex didn't live there. They weren't a Greyson, but Sadie would be. She would be a Greyson and a Trikru, and she would have a big family because Ryder said he was going to be in her life. They didn't get a say. Ryder said he wanted to be there, and Dilynn didn't say no. She wouldn't because Dilynn didn't turn people away.

They lived twenty minutes away. Sadie's case manager wasn't happy they were together. At the same time, the older woman was upset that they didn't live with Dilynn. They had to explain pronouns to her. Explain them to her and Ryder. Ryder would tell their parents.

They left California. Moved a state a way. It wasn't far enough.

Alex drove Dilynn to the store. It had so many options. Dilynn stressed about the choice. She didn't have the measurements, and Alex couldn't help her. They hadn't seen Evie's bedroom. Had no intention of seeing Evie or Sadie's bedroom.

They had never shared a room before. It wasn't allowed because Ryder was a boy and they were supposed to be a girl. That's why they ran away.

Ryder found them.

Nine years he looked. They ran and they hid. It wasn't far enough. Ryder found them, and he'd called Colonel. Ryder was a rat, and he would have told him. Colonel knew they were there. Mom would know, too. Everyone would know about pronouns.

> *They know you're a freak.*
> *Nothing new there.*

Mom would hate Sadie.
Colonel will try to fix her.
Ryder will rat her out.

Their eyes shot up. They were at the school in Landon's truck. They didn't remember driving there. It was unimportant how they got there. Alex needed Dilynn to know.

"He's going to bring Colonel to the game," Alex said. They turned to Dilynn. "I promised I would go. I told her I would go. And he's going to be there."

Dilynn's eyes scanned the back of the gym. She had on her thinking face.

"We don't have to talk to him," Dilynn promised.

"But he's going to be there," Alex said again so she would understand. "He's going to see Sadie. He's going to see her and when he finds out about her... they will fight you. They will fight you and try to fix her."

Dilynn looked back at the school. She understood. They knew she understood because she was Dilynn Greyson. She was a genius. She could figure it out.

She would have to because they were spiraling. Their thoughts had been spinning so fast; they could feel the whirlpool in their body. It swayed and they needed to puke, but they hadn't eaten to puke.

"I can run interference," Dilynn said. "We can call Simone. She can... she's good at making people leave."

Alex stared at the school. They still weren't even sure how they ended up back here. They looked around the truck. They thought they'd left and come back, but they couldn't remember.

"Did we... did we get the bed?" they asked.

Dilynn rested her hand over their cast.

"Yes, we went to the store. We bought the bed and you set it up. Said you didn't want me to break a nail." Dilynn huffed out an annoyed breath. "Possibly the most dude thing I have ever heard you say."

They had gone to the house. They remembered now.

Evie's room smelled like dirty socks and vanilla. They scraped their teeth over their tongue because Evie's room was gross. The bed barely fit, so Dilynn said she needed a bigger house. She went across the street. They remember commenting on the 'for sale' sign outside.

Dilynn was going to buy a bigger house for her and the girls. Her family was growing. And Alex's family was back. And they were coming tonight.

"Sadie's case manager doesn't like me," Dilynn said.

The case manager came when they were still assembling the bed. They were tightening bolts and the not-blonde-like-Dilynn lady had looked at Alex the way their mother had. She didn't argue about pronouns, but she didn't like them.

She didn't like a lot about Dilynn's house. She looked through every cabinet. Even went through Dilynn's bedroom drawers. It upset them, but Dilynn said it was fine.

"I want to change my name," they said quickly. Turning to Dilynn, they needed to tell her again. "I need to change my name. I can't. I can't go back. I can't let them make me feel like I have to go back."

Dilynn ran her finger over Alex's cheek. "I think we should get your name changed. I can fill the paperwork out for you. I have a friend with a really good lawyer. We can take care of it. We can call you, Dumpling."

Alex's eyebrows cinched together. They chewed on their lip. Their name was Alex. It needed to be changed to Alex because that was who they are.

"No. I need to change it to Alex. I need to be Alex. Not Alexis. My driver's license still says Alexis. I don't want to be Alexis. I don't want them to make me be Alexis."

"I was trying to make you smile," Dilynn said. "I know what you mean."

They looked at her again. "Dumpling?"

She smiled and shrugged. "You called me pumpkin and cupcake."

"But you're sweet. And white. Like, really white and a girl. So, pumpkin like a pumpkin spice latte."

Dilynn looked completely disgusted by them. They didn't like that face on her. That face was too much like the one the not-blonde-enough case manager had.

"You make me sound like a basic bitch, as Evie would say," Dilynn said.

She had to know they didn't think that. No way, they could believe Dilynn Greyson, the creator of worlds, was basic.

There were a lot of words that were needed to explain how they felt. So many feelings, and Simone would laugh at them for their feelings. She didn't do feelings, but Dilynn did. She understood feelings. She also misunderstood them.

So, they didn't explain the feelings. Only one. One feeling.

"I'm scared," they confessed. "It's been nine years, and I wanted to make it ten. Then fifteen. Then forever."

"I can explain it to Sadie," Dilynn offered. She sighed. "I know you don't want the girls to know because of work, but I think you need to reconsider. They will respect you, and Sadie... if Sadie feels like you feel, then you can help her feel okay about it. She will understand and she will still love you."

"They are going to fight you," Alex said again. "Colonel. He is going to fight you for her. He's going to say we can't because we are not normal. He will say we are not good enough because we are not normal."

"He has as much claim as you do," Dilynn stated. "If you and I did this together, instead of just me."

Alex couldn't put together subtlety. They needed her to speak clearly. Not in riddles. She always said some things, but not everything. They couldn't put the puzzle pieces together when the table was moving in a circle though.

"What are you saying?"

Dilynn took a deep breath. They could hear the fear in the way it sucked in and came back out. She was scared too, and that made everything scarier.

"If you and I were more. If we were together. Lived together. As long as you don't run away, they can't fight me then. As long as you stay with me."

"I'm going to want to run away tonight," they said.

Dilynn nodded. "I know. Your leg has been moving a mile a minute since we met with Sadie's case manager."

They realized they weren't imagining everything shaking. Everything was shaking because they were shaking. They were shaking the whole car, but they couldn't make it stop.

"I have a plan, but you have to trust me." Dilynn sounded so sure. "You have to trust me to take care of everything."

"I do. I trust you," Alex whispered. They at least wanted to believe Dilynn could make it happen.

The parking lot began to fill with students when the last bell began ringing. They sat in the car until Landon's head bobbed over the smaller students. His smile was as big as usual.

"Wait here," Dilynn said.

Alex watched Dilynn have an animated conversation with Landon. She waved her hands in the air, and then gestured to the school. It looked like they were playing a questionable game of charades, but Landon was nodding.

When Dilynn came back, she opened the door for them. They hadn't realized she'd changed her pants. She was at least still wearing their shirt, and it made them feel a little better. She was still theirs, even though she'd covered up the mark with a lot of foundation.

They smiled slightly because it also covered up the stupid tattoo.

"Come on," she said, taking their hand in hers. "We got you. Landon is going to get Simone and she is going to sit on one side of you. Landon is going to run interference at the end of the bench, so your brother doesn't sit next to you or talk to you."

The guilt began to gnaw at their gut. It shouldn't be Dilynn or Landon's responsibility to do this for them. It was too much to ask of people that barely knew them. Plus, Simone and they hadn't talked in a week.

"I should—"

Dilynn placed a finger over their lips. "You need time to process everything that has happened. We will not be able to do this forever, but we can do it tonight. We're going to do it tonight."

Alex gave in. They had to because they couldn't come up with a different plan. They'd tried to find Morgan inside them, but Morgan didn't have a voice in any of Dilynn's stories. She never told them how Morgan thought, so they couldn't know if they were doing it right. If they were being the person, she thought they should be.

The gym was abuzz with anticipation. Sneakers squeaked against the polished floor. Sadie's team wore their JV hand-me-down white uniforms. The jerseys were probably ten years old and most of the girls were swimming in them. Alex could pick which of the kids came from stable homes because they had under armor shirts under their jerseys and shoes with the Nike swoosh. Sadie carried in chairs from the equipment closet and set them up to make the home team bench. Alex smiled at the shirt under her jersey. It was Nike and clearly a hand-me down due to its size. They knew it probably came from Evie because Dilynn would have gotten her one that fit.

There were a lot of reasons to be frustrated with Evie. She was mean more often than Alex liked. But the girl had taken care of Sadie before anyone else gave a damn. The selfish brat that Evie so often displayed seemed to melt for the younger girl who had so little.

The rhythmic echo of basketballs mingled with distant chatter. In high school, Alex had loved this type of space. They were athletic, and it carved a place for them in the school with eight hundred other names.

Alex had been on the basketball team when Ryder ratted them out. A junior and a starter on varsity. They remembered how excited they had been that night. They'd stolen a kiss from Katie on the playground in the neighborhood, then come home to find their new shoes in the mailbox. They'd run in front of the mirror to see if their first pair of Nikes really could make them faster. When called for dinner, Alex jumped down the stairs, rattling the pictures on the walls.

The shoes were a size too big, but it didn't matter. They were excited to show Colonel that the years of saving birthday money had paid off. They didn't get the chance when the fight broke out over dinner and Colonel's hand collapsed against the table. Mom's wine spilled and stained the linen tablecloth.

The shoes were only for the court, but Alex had worn them when they ran out the door. Before the gray man could say they were going back to the closet in the facility. Go back to the pads stuck to their hair line as images of women in seductive poses moved across the screen.

They left the chair tipped over behind them in the shoes that were fresh from the box. The shoes crushed the lawns of their neighbors as they cut through hedges.

They hid behind an oleander when they saw the Colonel's car coming down the street. Heard his stoney voice calling for them like a lost dog. They'd torn their sweatshirt hopping the fence to go through Katie's backyard. Ducked behind the shed when they saw her sitting at dinner with her parents. Katie was just as scared of her parents, so they couldn't stay there. They said goodbye, even though she couldn't hear them.

After what felt like forever, Alex slipped from Katie's yard. They managed to make it across the highway without getting hit by a car or seeing Colonel again. He didn't look for them after that night and it wasn't until college that Alex had the courage to buy themself a brand-new pair of shoes.

Sadie didn't have new shoes. Another hand-me-down, probably from Evie's closet also. Dilynn would fix that though. Evie didn't wear hand-me downs, and Sadie wouldn't either after today. Not now that she was officially Dilynn's kid.

The guilt clawed out of their gut and up their throat. They should have been more worried about Sadie having clothes than their budget when they were at the store with Dilynn on Wednesday.

They had watched Dilynn buy Sadie new clothes. Worried about their own financial security as the woman went through the store making sure Sadie and Lyra were clothed.

Dilynn had stepped up like Nina had when they showed up at her door with nothing. Nina gave them a couch to sleep on. Brought some of Alex's clothes from the house when she went to work the next morning. She took responsibility for Alex. Like Dilynn did for Sadie. Took responsibility when Sadie should have been their responsibility.

The kid knew it, too. She knew immediately when they'd met. She'd looked at them for approval while they did the math to figure out how far away they needed to run.

They'd asked her if she had a last name. It was meant to be funny. The joke was on them though. She knew it wasn't the time to tell them. Too young to be so smart. And yet, she'd left so many breadcrumbs for them to find.

"Trikru!" the freshmen coach called to Sadie. They saw Sadie's head pop up from the bench where she was tying the laces into double knots. "Go get your hair fixed."

Sadie Trikru.

They liked that her name didn't start with Alex. Wasn't just another derivative of the rest of the bloodline. Maybe it meant she would have a better chance than they did.

She didn't though. They'd heard her story. Apparently, being a Trikru meant tragedy followed by living with the trauma of Colonel's choices.

He'd known he had a daughter. Been around long enough to name the girl after himself. They wondered if he visited her. If she had filled the gap they left when they said no to the dress for the Christmas photo.

Sadie jogged across the court towards Alex. She had several hair-ties wrapped around her wrist. No one had known she existed, which meant Colonel didn't know Alexandra. He made her. Named her. Walked away from her, just like he did to them.

"Can you do my hair?" Sadie asked when she came to a stop in front of them. The toes of her shoes didn't touch the floor. They were creased where her toes actually were. They decided tonight they would order her new shoes. Expensive shoes and an under shirt. It didn't matter that it was the last game. She could use them to practice in for the next season.

Alex tried to smile but it was forced. So, they guided her down to the bench where she wouldn't see their face.

Hair was something they could do. They had taught themself because Mom didn't know what to do with hair like theirs. They learned though, and they would make sure Sadie learned. And until she did, they would do it for her.

"I've been practicing what you said. Dribble towards the defender. Don't go to the side," Sadie rambled. "I worked on changing hands, and I made 28 of my 30 lay-ups this week."

They thought about last week. Thought about the girl asking about where their hair came from. They'd given her the list of their origins, and she'd repeated it. Another breadcrumb.

"Evie asked Ms. Greyson for a hoop for the house. I can practice and get better if my case manager says I can live there, because Evie said Ms. Greyson was going to get a hoop. I really like basketball. I didn't think I would because of all the running but I do. I do like it."

She ran her hands over her knees.

"I've never had... I mean, I have always lived in a group home. I mean, there was a foster home. They didn't like me though. I wet the bed because I had nightmares and they... they made me wear diapers, so I ran away because I wasn't a baby and after that... no one wanted me because they said.... They said I was dumb and that I wet the bed and that all went into the file, and..."

Alex's hands shook so much at Sadie's confession they accidentally dropped part of the braid. They had to start over. They decided to do two braids instead of one because of how thick the girl's hair was.

"I don't... I don't have accidents anymore," Sadie whispered. She tugged at the hem of her pants. "I make sure I don't drink a lot, so I won't make her mad at me. And I don't eat a lot. The lady said I ate too much, but I don't anymore. Do you think she meant it? That I could come there... forever? After they told her.... Do you think she'll still let me come? Or do you think I need to tell her? Tell her that I won't run away, and I don't eat too much, and I don't wet the bed anymore?"

Alex stared at the kid's collarbones, then her arms that barely had any form to them. They'd thought she was just lanky from going through a growth spurt. They'd been so wrapped up in Dilynn finding out about them, they'd never considered Sadie wasn't getting enough to eat.

"Dilynn will want you to eat until you are full," Alex said. They were trying to think of something to say to reassure Sadie that Dilynn wouldn't have changed her mind, but Sadie began to speak again.

"I been trying really hard in my classes. I used to.... I didn't think there was a point, but Evie is so smart, and Lyra got a perfect score on all her GED tests, and I don't want to be too dumb. I don't want Ms. Greyson to not want...."

"Sadie, she wants you," Alex said as confidently as they could with a broken heart.

"Do you think... do you.... Will she be okay if I call her mom?"

"I think... I think you should ask her that. Not because I think she will say no, but because that... that is a special conversation, and I don't think she expects you to want that from her. Something... maybe you should know about Dilynn is that she doesn't... she doesn't expect you to love her or want her. Kind of like you." Alex told her as they parted her hair as straight as they could. It was cleaner this time, and Alex could tell she tried hard that morning to do what they told her to. "I put together your bed."

"I have a bed," she whispered.

"And two pillows. I remember when I lived in the shelter. The pillows were always flat, and I was only given one. So, I put two pillows on your bed. And Dilynn... she said she would take you to pick out your sheets and a comforter that you want."

Sadie sat very still while they finished the first braid.

"Evie said she has a tournament this weekend," Sadie said. "They need a pick- up player, someone to play outfield. Do you think... maybe Ms. Greyson will let me play?"

Alex cleared their throat. They weren't the person to ask. They had given up that right when they said Dilynn would take her home. They should have done it. They had an extra room. They could have bought the bed and took her home, but they didn't think.

Ryder had been willing. He had come to take her home. Maybe he was a better person than they were. He'd shown up ready to love Sadie no matter what, while they pushed her toward Dilynn.

"You should ask her. She's... uh... she's your guardian now. I watched her sign all the paperwork."

Sadie's fingers played with the hem of the shorts. They were too big for her too.

"Do you think Ms. Greyson will adopt me, like she did with Evie? Do you think she would want to be my mom?" Sadie asked. "She said forever. She told your brother she was taking me home forever."

Alex secured the hair tie at the end of the braid. They were confident the answer was yes. It wasn't their answer to give though.

"You and her should talk about it," they said.

"Do you... uh... would you maybe want to adopt me? If you and her are together? Would that mean you both would be my parents?"

Their responsibility. They knew Sadie was their responsibility, but they didn't know how to answer. They wanted Dilynn, they knew they wanted to marry her, but they still didn't know if Dilynn wanted them.

"Uh... Dilynn and I... we...."

"It's okay," Sadie whispered. "You don't have to... I'm just happy you're here."

Sadie smiled softly up at them. She didn't have fake smiles and it hurt their heart. They should have told her yes. It should have been an easy answer. They would adopt her. They couldn't say that though. Not when they hadn't even told the case manager Sadie could come home with them.

She was happy with Dilynn at least. Happy to be one of Dilynn's kids. She hadn't asked them to be her parent even when she thought they were her mom. She'd thought they had given her up. Believed Alex to be her mother and hadn't asked them to take her home. Just asked them to be there.

Alex was her family though. They knew the moment they looked into her eyes. She could have easily come from them or Ryder or Colonel and Mom. They all were her family.

The fear filled their lungs again. Sadie was just like them. Maybe more like them than they knew yet, and that meant she was in danger.

"Sadie," Alex said, not sure if it was the right time. They had to tell her though. They dropped to their knee to look at her when they told her. "I have to tell you something. I don't want you to feel bad about it. I don't want you to think that who you are isn't okay."

Sadie studied their face carefully.

"I know... uh... I know about Casey and the other girls."

Sadie's face flushed and eyes dropped to the ground. "I was just... I..."

"It's okay, Sadie." They gestured to themselves. "It's okay to love anyone. No matter what gender they are. But... don't tell my brother that you like girls. My father... he may come tonight. I don't know, but if he does. He can't know either. No one with our last name can know."

"We don't have to talk to them," Sadie said slowly. "If you don't want me to. I don't... I just want to be with you. With you and Ms. Greyson."

"I know," Alex said because they did know. They would have to learn to stay for Sadie. Learn not to run for Sadie. "So, it's very important. Don't tell them anything."

They returned to Sadie's hair. The second braid was easier.

"If I tell them, they might try to send me away. Like they sent you away," Sadie whispered.

"Yes," Alex confirmed. "And that can't happen. It... I won't let it happen."

"He's here," Sadie said. "Your brother. He's here with his daughter."

Alex's eyes rose to the door. Ryder had changed from his uniform. He looked the same as he had in high school. Same haircut. Same boot cut jeans. And Ryder wasn't lying. Sadie looked just like the little girl bouncing by his side.

He was smiling and waving at them. He was happy, had been happy. It showed in the crinkles around his eyes. Fatherhood looked good on him.

The distance between them was closing, but Landon stopped him. He held his hand out. They couldn't hear the introduction, but they watched Ryder pause. Landon was talking and he was big. The boy was as big as Ryder was, and he was between them, protecting Alex.

It shouldn't be like this. They were the adult. They should be protecting the boy because he was still a boy. It shouldn't be his responsibility.

Ryder glanced over Landon's shoulder, but he nodded. He nodded and moved with Landon towards Evie. There were more introductions. Ryder was meeting Dilynn's daughter. He was getting acquainted with the family that was supposed to be theirs.

Ryder's daughter didn't follow her father. She ran over to them. Her bouncing didn't stop when she got to them. She was jumping so much they thought for a moment that the room was moving again.

"I'm Alexis," the girl said loudly. She had a loud voice like her father. "I knew it it's you because there are pictures of you all over our house and Papa's house, and Daddy said he made a mistake. He says you ares not my aunt. He says you is not a girl and that I can't call you my aunt because it will hurt your feelings and I don't want to hurts your feelings so I have to just call you Alex. That your names. Alex. You's my Alex. Just my Alex and I'm your Alexis. I don't like that name though either. Daddy calls me Allie. So, I'm Allie and you're my Alex and we are family."

The girl stopped bouncing when she ran out of words. She stared at them, and they stared at her.

Alex needed to say something. They hadn't spoken to a child this young in so long. Let alone one that wanted to talk to them.

"It's nice to meet you," was all they could come up with. It was enough though.

Allie launched herself towards Alex. Her arms wrapped around their neck, and she pressed sticky lips to their cheek. When she leaned back, she smiled. Her two front teeth were missing but it didn't seem to hinder her from spilling details of her father. She was as much of a snitch as her father.

"My daddy is sorry. He told me he is sorry that we just getting to meet because he saided that it was his fault, but he said he's going to fix it," she explained.

Allie's hand pressed sticky fingers against their cheek. He must have fed the kid a pound of sugar on the way to the game.

"And he talked to Papa and he was yelling, but he said Papa is going to make things better, too. They's going to tell you that they are all sorry."

Her body jumped in their arms, shaking them some.

"And Daddy says that I have an auntie. Is she here? Is my Auntie Dilynn here? I wants to meet her and stands up tall and tells her that I'm her niece and that I want to meet my cousins. Daddy says I have cousins and I am so excited because I have never had cousins because my mommy went away and she didn't want me or daddy anymore so I never gots to know if she had brothers or sisters or cousins but I have cousins from Auntie Dilynn and I have an Auntie and an Alex and there will be more family. I can have more family in my picture on the wall at school instead of just me and Daddy and PaPa. We have to take a picture to school for the family wall and everyone else has families but I just has Daddy and I always wanted more people in my picture."

They took a breath for her because she was still talking. She spoke so fast they couldn't make sense of most of what she said, but her attention had turned to Sadie.

"Woah," Allie whispered. She reached out and pressed her hand to Sadie's cheek. "You look like me. Daddy said my cousin Sadie looked like me and that my Alex looked like me. You are my cousin. You're my cousin Sadie and we could all be twins."

Sadie mirrored Allie's touch. She ran her thumb over Allie's cheek. "We could be. And I will be your best cousin. I will teach you how to play basketball and softball and I will make sure nothing ever happens to you. I will keep you safe."

Alex felt Sadie's words in their core. They would have to protect Sadie and Allie. They would have to keep them safe.

"Allie," Ryder called from his seat next to Landon. "Come here. Sadie needs to get ready for the game."

Allie followed instructions as well as her father did when he was kid. She didn't move immediately. When she did, she dragged her feet against the polished floor. Alex could hear her grumbling the whole way to her father's side.

"She's cute," Sadie whispered. "And maybe she's telling the truth."

"Maybe," Alex agreed.

They scanned the gym in search of Dilynn. She'd left them with Landon so she could go grab something. They didn't find Dilynn in the space, instead their eyes fixed on the man who stepped into the gym.

Colonel had aged well. Alex hated that he still looked like the same Colonel. The same person who stood straight in every family photo with his nose parallel to the ground. His eyes roamed the room until he found them.

"Is that your dad?" Sadie whispered. "He looks like your brother only grey."

Alex nodded because words didn't work. A hand rested on their bicep. It tore their gaze from the Colonel's cold stare to blue eyes. Blue eyes that knew they weren't okay and came to rescue them.

"He's here," Alex whispered.

Dilynn's gaze shifted to the man still hovering by the door. She nodded, "Okay. We knew that might happen. And it's going to be okay."

She pointed towards the door, not being subtle at all. "Simone, Alex's father is by the south door. Landon is taking care of Ryder, so you are on Daddy Dearest Duty."

Simone stepped to Alex's other side. She gave them a nod, then said, "You look like shit."

"Sadie needs to warm up," Dilynn reminded Alex. She gave Sadie a slight shove and told her the same. "Go warm-up. We can't have you getting hurt before you play in the tournament this weekend."

Sadie's eyes grew wide. "I can play?"

"Yes, honey. Evie's coach called me. She's going to bring you a uniform and Lyra is picking you and Evie up some cleats from the store, then she'll be here."

Sadie leapt into Dilynn's embrace. "Thank you. Thank you so much, Ms. Greyson."

"Dilynn," Dilynn corrected her. "Or Momma G, or whatever you want to call me. You'll figure it out when you're ready, just no teacher name. We're family now."

Sadie left with another slight shove. Sprinted on to the court and joined the team running warm-up laps.

Once she was gone, Dilynn gestured to Simone by her side. "This asshole is here to be your bodyguard."

Simone's eyes rolled dramatically. Her arms folded over her chest, as she growled at Alex, "I have to be civil, but she can call me an asshole? That's some bullshit."

"I don't need you to be civil," Dilynn said. "I need you to be the feral dickhead you are at your core."

"And people say you're the nice one," Simone said.

"I am nice and you're an asshole. And I'm done being scared of you," Dilynn declared. "I'm either going to be your boss next year or I will be gone. Neither of which matters because this isn't about you and me. You're here for Alex, who you said is your best friend."

"You don't have to leave just because I'm your new boss," Simone stated. She raised her chin so she could look down at Dilynn. "I am going to be a great AP."

"You would be nothing short of a dictator, which is why I am the better choice," Dilynn countered.

The blondes' fight was almost distracting enough to keep Alex's attention. Just not enough to stop them from feeling their father's heavy stare. When they turned to look at him, his eyes were no longer on them. He was watching Sadie warm up.

They wanted to yell at him. Wanted to tell him to get away from her. Alex didn't get a chance.

"Come on." Dilynn pulled at their arm slightly. "We should get settled in our seats."

They did as they were told. Followed Dilynn to their place in the center of the bleachers. Colonel didn't come to sit with them or with Ryder. He stayed by the gym door, and watched the game like it was field day on base.

Sadie did play more. She was given only three minutes rest by half time, but she was killing it. More than half the points on the board were scored by Sadie, and Alex got lost in the game.

Lyra squeezed in behind them just at the start of half time. She pulled a bag of microwave popcorn out from her backpack and passed it to Evie. "Here's your snacky. I got the shoes and the bags in the car. Sarah said she will be home all weekend, too."

Dilynn leaned back and squeezed Lyra's hand. "Good. We are leaving right after Evie's game. Sadie and Evie will sleep with the rest of the team, but I got you a room if you want to come."

"You mean, like come with you?" Lyra asked.

"Yeah, if you want to," Dilynn said. "We will be there all weekend. The tournament is basically all day, but we can do dinner and shopping in the evening. Maybe catch a movie."

"I mean, I don't have anything else to do," Lyra said.

"Where are the games?" Ryder asked. "I would like to come and support Evie and Sadie play..."

"Softball," Evie supplied. "We play softball. Basketball is just a filler sport for us."

"Cool." Ryder leaned forward and looked at Dilynn. "I would like to come. I have missed too much."

"Tucson," Dilynn said quietly. "We are going to Tucson."

Dilynn licked her lips. She turned her head towards Alex, and whispered, "I'm going to have to play the long game if I don't want him to fight me for custody."

They understood, but they hated that Ryder would be spending the weekend with Dilynn and the kids. They weren't even invited to the games that weekend.

Lyra reached over Dilynn and grabbed a handful of popcorn before Evie snatched the bag away. "So, what did I miss?"

Evie covered the bag like it was the only food on a deserted island. When she was confident her snack was safe, she gestured to the other side of Landon. "That's Trikru's brother. Said to call him Uncle Ryder like we are all sooooo excited about this reunion that has us playing a game of keep away."

Alex could always count on Evie to come in with the passive aggressive commentary. Landon was great as a shield, but Evie was a sword with a serrated blade. "Oh, and we don't like him even though he says we are going to. Trikru said the same shit on Wednesday though, so apparently, they pull their lines from the same book. The kid is cute though, so we are going to keep her. Can't blame her for being caught in the middle of all this bullshit. Oh, and apparently Mom and my coach are speaking again, but I heard them calling each other names the whole way across campus so I doubt that shit is going to last."

Ryder leaned back and held out his hand. Alex peeked around Dilynn to see his giant stupid smile.

"I'm Ryder, and you are Dilynn's oldest?"

Lyra looked at the hand, then at Dilynn.

"Yes," Dilynn said. "Lyra is mine and she is the oldest. Her birthday was last week."

"You'll like me," Ryder said from the end of the bench. "I give great Christmas presents. Plus, I need to make up for a missed birthday," Ryder stated with a smile. "I guess I can start proving that I am the best gift giver."

Alex's eyebrows tried to touch in the middle. He planned on being invited to Christmas.

Lyra slapped Ryder's hand instead of shaking it. Then, she leaned in closer to them. She didn't whisper when she asked Alex, "¿Lo odio? ¿O me comporto amablemente?"

Alex glanced over at Ryder. Watched the cocky grin spread over his face before they answered, "Él te entiende y ella descargó un traductor para saber lo que estamos diciendo."

"That's stupid," Lyra stated. She stomped her feet against the bench, then looked over at Ryder. "I want a blow torch. You know, in case I need to turn your car into a lawn ornament."

Ryder's laugh hadn't changed. It was still deep and full, and a part of them had missed that about him. He had always been able to make their mom less angry with his jokes and his laughter.

"What is with you and cars?" Dilynn asked.

She didn't get an answer though. Her attention was turned to Evie, who was hitting Dilynn in the leg repeatedly.

"No hitting," Dilynn whined. "What is your deal, E?"

Evie pointed to the door where Colonel was still standing. He wasn't alone anymore. Beside him stood a very tall woman with a handbag even Alex knew was expensive. Her ice blue eyes were moving between Dilynn and them, she seemed to snarl at their intertwined hands.

"Why is Sylvia Winters here?" Evie asked. "And why does she look like she is going to storm over here and yell at us?"

Dilynn tucked her hair behind her ear. She gave Alex a squeeze on their knee and smiled at them. It was a weird smile though. Not a real one. Uncomfortable. That was all they could come up with. She was just as uncomfortable as they were, which wasn't good because they were trusting her to keep everything together.

"I spoke to her a few weeks ago about some business plans we made together a while ago," Dilynn explained.

She turned back to Alex, "I mentioned Evie was playing basketball. It was before you and I started... and basketball is her... thing." Dilynn pulled at the shirt she was wearing. Clearly Sylvia was as much a problem for Dilynn's confidence as the stupid ex was. "I didn't know she would just show up. She was overseas when we spoke. I just... I will deal with this."

Sylvia Winters walked like she owned the gym. Her heels could be heard as the foul shots were taken by the other team. Dilynn tripped over the last step. Ryder caught her before she faceplanted.

"You sure you can trust her?" Simone whispered too close to their ear. "You know, they were together for years. Had a very intense relationship."

Alex felt ants crawling under their skin. If Simone knew about Sylvia, then it wasn't as secret as Dilynn had made it seem.

Dilynn made her way to meet Sylvia. She had to stand on her toes to hug the woman. The woman who smiled at Alex as she picked Dilynn up with ease.

Alex wasn't sure if Dilynn was playing interference or not, but several of the players on the court, including Sadie, were distracted by Sylvia's presence. Sadie's eyes watched Dilynn and Sylvia closely, then looked at Alex. She was worried, too.

"Why does everyone know her?" Alex asked Simone.

Evie was the one to answer though. "She plays for the NWBA. She's one of the highest shooting wings in the west. That's why Mom knows so much about basketball. She used to have box seats and half of her closet is still Devils gear."

The teen got up from the bench, leaving only Landon as the barrier between them and Ryder. Alex knew that smile on the girl's face. It was the one she'd used before she realized Alex wanted more than a working relationship with Dilynn.

Evie stayed with Sylvia and Dilynn longer than Alex liked. Alex knew part of the reason the conversation took so long was because Dilynn wasn't actually talking to Sylvia. She was watching the game, putting Sadie first.

Her body bounced as she yelled at the ref from the sideline. She screamed so loud the ref actually turned and said something back to her. Something that had Sylvia pulling Dilynn back by the t-shirt. Alex's t-shirt.

They smiled at that.

Sylvia may be standing there with Dilynn, but Dilynn was in their clothes. Their clothes were covering the marks they'd left to claim her last night. All night, she'd said their name. Looked in their eyes as she came apart.

"Does she have a giant hickey on her shoulder?" Simone asked.

Alex's smile grew. That was one Dilynn hadn't covered. And if Simone could see it from here, then Sylvia would have seen it too. She would know Dilynn was theirs.

Their eyes returned to the game as Sadie brought the ball down the court. She didn't move to the corner. Instead, she drove into the defender. Sent the guard back several steps as she crossed over and split the defense for a layup. She hit the ground hard when the center missed the ball and smashed Sadie mid-leap.

The ball bounced on the rim, then rolled in when the whistle blew.

Sadie went to the line with a subtle smile playing in her eyes as she looked at Alex. Alex gave the kid a thumbs up, and the smile grew across the kid's face.

"She plays like you did," Ryder said. "Just goes in headfirst, drawing the foul."

They took it as a compliment. If Dilynn did get a hoop, they could work with her. Teach her how to switch hands so the ball would be harder to defend.

The foul shot hit the backboard before bouncing away from the hoop, and Sadie fell back into defense. They would work on free throws, too.

The game ended with a win for the freshmen team. After the teams slapped hands, players from both sides swarmed Dilynn and Sylvia. Basketballs were signed, and Sylvia took time to speak with Sadie. Their Sadie, and the girl was smiling at Sylvia like she smiled at Alex.

Ryder leaned forward with his eyes locked on Dilynn and Sylvia hugging. He asked, "¿Podemos odiarla en lugar de a mí?"

Lyra placed one hand on Alex's shoulder, and she reminded them, "Evie said she doesn't want kids. Dilynn won't take her back because she doesn't want kids."

Sylvia's hand rested on Sadie's shoulder. For someone that didn't like kids, she hid it well. It could just be a game. Dilynn was constantly worried about them playing games, which means someone played games with her heart before.

They couldn't just accept Lyra's explanation. Not when Sylvia looked at Dilynn like she was the last cookie on a tray. Whether Sylvia wanted children or not, it was clear she still wanted Dilynn. She'd come to see Evie play in a basketball game, which was something they only did because she was Dilynn's daughter.

Alex turned to Ryder, now having processed what he had said. They studied their brother staring across the court.

"Why do you care?"

Ryder met their gaze. It was strange looking at him and seeing him, but it was a different him.

"I'm your brother. It's my job to be on your side."

Alex felt the pain return. The betrayal of being outed not once, but twice, by him. He got the happy ending, and they got trauma with an added bonus of more trauma.

"Since when?" they snarled. "You weren't on my side when you told them I was gay. You weren't on my side when you would let me take the brunt of Mom's anger for every little thing. Where is Mom even? Plotting how to get me committed."

"I've always been on your side," he said. "I didn't know."

Ryder pushed up from the bench, and they realized their mistake. With so much going on, they'd forgotten to watch Colonel. Lost track of him while they were busy trying to kill Sylvia with their eyes.

Before the Colonel made it to them, Ryder turned just over their shoulder, and said, "And Mom divorced him. They fought constantly after you left. She left him because we didn't stop looking for you."

Alex chewed on their parents getting divorced. It would make more sense if their mother had died than left. She was devoted to Colonel. Even when he was stationed overseas, she would write him every day.

Ryder stood before them with Landon by his side. The two created a wall while Alex tried to climb higher into the stands. They needed more time to process. Lyra got stuck behind them. They leaned against her, pinning her foot down.

"¡Whoa! Demasiado cerca," Lyra cried out.

They were stuck with Lyra pushing them and the guys blocking the path forward.

"I told you not to come," they heard Ryder say.

"Son, I need to see my..." Colonel took a breath. "My child."

Colonel's voice had lost its bark. Time hadn't changed his face much, but his voice sounded human instead of like a villain in a superhero movie.

They opened their mouth, but shut it again when Dilynn stepped in the middle of the standoff. She stood dwarfed between the men like nothing could hurt her.

"Alex." Dilynn said, pulling the Colonel's gaze to her. "Alex isn't ready to see you. There is a lot of fear and a lot that needs to be said, but today has been too much. You can understand that I'm sure."

She pressed her hand to her chest. "I'm Dilynn. I'm Alex's partner and your granddaughter's guardian."

She held Sadie's hand and gestured to her. "Sadie would like to meet you. Let's do that today and let's give Alex time."

"Hi," Sadie said. She pressed her jersey down. After a moment of silence, Sadie asked, "If people put in their two cents, but you only pay a penny for a thought, what happens to the other penny?"

The old man's chin dropped. His mouth worked over an answer.

"I think the difference is someone pays to say something, but when you want something from someone else, you have to pay them for it. Like, you pay someone to listen to you, but you pay someone else to tell something."

Sadie's face scrunched up.

"Does that mean your contribution is worth less when it is asked for?"

"I think so," Colonel said. He reached into his pocket and pulled out his wallet. He pulled out a penny. Held it between his finger and thumb as he studied it.

Colonel's gaze rose over Ryder's shoulder. He stared at them, before raising the penny to Alex.

"A penny for your thoughts, Alex," he said.

Nine years of hiding, and the game had ended. Hiding wasn't an option anymore. It had to end because Dilynn wouldn't want them if they were a coward.

Alex stood and showed the man who'd sent them away to be broken that he didn't win. They grew up in spite of him. Learned to love when they had never been given any.

Ryder moved when they put their hand on his shoulder. There was still so much to tell him and a punch to be thrown, but for now he was on their side.

Everyone was there for them, so they needed to be strong.

"You didn't break me," Alex said to their father.

They took Dilynn's hand in theirs. Drew strength from her when their father placed the penny in their casted hand. He pulled out a nickel from his wallet and added it to the penny.

"I went to your track meets," he said. "I knew you didn't want to see me, but I was there for every one of them. I watched you graduate from high school and again from college."

The man reached over and squeezed Alex's bicep. It was the closest thing to affection he'd ever shown Alex or Ryder as children. His eyes were watery, but tears did not fall.

He looked down at his wallet. From within he withdrew a quarter and placed it in their hand.

"That should cover the next time. When you have had time," he said. "I know I can't fix the past, but maybe I can fix the future. Maybe I can fix us."

Alex chewed on their lips. They held out their cast and dropped the change back in Colonel's hand.

"I never needed to be fixed. I was never broken." Alex squeezed Dilynn's hand. "I'm going to go. I will see you when you get back."

25

As Dilynn pushed open the door to her hotel room, a wave of exhaustion washed over her. The long day at the softball field had taken its toll, both physically and emotionally, and she was grateful for the chance to finally retreat to the comfort of her temporary sanctuary.

The room greeted her with a cool blast of air conditioning, providing some relief from the sweltering heat outside. Dropping her bag by the door, Dilynn winced as she peeled off her sweat-soaked clothes, revealing the angry red patches of sunburn that marred her arms and shoulders. The constant exposure to the scorching sun had left her skin tender and raw. Why Ryder had believed Sylvia showing up with bats for the girls would be a threat to Alex was beyond her when she looked in the mirror.

Dilynn and sunshine were not friends. Even sitting under the shade with an entire bottle of sunscreen on her hadn't protected her from turning an angry shade of red. The girls won every game, so at least they didn't have to be back at the field early Sunday morning.

The door between her and Lyra's room swung open. The young woman held up a white towel with an unimpressed scowl.

"Movies make it seem like hotel towels are worth stealing but this feels like sandpaper."

Dilynn waved around the room. "This ain't that kinda hotel. With the team, we always stay in cheap places because club ball is already expensive."

"So, you said dinner," Lyra stated, tossing the towel back into her room. She launched herself onto Dilynn's bed. "Are we ordering room service or going out."

Dilynn followed Lyra to the bed face first. The comforter also felt like sandpaper against her skin. She prayed that she remembered to pack aloe, since she hadn't needed it the last few tournaments with it being so cold.

"Everything hurts," she whined. She shoved her hand in her pocket and pulled out a wad of cash. She put it in Lyra's hand. "Take the girls to whatever you all want. Make sure they drink water before soda, though."

"You sure you don't want to go?" Lyra asked, running her fingers over the cash.

Dilynn waved at the door. "I think at this point the moon will burn me."

Lyra's snickering wasn't helpful, neither was her need to hang around after being dismissed. Hovering wasn't a new character trait for Lyra, but Dilynn thought it would fade since the girl stopped sneaking out every morning.

"Why did you get me my own room?" she asked. She scrunched the money in her hand. "There're two beds in my room. I wouldn't have tried to like crawl into your bed or anything."

Dilynn covered her face, not sure she could explain the intricacies of the decision without crying.

Lyra didn't take silence well though. She cleared her throat, and added, "I mean, seeing you covered in Alex's hickeys is clearly a giant turn on an all, but... you coulda saved some money."

The king-sized bed was a ridiculous amount of space for someone as small as Dilynn. Lyra had asked last night when she knocked on the conjoined rooms why Dilynn hadn't just gotten one room. Dilynn hadn't answered the question then either, but it was clearly still on the girl's mind.

"Simple answer, I didn't know Sadie would be playing and rooming with the team when I made the reservations," Dilynn said.

She sat up and came face to face with the lost battle she'd fought that day. Her nose was an angry shade of pink. Not red enough to be burned, but pink enough to give her reason not to leave the room.

"What's the complicated answer?" Lyra asked.

Dilynn glanced at the girl from the corner of her eye. It would be easy to say she had been overly confident that Alex would be there with her. She'd held out hope the whole night that they would change their mind and show up to apologize for running away. It still wasn't the answer though.

She took a deep breath, and decided to trust the girl she still didn't know much about.

"When Evie came home, she was terrified of me," Dilynn said just over a whisper. Her legs tucked up to her chest and she rested her cheek against her knee. "She's a lot like you. Thinks that everything comes with a price, but she didn't..."

"She doesn't want to pay it," Lyra finished for her. She shoved her hands in her pockets. Her head nodded up and down slowly. "I don't like what I did."

"I know," Dilynn promised. "I'm not worried about it. You trying to... with me. I just don't want anyone else to worry about it either. And not just with you. I don't share a room with Evie, and I will not share a room with Sadie. It just keeps the lines very, very clear."

Lyra licked her lips. Her eyes rose even though her chin was still tucked under. "When you told Alex's brother that I was your oldest, what did you mean?"

"That you're mine," Dilynn said quietly. "I mean, you don't have to be. But you could be. I know you're, like, an adult now and everything, and I know I'm not much older than you are, but if you wanted to be family. Wanted the girls to be your sisters... we could make that happen. It will cost a couple thousand bucks, but we could make it happen legally. That is, only if you wanted it though."

Lyra's weight shifted back and forth. "Why would you want that? Want me? After everything?"

Dilynn let her feet drop. Her fingers scrunched the comforter into small fists. "I can't honestly give you a reason. I just feel like you belong with us. You belong with the girls, and if I can give you permanence, I want to do that for you."

"What does permanence mean? Like, you become my mommy?"

Dilynn's eyebrows rose. "Yeah... uh... let's not go with that one. I could adopt you though. Adult adoptions are a thing, and I could do that. Be your mom like I am to Evie. Just think about it. We don't need to make any decisions tonight or next week or anything. I just wanted you to know that you have a home. If you want it."

"Yeah, okay," Lyra said. Dilynn was pretty sure it was another Lyra lie because everything about her stature said she wasn't okay.

"You should go," Dilynn said. She waved to the dresser where her key fob lay. "Don't let Evie drive my car. Last time I let her drive, she turned down a one-way street."

Lyra nodded as she retrieved the key. She paused at the door.

"Can I ask another question?"

"Just did," Dilynn said mid-stretch. She waved her hand in the air once she was done. "What's up?"

"Is Alex, like, transitioning? Like I should be calling her him instead of her."

Dilynn tried her best to school her face. It wasn't her story to tell, especially since they specifically told her not to tell the kids.

"Sadie said she heard Alex tell her brother that Alex isn't a girl. She asked me what that meant, but I... I mean, I don't know what to tell her." Lyra ran her hands over her face. "I never really thought about any of this before. I didn't even know that I might, like... like girls until I was trying to convince myself I could go down on you. And then it was, like, I thought about it more and..."

She looked at Dilynn with the apology painted on her face.

"I don't think about that and you now. I just... I was looking at you and I was trying to hype myself up and I just thought it wasn't something that I was opposed to. Not like with him. I'm not saying he raped me. It was just like, this is the expectation, not really something I wanted to do, but then I was thinking about you and then thinking about girls and it wasn't something that felt expected of me. It was something that maybe I would like to do with someone.

Someone else. Not you. I don't want that kinda mommy. The whole mom thing, I think I could get on board with, but you know what I'm saying, right? Like, I—"

"Take a breath," Dilynn said. She got up from the bed and closed the distance. Her hands hovered over Lyra's arms. "I'm going to hug you now because I want to thank you for sharing with me how you are feeling. I understand what you are saying, and I don't feel weird."

Lyra held up her arms. She didn't just let Dilynn hug her, she hugged Dilynn back. And Dilynn was grateful because she desperately needed a hug, too.

"Alex was stupid for missing the chance to come with us," Lyra said squeezing Dilynn's neck tightly.

Dilynn sucked back her emotions. She held Lyra tighter and remembered the girl's question.

"You should ask Alex that thing you asked me," she said. "When we get back... you know. When you see Alex. I think Alex is the person who should answer questions about their identity."

She felt Lyra nod, but her arms continued to hold Dilynn.

"You can hug me," Lyra said. "I'm not Evie. I'm not scared of you, and I like hugs. So, you know, if you need a hug in the future. You can hug me."

The moment with Lyra made Dilynn realize that was the expectation she'd had when Evie arrived. Made her wonder if Lyra would like cheesy Christmas decorations more than Evie did and possibly want to bake cookies with her with just a teaspoon of salt instead of a tablespoon.

"How do you feel about Christmas?" Dilynn asked when they parted. "Like, lights and decorations."

"Always wanted a tree," Lyra said. She killed an imaginary bug on the floor. "Last year, I got one of those little ones from the Food City. I wrapped up Brandon some socks because you know socks are... they are important, but I didn't get to see him open them."

"And1 brand?" Dilynn asked. "Grey ones that are like the tall ones."

Lyra's eyebrows knitted together. "Yeah? How'd you know?"

"He gave them to me for Christmas," Dilynn confessed.

Lyra stared at the ceiling for a minute. Then dropped her gaze back to Dilynn. "Did you get him a drill? Like, in a lime green."

"That was one of the things," Dilynn said.

"Yeah. He was a bastard," Lyra cast Dilynn a smile. "But I really do love that drill."

"So, tools. That's what you like?"

"Sounds a lot like you're asking questions, Mommy Dearest."

"Yeah. That sounds so weird from you."

Lyra chuckled and shoved the key fob in her pocket. "Tools make work easier because then I don't have to borrow from the guys I work with. I like books, though. Cars, but not motorcycles. Punk rock music, and I kinda want to dye my hair blue."

"You'd look pretty badass with blue hair."

Lyra twisted her ponytail. "If you wanted to maybe get me something for my birthday... I always wanted..."

Dilynn waited as Lyra shifted her weight to and fro.

"Don't laugh."

"Promise."

"It's not something I need, so I can't bring myself to buy it. But I always really wanted to learn to play the guitar. They sell them for cheap at the pawn shop and it doesn't—"

"Done." Dilynn wrapped her arms around the girl. "We can go sometime this week and you can pick out the one you want."

Lyra was smiling when she stepped out of the hug. "I promise, I'll learn how to play, and I won't torture everyone."

"I have no doubt you will."

When Lyra left, Dilynn showered. She tried to scrub away the frustration still lingering with Alex's sudden departure. Attempted to focus on Lyra opening up. But Alex's marks had only intensified with time. Between the hickeys and the fingerprint bruises, she looked like a leopard.

Pressing around the hickey on her neck, she was momentarily grateful Alex wasn't there. The bruise didn't cover her tattoo the way Alex had hoped. The snowflake was more vibrant with a dark background due to the blue being initially pale.

She wrapped herself up in the satin housecoat she kept in her travel bag. She'd packed it since she planned on being naked while she was here with Alex. She also hadn't realized she'd forgotten to bring basic sleeping clothes, which just added another layer of humiliation.

Wandering the room, Dilynn touched everything. Jotted mental notes about the smooth finish and shaded grain of the pale bedside tables while the blower of the AC suggested the need for maintenance. These things she kept in different files in her head. She might not talk about the hotel room, but the table might be an end table in someone's home. Like Morgan's home.

She hadn't written going to Morgan's home. She was twenty chapters in, and the characters seemed no closer to having a happily ever after than they were at the start. Morgan was still playing a game of freeze tag like a five-year-old because every time Priya got near her, Morgan announced she wasn't playing anymore. Or even better she needed a time out.

The only thing worse was that Alex seemed to be playing the same game. Dilynn knew that it was partially her fault. She was chasing after Alex every time they tagged her. She didn't shout that shit was unfair when they would call a time out like last night and run away.

A part of her wondered if she didn't chase Alex would they really come back? They said they would come back. Promised it was just them working through their trauma, and they would come back. She didn't know though.

Morgan seemed to always come back to Priya, but Dilynn didn't know yet why. She'd avoided interviewing Morgan in her head when she wrote the story because this wasn't Morgan's story. It was Priya's. Dilynn knew that was bullshit. It was her story. In her character. A dirty imagining of what Alex wanted to do to her, and all the ways they would hurt her. Had hurt her.

She opened her computer and read through the latest act of betrayal she'd posted last night. She didn't place the story in the gym. She didn't write about meeting family. Just Morgan running away in a public venue after Priya told her ex that she was with Morgan. That was the root of the hurt after all.

She'd told everyone that she was Alex's partner. Told their family and Simone. Told her kids all standing beside her. Told Sylvia when she'd said she was ready for more last night.

Alex walked away though. Stared at her blankly when she suggested moving in together. Then walked away when she declared they were together.

She finished reading the chapter without tears this time. Every time Alex walked away it was getting easier not to cry. A little easier not to hate herself over it. Not because she didn't blame herself. Because she knew it was real. No one would ever stay for her.

Her father's voice whispered to her from a picture on his shelf in her head. 'When someone shows you who they are, believe them.'

He used to tell her that a lot. Every time Sylvia came for a few days, only to leave like the townhouse wasn't in her name and her face wasn't in every picture frame.

It had taken Dilynn years to understand what he meant with Sylvia. She had shown Dilynn repeatedly, Sylvia wanted her for nothing more than her cunt and tits, yet she still tried to give Sylvia her heart. Sylvia at least had the courtesy to wrap it back up for her and give it back to her.

Dilynn hated Sylvia for showing up and asking for more. For talking to Evie and Sadie and making them like her. Sylvia was good at that though. Way better than Alex when it came to talking to the kids. Sylvia had always been that way though, and Dilynn had added that into the last chapter.

Runner had hated it. The disdain dripped from their comment she'd not bothered to respond to.

RunnerAT89 on Chapter 20:
Morgan is Priya's one true love. How could you even question that? Yeah, Morgan ran away, but Priya just paraded her ex in front of Morgan like Morgan didn't matter. So what, Morgan ran away. Who wouldn't when they were finally opening up to her and the person they loved might as well have been making out with her ex. Priya says she doesn't love that woman but then why hang on her like a bitch in heat. Morgan just fucked her senseless and Priya is letting that bitch pick her up in front of everyone. People don't hug people like that. Its fucking weird. Morgan doesn't even do that. They pick her up only when they fuck her because it's weird. It's like you are trying to make me jealous.

Dilynn set the computer down. The minibar was filled with overpriced snacks and vials barely big enough to equal a shot. She needed a shot though.

The vodka burned like it always did. She walked the length of the bed, dragging her fingers over the comforter. She'd planned on being naked under those covers, and instead she would sleep in a sea of blankets and hope they didn't attempt to suffocate her.

There was only one other bottle in the fridge. Room service would bring her more if she called them. There wasn't a reason to stay sober tonight. No one was there to watch her. She could even get some extra to slip into her thermos for tomorrow.

She shook off the idea when she remembered Alex's brother would be there again. He hadn't inherited the running gene that Alex and Sadie had apparently.

Getting drunk wasn't the answer, and she'd made herself promise to not lose herself in booze when shit got too hard this time. She needed to use the frustration and pain to move the story along. If Priya's ex had come back to make Morgan realize Priya wasn't someone she could just walk away from, then she would figure that out.

Words filled the page. They weren't good words. She didn't even follow her normal process. She just typed the feelings out. The reasons Priya was feeling them. Gave her a couple flashbacks to help her process. It wasn't close to being publishable. There needed to be a conversation, she wasn't there yet though.

She flipped back to the story. Read through Runner's comment one more time. She determined Runner really did see themself as Morgan, enough to switch pronouns from her to they. But there was something else there.

When the knock on the door came, Dilynn checked the time. She should have ordered room service because her stomach was angry now that she knew it was 9pm. The knock came again, and she pushed up from the bed. Lyra must have forgotten her key.

"Coming," she called. She wrapped the silk ties to her house coat around herself.

Lyra stood on the other side of the thrown open door with a Styrofoam container held out and a sheepish social studies teacher beside her. Alex's head hung, but they looked up with those frustratingly green eyes.

"I found this in the lobby," Lyra said jabbing her thumb at Alex. "Figured I would save the front desk some time."

Lyra looked Alex up and down and pointed to her room next door. "If she kicks you out, she got me a room with two beds. Why we didn't just share a room... well, I guess we know now."

"You didn't speak in code," Dilynn said, holding the housecoat tighter against her.

"It's not code, just the language of my people," Lyra said. She didn't hang out to listen to their reunion. Just pushed the food container in Dilynn's hand and walked away.

Alex tugged the strap of their backpack up their shoulder. "I messed up," Alex said once Lyra's door shut. They flipped the backpack strap up and down. "I told you I wasn't going to run away and then I left."

"You left," Dilynn repeated.

"I... I just kinda freaked out," they said. "My father was there. Ryder invited himself, and your ex. You know your ex still loves you, right?"

Dilynn's head leaned against the door. "Yeah, you don't know Sylvia. She doesn't love me."

"Well, she was definitely jealous," Alex said.

Dilynn's eyes rolled. She had heard the same speech from Sylvia when the woman picked her up solely to piss Alex off.

"You know, it doesn't really matter how Sylvia felt," she said. "The only person you should be concerned about is me. Sylvia can feel however she wants. However, if you are worried so much about her, you should know she wouldn't have left me to manage her family after I told them we were together."

"You're right, I shouldn't worry about her." Alex said. They rolled their shoulders back in a circle. "But you didn't shove her away. You shove me away all the time."

Dilynn let the yawn take hold of her more dramatically than necessary. She pressed her hand to her lips, signaling she was very bored with this conversation.

"When do I shove you?" Dilynn asked.

"When I tease you," Alex said, their head dropped again.

"So, why do you think I shove you?"

Alex's jaw chewed over their words. They had a lot to say, but only provided Dilynn a short answer, "Because I told you not to."

A wrong, short answer.

Dilynn reached over and shoved Alex's shoulder some. She did it again in the chest. "What happens when I shove you?"

"I tell you... if you don't stop, I'm going to make you pay for it," Alex said. Their eyes rose to her, a shade darker than she remembered.

Dilynn reached over to shove them again, but her wrist was caught in their hand. They tugged her body forward enough that the door almost closed, locking them out. A position Dilynn didn't want to be in when she only had a satin robe on.

"You like to push my buttons," Alex stated. "Tease me by shoving me, knowing I will do something about it."

Dilynn squeezed her hand into a fist and tried to pull away from Alex. She couldn't get free so she gave in, and gave them more details. "And I didn't shove Sylvia."

Alex's eyes narrowed at her. "You said... you said you have a type. So that means Sylvia is like me."

Dilynn nodded and glanced at their lips. Quietly, she said, "If I shoved her, she would have called me a brat, and taken it as an invitation. We're friends now. That's it. Even if she wanted more. It doesn't matter."

Alex dropped her wrist, only to cup her cheek. Their thumb caressed her burnt skin, then grazed over her lower lip. "Because you're mine."

She pulled out of their touch. Left Alex's thumb hovering where her lip was when she asked, "Am I?"

It was a genuine question she needed answered.

"Do you want to be?"

"I think I made myself clear with what I wanted," Dilynn said, taking another step back so she was in the room, while they were still outside. "You were the one who made it pretty clear you weren't sure what you wanted."

Alex's hand dropped. They studied the ground like the questionable carpet in the hallway would give them any answers. She knew they were plotting their escape though. The lines all lead to the elevator, which would take them to the lobby, and the sliding doors to the exit.

"You said no games," Dilynn said again because, apparently, they forgot.

They rubbed their face but stopped to look at the cast. The hands dropped to hold out no evidence again for their claims. Just a place to catch the words that fell from their lips.

"I wasn't playing a game. I was scared. There was so much happening all at once." They dropped their hands to their sides. "And I didn't know I was supposed to come. You didn't exactly invite me. You just said you were going. No one has ever wanted me before. I think that was pretty clear yesterday."

She realized she hadn't invited Alex. She'd just assumed they would be with her. Would want to share this weekend with her and the girls.

"You're right," she admitted. "I just thought you would come."

"I came," Alex said. "I got home yesterday, and I just walked in circles around my apartment. And everywhere I looked I saw you. On my table. On my couch. I couldn't even take a shower because... okay, well that wasn't because of what we did in there. That was because you left, like, a hair painting on the wall apparently, and when I was gathering it up, I kept thinking this is weird. Like, am I supposed to make a voodoo doll or something so I could cast a spell on you and make it so you would never look at your ex again without wanting to puke."

Dilynn's head fell back and hit the door. She pressed her fingers against her eyes, but she couldn't hold back the laugh.

"Look, I realized I messed up, but it was too late last night to do anything about it," Alex continued. "So, I had to wait until this morning, and I couldn't just text you. I needed to tell you this to your face. So, I had to call Simone to find out where you were staying."

"Why would Simone know where we were staying?" Dilynn asked. She felt the need to glance down the hall to see if Simone was standing there.

"Well, she didn't. But she has Casey's number and she had to text Casey. Casey didn't answer though because---"

"There are no phones during the games," Dilynn supplied.

"Yeah, so I guess the girls played like three games back to back—"

"I was there."

"Yeah, well... I had to wait for Casey to give Simone the address, and... and then she called me back. And it's Simone." Their head fell back, and they let out an exasperated huff. "She wouldn't just give me the address. She made me listen to how she is my best friend and that I let you be mean to her and call her names while I told her she couldn't call you names. She told me I was a shit friend and that I don't even hang out with her anymore. So, there were apologies and groveling. She made me buy her a case of beer and only then did she tell me where you were staying."

"You coulda just called me," Dilynn said. "You know, call me, so I don't sit here thinking you were going to run away. Leave me with Sadie and your family up my ass all weekend. Because they were up my ass all day. Ryder wanted to talk, and Lyra wanted to talk. And there was so much peopleing."

Dilynn waved to herself. "I'm not a people person. I just... I like to feed them, and I like to avoid them because they just want to talk and talk and talk."

"Well, I wanted to surprise you," they said. They raised their hands in the air. "Surprise."

"I would have rather had some notice," Dilynn stated, folding her arms over her chest again.

"Oh." Alex's eyes flicked to the room next door. "Well, I can go get my own room."

"All booked. And you're not staying in Lyra's room. That's weird since she slept with my ex. Not that I think you and her would... but it's still. I don't even want to think about it."

"Oh." Alex took a step back. "Well, I should probably—"

"Go?" Dilynn watched them carefully. "That's just what is always going to happen. You're just always going to need to go."

"I know." Alex shook their head. "But I came. I came to..."

"You shoulda been here hours ago," Dilynn said. She grabbed the waist band of their pants and tugged them into her. "Shoulda already been finishing what you started yesterday."

Alex glanced down the hall with their hands pressed against the door on either side of their head.

"Unless you don't want to," Dilynn said, trying not to appear crushed. She released the waist band of their pants. Let it snap against their abs. "You probably have to head to the outside of town. This is a big tournament, so most hotels are booked."

Alex pointed at the door next to Dilynn. To the room Lyra disappeared into. "I just gotta... just give me a second."

Alex moved to the next door. Dilynn watched Alex reach into their backpack and hand something off to Lyra.

"Yeah. I definitely appreciate that," Lyra said, then shut the door in Alex's face.

Dilynn's eyebrows tried to touch in the middle as Alex came back with a huge smile on their face.

"What did you say to her?"

Alex swooped down and picked Dilynn up. Pressed her against the door before stealing a kiss from her. Dilynn's legs wrapped around Alex's hips and let them grind against her core. She felt the thick protrusion tucked against their abs immediately.

"Are you strapped?" she asked, even though she felt the answer.

Alex jogged their hips against her. "Surprise," they whispered.

"What did you give Lyra?" Dilynn asked, hoping a different question would get her an actual answer.

"Ear plugs," Alex said. "I heard you tell her you got her a room. Assumed it would be close by, so I wasn't taking any chances. I still need her to like me, and I am pretty sure her listening to me defile her mommy would not help my cause."

"Defile?" Dilynn mused. "That sounds rough."

Alex's lips worked against Dilynn's throat as they hummed. "Your ex was hanging on you last night. Her arms were around you."

They pressed their nose to her pulse point and inhaled deeply. "You smell different."

"I smell like hotel soap and sunscreen, you weirdo," Dilynn said pushing them away from her.

They growled lightly and nipped at her bottom lip. "I don't like her touching you."

"Clearly," Dilynn said as the elevator beeped down the hall. "You know I didn't know the big bad wolf was so—"

"Oh. My. Fucking. God." Evie yelled from down the hall. She stood just outside the elevator with a group of her teammates and Sadie. "You are so embarrassing. Do you even have clothes on?"

"We need to move," Dilynn hissed, trying to hide herself. "Because I do not have clothes on, and all these teenage girls do not need to see me naked."

Alex didn't wait for further instruction. They carried Dilynn into the room. Let the door close on its own behind them while they dropped her on the bed.

There was a hunger in their eyes that only grew more ravenous as the satin tie was pulled undone. There was no question in this moment they were the predator and she was the prey.

Alex didn't take their time like they had the Thursday night. All their patience must have been burnt through on the drive with the silicone pressing against their clit. She pushed against their chest and tugged at their shirt, needed it off. Needed to feel Alex's skin against her own.

No undressing took place though. Dilynn's hands were grabbed and secured above her head as they growled, "I told you not to shove me."

The moan came from the most primal part of her. She knew she couldn't fight them. Knew she didn't want to. She wanted what they were giving. Wanted to be completely dominated. To be at their mercy.

They released her just to get off her. She didn't have a chance to move, before she felt their hand around her ankle. Her body flipped over like she weighed nothing.

With her ass up, she felt the shock of the slap. Her face flew up, but she couldn't go anywhere because Alex's body fit between her legs. She was certain

Alex didn't even bother to fully drop their pants before they pulled back. The extension of themself parted her lips and bumped her clit.

Her face dropped to the bed as she waited for them to fuck her. She turned her head, preparing for the stretch. She'd taken their dick two nights ago and knew she would feel every inch as it opened her.

Her eyes locked in on the story still open. She'd written a scene like this. One where Priya was brutally fucked over her desk. She didn't know how Alex managed to know every fantasy she had but they did.

The cool lube dripping around her entrance shocked her system. She was certain she didn't need any but appreciated their consideration. It caused her pussy to pucker and her eyes opened wider.

The computer was open to the comments section. She'd been reading Runner's comment.

"You're mine," Alex growled. "Hugging your ex. You knew it would make me crazy. No one else should be picking you up. Especially her."

Had Dilynn actually known hugging Sylvia would turn Alex into a horny animal, she would have hugged her twice. Except she didn't know that Alex would be jealous. Just like Runner wouldn't know that Sylvia had hugged her.

She hadn't written Priya hugging her ex. She'd written that she was there. That was it. So, the comment before her eyes only made sense if...

Dilynn was putting together pieces that she didn't want to align. Like, Alex was preparing her to fit a piece of whoever they were within her. The pieces of betrayal all fit together. They fit the story of the corporeal figment of her imagination preparing to fuck her.

"Hey, where you at?" Alex whispered. They grazed their hand over her bruised ass and released their hold on her hips.

With Alex barely touching her, Dilynn took the opportunity to escape. Her body propelled across the bed, and she gathered the blanket to cover herself. To block them from seeing her.

"I'm so sorry," Alex whispered. Their hands were up but shaking just like the cock still poking out from the waist band of their pants. "I didn't mean to—"

She couldn't stop the tears from falling but she wiped them away. Over the past several years, she'd been the butt of a lot of Simone's cruel jokes. Brandon had humiliated her. Sylvia enjoyed breaking her into pieces just to feel like a creator when she put Dilynn back together. And somehow this was worse.

So much worse.

"Dilynn," Alex whispered. They gestured to themself. "I thought... You said... you said you liked it rough."

"I said it or you read it?" Dilynn slapped the computer towards them.

Watched their eyes scan over the screen. "Who are you, RunnerAT89?"

She knew just by the look on their face that they knew before this moment. Used her story to manipulate her into believing they liked her while they treated her like shit online. Had always treated her like shit online when they didn't have to look at her.

"Did you just come here because I'm a stupid bitch in heat?" she cried.

Alex's eyes opened wider. They seemed to be choking on air. A catfish stuck on land.

"I'm so stupid," she whispered to the bed. "You've been playing me since the beginning. You started messaging me last semester. Tormenting me online and calling everything I write trash."

"It wasn't... I didn't—"

"You're a fucking liar," Dilynn said. She threw the pillow at them when they tried to move towards her. "Don't fucking come near me."

Alex took a step back. They looked down and shoved the dick into their pants just like Morgan did before she walked out of the classroom after fucking Priya.

"Now is the time you run away, troll," Dilynn growled. She chucked another pillow at them. "That's what Morgan would do, so that's what you will do."

"Please, just let me explain," Alex begged. "I found out at pizza night, and I thought—"

"You would use my story to fuck me. Take every dirty fantasy and make it real."

Alex pressed their hands to their chest. They were shaking their head, and words were coming out, but Dilynn couldn't hear any of it through the blood pulsing in her ears.

The room started to tilt to one side, and she felt like she was going to fall over, so she scrunched down lower. Held on to the mattress to keep from falling off the edge. It was only when the door shut behind Alex did the sobbing become uncontrollable.

The comment was still taunting her. Laughing at her for being a whore. For thinking she could be more than a sex toy for other people's amusement.

The laptop flew through the air. She didn't need it anymore. Never should have needed it to begin with. When it hit the wall, the screen shattered. It landed next to the purple shoes Alex had kicked off and left without.

She wasn't sure when the door opened again. Didn't hear it over her sobs. There were just hands too close to her. Hands she tried to push away.

Pulling the blanket over herself, Dilynn tried to shield herself from Alex seeing her, but she looked up to find dark eyes instead of green.

"Hey," Lyra whispered. She crawled on her knees towards Dilynn. Pulled her against her chest and wrapped Dilynn in her arms. "It's okay. It's gonna be... I got you."

"Alex...is... the troll," Dilynn sobbed into Lyra's chest. "Played... me."

26

The soft glow of dawn filtered through the windshield, painting the interior of the Audi with hues of amber and gold. Alex gradually awoke to the gentle warmth seeping through the windshield. They'd reached over, hand searching the air for Dilynn. They opened their eyes, realized they were still in the back seat of their car. They'd curled up across the seat, trying to shrink into a ball.

The sweatshirt they'd used to cover themself with fell to the floor. They stretched and blinked away sleep as the scent of creosote bushes and desert sage whispered to them on a faint breeze through the cracked window. Sleeping in a car wasn't new for Alex; sleeping in the Audi was though. They'd thought they were past the point of being locked out of a room. Apparently, they'd been wrong. They'd been so wrong about so many things. But they'd known Dilynn would get hurt when she found out about their comments.

They should have stopped responding. Deleted their account. So many 'should haves' now flew in a circle around their head like vultures, occasionally diving down to take a test peck at them.

The outside world knew their wants and dreams were insignificant in the grander scheme of things, so it awoke with the chirping of birds and the rustle of palm fronds in the breeze. The distant silhouette of the Catalina Mountains stood against the morning sky, their peaks catching the first light of day. The air was crisp, yet promising, hinting at the warmth that would soon envelop the desert landscape. The same heat Dilynn had been burned by the day before. They wanted to be the one to put the sunscreen on her today, but they would have to earn the right to touch her again.

The sun was halfway over the mountains and the clock on the dash read 6:30AM when they got out of the backseat. They tapped their fingers to the steering wheel, singing along with Lincoln Park as they tried to plan out how to get Dilynn to listen to them. They had made it through half the CD when the hotel woke.

Girls of all shapes and sizes in knee-length softball pants and colorful jerseys began to trickle outside with prizes from the continental breakfast. Dilynn hadn't been lying when she said the tournament was large, because several of the kids looked only a year or two older than Ryder's daughter. After a few minutes the girls lugged heavy bags, darting between cars while groggy parents called to their offspring to hurry up.

Alex hadn't gotten to play club sports, not like this at least, and they briefly wondered if the clans and their colors in Dilynn's novel came from the woman sitting at a softball field. Alex smiled at the thought of Dilynn turning baseball bats into swords in her head, softballs into arrows, and gloves into daggers. It was something she would do, they decided, and they envisioned her sitting along the fence with her laptop, describing a game as a battlefield.

The smile fell from their lips as they realized just sitting next to Dilynn wasn't an option. She would probably never let them read her writing again once they got her to take them back. That might even be part of the negotiation for a second chance. They would give up on the hope of ever seeing the sequel in print. If she didn't take them back, then they probably wouldn't want to read Alex the Troll being hacked to pieces by Priya. Or worse Morgan, but that would make sense she'd have the character they idolized murder them.

That would be if Dilynn even put them in the book. She hadn't written Simone as a bully in the story, so they would probably not be immortalized on the page, even as a troll.

They began to search for any sign of Evie, Sadie, and even Casey in the rainbow of uniforms. They weren't even sure what color they were looking for, which made it harder. After the caravans of cars began to leave, a new wave of kids exited the hotel. They had the location of the fields where the girls would play, but Simone had said the start time would depend on whether the girls had won or lost. There wasn't a chance to ask about the girls before she had thrown the pillow at them.

When they couldn't find the girls in the second wave of parents trying to leave, they figured that meant the team had won and they started later.

That was good, they decided.

With everything else already a mess, being late to the game wasn't an option. They needed to show up on time with a coffee for Dilynn. They'd be there, and they would wait until she was in the stands behind home plate. They would have to get there before she started yelling at the umpire and they would sit next to her.

That would be the plan.

They would sit next to her quietly on the bleachers and hand her a Chai and an iced coffee. She could choose which one she needed, and they would hold her second drink until she was ready for it. The straw in her mouth would keep her from yelling at them.

They nodded their head in agreement with the plan as they drove through the Starbucks drive thru. They knew what they needed to do, and they took the time to plan out what they would say. Practiced various configurations of words while waiting for Dilynn's happiness to be handed to them.

They looked at the cup, realizing the only thing she would enjoy about this morning was within it. She wouldn't want them to be there, like she hadn't wanted them in her classroom after Simone had harassed her. That could change though. They would go to her because driving their car off the road wouldn't be an answer. Punching a wall had already almost ruined things for them, so this would have to work because Dilynn didn't like attention, which was something they knew. They knew it from being with her, not from reading her story. Okay, maybe that was a little bit of both. But they knew Dilynn wouldn't yell at them in front of the kids. She would let them apologize like they had in their apartment.

'Speak in Español,' something inside them said. They knew it wasn't the voice that hated them, so they decided to trust it.

As they followed the GPS to the field, they considered what to whisper in Spanish to her. Wondered if it even mattered if they were being romantic. Dilynn didn't seem to know the difference, so they weren't going to go all out with their love in a language she couldn't understand. They could practice their apology in Spanish first though. They would say it in Spanish, then in English.

Pulling into the sports complex parking lot, they searched for the white Prius. When they couldn't find it, they decided to sit in the car and wait until they saw her. Watching her had always given them clues as to how she was feeling, so they would wait to see if she was still mad or if she missed them. They kept their eyes fixed on the gate where two older women sat taking entrance fees from grumbling parents as kids wheeled in bags filled with their expensive gear.

They needed to get Sadie a bag like the other kids had. Maybe after they apologized, they could convince Dilynn to let them pay for Sadie's softball stuff. Basketball was over, but softball tryouts were in a few weeks and Sadie should have new equipment. It would require they adjust their budget, but Dilynn shouldn't shoulder all the financial burden for Sadie. They could step up and show Dilynn that they would help her. Not that she needed their help, but they could help her.

There were tons of bags being carried and rolled into the field. Alex was searching the different brands on Amazon when their car window screamed.

They blinked several times as Evie's two middle fingers were pushed against the window. Even when she pulled them away, the oil from her hands was still there. That was the point they were certain getting out of the car meant taking her lopsided punch to the face.

Her laughter was just as cold as her gaze. They remembered they had messed up again on Friday by leaving before Evie's game. Both games they'd been invited to, they'd bailed before Evie played, which they knew showed the girl that they didn't care about her. Just like not coming to the tournament yesterday had been another time they hadn't bothered to show up for her, and it was something their father used to do. He'd never missed Ryder's football or basketball games, yet never managed to make it to one of theirs.

Their shoulders fell as they catalogued all the times they'd messed up with Evie. They hadn't made it in time in the mall to keep her from getting shoved by Dilynn's ex. They'd missed both her games. Getting out of the car this time was a requirement. It had to be.

Evie walked backwards staring at them as she made her way to the field where Dilynn hadn't even looked back at them. She hadn't looked, but Ryder was looking at them.

Ryder, Sadie, and Evie were all staring at the car as Dilynn withdrew cash from her wallet and exchanged it for wristbands. Evie tugged on Sadie's arm, and they realized they didn't need to get the girl a bag because she had one already that matched Evie's.

Of course, she did.

Dilynn didn't need Alex. She'd wanted them, and they ruined it. Ruined it like Simone had ruined things so Dilynn didn't let their friend see Evie anymore. Which meant there was a chance she wouldn't let Alex see Sadie or Lyra. Wouldn't let them teach Evie how to punch someone. She should get to punch Alex for hurting Dilynn, they decided, but it was too late. They hadn't gotten out of the car with Ryder still standing guard at the entrance to the field.

The expensive Starbucks beverages sat in their cupholder untouched as they put the Audi in drive and pulled out of the parking lot. By the time they reached the outskirts of Tucson, the drinks were ruined. Just as ruined as their fledgling relationship with Dilynn.

And there was no going back. By the time downtown Phoenix was in sight, the check engine light came on. A light that forced them to take another Monday morning off to get it checked out.

There were no open appointments available at the family-owned mechanic shop. With only a promise from the shop owner to fit it in, Alex brought the Audi in mid-morning and sat in the stiff pleather chair. They didn't have anyone to come get them, so they were forced to wait for the car to be done as the pain in their wrist had sweat gathering at their temples.

This would be part of their punishment for hurting Dilynn, they decided. Not taking the pain meds would make them feel as horrible as they'd let the woman they wanted to marry feel. It wasn't the pain of betrayal, but it was pain, nonetheless.

The single window in the lobby provided Alex a view of their car parked just inside the entrance. Two lanky brutes tossed dirty jokes back and forth as they drained cans of Mountain Dew and built themselves towers without touching Alex's car. There seemed to be only one person working, but whoever it was kept their head under the vehicles.

Cars and customers came and went. The business was clearly good and the tall blonde behind the desk greeted everyone like family. She'd tried to start multiple conversations with Alex, but they weren't good at small talk, so she eventually gave up.

Alex heard the tower of cans collapse shortly after the grease covered men left for the afternoon. The magazines were all read, and their phone was on its last 20% so they couldn't get lost in a fic by a writer who wasn't Dilynn. Not that they wanted to. Dilynn's stories were the only ones they wanted to see, even the sappy ones that they'd bashed before, but nothing new came. They'd checked hourly since Sunday night to see if Dilynn would share with them how to fix things. If she would show Priya's reaction to Morgan messing up once again.

The small shop's owner came into the lobby with her phone pressed to her ear. A box slapped against the counter and the woman loaded the empty plastic holder with new business cards.

"Audi next?"

Alex's head popped up at the familiar voice. Their smile immediately dropped from their face when they realized this was the last person they wanted touching their car.

Lyra hadn't noticed them, or if she had, she ignored their existence. She walked behind the high-top counter and pulled their keys from underneath. She studied the form as the owner continued talking.

"So, is the rim bent, because if she hit the curb too hard... okay good. Maybe don't let your kid drive your car anymore."

Alex chewed on their lip. They could change their mind, grab the keys to the only thing they had left that meant anything to them before Lyra grabbed her blow torch that she did, in fact, have access to.

The girl's onyx hair fell over Lyra's shoulder, and Alex could see the exhaustion on the girl's face. Her eyes rose from the sheet to Alex, and it was too late now. She could get the torch before they would get the keys from her.

"Tienes suerte de que necesito este trabajo," Lyra stated, before walking back into the shop.

She was already in the car when the owner was off the phone. Shaking her head, the woman set her phone down.

"My best friend," she said, gesturing to the device. "She knows nothing about cars and calls me with questions like, 'My tire is going bump bump bump. What's wrong with it?'"

The woman's laugh was a mix of amusement and annoyance. Alex could see the love there though. Something they would never find on Simone's face when she spoke of them.

"She has a lot of faith in you," Alex said.

"More than she should," the owner answered. She pulled out an envelope from a blue bank bag. "Hey, Lyra! Come here!"

Alex dipped their chin to their chest, trying to shrink into the pleather seat when Lyra came back in from the shop. She had a grease streak on her cheek, and wiped her hands down the jumpsuit tied around her waist.

"Thanks for giving the boys a break. I won't lie, it's nice not to hear them bickering like old maids this afternoon." The owner held the envelope out for Lyra. "I won't be here tomorrow, so I wanted to make sure you got paid."

Lyra thumbed through the envelope. A small smile rose up her face as she folded the envelope in two and tucked it in her pocket. "Thanks. My little sister's birthday is in a few weeks so now I can get her this tortilla blanket she wants."

"That's super cute," the owner said as Alex tried to figure out whose birthday was coming. Whose birthday they would be missing. "How old is she turning?"

"Fifteen, I think," Lyra said wiping her arm over her cheek. "Maybe fourteen."

The woman looked at Lyra with a questioning gaze, and Lyra added, "My mom calls us a found family, and it's still kinda new so we are still learning some things that normal families would know. But Sadie is a freshman, so it's fifteen or fourteen."

Sadie's birthday. Sadie was turning fifteen and they were going to miss it.

"Alex's is the last car today," the owner supplied.

Lyra twisted the hair in her ponytail and tossed it over her shoulder. "Scanner says it's the O^2 sensor. I checked, and we have one in stock. Should be a quick fix."

"Sweet, I'll cash Alex out, and then I'm going to head home. Can you lock up when you're finished?"

Lyra cast a glance in their direction, then nodded. "No problem. My mom's friend had me borrow her car today, so I don't have to take the bus."

She didn't wait for them to pay the bill. Ducked back into the shop without looking at them.

The footsteps echoed in the quiet shop as Lyra moved around the space. With their phone officially dead and the lobby casting spooky shadows around the lobby, Alex found themselves standing in the doorway to the workshop.

"How is she?" Alex asked, knowing if anyone would tell them it would be Lyra.

Lyra slid out from under the engine. She went to the sink and began to scrub the grease from her hands with the gritty cleaner. With clean hands, Lyra squeezed the edge of the sink.

"They all saw you there, then watched you drive away. And she won't tell Sadie why you left. Won't let me tell her either."

Lyra dropped her head to the side. Her dark eyes stared into the mirror over the sink with an anger that they'd never seen before. "Always protecting everyone. Always being there for everyone. Always making sure everyone else is okay."

Her head turned to them slowly. Her jaw ground back and forth before she said, "You were supposed to take care of her. And instead, she's taking care of you. But you knew that's what would happen, didn't you? You knew she would make sure no one talked shit about you even though you broke her heart."

Alex felt like Lyra's words were stones being laid atop their chest one by one. Each breath was becoming more difficult, and they flinched when Lyra kicked at the cabinet under the sink. The hubcap mirror hanging on the wall shook. She didn't seem to care, and she kicked the cabinet more. The steel toe of her boot would do damage when she decided Alex was better to kick.

"I took out the earplug because the wall shook. I was going to say something shitty and then I heard her." Her knuckles paled as she squeezed the sink again. "It was the kind of crying that just makes you know something is sooo wrong."

She stared at her own reflection in the mirror still trying to find its resting point. "I've only heard it that bad once before. Heard it when my mom's drug dealer showed up. She was crying and begging him for just one more hit. Just give her one more hit."

Her arms wrapped around herself tightly. "He'd told her to piss off because he came for his money. And she didn't have it. She didn't have his money, so she traded me. I was ten and she sold me to him, and she was crying on the floor because he wouldn't just give her a little more for me. She didn't even try to stop him from taking me away. Just laid there crying."

Alex stood as still as possible. They'd survived Colonel's wars. The closet under the stairs was horrific. The burn of the electrodes was unbearable, but nothing compared to Lyra's story.

Then, they thought of Sadie. Remembered how Sadie's voice didn't waver until she broke as she told them what had happened to the sister they'd never known. Sadie had watched her mother be murdered and her father kill himself in front of her.

And Evie... she'd been abused, too. A story they didn't know, but it was probably just as bad.

Each of the Greyson girls carried more pain than Alex had ever tried to imagine. But the girls didn't carry it alone because they had Dilynn. The petite woman, who carried her own demons with a smile on her face, walked behind the girls, holding up their baggage so it wouldn't weigh them down. And she'd done it for them, too. Put her body between them and the people they were scared of when they'd been stupid enough to think they were the protector.

"I defended you," Lyra hissed. She stood up, turning to face them. "Evie backed off you because I told her.... I told her you would treat her well. And you made me into a liar when I was trying not to lie to her. I was doing what you said to do and then you left her on the floor in a puddle of her own tears. And I had to pick her up just like I had to hold her when Brandon cheated on her with me."

Lyra picked up a wrench. It hung by her side, shaking slightly.

"When I showed up on her door, she answered with a fucking knife. And I thought... I thought this white lady is going to gut me like a pinche fish on the doorstep and not a single person on this shitty planet would even notice I didn't exist anymore."

Lyra squeezed the wrench that seemed thicker than her forearm.

"She took me in. Let me lie to her over and over again, and she knew I was lying. I know now, because she makes this face when she knows someone is lying to her, like she knew Evie was lying to her about Sadie staying at the house."

Her eyes rose but she didn't move forward.

"How could you hurt someone like that?" Lyra demanded, pointing the wrench at them. "How could you look at her and know what she does for everyone and just fuck her over?"

"I wasn't trying to hurt her," Alex spit out before the girl attacked. "I had a massive crush on her, but I thought she was just my coworker. I didn't know she was the author of that story until that night I met you at pizza."

"Did you even think about what could happen when you left?" Lyra practically yelled. "Did you even think that you could break her and then what happens to me? Or Sadie. I know, I know I don't fucking matter. But did you even think about Sadie? She's your fucking niece and, you know, she worships you."

"I didn't think," they whispered, as they thought about it for the first time. None of the kids had been a thought because they weren't Dilynn. Just like when they could have taken Sadie home, they didn't. They told Ryder Dilynn would take her home because they only knew one thing.

"I love her."

"You don't love her," Lyra snapped. "Evie loves her. Sadie loves her." She tapped the wrench against her chest. "I fucking love her."

She held the wrench towards them like a sword and stabbed the air. "You...

you didn't even care."

"I messed up. I tried to come back, but then Evie.... I thought she knew and that she was going to hit me, so I left." Their hand pulled at their neck. "Why am I telling you this?"

"I don't know," Lyra said tossing the wrench onto a pile of tools. She fished the Audi keys out of her pocket and threw them at Alex. "Your car is done. Probably want to get it out of here before I make it blow up on the freeway."

Lyra moved to the pile of tools. She had a clear routine of cleaning up the mess. Each wrench was meticulously wiped down before she put them back in the toolbox. She studied the blowtorch in her hand a little too long for Alex's taste.

"Dilynn doesn't write people off." She lit the blow torch and stared at the flame. "Even fucking catfish. So, if you care like you say you do... if you love her, then you got to make an effort. If nothing else, then you need to go back and make peace for Sadie. You can't... Sadie wants you, so Dilynn will give you another chance to at least be in her life. I'm not going to help you this time though. You ain't shit to me anymore, but Sadie doesn't hate you. And she needs you."

"How?" Alex asked, equally mesmerized by the flame. "She'll make sure our paths don't cross."

"I'm not one to try and fix things when I fuck up. I just go about my life," Lyra admitted. She took the torch to the tool bench and set it down. "I guess that's why I know... I know, you probably have no intention of coming back, but Sadie isn't going to understand. Evie won't give a damn, but Sadie... she fucking worships you. So, Dilynn is gonna let them think you are still just freaking out about the whole family thing. And you know she is blaming herself. Thinking she is the one that sucks instead of you."

Lyra glanced in their direction again. She shook her head and let out a heavy sigh.

"She left you a window to crawl back in," Lyra said. "And if you're going to try, you need to do it quickly."

Alex's head popped up from the ground their feet had finally managed to root into.

"Why do it quickly?"

Lyra's chest raised in a single, 'Ha!' She put an impact drill into a case before putting the case on a shelf.

"After you fled the parking lot, that blonde lady from the game showed up to 'support Dilynn's daughters.' She'd already been there Saturday and she'd brought them bats that apparently haven't even been released yet. But Sunday... she had new catching gear for Evie and a glove for Sadie. And your brother was pissed."

Lyra's fingers ran over the handle of the blow torch again.

"I bet she didn't tell you he got in Dilynn's face on Saturday because of the bats, but it was worse on Sunday. He started yelling at her so loud that Evie ran off the field in the middle of an inning, and he accused her of cheating on you." She sucked in a deep breath. "He was yelling at her, and she didn't tell him. She didn't tell him you were the fucking reason she hadn't smiled all goddamn day. And her ex... Sylvia stood up for Dilynn. She didn't even say anything, just stepped between them when he was yelling at Dilynn and his spit was hitting her. And she stood there protecting her. Protecting her when you were supposed to be there to protect her."

Lyra wiped the back of her hand over her face.

"Maybe Sylvia is the person who should have her heart though. She's there for Dilynn, and Evie said she's always been there. Always sent Dilynn birthday presents and calls her to check in."

Lyra finished wiping down the rest of the sockets for the drill she'd already put away.

"You leave her. You don't text her or call her. You don't apologize. But Sylvia... she doesn't make Dilynn fend for herself." Lyra waved to the parking lot where a large truck sat. "Sylvia even had a car dropped off at the house so I didn't have to take the bus. Said it would make Dilynn's life easier, and I didn't want to drive it, but she's right. Not having to pick me up from the bus is easier for her."

Alex left the shop before Lyra could say anymore. They tried to find a way to fix things as they drove straight to Dilynn's house with the check engine light no longer on. The car didn't blow up on the drive over. The tires didn't go flat as they crunched the gravel of the private road leading to Dilynn's house.

The apology needed to come first. They would do it on their knees so she could see that they weren't walking away. They would kneel before her and promise to never walk away again. Everything would be explained, and they wouldn't make excuses for what they had done. They would commit to her like she wanted. All those plans were lost when Alex saw the pristine sports car parked alongside Dilynn's Prius.

It was the kind of car they would never be able to afford. One that probably turned Dilynn on more than their SUV. They didn't need to read the license plate with Sylvia's last name to know it was her car, but they read it anyways. They read it and they drove away because whatever window Lyra said was open, Sylvia was already inside trying to close it.

27

Cabinets slammed, then a drawer. Reaching out to the bedside table, Dilynn tilted the phone to see the time. It was too early to be up on a Saturday with no tournament.

She pulled the blanket over her head to block out the sun, wishing she would have shut the door last night. No amount of darkness would stop the slamming in the kitchen. Had anyone told her becoming a mom would equate to being woken early on weekends to every item in the kitchen being slapped, slammed, or dropped, she probably would have passed.

Nerves on edge, she waged a war against the sheet that had wrapped itself like a snake around her ankle. No amount of kicking managed to help her escape. The comforter poised its own sneak attack by slowly cutting off Dilynn's access to oxygen.

Thrashing wildly, Dilynn futilely battled the bedding. She did not win the war. Her rescue was as violent as the attack. Cold air bit her bare arms and legs. The light blinded her, and she found herself blinking at three overly amused and awake faces looking down at her.

"Bad dream?" Lyra asked, her tone too knowing. She'd avoided eye contact with Dilynn since the deal was struck to not tell Evie and Sadie what happened.

Evie tugged at the neck of her shirt, then said, "I know Trikru is still tripping about having, like, family and stuff, but you know I could like Trikru, I think."

Her daughter had been on edge since Sylvia showed up, and the fact that Sylvia was stopping by the house practically daily with over-the-top gifts for the girls had turned Evie into Team Alex alongside Sadie.

The only benefit of Sylvia coming around was she walked the house across the street with Dilynn. It was five bedrooms and had a guest house atop a garage large enough for Evie and Lyra to both be able to have a car. Sylvia promised to have her appraiser stop by to see if the property was worth what the older couple was asking, but not before Dilynn made the woman promise not to just buy the house.

"You could, you know, ditch us to freshen up the hickeys today," Evie said, walking over and pressing her finger against the mark that was fading around Dilynn's tattoo.

Dilynn smacked Evie's hand away, then covered her face. "Oh my god, stop."

Evie plopped down on the bed like she hadn't been terrified of Dilynn for years. Sadie the Shadow followed suit on the other side. The two girls no longer seemed to have any boundaries with physical contact when it came to Dilynn, which at least meant she wasn't going hugless anymore.

"We have no food," Evie said. She spread her arms and legs out like a starfish, clearly not caring that she already occupied more than half the bed.

"There's food," Lyra clarified as she stepped towards the girls.

"Not food food," Evie whined. "Everything is, like, something that we would have to cook, which will just be a disaster."

Dilynn's arm covered her face. They were not going to let her go back to bed and hide out for the entire day. "So, you all want to go to breakfast."

"And the mall," Evie added. "And a movie. And pedicures. Sadie and Lyra have never had a pedicure, so you know that's a thing that we have to change."

Sadie was watching the fan oscillate. "Maybe we could call Alex and see if Alex wants to come. Maybe seeing us would make things less scary."

Dilynn hadn't seen Alex all week, but she knew Sadie had been to visit them daily. Spent a half hour in their classroom doing her homework before softball tryouts each day.

She prepared an excuse for Alex to protect the kid. "I don't think Alex is—"

"I could use some new work boots," Lyra said from her perch against the door. "There's a store in the mall. And Evie said they need purple socks for softball. Maybe we could go... uh... shopping. If you want to, Mom. Or I could take them so you can just sleep, if you want."

Dilynn sat up on her elbows. She studied the girl's downward gaze, trying not to celebrate being called Mom. A genuine Mom, not a sarcastic Mommy.

"Are you going to force me to watch you pay for them yourself, daughter?" she asked, not able to hide the grin spreading over her lips.

Lyra's heel tapped the door. "Maybe... maybe not. Or I could just walk out of the store and pretend you didn't pay for them."

Dilynn gave Evie a shove, knowing better than to try to climb over the top of her.

"Move," she said when her shove barely shifted Evie. "We have to hurry before Lyra changes her mind."

When Evie didn't move, Dilynn rolled to the other side. Sadie was half the size of Evie and rolled to the ground with less effort.

"Ow!" Sadie cried out after she bounced off the hardwood. Her head popped up with eyebrows scrunched in the middle. "What did I do?"

Dilynn hopped over her and ran towards the bathroom. "You were just easier to move and I gotta pee."

Evie rolled off the bed and chased after her. Dilynn barely got the door closed and locked before the girls followed her into the bathroom. Evie's fingers curled under the door as Dilynn sat on the toilet.

"Why don't you love me?" she heard her daughter whine.

She threw a roll of toilet paper at the fingers still pawing under the door. "Stop being weird."

"But I need to raid your closet," Evie said. "None of my clothes are clean."

"Oh my god. Go away!" Dilynn cried out again.

Evie's laughter flooding under the door made Dilynn feel momentarily like she wasn't a failure. She'd screwed up a lot of things in her life, but that kid, she did right. Even with the slamming, she knew she did it right.

The distant bickering and yelling let Dilynn know the girls had vacated her bedroom. At least she would get to shower before she had to pretend she was just waiting on Alex to come back like they said they would. She flipped on the tap to the shower but avoided the mirror when she got undressed. She didn't need to see the progress of Alex vacating her life.

Hating them would be better, but she couldn't find a way to hate Alex. No matter how much she was hurt, she still just wanted answers. She'd been here before though. Stood in the bathroom mirror searching for answers that never came.

The water burned, and it was something she always loved. Showers that were too hot. She'd barely rinsed the shampoo from her hair when she heard Evie call out from the living room, "MOM!"

It wasn't a playful cry. Not something that she could ignore to finish her shower. With the same clothes she'd slept in put back on, she bolted from the room.

Her daughters stood together, creating a wall before the open door. None of them were tall enough to block the buzzed heads of the Trikru men standing on her porch.

"Oh, hey," she said, hoping they wouldn't hear the fear creeping up her throat. She pulled her fingers through her hair to break up the knots some. "Girls, let them in."

Sadie stepped behind Evie, but Lyra didn't move. Her arms were folded over her chest, and she didn't turn from the men.

"Not until he apologizes," Lyra stated. "You don't get to talk to her like you did and then just show up here. You tell her you're sorry, or I'll make you sorry."

Dilynn squeezed through the barricade. The sealed envelope in Colonel Alexander Trikru's hand immediately pulled Dilynn's gaze.

"Dilynn." Ryder said her name in a way that told her what was in the envelope without it being handed to her. "We came to—"

"This is a summons," the older man said with a formal clip to his voice. The envelope jutted out from the senior's hand. "I spoke to Sadie's case manager, and she and I are in agreement that this is not the best environment for Sadie to be raised. She has filed a petition for a.... what is it called, son?"

Ryder's eyes dropped to the ground. "A change in placement."

"I don't want to go with you," Sadie said so quietly, but Dilynn could hear the tremor in her voice. "I won't go with you."

"Mom will take care of this," Evie promised, but Dilynn heard the truth buried in her daughter's voice too.

Dilynn took the envelope, not needing to open it. She'd seen these types of forms before, when Evie's case manager showed up to move her. It had taken months for Evie to come home because her foster license had originally been approved for Sylvia's townhouse. The paperwork wasn't like this though. It was just waiting for the Office of Licensing and Registration to come approve the new house, then two more months for Evie to tell her case manager that she didn't hate Dilynn for breaking her promise that Evie wouldn't have to leave after the first time she came home. That was right before the first Christmas, and Dilynn hadn't known Evie's abuse began on Christmas Eve.

"I don't understand." She tried to meet Ryder's gaze, but he was looking everywhere but at her. "We talked about this. You said—"

"My son told me he was under the impression that you and Alexis were in an established relationship," the colonel stated. "I don't know who Sylvia Winters is—"

"You're about to," Evie interjected quietly.

Dilynn looked through the crack between the Trikru men in time to see Sylvia's car slowly pulling up to the house. Sylvia was on the phone and hadn't appeared to notice the gathering on the porch yet.

Colonel Trikru cleared his throat and adjusted his stance to be even more mountainous. After opening his mouth, words didn't come out right away. He cleared his throat again before he said, "It is clear your relationship with Alexis is not—"

"Alex," Dilynn corrected, cutting the old man off. "Their name is Alex. And I won't call Alex to force them to talk to you."

Dilynn's eyes narrowed at Ryder. She waved the papers toward the men.

"And that is why Alex was not at the game. They left because you were there, because you were only supposed to be there Saturday, and they saw you and they left."

It was a lie, but he hadn't apologized for yelling at her. She still remembered him standing over her as Evie ran off the field. Her daughter came charging like the warrior queen she'd written, but she didn't have to hit him because Sylvia stepped between her and Ryder. Sylvia was bigger than he was, and she created the wall Dilynn needed until he'd stormed off.

"And you are the one that said Alex and I are not together." She tapped her chest. "I didn't say that. Alex didn't say that. That was you, making up stories because you can't accept that they don't want to see you."

That was at least the truth. She hadn't said Alex broke up with her, because that didn't happen. She'd not even told Alex that they were over. She had just thrown pillows at them until they left, but they'd come back like they said. She'd told herself Alex had come back, but left because they saw Ryder. She'd thought Alex would explain since they would be in public. Thought they'd come to talk to her when she wouldn't yell at them.

It had been a week of silence though, so she couldn't tell the Trikru men that they were still together. She couldn't call up Alex and ask them to come when she couldn't handle the thought that they had lied to her when they said she was theirs. That all the promises they'd made to her were broken. That they hadn't made love to her that night they'd spent together.

Ryder's shoulders stooped, making him smaller than his father. He was either a remorseful traitor or a knowing pawn, but she would write him as a traitor in the book. Scratch that. Dilynn decided to make him and Colonel Homophobe the invaders that ruined the peace Atlas had finally found. A patriarchal invasion in a female run society. And she would crush them.

"Look, Dilynn. I don't know where Alex is. I don't know how to reach her... I mean, them." Ryder pulled on the back of his neck, and Dilynn thought of Alex. "When I asked you why they left, you wouldn't answer any questions."

"What questions?" Lyra snapped. "You were yelling at her. Spitting on her. You pinche carbone."

Ryder's eyes fell back to the ground. "All I know is Sylvia was there and Alex was clearly uncomfortable with her coming to the game on Friday. And I know you two have a... uh... history, but it just feels off. And we don't want to lose Sadie or Alex. How about you call Alex, and we can clear this whole thing up, because, like Colonel said, we just want Sadie to be with family."

Dilynn glanced back at the girls. They looked between each other, and Dilynn knew this would be just the first challenge of many when it came to explaining to people that family didn't have to look alike. That a family could be mismatched patches sewn into a quilt that was worth being hung on a wall, but would always be ready to wrap around someone that needed to know they weren't alone.

"Let me explain something to you. Family isn't where your DNA came from." She waited for his eyes to meet her. "Sadie is home. She is home and with her family. The one that loves her unconditionally. You know that thing you and Alex have no understanding of."

Sadie stepped up to Dilynn's side. Her fingers intertwined with Dilynn's before she said, "We don't have to not be family. I want to be here, but we... we could all just--"

"*We* are your real family," the older man declared. He gestured to himself and Ryder. "We are blood and that's what matters. They are just a random group of dirty mouthed girls that live together. It's different and when you come home with me, you'll understand."

Sadie squeezed Dilynn's hand tightly and she reached back to take Evie's too. Evie grabbed hold of Lyra's until they were a chain. It would take a lot to survive the game of Red Rover that the Trikrus were attempting to play, but Dilynn was ready to send whatever they threw at them back across the threshold. She opened her mouth, but Sadie wasn't done yet.

"You are some random guy that says I have to come live with you, but you don't even know me. Like you didn't know my mom. You know, the one that wasn't good enough for you, so you abandoned her." Sadie's chin rose as she stared defiantly at the man who flinched just slightly from the words she'd shot at him. "I don't want to go with you. I won't live with you. I'll run away. I'll run away just like Alex did, and you won't find me."

The old man studied the girl carefully. His eyes were colder than a mossy stone, and Dilynn understood why seeing him brought Alex's fear to the surface. "I didn't get the chance to know your mother, but I will not let some... stranger brainwash you. She will not keep you away."

"Who is keeping you away?" Dilynn asked. She thrust the papers towards the inside of the house. "I never said you couldn't see Sadie. I was the person that introduced you. I never closed the door to her having a relationship with you. Hell, I want her to have a relationship with you."

She practically spit at Ryder, "Did I tell you that you couldn't come to the game? Did I tell you not to come to the tournament? No, I did not. I gave you the goddamn address to my fucking house. Invited you to dinner on Wednesday and we, you and I, are supposed to be planning Sadie's birthday."

"You tried to keep me from my child," the colonel said, raising his chin until his nose was parallel with the floor.

"She tried to protect Alex from you," Lyra said with spit covered words that hit the man in the chest. "Alex didn't want to see you. And this pinche pendejo knew that. He told you not to come. I was there. I heard him tell you that you were told not to come, and you didn't care. Neither of you care about Alex."

Ryder shook his head. "I have always cared about Alex. I have been looking—"

"Yeah, you looked for them," Lyra snapped, cutting him off. "But you didn't give a shit about the fact that Alex didn't want to be found by you or him. Just like you aren't here for Sadie. You came because Alex doesn't want to have anything to do with you. You're here to force Dilynn into giving you another chance to fuck up their life again. And you're doing it by fucking with Sadie's life. All of our lives, to get what you want."

The colonel's eyes settled on Lyra. He blinked a few times while his teeth chewed over his words like a cow. His gaze settled back on Dilynn before he spoke again.

"She's my granddaughter."

"She's my daughter," Dilynn said, stepping forward. She stared up at the soldier who wouldn't look at her. She crinkled the papers in front of the man's face. "I will fight for her harder than you ever fought for any of your children. And I'm not some scared kid that is going to be bullied by a couple of men. In fact, I am about to become your worst nightmare, because you came to my home and threatened my family."

"I would expect nothing less," the colonel stated. "This is not a fight you can win though."

"Never in my life have I let some old man tell me what I can and can't do," Dilynn bit back, then turned to the younger looking at her. "And there's no way in hell I'm going to start now. Now get the hell off my property."

The colonel didn't say another word. He walked away like a soldier on a mission, while his son lingered in his wake.

"Dilynn, we just—"

"You can go fuck yourself," Dilynn spat. She raised the papers to the house. "This whole thing. This whole family, you could have had it all and been the fun uncle."

Ryder studied her face, then looked over her head to the house.

"You should go, little shadow." Dilynn made herself as big as possible. Tried to fill the doorway to keep him from seeing within.

Ryder's shoulders fell, but he didn't move.

"Go on." Dilynn goaded. "Your daddy needs you to run his errands for him."

He took a deep breath. His mouth opened to say something, but his words were cut off by Sylvia walking up the porch. Her heels clicked against the porch steps, and she carried herself with her chin raised to remind everyone there that she was in charge.

"Everything okay here?" Sylvia asked coldly. She knocked into Ryder's shoulder as she walked into the house.

"No," Dilynn said, feeling her whole body begin to shake. She handed the papers to Sylvia.

Sylvia tore open the envelope as she said, "Well, this looks familiar."

Dilynn couldn't pull her eyes from the man who'd promise to not interfere. She could just tell him why Alex really left, but that would mean telling the kids. And she couldn't do that.

"I believe I heard Dilynn ask you to leave the property," Sylvia stated. Without waiting for a response, Sylvia slammed the door in Ryder's face.

When she turned back to the family gawking at her, she smiled at them. "And that is what we do when people don't leave when we ask them to."

She looked down at Dilynn still staring at the door, trying to activate her x-ray vision. Her hands rubbed over Dilynn's arms. "It's okay, Princess D. I am going to call Simmons and we are going to get everything put into place so that they can't fight us."

Sylvia's pale eyes scanned over the first sheet, and she flipped to the second. She would spend more time going through them line by line like she had when Evie was moved. She'd come that time Dilynn had called her in tears. Got on her jet and flew to the rescue.

"Don't worry, Sadie. I'll call my lawyer, and we will get this all sorted out," Sylvia stated. Sylvia shifted her gaze to Evie and said, "Right, Evie?"

"Yeah." Evie hung her arm over Sadie's shoulders. "Sylvia will save the day. She's why I got to come home when my case manager pulled some shit like this."

Evie glanced over at Sylvia. "Does that mean that you're going to be hanging around more?"

Sylvia's smile spread over her face. She put her arm around Dilynn and looked down at her. "I have always been here, Evie. You know that. Every birthday and Christmas. I mean, obviously I wasn't here because of that mole with the bad breath, but I was here. And now that he is gone. I will be here in the flesh."

Sylvia released Dilynn, then pulled a small box from her purse. She flipped it open and revealed a large diamond ring.

"I planned on waiting until a more ideal moment, but the hearing is in a week, so we will have to move faster. They would prefer we were actually married, but I know you always dreamed of a fairytale wedding." Sylvia didn't wait for a response. She pushed the ring up Dilynn's ring finger as the girls all stood around her equally stunned into silence. "And I want to make sure everything is exactly how you want it, Princess. But this will all go away. Between our engagement and my last name, there will be no question that Sadie's future is more secure with us than some grumpy old military brute."

After a simple kiss pressed to Dilynn's unmoving lips, Sylvia pulled her cellphone from her pocket and walked further into their house. She held the phone to her ear and immediately began detailing her demand.

"Simmons, I need you to put the development on hold. Get the shadow team to start digging on a..." Sylvia looked at the papers once more. "Alexander Trikru. Everything they can find. Financials. Properties. Every skeleton needs to be..."

"Mom?" Evie whispered. She ran her finger over the large diamond, then looked up at Dilynn. "I don't want to Flowers in the Attic. I don't want to have to make out with one of my sisters."

"Not it," Lyra said quickly, while Sadie stepped out of Evie's arm reach.

"I'm not kissing you either," she whispered. Then she looked at Lyra, "What's Flowers on the Attic?"

"Dunno," Lyra said, taking Dilynn's hand to look at the ring next. "But I don't think I wanna know either. And I have a feeling that comes with a lot of expectations. Like the type of rock that comes with some really heavy debt."

Dilynn stared at the ring on her finger. Two years ago, she would have been elated to be given the rock that would tie her to Sylvia. She would have been anything Sylvia wanted. And maybe that was the problem. She had done everything people asked of her.

Given up the tiny baby.

Lived in Sylvia's lavish closet.

Bought Brandon a building.

Protected Alex's secrets.

Everything anyone demanded of her, she'd complied like a weak and broken people pleaser. That was the problem, and Dilynn hadn't realized there was a name for people like her. Alex had known, and they told her what she was. She was just a MarySue, and she probably should have driven her car off the road a long time ago.

She continued to stare at the ring.

Sylvia hadn't even asked.

And Dilynn still hadn't said no.

"I don't care that he knows your ex-wife," Sylvia half-yelled at the phone. "Call her and tell her I will pull her funding if she doesn't back the hell off. Plus, it's kiddie court. We have to have a judge that we paid for in there."

Sylvia wrapped her hand around her ponytail and pulled it flat over her shoulder.

"Then get me a judge. The election is next year." She looked at the papers again. "Find out if this Maguire is up on the ballot and I'll meet with her to discuss my contribution."

She pinched the bridge of her nose.

"You will make this happen, Simmons. She is my fiancé, and you will not be the reason her kid gets moved."

Dilynn stood in the entryway still listening to Sylvia rant.

"Yes, she has more than one kid." Sylvia licked her teeth and looked over the girls one by one. "No, this is not the same one. There's three now."

Dilynn had promised herself she would never let Sylvia use her money or power to fix her problems after last time. Last time, she'd spent the majority of her summer break completely trashed as she waited for Sylvia to bring Evie home. Had promised the woman she wouldn't call her to fix something for her again. Nevertheless, Alex wasn't coming back to help her. She couldn't fix it without them or Sylvia. And Sylvia was there, while Alex was done playing games with her.

She swallowed her sense of worthlessness. This was her life now because it would mean Sadie wouldn't have to leave. She would be whoever Sylvia needed her to be, because the kids came first.

28

Routines made breathing possible. A new morning routine was created by getting to school a half hour earlier than Alex used to. It wasn't difficult when sleep didn't last with all the thoughts in their head. They were exhausted so often that they'd become pretty effective at student-led teaching because they wouldn't have to talk much. There weren't copies to make with student led teaching, so they didn't have to look at the coffee pot. And they stopped coming out of their room, unless it was to go to the bathroom at the tail end of lunch when everyone else was socializing.

The lack of adult conversation wasn't actually the worst thing to happen to them, and they'd given up on reading any stories that would remind them that once upon a time they had held the real Priya in their arms.

The only part of their day left to remind them of Dilynn slipped into the quiet room just after the last bell. Sadie set her backpack down, while Alex shifted through a new pile of essays.

"Dilynn has everyone grade their own essays," Sadie said, getting her notebook out of her bag. She set it on the desk like she'd done every day since they saw Sylvia's car parked in the woman's driveway.

Sadie had been their only non-student visitor in three weeks. Coming for a half hour before practice to tell them about tryouts or that she had gotten a B on her math test. She'd never had a B before, and she asked them to hang it on their fridge. It was still in Alex's desk though. They couldn't bring it into the apartment where there had been a room they could have offered her. Should have offered her.

"We talked about this Sadie," Alex said, flipping their pen between their fingers. "Dilynn and I... it just didn't work."

Their eyes wandered to the small calendar on their carefully organized desk. It was Wednesday, and they'd promised after last week that they wouldn't drive to Dilynn's house again just to sit in the car and stare at whatever foreign vehicle Sylvia had parked in the driveway like she owned the house.

They glanced up at Sadie, then back to the essay. They had to look again when something didn't seem right. It took a moment for them to realize the girl wasn't dressed right.

"Why aren't you ready for practice?"

Sadie's pencil paused on the composition book she used for doodling and journaling. Something she'd shown them that she'd gotten from the therapist

Dilynn had her seeing. Therapy at least seemed to be working for Sadie because she was using fewer strange questions to deflect from attempting actual conversations.

She didn't look up when she said, "I don't have practice."

Alex studied the girl to see if the color rose in her cheeks like it always did when she lied. That was something they'd learned from the afternoon routine. They'd seen Simone going over notes for practice when they had stopped in her room to find out when the juniors were taking their mandatory state test. They hadn't been paying much attention and Sadie's cheeks weren't flushed so Simone must have been planning for another day.

"You should try to talk to her," Sadie reminded them, like she did every time she came in. "Dilynn is—"

"Sadie."

"I know. I know," Sadie snapped. It was the harshest tone the girl had ever used with them. The closest thing to an attitude she'd ever had, as well, which meant she was finally learning how to be a teenager from Evie and Lyra.

Alex flipped the page to read the same information in the same paragraph as all the others. There had to be a better way to do this, and Sadie was right, Dilynn would have an answer.

"Is Sylvia still hanging around?" Alex asked, before they could stop themselves. They dug the pen's tip into the desk. Maybe if Sylvia was gone, they could go to pizza night. The woman might not have found the window Lyra was talking about.

When they looked up, Sadie was chewing on her lip. They wondered if she hadn't heard the question, but her eyes rose to look at them.

"Why would it matter if she is?"

Alex's carving motion paused. Their brow furrowed, and they needed the girl to answer questions with answers, not more questions like Dilynn would.

"What does that mean?"

Sadie shut the notebook with a slap and thrust it back into her bag. When she looked at them once more, her eyes were set in a stony glare Alex had never seen on the girl before. It was still a familiar look though. One they'd seen their entire life when their father or brother were pissed at them.

"It means it doesn't matter if Sylvia comes around or not. At least she's there. And she talks to me like I'm a person." Sadie waved at them. "You just sit behind your desk and ignore me. Evie said I'm being stupid and that I shouldn't keep coming here since you just dumped Mom and us. I mean, Dilynn and us. And Lyra knows what really happened. It happened at the softball tournament because I saw you and Evie saw you. You two were making out in the hallway but you weren't there in the morning when Evie came to make fun of you guys.

But Lyra knows because she was there. She knows, and I know she knows, but Lyra won't tell me or Evie what happened, but I know. I know it's your fault. You messed it up because you just left. And... and... they're making me move again because your dad said I need to be with family, and no one cares what I want."

She pulled the backpack up her shoulder.

"Not like you care anyways. You never wanted me. Mom... I mean, Dilynn. She's not going to be my mom. But she says when people show you who they are to believe them. And I shoulda believe it when you said you didn't want me. But I'm not stupid anymore. I'm not stupid anymore to think that anyone with a Trikru last name is worth shit in this world, and I just... I just wish my dad would have killed me, too. I wish he would have shot me when he shot my mom so I wouldn't have to be a stupid Trikru anymore."

The kid was at the door before Alex recovered from the verbal lashing. They were trying to still think of something to say when the door closed behind her, leaving them in the room, alone again.

Alex was on their feet just after the latch clicked. They couldn't have given Sadie more than a half a minute head start, but the girl with legs and arms too big for her body was already gone from the hall. Without knowing which way she went, they sprinted down the hallway to the woman who would have all the answers.

Dilynn's classroom door was unlocked, and they didn't wait for her to kick them out. Words came out immediately and loudly because their voice had been silenced for too long.

"Why is Sadie being moved?"

The blonde jumped back from the student desk she was standing over. Her body fell into a question mark like stance that didn't look up at them. The bags under Dilynn's eyes were heavier than normal though and the edges were red. Her cheeks were wet from the tears she'd been shedding before they stormed in.

"I tried to fight it," Dilynn said to the handwritten pages. She took a deep breath, but a tear fell from her chin to the pile. "I went to court, but she'd only been with me a month. The judge... she said it was better for her to be with family than someone Sadie barely knew."

"How could you let this happen?" Alex demanded. Their hand raised to the door. "She doesn't want to go. And you know... you know, what he is going to do to her when he finds out."

They shook their head, trying to calm the anger boiling their blood.

"It will eat her alive trying to stay in the closet when she was allowed to be free," they tried to explain to the woman that couldn't know. She hadn't had to live in a closet. "The things she will do to herself will be just as bad as the things they will do to her there."

Dilynn lips set in a straight line before her gaze dropped back to the pile of papers she was sorting. She slapped the essays against the table. Then, she picked them up and hit them again, but it wasn't enough.

The whole pile flew through the air at Alex. Packets broke free and single page rubrics fell from the sky like the kind of warnings the military would drop over towns before they were bombed during World War II.

"You think I don't know that?" Dilynn hissed. Her hand hit her chest. "I did everything I could. Every single thing I was capable of doing."

She curled up into herself again. Wrapped her arms around her middle as she shook. Her words came out in waves of pain, as she explained, "He's fucking withdrawing her from school here to make sure that I can't talk to her. I can't see her."

Her tears continued to flow until she ran out. Sucking in a deep breath, her finger pointed at them. With teeth bared at Alex, she delivered the assault on them in rapid fire.

"You knew what could happen," hit first.

"You had to stay with me," came next.

"You said you would protect her," which was true.

"You fucking promised," and they had.

"You fucking lied to me," and they did.

"And to her," and they couldn't fix it.

"You just left," because it was safer.

"You fucked me," but she forgot to add 'over' at the end.

"You broke my heart," and theirs.

"You abandoned her," which was another truth.

"You just gave up," but they hadn't.

"You didn't text," because there was nothing to say.

"You didn't call," because there was no way to make it right.

"You just vanished," but they hadn't.

"You just had to tell me," which may have been true.

"You made me love you," and they blew it.

"You're so stupid," but they knew she wasn't talking to them.

The guns had changed directions.

"You were just acting like a whore."

"You just dropped your panties."

"You shoulda known."

The side of Dilynn's fist hit the tabletop over and over again. Her cries carried to them what Lyra had warned them would happen.

"It's my fault. I was supposed to go that day."

She hit her fist to the surface again.

"Instead, I threw myself at you."

She held her fist to the desk but didn't hit it.

"If I had gone to see Marcus… he never would have found her."

Dilynn wrapped her arms around her chest.

"Do you have any idea?"

She took another breath. Her grasp on her middle shifted, and her hands held her ribs as she tried to breathe.

"What you did? How you used me?"

Alex stepped forward, but Dilynn shook her head. Held a hand up to keep them back. She was trying to breathe through the tears, and Alex understood what Lyra meant by an unmatched cry of pain.

"I loved you, Alex. I fucking loved you and now… I don't even know who you are? You… you catfished me, and I still don't know… I don't know why you would do that to me? Like what did I do that was so wrong? What did I do that you needed to hurt me so badly?"

Alex tried to swallow around the stone in their throat. They hadn't meant to hurt her. Never wanted to hurt her. Only ever wanted to protect her.

"I lost everything that night," Dilynn said between gasped sobs. "I lost my ability to trust anything. Anyone."

She held her hand in the air. The rock was too big for her finger. Bigger than anything they could possibly give her.

"Sylvia asked me to fucking marry her. And I… I know it's just a lie. She never wanted to marry me. Shit, she didn't even fucking ask. She just put a ring on my finger and said we are engaged. And I just let her put the ring on my finger because I couldn't even trust myself to tell her no. I can't even trust myself to know what is real and what is fake so I just… I just…. just can't stop thinking you had to care just a little. Care enough to read every word. Make every fucking scene come to life."

She paused only long enough to suck in a breath, but not long enough for Alex to speak.

"I don't know why but for some reason I still believe that this isn't Simone. She's just not that smart. Evil and cruel, but this… this required an effort, and she doesn't put effort into anything. But you… you were invested in this. And just… why would you do that?"

She didn't wait for an answer.

"Was it really just a joke? Like a cruel joke? Like a sick and twisted joke? Like, you laugh as you torture someone because you can. You make me crazy and then you see how I feel about it, and then you just do it again."

They tried to make words again, but her tormented laughter painted the room.

"It's pretty funny," and she's smiling, but it's not a smile. "You know I should write it up. The readers would get a kick out of it. Make the dumb blonde crush over the social studies teacher that never gave a damn about her. Oh wait, I did write that. And stupidly, I tried to give them a toxic happily ever after."

"It's not funny," Alex said too quietly to be heard over Dilynn's own analysis of her story.

"I get hurt, and the stoic social studies teacher gets a rally chant from commenters cheering them on to find new ways to break the idiot's heart over and over and over and over again because she is too stupid to see what's in front of her the whole time. Like, just fucking stop. But that can't happen. No, they have to have a happy ending that is coated in slimy green toxic waste. Then people are happy, right? That's all you want, isn't it?"

"I don't want to be a toxic romance," Alex said louder this time. "I want forever. I want forever with you."

They stepped forward. Her hand shot up, but they couldn't let that stop them. They'd run away every other time she felt like she was losing her mind, but they wouldn't do it again.

"I know, I screwed up. I found out... I found out you were the author of the story, and I didn't tell you. But I didn't tell you to use it against you."

They pressed a finger to her lips when she opened them again.

"I thought Morgan was Simone," they admitted. "And I didn't tell you because I didn't want to screw it up like Simone did. Whatever she did, I wanted to make sure I didn't do, and when I realized you were writing it, I thought... I thought it was about her. I thought it was why you hated her, because Morgan is fucking terrible. And I wanted to do it differently. So, I read it. I read every word and the stuff that Priya liked, I memorized because all I wanted... All I ever wanted was to be what you wanted."

"That is just so much bullshit," Dilynn cried out. "You wrote to me after pizza night. You wrote to me knowing it was me. You told me to drive my car off the fucking road. You said I was desperate. You said I was stupid for chasing after someone that clearly didn't want me. You told me I was a bitch in heat."

Her eyes roamed over their face like she was looking at them for the first time.

"You told me you needed chapters from Morgan's point of view. You needed me to tell you what to think so you could use that, too. So you know what angle to play to make me sympathize with you. Well, here's the truth, Morgan is a cold-hearted fucking monster." She smacked her hand against her chest. "*My* cold-hearted monster. The one who just wants to treat people like shit because she can. The person I never get to be."

She shook her head again. "But you... I don't even know who you are. It's like I look at you and I don't even know who you are. Alex, you were inside of me! I didn't even let your fucking friend kiss me, but I... I trusted you. And you are just an avatar. Who are you?"

Their hand pressed to their chest.

"I'm just Alex. Just Alex. Just non-binary teacher down the hall that is terrified of the world knowing who I am, so I take out my anger on strangers online. And I am so in love with you." They reached out and touched her cheek. "I am so in love with you, Dilynn Greyson. I was in love with you before I knew you were the author of my favorite book. Before I knew you were the writer of some of the sweetest and most delicate stories of two people that just loved each other. Before I knew that you had darker desires that matched my own. I was in love with you. I loved you before you even spoke to me, so I came up with ways to love you in silence. Made you coffee every morning and paid off the math teacher that got your name in the Secret Santa drawing so that I could be the one to make you smile."

They stepped into her bubble.

"I am the person who was withering away to nothing, but you saved me with a hug," they whispered. "The one that never wanted to hurt you. It was me making love to you. I wasn't fucking you. I wouldn't... do that, because you are everything to me. I was granted the privilege of making love to you, to fulfill desires that I don't know if you ever would have told me, but I betrayed your trust. I know I did, and I am so sorry."

Her hands rested against their chest but didn't shove them.

"You're not broken, Dilynn," they whispered, tucking a strand of hair behind her ear. "You shine like a star, and stars don't break. And you are the brightest star in my universe."

The blue eyes didn't raise to look at them. They remained fixed on their chest where her hands still sat.

"They implode. Stars don't break. They turn into a black hole, and they implode into pitch black nothingness," Dilynn said, looking up at them with her tearstained face. "They burn up internally and they collapse within until there is nothing left. And when they shine and they are so bright, it's because they are already dead."

She didn't shove them. She didn't give them an invitation. She turned away instead. Closed herself off against the whiteboard. Her fingers pressed against the board as another round of sobs shook her.

"They are making her move Friday. I don't even get to celebrate her birthday with her," Dilynn choked. "She... she started calling me Dilynn... she... she...

she... she said... she said... that... she said that it would be easier... that it would be easier... that I won't get to be her mom."

Alex wrapped their arms around Dilynn. Pulled her back against their chest. She clung to their arms tightly as her legs gave out.

"I'm going to fix this," Alex promised. They didn't know how but they promised her again and again. "I'll fix it, Dilynn. I will do whatever they want, so she can stay. I'll fix it. I promise, I'll fix it."

When Dilynn ran out of tears, she turned into their embrace. Her head rested against their chest, like they hadn't betrayed her.

"Don't marry Sylvia," Alex whispered, wanting nothing more than to rip the ring off Dilynn's finger. "She'll never love you like I do."

"I don't think I can ever trust you," she said. Her finger ran over their bicep. "I know what I am getting with her. She'll never love me, but I don't think I was ever meant to be loved."

They used their finger to raise her chin. Forced her back to the perfect position to kiss.

"I can't do this," Dilynn whispered. "I can't let you hurt me again."

"I won't," they promised. They leaned in closer. "I won't hurt you. Not ever again, if you will just give me a chance. I can make it better."

They pressed their lips to hers. She didn't kiss them back. She didn't move, so they pulled back.

Alex knew why she didn't push them away. Why she didn't stop them from kissing her. She didn't push them away because it would have been an invitation. She'd already explained herself. Told them everything when they kept everything hidden.

She pressed her face to the tie she'd given them. "Just hug me like you used to. Let me pretend for a just another minute that it wasn't all a lie."

They tucked her head under their chin. She still smelled just as sweet, but her body didn't relax against them. Her frame trembled and their shirt soaked through with tears.

When Dilynn stepped back, her mask was in place. She quietly moved about the room, gathering the papers while they left in silence.

Alex's brain was anything but quiet. Every thought was trying to be heard at the same time, including the one voice laughing at them for their failure.

Happy endings only exist in fairy tales.
And princesses marry princes there.

29

Dilynn wandered through the house Friday afternoon finding memories of Sadie everywhere she looked. The knock had come too early that morning. Goodbyes were barely allowed to be said and only a single bag was packed because the agreed upon plan for Sadie's transition was tossed out the window. What was best for Sadie didn't matter when the homophobic case manager wanted to close out Sadie's case. She'd shown up with paperwork she declared needed to be signed immediately because she was being reassigned to a new unit.

The photo of the kids was all Dilynn had left of another family lost. She touched the corner of the couch Sadie had claimed as her own. The girls had left for Casey's shortly after Evie got home from school, unable to handle Dilynn's tears that kept infecting them.

"Dilynn?" Sylvia called from the front door that closed too hard. Sylvia always closed doors too hard. Shook the walls that were supposed to be steady.

"You said you would fix it," Dilynn said as she wiped away the tears. She threw her hand up in the air. The ring didn't sparkle in the unlit house of mourning. "You said to put this on, and they wouldn't be able to take her."

Sylvia set her purse on the table. Her head hung with her failure, something Dilynn rarely saw when they were together.

"I did what you said," Dilynn said to the picture. "God, I'm so stupid. I always do what you say, and I always end up here. Crying on the couch waiting on you."

"I tried," Sylvia said quietly. "I offered to finance the judge's whole campaign to retain her seat. She wouldn't take my money."

"He just took her," Dilynn said, falling to the couch. "Just took her even though she didn't want to go. It's like it's happening all over again."

"Dilynn, I got Evie back." Sylvia tapped her chest. "I brought her home. I know it took some time, but Evie came home to you. And now I came home to you. And I will bring back Sadie the Sassy."

"Why are you here?"

"I didn't want you to be alone."

Sylvia lowered herself gracefully to the couch. Her arm wrapped over Dilynn, but Dilynn leaned away.

"Not right now." Dilynn licked her lips, unable to shake away the fact that Sylvia's kisses didn't taste sweet anymore. "Why did you come back at all?"

Sylvia cupped Dilynn's flushed cheeks. "Because I'm ready to do what I should have done two years ago."

"What? Put a ring on my finger without even asking me?"

Sylvia sat back. Her hands folded in her lap, and she stared her own reflection in the television. "I told you... It wasn't how I planned it."

"What did you plan?" Dilynn pressed, realizing everything was an exchange. That Alex and Lyra had been right, but she had been too sheltered to understand that when Sylvia's father had called her a concubine, he wasn't wrong.

Sylvia shifted in her seat. She tucked a leg under her, and Dilynn recognized Sylvia's negotiation stance.

"I got your text." Sylvia's head lulled to the side. "I could tell you were drunk, which is something we need to work on. You have been drunk a lot lately and alcoholism is not attractive. However, that night I was, too. I was at the Escape, and... I knew it wasn't time yet."

"You didn't answer me." Dilynn rolled her eyes. "You called me a week later for a booty call and then fled the states the next fucking day."

"I needed to give you time. Time to grieve that hideous human that you brought into *our* house. The house I would have come back to if you'd given me time to manage this whole new Mommy Dilynn you wanted to be." Sylvia sighed. "If I came that night, you and I would have fallen into old habits, which wasn't what either of us needed. So, I went to Italy and I strolled along the streets as I waited for the ring to be ready."

Sylvia's tongue ran over her teeth. There was more to the story, but Dilynn doubted Sylvia would tell it to her willingly.

"I didn't know you would hook up with the Morgan action figure, or I would have come then," she confessed. "I just wanted a fresh start. Not a one-night stand like the last time you texted me."

"You don't love me."

The ice blue eyes shifted from the television to Dilynn. "I do love you."

"Not like that." Dilynn held up the ring. "Not like this."

Sylvia took Dilynn's hand in her own. She adjusted the heavy diamond to sit straight on Dilynn's finger. "This is a commitment. No different than the one I made to you that first night."

"You told me you wanted one night to stop pretending who you had to be," Dilynn reminded her. "Took me to a hotel and covered my body in your hand prints."

Sylvia's eyebrow rose. She held the ringed hand between her own. "And one night turned into three."

"Because you couldn't just have me walk out with your fingers prints on my neck.”

“Three turned into weeks.”

“You at least took me to the townhouse.”

“Weeks turned into years.”

“We weren’t together.”

“Good years.”

“Years of being your sex slave. I wasn’t your girlfriend.”

Sylvia’s eyes rolled, before she locked eyes with Dilynn, “You know we were. Together. I wasn’t with anyone else. Only you. You were mine.”

Dilynn scoffed and let her head fall back to the cushions. “You introduced me as your friend at every event you paraded me through in one of those skanky gowns.”

“Friendship is the foundation to every good relationship.” Sylvia rested her cheek against her hand. “I won’t say you were my best friend because that’s Emma. But you were my friend.”

“We were friends,” Dilynn mused. “You were my only friend because I wasn’t allowed to tell anyone anything.”

“We were friends,” Sylvia affirmed. She tucked a stray hair behind her ear. “Still are.”

“Why are you here?” Dilynn asked again.

“To give you what you want,” Sylvia answered. It was a partial truth, like Lyra always gave. “And in turn, get what I want.”

Dilynn knew she needed to address both parts of the answers. They were separate topics since Sylvia never wanted what Dilynn wanted.

“And what have you decided I want?” Dilynn asked.

“Your school.” Sylvia smiled widely. “I am going to build your school and you are going to marry me.”

“Why do you want to marry me?”

Sylvia patted the top of Dilynn’s hand. It was cordial and frustratingly business like. Nothing that fit into a conversation about marriage.

“It’s rather simple, Dilynn,” Sylvia stated in a way that made Dilynn know it was anything but simple. “You want the life that I never imagined for myself, even though I need it. The family. The kids. So, I am going to give you the poor people school. Give you the family, including Sadie.”

Sylvia’s face flushed slightly when she looked down at the picture in Dilynn’s lap. “I’m going to be honest. She’s my favourite of your rescues. With her questions and her, just, quirkiness. Who makes cereal by putting milk in first?”

“That is one of her weirder things.”

Sylvia chuckled, then said, “May have to pay off a jury if she grows up to be a serial killer, but you know, anything for the kids.”

Dilynn didn't have a chance to tell Sylvia it wasn't fair to play favourites. She couldn't when Sylvia inched closer and tucked a loose strand of hair behind Dilynn's ear.

"You are going to be their mom and a principal and anything else you desire. Just tell me and I will make it happen," Sylvia offered.

"Like you made it so Sadie could stay?" Dilynn jerked her hand away from Sylvia's. Pulled her legs to her chest and trapped the picture against her pounding heart.

"Dilynn, I already got the last case manager removed due to her clear prejudices." A mean smile curled up Sylvia's lips. "And Grandfather Trikru has quite the closet of skeletons. Did you know he sent your action figure to a conversion camp? Simmons is currently working on getting access to the camps files to prove he sanctioned some god-awful treatment for Alex. It will demonstrate he is a danger to Sadie."

Dilynn's eyes shot up and every muscle in her body locked in place.

"I can see the steam coming from your ears," Sylvia said, rubbing a circle against Dilynn's earlobe. "We will do it quietly. No court summons. And we won't out Sadie."

Dilynn closed her eyes. After several deep breaths, she decided to attack the other answer.

"What do you get, Sylvia?"

Sylvia placed her elbow on the back of the couch. She leaned her head against her hand once more and smiled. It was a different kind of smile. One Dilynn wasn't familiar with. Almost dreamy.

"You taking care of our family."

It was a puzzle piece that didn't match the picture of Sylvia's desired life. Like a hint of a rainbow in her world of black and grey sharp lines. Then the words settled in her head. Sylvia had said 'our family.' Over the past month, Dilynn's kids were referred to as many things, primarily Dilynn's rescues. Never as theirs though. Sylvia had always been adamant there would be no kids.

Dilynn stared at Sylvia, trying to tap into her wavelength. It wasn't a gentle or steady flow. It was a laser that sliced through Dilynn's torso to her womb that Sylvia didn't want but needed.

"You want me to carry your baby? You want me... to have your baby?"

She blinked a few times waiting for Sylvia to say something. Anything. Answer the question so it would make sense.

"I read that your dad's sick. You have officially taken over as CEO of the Winters Group, which means.... You need to give him an heir, and... Jesus." Dilynn squeezed herself tighter into a ball, thinking how all of that could go wrong so fast. How the woman put a ring on her finger for the sole purpose of using her as a surrogate. "Fucking hell, you don't love me. I'm just a goddamn incubator for your child. Not our child. Yours. A Winters baby."

The smile fell from Sylvia's face. She rolled her eyes dramatically, and the dream dissolved before Dilynn's eyes. A dream Dilynn had offered to give Sylvia when the woman learned there would be no heirs of her own creation, and she'd laughed in Dilynn's face. Said Dilynn wasn't going to cast off the smell of new money that easily.

"I won't lie to you, eventually that would need to happen," Sylvia stated coldly. "We would need to do an egg transfer so that there wouldn't be issues with legitimacy, but not now. I think four teenagers will keep you busy."

Slugs moved around Dilynn's guts. She'd wanted to be a mother like that again. Wanted to give birth without knowing the infant would be taken from her arms. That would be what happened though. Another child would come out of her womb and placed in another woman's arms to call her own. She'd be given a second chance to do it right, but it wasn't right because that child would be Sylvia's, making the dream felt slimy now.

Then she processed the rest of the sentence. Dilynn's eyebrows scrunched together. "Sylvia, I know you can count."

With a slight huff of breath, Sylvia nodded her head. "Yes, counting was something they taught me how to do in primary school. I'm sure my father would have had a lot to say if he spent 40 grand a year, and then put me through Oxford without being able to count to four."

"Then you know Evie, Lyra, and Sadie make three. I have three kids."

Sylvia didn't speak. She simply stared at Dilynn, like the teacher would do to a student when she was waiting for them to catch on to something. And Dilynn did catch on.

She took a deep breath of understanding. "Did your sister's dad vanish again?"

"My sister." The phrase was tainted from their last conversation of the kid. "Kayla is possibly more of a hellion than your Evie. Got kicked out of boarding school. Crashed one of my cars that she decided to take for a joy ride."

"Where is she now?"

"Our townhouse," Sylvia said, like Dilynn's name was on the deed.

Dilynn looked at the ceiling, and then at Sylvia, "*Our* townhouse?"

"I bought that place for you, Dilynn. That's why we had to stay at the hotel for three days. I bought us a house because I knew you were mine after that first night. It may be in my name, but it was always ours." Sylvia let out a deep breath. "Father won't let her stay at the house. You know how he felt about my mother's affair. But Kayla just needs.... She needs you, Dilynn." Sylvia gestured to herself. "I can't be her mother. I could with yours maybe, with Sadie. But Kayla... she's my sister."

Dilynn sucked in as much air as she could, and let it out with her paraphrase, "So you came back and put a ring on my finger because you want me to raise your sister."

"Raise is a little much." Sylvia's face scrunched into a look that told Dilynn she should know these things. "She's thirteen. She's at the point that she knows everything and hates everyone. But you... you're good with kids like her. Kids that have lost their parents. Just look what you did with Sadie. Within a month she was calling you mom and doing chores."

"Sadie is nothing like Kayla," Dilynn stated.

She'd met Kayla a few times during their seven years together. The kid hadn't hated Dilynn, and Sylvia wasn't wrong that she could care for Kayla in a way that Sylvia would never be capable of. However, she'd watched her throw a tantrum over Sylvia's refusal to buy her a diamond tennis bracelet from Tiffany's when Sylvia had taken Dilynn out to get appropriate accessories for a gala that she was told she would be attending.

"Because Sadie has you," Sylvia stated.

"No, because Sadie isn't a spoiled rich brat. She doesn't have that sense of entitlement Kayla has. She has seen actual shit. Like her parents dying in front of her."

"Kayla and I were the ones that found my mother murdered in her home," Sylvia reminded Dilynn. Sylvia's gaze fell for a moment, and Dilynn remembered. Remembered Sylvia walking into the house still covered in blood. It was the only time Sylvia broke in her arms.

Dilynn steeled her nerves and declared her truth. "Sylvia, I'm not going to marry you. And I'm not going to play mommy to Kayla so you can go about your life."

"Dilynn, don't be ridiculous. You get everything you want from this arrangement," Sylvia snapped. Her leg dropped from under her. "I will make sure your girls will have more than a generous future whether I am alive or not. I'll put my name on the papers even. I will give them my name. And I can also promise I will be there for all the major events. Do all the family things you enjoy like the Christmas cards with the photos. Be there on Christmas morning. Thanksgiving. All the holidays."

She gestured to the house. "I will, of course, move us to a bigger house. Not here. We need to go to Scottsdale. Or if you want, we can even go back to Seattle. I still have the cabin in Prescott, if you want. But this... well, it was fine when you me told you just wanted the one girl."

Sylvia looked at Dilynn with utter disappointment. "Honestly, you should have called me when you decided you were going to be running a shelter because you know I would have upgraded you months ago. You know I've always taken care of you."

She held up her hands when Dilynn opened her mouth. "But it's fine. Honestly. We will get it all sorted."

"Sylvia."

"Dilynn, please don't make the house a thing. I know you weren't happy that I bought this one, but it felt strange having you move the kid into our townhouse. I mean, we had sex in every room. Even the kitchen. And she would have been right next door and heard you getting your ass whipped for shoving me like you know is naughty. I couldn't do that to her, so I got you a house with rooms on the opposite sides so when I... when I was ready to do this with you, she wouldn't have to hear you making all those wonderful pleas."

"Sylvia."

The woman's head rolled like the bones in her neck turned to gelatine.

"Okay, you can pick the house this time. Just please, make sure our room is on the other side." She looked at Dilynn with a devious smirk. "You know how loud you can be, and it is just uncomfortable if they are close by."

"Sylvia!" Dilynn cried out. She dropped her legs to the floor but kept the picture clutched to her chest. "I'm not going to marry you."

"Fine, if you really need the rooms all on the same side, then we will just soundproof them all. It will take a few weeks but whatever house you choose, I can get a team in to make certain—"

"There will be no house, Sylvia." Dilynn snapped. "I. Am. Not. Going. To. Marry. You."

Sylvia's mouth snapped shut. She studied Dilynn's face, then the room she'd quickly begun to infiltrate with her own preferred décor: a new television, a tri-panel painting that cost more than she would have paid, and pictures of her and Dilynn that had been packed away since she'd moved.

She tried out a few sentences, but none of them made it past her gritted teeth. Slowly, she turned her gaze back to Dilynn, "Why?"

"There are a hundred reasons," Dilynn whispered. "A hundred reasons why I can't and won't marry you."

They sat in the home Sylvia had provided for her. Dilynn knew what Sylvia was offering was nothing less than everything. Well, one thing less. The thing Dilynn knew the other woman would never give her.

"The Morgan look-a-like," Sylvia said, like she was always tapped into Dilynn's brainwaves.

She stood up and walked to the fake fireplace. Hit the button that brought the flames to life. The new softball glove Sylvia had bought Sadie was still sitting there. In the place she'd put it down when they'd lost in court. Sadie wouldn't get to play this season with the school change. Too late for tryouts, and Colonel Trikru didn't give a damn about what she wanted.

"I saw the way you were looking at her at the basketball game." Sylvia held up her hand. "I mean them. I'm sorry. That wasn't a dig at them. Just something new."

Sylvia let out a heavy breath. "You know, I thought the bitchy General was supposed to be me when I read the book. The obvious tension between her and the little mommy you wrote about yourself. Then I saw Alex sitting next to you, and... I almost left."

"You read my book?"

Sylvia's eyes rolled so hard Dilynn felt Sylvia could give Evie a run for her title of the Queen of Drama.

"Of course, I read your book." Sylvia picked up the glove and punched the leather. "I ordered over a thousand copies."

Dilynn's jaw dropped open. It took her a second to recover, but she still sputtered as she said, "You bought... a thousand... one thousand copies of my book."

"Well, not all at once." Sylvia gave the glove another punch, before she set it back where Sadie left it. "It was 10 here; 25 there. I had a whole team working on it. A lot of individual purchases that were sent to libraries."

The pride Dilynn had felt for her accomplishment fizzled. "You forced it on to the best seller's list."

Sylvia's eyes shot up to Dilynn's. She pressed her hand to her chest. "I didn't force it. I made it so people were paying attention."

She began to walk around the coffee table as she explained, "I put my publicity team on it. They infiltrated some key markets, and I have a few talented interns that liked it. They said to create a buzz we had to get people talking about it on social media, so they composed some fan fictions about it and posted it on some of those sites with all the words. Tumblr and quotes on Instagram. One drew some comics. All of the normal stuff that would happen when something becomes popular."

"So... people didn't actually read my book and like it," Dilynn said, squeezing the frame tighter.

Sylvia's eyes rolled again. "People love your book. I have an intern that worked out a draft for a movie. They pitched it to a few directors. Several want to take it to production and you should be getting a call in a month or so."

The older woman stopped pacing and sat on the coffee table before Dilynn. She folded her hands as she leaned forward. "Look, I know where that brilliant mind of yours is going. However, I didn't make your book popular. Your story did that on its own. I just got it into people's hands."

"Why would you do that?" Dilynn asked.

Sylvia's hand jutted out from her body. "Because you wrote an amazing book and people should read it."

"You bought 1000 copies, and you hadn't read it," Dilynn reminded her.

Sylvia's head fell back. "I told you I read it."

"Before or after you bought 1000 copies?" Dilynn asked to prove her point.

"Well, that's not fair," Sylvia stated. "My team worked very quickly, so the first 1000 copies were purchased in pre-orders before my copy arrived. Plus, I own a hefty share of the publishing company so it isn't something I wouldn't necessarily do for any other book we were trying to promote."

"You're unbelievable," Dilynn said.

Sylvia slowly dropped to her knees. She pushed Dilynn's legs apart and slotted herself in the space. Her hand cupped Dilynn's cheek as she said, "Unbelievably in love with you."

Dilynn's eyes narrowed as Sylvia inched her way closer to Dilynn's lips. "You're unbelievably full of shit."

She smacked Sylvia's hand away with a sharp turn of her head.

"And Alex is not Morgan. If they had been, then Morgan wouldn't have been a girl. And you are also not Morgan."

"Dilynn," Sylvia said. Her fingers walked up Dilynn's thigh. "Half the lines out of that woman's mouth were things I said to you."

"Well, yes, I definitely used your go-to lines for when you weren't listening when I spoke. Like you are not listening now. I am not going to marry you."

Sylvia dropped back on her heels. Her face scrunched up in distaste, but she nodded to herself.

"Okay. Okay. You win," Sylvia said. "Since you want Alex, we can figure that out."

"Sylvia."

"They are very attractive, and I get it. I could get on board with that addition. But you know how things work for people like us. Marriage is a financial contract, and if you need them to fulfill those softer fantasies you have, then so be it. It would have to be discreet, but I know you're capable of that. I know I sometimes—"

"No, Sylvia."

"No to what? The open marriage?" Sylvia's lips pursed. "Dilynn, it's hardly fair that you get to keep yours on the side and expect me to—"

"No to marrying you." Dilynn put the picture down. "I'm not going to marry you. I'm not going to be Kayla's mother."

"Dilynn, darling."

Sylvia reached towards Dilynn once more, but Dilynn was done with the touching. She snapped at Sylvia's hand, letting her teeth smack against each other.

Sylvia pulled her hand back, blankly staring at Dilynn for a moment.

"Did you just try to bite me?"

"It was a warning," Dilynn said. "I can't push you without my shirt becoming a set of cuffs, so if you try to touch me again, you're going to lose a finger."

Sylvia cupped her favourite hand to her chest.

"Well, that's just mean."

"Touch me again, and I'll show you all the tricks Evie has taught me." Dilynn pointed to the house rules sign. "There is a reason we have rules for no biting, hitting, kicking, spitting, or yelling."

Sylvia's gaze followed Dilynn's finger to the sign. A smug smile spread over her face.

"I know for a fact that all of those things make you wet enough that lube is not necessary."

"I know having all of those things done to you, makes you drier than the Sahara," Dilynn reminded the woman.

Sylvia's eyebrows cinched in the middle. After a moment of recalibration, Sylvia launched another attack.

"Dilynn, I know you're hurting. I know you're angry with me for promising you to make it so Sadie didn't have to leave." She rested her hands on Dilynn's knees. "I truly thought it would be simple, but I told you I would make it so she comes home. And you know, when I say I am going to do something, I am going to do it."

Dilynn's gaze dropped to the picture of herself with the girls. Sadie had been smiling. Really smiling that day at the field after she'd hit her first homerun.

"We didn't lose, my darling. This is just a road bump. Just a little pothole, but I'm taking care of it. I always take care of my princess, you know that."

"Sylvia, I want more," Dilynn whispered.

"Name it. It's yours. Whatever it is. I can afford it."

"You can't buy me. I'm not for sale."

"Of course you're not for sale. You're not a prostitute. I will buy anything for you though. You want a prostitute, I will get you one. You want a house on the beach. Done. An island. Yours."

"No, Sylvia."

"Dilynn."

"I know you hear me."

"I hear you just fine."

"Then the answer is no."

"I didn't ask a question."

Dilynn stared at the master manipulator. She'd been a pawn in so many of Sylvia's games, it was stupid for her to pretend for weeks that this was something more than another game.

"You knew I would say no."

It took a moment for Sylvia to get up from the ground. Even with personal trainers, playing professional basketball had done a number on her knees already.

"I knew there would be push back," she said, pressing the wrinkles from her linen pants. "After last time, I knew it was the wrong time. I knew I had to let the whole nasty situation play itself out."

Dilynn's head fell to the side. "You knew? You knew he was cheating on me."

"Dilynn, I make it my mission to know everything about everyone that I care about. I know everything, Princess."

Dilynn searched Sylvia's face that had turned completely serious.

"Everything you ever tried to hide from me," Sylvia confirmed with just a phrase that Dilynn had never had secrets from the woman.

"And I know there is something else you want. And I will give that to you. I would have given that to you years ago, just like I gave you Evie."

Her shoulders seem to lift, like this secret had been weighing her down.

"I was just waiting for you to ask because I wasn't sure you were ready. But when I moved all of your stuff, I saw. I saw the boxes with the gifts. But you didn't ask. And then you had that bastard move in and you were pretending to be happy and in love. And you put on that dingy, disgraceful diamond, and.... It doesn't matter because it wouldn't last. But I knew you wouldn't listen to me. The whole not-talking-poorly-about-people is your greatest and most frustrating quality."

Dilynn popped up from the couch. She shoved Sylvia away from her. "I could have gotten an STD."

Sylvia shook her head. "It was only the girl. The one that doesn't like me."

"Lyra." Dilynn said. "Her name is Lyra."

"Yes, that one." Sylvia's gaze rose to Dilynn. "Why doesn't she like me?"

"Oh, I don't know." Dilynn held her hand in the air, so the rock was at Sylvia's eye level. "Probably because you put a ring on my finger without asking me."

"She's the adult, right?" Sylvia asked. "The one that just turned 18?"

Dilynn's hand fell. "Yes."

Sylvia nodded to herself. She pulled her phone from her pocket and began typing. "She needs a car. I will get her a car. She'll like me then."

"She'll hate you more," Dilynn said, stepping around the couch to put some distance between them.

With a scoff, Sylia asked, "Who hates someone that buys them a car?"

"She's not me, Sylvia." Dilynn gestured to herself. "I let you buy me a car because I wanted to be tied to your bed. But Lyra. She doesn't want that, and if you buy her a car, she will think that is what you expect from her. She isn't going to take your present without thinking bad things. Shit, I should have known taking your present meant indenturing myself to you, but that was different because I wanted that. I wanted you to own me."

"You're still mine, Dilynn," Sylvia said. She waved in Dilynn's direction. "That's why you didn't get your tattoo removed. You want to be mine."

"No, I didn't get it removed because I wanted to remember not to do stupid shit like that in the future." Dilynn shook her head slowly. "Do not buy Lyra a car. It will hurt her, and I am working so hard to make her believe she isn't her past."

"Why are poor people so complicated?"

"Why are rich people so fucking dense?"

"You say that like you're not rich," Sylvia stated. "I mean, you are just baby rich, but still rich."

"When people say eat the rich, they are not talking about me."

Sylvia's eyebrow cocked in Dilynn's direction. "You always seemed to enjoy eating the rich. At one point, you told me that if I stayed you would eat me all day."

Dilynn folded her arms over her chest. "And you left."

The ice maker dropped a tray of cubes into the bin, pulling both their gazes away from the stare down. The house was too quiet with the girls out at Casey's party.

"I shouldn't have left, but you... what you wanted. I couldn't give it to you then." Sylvia stood up straight. "I am stronger now. Braver, and I told my father. I told my father that I am not going to share his closet."

It was Dilynn's turn to be surprised. She'd known Sylvia's dad was gay. Sylvia's dad knew Sylvia was gay. Had even sanctioned the townhouse where Dilynn had unknowingly opened the door to an ambush. The non-disclosure agreement was slapped into her hand, as the man appraised his daughter's choice of sugar baby.

"How did that go?"

Sylvia shrugged, and the smile was weak. "He told me there are seven closets in Scottsdale, and I should choose one of my own."

"I'm sorry that he said that to you," she whispered. "If it makes you feel any better, he told me to always answer the door in lingerie for you so you wouldn't go find some other concubine to fuck."

"Don't apologize for him." Sylvia's fists shook at her side. "He's the reason I didn't do this sooner."

"You didn't do this sooner because you didn't want to marry me." Dilynn looked down at her chest. "You don't want to marry me now. You just... you just want to get married."

She looked up. "Why? Why do you need to get married? And don't tell me it's because Kayla needs a new mommy."

Sylvia dropped back onto the coffee table. "I need to think about the future. I need someone I can trust by my side, and love... love just isn't in the cards for me."

"You fell for someone." Dilynn studied the way Sylvia's whole body collapsed inward. "Like, you actually love someone."

"No. I had a crush. First crush since you, and she committed to some bitch. She got married to some stupid cunt that... that treats her like crap. And she's... she's just like you. Too loyal to accept that her bitch of a wife is cheating on her constantly and is just... she fucks teenagers. But I can't tell her that because she wouldn't believe me."

Dilynn looked around the house. She wouldn't have bought this house. It had always been too big for her and Evie, and now it was too small for everyone.

"So, you came back to me."

Sylvia ran her hands over her face. "It's not like that. She's married now... it was just a reminder of what happens when I am too scared to do something. And I realized, I feared being with you, actually being with you because you are amazing."

"I can't believe you didn't tell me. You didn't even tell me when you came that time he left," Dilynn whispered.

"You were very intoxicated," Sylvia reminded her.

Dilynn's head shot up. "Why did you come? You never came over when I was drunk, but that night you came over."

"Dilynn, when have I not come when you called me?"

"Uh... like ninety percent of the time we weren't together, but were together," Dilynn hissed.

"Dilynn, it's really hard to just leave Oxford because you missed me." Sylvia licked her lips. "Look, I came when it mattered. When you called about that cunt trying to take what was mine in my own damn house, I was here in eight hours. I got on my jet, and I was here."

Dilynn remembered making the call to Sylvia. Simone had taken her home because she was drunk. She had never let anyone into their townhouse before, but she had drunk too much. Was stumbling around the room, and Simone had seen all the pictures of Sylvia and her together.

"Was she wrong?" Dilynn asked.

Sylvia looked up at her. "Wrong about what?"

"Simone," Dilynn said. "She told me you didn't give a shit about me. She said you had your eyes on someone else. Someone else that you spent practically every night with all that summer when you were in town. You would go out with your team, and she said you were always there. But it wasn't like with me. She said you just hung out with this girl. She saw pictures of you and her together. Simone's girlfriend. They just got married. That was the girl. The one that got married. She's a barback at the Escape."

Dilynn sucked in a breath, as she put the pieces together. Brandon wasn't the only person who'd cheated on her.

"Simone... she kissed me because she wanted to get back at you. And she... she threatened my job because you were flirting with her girlfriend. But you weren't just flirting. You wanted that girl, and I was just..." Dilynn's eyes cinched shut. "I really was just your fuck toy. You wanted that kid, and I was who you settled to come back and fuck when she turned you down."

"It wasn't like that. Echo was just sweet. And she was a fan. I took pictures with her because she asked. She took pictures with everyone."

"But you love her." Dilynn's hands shot out from her chest. "Don't fucking lie to me. I can see it on your face. She's the girl, and Simone was pissed, and she tried to fuck me, and I was just... I was just a fuck toy. She knew it, and she tried to fuck me because why the fuck would I say no. It's not like you gave a shit about me."

"You were mine," Sylvia snapped. "She should have never touched you because you were mine. I didn't touch her girlfriend."

"I was Alex's," Dilynn growled. "And you put a ring on my finger."

"The one that hates me said you two broke up," Sylvia stated.

Dilynn's eyebrows scrunched together. "Lyra said we broke up?"

Sylvia's head moved around like a bobble head. "Technically, she said you had a fight and that she told Alex that you left a window open for them."

"A window?"

"Yeah, you know." Sylvia waved in Dilynn's direction. "Savior Dilynn, always giving people second chances. Apparently, for everyone but me."

Dilynn looked at the rock on her finger, then at Sylvia.

"So, you put a ring on my finger so Alex would stay away."

"No, I put a ring on your finger because you are going to marry me and I am going to bring your kid home," Sylvia said, rising to her full height.

Dilynn sucked her teeth as she looked at the ring again. Shaking her head slowly, she pulled it from her finger, and tossed it to Sylvia.

"You're going to bring my kid home even if I don't marry you," she stated with the ring now back in Sylvia's possession. "Just like you are going to help me build my school even though I am not marrying you."

After another dramatic eyeroll, Sylvia asked, "Why would I do that?"

Dilynn smiled like she would at her students when she knew they would comply with her requests. "Because you said you would. And when Sylvia Winters says she is going to do something, she does it."

She could hear Sylvia breathing in deeply. The rose tinge to her cheeks only spread to the rest of her face, and Dilynn knew. Knew she had called Sylvia's bluff.

"I'm not marrying you," Dilynn said again. "Now, go get my daughter and bring her home."

Sylvia pushed the ring in her pocket. She was clearly mimicking Dilynn's demand under her breath, but she looked up at Dilynn when she was done. "Only because she's my favourite."

Dilynn bit her lip, and a soft chortle fell from her lips. "She really is awesome."

Sylvia picked up the picture and set it upright on the coffee table. "Maybe I'll adopt her. Then, you'll be tied to me forever."

"I'm always going to be tied you." Dilynn gestured to the house. "You already made sure of that. She'll be a Greyson, not a Winters."

Sylvia returned to her purse. She ran her hands over the straps before pulling it up her shoulder. "I'm going to go."

She paused, looking out the front window. "Maybe open the front window, so the action figure sees it."

Dilynn took her turn to roll her eyes. "Fuck off, Winters."

Sylvia licked her lips. She looked over her shoulder at Dilynn, "We could... for old time's sake. I mean, you being all feisty has me—"

"You know where the door is," Dilynn said.

"Probably don't tell them I own half the house," Sylvia said when she reached the threshold.

"Alex isn't coming back," Dilynn whispered. "We... we did break up."

"They will be back," Sylvia stated with such a certainty that Dilynn looked at her once more.

"How do you know?"

"Because they have been sitting in the car outside for the last twenty minutes."

Dilynn moved to the front window. She parted the blinds, only to find the Audi SUV sitting across the street. "Why didn't you tell me?"

"I didn't think you were going to break up with me."

Dilynn moved back to the entry way. "We were never together."

Sylvia's finger grazed the handle of the door. She gave Dilynn that devious look over her shoulder once more. "They are very handsome."

"No."

Sylvia turned back to the door, and the smile was still in her voice as she said, "We'll see."

30

The sun disappearing from behind the large trees pulled Alex from the car. It had been high in the sky when Sylvia cast them an icy glare upon her arrival. Their stomach sank, taking with it the hope Dilynn would break off the engagement to someone she had loved for them. She knew Sylvia. Trusted Sylvia.

Alex wished they would have been mid-knock when Sylvia, with her flawless complexion and straight blonde hair, threw open the door. Even if they had broken her nose, Sylvia's sharp angled jaw and symmetrical lips would be more than attractive. The meticulously tailored outfit only added to the litany of reasons Dilynn would choose her over them.

"I don't like you," Sylvia said once Alex's fist dropped to their side.

Alex stood in the middle of the welcome mat like a statue. Slowly, they said, "The feeling is mutual."

"Go away, Sylvia," Dilynn said, pushing Alex to the side so Sylvia could leave.

The stare down continued until Dilynn slipped sideways through the door. They thought she was going to walk right past them. That was, until she shoved them back against the wall to create a path for the woman. The stucco prodded them through their shirt, but Dilynn's back pressed against them.

"I'll be back," Sylvia told Alex, then her gaze dropped to Dilynn, "I love you, Princess."

"I'm not a fucking princess," Dilynn snapped at her.

Sylvia's thumb grazed over the snowflake. "You'll always be my snow princess."

Dilynn's body leaned back against Alex because there was nowhere else to go with Sylvia touching her again.

"You really want to lose that finger," Dilynn hissed through her teeth.

Alex's fingers dug into Dilynn's hip bone.

"I am going to need my fingers to get your kid back," Sylvia said with a smile. "But we can talk about your need to bite something at another time."

Dilynn held her hand at Sylvia's eye level to signal her to stop talking. Then she pointed to the street. More words were spoken between the two blondes, but Alex was focused on the silent cue immediately. The short, thin finger was unhindered by the weight of Sylvia's over-the-top engagement ring.

She'd taken it off. Taken it off and given them the invitational shove, while at the same time avoided touching the other woman in their presence. They knew it had to be intentional. A declaration to everyone present, so they took advantage of her body against them to lay claim to her while Sylvia continued to transmit a silent warning to them with just her eyes.

"I need my brother's phone number," they said. "I came... I came because you weren't at school, and I need his number."

Dilynn didn't smell soft and sweet like normal. Sadness seeped from her pores, but Sylvia's jasmine and ginger perfume lingered on the porch even after her heels clicked against the concrete and the driver's side door shut to the latest sports car she was driving. They tried to scrape away the flavor of wealth from their tongue with their teeth while Dilynn's hair tickled their nose.

"My phone is inside," Dilynn said.

She stepped out of their grasp. Their fingers balled up into a fist. They didn't have a right to touch her after causing her so much pain. Might never have the right to call her theirs again.

Dilynn's socked feet almost floated as she moved like a ghost through the space that once felt so alive and warm. They followed her to where the battle between porch light and the dark house was at a standstill.

The magic of pizza night with fairytale music was gone from within the home. Dilynn hadn't bothered to turn on any lights even though the sun had vanished from view of the window, so the furniture sat in solemn shadows with only the glow of the fake fireplace flickering. These were shades of the black soul Alex carried with them everywhere they went, and they worried they'd darkened Dilynn's world by ever walking through the doors.

With Dilynn's world shrinking into a black hole, they began to turn on the lights. If they had brought darkness, they would chase it away. The kitchen was first. Then the ceiling fan's light resuscitated the living room. They illuminated the hallway bulb they had replaced when they had a job in the house.

Dilynn returned with her phone. She'd barely opened the screen when the quiet was broken by an eerie, high-pitched tune, signaling the potential arrival of Michael Meyers. She held up the phone so Alex could see Ryder's name.

"A fitting ringtone," they mused.

"Do you want to answer it?"

This wasn't part of their plan, but they took the phone. They were supposed to get drunk first. Get angry like Mom, enough to not give a damn anymore.

They connected the call and breathed out, "Ryder."

Alex checked the call was in fact connected when Ryder said nothing. They had barely gotten it back to their ear, when they heard, "*Alex?*"

"Yeah, it's me."

"*I thought I called Dilynn.*"

Alex's eyes rose to Dilynn's questioning gaze.

"You did."

"*Is she... is she with you?*"

"No. I stole her phone," they said. When Ryder didn't respond, they said, "Of course I'm with Dilynn, gillapollas. She was... going to give me your number, so... so I could call you and tell you that I hate you. That you're the same selfish asshole from when we were kids."

Dilynn rubbed her face. Her nose scrunched up as she said, "Probably should have saved that last bit for after he helped you."

Ryder was laughing though. Laughing at them hating him.

Their molars ached from grinding them. They tried to come up with something else to say but his laughter fizzled first. "*I'll let you punch me after we deal with the situation. Can you put me on speaker?*"

"You think you are going to *let* me punch you," they said before handing the phone back to Dilynn. "He says put him on speaker."

She took her phone back and held her finger up. "You have the same phone," she said as she dramatically pushed the speaker button down.

Her gaze dropped the device resting atop her palm. "What do you want, traitor?"

"*Do neither of you know how to say hello?*" Ryder asked.

Alex cracked the knuckles on their left hand. They hit harder with their right, but Ryder wasn't getting punched once. He was going to sport a broken nose every day for at least nine months. One month for every year they spent on the run because of his big mouth.

"Hello is a greeting; it's meant to be polite," Alex rattled off from some unknown source of random definitions. "Neither of us owe you a polite greeting, so no, we do not know how to say hello."

Dilynn rolled her eyes, then poked Alex hard in the chest. "That would have given your lying ass away."

Alex's eyes rose from their hand still trying to rub away the stabbing pulse from the jab. Poking should be on the same level as shoving, but this wasn't the time because Dilynn's eyes were shut, and her fingers pinched the bridge of her nose.

"What dictionary.com means is, what do you want?"

"*Is Sadie there?*"

"She left with the geriatric general this morning," Dilynn said shaking her head slowly. "They were supposed to come after school, but the homophobe showed up with him at 7am and took her."

"Don't give him a promotion," Alex said. "Generals are the highest-ranking officers."

"I don't care if he is the fucking president," Dilynn hissed. She turned back to the phone. "I want my fucking kid back, asshole. So, unless you are calling me to tell me you are going to help Sadie come home, leave me the fuck alone."

"*I can't bring her home,*" Ryder said the timbre of his voice no longer light. "*Sadie ran away.*"

Dilynn's eyes darted around the room faster than she moved. Carrying the phone with her, Alex followed her to the threshold of Evie and Sadie's bedroom. Their names hadn't been on the door last time. It brought a smile to their face to see Sadie claim a space. The smile dropped when the slamming of dresser drawers began.

Alex expected to see half of the dresser empty and tons of empty hangers. Everything was full like the girl had never left.

"When did she leave?" Dilynn asked.

She flipped the bedding from one bed to the other. Dilynn tossed a room more effectively than any guard in any prison movie they'd ever seen.

"*Colonel said she went to her room this morning when they got back. He wanted to give her some space, but she didn't come out after being called for dinner so he went to look for her and the screen for her window was cut open and she was gone.*"

Dilynn's hand dug between the mattress and the box spring. She pulled out a wad of cash, then a photocopy of Sadie's birth certificate folded into a tiny square that was rubber banded with her high school ID and a picture of Sadie and her mother. When Dilynn handed them the photo, they understood why Sadie was confused when she saw them. It was like staring at the feminine version of themself.

Dilynn kept digging until she pulled out a pack of individually sealed pills. She studied them for a minute, then tossed them at Alex. "That explains why she never gains any weight."

The woman dropped to her knees. With one arm, she scooped everything out from under the bed. Moldy dishes and an entire trash bag worth of food still in wrappers came out in the first swoop. Their gaze shifted back and forth between the pills and the unopened food packages.

"I shoulda gave her a bin to store under her bed so she would have a security stash when she was hungry," Dilynn said. She rubbed her hands down her face.

Alex waved the packet at Dilynn since words weren't working.

"They're laxatives," she said, moving on from one room to the next. "Some foster kids... they binge eat until they are going to puke. That is just the next level to make sure she doesn't gain weight."

Dilynn used the same arm scoop under Lyra's bed with a similar result. Where Sadie had hid granola bars, Pop-tarts, and chip bags, Lyra hoarded ramen packets and half eaten jars of peanut butter.

"I swear, I just told them to get all the fucking spoons from their rooms and they swore they didn't have any," Dilynn growled. Alex counted seven spoons and three forks that came out from under Lyra's bed. "I literally just ordered new silverware on Amazon because all the utensils fucking vanished."

Dilynn pushed the clothes in Lyra's closet from one side to the other, but Sadie wasn't hiding in the closet. She stepped back and closed her eyes.

"She probably left right away," Dilynn said to both Alex and the phone.

"Do you think she will try to make her way back there?"

"She's coming back," Dilynn said with a confidence that made Alex's heartbeat harder. "She must have stuffed her bag with just enough stuff for her to carry when she bolted."

"Why would you tell him that?" Alex whispered with their hand over the end of the phone. "He's going to come here now and look for her."

Dilynn didn't seem to care that Alex was asking questions. Not like she ever answered questions unless it was with another question to prove she was smarter than they are.

"I need to find my keys," Dilynn stated when she was already walking out the door.

Alex looked at the mess that was Lyra's room. They started to kick the stuff back under the bed so the older girl wouldn't feel like her space was violated, but Dilynn yelled at them from the living room. "Don't return my silverware to Narnia."

The forks stared back at them from the ground.

"That punk can clean that shit up just like Sadie can clean up her mess when she gets back."

They studied the mess again, and decided Dilynn was their mother and what she said went. It was the least they could give her.

"I can't believe I didn't fucking see it. Of course, they had a plan. Those fucking shits."

Dilynn was walking through the house picking up everything resting on a surface they could be hidden under while the keys sat in plain sight on the kitchen table.

"Found your keys," they said, letting them dangle from their finger. When Dilynn made a grab for them, Alex dropped them in their pocket. "I'll drive."

"You are stupid if you think I have any issue sticking my hand in your pocket to get my damn key, Alex Trikru." Dilynn said.

She reached out to shove her hand in their pocket, but they caught it by the wrist.

"You are not driving," they said. "And if you stick your hand in my pants, it will not be to dig in my pocket."

"*I don't need to hear this,*" Ryder groaned from the phone scrunched in Dilynn's other hand.

"What makes you think I would ever get into that car with you again?" Dilynn asked as she tugged to get her hand back. "You played me in that car."

"Played you like a guitar," Alex reminded her. They ran their finger down her cheek. "Had you singing my name over and over again."

"*Should I hang up?*"

"You love my car," Alex reminded her. They pulled her hand up to their mouth. Looked at it briefly before forcing her jabbing finger up. They bit the tip of it just hard enough to leave light teeth impressions. "And poking is just as invitational as shoving."

There was loud gagging coming from the phone still clenched in Dilynn's hand. "*Guys, we need to find Sadie.*"

"You know where she is. I'll take you. Bring her home with you like I promised. Stay with you like you asked. I can do better," Alex said putting Dilynn's finger back against their lower lip.

They were preparing to tease her once more, when their jaw was yanked down with the sheer strength Dilynn possessed in her single finger. She dragged them down to her level, practically prying their jaw from their face.

She dropped the phone still connected to Ryder's call in their pocket and retrieved her key fob.

"Oh look, I hooked a catfish," Dilynn said dryly. She popped her finger from Alex's mouth, then wiped it on their shirt. "She's at Casey's."

Alex worked their jaw back into place as they followed Dilynn like a puppy. They almost stepped on Dilynn's freakishly small feet when she stopped and turned suddenly. While they managed not to stomp on the cute little dinosaurs covering her toes, they did not have the ability to stop their body from collapsing into her.

"Didn't realized you were still hooked," Dilynn whispered, smooshed between their body and the front door.

"You took the ring off," Alex said, grazing Dilynn's finger.

"I told her it wasn't going to happen."

They raised Dilynn's chin. "I almost broke her hand for touching you."

"She wants you," Dilynn said with her eyes on their lips. "Whatever voice you said you heard in your head, it's wrong. And I'm not the only one that sees how handsome you are. There will be others. If you show them who you are. The real you. That person that brings flowers that mean something. You could probably even get Sylvia Winters to propose to you."

Alex's pocket was talking, but none of that mattered as Dilynn's hands rested on their hips.

"No one else will ever matter to me," Alex said. "Just you."

"Last time I got in your car, I forgot what's most important," she said raising her gaze. "So, get out of my way before I do something I have never done before."

They held their breath as their heartbeat pulsed with no real rhythm. "What is that?"

Dilynn shoved her hand into their pocket as they stood with their hands out. She pulled her phone out.

"Shut the door and every fucking window in my house."

They stepped back. Gave her the space she deserved, because she wasn't shutting them out. She was promising them a window if they played this new game by her rules. They just needed to learn the rules that she never seemed to share.

"Get your father and bring him here," Dilynn spoke into the bottom of the phone. Her eyes didn't move from theirs. "We are going to get Sadie and bring her home. You have until we get back to make him understand that she will not be leaving."

Dilynn didn't wait for Ryder to respond. She ended the call and waved her key in the air. "Let's go. You are not running away this time."

From the outside, Casey's house looked like all the rest on the street. There was no sign a party was taking place within. It was a far cry from the abandoned house parties of their youth.

"Have you ever met Casey's parents?" Alex asked as they got out of the car.

"Her father is an educational consultant. He travels about 60% of the year, and since Casey is 17, her mom travels with him now. Super conservative and the most miserable humans I have ever met." She sucked her teeth. "I want to build a school that will take kids like Casey away from parents like hers and like yours."

Alex swallowed the knowing. They'd never heard of anything like that, but they would do what they could to help. Anything she wanted to make that one thing a reality.

Dilynn didn't bother with the doorbell. She walked into the house, drawing a rainbow of irises towards them. With a hand over her eyes, Dilynn declared, "We don't see anything, and we were never here."

The teens within view barely paused, before they returned to the cups in their hands. Alex held their breath as they walked through the smoke rings from a hookah being shared in Casey's living room.

Alex scanned the space but did not find a single Greyson girl. They caught up to Dilynn making her way to the back of the house and was surprised to find another living room.

They were more surprised to find Lyra being straddled by a girl they vaguely remember from a pizza night. Alex hadn't realized Lyra was gay, but her hands holding on to the girl's ass in her lap was a clear sign she was not straight.

Lyra's mouth was working its way down the girl's throat, when Dilynn stepped alongside her.

"18 means she is jailbait, and you are too pretty for prison," Dilynn told Lyra.

The dark eyes shot open as she shoved the startled girl from her lap. Lyra popped up from the couch.

"Where's Sadie?" Dilynn asked, nodding her head at the younger girl to go away.

Lyra's brow furrowed, but she glanced at the stairs.

"Get Evie," Dilynn said without waiting for a verbal answer to the first question.

Lyra's eyes moved back to the stairs once more.

With a shake of her head, Dilynn said, "You are still going to get her. I do not want to see her and Landon—"

"I don't want to see that either," Lyra whined. "I mean, that... that could scar me for life. Plus..." Lyra swayed slightly. She looked up at Alex when they caught her. "I don't think stairs and me are a good idea."

Dilynn's eyes rose to the stairs. "Is Sadie with Casey?"

Lyra's chin dipped, then she nodded her head. "She waited for Evie to go upstairs with Landon, then said she couldn't come home yet so she needed to make it so Casey would let her stay."

With a sharp intake, Lyra cast a guilty look towards Dilynn. "I'm sorry. I just... I knew what she meant but I couldn't... I told her it wasn't the way but she... she really does like Casey. Said Casey is the only person that never lets her down."

Dilynn licked her lips.

"Stagger your ass to the car. And don't you dare run away because I swear if I have to chase your ass tonight, I'm going to hit you with it before I let you get in and we are not going to the hospital. I will staple whatever is bleeding back together myself." Dilynn turned Lyra towards the door. "We are all going home together and tomorrow we will be having the lesbian safe sex talk, so yay!"

Lyra cast a glance at Alex, before she pushed past them. For someone so thin, her shoulder felt like a blunt sword when it struck them in her walk past them.

Alex wanted to go with Lyra and avoid whatever was happening upstairs.

Dilynn didn't give them the option to leave though. The tie hanging from their neck became a leash, and Dilynn dragged them behind her as she climbed the stairs.

She stopped at the first bedroom and knocked on the door.

"Taken," Landon called out.

"Well, you're being evicted," Dilynn called through the door. "Tell my daughter to get her ass in the car before I come in there and make a scene."

There was a lot of thumping on the other side of the door, but it opened quickly.

Alex breathed easier when Evie's clothes were, at last, all on. The eyes of every color narrowed at Alex.

"What the hell are you doing here, troll?" Evie hissed.

"Car, now," Dilynn said. "And leave the middle seat open for Sadie so she can't jump out while we drive."

Evie took her swipe at Alex as she pushed past them. Their shoulder was going to be bruised by the time the girls were done getting their shots in.

Landon hung out in the doorway of what was clearly the master bedroom. He ran his hand over his head as Dilynn crossed her arms over her chest.

"Show me," Dilynn said. "Give me peace of mind that you are at least using protection because I don't care that she is on the pill. You know that is not always 100% fool proof."

The boy's eyes grew wide. He waved in the space between them. "It's not what you think," he said slowly. "We weren't.... we don't... not yet. We just sleep when she gets tired of the party. She... she didn't want to leave because she said Sadie couldn't go back yet. And she... she wants to wait and, you know... You know, I would never try to... not until she's ready. Like really, really ready. So, I don't... I don't carry that... stuff. Because even if she says... you know, that she wants to... I just want to give her time to think about it and then I will... you know, get some, so she has... you know, time. Make sure."

Dilynn pressed her hand to his chest so he would stop talking. She patted him a few times and smiled at him.

"I didn't know that," she said softly. "And thank you. Thank you for being a good man, Landon."

Alex didn't echo the sentiment, but they felt a sense of pride fill their chest. As Dilynn moved on to the next door, they met Landon's gaze. With words not being their thing, they extended their hand to the boy on the verge of manhood.

Landon took it and they shook. A silent understanding was shared between them, before he followed Evie's trail of vanilla perfume. They appreciated knowing they weren't the only human on a Greyson leash.

Dilynn made it through all the doors and stopped at the last down the hall.

They didn't follow her. Couldn't bring themselves to face what Dilynn walked in on, but their heart tried to drown alongside their stomach when Sadie came out of the bedroom still trying to get her shirt on. Her gait matched Lyra's, as she leaned against the wall to hold herself up.

She locked eyes with them before her gaze fell to the ground. Her arms wrapped around herself as her frame began to shake. Tears were already falling down her cheeks, and the hickey on her neck that hadn't been there before filled them with a different type of rage. Not the kind they had when Sylvia's finger pressed against the mark she'd left on Dilynn. It was an anger fueled by a love they never thought they would possess. And anger that was matched by the woman shouting down the hall.

"I don't give a damn what she said, Casey!" Dilynn was yelling. "You brought her up here and she is still drunk!"

Alex took a step forward, but stopped to keep themselves from murdering a child. A child that was falling through the cracks in a world she was ill prepared to enter.

"Who the fuck do you think you are talking to?!" Dilynn shouted. "I'm not one of your little friends. And since you won't listen to Evie, you're going to hear it from me! She is fourteen! She is a fucking child, and you have no fucking right to take advantage of her! Stay the fuck away from my kid, Casey!"

Dilynn stomped out of the room, and her arm pulled Sadie against her side. "We're going home, and you will not be seeing Casey anymore."

Casey chased after them in a stage of undress that had Alex's blood boiling. The fact that Casey was still a kid was the only thing that stopped them from attacking her.

"Momma G," Casey called out. "I'm sorry. I just... I was just... she threw herself at me."

Alex didn't wait for Dilynn to escort Sadie past them before they stomped down the hallway. The tent in Casey's sweatpants let them know exactly what the girl planned on doing to Sadie.

"I was her kid, too," the girl said, but her hands were up when she met their eyes.

With an arm against Casey's chest, Alex pressed the kid against the wall, and closed the minimal space between them. Spit speckled Casey's face as they growled, "You like taking advantage of little girls."

They let up on Casey only enough to push her back against the wall once more.

"You touch her again, and I'll make sure you never touch anyone with that hand. I don't care if I go to jail for the rest of my life, I will make you watch as I take it off."

Tears streamed down Casey's face. "I'm sorry. I'm sorry."

Alex moved so their face was less than an inch from Casey's. "You will not touch her again. Do you understand me?"

Casey's head bobbed up and down.

"Say it!" Alex barked.

"I understand," Casey cried. "I won't touch her."

"And you will stay away from her."

Casey's head bobbed again but she didn't have to be told to answer. "I will stay away from her."

"Alex." Dilynn's voice was like a tug on that leash she had on them. It pulled them back, causing their cast to give Casey space to move.

The teen slid down the wall, tucking her body into a ball. She looked up at them, face red and wet.

"I'm just a kid, too," she whispered to no one, but they heard it. Her hands clenched into fists. Her hand hit the side of her head. "Stupid fucking freak."

Alex stepped back, looking down at the girl. They couldn't be the one to pick her up when they were the monster that sent her to the ground.

"Let's go," Dilynn said in nothing less than a command.

They trailed Dilynn down the stairs. Their head hung as they felt a wave of shame wash over them for what they did to the kid left upstairs. They had been that kid, scared of an adult.

Alex swallowed the rock in their throat. They were about to face the person that taught them how to hold someone against the wall. And running away wasn't an option this time round. There would be an actual conversation. A promise of continued contact for the safety of the girl tucked in the center seat of the Prius.

"You have to stay," Dilynn said coldly from her side of the car. "I don't care if you have to glue your fucking feet to the floor. You have to stay."

31

The house felt different when Dilynn shifted into park in the driveway. Once, it felt so large and overwhelming. Sylvia was right about her hating it. Now with a car stuffed with drunk and cranky teens, it seemed small. Too small because her world had grown so much.

"Everyone inside," Dilynn instructed, not sure how her plan would work with Sadie and Lyra trashed. She walked behind the entire group like a cowgirl trying to wrangle in a nervous and sick herd. No one moved like they wanted to be there, and she found herself weaving behind them.

She'd at least expected Evie to be huffy, but the rage radiating from the girl was bound to be more than Dilynn bargained for on a night she needed her daughter to show they were in it together.

Dilynn met Alex at the passenger's side door. She blocked the path to their SUV, and she locked her arm in theirs, forcing them forward. The soles of their boots had solidified into concrete blocks on the drive back to the house. Cognitively, they were just running through the motions as they barely lifted their foot for each step while Evie was trying to run behind Lyra, who singlehandedly stopped the procession.

Lyra held herself up against the railing of the porch to empty her guts in the flowerbed. The youngest of the herd followed suit with just the sound of the eldest puking. Evie stopped short to avoid being hit with any splatter, but took the first window available to bolt past the other two girls.

"Hold on, E," Dilynn called out before the girl could disappear into the house and lock Sadie out of their bedroom.

"I am not carrying either of their drunk asses inside," Evie said with her arms crossed. Her face pinched as Sadie puked again. "She needs to sleep on the couch, or they can sleep together because I shouldn't have to stay up all night as Sadie pukes her guts out. In fact, I was here first. I shouldn't even have to share a room."

"Sadie can have my room," Lyra said, dropping herself to the steps. "I'll just—"

"Yeah, you would just leave," Evie growled. "That was your plan, anyways. If Sadie couldn't come home, you and her were just going to leave."

Dilynn's eyes went back and forth between Lyra and Sadie. Their faces told her Evie wasn't lying. It was a plan. Not the first plan, but a backup that would always be there.

"No one is leaving," Alex said. "No one is running away."

"Really, troll?" Evie snapped. She threw her head back as she cackled like the witch she so badly wanted to be. But it cut off dramatically and she focused all her hatred on Alex. "Lyra told me all about you and your game. Mom told her not to, but I was trying to stupidly fight for you over Sylvia. I know, shocker! But I didn't believe her. I didn't think you would do something like that to her when you fucking promised me to treat her right. So, I went into her email and read all the comments you sent her. Found the one about pronouns. But my favorite was the one that you sent the day after Christmas. You know, when she got her heart broken and you were there."

Dilynn let out a heavy breath and gave up on the idea of making it into the house just yet. She tightened her grip on Alex's arm, who was trying to turn away.

"Guys, we can't do this now." Dilynn glanced down the private drive. Searched for headlights, but found none. "Alex's father and brother are on their way here. And we are going to have a family conversation about what happens now."

"What family?" Evie spat. Her hand shot out to Alex. "Are you just calling everyone family now? Is that the model I should follow? I mean with that logic, Sadie and I should just both go and fuck Casey. Sound good, Sads? You can learn first-hand exactly how to do it so she will be hooked. I mean, she treats us both like sex toys anyways, or do we not care about Casey anymore?"

Evie tapped her finger to her lip, "Oh, maybe I should call Brandon. He loves some teenage twat, right Lyra?"

When Lyra didn't acknowledge her, Evie stabbed the air with a single digit. "This asshole is no better than the last douche bag. And don't even get me started on Sylvia."

Dilynn felt a wave of exhaustion rush over her. Her head fell back because the thoughts were too heavy to hold up anymore.

"No." Evie folded her arms over her chest. "I say no. No more. There's no more room at the Greyson house. There's not enough room for the people who already live here."

"Evie," Dilynn sighed. "We don't turn people away when they need—"

"Mom, seriously. You have to stop. You can't save everyone. This isn't one of your books or stories where everyone is just going to be family because they need a place to go."

"Evie."

"Stop saying my name," the girl snapped. "It's not going to change that I'm pissed off at you. Or that I hate sharing my room. Or that I'm tired of being here with all of them. Or that Trikru and their fucked up family has me feeling like Dorthy in the tornado."

"Me, too," Sadie whispered. "I'm tired and pissed, too."

Evie's hands pulled at the roots of her hair as she screamed at the porch covering. Her head dropped as her finger raised to Sadie.

"You don't get to be me. Stop trying to be me. God, you are just like that fucking catfish." Evie sucked her teeth and shook her head. "Does it, like, run in the blood? Like, you just find someone else's life and just put it on and wear it for a while to get what you want? I mean, if you're going to play me then do it right. I didn't try to starve myself and then take a pill. I cut myself open."

Sadie's gaze studied Evie carefully, and Dilynn studied Sadie, trying to make sense of what Evie meant.

"She would let you stay even though you are not me," Evie declared. Her finger shifted to Alex. "She's going to let a cyberbully stay. So just stop pretending to be me. Just... fuck, put on Lyra's personality for a while. Mom seems to like that one. And Trikru, you should do some digging into Sylvia because Mom fucking loves her."

Evie tugged at the top of her shirt like it was trying to choke her, then screamed again. "I'm sorry. Fuck! I'm just mad. I'm sorry, and I get it. I get why you went after my ex and why you follow me around. I get what it's like trying to get out, but FUCK! I don't even have a room to escape to."

"I told you, she can have my room," Lyra said again.

"And where you going to go?" Evie hissed. "This your passive aggressive way of saying you're leaving next?"

Lyra raised her middle finger to Evie and didn't answer the question. The silence itself was an affirmative answer.

"Well, it probably doesn't matter who sleeps where." Evie's eyes rose to Dilynn. "Not since Sylvia is back and you are getting married. Or is that not happening now because we are having family conversations with the Trikru Terrorists?" Evie didn't wait for Dilynn to tell her Sylvia was gone. "No, Sylvia's not gone. She's never gone. She's just avoiding the drama. Avoiding us. Probably plotting on sending me and Sadie to, like, boarding schools like she sent her sister to. She doesn't like me though so I'm gettin' crated to Russia while Sadie is headed to some place cool like France, and Lyra... you don't even get to go because you can't even pretend to be nice to Sylvia. She's going to kick your ass out as soon as Mom is too fucked to think straight. Not that you were ever straight."

"Fuck the rich!" Lyra said. Then pointed at Evie. "And fuck you, too!"

"The phrase is eat the rich," Evie said, "But I bet Mom has that covered for us. You're just, what, a sugar baby that fucks trolls on the side?"

"Evie," Dilynn swallowed the rest of her sentence.

This wasn't what she signed up for. Not what she thought parenthood would be like. None of it had been, and Dilynn felt the cold air seeping into her bones. The doubts that had always swirled in her head were the loudest and they beat against her skull trying to escape.

Dilynn wasn't sure anymore if she was holding Alex there or if Alex was holding her up, but she was tired. Too tired of fighting with and for every single person she loved to just stay together.

Maybe her Mom had been right. She wasn't meant to be a mom yet.

Her fingers worked at the frayed hem of her shirt. She loved the shirt, and it was falling apart like the fake family that she couldn't sew together properly.

"Look, I'm just gonna..." Lyra started but the rest of her sentence dissolved in the alcohol being retched into the yard once more.

"Then, I'll go with you," Sadie said. "We can go, and Evie can have her life back. Go before they get here."

And there was the truth. Everyone was always ready to leave.

"Yeah, just run away when shit gets hard," Evie said as she gripped the porch banister. "Never wanted sisters, anyways."

Dilynn needed to do something. Needed to say anything to make them stay. To be the good mom everyone told her she was. Be the person that made things okay. The Mary Sue that would put the pieces back together.

"No one is leaving," is what she came up with, and it came out as weak as she felt.

Gravel crunched and Ryder's brakes squeaked. The girls ready to leave were trying to gather their wits, but the adults now outnumbered the kids.

Dilynn heard the driver's side door close.

"Oh look, Uncle Creeper has arrived with Grandpa Trauma. Did you bring some cool present that I should open while I sit on your lap?" Evie called from her position on higher ground.

Ryder's steps stopped, and Dilynn cast him a defeated glance. When she turned back to Evie, the girl's cold stare cut through Dilynn as she waved to her bare mid drift.

"Should I go put on some more clothes and pretend that they don't creep me out like you had me do with Brandon?" She raised her arm in the air and took a deep inhale. "Shit, I remembered to shower and put on deodorant today."

Dilynn turned slowly to find a very wide-eyed Ryder. He raised a hand in the air and started to speak, but he was cut off when the even stepped-man came around the front of the car.

"Sadie," the old man said upon his approach. "I'm so glad we found you."

Sadie's head tucked into Dilynn's shoulder. Dilynn could feel the girl holding on to her sweatshirt, and the pleas coming so quietly from the girl's quivering lips were like a nightmare repeating. "Don't let him take me back there. I'll leave after like I said I would but please, please don't make me go back there."

"I was so worried about you," the old man said too close for the child shaking against her.

"We both were," Ryder added. "You had us very worried, kiddo."

"Guys, I think—" Dilynn began.

"I'm gay," Sadie said into Dilynn shirt.

"Sadie," Alex said, shaking their head desperately. They reached out but stopped before they touched her.

"No," Sadie said, wiping the tears from her face and pulling out of Dilynn's embrace. She looked over at her grandfather. "I can't stay with you because I'm gay. And I'm not just saying that. I don't like boys. I have never liked boys. I have sex with girls and I'm not going to pretend to be straight like Alex did."

Colonel Trikru froze. He looked from Sadie to Alex.

"I..." he breathed out.

"Alex told me not to tell you." Sadie held on to herself. "Said if I told you that you would send me away like you sent them to that... to that place. My girlfriend was sent to one. She said it was terrible, said they do horrible things to you, and I'm not going."

"Sadie, I..."

Sadie glanced back at Evie and dropped her chin down. "You won't want me, now. Just like you didn't want Alex, so you can... you can just walk away. Walk away like you did on my mom. Did you know my mom ended up in foster care just like me. She met my daddy when they were in high school. He was a foster kid too, and they had me because they wanted a family, but he killed her."

She nodded to Ryder. "Did he tell you? My daddy killed my mom and then himself. And I was there but told myself that it was just a bad dream. That my mom was just scared, and she gave me away, so I... I did things so that I could get a new mom. Thought I could pretend to be Evie and that Ms. Greyson would want me, too."

Going from being Mom to Ms. Greyson in heartbeat made Dilynn feel like she was flatlining.

"But... it was all a lie. And all of this... I just wanted to have a family so badly that just loves me. Loves me and lets me be... me."

"Sadie," he whispered again, stepping towards her.

Sadie held her hand out and stepped back.

"I'll run away. If you make me go with you, I will run away." She took a deep breath. "I have been running away from foster homes since I was seven. Group homes were harder, but I figured it out, and they put bars on the windows."

"There's always a way out," Lyra said. "And the things that you have to do... the choices you have to make—"

"No more running," Alex whispered to the ground. They raised their chin and said it louder for everyone. "No more running."

Dilynn wanted to echo the call that dissolved into the cold air. She wanted to scream it so that it sunk into the girls' thick skulls.

"Two girls..." Alex cleared their throat. "They were killed trying to run away. They say... they said they drown trying to cross the river. The river was the only way out. The fence was electric and they... they chose to try and cross a river at night. I don't think they drown. Not on accident."

They pressed their cast to their head and tapped it against their skull. "I don't think... I don't think it was an accident because they went after them with rifles. But... I couldn't run away."

They looked at their father, while Dilynn thought of the kid four miles away left on the floor.

"Did you know?"

The older man's face had lost most of its color.

"Did you know that if I tried to leave, they would come after me with a gun?"

He blinked a few times, then shook his head.

"You never even asked," they said. "Not when I came back. You never asked what... what they did to me."

Dilynn watched the old man closely. Measured the way he leaned away from each question. Tried to find where the lines of understanding were less black and white.

He licked his lips, before he said, "You didn't say—"

"What was I supposed to say?" Alex's chest shook with a pained laugh. "I woke up every night trying to scream, but nothing would come out. I would just scream and scream, but there was no sound because I was drowning. Like it was me that tried to cross the river and I didn't make it."

Alex started to step towards him, but they barely made it a step with Dilynn's grip on their arm still in place. They looked down at her, and she could see the war being fought.

Green eyes rose over Dilynn's head, forcing her to turn back to their father.

"I thought about it when I ran across the highway. That I was just crossing the black river. That I wasn't going to make it, and I was okay with that. I understood why those girls would be willing to do it. And I ran. I ran because you might as well have been carrying a gun."

They wiped their face as Dilynn tried to catch her breath. All the anger she had still simmering about how they'd hurt her seemed to be cooling. Everything she'd been through was so basic.

Alex gestured to the girls lingering in their own space. "I don't think the girls should—"

"I couldn't run away, so I used to cut myself," Evie said, stepping down the porch steps. She pulled the band of her jeans down, revealing the starburst scar on her hip bone for the men in the grass. "After my stepfather started molesting me, I tried to run once but that ended me up at a party with my best friend's hand down my pants. And I realized that was just the reality. That this was what my life was, so I stopped showering. I thought if I was gross enough, he would leave me alone. It didn't work and the kids at school made fun of me, so I started cutting because I was so... angry. When I wasn't cutting, I was drinking. Pills. I told myself when my friend was fucking me that it was different. And when no one was trying to have sex with me, I beat the shit out of my classmates."

Evie cast a glance at Lyra. She took a deep breath and gathered more pain to share. Words were her weapons, and Dilynn realized her fists hurt less.

"I hated everything, and the truth was... I was trying to get kicked out of school. Then he would have to send me away, or they would take me away. But even when they showed up... it didn't happen."

Lyra looked up at the old man. Her head lolled to the side, and she rolled her eyes. With her hand raised in the air, she continued to paint the yard with another layer of pain.

"My mom sold me into prostitution when I was ten to cover a drug debt. I got away in the parking lot. There were tons of people there, but no one tried to help me, so I just ran."

Dilynn's fingers dug into Alex's arm.

"Couldn't go back. So... I just set out on my own. Went to school for the free food and no one asked questions." She looked at Alex, then at Dilynn. "Hey Sads, you left your group home two months ago? Any one at school ask any questions?"

Lyra stared at the old man with a half-drunk smile that grew when Sadie said, "No. No one noticed I had the same clothes on for a week."

Lyra nodded aggressively. "It's really not hard. The whole running thing. Summers though, and holidays. I started shoplifting because there's no breakfast or lunch during summer vacation."

She looked up at Evie. "That's how I know Landon. His mom caught me the summer before my freshman year. She hooked me up. Got me a backpack and notebooks and the clicky pencils all you popular girls liked. And I won't lie, all that shit gave me some of that toxic hope. Like, maybe I could make it on my own.

"I learned quick to avoid the new teachers. They were still trying to save the world and thought they were, like, doing shit. I guess it was lucky for all of us that you started the year after I did." Her gaze wandered to Dilynn. "It's because of you that I stopped being able to stay at school. You, like, never left campus that year. Always there late with that bitchy blonde teacher. Had her for a hot minute. She avoided me though. Sat me at the back of the room as far away from her as possible. But you... you were so happy, and I thought... you know, I'm going to get out of here and do you. I'm gonna get myself a college degree and I'm gonna teach and just smile."

Dilynn watched Lyra force another smile on her face. Everything she knew shook as more pieces into the puzzle of them fell into place.

"But well, that didn't happen. But, hey, I got a GED, and you know a couple blow jobs later, I had a job. Then I met a jackass and he said he could help me. Didn't have to give that piendejo nothing. I mean, I wasn't raped like most girls. I told myself, you know, I slept with him because I said so, so it wasn't what was happening. Not to me. I wasn't a prostitute, and I wasn't a whore. I was just the girl he slept with on the side, and of course it was you."

Lyra's smile dropped, and she leaned forward once more. She studied the sky before looking at Dilynn. "I lied when I said I wasn't a thief, but you know, this whole family thing, it never really was for me. Nobody ever even noticed. I made it to eighteen and I'm out. So, you know, I'm gonna be okay now."

"Colonel," Ryder said, resting his hand on the older man's shoulder. "They are telling you these things to—"

"To warn me," Colonel finished. "To tell me what happens when kids run away, like I don't know. Like I wasn't sixteen when I enlisted. I know that life is hard, and I have seen things that no one should see, which is why I need to give Sadie a better life. Be a better man so she doesn't think that all men are—"

"Rapists," Evie said.

"Liars," Lyra added.

Dilynn chewed on the inside of her lip. She knew the studies. Knew that the girls needed good men in their life.

She pressed her hand to her chest. "I had a great dad. He was my rock, I was lucky."

She wasn't sure where she was going with this. She needed to circle around to just having men in Sadie's life, but that they didn't need to be her dad.

"You weren't a great dad," Alex said. They took advantage of Dilynn's surprise to pull out of her reach. "You weren't even a dad. You were the colonel, and we were your soldiers. And Mom... she was drunk. Always drunk so she could deal with your anger."

They took a step closer to the man, and their boots knocked a stone from the sidewalk to the grass. They watched it roll, and said, "We learned to listen to how you walked so we knew if we had to hide because you were terrible. Abusive, even. Today, they would lock you up for what you did to us."

"Stop, Alex. I—"

"No. You don't get to shut me up." Alex's hand slapped against their chest. "I am not going to be silenced anymore. I'm not going to pretend not to exist anymore because it will make your life easier. Because... Because I ran away to make your life easier. I knew you would send me back, just like I knew if Sadie ever told you she was even somewhat like me you would send her away, so I told her to stay quiet. But she doesn't have to be ashamed of who she is."

They stepped within striking distance. Dilynn wasn't sure who she should be afraid of throwing the first punch, so she placed a hand on their arm to hold them back.

"You sent me away to be fixed. That's what you said when I was begging you not to make me get into that van. You said that it was just camp. Just camp to help me fix my broken relationship with God. But I wasn't." Alex's arm was shaking and their fists clenched. "I wasn't broken until you sent me there."

Dilynn's chin fell to her chest. She had heard Casey tell her a similar story and hearing it from Alex made her realize she needed to call Sylvia. Needed to stop stalling when so many kids were being hurt.

"You had them break me into a thousand pieces, and then they used super glue to put back the parts that they wanted me to have. They poisoned me and left all the shards they didn't want me to have still there so that everything would always hurt."

Alex sucked in a deep breath. "And those pieces... they tore their way through me until I couldn't breathe. I couldn't breathe and I knew... I knew, you would never protect me. I knew... I knew, you would never love me. Never love me. Never protect me."

The old man was barely breathing as Alex stood tall enough to be at his eye level.

"But you come here. You show up and act like you... you are this super dad. But you shoulda never been a father. Not to Sadie's mom, who you left. Then, you left Ryder and me while you climbed up the ranks and brought home wars instead of hugs. You have never hugged me. Never in my life."

They slowly raised their hand in a salute. "But I know how to salute. I learned to do that for when you came home from war. I was three and knew when the other dads were running to hug their kids that I needed to salute you, Colonel. You never hugged me or Ryder, but you knew I needed to be a soldier."

Their hand dropped to their side. "You weren't a father but you took Sadie from Dilynn for what? A new punching bag for the flashbacks?"

"I just wanted..." he swallowed.

"Answer me," Alex cried out. "I deserve answers. I deserve to know why you hated me so much that you let them electrocute me. Why you sent me away to be raped and locked in a closet."

Tears fell from their chin. Each drop plunked against the concrete, and Dilynn realized Ryder's face must match Alex's.

"Why you never came to see that I was okay."

They pulled away from Dilynn.

"Why you never called. Never wrote."

Stepped within the old man's reach.

"Why I was so unlovable."

Their whole body was shaking.

"Answer me!"

Dilynn held her breath, as she waited for the man to cease chewing on his words.

"I... I don't have answers to your questions," he said like a man speaking to a platoon. "I have asked them. The questions. I have asked them over and over again. I asked them so many times. And your mother, she said we did what we were supposed to."

He shook his head. "I should have known. I should have never..."

He stepped back but ran into his son. The man who'd brought all this pain to Dilynn's home not once but twice. Brought him into their lives for some reason none of them would probably ever understand. Maybe trying to fix things himself.

"I was confused because I didn't know how to be what you need. The gay thing... we weren't supposed to talk about it. I couldn't ask anyone, and felt I failed. That I did something wrong, and I did. What I put you through was wrong." He reached out but stopped just before touching Alex. "I will never be able to take it back, and I will never be worthy of your forgiveness."

"I will never forgive you," they spat. Slowly shaking their head, Alex looked up. "But I don't want to carry this hatred anymore. I can't carry it because I need... I need to move on. I want to know love, but that means I have to be me. I have to stop being afraid to be me."

"I... I love you," Colonel said. He turned to Ryder. "I love both of you, and I don't want to be the cause of any more of your pain."

"Then let Sadie stay with Dilynn," Alex said. "Spare her from your pain. Let her stay with Dilynn. They are a family. A real family. They are my family."

"No," Evie said loud enough to temporarily silence the crickets. Dilynn's neck practically snapped in the direction of her daughter. "We are not your family. Or their family. This is the Greyson house, not the Trikru house."

"Evie," Dilynn breathed out trying her best not to yell.

"No, Mom. No." Evie said. "Trikru can't declare themself part of this family. They didn't even make it into the house like you told them they had to. And Lyra hasn't unpacked her shit because she doesn't want to be a part of this family. She just called you Mom to make you feel better when they broke your heart. And Sadie. Sadie is hooking up with Casey because she is desperate for someone to love her because she knows this isn't a fucking family, that she knew she couldn't even come home. And I... I read the fucking story that Trikru read. I read that you are just waiting for me to leave after graduation, and I realized that is why you just keep throwing yourself at these losers. But I'm not going anywhere."

Dilynn opened her mouth, but she felt like a witch had stolen her voice. Like maybe Evie had worked out her spells and finally found her way into Hogwarts. Maybe Sylvia could send her there and complete the self-fulfilled prophecy Dilynn had been preparing herself for.

"Don't! Don't defend what that troll did to you. And stop pretending that whatever happened with Wyatt didn't fucking hurt so much. And where is Sylvia?" Evie threw her hands in the air. "Another person that said she wasn't going anywhere, just like that fucker said they weren't going anywhere, and yet she's fucking gone. And you do this. You do this with those losers over and over again. You just let people back in and it doesn't matter how bad it hurts you. And you're going to let these people into our lives, and we don't know them and they already hurt us so much. We don't know them!"

Evie tossed a thumb towards the old man standing like a stone.

"And this guy basically said who all of us are sucks in court. Said we were unstable and not a family because all he has seen is this bullshit. All they have done is turned our world upside down, and it was finally good." Evie wiped her hands over her face.

"Evie," Dilynn whispered, not even sure it came out.

"No is a complete sentence, Mom." Evie took Dilynn by the hand and gestured to the other two girls now standing like they were ready to disappear again. "And I say no. Everyone just needs to chill the fuck out. And they..." She moved her finger around the Trikru bunch. "They all need therapy. They need therapy and we are tired, and they are drunk because of all the emotional trauma the Trikru Trolls have caused us. Like, it's too much. It's too much."

She pulled Dilynn towards the house. Made enough space that she dropped the leash. "Let Trikru fight their own battles because it's not your job. It's not your job to fight battles for them when we need you. All of us need you. Just you."

Dilynn swallowed and turned to the man still standing in the yard.

He looked from Alex to Sadie, then nodded towards the house. "You girls should go to bed. It's late."

Evie rolled her eyes. "It's barely eight, Grandpa Geezer."

"E, seriously," Dilynn hissed.

"I am pretty old," Colonel said to the ground. "We get up early—"

"Is this going to take long?" Evie whined. "Like, I just said a lot of words and I wasn't kidding about being really tired because no one has slept in this house in like a month, thanks to you. And I just want to go inside."

"No, Ms. Evie." He looked at the girl with a softness that Dilynn couldn't quite understand. "I shouldn't have... my son told me the whole way here that Sadie belongs here. But as a grandpa, I wanted her with me. I wanted to be a grandpa because I'm good at that. Ryder told me I'm good at that."

"Great, then buy her a pony for her birthday," Evie said. "Can we go now?"

Colonel shifted his feet, and Evie sighed loudly.

"Dilynn," he said cautiously. "I was worried about what would happen when Alex left. I was scared that you would cut me out because I made Alex run away. And I came to force you into a predicament that would require you to surrender Alex's contact info."

He ran his hand over the back of his buzzed head. "I didn't want to lose Alex again, and I ended up just proving to be exactly who they thought I was."

He looked at Alex. "If I hadn't come to the game, would you and Dilynn still be together?"

Alex's gaze dropped, and they mirrored their father's motion.

"No," Dilynn said before Alex could answer. "We wouldn't be."

She cast her eyes to the sky, then to Alex. "E's right. I can't keep... keep throwing myself at you and expecting you to step up and be the person I need. She's right. If I hadn't gotten you out of the car, you wouldn't even still be here. You'd have bolted and left me to deal with them again."

She stepped away. "I need to stop. You all need to talk and Evie's right, today has been too much. It's just too much. This is too much."

Dilynn turned to the colonel. "I know you have a court order, but she stays here. She stays where she doesn't feel like she has to run away. You did this to back me into a corner, but no more. You and Alex... that's not mine or Sadie's problem. So, she stays here where everyone knows she is safe. She stays with me and with Evie, and with Lyra if she wants to be here. But you all, you all need to go."

Dilynn ushered the girls up the steps and into the house. She turned when she heard Alex's broken timbre sung with the cricket's violins.

"I... lied to her. I couldn't believe anyone... that I could be wanted, and I lied to her. I lied because I wanted her to love me so badly that—"

Dilynn shut the door on Alex's sob story. She needed to hold on to her anger with them, so she didn't let them back in again. She needed to move forward. She needed to show the girls that this wasn't what love looks like.

Love was not enough when the person she loved would always walk out the door. And right now, she needed to nail the doors and window shut to keep the kids from following their lead.

Turning to said children now watching her, Dilynn let out a heavy sigh. "Why didn't any of you tell me?"

"Because you can't know things," Lyra said with a heavy head. "There are things that are better that you just don't know. It makes it easier that way to be you. Because this... this darkness that we all have... you don't want it. You think you can hold it for us, but it's too much. It's too heavy."

Dilynn's mind ran through their stories and felt the bricks being added to her backpack. Felt the weight of their pain in her gaze on them. And knew it wasn't what they needed. They didn't need to carry it all either.

She was their mother. She couldn't let them lug it through their lives alone. Vowed to never let them be alone.

She dug through the drawer until she found the chalk board marker. She tossed it to Lyra and pointed to the board.

"No secrets," she said. "Add it to the house rules."

Lyra dragged her feet against the wood floors and scratched the new rule on board. After stabbing the marker into the board to punctuate the new rule, she turned and threw the marker back at Dilynn.

"Well, birthdays are going to suck," She said, and Dilynn caught her grumbled, "not like they haven't always sucked."

Dilynn silently conceded there would be secrets, just like there was still hitting, biting, and yelling. After a few measured breaths, she chose to silently celebrate that the girls at least worked together. Like they worked together to steal all her silverware.

"Now to the family business. First, you all will go get all my silverware from under your beds. Then, we are going to have a chat over some pizza about what we need in a new house. A bigger house where everyone has their own room."

She pointed to the hallway, "But first, go to Narnia and get my silverware."

The groans from the girls were like music to Dilynn's ears. Along with the cries of betrayal for their rooms being destroyed. They returned with an entire sink worth of moldy dishes as she ordered them each a pizza.

"Done?" Dilynn asked. "Or should I go do another arm swoop under everyone's bed?"

"We got it all," Evie said. "Can we, like, not do house talk tonight? Like, everyone is pissed at me right now, so, like, can I just go to bed?"

Dilynn pointed at Evie. "You two mad at her?"

The two girls shared a look, then looked back at the ground.

"Okaayyy" Dilynn sucked in a breath. "Change of plans. We need mattresses, blankets, and pillows all in the living room."

A small smile rose up Evie's face. "Hunger Games?"

Dilynn nodded, "The Hunger Games from this point forward will no longer be an annual event, it shall be a monthly event. No boyfriends. No girlfriends."

"No they-friends," Evie added with a grin.

"We should call it the Greyson Games," Sadie whispered.

"You don't even know what they are talking about. And we're not Greysons," Lyra said, causing Sadie's chin to fall. "Right, Evie? This isn't a family."

"That's not what I meant," Evie said. "I just wanted... You know what? Fuck it. You're not a Greyson. And Sadie isn't one either. But it doesn't have to be that way. You could unpack your shit, but you're not going to because you hate me. But you know, you could hate me and still unpack your shit because I love you and I hate you, which I think is what it's supposed to be like having a sister. So, just unpack your shit and commit to the goddamn Greyson Games."

"That is a terrible name," Lyra said. "And... I don't even know what it means."

Dilynn reached into her pocket and threw her keys to Evie, who was apparently the only kid that didn't drink in the house. "Evie, let's go with Gilmore Girls. You two go get the supplies while Sadie and I move the beds."

"But like, what is it?" Sadie asked.

"Oh, you'll see, Saddie Bear," Evie announced. She shoved Lyra towards the door. "Let's go Liar Bear."

"Okay, Egotistical Bear," Lyra said, but stopped in the doorway. "Uh... hey, Mama Bear?"

Dilynn swallowed the hope before she turned to find Lyra chewing on her lower lip. Those dark eyes raised in that bullshit innocent gaze. "Can we... uh... can we get some money? For the supplies?"

32

The door to the house was as shut as it had been two weeks ago when Dilynn walked inside. Alex tapped on the steering wheel to the beat in their head. It was just their heart moving too fast like it had every time she walked past them in the hallways.

Whether Dilynn was purposely trying to make them miss her, they didn't know. She was out of her room though. At lunch, she walked through the cafeteria. Between passing periods, she was in the hallways instead of hiding in her cave. And on Monday, she walked through the halls in tailored slacks, with a blouse that said she was their new boss. It was the first time Dilynn presented herself as a businesswoman, and they loved the smell of confidence she left in the hallway as she walked past.

There was no engagement on Dilynn's part with Alex, which was why they sat in the car on Wednesday night when all the people she was expecting had already arrived. Alex knew she preferred notice over surprises. They even tried to give it to her, but she'd been pulled into a civil back and forth with Simone over who was going to be the Assistant Principal next year. One that had kids hollering out Team Greyson vs. Team Wyatt.

They were Team Greyson, but couldn't yell that when Dilynn wasn't talking to them. She would talk to them if they went inside though.

The very closed door hadn't opened in a while, so everyone expected was already inside. Alex needed to get out of the car. Needed to just go in and sit down.

'Everyone's invited so that means I am not a stalker.'

Looking at the flowers in the passenger's seat, Alex second guessed their selection. They'd chosen a flower to apologize; now they thought it would have been better to go with a new beginning bud. Briefly considering a quick run to the store, they shook the idea away.

Already late, Alex left the flowers on the seat rather than taking them in. They would be an ineffective shield, and in their mind, now felt more like a weapon they'd once yielded. Eventually they would change that, because Dilynn smiled at the previous flowers.

The door to the car was heavier than Alex remembered it ever being. Harder to push. So difficult that when Alex squinted to tolerate the low sun, they felt a sense of freedom. Liberated from the confines of the vehicle still standing on the opposite side of the street from Greyson's house.

Deep breaths in and out helped Alex find a center. They focused on the door, because last time they walked across her yard, it was because she was dragging them with her. They don't tear their eyes from the door, because running away wasn't an option.

"I'm going to go in," they told themselves aloud to stop from hearing the voice in their head. "I'm going in."

With each step, they feel a little more confident. A little proud for not turning away. They made it halfway across the gravel road, and there was nothing stopping them.

"I'm going in."

The confidence boost of getting out of the car and halfway across the street was enough to keep them still standing when Evie burst through the front door with Landon chasing at her heels. While each step Alex took felt like minutes, the kid's took less than three seconds before she was within striking distance.

"What the fuck are you doing here?"

Sucking in as much air possible, Alex attempted to steel their expression. It was weak, but not as feeble as the attempt to not let their voice crack. "I'm here... I'm here to show her she matters to me."

Their gaze dropped to their shoes. Sneakers were the wrong choice for someone trying not to run away.

"You don't get to come here. You don't get to hurt her again," Evie spat as she moved closer. "I was nice the last time you were here because I get facing your nightmares is hard. But they aren't here. And you shouldn't be either. Just let her move on."

Alex prepared for the fight. The fist she'd try to use, since her eyes are the same shade of angry as not too long ago when she looked at the man that broke her mother's heart. Landon's hand enclosed around her arm to keep her in place, and the strike didn't come. Alex wished it had. Wished for the fist against flesh to avenge Dilynn.

Evie can't offer them atonement. Only Alex could achieve that now that they realized they were the villain of Dilynn's story. They'd managed to become Morgan and, as she foretold, brought all her nightmares into reality.

"Open doors are for everyone. Even Alex." The words are soft but stern. A mother's tone setting the rules came from behind the young couple.

Alex couldn't see Dilynn through Landon, but they could feel her. Subtle quakes in her words created waves of pain and confusion that crashed against Alex. They took a breath. It wasn't like Alex hadn't seen her since they finally punched Ryder in the face with their left hand and told Colonel to go to hell. This time, she couldn't just give them a co-worker's smile; she would have to talk to them.

Except she didn't talk to Alex.

They're left to watch her be the mother. Her focus only on Evie, her eyes never glancing their way, even though they came for her. Came as themself.

"Open door means everyone. You know that."

The breath Alex held released. To Dilynn, they were just another loser ex, which really never was a thing. Just a first date, a one-night stand, and a heartbreak.

"Mom." Dilynn shook her head and Evie's shoulders slumped. "Trolls don't stay the night."

Old habits do not die, and Alex found their feet retreating, and the words, "I should go," fall out of their mouth once more.

They turned back toward the Audi, feeling stupid for thinking they still had a chance. There was no one to blame this time. She didn't reject them. They rejected themself and let her suffer the consequences of their own self-hate.

All those years, Alex pretended to stand up for being themself. They stood for nothing though, because they never stood for themself. Every moment they chose to run from rejection flashed in their mind.

"The door is open if you change your mind."

The words barely broke through Alex's own heart beating out a call to retreat. They concentrated on her voice to block out each of the times Alex told themself to leave because they weren't normal enough.

Alex studied the grey shades of gravel under their feet. The ground protested with their shifting weight. The problem was, no matter which way Alex moved it grumbled, and they just wished it would be quiet in one direction to show them the right path to take.

Gravel didn't really grumble though, and to imagine their life as a fantasy with non-sentient communicating things was a waste of time. Dilynn didn't even write that kind of stuff in the original novel. Time passed that they could use to fix things, but Alex wasn't fixing things because they were still standing in the middle of a fucking road instead of doing what they came to do.

Alex looked at the house. The light inside now brighter than outside, let them see Pizza Night going on as though they didn't exist. That Alex could walk away, and nothing would change.

Nothing would change if Alex got in their car and left.

Nothing could change.

Landon took a step towards them with a hand extended.

Everything changes.

Everything could change.

Everything would change if Alex walked into the home.

Moments were all it took to follow the boy who was still holding the door open for them. Landon didn't seem fazed by their fear and offered them the same smile he always had for them. It was unlikely he didn't know, but they wanted to be like him when they grew up.

The dough thudded against the counter. No one appeared even fazed that Evie and Dilynn had run out, or at least they were all doing a good job of acting normal. Dilynn dropped the dough on the counter and wiped her hands on her apron.

They didn't have time to even process Dilynn coming towards them until her arms encased Alex's middle. Her perfume was sweeter than they remembered, and they found themselves pressing their nose to the top of her head.

It was all too normal. Almost the same as the first time they walked through the door, but they felt warm for the first time in weeks.

Sadie followed suit, closing the distance. She squeezed them tightly, then stepped back. Her hand rubbed the back of her head, and she said, "I really love my new softball bag. I thought you forgot my birthday was coming up, but Mom said you left it in her classroom."

"I can't wait to see you hit a homerun," Alex told her. "First game is next week, right?"

Sadie nodded. "Yeah. I'm glad you're going to come."

"I wouldn't miss it," Alex promised. It would be a hard promise to keep when they knew Ryder would be there and probably Colonel, but they had to. They had to show up.

Sadie left them in the entry way. Returned to her spot at the table beside the girl that wouldn't look at them. Casey's sandy blonde hair fell around her face, but Sadie pushed it back behind her ear. Whatever sanctions had been made for the older girl would not replace the apology they owed the kid fighting off demons.

Alex stalled in the middle of the room. Glancing between the table with the kids, the living room with the adults, and the kitchen where Dilynn stood alone, they debated where they belonged. They didn't come for coworkers they didn't talk to on campus, and the kids were engaged in a debate over whether fruit loops had individual flavors that Alex didn't want to weigh in on.

They started to make their way to their post beside Dilynn, but paused when Jordan called out, "Hey Dilynn, did HR call and tell you that you're going to be our boss next year?"

Alex studied the top of Dilynn's face. She sucked in her lower lip. When she released it, she chewed on it until she gathered the courage to tell everyone what Alex already knew.

"Uh... yeah... I got the call today."

The room went quiet as all ears tuned into the conversation.

"Wyatt got the job." Dilynn slowly spread the marinara over the pizza dough. "They wanted someone with more teaching experience. Said that I've done a lot of great things, and that in a few years I will have more experience."

"That's bullshit," Casey practically shouted. "There's no way that Wyatt should ever be—"

"Casey," Sadie said quietly. She shook her head. "Now isn't the time."

"So, what does that mean?" Evie asked. She laced her fingers with Landon's and held on like he was her lifeline.

"You're leaving," Alex answered for her.

Dilynn's eyes rose from the pizza to them. She didn't say anything, which brought the room to a roar of outrage. Battles were plotted, and pleas were made from the kids. No one was happy about Dilynn's decision to leave, but no one had a reason for her to stay other than the kids.

"Are we moving?" Evie asked, bringing the room to an eerie quiet once more.

Dilynn tucked her hair behind her ear. She nodded towards the street. "I.. uh... put an offer in on the house across the street. It needs a lot of work, but I am not going to be working next year while I... I'm going to chase a dream I've had for a while. It's time because I can't stay and work for her. So, I am going to open a school. I... um... I spoke with Sylvia this afternoon because we made this agreement many years ago that when I was ready, she would invest in a school for kids that the system is failing."

"What kind of kids are we talking about?" Marcus Thompson asked. He swiped a handkerchief over his head.

"Kids in the system. Juvenile Detention." Dilynn cast a glance towards Evie. "I'm... uh... going to build residential facilities on campus and we are going to offer it as alternative placement to group homes and juvenile detention. Set up more of an independent living situation so that I can help kids without bringing them home. Next year will be focused on building, making connections, and getting ready to open the following year. So, yeah. I am going to open a school. And it's going to be a good thing. Good for me. Good for the kids that need something different."

"Count me in," Marcus said, getting to his feet. "I want to help. If you want, I mean. I haven't signed my contract for next year."

"Are you going to start small? Like, just with freshmen?" Jordan asked. "I am certified for Bio and Chem, so I can handle the science department if you want. I mean, I'll stay at Cactus next year, but I'll come work for you, D. You know, I got your back."

Dilynn's face flushed slightly. "I would really like that. It's going to be a small school, but we are going to open to all grade levels. Most kids come in deficient in credits anyways, and I plan on still teaching the English courses to start with so that we can get off the ground."

"You'll need a social studies teacher," Alex said quietly. They tapped their chest. "I... can take the tests. Get certified for all the subjects, if you wanted."

Dilynn studied their face carefully.

"Yeah. I would like that." She tossed pepperonis onto the pizza. She cocked her head slightly to the side as she looked back at them. "I mean, I already put in a lot of work training you."

Alex's head dipped before they said something back. Something inappropriate. Didn't stop them from thinking about the type of work Dilynn would train them to do as they washed their hands to help. They didn't have a real job, but they didn't want Dilynn to have to manage them or wait on everyone.

They grabbed one of Dilynn's aprons and put it on, then flipped the light on to the oven. The pizza within was gradually shifting, and they decided this was a job they could handle. They'd watched last time like they used to watch Dilynn make her coffee.

"What are you doing?" Dilynn asked when she turned with a pan in her hand.

"Cooking pizzas." Alex took the pan and placed it in the oven. "It's twelve minutes, right?"

"Uh... yeah." Dilynn's eyes studied them closely. "What if I don't need help cooking pizzas?"

Alex stood up and looked Dilynn directly in the eyes. "You are the most capable human I have ever met. You don't need anyone to do anything, even reach the top shelf of your kitchen. But sometimes it might be nice if you didn't have to do it all, like now." Alex nodded to Dilynn's prep area. "You do the magic, and I'll just try not to get burned."

"This wasn't in a story."

Alex tugged on the back of their neck. Then they realized their mistake and returned to the sink and washed their hands again. As they scrubbed between their fingers with the soap, they said, "I know. This is... me."

They looked up hoping to find something else to say. They were met with a murder scene on the ceiling.

"Uh...." Alex pointed at the ceiling.

"Don't ask," Dilynn said before turning back to her dough.

"Why are you helping?" she asked barely over a whisper.

Alex decided not to point out the hypocrisy of her always refusing to answer a question, but never failing to follow with a question.

Offering Dilynn a light shrug, they dried their hands on a dish towel. Turning back to her, Alex gestured to the room. "It always bothered me, you waiting on me. The whole master-slave thing, not really my thing."

They watched the flush rise up Dilynn's face, and they awarded themselves a point in her game with no rules.

"Anyways, I can't just sit here while you wait on everyone, and this... this is a job that I can do with minimal babysitting."

Dilynn's eyes narrowed. "I feel like you are going to burn my pizzas."

There was the potential of burning the pizzas, especially if they got distracted by the way Dilynn's V-neck hung a little lower than usual. They blinked twice and pulled their eyes to the unamused crystal orbs staring back at them.

"Uhm," they listed things Dilynn loved in their head. Kitchen supplies. Dish towels with puppies on them. Books. Writing. Writing was a fitting punishment for messing up. "If I burn a pizza, I have to deliver a stand up poem next week."

With a hand on her hip, Dilynn's head fell to the side. "You write poetry?"

Alex clenched their teeth together and smiled. Then they said, "I do not. Which means it will be very, very bad. Or I could surprise you."

"I don't like surprises," she said. She punched the carefully crafted circle of dough.

Alex pointed at the oven.

"Then I better pay attention to the pizzas."

Six unburned pizzas later, the house emptied of adults and half the kids. Dilynn's kids were engrossed in a game of Monopoly as Alex scrubbed the stove down. There had been little time to talk, but the quiet gave them a chance to ask about the ceiling because they answered her questions, so they deemed it fair to get at least one answer to one question.

"What happened up there?" Alex asked pointing to the blood-like splatter covering the ceiling.

Dilynn bit her lip, and she looked away from them. "Uh... I bought myself one of those fancy pressure cookers for my birthday and... I uh.... I tried to make my own marinara for pizza night. But it—"

"Hold on," Alex said. "I missed your birthday."

Dilynn dropped the left-over pizza into Tupperware containers. "Technically, you showed up just in time."

Alex's head popped up and scanned the room. Nothing suggested this was Dilynn's birthday party. No one had said anything, and there definitely wasn't cake. And they actually liked cake. They would have remembered cake.

"You didn't tell anyone," they whispered. They glanced at the kids in their own world. "Not even Evie?"

The kid's head shot up at the sound of her name. "Not even Evie, what?"

"Don't," Dilynn hissed with her back to the kids.

"Your mom didn't tell you that... uh... she's uh... thinking about getting a new tattoo."

Dilynn's arms crossed over her chest. "I hate you."

Alex's smile spread. "Yeah, something cool like a sword."

Evie rolled her eyes, while the table came to life with conversations of future ink the kids wished to get.

"Why?" Alex asked Dilynn, knowing they were pushing their luck on the questions. "Look, I don't tell anyone because there literally is no one there, but the girls...one day they are going to grow up and think, Mom doesn't have a birthday. So, what do they do when they have kids? Do they give up their birthday because that is what Mom did?"

Dilynn chucked a towel at them, "Save the parenting advice. You don't even want kids."

Alex shook their head. With a hand on their heart, they said, "I didn't think about having kids. There's a difference."

They reached out to touch her but paused. The forcefield around her kept them away.

"Look, it just makes it easier. You know, like no disappointment when no one remembers," Dilynn whispered. She glanced over at the kids.

"We should have celebrated," Alex said. They gestured to themself. "I could have cooked the pizzas."

"You did."

"But—"

"Alex." Dilynn waited for them to close their mouth. "Please, don't. Just don't make a big deal about this. It's self-preservation. After Christmas, I just... I didn't want to do it again."

Their eyes narrowed at her. "What happened at Christmas?"

"It doesn't matter?"

Alex licked their lips. "Evie."

"Alex."

"Troll?" Evie called. "Why are we all saying names again?"

Alex stared at Dilynn as they took control of the game. "What happened at Christmas?"

The girl looked up and blinked a few times at them. She looked between Dilynn and Alex before she shared, "I assume you mean what happened on actual Christmas and not the day after."

"Yes," Alex said, now staring at the back of Dilynn's head.

"Let's see. Brandon forgot about Christmas and gave Mom a pack of men's socks for her toddler feet. Then he was a dick and made fun of dinner. And so, I picked a fight with him. And no one really talked after that."

The kids were ranting about how much they all hated Brandon, while Alex attempted to compartmentalize their feelings about this entire thing.

"I got myself a MacBook Pro," Dilynn said, turning back to Alex. "You don't have to feel sorry for me. It's done. He's gone. But I took care of myself because I learned after the first year that was how it was going to be. So, I got myself a computer and last weekend I bought the pressure cooker. And both are trash now, so the reality is I shouldn't have gotten myself anything and I just shouldn't tell anyone anything."

Alex chewed on the inside of their cheek. They glanced at the desk and noticed the sticker covered computer in pieces. They knew Dilynn was klutzy, but she had always cradled her computer like it was a newborn when she moved it from one area to another.

"What happened to your laptop?"

She glanced over at the desk. "It got in a fight with a wall."

Dilynn didn't have to say it was their fault. They knew it was.

"And the pressure cooker?" Alex looked at the ceiling once more.

The quiet chortle broke the tension. Dilynn's eyes crinkled in the corners as her face flushed a vibrant red. She flicked her finger in the air. "You have to push a button to release steam before you open it or it explodes."

Alex's mouth dropped open as the word leapt from their mouth. "It explodes?!"

"Big boom," Sadie said from Casey's side. She pointed to the ceiling. "And no one is tall enough to reach that part."

Alex took the kid's hint. Without a word to Dilynn, they went into the garage and learned Dilynn was a hoarder. They walked through lines of boxes stacked atop each other. Most had Dilynn's careful print across the side detailing the contents within, and Alex found themselves laughing at Dilynn's clear disdain for whoever runs Goodwill. They moved through the lines in search of the ladder. Their face scrunched at boxes labeled with Brandon's name. Shaking their head, they decided this was a project for another day.

When they found the ladder, they were disgusted that it looked as brand new as the tools in Brandon's toolbox. They would be different from him when Dilynn took them back. Their tools would be used, and birthdays would be celebrated. And the tree would be filled with presents for Dilynn and the girls.

Alex started making a list of things they would get the girls and Dilynn as they carried the ladder into the house. Dilynn rolled her eyes at them, before returning to the dishes. They hated that she was doing that, but one thing at a time. They would get the ceiling clean first, and next time they would do the dishes before they left.

Cleaning took twenty minutes. Their arms were exhausted, but they managed to get all of the sauce from the ceiling. The paint was stained, which added a new task to their list of they-jobs. Plus, if she really was selling the house, then it would need to be painted. Then it hit them, Dilynn was selling the house.

"When is the house... when is it going up for sale?"

Dilynn glanced over at them. "It's not."

Alex looked around. "I thought you said you all are moving across the street."

Dilynn nodded. She scrubbed the bowl to the mixer. The mixer that was too small. Alex wanted to kick themself. They were supposed to get her a new mixer for her birthday.

"Sylvia refused to let me sell it," she said.

Alex's eyebrows cinched together. "Sylvia?"

"She owns half the house. Bought it for me when I finished my foster parenting classes. She didn't want Evie to come live at the townhouse that we... uh... shared."

They locked away that tidbit of information to think about later.

"Plus, Sarah and Trisaya live out back, so I don't want to disrupt them. So, I'm just going to rent this place out to Ryder actually. And one day, it will be Evie's because that way she will always have a home." Dilynn gestured to the front window. "I plan on owning the whole street someday. That way they never have to feel like they're alone."

Alex picked up a towel and began drying the dishes. They didn't know where anything went. but didn't want to ask. Each time they opened a cabinet and found the top shelf empty, they silently chuckled.

"They make cabinets with a step stool that comes out of the bottom," Alex said as they slid the pizza platters on the top shelf.

"I can't reach those," Dilynn said with a huff of annoyance.

"That just means I will have to come back next week."

"Or that I break my arm when I fall off the counter because you decide not to show up."

Alex felt the jab dig between their ribs. It was deserved, but didn't make the pain any less.

"Thank you for letting me come in, and for dinner," Alex said, adding another dish to the top shelf.

"You didn't even eat," Dilynn mumbled as she scrubbed the sink.

"Oh." Alex slapped the towel over their shoulder and popped open a container. Grabbing a piece of cheese, they tried to stuff the whole square into their mouth. The pizza was amazing as always, and the flavors caused a quiet moan to escape. They hadn't realized how hungry they were because of the knots tied in their guts.

"Thanks for dinner," Alex tried again with a mouth still full of pizza.

The reward for their effort was half a laugh, the kind where only one *ha!* was trapped within her chest.

"You're welcome."

Her eyes shifted back to the counter. It was clean, and there wasn't any reason to stay in the kitchen. They tried to find something else to do. Unfortunately, even the kids were winding down their game.

"Why did you come tonight?" she asked quietly. "It's been weeks. No words, and then you just show up."

Alex pointed to their mouth. They continued to chew as they tried to come up with a way to tell her that they wanted to give her time. That they called a therapist and they needed to see that first step through before seeing her.

The door opened before they finished chewing on their words and pizza. They nearly choked when the tall blonde walked through the door. Pounding their chest, they looked to Dilynn for help, but she was standing idly by watching them potentially die once more.

They wiped the tears from their face as Sylvia crossed the space without hesitating. She smacked Alex hard on the back, then made approaching Dilynn look so easy. She held up a thick cylinder in one hand and a giant bouquet of lilies in the other.

"Happy birthday!" Sylvia almost shouted, giving Dilynn no time to ask her also not to say anything.

Sylvia knew when they hadn't, and they hated her for it. The expressions of horror on the Greyson kids' faces told them, the kids felt the same.

"It's your... birthday?" Lyra asked. She reached across the table and punched Evie in the shoulder. "Why the fuck didn't you tell me it was her birthday?"

Evie rubbed at the place she'd been hit. She didn't hit Lyra back as she stared at the table. She whispered, "I'm just as bad as he was. A fucking Starbucks card."

Sylvia didn't seem to care about the argument taking place at the dinner table. She held the container out to Dilynn, and said, "I had these drawn up after that night we had too much champagne. I think I have everything you said you wanted but we can have them redrawn. It has been three years since you told me what you wanted the school to look like, so I suspect you have some changes now."

Dilynn didn't hesitate at the offering. She took the container practically bouncing on her toes and began to tug it open. Sylvia placed her hand atop

Dilynn's.

"There's one more present, so maybe look at these after."

Dilynn's eyes flitted to the canister, then the blue eyes rose back to that annoying, bright smile. "This is already too much."

Sylvia shook her head. "No, this is what I said I would do. It's the minimum. Not even your present."

Sylvia's chest puffed up proudly, "Your present is something you said you wanted long before you ever talked about opening a school."

"I never—" Sylvia cut off Dilynn's words with a finger over her lips.

"This one is technically from me and Kayla."

Nails clicked over the hardwood as an auburn dog pranced into the house with a gangly kid clutching to its leash. The kid, who Alex assumed must be the sister Evie said was sent to boarding school, gave Dilynn a broad smile, and led the dog over to her.

"You told me you were never allowed to have a dog because your mom was allergic," Kayla said. "Via wanted to get you some crazy German Shepard guard dog, but I told her you said you wanted to rescue a dog."

The kid dropped to a knee and scratched the smiling pup behind the floppy ears. "We found this guy at the shelter. He was on death row because he always hid when people came to look at him, and we thought that's Dilynn's dog."

Dilynn sunk to the ground and the medium sized mutt crawled into her lap and leaned his body against her. Her arms wrapped around him and held him so tightly.

"He really was so cuddly, and he really liked hugs." Kayla tucked her dark hair behind her ear. "You always gave the best hugs so I thought, he would be perfect."

Sylvia stood beside Alex, and quietly said, "I tried to wait for you to leave, but then you were on a ladder. We went to Starbucks and came back, and he started to whine so I couldn't wait any longer."

Alex chewed on their lip. "She didn't tell anyone."

"I figured she wouldn't," Sylvia whispered. "You know now. So, you don't have to miss another one."

"I can't compete with a dog that she always wanted," Alex said, watching Dilynn fall in love with the pup whose tail made his whole body wiggle against her.

Sylvia nudged them lightly. "We're not in a competition. Watch her eyes. She's not looking back at me. She's looking at you, Action Figure. Trying to figure out how you feel about her having a dog. I mean, she knows how I feel about dogs and hair."

Dilynn glanced back at them with a giant smile on her face. She held the dog close to her chest, and asked Alex, "What should I name him, Wikipedia?"

Alex ran their hand over the back of their head. "Uh... Pumpkin?"

"You never get to name anything," Dilynn said.

The kids began rattling off names as they gathered in a circle around Dilynn and the dog. They clearly loved the addition.

"We should call him Brother Bear," Sadie said. Evie and Lyra vetoed her, and the debate began again.

"So, you're back," Alex whispered with their gaze still locked on the dog.

"Action Figure, you're the future. Me? I'm the past. I'll always be here, like this. Don't make her choose, and I won't either."

"You say that like you have any idea what happened."

Alex followed Sylvia's eyes to Sadie. "Your niece was the only one that didn't shun me, which surprised me because... well, I took your place in her bed."

Alex's whole body went rigid. They searched Dilynn for any mark Sylvia left on her.

"Calm down, G.I. Morgan. Nothing happened. I mean, I tried of course because D is one of a kind, which I know you know, but when I kissed her, she—"

"Closed her eyes, and you knew it wasn't you she was thinking about."

"Yep." Sylvia shook her head. "She chose you. That day on the porch. She chose you, not me. And you're here. So, wear the broody one down by climbing up the ladder so D doesn't break her ankle again. Go to the games. Do all the things I should have done without... and this is the real challenge, do it without putting your hands on her. Let her come to you because when she does. You'll know it's time."

She left them to pull a bottle of wine from the cabinet. After pouring herself a glass, she leaned against the counter and met their gaze.

"Anyways, back to little Sassy. She told me everything. Perks of being the fun auntie figure. Probably the one thing I will truly miss about not convincing D to keep that ring on her finger is spending time with her. She's fun. A lot of trauma there, which I know you know, but she's a good egg."

Sylvia gestured towards Casey. "Is that the girlfriend?"

"Yeah."

Sylvia hummed to herself. She took another sip of wine, before she said, "Well, if you fight it, then she's just going to hide it like I did. I would suggest just supporting her so when that one goes to college, Sassy knows she can tell you she got her heart broken."

Alex watched the kids roll around the floor with the pup. They hated that they agreed with Sylvia about the dog hair, but they would love the dog because Dilynn's smile told them she loved that dog.

"I'm headed to Italy tomorrow," Sylvia said. She nudged Alex slightly. "That means you are the person that has to be here for her. Show her she can depend on you to be here."

"Why are you telling me this?" Alex asked, now genuinely curious as to why Sylvia cared anything about them. "I did nothing but hurt her."

"I like you," Sylvia stated blandly. They could feel her eyes on them even though she was still facing forward. "You are a unique human."

"You told me two weeks ago you didn't like me."

"I just got dumped," Sylvia said, studying the wine in her glass. "I may pretend to not have feelings, but I do. That's done for now, though."

"For now?"

Sylvia raised her glass to her lips. "D is one of a kind with very intense and sometimes dark fantasies. One day, you're going to ask me to help make one of those fantasies come true."

Alex eyes widened, and they turned their head to actually look at the smile preparing to take another drink.

"One day," Sylvia whispered into the glass. "It would be better if it was me than someone else. Afterall, you know I am not trying to steal her away from you."

"I don't share what is mine," Alex stated.

"We'll see," Sylvia said, leaving them to spread the plans for the school across the table. "Dilynn, come look at your school while the kids take that mutt outside so he doesn't ruin the floor."

With Dilynn leaning over the blueprints and Sylvia too close for their own comfort, Alex took it as their cue to leave. They didn't want to disturb the business meeting taking place. They slipped out the front door as quietly as possible, only to jump when the door was thrown open.

"You're just going to leave again," Dilynn said louder than necessary for the fact they were still standing on the porch.

Alex couldn't turn around and see her betrayal. They already had it engrained in their brain.

"I didn't want to disturb you while you were planning," they said. Their grip on the banister tightened. "It's late, so I should go."

They could hear her sigh. Knew her chin was probably tucked to her chest.

"Happy... Happy birthday, Cupcake," they said. Then they walked away before they pulled her against them and forced her into a hug that she wasn't ready for.

Dilynn was still standing on the porch when they drove away. There were two ways to get back to their apartment. Neither felt right because a part of them knew they should go back instead of taking Sylvia's advice.

They kept driving, making the choice to trust the woman who at least knew Dilynn well enough to know it was her birthday. Without Dilynn's story, Sylvia's words were really all Alex had if they were going to fix things.

33

Most of the posters in Dilynn's classroom were from college. She'd made them during her student teaching while Sylvia teased her from her perch on the stiff leather couch as she read her serious papers with charts and stuff Dilynn had no interest in.

Three years of her life had been spent in this room. She'd hid in this room more hours of the day than she spent anywhere else. Her guts twisted into knots of what the future would hold. This was always the plan, but it didn't make anything less scary.

Dilynn sat in the beat-up armchair. She'd miss her freshmen gathered around her feet weekly to listen as she read them a children's book. *Rainbow Fish* was always the students' favorite until they realized the message was to give away all the special parts of yourself until you had nothing left to give, but people will like you then. Each week they dissected the societal messages used to condition their understanding of themselves and people around them. She wasn't sure if she would miss story time or listening to the kids talk about the books they read together.

She glanced down at the resignation letter on her laptop. So much change had happened so fast. More change than even when Sylvia had Dilynn's stuff moved into the garage of the house. She'd come to what she thought was home to find a break-up letter on the counter of the townhouse she didn't belong in anymore because she was a mom.

Marcus had been her saving grace. Called her to let her know Evie was getting released from juvenile detention early and he was going to go with her to get the kid. She'd worried he would judge her when he came to find her crying on the floor, but he sat down beside her while she cried her weight in tears and offered her his sweat soaked handkerchief. He wasn't a dad, but he had never believed what Simone had told everyone about her.

She picked up the phone and sent a text to Marcus: ' Staring at my resignation letter and I feel like the ground is about to swallow me whole.'

The ellipses appeared almost immediately. Marcus took his time typing out a response. Texting wasn't one of his strengths, but talking on the phone was something he dreaded. Dilynn stared at the phone trying to predict what he would say. She laughed at how his gruff voice sounded with her overly feminine dialogue.

'I just sent mine in so no backing out on me now. Paying for two houses is expensive as it is.'

Dilynn rolled her eyes. 'Did you hit send just so you could tell me that?'

She didn't have to wait long for the answer.

'Yes boss'

Boss. She'd never been a boss of anything or anyone. Never imagined herself being in charge of anything or anyone, even when she told Sylvia she wanted to run her own school. And now she was the boss.

Boss of a school.

Boss of a household of three girls.

She even had to learn how to be the boss of the dog with four names that loved trash more than dog food.

The room that always kept her safe was tilting on its side. She'd been here before. Knew even though it felt like she was having a heart attack, it was a panic attack.

She held the phone to her chest as she tried to catch her breath that kept racing out of her mouth. She hit Sylvia's contact, choking on air while the phone rang and rang and rang. When it went to voicemail, Dilynn called again with the same result.

Sylvia was dropping her again. Just like last time the world was falling to one side. She always flew away when the storm in Dilynn's head turned into a blizzard.

Her knees rose to her chest. She would take up less space when the storm buried her in snow. Her heart would slow down with the freeze. The ice would ease the fire burning up her skin.

She barely heard the door open behind her. Her limbs were shaking too much to move. The pounding in her ears made it impossible to hear who was coming but she clenched her eyes shut and prayed it wasn't Evie or Sadie.

"Hey," Alex whispered.

They knelt beside the grungy armchair. Their hands were warm and hard but smooth. Her hand was in theirs, then it was pressed against their sternum.

"I'm going to take a deep breath in."

Slowly she felt the pushback on her hand as they inhaled.

"I'm going to slowly exhale and count," which didn't make sense because she felt them exhale as they spoke.

Alex's perfect stomach extended and the calcium cage in their chest rose, as well. They closed their perfect lips for a moment, then they parted as they whispered their countdown. With eyes on her, they began.

"Ten."

They tapped a finger over her hand.

"Nine."

Another tap.

"Eight."

She tapped with them.

"Seven."

Their eyes smiled.

"Six."

She was pretty sure their stomach was flat again.

"Five."

They were definitely breathing in again.

"Four."

This exercise was faulty.

"Three."

She was holding her breath.

"Two, and one."

Alex placed Dilynn's other hand on her diaphragm.

"Breathe with me."

They counted down again. Dilynn's chest shook as she tried to breathe through it. She followed along as best she could. Repeating the breathing exercises until her lungs stopped trying to suffocate themselves and her mind was done laughing at how someone was supposed to count out loud while breathing out one breath.

She wiped away the evidence of the breakdown from her face. She locked away the fears. This wasn't the space to fall apart.

"Did Marcus...?"

Alex shook their head, then scrunched up their nose.

"Sylvia texted me. How she got my number was... confusing. Almost as confusing as the string of emojis. So, it took me a minute, but apparently snowflake, phone, and ambulance made sense to me."

Dilynn hated Sylvia's need to speak in hieroglyphics. She never did it before Dilynn started majoring in English, but then it became a game to the woman. Always a game with Sylvia, and the woman never gave her the rules to the game, so Dilynn could never win.

"Want to talk about it?" Alex asked.

She didn't want to talk, so she pointed to the computer. Alex took the hint and picked up the laptop. She watched their eyes move left to right. She could see the sadness in their gaze.

"I hate it," they admitted when they set the computer down. Their head fell back against the couch as they sat back against it. "Don't get me wrong. I think that what you are going to do is amazing. And I really do want to be a part of making your dream come true. But being here without you... I've never been here without..."

Dilynn looked at the screen, then back at them. She licked her lips to try out her idea, but it only tasted like the salt from her own tears.

"How much?" she whispered.

Alex looked around the room, then back at Dilynn. A crease cut through their brow as they asked, "To?"

She wiped her face again and moved to the edge of her chair.

"How much would it take for you to come with me?" Dilynn asked.

Alex blinked twice. Their lips twitched and they scanned over her face until she began to think she'd not said the words aloud.

"Maths. You know... I don't do the maths," Dilynn said. "And Sylvia will take care of the, like, building. Well, she won't because she also doesn't do the maths well either. She pays people for that, and I have money... so I could pay you to... do the maths for me."

They chuckled lightly with a hand up, "Stop saying maths."

"Well, how much?" Dilynn asked again. "I can match your salary."

Alex chewed on the side of their cheek. Their eyes stared at the ceiling, and Dilynn was pretty sure they were doing their own calculations.

"What if I did the books for you and kept my day job," Alex asked as they played with a fold in their slacks.

Dilynn's eyes narrowed at them, "You don't think I can afford you."

"No. I have no doubt that you can afford me, or Sylvia could afford me because I am sure she already knows you don't do math." Alex took a deep breath. "I... I feel weird taking your money when I..."

"Want to sleep with me?" Dilynn laughed when Alex's ears turned a vibrant shade of rose.

"Well, I guess we know who would win the hammering contest," Alex stated.

"You," Dilynn said with a single brow cocked at them. "I mean, you hammered me pretty hard and the endurance. I felt you for days. Took a week for the bruises to fully fade from my hips and thighs. Like, you must do a thousand sit-ups a day."

Alex sucked in their bottom lip. When it popped out, they dropped a mask on their face.

"So, I meant this game my family used to play. We took turns to see who could get their nail into a stump first. If you hammered your nail quickest, you won. It was a joke about hitting the nail on the head. Like a dad joke." They propped their head up on one hand and smiled. "But... I do work out a lot."

Dilynn rested her chin on her knee. She tried to make the face she used to describe when Priya was flirting.

"We could... practice hammering," she said, watching them carefully. "I mean, if that was something that you maybe still wanted to do with me.”

Alex’s head dropped from their hand. They seemed to be working through their breathing exercises again.

“Panic attack?” Dilynn asked.

Alex held up a finger as they continued to mouth off numbers.

“You good?” Dilynn asked, looking down at herself.

It was Friday and she’d already changed to go to Flagstaff for the girls’ club tournament. Maybe they didn’t like her in spandex.

Alex slapped their hands to their knees. Irritatingly beautiful mossy irises rose to Dilynn. Their mask was back in place, and she felt like a bloated fish sitting on land. “The question is, are you okay?”

Dilynn adjusted her shirt. Pulled the zippered hoodie tighter around herself. “Yeah. I was just... scared of change.” She tucked her hair behind her ear. “And sorry for like trying to seduce you with corny ass lines.”

Alex handed Dilynn the computer and moved closer to her side without touching her.

“Hit send,” they said. They pointed to the button. “Hit send, and I will send one, too. Be your maths person.”

Dilynn’s nose crinkled. “That sounds weird coming from you.”

“’Cause it sounds so different from you,” Alex retorted. Their voice raised an octave as they flipped their hands around. “I’m Dilynn Greyson the Queen of English Grammar, but I can’t do the maths.”

She fought the urge to shove their smug face to the floor. Even with the dirty suggestion, she knew she wasn’t ready to completely forgive them.

“Look Wikipedia, you need to update your site. Maths is a term used in Britain because the term math is singular and there will be more than one math. Like spread sheets with formulas and, like, geometry and, like, ordering.”

Alex pulled away on their own. They cupped their mouth, and called out, “We have a loyalist in our midst. Light the lanterns because the British are coming.”

“You know what,” Dilynn growled. “I’m going to give you all the shit jobs.”

“Careful,” Alex said with a waggle of their finger. “I haven’t sent my letter in yet.”

“You’re going to come with me,” Dilynn stated.

“I’m going to come with you,” Alex promised. “The work thing. Not the... u version of the word. Not yet.”

Not yet. The two words bounced around Dilynn’s skull.

“You still...uh... want to, like, with me?” Dilynn asked, needing things to be plainly spoken.

Alex got up. They moved around the small space between the chair and the whiteboard. With their back to her, Alex began to share more words than they'd ever strung together at once.

"I started seeing a therapist. I mean, technically she's an intern, but she is going to be a therapist in a year. She doesn't seem fazed by the gender dysphoria. And there's a lot that I have to do to get everything sorted because of the last therapy... Not therapy. Torture. They called it therapy, but she said when they shocked me that it gave me seizures and it kinda gave me PTSD." Alex shook their head. "No, she said it is definitely PTSD. She said that, basically, it caused the memories of the bad things to store in the part of my head that is the fight or flight. And so, when I want something like what I want with you... it's scary because they showed me pictures and videos of women naked and kissing and porn. They had me watch girl on girl porn as they shocked me. So, my intern therapist, she says that when I think about you it—"

"Activates your flight response," Dilynn interjected, watching them move in a circle around the room. "Like right now."

Dilynn took a deep breath. "That's why you are willing to come with me. Because if I'm not here, you think you will run away."

Alex moved faster along their self-created track. They moved their hands around like they were sorting their sentences in an essay only they could see.

"I just... I know I want you. Like, I know it in my core that I don't just want the sex, but the sex is so good. Sooo sooo good and I do." They stared at her, and their feet paused for a moment. "You have no idea. I want to rip your clothes off. Go all werewolf on you and pretend just for a moment it's okay to be a slave to my impulses, but only if you wanted that. But yeah. You and naked are... I..."

They held up their hands as though they could actually rip her shirt down the middle. The way their biceps flexed, she decided it could happen.

"And I want to do that thing from your story where I tie your hands up, and I make you beg because you sound so good when you are begging. Like sooo sooo good, and I don't know why I thought you would taste like coffee because of all the Starbucks you drink, but you didn't."

They held the back of their head with both hands. Their eyes were barely green anymore and their pupils were blown wide.

"I think your pussy is fucking meth," Alex said so suddenly. "Like, one hit and I was addicted. The only pussy I ever want to eat. And it's sooo sooo hard. Sooo hard to not just."

They clenched their hands into fists that shook. Then, Alex pointed to the door.

"I need to go. I need to go and quit my job so that I can follow you around on a leash." They laughed at themself while Dilynn was still trying to process.

"So, I'm going to go, like usual and contemplate why Greyson women are issued leashes for people like me and Landon, but yeah. I'm going to go because I... my teeth itch. I just want to bite you and I want to... I'm going to go. And I'm not going to think about you naked with a collar and a leash as payback for dragging me around on the one you have on me, but I am because you would look hot. So hot."

They tugged at the roots of their hair.

"I'm sorry. I'm sorry. You just... you don't know what you do to me. I know, I know I'm not supposed to use your story to make your nightmares come true because you said they are nightmares, but they are my fantasies." They pressed their hand to their chest. Their casted hand gestured to the desk that the castle would have to be removed from. "Like, I am twisted and dark and the idea of bending you over that desk makes me so... I'm going to go now. Like run away. Run like a sprint, not like a marathon before I say anything else... or take you up on your offer because you look sooo good in those pants and I could just...."

Their eyes ran over Dilynn, and they looked like the wolf they joked about. It gave Dilynn an idea for a twisted werewolf tale, but the idea was cast out of her head when Alex bolted from the room as promised.

Dilynn sat in the quiet. Tried to sort through the vocal waves Alex left bouncing off the walls. She shifted in her seat to ease the pulsing in her pants as she caught the echo of Alex's dark desires.

Her pulse was beating wildly, and she considered chasing after Alex once more to tear her own shirt off and lay atop their computer. She didn't get the chance when the door flew open again. She jumped up thinking the wolf in Alex had won the battle, but she stepped further in the room when it wasn't a stoic social studies teacher staring at her but a broody bottle blonde that barely fit through the door with her gigantic head.

"What did you do now?" Simone snarled at her. "Look, I know you think your fucking hot shit but stop playing with my best friend."

"What are you talking about?" Dilynn snapped.

"Alex just ran out of here," Simone said. "They were running down the hall, which means you fucking yelled at them again for nothing because you're insane. I can't wait to be in here every damn day next year so I can document how incompetent you are."

Dilynn's lips set in a straight line. Every fear she'd had about the future was drowned in the rage coursing through her veins. She grabbed the laptop from the couch and hit the send button. Once the email disappeared into her sent folder, she turned her cold gaze back to Simone.

"I just sent in my letter of resignation," Dilynn snarled. "And the running down the hall was Alex going to do the same thing."

Simone's head tilted to the side, then she cast a glance at the door she was blocking.

"You're lying."

"You can tell yourself that," Dilynn said, moving to her desk. She gathered up her stuff. "But the truth is you walking in was that final push I needed to send in my letter."

Dilynn picked up her phone and tucked it into her bag. She tried to move past Simone, but the woman stepped in her way.

"You're lying," Simone repeated, staring down at Dilynn.

The strap to Dilynn's messenger bag folded in her grip. She reminded herself that if she harnessed her inner Evie, she wouldn't even be able to finish the year.

"Get out of my way," Dilynn commanded.

When Simone still stood in her way, Dilynn decided she was done letting this bitch push her around. She shoved Simone to the side with her shoulder and walked out of the cage she let the woman back her into three years ago.

34

The classroom was basically empty anyways. Alex gazed around the space as they calculated how many copy paper boxes they would need to pack. Their room was just as vacant as their house, and they felt like a failure as a teacher.

There should be student projects on the walls. Inspirational posters like Dilynn had covering hers. Or college banners. Something that said this was a safe space instead of an institution. They had to do better at Dilynn's school.

The door to the classroom slammed open so hard, Alex leapt from their chair. They held the laptop up ready to throw it at whatever irate senior was coming after them after the latest progress report sent home.

"Don't you send that goddamn letter," Simone yelled from the threshold.

She stormed across the room and ripped the laptop from Alex's hands. Waving it in the air, she looked like she was going to cost them $1000 from their last check to pay for its destruction.

"Delete it," Simone demanded. "You can't just quit. You can't leave with... with her."

"Simone, I'm going." Alex said.

"No." Simone opened the computer. She hit the track pad repeatedly only for the lock screen to light up on the display. "You're my best friend, and she's... she's not even your fucking girlfriend. So, delete it. I'll delete it. What's the fucking password?"

Alex chuckled lightly.

"I swear if the password is her goddamn name, I'm going to kick your simp ass."

They watched Simone type in Dilynn's name, but the password rejected her. She tried Dilynn's last name next, apparently forgetting that the school district required everyone to use a number and a character in addition to letters.

She thrust the computer in their direction. "Delete it."

"I can't do that," Alex said.

They watched Simone's red face grow a shade paler. She slapped the screen shut and raised it in the air like she would actually throw it.

Alex only exhaled when the device didn't leave her hand, even though it would have probably gone through the wall with the force she fake threw it with.

"Why, Alex?" Her head fell back. She took several deep breaths, before she returned her death rays back on them. "Of all the women in the world, why did you have to choose her?"

"I love her," they said.

Simone's hand shot towards the window. "Hundreds of chubby blondes out there. Fall in love with someone else."

"I can't do that," Alex tried to explain as they fought the urge to hit the woman for talking about Dilynn like that.

"You send that letter and I'm going to evict you," Simone said. She dropped the computer on their desk. "Delete it."

Alex shrugged slightly and logged into the device. They pulled up their sent messages and turned the computer to Simone. "Guess that means I'm U-Hauling."

Simone's gaze ran over possibly the worse resignation letter ever sent. Her nose scrunched up. "No. I can't. I can't let that happen. It's bad enough that you quit, but I can't have you move in with her, too."

She started to pace around the room. Her fingers gripped the roots of her hair and she pulled. The pulling was apparently helping her problem solve.

"I'll just... I'll just fix your lease. Lifelong. Yep. I can just change the dates and you will never leave. A lifelong lease that locks you in. I can just type it up and do the window thing where I copy your signature from the last lease."

Alex rolled their eyes. They appreciated Simone wanted to keep them; however, there was no doubt in their mind about who they would choose in a contest between Dilynn and Simone.

"Dilynn would buy me out," they reminded their friend. "Don't give her that power to piss you off."

"No," Simone said, shaking her head. "You can't just drop everything you want to follow her around. She'll use her money to fuck with you. She's rich and she will try to buy you off and make things that are not okay, okay because she is going to buy you what you want."

Alex shook their head. "I didn't do this for money. Her money is her money, but if you try to back me into a corner, you know she'll try to buy my way out. And I don't want that. You don't want that. So just... let it be."

"You can't leave me for her."

Alex flopped back in their chair. They hadn't even had time to think about how they would tell Simone they weren't coming back next year.

"I'm not leaving you. I am just..."

"You didn't even talk to me about it first," Simone growled. "I'm your only fucking friend. When you quit your job, you are always supposed to consult your best friend first."

"I had to do it before I chickened out," Alex said quietly. "You know how I panic. But this is what I want, so I had to do it before I got scared and ruined it."

Simone kicked a desk. They knew it had to hurt, but she barely flinched. "Why her?"

Alex smiled at the thought of Dilynn. "She's special. And I love her."

"Love is bullshit," Simone snarled. "One day you're going to wake up and realize the whole commitment thing sucks."

A crease spread over Alex's forehead. "I hope you don't say stuff like that to Marissa."

"I'm not stupid," Simone snapped. "You are definitely the grand prize winner of that reward."

Alex ran their hands over their face. They tried to rub away the frustration, but having to repeatedly defend their feelings for Dilynn was getting old.

"You have to let me do this," they said.

"No. No, I don't," Simone said, shaking her head violently.

Alex tapped their chest. "She is good for me."

Simone's eye roll was intense, and the stare that followed was more so. "She treats you like shit."

"I can promise you, I deserved it," Alex said with a soft chuckle. "I have made every single step of things with her as hard as possible, and she still didn't lock me out. Didn't give up on me."

"I didn't give up on you," Simone said. "I do everything for you."

"My stove is still yellow," Alex reminded her.

"I told you I would replace it."

"When I order a U-Haul?"

Simone's finger tried to shoot a laser at them as she jabbed it in their direction. "You will not move in with her."

"Yet."

"She's going to hurt you."

Alex studied Simone carefully. This wasn't a new tactic for Simone. Playing off their fear of rejection had kept them at her side for longer than they wanted to analyze. They started to count the opportunities they could have seized if they hadn't believed her when she said it would hurt them. Talking to Dilynn in August was the first. They would have spoken to her before she started writing and saved themself from becoming a catfish smelling troll in her life. They could have gotten an undercut like they said they wanted, if they hadn't believed her when she said it would threaten their job.

They made it to seven when the phone rang.

Alex blinked a few times, realizing they were staring at Simone, and she was still talking. Their ears tuned back on when she hissed, "That's her isn't it?"

Alex looked at the screen and nodded. They tried to swallow the lump in their throat. Their mind ran through all the terrible things that could be waiting on the other end of the line.

"Are you going to answer it?" Simone demanded.

"She doesn't call," they whispered. "She texts. She doesn't call."

"Then answer it, dipshit."

They just stared at the phone. They hadn't seen Sadie that afternoon. Why hadn't they seen Sadie?

Simone took the phone from their hand as their heartbeat too fast. The call connected and Simone hit the speaker button.

"*I fucking hate you, you fucking piece of shit!*" Dilynn was yelling.

They were still trying to breathe correctly when Simone huffed, "This is the bitch you fall in love with."

"Don't call her a bitch or I have to punch you," they stated. Alex raised their casted hand. "I already have a broken hand."

"*Alex?*" they heard calling out to them.

They cleared their throat. "Uh... yeah, I'm... I'm here."

"*Are you, like, busy?*"

"Yes," Simone growled. She pointed at them. "You're going to take me out for drinks since you're a backstabbing best friend."

"*Is that Simone?*"

"Yeah," Alex said. "Did you tell her I was leaving?"

"*Only because she barged into my classroom yelling at me. Tell her she's a bitch.*"

"I fucking heard you, you twat," Simone said with the phone held close to her face.

Alex sighed and took the phone back. They locked eyes with Simone, and said, "You need to get control of yourself."

"*Alex?*"

Alex looked at the phone. "Si, mi reina."

"*Remember when you said that thing about me being able to do anything?*"

Alex's eyebrows scrunched together. "Yes."

"*Well, it turns out that you're a liar.*"

"Dump her," Simone demanded.

They ran their hand over the back of their head. They would get that hair cut this weekend.

"*Alex?*"

"Uh...." Alex swallowed. "Why am I a liar?"

"*Because I can't make my car start, and I'm late because the girls are already headed to Flagstaff for their tournament with your brother, and I just.... I just... need...*"

Alex listened to Dilynn choking on the request. A part of them wanted to help her over this hurdle by waiting her out. The other part of them wanted to show her, they understood her.

"I'm coming."

"*Are you sure? Ryder is—*"

Alex glanced at the phone, then the stack of papers on their desk that were supposed to be graded by Monday. "Yeah... I'm just grabbing my stuff and I'll drive you to Flagstaff."

"*Thank you.*"

"Of course, cupcake."

They rolled their eyes at Simone's gagging.

"Be out in a minute," they said, then hung up.

"Cupcake?" Simone choked. "You call her Cupcake?"

A smile spread over their face as they realized their car would smell like her. The car that made her want to drop her panties. Maybe she'd shove them today and they could repeat their first date.

"She smells sweet."

"She smells like betrayal."

"You smell like green Jell-O," Alex quipped, jamming their computer into their bag.

Simone's angry face scrunched up. "Green Jell-O?"

Alex nodded, as they shifted the essays like Dilynn did to make them easier to carry. "Yep, because you're so jealous that she wants me and didn't want you."

"She only didn't want me because she was too busy being a prostitute," Simone snapped.

Alex paused their sorting. They set the papers down because the pages were crinkling in their grip.

"What did you say?"

"She was a fucking concubine." Simone's hands shot out in front of her. She shook her head as she dropped her hands. "You wanted to know what happened, well the full story is she turned me down because Sylvia was paying for her pussy. I wasn't willing to pay for it because that's just.... She's a fucking whore. I told her I was going to report her to admin for being a prostitute, and she beat me to the punch by telling HR I kissed her and threatened her job. And I had kissed her, and she told me that I couldn't be anything to her because she was Sylvia's property. Anything I would say at that point was just me retaliating so I just kept my mouth shut, but I can't... Alex, I can't let you do this. Not for a girl that sells her body to the highest bidder."

Alex chewed on their lip until it split. They tasted the blood, and they needed more.

"That's the girl you fell for, Alex. She fucks people for money. That's how she got the house and paid for Evie's lawyer, so if she is leaving teaching it means she's back to being someone's whore." Simone licked her teeth. "She's probably still screwing Sylvia. And you deserve better than that. You're good, Alex. Too good and too kind to have to have your heart broken when you find out that the life you think you have is just a bunch of—"

Alex's left hand didn't hit as hard as their right, but Simone's jaw wasn't made of concrete. They left their bag as Simone was still pushing herself up from the desk she'd used to break her fall.

Every muscle in their body was locked as they stomped down the hall. They were ready if Simone decided to come out for a fight. They would fight her, and they would win because she was wrong. She was just lying.

Dilynn was still kicking her car when Alex made it outside. They watched her rage unleash on the car. After a very hard hit to the hood, Dilynn held her hand close to her body. Unlike them, she preferred her left hand.

They understood her pain.

She was doing some type of tribal dance trying to shake away the sting, when she stopped abruptly and studied them. Still holding her fist, she asked, "Should I call Simone an ambulance?"

A crease formed over Alex's forehead, but they let Dilynn take their hand in hers. Simone's face wasn't made of concrete, but her cheekbone had busted open their knuckles.

"You don't need stitches." Dilynn pressed on their tender fingers. "And nothing looks out of place or broken."

"You don't know the difference between CPR and the Heimlich. How do you know if bones are broken?"

"Did she swing at you?'

"I don't want to talk about it," Alex said, glancing back to the window of their classroom. "I just want to get out here."

"Okay, do you want me to drive?" she said playfully. She shoved her hand in their pocket and took their keys out.

They ripped the keys from her hand. They pointed to the passenger door. "You're a passenger princess. Never the driver."

She rolled her eyes when they wished she would have shoved them. It would give them an invitation to hug her. Some reassurance that they hadn't just ruined their only friendship for something that isn't real.

"Sylvia is not coming, right?" Alex asked. They knew she was supposed to be in Europe but today didn't feel like their day. Not with everything spinning out of control.

"Simone told you," Dilynn whispered.

Alex's eyes raised to the blue crystals. They could see they didn't need to answer her.

"She told you I was a prostitute. She told everyone that my first year after I kicked her out." Dilynn twisted the strap to her bag. "She didn't pay me for sex. I wasn't a sex dealer even though my vag is like meth."

With a forced smile, Dilynn looked at them differently. The part of the story she'd not wanted to share was clearly now out in the open. The part that had driven her into hiding.

"I told you that Sylvia paid for everything when we were together, but not together. We weren't together like that. I was always the friend outside of the house, but inside.... Let's just say after six years together it was clear we were more than friends. But it wasn't transactional like Simone wants you to believe. And Sylvia was pissed. She wasn't ready to be outed, but she was also ready to file a lawsuit to bankrupt Simone for slander. If I had gotten fired, I know Sylvia would have gone for blood."

"It doesn't change how I feel," Alex stated as they realized Dilynn had already told them what happened. That the two stories they'd been told had only left out the part of Simone bullying Dilynn.

Their hand hovered by her cheek. "I trust you. I'm just... I'm just angry. I'm angry that she—"

"She's jealous," Dilynn whispered.

She chewed on her lip. They wanted to pull it down just enough to tell her she's okay. She didn't need to worry. It popped free on its own, and she licked away the smallest hint of blood.

After a deep breath, Dilynn said, "She is going to miss you because you are her only friend. People... they didn't like that she was calling me a whore. A lot of teachers left because of it and admin was pissed. So, you are the first person to talk to her since my first year. And she is still mad at me. Mad that I went to HR to get a new mentor. Pissed that I couldn't let her come around Evie like she wanted because I knew she would tell Evie the same shit. Make Evie think that I was a whore and Evie was scared of all adults, which is why I stopped dating women. I didn't want her to think that I would be interested in her like that. So, I dated two men, and the third was everything Sylvia wasn't. Literally, the exact opposite of her. And so, just know it's not about you. It's that she will miss you, because the last two years people stopped listening to her. But you came and you were hers."

She paused, looking back at the school.

"One day, maybe you will tell me why you felt safe to tell her your pronouns, but not me."

It was a question disguised as a question. Something that Alex had never even considered as being something Dilynn would want to know. But they had also lived through Simone's brainwashing. Their decisions had also been impacted by Simone telling them what could or could not get them fired.

"She took me out," Alex confessed. "I didn't know she had a girlfriend."

Dilynn's eyes grew wide, and they could tell where she was going with it. They tried to wipe away the woman's thoughts with a wave of their hand.

"We didn't even get to the point she was trying to kiss me," Alex promised. "She tried to flirt, but I told her I wasn't a lesbian when she said we were the only two lesbians on campus so people will think we are hooking up. She had laughed at me and said I definitely looked like a lesbian. And... I just said I'm non-binary. She... she said okay but followed it with not to tell anyone because all the conservative parents would lose their minds and get me fired. And she said you were like that, too. But once she found out... she wasn't interested in me anymore. Which is good because she's not my type."

Alex ran their hand over the back of their head. "I don't know how we can still be friends after what she just did. She has manipulated me. Tried to control everything I wanted to do. Like, I want a haircut. I want an undercut, and I just.... I want to do it even more now because she told me not to."

Dilynn ran her hand over the back of their neck. "You'd look so dapper with an undercut."

Never had they been allowed to have short hair. They tried to imagine what it would feel like to have her run her hand over the buzzed area. Hesitantly, they asked, "You think so?"

"Yes, I do. Just like she thinks she's protecting you," Dilynn said. Her finger twirled a curl at the base of their neck. "So, let's not be one of those teen movies where you dump your friends for a girl, and then we get in a fight, and you have to run back to her. Just fix it when we get back."

"How?" Alex asked.

Dilynn shrugged. "I don't know how to fix a friendship that I don't understand to begin with. You'll figure it out though. You're brilliant."

Alex shifted their weight from foot to foot. "How can I be with you and friends with her when you two can't even be in the same room?"

Dilynn shrugged again. "I mean, you are not even with me. So, I guess fix your friendship first and just know that I like her wife. She's super sweet, so if we have to occupy the same space, then I can just talk to Marissa. Marissa knows I wasn't a prostitute."

"You know Marissa?"

Dilynn nodded and wrapped her hair up in a messy knot. The tattoo was now the only claim on Dilynn's body, and Alex hated that Dilynn was right. She wasn't theirs to carry their mark because they had been stupid.

"She's a barback at The Escape," Dilynn explained as though Alex didn't know Marissa. "She... uh... she always looked out for me when I was there. Walked me to my car a few times because it was late, and I wouldn't call us friends, but we could be under the right circumstances."

Alex nodded at the car. "We should go."

"Hey," Dilynn said. "Thanks for... defending me. No one has ever..."

The downward gaze told them she wasn't lying. It meant that even Sylvia cast her to the wolves. It may have made her strong, but also made her unable to believe in anyone.

They couldn't wait for her permission; they pulled her into a hug. Inhaled her forgiving aura and reaffirmed their internal promise to be the shield and sword to keep away the monsters.

"I'll always defend you, Pumpkin," they said, trapping her arms between them to make it so she couldn't shove them away.

"I can't with you," she groaned. Her head fell back, and they saw the annoyed smile playing on the corners of her mouth. The dimples were the sign of a real Dilynn Greyson smile, and they loved Dilynn's dimples.

She twisted out of their hug, huffing the whole five feet to her trunk. With a finger pointed at the compartment, she commanded, "Use your giant muscles and get my bag."

"So demanding."

They went and got the bag without putting up a fight. They would do whatever she said, and it wasn't scary. It couldn't be scary since somewhere in their brain filled with unstable fears, they knew she wouldn't hurt them.

35

After the girls lost the first game, Ryder insisted on taking everyone out for dinner before he and Allie drove back that night. The most Dilynn took away from the evening was at least no one got into a fight. There were grumbles and verbal jabs thrown across the table.

For the most part, the only person surly was Evie. Luckily, Landon had driven up to see her play and visit his grandmother while his mother was away for the weekend. His presence was like adding a base to her acidic temper, making her attitude partially neutralized by the end of dinner.

"Please don't take it personally," Dilynn searched for her hotel reservation in her email and clicked the address as Alex continued to scowl at the road. "Evie just hates to lose."

"She called me a jinx. Said she couldn't stop smelling fish when she was trying to catch," Alex reminded her.

Putting on her work smile, Dilynn offered, "Well, the bright side of her being off her game is that we may get to head home tomorrow if they lose again."

"Then she'll really be mad at me," Alex reminded her. Their fingers tightened on the wheel.

"Wait until she finds out you're not going to be her teacher next year," Dilynn said, thinking about the blow up that would come when Evie learned Alex was going to be spending every day with Dilynn.

"Do you think she is ever going to forgive me?"

Dilynn studied the map because it was easier than looking at them when she explained, "It's not about you. She hates everyone I date. That's the choice she makes though. Never chooses happiness, that one."

"What do you mean: a choice?"

"Everything is a choice. Evie usually makes a choice out of fear instead of trying to be happy. I hope one day she will choose to be happy and not hate who I'm with because it will actually be easier for her."

Alex's eyebrows created a canyon in the middle of their face. "So, she chose to hate Brandon?"

"Yes. Even though that one was valid, she still chose to hate him from day one. Then she chose to hate Sylvia." Dilynn set her phone on the console so Alex could follow the periodic verbal commands. "Evie was scared of Sylvia because she knew Sylvia didn't want kids. That's my fault because she used to use Sylvia as a carrot to get me to second guess being with Brandon, so I told her Sylvia didn't want kids so she would stop bringing Sylvia up. Didn't work. She literally said something about her on Christmas. Not the point. Just know that when Sylvia showed back up, she was scared, and she chose to make every conversation with Sylvia difficult. She always chooses to push and push and push until people break."

The tree lined streets reminded Dilynn of the small town her father used to drive them through on their way to go fishing. She hated those trips because she hated fish. Now, she wished this was just one of those trips, and she wasn't a cranky preteen just wanting to be cool.

"Again, it's not a you thing. Not even as much a me thing."

She studied an old wooden sign whose post had been devoured by a creeper vine. The paint peeled back from the family real estate logo, and Dilynn wondered if she would ever leave the desert for a life in a cooler climate.

Snow reminded her of Washington though. And Washington reminded her of her mom. The whirlpool twisted until she was thinking about the baby she didn't get to see grow up. The baby she replaced with Evie, who would always remind Dilynn that she hadn't known her as a baby.

"Evie's mom... she and I have a lot in common," Dilynn admitted. "The whole scared of being alone thing. Evie said once.... said that I was just like her mom because I could never just be alone. And going from Sylvia to Brandon to you to Sylvia to you... it's just scary for her. And she was scared of Brandon."

She tried to swallow the guilt rising in her throat. It tasted as vile as she felt. Disgusted with herself for begging him to stay when he clearly wasn't interested. For giving in when he was an ass because she just wanted him to want her, even though she didn't actually want him.

"He was not what I used to think he looked like when Simone said you had a douche bag for a fiancé," Alex said. "I pictured you with some overly buff frat boy."

Dilynn sucked back a laugh at the thought of someone like that being interested in someone like her. Then she cast her gaze on Alex, and tried to justify again why someone like them would want someone like her.

She tightened her hold on her sweatshirt. The feeling of inadequacy was creeping up. The desperate need for them to want her burrowed through her mind once more, but it felt pathetic. Like she would do anything for them to stay with her.

"She never backed down from a fight with him," Dilynn said more as a reminder to herself. An attribute she wished she'd had. "I think that it was to make sure she never gave him any hint of an opportunity. And everything with Lyra and him, well that just made her hate me worse for bringing him home."

"I would never—"

"I feel like she knows that."

She began to pick at her lower lip. Searched for a sliver of loose skin to pull away and bring just a tiny bit of pain. A sensation that would distract from the rising need to vomit.

Alex watched the road with a focus that made her feel like they were waiting for her. Waiting for her to explain more, but she didn't know how to say what she wanted to say without potentially hurting their feelings.

The more she tried to find a different way to say that Evie didn't fear Alex because they weren't a man, the more it sounded just like that. She gave up, deciding to lead with the truth.

"I don't want you to take this wrong. So please, know this isn't me trying to misgender you. But I don't know how else to explain it other than that she doesn't seem to fear people without penises now. When she first came out of detention, she was scared of me. So scared I would do what her stepfather did. I stopped dating women because I didn't want her to think that I would... that I would ever look at her like that. She was with Casey though, and she thought I would hate her because she was with a girl. That's when I told her about Sylvia to make her feel better. But yeah, she isn't afraid of you like that."

Alex tore their eyes from the road, and a playful grin rose up their face. "I appreciate not having a permanent penis. Also appreciate getting to choose my size when I have one. Or if I want two at one time."

"Two, huh?" The queasiness in her stomach didn't go away, but she silently chuckled at the thought of Alex sporting two dicks. Imagined them wiggling them around like some proud teenager. Then she caught up with their thought process. "That's mighty ambitious of you. I mean, usually when you read about two it's alternating motions, not two at once. Sounds very, very full."

"I doubt sporting two in equal lengths and girths would be advisable," they mused. Then an eyebrow shot up in her direction. "Not one of your non-vanilla fantasies?"

She shifted in her seat, thinking of Alex kneeling between her legs with two strapped on. "I could be interested. Logistics and such would need to be discussed of course."

"Interested or excited?"

Dilynn sucked her teeth and sat up a little straighter. "A lady doesn't disclose."

"Pretty sure you're a succubus; not a lady."

"I'm pretty sure you're the big bad wolf implying your intent to defile me," Dilynn quipped.

"You know, they sell them. The wolf shaped dildo. Wolf, tentacle, cat." Alex stated. "I would never buy one, but they sell them."

Dilynn's eyes grew wide. She was kinky, and that was never something she'd been ashamed of admitting. She wasn't sure she was that kinky though.

"And why do you know that?"

"Lots of ABO fics, and one day I was bored so I looked it up," Alex stated plainly. "I do that. Look up stuff randomly so that I know more things."

Dilynn didn't confess that she did the same thing, too. She had never looked up wolf dongs before, but now she'd be lying if she said she didn't plan on doing so when they got to the hotel.

She glanced down at the phone. The hotel was on the opposite side of town from the restaurant. They had another ten lights before they reached it.

"Anyways... back to the conversation about my kid." Dilynn licked her lip. "I think she's more worried about what happens if you run away again, and I rebound with someone that I don't like just because I need something so different."

Alex tapped one of their bruised fingers to the wheel. They licked their lips and Dilynn wondered how the sentence they were trying out tasted. She missed tasting their words. They were savory and rich as they unraveled parts of her that had been coiled up too tight.

"Sylvia and I...." The rest of the sentence made them grimace.

"Are cut from the same type of cloth," Dilynn supplied. Her head rolled against the headrest, mussing up her hair. "The girls have pointed out that I have a type."

"She told me you would want a threesome."

Dilynn's neck popped when she snapped her full attention to them. "She did not."

Alex nodded their head slowly, and they tried out the sentence once more before, they said, "She did. Said that you have dark fantasies, and it would be better that it was her than someone else."

Dilynn flushed just thinking about it. It wasn't the first time the image had popped into her mind. Her brain was short circuiting. "I...uh..."

"I hate that she is right," Alex whispered.

Dilynn's chin dropped. "I'm sorry. There is just something about the thought of you two..."

Dilynn knew she was red. She could feel the heat rising in the car, so she opened the window and let the mountain air wage a war against her body. She couldn't hear whatever Alex was saying on the other side of the car, so she rolled the window back up.

"Huh?"

Alex tugged at the tie around their neck. "Uh... I was asking... um... you said that your story was nightmares, does that mean you don't like... the rougher stuff?"

"I believe I told you I wasn't vanilla," Dilynn answered.

She fiddled with the zipper on her sweatshirt. The topic of the story was something she wanted to move away from. She wanted to pretend like they never read it and for them to not bring it up ever again.

"Yes, but then you said...."

Dilynn took a deep breath and exhaled through her nose slowly. She tried to slow her thoughts down, but they bulldozed out.

"I don't want to talk about it, but clearly you need to. So let me dissect the characters for you."

She took a deep breath and launched into a breakdown of her characters before Alex could interject.

"Priya didn't feel good enough for anyone to want her. She took Morgan's almost predatory interest to mean she was desirable. She didn't feel that way, so to get that physical attention made her feel valuable and pretty. But Morgan always left right afterwards, and that took its toll on Priya. Like, she thinks she's wanted, but it's only on a carnal level, and the psychology of it breaks her a little more each time because she doesn't want to be just someone to fuck. And that's the piece of me. To Sylvia, I was just someone to fuck. She is loyal to a fault, and she treated me very well, but I was just a toy to be played with and she would—"

"I don't need details."

"Okay... yeah. Well, the thing is once she was done, she would leave. So, when she stayed the night this last time I just couldn't stop thinking that she was going to leave like she always did. And I could hear Simone's voice calling me a whore, and then I heard Sylvia's dad tell me to be a good concubine, and I just realized this is what I had become."

Dilynn twisted the button again.

"When we had our night together— I mean you and me, not me and her— it was like déjà vu because you were leaving the first chance you got. And I was covered in your marks. Not just the obscene hickey, like, if I had been murdered, cops would have locked you up. You left enough evidence on me that there would have never been another suspect, which is great. I liked it and I didn't not like it the next day, except that I had to watch the imprint that you left on me just slowly fade away, and it just... it sucked. It sucked because I never wanted to be Priya. I never wanted to be the person that no one chose, and so I kept doing more and more and more to make sure you would want me. And so, I threw myself at you, and then I would remember that I have done this before and it didn't work, so I would pull back.

"I don't want to be crazy. I don't want to keep making the same mistakes, but then the only time I know you at least want me in that moment is when your hands are on me, and I know it's not right because it's not what I want because I want more. I want to be wanted for more than what I can do in bed, because even though I am heavier than I used to be, I know I'm a good fucking lay.

"I'm not a fucking pillow princess and I have skills. I have things that I can do with my mouth that will make you want to come back. Plus, a meth flavored vag apparently, but I just wanted more. I wanted cuddle conversations and the things in the stories that you hated because they were sweet, but when you're the sub and the toy you don't get the sweet, so I wrote the sweet in the stories you didn't like and you took the one that hurt and that was a nightmare because it was too true and you made that one real. That is one you made into reality and I just wanted to be loved. I just want someone that looks like fucking Morgan because it makes me fucking hot and horny, and I just want them to love me and do the other... other dirty things too, but the sweet things and the things that say I love you even though I spank you and leave you covered in bruises. I just wanted to be loved when I don't have to be a sub. And I just want... I just.... I... I'm fucking sorry."

Dilynn held up her hand when they opened their mouth.

"Don't apologize. I have heard enough apologies, and I just... I just... I need to be done with the whole thing. So, can we please just stop talking about my stories and what you thought was and wasn't what I wanted? Just, like, try to get to know me by actually talking to me."

Alex tapped their fingers against the steering wheel again. Their eyes scanned the road, and Dilynn briefly wondered if they had spaced out during her overly long explanation.

They followed the prompt to turn right, and even used their turn signal. The clicking sound was enough to irritate Dilynn's ears. She hated repetitive sounds, and Alex's routine tapping while driving only added to the problem.

"So, you are a sub," they said while merging into the left lane post turn.

"Yes. And you should know I am a bratty one in the bedroom, or the house, really anywhere I see potential of... you know." She raised a single finger. "But only in sex. Like, you said the whole collar and leash shit and I want to make it very clear that it would be in the bedroom and no place else, but I would do it. If you did end up liking the real me. But I am not into the, like, being a pet thing. Like, the whole puppy or kitten kinks are not my thing. And I will never call you daddy; that's a hard no. I don't want to be a sub every day, all day. It's like, I worked too hard to prove to Sylvia I was ready to be a boss. And I think that's why I wrote sweet stories because I have never.... It's never been.... I am the boss now, and I am figuring out how to be a boss."

"My boss," Alex mused. They tapped along with the music a beat too late. "You know, I am all in for that, but it's still like... I'm going to do the boss on her desk."

Dilynn's lips scrunched into a miniature duck face. She appreciated how direct they'd been about their interest in the future, but this was a new level of bold. A part of her wondered if Alex had missed half of what she'd said about wanting more than the sex. If they hadn't, then that would make sense though. No one ever seemed to hear what she was saying unless she was yelling.

"You are, huh?" she decided to go with, since they were for once actually talking to her.

"Absolutely," Alex said with a smug grin. "When you decide you're mine, I am totally fucking you on whatever desk you buy yourself. I can't decide if I will be begging for my job, even though I will be a great employee, or if you will be the bitchy boss that needs to be taken down a notch."

They cast their gaze on her, and she swore they sat taller in the chair. "I have a feeling it's going to be the latter."

"You are incorrigible."

Alex nodded their head and flipped on the left turn signal. "Definitely the latter."

"Well, I can be rather bitchy and bratty," Dilynn declared.

"Oh, I know how bratty you can be."

Dilynn shook her head. A part of her was still annoyed that they had taken everything she'd said and flipped it back to the sex. Annoyance didn't sit in her tummy well, so she decided to give them some of her own acid.

"So, to circle back to your original question about my darker desires... would I ever entertain the idea of both of you. Yes, I would. I trust her like I trust you to bed me well and make sure I don't leave with any real physical damage."

Alex's brow furrowed and they glanced away from the road for a minute. "What about the emotional... the emotional part?"

"Well, yeah that, too," Dilynn said, not figuring Alex would give a damn about the emotions when they'd just blazed over what she'd said.

"I'm safe with you. I am safe with her. And she, apparently, has decided I'm safe with you. So, I think that's why she said it would be better that it was her."

"I feel like I would be driven mad with jealousy."

"That's basically the fantasy," Dilynn said with a chuckle. "I mean, I wouldn't do it for some sappy smut that is dunked in glue and rolled in glitter. That is the other stuff I was trying to tell you"

Alex's face scrunched up. They turned to her when they stopped at the light.

"I really don't enjoy vanilla sex, even reading it, and the stuff you used to post was sooo vanilla."

"You could have read someone else's story then," Dilynn snapped, now more irritated that Alex just wasn't getting it.

"I did," Alex said. "Pretty sure I have read all the stories."

"Well, then you don't get to complain about my sweet sex scenes. Some people like that stuff." Dilynn sighed. "I didn't even write those for the sex. The sex was just a biproduct."

"Those people sound boring," Alex mused. "I mean, I heard you about the whole sweet stuff. We haven't really had a chance to cuddle, but I would... don't laugh okay."

"I'm not promising you something I can't keep."

Alex glanced over at her. They took a deep breath, and Dilynn hoped it wasn't something actually funny.

"I want to.... I went the other day and I was at Home Depot."

"How gay of you."

"Rude."

"Anyways, you were getting on your DIY queer."

"I saw these rocking chairs, but it was a two-seater. I think when you say you want sweet, it's like that."

"I don't need gifts."

"No. No. Not the gifts. I mean, sitting on the rocking chair. Together. You and me, hopefully. You could drink a hot coffee and you could put your legs in my lap. And we could just... I could rub your feet. And it would be, like, raining and I wanted to buy it. I'm gonna buy it when you are begging me to touch you again. Until then, I will just have to dream."

Dilynn licked her teeth. They were fucking with her. Frustrated with their focus on getting laid, she decided that domme Alex probably needed a reminder of who is actually in control.

"I think I would enjoy you begging as well," Dilynn stated. "You're so cocky about getting on top of me, I think I'll wait for you to beg."

Alex's laughter was sudden, and they didn't understand. She knew there was no way they could understand how serious she was at this point. Because she was determined to make them beg now.

"Not going to happen." They point to themself. "I don't beg."

"I think I could make you beg, little werewolf," Dilynn said in a voice she knew would work.

Their eyebrow rose once more. "Werewolf?"

"You called me little red riding hood and called yourself the wolf."

"Well, I'm not sure if you are in the best position to be threatening me with the idea of Sylvia touching you." They pointed to the full moon hanging low in the sky.

"Why? You going to go into rut?"

She was about to laugh when they quipped, "You smell like you're in heat."

She tried not to make it obvious that she was trying to suss out the unique smell that was her arousal. Failure was inevitable, and they found her failure hilarious.

"You are terrible," she groaned, wrapping her arms around herself.

They tapped their nose. "I guess I have the nose of a wolf."

The GPS provided an update on the upcoming turn. It repeated the perfect amount of time to be annoying enough for Dilynn to shut off the sound. She decided she would be responsible from that point forward for navigation. She just wouldn't tell Alex that her ability to focus on something like directions was on par with her skill of figuring out how to start her car with a dead key fob battery.

"So, you want me to get jealous over Sylvia touching you so that I, what, break her nose and then fuck you in front of her?"

Dilynn snorted, drawing her gaze from the now silent GPS. "No more hitting people, number 1. And number 2, if you want to know what I envision, it's more of a competition."

Alex narrowed their gaze at the road. Then chewed on their lip, before they asked, "What if I lose?"

"You wouldn't."

"We've had sex once," they reminded her.

"Well... I chose you. I gave her back her ring and I decided that waiting for you to want me is... better."

Dilynn hated how much she sounded like that goddamn story. She'd considered herself a lot of things, but pathetic usually wasn't high on the list. Now, it felt like it should have been outlined multiple times and a circle drawn around it.

"I never stopped wanting you," they said, pulling her gaze to them.

She studied them for any hint of shift in their mood, but they looked the same as they always did. Wonderfully put together, and like they would be cool to the touch.

"Coulda fooled me," Dilynn whispered as she turned her attention to the window. She realized they had been traveling down the road too long. The GPS was trying to reroute, but Alex was driving the speed limit and missing every turn.

"What does that mean?" they asked.

"Turn right at the next light," Dilynn said.

The turn signal clicked. She waited for them to take the turn before she decided to play the role of brat.

"I think, I could drop my pants right now and start playing with myself and you wouldn't even be fazed."

Alex's mouth dropped open, but they shut it with a snap of their teeth. If Dilynn had known flustering them would cause the tapping to stop, she would have done it hours ago.

"Well, I'm driving so paying attention to you," they swallowed, "touching yourself next to me sounds dangerous."

"That's what I mean." Dilynn glanced down at her cleavage. She wore the wrong shirt to play slut today.

"Did you miss my basic break down this afternoon?" Alex asked, glancing her way.

"No," Dilynn spread her legs. She inhaled deeply to see if Alex could in fact smell her. Then she added, "You just used to be very hands on. Now you seem like you are afraid to touch me."

"Blame your ex."

"Sylvia?" Dilynn rolled her eyes. "Sylvia told you she wanted a threesome, so you put in place a personal restraining order?"

"She told me not to touch you."

Dilynn's whole body turned in the seat.

"And you listened to her?"

They nodded.

"What if she was telling you that so that I would get frustrated enough to go back to her?" She turned away and decided to kick them with her spurs. "I mean, she at least tried."

"Oh, I thought about it." They ran their hand over their face, but quickly returned their hand to the wheel. "She told me that didn't work though. That you were thinking about me. And what she said seems to be working."

"Explain."

Alex smiled like a kid who couldn't keep a secret. She knew it was a lie, but she wished it was true.

Tapping on the steering wheel again, they shared, "You called me to drive you. You could have called anyone, and you called me and now you're telling me you want me to cuddle you and do all the things that I wanted to do the whole time and you're talking about touching yourself to make me want you, so I guess I can't hate her when she was right."

"You don't have a story to tell you how to play with my head anymore, so you got yourself an inside man."

"If Simone wasn't mean, wouldn't you ask her for advice?"

"No."

They narrowed their eyes at the road, and Dilynn realized they had missed the turn around point again.

Before she could tell them to turn around, they asked, "Why?"

"Because I enjoy the challenge of figuring shit out for myself," Dilynn said.

"You don't like asking for help," they mused.

Dilynn sucked her teeth and wrapped her sweater tighter around herself.

"You know what?"

"What?"

"I don't like you."

Alex's chuckle tickled her when she wanted to be grumpy. Their words then danced over her like a truth serum.

"But you want me to crash us because you're a wet mess every time you sit in my car." They cast their gaze on her as they stopped at the stop sign in the calm neighborhood they'd ended up in. "You weren't lying about dating me just for my car, huh?"

"I'm not a mess... just aroused," she said, staring at the route that would require a U-turn and a confession for getting them lost.

"And you want me to do something about it. Right now. While I'm driving." They didn't move from the stop sign. "Just unbutton your pants and push two in."

Dilynn buckled down on her need to appear unfazed. "I wouldn't stop you."

"And that's why I'm going to keep my hands on the wheel instead of putting them inside you," they stated. "You want sweet. I can do sweet. I can do sweet until you can't handle it anymore. Then, Sylvia and I will not be the same in your head."

Alex continued straight, making Dilynn believe they had to know she'd gotten them lost at this point.

"Two hands seems a lot. Maybe one, but it would take a lot of build-up," she said to regain the upper hand.

She smiled when they flexed their grip on the wheel. The casted hand moved to lean against the console like she wasn't tossing lit matches at spilled gasoline.

"You want to do it," she prodded.

"I want to do everything with you," they admitted. "However, I'm going to wait until you want me to do it."

Dilynn pulled her sweatshirt off and leaned back in her chair. "What if I just take off all my clothes, would you lose control?"

The bruise on Alex's hand paled as they gripped the wheel tighter.

"No."

"You don't sound so sure," she replied. Her t-shirt was next to come off since she knew there was still a tank top underneath.

"When you want me, you'll show me."

She kicked off her shoes. "And being naked is not showing you?"

"Sounds like you teasing me."

"Sounds like you're playing a game," she said while twisting her hair over her shoulder to put the tattoo beside her ear on display.

"You stripping down naked to tease me knowing I will be slowly going mad is the game, and you're the one playing it," they said through clenched teeth.

She ran her finger over the raccoon drawing on the cast. "So, you're just not going to touch me."

"Not until you want me to."

"And walking around naked is not me wanting you to?"

Alex sighed. They waved the cast in her direction as they took the moral high ground. "You should be permitted to be naked without me assuming that I get to touch you. I won't pretend not to look. I love seeing you naked. Like, your boobs are just... and your ass."

"Sounds noble, and painful for you," Dilynn poked, because she was already committed to the dirty route.

"Feels like you are going to torture me," Alex admitted.

"Probably."

"You really are a brat."

She smiled. "I am."

They stopped at another stop sign and turned to her once more. "You know at some point you are going to beg me to touch you and I am going to make you pay for your cruelty."

"You know that sounds like winning for me."

"Is it hot in here?" Dilynn asked, tugging her tank top just a little lower.

"What hotel are we looking for?" they said. "Because I am pretty sure we were supposed to be there long before you decided to get naked in my car."

"Yeah, we got lost, like, twenty minutes ago," Dilynn said. She turned to look at them with an upward gaze. "I just got so distracted thinking about that time that you had me for dessert in the backseat."

"Gimme the GPS," they growled, tearing the phone from her hand.

She laughed for the majority of the drive back to the Howard Johnson Inn. Dilynn had to redress to get out of the car, something Alex found amusing. The smile dropped from their face when she got back into the car and handed them a keycard.

"I got you your own room," she said. "I mean it's the least I can do since you drove me up here."

"I could have slept on a cot in yours," they said. "Or the floor."

She hated that they didn't say bed. That their commitment to not touching her extended to a willingness to sleep on the floor.

"Last time I just got one room, I ended up looking like an idiot," she explained.

Alex parked and retrieved her bag from the rear compartment of the SUV. They didn't hand it off to her when she held her hand out. Instead, they lugged it up their shoulder and they made their way up the single flight of stairs.

Dilynn pointed to the first door they came to, and said, "That one is yours." She gestured to the next door down. "And that one is mine. It has a door between them."

Alex rubbed the back of their head. They handed the bag to her, and said, "I didn't bring any clothes. I'm going to—"

"I have spare clothes," Dilynn offered. She didn't admit that she was scared of them driving away and freaking out. "Plus, I'm bigger than you so you won't look like you're doing the walk of shame."

They followed her into the simple room. The bed was too big again, but they didn't make singles with beds not prepared to swallow her whole. She made quick work of laying out a variety of tops and bottoms for them to choose from.

She watched them move from shirt to shirt, rubbing each between their fingers before they picked up the more tattered of them all.

"Is this one your favorite?" they asked.

Dilynn looked over the frayed hem and the barely visible lightbulb exploding. "Yeah. It's soft so it doesn't chafe the nips."

They crunched it up in their fist, and Dilynn realized there was a chance she would never see that shirt again after today. They looked at the pants and held up a pair of loose sweats.

"I think these would be capris on me," they stated.

"Beggers can't be choosers," Dilynn reprimanded them. She dug through the bag and pulled out the basketball shorts she'd stolen from Evie. Tossing them to Alex, she said, "Something to sleep in."

"What will you be sleeping in?" they asked.

Dilynn whipped out her fluorescent purple vibrator. Bringing it to life for a minute, she looked them straight in the face. "I sleep naked."

They were still trying to figure out how to breathe when there was a knock on the door. Dilynn stuffed the toy back in her bag, before she opened it.

Evie and Sadie were in a hushed argument, but they stopped talking to take in the scene.

Dilynn pointed to the door in the wall. "Don't worry. I got Alex their own room."

She noted Sadie's gaze falling to the ground. This was clearly Evie's mission to play cliterference.

"Landon stopped at Denny's for us before he went to his Gram's house," Evie said holding up a large bag. "We needed pie after that loss."

Evie looked at Alex. Her breath rushed from her like an overworked mule, but she dug through the bag.

"Casey asked coach and she said you like the pecan pie, which should be, like, a strike against you because it looked like a snot rocket after a really dirty play," she explained.

Alex sighed, and Dilynn suspected Simone knew they didn't like pecan pie. Even Dilynn knew they didn't really like sweet things. They'd told her at some point when she tried to give them a cookie in her classroom.

"And green boogers for you," Evie said, pulling out another container and handing it to Dilynn. "I'm pretty sure someone should do a study on serial killers. I bet they all eat key lime pie."

"They don't give foster licenses to serial killers," Dilynn stated.

Evie made her way into the room, bringing her post game stink with her. Sadie's raunchy feet weren't any kinder, and Dilynn found herself yearning for a room with a window that opened.

"Lies," Evie declared. "I knew a girl in juvie whose parents were legit serial killers and she said her mom was a baker at Frys and her dad was a mechanic. Plus, they give anyone with a pulse a foster license."

Sadie's face scrunched up. "I lived with one lady that looked more like a zombie than a human and she had a license."

"I got, like, six other pieces because Casey said Coach sounded like she was smiling when she answered and that she said she saw coach with a black eye before she left school." Evie held up the bag to Alex. "She say some shit about my mom?"

Dilynn started to intervene, but Alex nodded, then said, "She did."

"And you hit her."

With a slight shrug, Alex said, "Might be getting fired."

"Well, you can help Mom open her school then." Evie handed over the bag and took the pie she'd given them. "You can choose which one you want because Sadie said she likes pecan pie. I think she said she likes it because Coach said you did, but whatever, now she can eat it."

"Thanks," they said, gazing within the bag at the choices.

"Yeah... you too," Evie said, before she hopped atop the mattress and started flipping through channels like she wasn't sharing a room with Sadie on the other side of the hotel.

36

Water droplets ran down the shower wall. The metal faucet, set to jet, beat away at the tension between Alex's shoulder blades. The water rushed down the drain with the type of purpose they wished for, moving around or over obstacles without signs of distress.

Dilynn's words about choices slammed against the walls of their skull. Choices to stay or run. Choosing to be happy didn't make sense. Things happen. People hurt each other, and Dilynn acted like they just chose to get to be happy.

Happiness just seemed so easy for her. Her being made of water and fire, which didn't make sense. Water didn't choose to be happy. Water moved around anything in its way.

Alex's hand blocked the trail of water, and it found a way around. Dilynn couldn't be water, because she didn't move. She stood still, forcing obstacles around her. She was the hand, meaning she was earth. Evie was obviously fire, while Sadie and Lyra were wind whipping through the streets.

The faucet turned easily, cutting the water off. Stopped the spray from washing away the night. They'd barely made it through dinner by bouncing their legs with enough force to shake the whole table. Something else for Evie to make fun of them for. Another round of word shaped ninja stars that she launched at them. They couldn't dodge her blows because moving meant running away.

Running was the way of the wind. They had been the wind for so long, like Lyra and Sadie. To be with Dilynn, they couldn't be wind.

The mirror didn't tell Alex who was the fairest as they stood before it in their towel. Its honesty wasn't about beauty, but a reflection of what one chose to see. They could choose to see more than the wind. Choose to see more than something no one wanted. They had to choose.

"I'm worth it. I'm strong, and I'm not the wind."

They walked to the door that would lead them to Dilynn. She'd left it unlocked, another part of her game to drive them mad. They could just walk through, but that felt wrong.

It was late. Probably too late, but Alex needed Dilynn to be awake, so they knocked loudly enough to wake her up, in case she was sleeping.

The thin walls announced Dilynn's approach. They prepared for the scolding for not walking in. They didn't think to prepare for the naked woman to throw open the door.

Without saying a word, she twisted the handle on their side of the door. "Look at that," she said, pointing to the handle. She wiggled it again. "Your side of the door does work."

She carded her fingers through her hair as she waited for an explanation. A lone finger ran down her chest.

"Okay, that is cruel, even for you," they said, gripping their towel tighter.

"What are you gonna do about it?" Dilynn said, with her normally adorable gaze of playful innocence.

"Not you."

Dilynn's eyes rolled. Apparently, her brat was only contained by clothes, a detail Alex stored for later use.

"So, what made you decide to interrupt me?"

Their eyes wandered to the bed. The purple toy lay in the mussed sheets, and a familiar scent wafted through the door. They let it caress their senses for a moment.

"If you really want me to touch you, you just have to ask," they reminded Dilynn.

"And why would I do that, when this is so much fun."

Taking advantage of the height difference, they stepped into Dilynn's sexualized bubble. They looked down at her. "You'd have more fun holding on to my hair like a saddle horn as you ride my tongue."

It would be a lie to say they were disappointed by her indifferent duck bill.

"Well, that's rude."

"What can I say?" she shrugged. "I was almost two minutes from orgasming, and you choose to knock on the door instead of coming in and at least letting me finish. So, now you get the bitchy brat."

They stepped back with the new information. Put in a similar situation, they would be angry, too.

"I needed to tell you that I have only been in one relationship." They looked down at the towel, regretting the decision not to dress first. "So, I don't really know where to go since we already did the first date, but then you had someone else's ring on your finger three weeks later, so I don't know how dating is supposed to work, because I have never really dated. With my ex, we just kind of started being and that was that."

"Very gay of you."

Alex's eyes dropped to the ivory breasts. Breasts that would only look better with their teeth marks wrapped around her areola like a chain.

They clenched their eyes shut. "Why are you naked?"

"Testing your theory that you can keep your hands off me." She smiled, gaze dropping to her chest. "Full moon an' all."

Alex knocked their head against the doorframe. The blood rushing to their head temporarily sated their urge to forfeit the game.

Dilynn seemed to sense the shift. Her arms crossed over her chest, and temptation was further removed.

"Well, we can high school date or we can adult date," she offered.

Alex rubbed the back of their neck. "What's the difference?"

"Well, adult dating is where we go out and get to know each other. It is not exclusive, but rather open, so that if in a few dates you decide I am crazy and a slob, then you don't have to commit to me."

"But that means you could date others?" They licked their teeth. "Like Sylvia, who wouldn't bother with your game and take what she wants."

"Not going to happen with Sylvia, but yes." They tried to remain impartial under Dilynn's studious gaze. "And that threesome talk that would be the only way Sylvia would ever touch me again, and it would only be after an extensive conversation between all parties involved. Everyone's limits and desires discussed."

They chewed on their already raw and sore lower lip. When they tasted their own blood, they knew their truth.

"I don't know if I can handle the thought of you out with someone else." Their chin dropped. "I... I missed Sadie's birthday because I couldn't see you with Sylvia. I couldn't handle watching her be the person I was supposed to be. And when she showed up Wednesday, and it was your birthday and she knew."

They took a deep breath. "No. What's the other option?"

Dilynn reached towards them. She hesitated before taking their hand. She placed it over her sternum. "You feel that. That thumping. It's for you, and when I first saw you, I thought I had dreamed you into existence."

Each beat of her heart felt a little faster. They wanted to believe it was for them. Wanted to trust her.

They couldn't be as sure and steady as Mount Dilynn. They could be the air that made it possible for her forests to live. Move the molecules just enough to create the rain.

Dilynn didn't seem to notice their thinking face, so she moved on.

"High school dating is not dating. It's what you did last time. We decide to be exclusive and just make a commitment to jump right in. This is the type of dating I always yell at the kids about because it seems to end really quickly."

They tried to sort through their feelings. "So, you don't agree with high school dating, which means you want to adult date."

"Or we don't date," she said. Her hand pressed their hand tighter to her chest. "I don't mean we are not going to give this whole thing a go. Just more of let's not do the thing where we go out to all of these dinners or movies and ask each other a hundred questions. I mean, let's, like, just be us, and not the extravagant stuff that all those fandom writers swoon about."

"What's the label for that?" They shook their head. "Because that was not an original option. You said there were two types of dating."

She let go of their hand. Shifted her feet until she was more in their room than her own. Her fully naked self just standing in their room.

"Let's call it being. Like, let's just be in each other's company and let things develop in the way that they should." Her thumb ran over the valley just under their collarbone. "It will give you the chance to get to know the girls a little more, and me. I mean, we've known each other for just a few months, and a lot of those weeks have been off. What if you don't really like me?"

"I like you, trust me." They ran their eyes over her hard nipples once more. Patted themselves on the back for cranking up the AC before getting in the shower. They should have their lips wrapped around them.

"No, you like the idea of me." She walked her fingers along the terry clothed barrier. Then dropped her hand to the space just under her navel. "You don't know me, and I don't want to just jump only to find out in a month or a year that you can't really stand me. I've been through that. I mean, I'm weird and I don't look like you. And I could try and start running, but I have really no interest in exercising. I like to be home, and I spend most of my time writing. Does that make sense?"

"Yes," they said, wanting to take her hand away.

"How about you come over for dinner next week. Not Wednesday, I mean, yes, come on Wednesday since there are no games this week. But not for, like, pizza night. Like, come for dinner with just me and the girls."

"Yeah. Okay." They licked their lips. "Dilynn, please don't cover yourself. I like looking at you."

"I'm not like you."

"You're just not your type."

Her eyebrows tried to touch in the middle. "I'm not my type?"

Alex nodded and pointed to themself. "I don't want to be with someone exactly like me. I'm not attracted to people that look like me."

Their hands ghosted over the curves of her hips and her thighs. "But this, this is heaven. Something that makes me almost willing to drop to my knees and plead for the opportunity to touch you."

Her eyes rolled, but she chewed on her cheek. "I never thought about it like that before. I'm... I'm going to have to put that in a book."

"You should. Possibly help a lot of kids," they said.

Dilynn let out a long breath. She looked them up and down. Then asked,

"Is that all?"

"Do you have something you want?" they asked.

Dilynn narrowed her eyes at them. She tugged at the towel they held on to, dropping it to the ground.

"Look at that," she said. "We are both naked."

Alex knew the game. And tomorrow looking promising, they decided to play. They held the door frame and leaned into her space once more. Their chest was millimeters from grazing her nipples.

"Is there something you want, Cupcake?"

She dropped her chin. "Ugh, you ruined it."

They looked down at her slick thighs, then the toy, still on, laying atop her sheets.

"Looks like it wants to be ruined," they said slowly.

Alex didn't give Dilynn a chance to say anything. They walked to their bed and laid back, with the remote. They flipped through the channels casually, until they settled on the news.

Dilynn huffed out an annoyed breath, but she followed them to the bed. They hoped she would crawl up them, conceding her defeat like the desperate sub she was.

She tugged the blanket until they lifted their ass so she could pull it down.

"What type of heathen sleeps on top of the blankets?" she growled.

They held their breath as she crawled on the bed. Her skin felt like fire as she moved her leg over them. Rubbed her drenched core over their semi damp skin. But she didn't give in.

She crawled on to the other side of the bed, like the stubborn brat that she was. Upping the ante, she laid her head on their chest.

"I like to be the big spoon," she said, nuzzling into the crook of their neck.

"I like wearing you like a little backpack," they said, just millimeters from pressing their lips to her forehead.

"I better not wake up to you between my thighs," Dilynn said, pulling her hot flesh closer. Her leg wrapped over their thigh.

"Well, if you need to grind against me in your sleep, I will be than more understanding," Alex offered. "I know succubus need sex like normal people need air."

They started to move their arm to pull her closer, but stopped. Whispering into her hair, Alex asked, "May I hold you?"

"Please," Dilynn whispered.

They smiled and wrapped their arm around her. It was a sweet moment, until Dilynn jerked the remote from their hand.

"I go to sleep to old sitcoms," she said.

They bit back the comment about her coming into their room and taking over their bed and television when she tossed the remote away after turning on Nick at Night. They just held her until she fell asleep against them like they were her body pillow instead of the big spoon.

It didn't matter though. Even the tingling in their arm didn't matter, because she was naked in their bed. She was touching them.

It wasn't an invitation. They decided that would be when she shoved them. She said that was an invitation, and they would wait for it.

37

Every shift from the backseat of the SUV was followed by one of Evie's growly breaths. Even after back-to-back wins, the afternoon loss sent them back to Phoenix.

"Sometimes you have to lose," Dilynn reminded her daughter.

"They weren't a better team than us," Evie said, shaking her head again. "It's one thing to be out played, but they won on errors. And mostly my errors."

"It was one overthrow," Dilynn offered. "One mistake, and it happens."

Evie's only response was her hand hitting Dilynn's arm. A tap for attention that wasn't followed by words. Just tap, tap, tap, and a finger pointed to the Ford truck parked in the driveway. Parked in the same spot it always used to park when Brandon came home.

The car was moving slowly over the gravel, but Dilynn couldn't wait. She clicked the seatbelt and pushed the door open.

"What the—" Alex said as they hit the brakes, resulting in Dilynn running into the car door.

She bounced off it and took off towards the house, barely hearing Evie in the distance.

"Brandon's in the house."

Her ankle protested every step. She couldn't stop though. Not when Lyra was supposed to be home. She'd stayed to care for the dog with four names. An animal that demonstrated zero heroism.

She could hear Brandon yelling as she raced up the driveway. Knew the front door had to be open.

"You what? Come here and seduce her. Climbed into her bed and fucked her so she would give you a place to live. That's what you do isn't it. Fuck 'em until you ruin their life."

Dilynn willed her body to move faster. She stepped over a ruined bouquet, careful not to slip on the flower petals littering the floor. They weren't in the great room, so she had to pause. Had to use her ears through the pulse that made her still feel like she was running.

The dog was scratching at the door to her bedroom. He was locked in and whimpering to get out.

"Say something, you bitch," Brandon snarled, giving away his position in the girls' hallway.

"You're not... not supposed to be here," Dilynn heard Lyra stammer.

Picture frames shook with the sound of a body being slammed against a wall. Dilynn turned the corner of the hallway as the mirror in the entry way came off the wonky hook, shattering across the floor.

His arm held Lyra up by her neck. Spit flew from his mouth as he screamed in her face, "Like hell I'm not. This is my house. I live here. You shouldn't be here. You shouldn't be anywhere near here. I came back to fix things."

"There's nothing to fix and this sure as fuck isn't your house," Dilynn practically yelled.

A face Dilynn had never seen Brandon wear before turned to her. He blinked twice, then let go of Lyra. His snarling mouth quickly shifted into fake concern.

"D... I... I don't know what bullshit she's been telling you, but it isn't the truth." He gestured to where Lyra had been pressed against the wall. She'd managed to move out of his arm's reach. "She's a liar. She always has been. I was just trying to help her—"

"Okay," Dilynn said, trying to appear calm. She held her hand out as an offering. "How about we go and talk about it."

Brandon looked at the wall where he'd left Lyra, but didn't turn in search of her.

Speaking with just her eyes, she told Lyra to go into Evie and Sadie's bedroom. Flicked her gaze to the right, as though she could close the door with magic. Lyra seemed to get the message as Brandon's hand enclosed around Dilynn's.

His touch made her skin feel like bees were swarming in her chest. She could barely hear over the buzzing of her own insides, but she had to keep it inside so that she could get him away from Lyra.

"I'm sorry you had to see me like that," he said as he followed her through the wreckage. "Seeing her here, I thought...I thought she must have lied to you. She must have spun this story that I am some predator."

Dilynn heard the click of the door, and knew Lyra was safe. From the corner of her eye, she saw Alex jogging up the steps, so she dropped her mask. She didn't need to stay calm because Alex would protect her like Morgan always protected Priya in her novel.

"Explain to me how fucking a girl that just turned eighteen isn't you being a predator." She tore her hand from his grip, moving towards the couch so he would be forced to turn his back to the door.

"It wasn't my fault," he said in that voice he'd used to play her. When he'd told her something similar about Evie's behavior being not his fault when he'd triggered her.

"Look, baby, I messed up. I called your mom and she said that I need to fix this. You're right, I made you a promise and I made a mistake. It will never happen again."

Alex's jog turned to a slow stalk. Their being moved with a silent grace around the obstacle course.

"You're right," Dilynn said, wrapping her arms around herself.

He hadn't brushed his teeth in weeks. Dilynn could tell from the plaque build-up visible with his sick smile.

"Okay, so let's fix this then. Let's sit down and make a plan." He gestured to the couch like it was his and not hers. "We can fix this by just picking up where we left off. You know, we're supposed to be married in a few months. We can send out the invitations. And get Evie's college applications in so she can move out. And Bella, well, Bella can go wherever she goes. I don't care, but you can't keep her. She's a liar."

Dilynn glanced at the hallway. She knew Lyra was a liar, but to give her a whole different name felt weird.

Alex held up their phone to Dilynn. The screen showed a connected call to 911. If they were coming, they were taking their sweet time though.

"We're not going to fix this," Dilynn said, locking eyes with Brandon. "You don't get to call my mother and make her feel sorry for you. You need to leave."

His hand shot up to the hallway. "No, she needs to leave. She's the problem. She fucked with my head, and now she's fucking with yours. She's probably robbing you blind, too."

Alex's quiet steps ended, with the red and blue lights dancing over the floor like a disco ball. They smashed the glass under the heavy boots they'd worn all weekend.

Brandon's body turned suddenly, and Dilynn saw the gun tucked into the back of his pants. He had come to fix things with her or end her, and that knowledge changed everything.

"She asked you to leave," they stated. "I already called the police, so let's not make this worse on anyone. Just go home."

"Who the fuck are you?" Brandon turned suddenly. He waved his hand around the house. "This is my home and that's my fiancé. I don't have to leave. You are the one whose trespassing."

Alex couldn't be here to protect her. She wasn't a princess in need of saving. Alex needed saving as Brandon reached for the gun.

Without a weapon ready, Dilynn was forced to act without thinking. She picked up a cushion from the couch and launched it at him. It was the most ineffective tool at her disposal, since a pile of books were sitting on the end table.

It tore his attention away from Alex just long enough for the cops to enter the house. Dilynn recognized Ryder immediately, in full uniform, standing outside. His long arms held Evie and Sadie back, but he released them when Brandon was on the ground with different officer's knee on his back. They ran in at the same time Lyra came out from hiding.

Brandon's voice echoed off the walls, "You fucking whore. You ruined my life and don't you fucking think for a second that I'm not going to find you."

Dilynn closed the gap between herself and Lyra. She pressed her hands over Lyra's ears and told her, "Don't listen to him, baby. I got you. You're safe."

"Who was that?" Ryder asked, following the girls inside.

With the danger gone, a different type of panic rose in her. This was another reason for them to try and take Sadie.

"That's Mom's douchey ex," Evie stated.

Ryder's hand rubbed the back of his neck and cast a glance towards Alex. "You shoulda waited outside."

"And you should shut the hell up and leave me alone," they snapped.

Lyra moved out of Dilynn's embrace, disappearing down the hallway to her room. In between the latest Trikru family argument, Dilynn could hear the sounds of drawers opening and closing.

Evie's head tilted and looked down the hallway. She didn't care that she was tracking glass through the house. She just stomped through the pieces of mirror and threw open Lyra's bedroom door.

"What are you doing?" she said loudly enough to demand Dilynn's attention.

"It's better if I go," Lyra said quietly, but Dilynn still heard it. "I need to get out of here before anyone realizes, but it's safer this way. I need a head start. Like we did with Sadie, so just... just go yell at someone and give me a distraction."

Dilynn could see Evie shift her stance wider. She used her frame to block the door, which told Dilynn Lyra would try to go out the window.

"Can you two just stop fighting?" Sadie raised her voice. "Just stop because you both would have done the same thing. It's who you are. It's in our blood, so just stop fighting. Because fighting isn't genetic."

"Actually, take your entire conversation outside," Dilynn commanded. "There's glass everywhere and I need to make sure everyone is okay."

Alex looked at the door, then back at Dilynn.

"I'm not telling you to leave. I'm telling you to give the neighbors a show so they will move out and make it possible for me to buy the whole street."

Ryder's face twisted up, but Alex's lips curled into a smile.

"Can I hit him again?" they asked.

"Haven't you hit enough people this week?" Dilynn asked, flicking her eyes back to the bedroom to see Evie and Lyra having their own very quiet fight.

"Who'd you hit this week?"

Alex shrugged, "Someone that said something mean about Dilynn. I had already warned her, and she said it again. So... yep. I hit one person, and I'm ready to hit you again."

"So aggressive," he said, stepping towards the door. "So, since you don't have a gender does that mean the whole not hitting girls thing doesn't count for you?"

Alex slugged Ryder in the shoulder. "Apparently, I can hit girls."

"You are such an asshole."

"And you are..."

The name calling moved to the front porch. Sadie followed her genes, giving Dilynn the chance to listen in on the conversation.

"Look, you heard him. She knows now. She knows that I... that it was all my fault. I lied to you all. I lied to her and to you, and she's just going to throw me out anyways."

"How fucking drunk were you when Sadie ran away last time?" Evie growled. "You already told us all that you knew about her."

"But now she knows that I fucked him to stay. He didn't ask for it. She knows. She knows I was the reason she got hurt." Lyra slammed another drawer. "I have to go."

Evie's body moved an inch when Lyra tried to pass her, but she locked her hands around the doorframe.

"Get out of my way, Evie."

"No."

Lyra pushed her again, this time putting more weight into it.

"No, and I swear if you don't put the fucking bag down, then I'm going to scream so loud you'll be deaf before I even run out of air," Evie warned.

"Just leave me alone."

Dilynn walked down the hallway. She wasn't as big as Evie, but she did her best to fill the space in case Lyra managed to get past.

"E, go to your room."

Evie let go of the door frame, but she didn't move. She didn't even turn around when she started yelling at Dilynn. "Like hell I'm going to my room. I just watched fuckface get handcuffed. She's trying to bolt. And you know the Trikru trolls are going to get into another boxing match that I want to see. There is way too much going down to sit in my room."

"Lyra and I need to talk."

Evie stepped out of the way, but she still didn't leave like asked.

The bag on Lyra's shoulder had her looking like a cross between a question mark and an exclamation point. Dilynn found both fitting, and she wasn't sure with Lyra what reaction she would get trying to talk to the girl. She had to try though, so she walked into the room and sat down on the bed.

"What do you want to know?" Lyra asked, scrunching the backpack strap in her fist.

"How about your name?" Dilynn asked.

"Lyra."

Dilynn looked back at the living room. Replayed Brandon's sorry excuse for an apology.

"Then who's Bella?"

Lyra shifted her weight to balance the bag until she no longer looked like a question mark.

"I was sleeping in shelters when we met, but one day I got there too late because of the monsoon and there weren't any beds left. He gave me a key to his place. Said he would be at the shelter all night. I make questionable choices, but I wasn't about to give some strange guy my real name."

"But you gave it to me."

"Well, I lived that skin for two years and it wasn't mine." She tugged at the strap again. "I realized I had to stop pretending to be someone that I'm not. So, you got my real name, but I let you believe that it was him. It wasn't though. He came back and he told me about you. Showed me your picture and I knew it was you and you were the reason I didn't have a place to sleep at the school, but he had a roof and a bed. So, I waited for him to get drunk and I gave him head so I could sleep in that room again."

Dilynn hated that Lyra thought this information would cause her to hate Lyra. That after four months, Lyra believed she wouldn't be able to see that Lyra was probably fifteen when she was backed into a corner. That she wouldn't blame herself for forcing Lyra from the school to the street that ended up with her needing that key to Brandon's apartment to begin with.

"I was seventeen when I met Sylvia," Dilynn stated, not sure what else she could give the girl. "I was seventeen and I had dropped out of college. I was about to be kicked out of the dorm in a week when Winter break started. I was going to be on the street and I met Sylvia and I let her take me to a hotel. I had never been with a girl before, but I let her take me to that hotel and did every single thing she asked me to do."

She glanced back at Evie still standing over her shoulder, listening to her confession.

"Sylvia did what Brandon did. She was an adult and she took me to her house and she kept me there like a pet," Dilynn added.

"I did it to get back at you," Lyra stated.

"And I did it to get back at my mom."

"I need to go," Lyra said, holding her hand to the door. "You heard him. He is going to come back here. He is going to come after me for fucking up his life with you, and if I'm here then you all are in danger."

"I won't let him hurt you."

"I don't give a damn about me," Lyra said. "I have to go so you are safe. Just like I told Alex to come back so you would be safe from Sylvia. I knew she was no good for you. But you got out. You got out and I couldn't let her make you be like me. You're too good, but I'm... I'm the problem."

There were a hundred holes Dilynn could poke in Lyra's statement. It wouldn't change the girl's desire to leave. This was what she decided she needed to do.

"What's your plan now? You have another place to stay?" Dilynn asked.

"Don't worry about me. I've always been on my own. But thank you. Thank you for doing what you did."

Dilynn stepped into the room. She picked up the black comforter from the floor and set it on the bed. The guitar Lyra had asked for leaned by the bed. The one she'd picked out at the pawn shop because Dilynn knew the kid wouldn't let her buy one from Guitar City like she wanted to. She knew Lyra wasn't going to stay because Dilynn wanted her to, but she was doing what Sadie did. Leaving pieces of herself here that she would want to come back for.

"Evie, go get one of those duffle bags from the hall closet. Oh, and a sleeping bag," Dilynn commanded. She turned to Lyra. "I'll pack up some food."

Evie blocked the door again. "You're just going to let her go?"

"She's not a prisoner," Dilynn reminded the girl. "You seriously need to stop watching so many Disney movies. We can't just give her Stockholm Syndrome."

"But she can't just leave. You rescued her."

"Again, not a puppy you picked up on the road or adopted from the pound. If she wants to go, then she has the right to go."

Evie's eyes stared into Dilynn; her body still too much in the way.

"What the fuck is wrong with you? We are supposed to be family. We can't do that if you just let her leave."

Dilynn cupped Evie's face. She held the girl's gaze as she tried to sooth the blow of Lyra needing to leave.

"Look, I know you hate this. I know, baby. I know that when people leave it sucks, but she's an adult."

While Dilynn gathered up the entire pantry of dry foods, Evie did as instructed. The bags were too heavy to be carried for a long period of time. Lyra seemed to know it, too, but Evie had disappeared into her room with a slam of her door.

"I guess she'll be happy to get her own room back," Lyra whispered.

Dilynn chose not to acknowledge Lyra's attempt at making light of the situation. "So, if you run out, or you just want pizza, then come home. The door will always be open for you, Lyra. You can always come home. And when we move across the street, your room will be waiting for you. I will put your stuff in there when you are ready. When you feel like you're safe."

Lyra's eyes were locked on her boots. The new boots fit her feet because Dilynn did that. She did at least one good thing for the kid because the guitar wouldn't be able to be carried with everything else.

"Why are you doing this?" Lyra asked.

"I can't let you just leave without doing what I can, and this is the bare minimum." Dilynn tapped the table until Lyra's gaze rose to her. "You don't have to go. Like I said, this is the bare minimum. I can keep you safe."

"It's better this way," Lyra said.

She made her way to the door. Her body was scrunched into a question mark again.

"Thanks... for everything," Lyra said, looking at the wall where the mirror had been the first time she came inside.

"Come back for pizza, please," Dilynn said following Lyra on to the porch.

The girl raised her hand just enough to wave awkwardly with the sleeping bag. Then she walked down the dark street while the Trikrus watched.

38

The argument turned into play-fighting with Sadie being bounced back and forth between Ryder and Alex in the front yard. The smile fell from Sadie's face first, then the older Trikrus as Lyra walked down the steps carrying too many things.

Alex knew it was all the things she probably owned. Except the sleeping bag she waved at Dilynn. Sadie started to follow Lyra, but Alex caught her by the wrist.

"Don't," they said.

Sadie looked at Ryder, then back in the direction that Lyra was heading. She whispered, "We had a deal. We wouldn't go alone."

"I'll go," Alex promised. "She won't be alone. If she doesn't come here, then I'll take her to my place. But Dilynn needs you."

They glanced up at the woman as the house began to rumble with music too loud. Dilynn was using the porch railing to hold herself up.

"I'll go, too," Ryder said. "If you go inside, and promise to stay inside, then I'll go with Alex."

Sadie studied the house.

"That's Evie's angry music. She's not going to let me in the room."

"She's going to need you," Ryder said. His hands ran over his face. "When Alex left and I was all alone, it was terrible. She just lost one sister. Don't make it two."

Alex never considered Ryder's life being more difficult when they left. They weren't close growing up. Each was expected to live in their own sphere of gender-specified existence. However, those spheres overlapped within the house filled with emotional IEDs planted under the carpet.

They ran their hand over the back of their head, then looked down at the girl who still seemed unsure. "You don't have to talk to her right now. Just go take a shower or watch TV in the living room. Sleep on the couch, just promise me you will not run away."

"You should probably hang out for the noise complaint that I am sure is coming," Dilynn called to Ryder from the porch. She locked eyes with Alex, "I need to help Evie through this."

The weight on Dilynn's shoulders was pulling her to the ground. Even though she'd slept through the night in constant contact with Alex, she'd spent all day screaming at the umpires. She seemed to remember Sadie had come outside, when she reached the door.

"Uh... Sadie, come inside when you're ready. You can... uh... sleep in my room tonight, and... I'll take the couch."

Sadie nodded, but her feet didn't move.

"Just go inside and watch TV," Alex said, pushing the girl towards the door. "I promise, I won't let her be alone."

"And don't take your mom's bed," Ryder said. "It's just a respect thing."

Sadie shifted her gaze between the siblings. She still hadn't moved, when the young woman who lived in Dilynn's guest house appeared.

"Hey, Sadie," the woman called from the porch with a small baby in her arms. "I just spoke with Dilynn. Do you think maybe you want to come play video games with me. Lyra brought the Xbox from the house out back last night. It's still there because we thought you all would still be up north. Would you, maybe, wanna come play Assassin's Creed with me. Lyra said you're better than she is and I need all the help I can get. And you could... escape Evie for a while?"

"I wanna go play Xbox," Ryder said. His radio went off, and a garbled female voice ran through a series of codes. He tucked his chin in and responded, "912J. I copy the info. I'm near that 20. Can you send me the 415E call, please?"

He scanned the neighboring houses as the dispatcher relayed another complex series of codes. "She wasn't joking about the neighbors calling the cops. Is she really trying to buy the whole street?"

Alex shrugged, then offered, "Probably. Every time she's says she's going to do something, she finds a way to make it happen."

"So, she wasn't kidding about being rich?" he asked with his eyebrows trying to touch his hairline. "What is the non-binary term for a sugar baby?"

"What's the term for an asshole cop?" they threw back.

"Cop," Sadie said. She was already halfway to the house, before Ryder managed to shut his mouth.

"That's you," he said, pointing at the back of the kid's head before she disappeared into the house. "You just walked out of her mouth."

"Better me than you," Alex stated. They crossed their arms over their chest. "And you are not coming with me."

"You could have been shot tonight," he argued. "Just let me go in and tell my niece to turn the damn music down. Then I will go with you."

"No."

"Don't do this. I told her I was going to go, too."

"First, Lyra isn't going to talk to me if you are there." They looked down the street, but the absence of streetlights made seeing the girl impossible. At least she was carrying her body weight in belongings. That would slow her down.

They turned back to their brother.

"And two, you have to sit post here because if I can't get Lyra to come back, then Sadie is going to try to sneak out."

Ryder looked at the house, then down the street.

"You think she'll come back."

"I think if anyone knows what she is going through right now, it is me. So, that means she's not going to trust you. I don't even trust you."

"Alex."

They tried to take a deep breath, but it wasn't enough. Their lungs screamed for more oxygen, but their chest didn't want to move.

Even after a moment of what could have been normal, they felt their walls going back up. He was still the same person. Still thought he knew everything. Only he was taller, and his voice had the same timbre as Colonel's.

"I can't do this," they say. "Why can't you just respect that I can't do this with you? That you in my face and wanting to pretend that everything that happened didn't happen.... You just don't seem to understand that I can't just go back. I can't just pretend that you didn't out me twice. That you weren't the reason I was sent there. You ruined my life."

"Please don't do this again," he pled.

His phone was fished out of his vest pocket. The screen was too bright for the darkness of the night, forcing Alex's eyes to adjust. The little girl had his eyes and Sadie's curls. Their eyes and curls.

He let the screen go dark and the smiling face disappeared.

"I want her to know you," he said. "I can't make up for the past. But it's the past, Alex. I was a kid, trying to survive the same war zone you were living in. And when it happened, I hated myself. I hated what I did because it ruined our relationship. You never spoke to me again."

"How could I?" Alex gestured in his direction. "You were the biggest threat to my survival. And all I was trying to do was survive."

Ryder's eyes traced the sky. His phone disappeared into his pocket.

The radio blared again, and Ryder listened. He didn't respond like they wished he would. Wished he'd have to go somewhere else right now.

"I shoulda defended you."

"Maybe, but it won't change what happened. That night was just the last straw because they were going to send me back," Alex said again. "This is why I don't want to see you. I have to keep going back to that point in time where I had to run away because you needed to be the golden child, and that could only happen if I was their problem."

"Alex." He reached out, but Alex couldn't let him touch them.

Their fingers clenched in a fist. They tried to fight the urge to hit him for turning their life into a living hell.

"I didn't know," he whispered. "I was a kid, just like you, and I didn't know. And I'm sorry. I will never not be sorry, but I'm not that kid anymore."

"I have to go find Lyra," Alex said, understanding what Dilynn meant last night when she demanded no more apologies.

"Alex."

"Just give me space. You're already in my life because of Sadie. That's as good as you get right now. Just let that be enough," they said. "I'm seeing a therapist, and I am working through my stuff, but I need you to just give me that. It's literally all I have asked of you, and you need to listen. You need to hear me when I tell you that I do not have the capacity to be your sibling, yet. I do not have it in me to laugh with you without wanting to beat you to a pulp. So, just back off."

The words must have stung because Ryder took a step back. His hands were spread from his body, and he took another step back.

"I'm still going to say hi to you when we see each other."

"And I'm still going to call you an asshole."

His lip curled over his teeth. "Well, that's rude, but at least it's words."

"I'm going to get Lyra."

"And I am staying here to make sure Sadie doesn't run away."

"Move your car down the street so she thinks you left."

"I know how to do a stake out."

"Don't follow me."

"Just go," he said.

So, they left.

The gas light came on as they slowly drove through the small private community. They scanned the yard of each house they passed, knowing she had to be there somewhere. She was carrying too much stuff, and she was on foot.

They hadn't seen the stuff left by the road, but Lyra could have tucked it into a bush. That would have taken time. It would have slowed her down more, but her pace should have sped up once she had less stuff.

Nestled at the end of a street lay a dimly lit park. Under the single light was the silhouette of a girl holding her head on a bench. Her bags surrounded her feet in piles, while the weight of survival pulled her towards the ground.

Bringing the car to a stop beside the park was easy for Alex. Getting out was even easier. Facing the kid, well, that was the hard part. Even though she didn't look like them, it was like facing themselves; it was like preparing a pep talk that they wouldn't have listened to.

But they had to get her to listen.

She had a home. She had a family.

She wasn't them, and they would make sure she didn't have to walk through the same alleys in adulthood.

"I was homeless for a long time," they said, still standing on the other side of the car.

"Did she send you after me?" she asked without looking up.

"No."

Alex didn't have to see her expression to know she didn't believe them.

"I've been where you are," they said walking around the car. Their fingers ran over the hood, but stopped. "That's actually a lie."

They tapped their finger against the hood.

"We're not the same. But I know that the park benches have spiders so the best place to sleep is just above the slide." They pointed at the structure. "But that one looks small."

Lyra glanced back at the playset. Barely over a whisper, she said, "I can't go back."

"She didn't ask you to leave. I know she didn't." They closed the rest of the distance, then sat beside her. "She doesn't blame you for what happened."

"May not blame me, but she'll never trust me." The girl held her face in her hands. "She shouldn't."

The crickets told a slow tale of trudging through the street. A kind of background music meant for heavy steps that didn't have a place to go. Cherished by one culture, crickets were pests in western places. No matter where the kids were walking, there would be crickets and shadows that swallowed the wander whole. Too many kids walked to the beat. Some fled with a faster rhythm, like Alex had but the crickets knew their role well. Creatures that only sang in the dark, would draw shrieks in the daylight as they moved about. Alex wouldn't let the world stamp out Lyra's ability to live in the light..

Alex studied the houses lining the street. Lights on in each with people living instead of surviving. But maybe not so much. They'd lived in a house. Still do.

They pointed to the house closest, and told Lyra, "Two kids. Hetero parents. Kids locked in their rooms playing video games. Parents fighting in the backyard. They use their whisper voices, but they are talking about getting divorced."

When her dark eyes looked at them like they'd grown another head, Alex pointed to the next.

"Elderly couple. Had three kids, all a mess. They thought they would get the big house and the kids would visit. But no one comes."

"What are you talking about?"

Alex shrugged and leaned back against the bench. They held their hand up to the street. "I used to walk through streets like this in the evening. Not at night because I didn't want to get caught by the cops, but around dinner time I would glance through windows and pretend to know what was inside. And I would make up stories."

"Your stories are depressing," Lyra stated. "Keep your day job."

"I wanted them to be real." They licked their lips. "You know as well as I do that it's not happiness and butterflies inside."

"It was there," Lyra whispered. "Even living with Evie could be described as living with butterflies. She might be a moth, but she likes them. Butterflies. She wants us to all get tattoos when we are old enough. Butterflies."

She snorted and wiped her face with the back of her hand. "I'm not a pinche butterfly."

Alex watched the largest moth they'd ever seen flying around the streetlight. They didn't tell her that even the house with open doors has walls painted in pain that were textured with angry words. That the home waiting for her was getting a fresh coat of rage as they sat there.

She kicked the bag Dilynn packed for her. "I was so fucking stupid. Stupid to think I could stay there, and that she wouldn't find out."

"You were trying to survive."

Alex could justify the lies for the girl. They weren't exactly innocent, and Lyra had told them to go back.

"I get it," they whispered. "She's a safe place in a world that really doesn't have any. There are so many that pretend."

"The only person pretending is me. Pretending that I could be something bigger than this."

"So, did I. I lied to her. I pretended because I wanted her to like me. Sadie did it, too. I hurt her... and you told me to go back." They folded their hands together in prayer but uttered no words to any entity. "You would tell Sadie to go back. Wouldn't want her out here."

"Sadie doesn't belong out here. She's still good. She's not a whore yet."

"How many people have you been with?" Alex asked.

"Creepy," Lyra said, scooting farther down the bench.

"But really? You say, you're a whore. What's the number?"

They could see the reflection of the light in her eyes.

"Do blow jobs count?"

"You decide."

"Then one."

"And Sadie?"

Lyra sucked her teeth. "Mas."

"So, is Sadie a whore?"

"She's a kid," Lyra hissed. "Doesn't matter how many people she'd slept with. She's a kid."

Slowly, Alex said, "And so are you."

Lyra looked up at the sky. She was good with math, and they wondered if she could calculate the stars with just a glance.

"Is that why you're here?" She turned to actually look at them. "To tell me to go back?"

Alex shook their head.

"I don't think I need to tell you that. You know you should. You know you want to be a part of them."

She kicked the bag again. "I'm too fucked up."

"Aren't we all?"

"She can't save me like she did with Evie and Sadie. But she is, like, talking about adult adoption and shit."

Alex reopened their lip with their teeth. That was the hope, wasn't it? Sitting on a bench with a backpack and no place to go. There was only one hope plausible and that was to wish for someone to save them. Maybe that was the real Superman complex. Not to be invincible, but to be saved by a hero.

"Do you need to be saved?" they asked.

"Sometimes it feels like it."

They looked down at her boots. Dilynn had put them on her feet. They knew because Sadie had told them that Dilynn took them all shoe shopping and that Lyra got boots with steal toes.

Her foot kicked at a small stone. It bounced along the sidewalk, only to find rest when surrounded by its own kind. Funny that a stone can find a space with others, but the two souls on the bench felt so lost in a world looking for their own kind.

"I think that we figure ourselves out through our relationships with others. Our environment shapes how we see ourselves." They pointed in a general direction of the Greyson house. "When I'm with them, I feel like a person. When I'm home in my apartment, I feel like a freak."

"I'm not you," Lyra reminded them.

"I know. You are not me, and you have a chance that I didn't have. One that I'da killed for."

Lyra's eyebrows cinched in the middle. Then her head dropped to the side as she said, "You ran away from them."

They tapped their chest. "No one gave me a chance. Nine years of doors slammed in my face. Of people telling me I'm not normal; proving what my family told me."

Lyra's laugh weaved down the road. They could hear it wobble over the gravel drive even after she started talking again.

"So what, I just go back? After everything tonight? I just walk back and knock on the door?"

Alex wiped away the first sentence that came to them with their hand. The second was a question. The type of question Dilynn would ask if she was there.

"Well, what did you do the first time?"

"Sat in my boss's truck for an hour," Lyra said quickly. "And then on the porch long enough to name the pinche spider by the light."

"And?"

She rolled her eyes.

"And I rang the doorbell."

"And?"

A smile pulled up on Lyra's face. "She opened it with a knife. She threw her ring at me."

Lyra opened her fist. The small diamond on a plain band sat in her palm.

"She didn't take it back even when I gave it to her. Just left it on the counter, so I put it in my bag for when...." She swallowed the rest of the sentence and started a new one. "He was a cheap fucker. Probably only worth $100, if I'm lucky."

"What happened next?"

"She let me in." Lyra's head bobbled from side to side. "Technically, she left the door open, and I walked in. And I tried the shit I did with him. I tried to make her want me because I didn't want to come back out here, and... I'm an idiot."

Alex's laughter came from a place that wasn't happy, but it tore free. Once it started, it didn't stop easily. It only grew louder when the girl began to glare at them.

"Me being an idiot is funny to you?"

They choked on more laughter. With their hand up, they tried to calm themself enough to explain. It didn't work.

"Stop laughing at me."

"You told me about second chances," Alex said, when the wheezy laugh subsided. "You're so worried about forgiveness, but you know. This is where you don't want to be. You were willing to sleep with her not to be here. She let you be there, and you walked out here."

"It's not funny."

"No, but it kinda is because she knows how smart you are. We all do. So, go and take your second chance." They gestured to the car. "I'll go with you, and we will create a new worst thing. And that will be going back to my place where there isn't color and there isn't cable. Just a stiff couch and a punching dummy named Gerald. It's not a home, but it's better than a slide where the roaches are crawling around under you."

Lyra looked at the bags. She kicked the bag again, then said, "Gerald is a name that should be punched."

"Gerald is a person that should be punched," they said.

"So, I just go back?"

"Dilynn told me about the hero's journey when we were on our date. I didn't know what she was talking about, so I looked it up. Something interesting I found was, it says you have to end a journey where you began."

Alex drew a circle in the air. Then wiggled their finger at the top. "You started on the porch. You need to end at the porch."

"I ain't no pinche hero."

"Me, either," they promised. "Maybe if you go back to that porch and say hi to.... What's the spider's name?"

"Jose."

Their head dropped to the side.

"So many names and you picked Jose."

"You named a dummy Gerald."

"Gerald was a dummy that needed to be punched."

"And Jose was a spider that came to pick up a ten-year-old to sell her on a street corner," Lyra hissed.

Alex took a deep breath. "Okay. Maybe squish Jose, then you'll start the sequel."

Lyra looked around the park. "What if the new book is worse than the last?"

Alex got up and slung the larger bag over their shoulder. With the sleeping bag in their hand, they said, "What if it isn't?"

39

The music was turned down, but that didn't mean Evie could hear Dilynn. She could have headphones in or be cutting again. So many things could be happening that made Dilynn too scared to leave.

Dilynn's head hit the girl's door repeatedly because her knuckles had no more knock left in them. She was in the process of falling back against the door once more when it opened.

The carpet didn't hurt as much as the wood. She blinked a few times trying to remind herself that the world had not flipped upside down even though Evie's eyes looked at her from the wrong angle.

"I can't make her stay," she said for the sixth time. This time to the girl, instead of the hallway. "I can't force her to want to be here."

"You made me stay," Evie said, pointing out her mother's hypocrisy.

She paced the narrow line left between the piles of rank clothes Sadie and Evie left everywhere.

Dilynn held her head, not bothering to get up from the floor.

"You were a minor," Dilynn reminded her. "I couldn't just let you leave because you were mad at me."

With fists at her side, Evie glared at her. "You said family is about being there for one another."

"Pretty sure that's from Lilo and Stitch," Dilynn corrected.

"Well, you said family means fighting for each other. Was that just a lie or did you just lie when you said we were going to make everyone family?"

Dilynn took a deep breath, then gathered her energy to push herself up from the floor. She didn't bother trying to stand with her weak legs.

Tonight was supposed to be good. They were supposed to come back and get Lyra. They were supposed to go to Olive Garden and have dinner together. Tonight was supposed to be a step forward together.

She leaned against the door frame and closed her eyes to hold back the tears. Evie didn't need a pathetic Mary Sue. She needed a warrior.

"E, if I could've made her stay I would've."

Evie sat down on her bed. Her breathing was shaky, and Dilynn could hear her daughter's attempt to be like her.

Every inhale burned, but Dilynn held each in turn. Tried to imagine her heart slowing down, so her mind could work through a better way to explain to the girl that she thought Lyra would come back.

"Would you've let me go without going after me if I was 18? If I said I'm leaving?"

Dilynn picked at her lower lip. It was dry and cracked because she hadn't drunk enough water while at the field.

"You said you read the story." She met the girl's gaze. "I never thought you would stay. Figured you hated me enough to leave the first chance you got. Just like you did that first time."

She still remembered falling asleep at the kitchen table. The agreed upon time had come and gone, and Evie hadn't come home. But Dilynn had waited, and waited, and waited. Waited until Evie stumbled into the house with Casey. Both were too young to be drinking. Too sexually active to be sleeping in the same room with each other. But Dilynn made concessions for the kid who'd been doing all of those things since before she met her, because she came home.

"My dad..." Dilynn started. She tried to swallow around the pill of grief stuck in her throat. It wouldn't go down, though. And Evie was waiting for her to finish. "He said.... He believed in waiting someone out."

A picture of a man too young to be a grandfather came to the front of her mind. She could have looked down the hallway and seen him standing there. He should have been there. Should have known his granddaughter. All four of them.

There would be four daughters in her house if he'd lived. She thought about that for a minute and realized that would be a lie. Had he lived she wouldn't have met the baby's father. There wouldn't have been a baby to chase to Arizona. She wouldn't have punished her mother with Sylvia. She wouldn't have been at Cactus High, so she never would have met Evie. Evie wouldn't have gotten out. Lyra would have been still sleeping at the school and not met Brandon. And Evie never would have brought home Sadie, which meant she would have ended up in juvie or the group home where Brandon worked.

"Why don't you talk about him?" Evie asked.

"Because he was amazing, and it hurts." Dilynn held a hand to her chest to keep her heart from breaking free of its cage. "Kinda like you never talk about your real mom."

"I would've liked him, I think," the girl offered.

"He would've loved you. He would've loved Lyra and Sadie." She wiped her face and cleared away any paths for tears. "And he would've packed her up too much stuff to carry very far. He would've reminded her that there would be pizza on Wednesday, and he would've reminded her that the door will always be open, and she would've known that it was true because she would've tested it already. Like you did."

Her fingers played with the carpet fibers.

"He said keep the doors open. Closed doors are easy. Locked doors feel safe." Her tears found a way out. "He said... he said that locking a door may make you feel safe but... then no one is there to help you fight away the real dangers. The ones that lock you in your own dungeon."

Dungeons of the mind. Dungeons of torture where the only trickster was herself. Dilynn wondered if Lyra was in her dungeon, and if she knew how to pick the lock of her self-created cell. She was brilliant, but that meant her locks would be as complex as her mind.

"Why'd you fight for me?" Evie asked, pulling her legs up to her chest.

"Because you're worth it."

Even cradled into a ball, Evie managed to roll her eyes. "What's the real reason?"

"That is the real reason," Dilynn stated.

"There has to be more. You didn't have to. Your life with Sylvia was good. It sounded like it was pretty easy."

Dilynn raised an eyebrow to Evie. "You want the thought process?"

She nodded.

"There's not just one reason," Dilynn said. "And when I made the decision, I didn't go through a process. It was just something I was going to do. Something, I knew I had to do."

Her head fell back against the door once more. "My dad wanted to foster, but my mom was against it."

Evie groaned, then said, "Surprise, surprise."

"My mom is driven, and I don't think she ever wanted to have me. I was a tool to keep my dad because he wanted kids. He wanted a big family because he was an only child. My mom, she wanted to be a doctor, and being a surgeon wasn't conducive to being a foster parent."

"So, you did it because your dad wanted to, but couldn't?"

Dilynn shook her head. "I wanted to just give you some place safe."

"Did you want to be a mom?"

Dilynn played with the zipper of her sweatshirt. Pulled it up, then down. She'd been wearing one like that when she told her mother she was pregnant.

"I'm going to tell you something that I don't want anyone else to know. Not Sadie, and not even Lyra when she comes back."

Evie rested her chin on her knees.

"You don't get to use this against me, when you're mad at me. You don't get to throw it in my face. It hurts enough without you weaponizing it."

She waited for Evie to decide if she could handle the information. Wait for the girl to acknowledge the request.

"I won't bring it up," Evie said. "Ever."

"When I was just a little older than Sadie, I got pregnant."

Evie's eyes opened wide, but she didn't say anything.

"I was fifteen and Dad was gone, and Mom, well, she didn't want me, let alone my baby." Dilynn pulled up the zipper again. "She arranged for a private adoption. Told me if I didn't follow through with it that she would kick me out, because Mom... Mom never believed in open doors. She wanted them all closed."

"Am I the replacement?" Evie asked. "Did you bring me home because you couldn't find her?"

Dilynn shook her head.

"When I met you, I didn't see the little baby that I had to hand over to the social worker. I saw me. I saw a kid who'd lost the only parent that matter to her. The girl who was having sex too soon and would end up on my path. A girl who was beautiful and would get taken advantage of in this world if someone didn't do something. So, I did something."

She licked her lips.

"That's why I didn't have a process. It was a decision. I was going to give you the life no one gave me. I was going to give you a home with no closed doors, and I was going to support you no matter what you did."

"So, you didn't want to be my mom," Evie whispered.

Dilynn felt herself let out a slight chuckle. "At first it was like... I was your teacher and I loved you, and I wanted you to be safe. I knew I could do that."

She gestured to herself. "I didn't have a mom. I didn't know what a mom was supposed to be like, and the only person I saw as a good mom was Loralie Gilmore."

"The teen mom."

"Yep. But... when I was writing the adoption letter... that made me realize I did want to be your mom. I wanted to be a mom like Loralie. One that loved her kid and that her kid loved back."

Evie's eyes scrunched together. "What letter?"

"I didn't give you the letter because right before the adoption you told me that I wasn't your mother and you didn't want another. And every time I thought it was time, you'd remind me that I wasn't your mom. Just like Lyra doesn't want me as that role in her life. And Sadie probably won't either once the honeymoon period is over."

A knot in Dilynn's stomach started to tighten. She felt the bile rising up in her throat.

"It's funny when you look back at things that you once thought were good. Like the Gilmore Girls. Loralie was a great mom to my teenage self because she had the courage to run away with nothing and give her kid a good life. But she wasn't a mom, she was a friend. A big sister. And when we watched the show the other night, I realized I screwed up with you and I would do it with Lyra and Sadie, because that's the only version of motherhood I know."

Evie clenched her knees tighter.

"I remember Brandon telling you, you weren't my mother. I remember him talking about when you two had kids. His image of what your family would look like. It was easier to reject you."

"Closed doors," Dilynn said.

"Closed doors."

Dilynn shut her eyes.

"I used to cry in the shower because you hate me so much. It hurt so badly because I do love you like you're mine. I can't imagine my life without you being my daughter, but when you asked if I would let you go at eighteen, then my answer is, yes. I would let you go because you had to decide at that point to stay."

"I'm sorry." Her voice was barely higher than a whisper. "I'm sorry I was so cruel to you."

"I know," Dilynn said. "I know how scared you are. It's easier to close those doors because if you don't have to see people leave it's easier. But if you stand with the door open, they usually look back to see if they have the option to come back."

"Did you walk Lyra out?"

"I did. I left the door to the house open, and I stood on the porch. And she looked back. She didn't want to leave."

The house didn't talk to them as Evie crawled down from her bed. She leaned against Dilynn, and let the mother hold her against her chest. They stayed that way until the door to the front of the house opened.

40

The daddy long-legs spider hanging above Dilynn's front door stood as an idle watchman. He remained at his station in the middle of the web watching Alex walk Lyra to the door. There wasn't any need to fear the spider, but the girl's eyes had stared at it for longer than she stared at the handle.

"It's quiet," Lyra said, once Alex set the sleeping bag and the duffle bag full of food on the ground.

"Which means Evie has calmed down," Alex said.

"Or she murdered everyone," Lyra stated as she glanced up at the spider again. She licked her lips, then shared, "I know those kind aren't poisonous. It's just... he had a tattoo of a spider across his throat and when I first came here, I saw it up there and I just thought, I never really got away from Jose. He found me and he's here to make sure I still pay off my mom's debt."

"You don't look like me," Alex offered, hoping it would make the girl laugh.

She gave them an annoyed side-eye stare that only a teenage girl could deal so painfully. Then her face pursed as though they smelled sour, and they understood now what Dilynn meant when she said she was getting tired of being called old.

"I just meant—"

"Neither did Brandon," Lyra interjected. "But I know what you meant. It's just weird. Like you and Sylvia. Yeah. Just weird but I guess, we all have a type, and I dunno how she ended up with Brandon, but... yeah. I'm not her type."

They continued to stand on the porch. Lyra touched the handle twice but pulled back like it had burned her. At one point they considered pulling Dilynn's move and hitting the handle just to prove to the girl it was still unlocked.

"Last time she had a knife," Lyra whispered.

"I bet this time she has open arms."

"Are you going to come in?" Lyra asked, holding on to the handle that she didn't click open.

"No."

"Are you going to come back?"

"I plan on it."

Lyra let go of the handle. "That wasn't a yes."

"I'm going to marry her," Alex promised.

They didn't like the eyeroll, or the fact that Lyra said, "Sylvia said the same thing when I told her to go away."

"Go inside, Lyra," Alex said, not wanting to rehash the whole Sylvia thing.

"That almost sounded like one of those angry parent moments," Lyra snarked. Then she smiled softly. "But if you do... marry her. Sadie and I looked up some names for, like, parent in different languages because it's different when you say it in a different language. Like, if I said this is my Mom and Parent it would sound weird, but if I said this is my Mom and Obi it would just sound like a name or a title."

"Obi?" Alex asked. "Like the Star Wars guy."

"No." Lyra shrugged a little. "Sadie found it, and Evie didn't hate it. It means parent. Not like mom or dad, but just parent. So, you could be Obi. And maybe I could be a Greyson-Trikru. And the next book would be different."

They'd never considered being more than just Alex. Never thought any of Dilynn's girls would want someone more than Dilynn. But they'd found a name for them. Found a name to call them as a parent if they didn't run away.

Alex looked at the door handle wanting to go in. They could go in and tell Dilynn that they had a name that wasn't Alex. But then they looked at the kid still not walking inside. The one that was no closer to walking through the door than she had been since they got back.

Their eyes narrowed at the innocent tilt of her chin. "You're stalling."

"I... I was just saying..." Lyra ducked her head. "Yeah, okay. I'm stalling. But—"

Alex didn't wait for the girl to come up with some other story. They took the step for her by hitting the door handle as Dilynn would. Then they did what they thought Sadie would do and hugged Lyra for just a moment before they shoved her through the door like Evie would. The bags were tossed through the doorway and Alex hit Lyra with each one.

"Go to bed, Lyra Greyson-Trikru," they said, then closed the door before she could run back out.

They justified the treatment as fair revenge for taking a moment that felt so good and turning it into something else. But they tried their future name out and didn't dislike the way it tasted.

After walking Lyra to the door, Alex searched Dilynn's yard and shrubs praying to not get stung by a scorpion. They could feel Ryder laughing at them from the police car down the street. They were surprised he hadn't come to shine his spotlight on them and taunt them as they searched the ground for a stick to get the spider down from the entry way.

After hearing Lyra's story of Jose, they needed to take away that reminder. Having said that, finding a stick to reach the spider was harder than Alex expected. They finally found one, but they had to stare at it for a long time to make sure there were not any insects that wanted to poison them on it. After several examinations, they assessed Dilynn probably had a pest service since she had a landscaper.

That stick was too small though. It wouldn't reach the spider that they needed to execute for Lyra. They ended up having to partially climb the tree in Dilynn's front yard to break one off. There was no doubt Ryder was laughing at them now. He'd probably gotten another call to go back to Dilynn's house for a potential break-in. But they had a stick and they used it to pull the spider down and take it to the driveway.

As it crawled towards the yard, Alex prepared to crush it. They wanted to do it so Lyra wouldn't have to be reminded of Jose the real spider or standing on Dilynn's porch when she thought she didn't belong there. They couldn't kill the daddy long-legs once he was on the stick, and they wondered if the part of them that wanted to be Morgan was changing. Everything else was changing, and maybe Dilynn could write a them in the sequel.

They couldn't see Jose once they dropped the stick in a bush on the far side of the house. It had to be dropped though, because Jose was climbing towards them. Of course, they weren't scared of spiders. They just didn't want spiders near them, just like they didn't want Jose near Lyra.

Happy they'd done what they decided was a 'they job', Alex got into their car and drove down the road. They wanted to just pass by Ryder's cop car, but they also wanted him to get away from Dilynn's house. He would be living too close soon enough, so the more space they could put between him and Dilynn for now felt more comfortable.

They rolled down their window and stopped beside his car. Unable to look at them, they spoke to the road that they were all too familiar with, "She is back, so you can go."

"Good job," Ryder said. He wiped his face. "I want you know that I'm not going to tell Colonel about this."

It had been a concern for Alex, and to not have to ask made them feel just a tiny bit like Ryder was finally starting to understand. They nodded, then said, "Thank you."

They studied the street the woman intended to own. There was no doubt in their mind she would accomplish that goal. With eight houses on the private drive though, they wondered how many kids she would want. She'd said she wanted one for each kid, but did that mean she would want more?

"Dilynn's a great woman," Ryder said, still sitting in the car typing on his industrial strength laptop.

Alex felt an uneasiness crawl under their skin. The first time they'd kissed a girl was Ryder's girlfriend. They hadn't known the girl, who had slipped into their room and crawled atop them. Hadn't realized she would end things with their brother the day after and tell him that she'd kissed Alex to figure out if she just didn't like him or if it was because she liked girls. And hearing Ryder talk about Dilynn brought it all back.

"Where's Allie's mom?" Alex asked, needing to shift Ryder's attention from Dilynn to something darker. To stop him from thinking about Dilynn as a good woman. She was, but not for him.

"Katie left me," Ryder said, closing the computer. He leaned back in his seat and rested his hand on the neck of his vest.

Alex's head snapped to their brother. "Katie? My Katie from high school. The Katie that you outed me about."

Ryder licked his lips and nodded. "Yeah. I had a crush on her since she was a freshmen and I saw you two kissing and I was just.... I was pissed because I know you kissed Dana. I know, that's why she broke up with me, and so when you left, I was fucked. And Katie was too though. She was always awkward and shy, but after you left it was like she decided she wasn't going to sit on the outside of the group anymore."

Katie was shy. The type of quiet observer that they appreciated. Her goals had been similar to their own. Graduate high school and leave everything behind. Movies had promised them both that college would let them be free, and they made a plan to go together.

"She started going to parties and drinking, and we ran into each other at one and I got my revenge I guess for Dana but... it wasn't revenge. I really did like her. She hated me though. Hated that one time got her pregnant."

Alex turned to face their brother once more. He ran his hands over his face, then stared out his windshield toward Dilynn's house.

"The trauma of losing you was what brought us together, and then we lost the first baby and we kinda hit a point that we could do this. We were going to be there for each other no matter what. But then Allie came, and I didn't know that naming her after you would.... I don't even know what happened to her, but Katie couldn't shake off the tears. She cried every time she held Allie until she stopped holding her. She just withdrew from everything and everyone and I didn't know what to do and I was mad because this was our daughter. Our parents had sucked, and this was our kid and we were supposed to be better because I wasn't Colonel. I was a dad and she was supposed to be a mom."

"She never wanted kids," Alex shared quietly.

"She left a note when she disappeared. She told me that she only slept with me because she missed you. The whole time we were together she wanted you.

And I think I knew that because she was the person that pushed me to keep looking even after I had given up."

Alex looked over at them. "I saw Katie three years ago. She was working at State U in the bookstore. I went to pay for my books, and she looked at me like I was a ghost. She wrapped her arms around me, but I didn't recognize her."

A soft smile pulled up his face. "She always wanted to go to college, but her mom had said she couldn't do it and take care of Allie. I told her anything was possible, but she was pissed and she said I ruined her life."

Alex squeezed the steering wheel. He'd outted them twice because he wanted the girl they were with.

"Stay away from Dilynn," Alex growled. "She's mine."

"Pretty sure I have learned to not go after the girls that love you." Ryder sighed. "I'm, apparently, the ugly Trikru."

"Your head is the size of a soccer ball. Of course you're the ugly one," they snapped at him. It wouldn't hurt his feelings though. It was a throwback to their childhood. A timeless taunt that they would throw at Ryder when he started to care what people thought about him in middle school.

Ryder ran his hand over his giant head and smiled. Then he looked over at Alex. "At least I don't look like a Q-Tip."

They ran their fingers through the curls at the bottom of their neck. Tomorrow they would go to the barber and have them fade the bottom. Dilynn had said it would look good, and they wanted to show her they were making changes.

With everything else changing, they needed to be part of it. They couldn't keep standing on the outside with everyone moving forward.

"I don't like that you're moving into Dilynn's house when you always try to go after the girls that like me."

"I knew you wouldn't." Ryder sighed. "But she offered. I know she only offered because it was when you two weren't together and she was trying to keep me happy, but the rent was something I couldn't pass up."

Ryder cranked up the AC in his car.

"Look, Allie needs people. She needs girls around her and Dilynn's kids are good to her. Plus, with all the new information... I don't want her to have to stay with Colonel so much and Dilynn said she would make Allie up a bed in the new house so she could sleep there instead of me having to drive across town to pick her up and then bring her back to school."

The radio in his car startled Alex. They decided he must be going deaf with the level it was turned to, but Ryder listened to the dispatcher carefully. He held the radio close to his mouth and relayed that he was on his way to the next call.

"Allie's birthday is next month," Ryder said, setting the radio back on the holder. "She asked me to invite you."

"I hate you," Alex said because that still needed to be a part of every conversation. "But I will come. For her. You will leave me alone though."

"I will give you the space you asked for," Ryder verified. "I heard you. You need time, and I will give it to you."

They didn't say goodbye when they drove away. It wouldn't be a goodbye, anyways. It would have been a 'see you later,' and they weren't ready for that.

They drove to the apartment that didn't have anything that they wanted. The number of times they'd run back here felt ridiculous now. It wasn't where they wanted to be, especially now that they knew what it felt like to sleep alongside Dilynn and the kids had given them a name.

The apartment was everything wrong with them, but they fell into the normal routine that they'd had for Saturday nights. They cooked themself a chicken breast and sliced it into thin pieces before they harvested the lettuce from their garden. The laptop loaded the fanfiction site, and they navigated through the stories. Each one they opened made them miss Dilynn's story.

After they showered, they pulled the shirt they'd stolen from Dilynn back on. It defeated the purpose of showering, but it still smelled like the woman. Burying their nose in the material. They were almost asleep when their phone went off.

It was practically midnight, but Dilynn was up. She was up and she messaged to tell them: 'I wrote a new story about my big bad wolf.'

Alex didn't respond, instead they opened the fanfiction site on their phone. The first story was new, but Alex's eyes grew wide when they saw Dilynn's username. She really had written a new story. Another alternative universe of Priya and Morgan with an explicit rating and a werewolf tag.

The air was trapped in their chest as they realized she hadn't just written a story. She'd written a non-binary character like them. Made them into a werewolf that didn't belong.

They sat up in the bed to read.

> Morgan dropped the thick rope and reminded themself that tonight would be no different. Bringing a fire to life, they put on the kettle to brew the herbs. They scraped their teeth over their tongue, already able to taste the putrid mixture that wouldn't stop them from transitioning. They would drink it though. It was the only way to keep Priya's stubborn ass safe.
>
> Safety wasn't something Priya concerned herself with, which drove Morgan mad. Where Morgan was measured and calculated, Priya was carefree and impulsive. The

woman cared nothing for their warnings, which was why they had snuck out of the village even earlier than usual to keep from her seeing them.

Their head turned at the subtle gasp from the clearing. They rolled their eyes at Priya's inability to just let things be. Because of course it was her. It was always her chasing after them. So, they hid like they used to when she would chase them as a child. She'd never been scared of monsters. Didn't care that as a young girl they could have torn her in two and eaten her like they had done to the boy who'd put his hands on her. That should have been enough to scare Priya. It had been enough to bring the villager's tales of shapeshifting wolves back into the pub.

"I know you're here," Priya called out, stepping on to the porch. "I might not be a tracker, but it's like I can close my eyes and follow my feet and I know it will lead me to you."

They rolled their eyes at her cheesy lines. She was lucky she hadn't walked off a cliff with how oblivious she was at times.

"Are we playing hide and seek now?" she asked, cupping her hands against the window. Morgan watched her from their position on the floor. It was still too dark for her to be able to see in, and they checked that the latch to the door had been secured to keep her out. To keep everyone out.

A part of them loved that she seemed to understand them. They liked seeing themself in Dilynn's work, even though she'd made them into a monster. Notwithstanding, she'd also written it as though they were the one who didn't want her, and they wondered if she was still scared of them.

They continued to read, pulling the shirt back over their nose. They imagined the words in her voice. Tried to hear her reading it to them, but this wasn't Priya's story. It wasn't Dilynn's voice. She'd finally written something from Morgan's perspective, and it was their own voice they heard when Morgan shifted into the monster they feared for Priya to see.

When they were able to stand once more, they could still smell her presence. Their claws dug into the floorboards, and they knew the stubborn human wouldn't just leave. Wouldn't heed their warning.

"I want your mark," Priya said in an even tone as her

fingers ran over the slick soft fur that lay over their back.

"I'm a monster," they said, gnashing their teeth, but not turning to her. "You can't want a monster's mark."

"You're perfect," Priya promised.

Her arms wrapped around their torso as they stood like the mutated monstrosity the moon created in mid-day thanks to the stupid eclipse. The touch lit their skin on fire, and they fought the need to do what biology demanded of them. Give the human what she claimed to ignorantly want.

"I can't control it," Morgan growled.

"Mark me," Priya said again. "Mark me and make me yours. I just want to be yours."

Morgan pulled the woman's arm off them, shoving her away. They tried to hold their breath, but they could still taste Priya's scent in the air. Her arousal said the same thing that her lips did, but she didn't know.

They stood, leaning forward just enough to keep their head from hitting the shallow roof of the cabin, and they turned. Turned to show Priya what she was asking for. She would never love them when she knew what they were.

Alex looked out the window for a moment. When they'd asked for Morgan's perspective, they had wanted to know what Dilynn saw in them. Now she had hit the nail on the head, they weren't sure how to feel about her knowing the darkness that lay in their mind.

The worst part was reading Morgan run away. The werewolf hadn't gone far, but they'd left Priya tied to the bed for her own safety. Left her while she cried out for them to come back. Shouted at them that she wanted to be theirs.

Their lower lip had no flakes of skin left to chew, but they chewed on it, anyways. Dilynn had sent them back into the cabin, and they felt a tiny bit of hope that she understood they would always come back. The almost sex was hot, and it reminded them of how Dilynn couldn't keep her hands off them, even in her sleep. She gave them the control in the story that they'd had last night. Even as she tortured them, they'd kept their promise to wait for her to be ready.

"I thought you would want me, if I came," Priya whispered, her face now wet from her tears. Her eyes closed, and she turned her face into their neck. They heard her take a deep inhale, before she pulled back. "I'll do as you ask. Go home to my mother and wait for you to come. I will wait for you, Morgan. Until you are as ready as I am."

She pulled her camisole on and wrapped the skirt around her waist once more. They leaned against the wall watching as she didn't leave immediately. The herbs for the tea were gathered and dropped into the kettle. She watched them simmer for several minutes, before she gathered her skirt in her hand and pulled the metal handle from the holder.

The tea was poured and left to cool as the sun drifted to the point that Morgan could see the orb through the window. Priya left the door open when she walked outside. Looked back at the house where they knew she couldn't see them.

Their heart broke when she looked down at herself. They knew the look. They gave themself the same one every time they stopped at the lake to drink under the moon. She had come thinking she was desirable and left feeling grotesque. And it was their fault.

They looked at the steam rising from the cup. If drunk, it would stop the full shift from happening when the sun dropped behind the mountain. It would keep their teeth from extending to a mating tipped point. It would make them too tired to fight the rope so they could go after the woman.

They couldn't see her in the trees anymore. She was going home to her family, a place they couldn't belong. This was where they belonged. They got up, running their finger over the scratched post. The notches of life lived as they had grown before the world flipped upside down. Before the grey buildings tumbled and the forest took over its rightful ownership of the land again.

They had seen the fall of humanity. Watched it struggle to survive as they fled the disease that didn't discriminate between beast and man. There weren't many of Morgan's kind left. Lone alphas scattered across the continent, each searching for a mate to bring their kind back. They'd abandoned hope of that until now.

Priya would have time to think about it if they drank. If

she came back, it wouldn't be a foolish little girl that didn't know what she asked for. She could come back and make the request again. The request they wouldn't deny her.

Or she wouldn't come back.

Morgan's eyebrows scrunched together. They glanced at the tea, then the trees.

What if she'd brewed the tea to give them the same choice that they had given her. Take the remedy so they could resist her, since they'd said they couldn't control themself. They hadn't told her they wanted her. Feared it would just become part of the pheromone fog that had lured her to them to begin with.

The sun crested the ridge as they held the cup in their hand. The liquid wasn't steaming any longer. It was time to drink, but she'd said she wanted them. No one had ever wanted them. Not even her gram, who'd said she loved them. She'd stopped loving them when she heard the tales of the shifter. Shifters frightened her, but Priya wasn't afraid.

They listened for the sound of her footfalls in the forest to hear if she needed them. They were the one who was afraid. Afraid knowing what it meant to not be alone.

Morgan licked their lips and watched the last of the sun fall behind the trees. Theor bones cracked once more, and they heard the twig snap at the edge of the tree line.

Nose held up high, they inhaled the woman's tulip scent as rain began to plunk against the weathered roof. They closed their eyes and listened for her heartbeat. They found it to the left and looked the shadowed trees.

"Better run, little red riding hood," Morgan called out. "Because I'm coming to eat you up."

Priya's head popped out from behind a tree. Her smile spread across her face, as she called out, "I'm not scared of you, wolfy. And I bet you can't catch me!"

Morgan licked their sharp teeth that they would use on her at the end of this game. They would make the bond and tie their lives together. That would come at the end of the chase. They pulled off the rags, and felt the rain wash away the shame of who they were born to be.

With a deep inhale, they picked up her scent, running

the opposite direction of the village. Towards danger that she knew nothing of. Their eyes shot open, and they took off through the trees to stop her. Stop her from running into monsters worse than them.

There wasn't a next chapter button. It stopped before Morgan caught up to Priya. Another fucking cliff hanger instead of a happily ever after with her in their arms.

They returned to Dilynn's message. Typed out a demand to know, 'Where's the rest of it?'

They could hear Dilynn laughing at them. Knew she'd messaged them specifically to further torture them.

'TBC, Morgan!wolf.'

They stared at the ceiling. If they had just gotten on their knees and asked to fuck her, she wouldn't be torturing them. That was why the sex scene wasn't complete. They shook their head, knowing the devious brat Dilynn was wouldn't have wanted them a begging mess. Dilynn wanted nothing to do with someone who didn't command her in bed. She'd said so.

Plus, this wasn't a story from Priya's perspective. She'd given them Morgan's view of things, finally. Made a Morgan wolf who was a them instead of a she. A them who was different from everyone else, and Priya still wanted them. Dilynn still wanted them. She was showing them what she wanted. She wanted them to play the game.

They got up for water. Needed not one bottle but two to wash away the need to taste the woman. They pulled the shirt up to their nose, and breathed her in. A subtle shake of laughter rumbled in their chest as they thought smelling the woman's shirt was something a werewolf would do. Yet, the laughter subsided because they needed to find a way to prove to the woman they were invested in not just a few moments with the woman, but the long term. They needed to show her and the girls that they wanted to be Obi and not just Alex.

There was a single truth they knew of Dilynn. She was a giver. And she gave them this story for a reason, and it wasn't just to play a game. She asked for no games and no secrets, but they knew she had wants.

She had wanted a dog, but Sylvia had done that for her.

Wanted a school, and Sylvia had done that too.

They searched their memories for something Dilynn had said that would provide them a hint as to something they could give her. Something Sylvia couldn't steal from them.

It hit them like lightning. Well, it wasn't painful and it didn't tattoo their skin, but it made all their neurons fire.

Christmas had been ruined before the mall. Sylvia had said birthdays were always ruined. So, they would give Dilynn a holiday. A family holiday would start a new chapter. No, it wouldn't be a new chapter. It would be a whole new story. The story of Dilynn and Alex together, and it would begin with a holiday that didn't suck.

It would begin with Easter because Halloween was too creepy and Christmas was too far away. Easter was next week though, and Dilynn would be scared to celebrate it because she'd only ever been disappointed. All of the Greyson girls had only ever known holidays as disappointments.

But the new story of Dilynn and Alex's family would be different. It would be a story of good holidays, because they were going to start a tradition. One that would make sure no one was forgotten. They sat down at their desk and searched through their drawers until they found the box of Christmas cards they'd purchased to hand out to their coworkers. More specifically Dilynn, but that would have been weird, so they got a big pack to give one to everyone on the floor. They didn't do it, but that was a good thing because they needed the envelopes.

Secret Santa had been the first present where Alex felt seen. They wanted to share that feeling with the Greysons, and maybe the girls would see them. Maybe Evie would see they were trying. Sadie would see they wanted to be there. And Lyra would feel a part of something.

They looked at the names they'd written on each of the envelopes. This wouldn't be for Dilynn. It was something for all of them. Something for the family they'd been running towards for nine years.

41

The next morning, Dilynn woke to the sound of the toaster popping and the buzz of her phone. Two sounds signaling two people were awake. Too awake for it being a Sunday in a non-church going family.

Her growl was low and hungry. She wanted what was in the toaster and wanted to throw the phone through the window. Eating required getting up, so she chose to find out why Alex chose to commit this vicious act of terrorism.

'good morning queen of the sun i was hoping you and the girls would come to the mall'

Murder was too kind for the human tormenting her. She typed out several responses, deleting each because she needed coffee. She needed coffee to make decisions.

A thought popped into her grumpy, grumbly head. Alex knew she hated morning. They knew she did her best not to speak before coffee. They knew she would flip over that message.

This was payback. A type of psychological warfare. They were trying to get a reaction from her because she had only given them a single chapter.

Well, if they wanted a war, then she would give them a war. She moved the sheet to hang just below her hips. Angled the camera to show only her hand placed above her core, hiding below the sheet.

She sent the photo with a message to follow. 'Only educated people get to touch the kitty. I guess, I'll be touching myself.'

She lay there for a moment. Pressed her thighs together enjoying the pulse at the thought of Alex getting all flustered. It faded after a moment, and the toaster popped once more.

Whoever else was alive at this inhumane hour was eating all the waffles she just replaced, and she needed one. Needed something in her stomach after not getting dinner as planned last night.

She rolled off the bed and tiptoed to her door. There was no hiding from Four, the dog with four names. He pranced around her feet, zooming through the living room to give Lyra a giant doggy hug.

"I made you a waffle when I heard you growling," Lyra said from the kitchen. She put the plate down on the table.

"You woke me intentionally," Dilynn stated.

Lyra sat at the table and began flipping through the pile of essays Dilynn had left without on Friday morning. Her eyes ran over the first page of the top essay, then she set it aside and went through the next. She made it through six essays before Dilynn sat across from her with a cup of coffee and her phone going off like Alex was giving her a play by play of their sexualized breakdown.

A small dribble of milk escaped the corner of Lyra's mouth. Wiping it with the back of her hand, Dilynn worried for the essay still clutched in her hand. Lyra held up the unblemished paper though.

"This one is the first one that isn't utter crap."

Dilynn's chest vibrated, though she didn't laugh. She pointed to the pile. "They are freshmen. To be honest, there are rare cases that what's inside is actually insightful."

Lyra looked back at the paper.

"Were they supposed to write about the hero's journey thing?"

Dilynn picked up a waffle from her plate. They were the perfect level of toastiness. She slowly chewed it, one row at a time. Careful not to disrupt the next line. After she made it through two rows, she decided to just roll with Lyra's aversion to talking about last night.

"Yeah, they had to write about a completed journey of their own. Basically, where they began, the call to action, the task, the abyss, transformation, and finally what it was like going back to where they began." She looked at the next row of the Eggo, but paused.

"You know about the hero's journey?"

Lyra continued to study the paper in her hands. "Alex told me about it last night. Said I had to come back to where I started. It was weird because when I came back it really was like coming in that first time, just without the knife."

"I think these last few weeks have kinda been a journey for us all. I know it has been for me," Dilynn said, before working on another line.

"Evie said your book was about a warrior teenager." Lyra crunched on another bite of waffle with her mouth open. "Do you write about your journeys?"

Sadie may be the serial killer, but Lyra was a heathen like Evie.

"No; really, I just write dystopian fiction, but maybe someday I'll write this whole story down. I kinda started a story about Alex's mean comments a while back, and maybe I'll finish it someday."

"I heard you typing last night," Lyra stated. "You know, normal people sleep when the sun goes down."

"I had an idea that wouldn't let me sleep," Dilynn shared. A blush rose up her cheeks as she added, "And it was a story to drive Alex crazy, which worked."

Dilynn nodded to the phone that was still trying to dance its way off the table from all the text messages Alex was sending her.

Lyra returned to reading after shaking her head. Milk ran down her chin once more.

"So, are you guys going to U-Haul now?" Lyra asked, wiping away the dribble with her hand again.

Dilynn's eyes practically detached from the optic nerve with how far they rolled back. "What is with you and Evie and the U-Hauling?"

"Well, you seem to collect broken people," Lyra explained. "And I'm pretty sure that next to me, Alex acts the most broken. So, are you going to try to fix them?"

Her candor was slightly jarring.

Dilynn looked down the hallway where Evie and Sadie still slept, then across the table. "I know that there is something there with Alex. However, for the first time I woke up and wasn't scared to be in my bed alone, so I need to own this right now. I mean, yes it sucks when at the end of the journey there's not the happily ever kiss, but that's the thing, I guess. Some journeys are more than romance, and the credits don't roll because you kissed the person you want. It's just not the purpose of the journey."

Dilynn nibbled more of her waffle. She hoped Lyra took note of how pleasant it was to not hear other people chewing.

"So, did your journey begin with breaking up with Brandon, or was that like a side quest?" Lyra shook the paper she was still reading. "This kid keeps talking about side quests."

Dilynn considered if this was all a side quest. Just a quest of many as she found the next real villain. And who that villain was.

Lyra was waiting for an answer, though.

"I think about that day a lot. I think about why I wasn't enough. I think about what I could've done differently." She pushed the hair from her face. "Honestly, that day began with me trying to convince myself that Brandon wasn't a loser. So maybe this wasn't about romance. I think the romance with Alex is another journey. I think, if I had to write the essay I assigned my students, I would write about codependency. I would write about myself as the villain. I would write about realizing my call to action wasn't to meet someone new, but how to be a better parent. Putting together the missing pieces of my family."

She poked holes in the waffle compartments.

"I think that really, getting to know Alex is something I want to do, however, these last few weeks showed me, I need to be the parent that I promised Evie I would be, but instead I jumped into a relationship with Brandon, and then if you think about it, like, I tried to do that with Alex. And that's not what I want for any of you. So, if you stay, then I need to be better for you. Show you how a relationship should look."

Lyra slurped down the remaining milk. Dilynn had to fight the urge not to cringe since the girl was clearly oblivious to the lack of table manners she didn't possess.

"So, Alex and you are like book two?"

Dilynn had written the story of her in relationships when she wrote Priya and Morgan. She couldn't see herself writing that story again, or something like it. She could only see herself telling stories of others. Let the story of Priya and Morgan play out in other people's worlds.

"I don't know if we will ever be a book," she admitted. "There are so many stories to tell, and ours will probably end up being side quests in other people's tales. Like your story or Evie's, or Sadie's. I think your stories will be far more interesting than if the Catfish Troll lands Princess MarySue in the end."

Lyra set the paper back in the pile. She grabbed a waffle from Dilynn's plate and bit into it without caring that there was a method to eating an Eggo.

"Do you think there's really happily ever after?"

Dilynn had never met someone with a happily ever after before. She couldn't find a way to tell the kid that though. To steal away her hope.

"I don't have an answer for you. I think there are shit times and there are good times. I think that the shit times help us enjoy the good times and force us down paths that give us more shit and more good. Happily ever after, I think, is when you just move on to the next challenge, but I don't think you can stay there."

Lyra's eyebrows rose. "So basically, no."

"I don't know," Dilynn said. "I'm twenty-eight. I can't cook and I don't know shit about most things that matter. So... I can't tell you yes or no."

Lyra took another giant bite of waffle.

"Chew with your mouth closed, or I will stab you with a spoon," Dilynn growled.

Lyra's mouth hung open with the waffle half mashed. She swallowed it semi-whole, almost choking.

After stealing a sip of Dilynn's coffee, she said, "Violent much."

"It's not even 8, and you and Alex woke me up," Dilynn stated.

Lyra shrugged and tore the waffle in her hand in two.

"Well, let's hope that book two ends with you in a momentary happily ever after, and book three does, too. Let's not live in books without happy endings," Lyra stated.

She got up, leaving Dilynn to read through the litany of Alex's perfectly grammatical resume of their educational accomplishments. It was followed by a resume of sexual skills and talents that would benefit Dilynn in various ways.

Red in the face, Dilynn confirmed she would get the girls ready and meet them at 10AM.

"We're meeting Alex at the mall at 10. Probably need to get your sisters up," Dilynn told Lyra.

Lyra set her cereal bowl in the sink, before running down the hallway. After slamming open the girls' door, Lyra yelled with her voice at full volume, "GET UP! WE HAVE TO BEGIN OPERATION QUEEN AND TROLL ROMANCE!" Her fist pounded against the door, even though it was definitely open. "GET UP! IT'S TIME TO PLAY MATCHMAKER."

The growl of Evie's morning call was followed by a thud and a groan. "Does no one know how to nicely wake someone up?"

Lyra's laughter was wicked, but she sprinted back into the living room. Hiding behind the couch as Evie came barreling out of the hallway only to lose her balance and slam into the wall.

"Mom! Evie hit me," Lyra said, pointing at the girl ready to kill Lyra without a knife or a spoon.

Dilynn added plaster and ice packs to her mental Target list.

42

Neon signs and vibrant menu boards illuminated the food stalls. Lines of customers snaked their way past the nylon strapped lanes and through the tables, eagerly awaiting their turn to place orders. Chatter on menu options, laughing, and enjoying the overstimulating space all hammered against Alex.

Alex had come straight from the barber shop. They were still getting used to the cold air on their scalp, but they liked how light their head felt. As they searched for a table, they hoped Dilynn would want to run her hand over their head. Hopefully she would like it, like she said she would.

The air was infused with the mouthwatering scents from global cuisines, blending cultural experiences into tantalizing hybrid options. Alex watched a family set a collection of purchases on a table. With a stroller parked at the end of one table, one parent of the two-mom family sat in wait as the other dished out money to teenagers of various races awaiting their share. Everyone had a different desire in the food court with so many options, but they would come back to the table where one mother sat posted scanning the space for dangers to her children.

The table Alex waited at rocked violently at the same pace as their leg. The ice clinked against the two Starbucks cups, neither touched as they watched the closest doors to the outside world. Last time they were here at the same time as Dilynn, the Greysons had disappeared through that door.

Sitting made it easier to move without actually going anywhere. Their legs bounced like they were racing towards something, and for once they felt like their life was on a trajectory that would be right. A place they wanted to be rather than a place that wasn't just someplace else.

They were smiling at the thought of the future when Dilynn came in like a lithium atom. The three girls circled her in their own orbits all chattering and shoving one another each time one got too close to the other.

Alex held up a hand just enough to catch the blue eyes scanning the crowds. She pointed to the Starbucks kiosk, but paused when her gaze fell to the table. She dug her purse from her bag and handed her wallet to Evie. There were obvious instructions being given, but the girls left with Dilynn's money as she made her way to the table.

Unsure if they were supposed to get up for the ritualistic hug in a very public space, they remained seated. Dilynn didn't seem annoyed with their choice, but she came around the table and pulled their head into a hug. Her fingers ran over the fresh cut because she yanked their head back by the bun they'd wrapped the rest of their hair up in.

"Very handsome," She praised, before she pressed a kiss to their cheek.

They knew they were still smiling at the reality that Dilynn had just publicly kissed them. It wasn't a kiss kiss, but her lips had been on them and it was a step forward.

When Dilynn took the seat across from them, she turned the drinks until she could read the labels. With a quirked brow, she asked, "Which one is mine?"

Alex sucked back their lips. They had purchased two drinks for the caffeine gremlin.

"Both," they said as the heat rose up their neck. "I wasn't sure if you were at the just waking up stage and needed your Chai or if you had hit the iced coffee time of day."

With a soft chuckle, Dilynn shook her head and grabbed the Chai. "I woke up to your text. Didn't want to take a chance that the mall would scare you away."

Alex found the girls still moving through the Starbucks line. "I'm really glad they came."

"Remember that when they roll their eyes at you," Dilynn said with the straw resting on her lower lip. She glanced at the cup and set it down. "Thanks for talking to Lyra last night. I know... I mean, I know between Brandon showing up and Evie blowing up.... It was a lot."

"I'm glad I was there," Alex admitted. "Also, glad Ryder showed up because I don't think—"

"I get it." Dilynn's finger ran over the circle of condensation. "How long have you been here?"

"Six songs, roughly eighteen minutes." Alex glanced around the space when Dilynn chuckled to herself.

"I count songs too, you know, when I wait." Dilynn held up her cup and shook it some. "I use these to consider if I should buy something. Each one is about $5, so when I am about to buy something, I consider if it is worth how many of these I may have to give up."

"Interesting system," Alex mused. They had never imagined Dilynn worrying about money when shopping.

"What's yours?" Dilynn asked.

"My system?" They played with the bottom of the cup Dilynn hadn't chosen only to gather moisture that they used to draw a sword on the table. "I count everything down to the dollar. I... uh... keep an expense journal. My car is the only thing I ever splurged on, but when I'm shopping, I struggle a lot with image so it keeps me from spending money on most things."

"Explain." She leaned back in her chair with her cup perched on the edge.

Alex pulled on their shirt. "Small example would be this shirt. When I must spend money, I ... I consider what the colors will say about me. I avoid things that make me seem feminine like flowers and pinks. I avoid things that make me seem masculine like baggy shorts and shirts."

Dilynn chewed on her bottom lip. They tried to prepare for whatever question they knew would be coming, and had to school their face when she said, "So, you don't have a gender, but you think colors do."

Colors didn't have a gender. They knew this. They knew that people assigned gender to colors. Colors didn't have a gender though.

"If Landon wore a pink shirt, would you think him a girl?" Dilynn asked.

Alex shook their head.

"And you bought me a blue sweater. Does that mean you think—"

"First, you scream nothing but big dick energy," Alex confessed. They held up their hand when Dilynn opened her mouth again. "And second, I see where you are going, but when people look at me, they see a girl."

"Well, once someone looked at a woman drowning and said, 'there's half fish-half woman,' and poof we have mermaids."

Alex's mouth opened and closed but they couldn't make words.

"I guess what I'm saying is fuck other people." Dilynn took a drink and stared across the table, daring Alex to challenge her.

"I don't really want to fuck other people." Alex looked away, then cast a devious glance in Dilynn's direction. Before Dilynn could retort, Alex added, "It's a me thing. For so long I felt like I gave everything up to be me in my own skin, but I don't really know what that means to be me. Like, do I have to be androgenous to be me? And I think that's why when you gave me that tie, I felt so seen. I always wanted to try one on, but I worried people would think I'm trans or butch, but really, I just wanted to wear a tie."

"You look very good in ties," Dilynn mused. "Bet you could pull off suspenders even better."

Alex's head fell to the side. They'd never considered suspenders.

"Like, the ones with buttons though. Not the clips. The buttons just add this tailored look to the whole thing."

"Sounds expensive," Alex whispered. They fondled the envelopes they were holding under the table. The cash within was already stressing them out, but it still felt right.

"When I first read your comment on my story about your identity, I sat there and tried to figure out what it meant to feel like a girl." Dilynn tugged at her shirt. "Then considered what it would be like to be male. Not going to lie I had some crazy detours in that thought process like what it would feel like to do the helicopter. And I didn't find an answer, but it did lead to some super hilarious conversations with my pizza night people."

"Like?"

Dilynn's face was a shade of pink they adored. She leaned over the table, as her eyes scanned the tables around them.

"So, first you need to know that when I am not making pizza, the conversations are always borderline inappropriate, which is why the adults sit away from the kids." She paused and looked over her shoulder at the girls gathering their drinks. "Anyways, I wondered if being in a different body meant you worried about different things when it came to mundane tasks."

Dilynn covered her face, only to peek through her fingers as she confessed, "I actually asked Jordan how he wiped his ass."

Alex took a sip of coffee to do something. It was a mistake because it tasted like watery nut juice with so much sugar. They tried to ignore the nastiness in their mouth as they choke out, "You what?"

She moved forward in her chair, eyes wide and shining.

"Well, first, I'm weird and I like to know things. I was going to the bathroom, and I wondered if guys had to move their junk to wipe their ass. I didn't have anyone else to ask. Thankfully, he was cool about it, but that led us down a rabbit hole to tip touching and Marcus turned so fucking red when Jackie Parker, you know, the SPED teacher, anyways, she started talking about her vibrator. Like his face was soaked and it was just... hilarious."

Dilynn took another sip of her drink and changed the subject entirely. "So, we are here for... what?"

The girls' voices were close by, and they had meant to talk to Dilynn about their plan beforehand.

"Thanks for bringing the girls with you," Alex said again.

A crease ran across Dilynn's forehead.

"Evie is PMSing and Lyra is exceptionally solemn today, so maybe don't thank me yet."

Eagerly nodding, Alex pulled out a pile of envelopes from under the table. They didn't have time to explain before the kids surrounded them.

"Sup, troll," Evie said, sitting as close to her mom as possible.

"Be nice," Dilynn hissed lowly. "Alex invited you here."

The girl rolled her eyes and leaned as far back in her chair as possible.

"Good morning, Evie," Alex said. They tapped the envelopes on the table. "So, I was just telling your mom that I'm glad you all were willing to come today because I have an idea, and I am hoping you all will be interested in participating."

"I like your hair cut," Sadie offered.

They didn't get to thank Sadie, before Evie sighed loudly. "So, what's the big idea."

"Uh... Easter is coming up," Alex fumbled. They gestured towards the entrance that the girls had walked through that was mostly blocked with the photo shoot area.

"Are we doing like photos with the creepy bunny?" Evie asked, shaking her head no already.

"Please tell me there are not photos today," Dilynn pleaded.

"No. No photos." Alex rubbed their face and looked down at the envelopes again. "Uh... holidays have never been something I particularly looked forward to, but I was thinking last night about the birthdays I missed and that we all seemed to have a crappy Christmas, and I figured we all have had some pretty bad experiences in the past."

"You can say that again," Lyra said.

"Fucking hate Christmas," Evie grumbled.

Alex looked at the first envelope with Dilynn's name on it. They wanted that envelope, but they handed it off to Lyra. Then gave Evie the one that said Sadie. They handed their envelope to Sadie, and Lyra's to Dilynn. They kept Evie's for themselves, replaying Sylvia's words in their head to wear the broody one down.

"Secret Santa this last Christmas was probably the best holiday I have ever had," Alex confessed. Their eyes flitted to Dilynn. "I was lucky and had someone that cared enough to do something special for me."

"Me, too," Dilynn whispered. She ran her finger over Lyra's name. "So, we are doing a Secret Bunny."

Alex licked their lips. "I don't think it really needs to be a secret. I mean, there are only five of us. I thought that we could just take the time to get one person something special and that way no one gets forgotten."

Lyra opened her envelope. "Fifty bucks?"

"Yeah." Alex tried not to stress about the cash they'd withdrawn once more. "I put $50 in each envelope and all $50 should be spent. No gift cards. It should be something you feel that person really wants. No needs. Your mom always takes care of the needs so no basics."

"Like socks?" Evie asked.

"Exactly," Alex said. "No socks. No hair care products."

"Can I spend more than $50?" Lyra asked, staring at her envelope.

"I... I can't stop you," Alex said. "But let's try to stay in the $50 range."

"This actually isn't a shitty idea, Alex," Evie said, shoving her envelope into her pocket.

They felt a stitch being sewn into the hole in their heart. Moving from Troll to Alex was a step forward instead of backwards.

"Thank you, Evie," they said.

"You know, most people don't feel the need to say people's names constantly," Dilynn added. "Like, the fact that you two do that is pretty weird."

"So, we are just all going to go shopping now?" Sadie asked. She looked down at her envelope, then ran her eyes over them. "How... are we going to keep it a secret?"

"We split up," Evie said. She glanced at her phone. "Landon should be here soon, so I'll go with him since I have Saddie Bear. Lyra and Sadie can go together, since they have you guys, and then you two can go pretend not to be dating."

Dilynn's eyes rolled, but the kids seemed to be in agreement and began to gather themselves.

Alex got up, taking Dilynn's second coffee with them. They walked through the mall, pausing outside of Sephora.

"I asked you here because of last time," Alex confessed as they paused alongside the railing that overlooked the first floor. "I kinda wanted to maybe come back here as, like, a start over."

"Why?" Dilynn asked. "Like, of all places to start over, why here?"

"I was coming to rescue you and Evie," they confessed. "I had this version of you in my head. Queen Greyson, and I would be your knight in shining armor, but instead of playing the hero, I was the coward."

They squeezed the railing.

"I have to close this chapter."

"Did you talk about books and chapters with Lyra last night?" Dilynn squinted at them, searching for the answer to her question.

"Yes."

Dilynn leaned against the railing. She finished off her first drink and tossed it in the trash bin not far from where they stood.

"I didn't think you were listening when I told you about the Hero's Journey. You honestly rolled your eyes so many times, but then you had moments of being sweet, so I figured you didn't realize you were doing it."

Flashes of their date played out in their head. They didn't even realize they were rolling their eyes.

"I'm sorry. I was listening, but I was also freaking out. That was my first date. Like a real date."

A bubble wrapped around them, drowning out the conversations and squeaky sneakers passing by them. It soundproofed even the music, so Alex didn't know how long they stood there waiting for Dilynn to say something.

"What's making the wheels in your head grind together so loud?" she finally asked.

"Your story."

Dilynn groaned and she ripped the second coffee from Alex's hand.

"Again?"

Nodding their head, Alex tried to come up with a way to explain. "It's the chapter I need to close. I read your story."

"You were a troll," Dilynn reminded them.

They hated that it was the truth. "I was a troll."

"Then a catfish."

"A catfish smelling troll, yes."

Dilynn didn't look up when she asked, "Why?"

"Morgan was the first time I saw myself in a book. I mean, she wasn't non-binary, but her anger and protectiveness... I just connected. She'd lost everything, and still built a world where Atlas could bring something other than war."

"The war is coming," Dilynn whispered. "Legend is going to lose a hand. However, that little shit made fun of my driving, so I don't even feel bad about it anymore."

Alex stood up straighter. Wars in books meant characters die and Alex didn't want any of them to die. Especially since they knew now that each character was a piece of Dilynn.

"Is there a way for there not to be a war?" they asked, tapping their finger on the railing.

Dilynn shook her head.

"Why can't there not be a war?"

She swirled the liquid around the cup in her hand. Lips smooshed in contemplation as she prepared some reasoning that would make sense, but they would hate it.

"People fight for what they think they are entitled to, and Atlas's world of unity just doesn't fit with human nature, so she is going to have to solve disputes amongst clans, which mean nothing when her territory becomes threatened. Atlas can't compromise if she doesn't want to be seen as weak."

"Compromising is not weakness," Alex tried, hoping they could change her mind.

"You say that, but when I wrote Priya trying to compromise, you called her a Mary Sue, so she has to be strong and Atlas has to be strong, which means following rules that she sets even when she doesn't like them."

The air in Alex's lungs rushed out. Dilynn can't let them go to war. The whole first book is about the pointlessness of war, and she has the chance to show that the world doesn't need war.

They ran their tongue over their teeth, then came up with a strategy.

"Do you follow the rules?" they asked.

"What rules?"

"Any rules."

She shrugged.

"I don't believe in rules. I mean, we have house rules, but they are really just there because it looked cool on a chalk board. There's still yelling, and hitting, and biting. You should see the teeth impressions Sadie left on Evie when they were fighting over the last Eggo Thursday."

She took another sip before leaning over the railing. She was so far that they worried she was going to fall off the edge.

"Rules create boxes we don't fit in, so we have to break them. When we break them, we have to serve the consequence. When we don't break them, we still serve a consequence. Example, you don't fit in the box society tries to put you in. You reject the rules, so if you don't believe in them to begin with, then the rules don't apply to you. I feel like you are so lost in the rules of who you should be that it's hard to accept who you are."

Alex watched the people walking around the mall like ants gathering whatever they could find. There seemed to be no reason or function to their movements, but Alex understood that it was all still part of the roles they were each cast in life.

"Do you always make everyone question everything?"

A rare real smile played on Dilynn's lips. She took a long drink from the cup, before she let them in on a secret.

"That's why my kids love my class. There are no rules they have to fit; they get to think and explore without fear because there is no right answer. Just like I don't know if there is a right answer to what it means to be a girl or a boy or neither. Most people though, believe they have the right answer, so they go to war for their beliefs."

She moved a tad closer to Alex. Just enough that their arms grazed when she swayed slightly.

"Atlas believes that love can rule a people. Morgan helps because she instills fear in the people. But the people that are coming in book two... they have no love for Atlas and no fear for Morgan, and they think they know the right answer. So, there will be a war and people will die. Many will die because that's what happens in war."

"Can you please not kill Morgan?" Alex asked.

She shook her head. It was subtle but the butterfly effect made them feel like an earthquake was hitting.

"Good news is you have expanded my understanding of people, so I am actively writing a prequel that explains how society flipped from a patriarchy to a matriarchy, and I am writing it with several characters that have no gender identity."

A book with characters like them. One that would explain pronouns in a way that, maybe, people wouldn't argue with them about being a they.

The world stopped spinning for a minute. They tried to imagine what a world with just theys and thems would look like. Alex had never met someone like them before, except in the comment sections of fics.

"So, you are okay with being with someone that is nonbinary?" Alex asked.

Dilynn tilted her head and studied them. Then without reason, she placed a hand on their arm and shoved Alex away from her. She went to do it again, but they caught her wrist and tugged her against their chest.

"Giving me an invitation?" Alex growled as they tucked her head under their chin.

"It's not about your gender identity," she said, ignoring their question.

They danced their casted fingers over her side just enough to make her giggle and wiggle before they released her.

She turned around and pressed her face to their chest. Wrapped her arms around them and hugged them like they mattered.

"I thought that was the point I already made, I want more, Alex Trikru."

Alex wanted to celebrate; except they knew a 'but' was coming. Dilynn always spoke in buts. What she wants, but what she thinks will happen instead.

They swallowed and waited for it.

She was still holding on to them when she leaned back to look at them.

"So, here's the thing: I'm not okay with RunnerAT89. They are not nice to people, and they are pretty cowardly. I get that shit sucks sometimes. I have days that I just want to yell, but it's like Evie screaming at me because she's in pain. My life isn't perfect, but people seem to think it is, so they dump their shit on me all the time. Taking your shit out on someone else isn't okay."

Alex tucked a lock of hair behind Dilynn's ear.

"In person, you are kind, attentive, and somewhat vulnerable. But..." Alex knew it was coming, "... the online persona is not someone I want my girls to look to as a role model."

Nothing prepared Alex for possibly being a role model to the Greyson girls. Yesterday was about just getting Lyra to go home because Alex knew what could happen if she didn't go back.

They licked their lips and attempted to think of something to say.

"Do you troll people often?"

They ran through a short list of all the comments they'd made. The list wasn't complete but it didn't need to be for them to know they were a jerk.

"I wish I could say no. I would tell myself I was just being honest. I did that when I considered if what I had said on the Christmas story was too harsh. I even tried to delete it. I don't think I realized how much an author puts of themselves into their stories until I read the last one. I remember reading it and telling you that I wished she would crash her car. I remember when I realized you were the author. I remember crying over you describing my life and realizing that you weren't writing about me, but about you. About your breakup. About being disposable."

"I write a lot when I'm drunk and in a lot of pain," Dilynn confessed.

"I can't blame you. I know I have felt disposable. Like people can just throw you away," Alex admitted.

Dilynn was about to speak but her eyes squinted at something over Alex's shoulder.

"Maybe we're all recyclable. Like maybe, it's not that people dispose of us but that we just become something new, sometimes something better. Sometimes something not better." Alex recognized Evie's voice.

"The word is worse," Lyra stated, leaning against the railing with a bag in her hand.

"Why are you both here?" Dilynn asked, then she looked around. "Where's Sadie?"

Lyra pointed to a group of kids in a circle at the food court below them. "Apparently, those are Sadie's friends from one of the group homes she was in. Turns out she was here the day after Christmas, too. They were at Spencer's when they heard the fight. She said that was when she was able to slip away from the group and take off."

Dilynn looked up at Alex.

"We were all here. That day. All of our paths crossed at the same time."

Alex glanced towards the spot they froze at. The place they'd been too afraid to help. It felt so long ago, but they knew it had only been a few months.

"It's time for a new book," Dilynn said, pushing against their chest. "Maybe one that doesn't have a princess or a troll."

"Let's just hope no one gets murdered," Evie contributed. "Unless it's a douche bag named Brandon and his dick gets cut off."

"I like murder movies," Lyra said. "And, like, crime. Maybe I will go to school to be a lawyer."

Evie scoffed and leaned against Landon. "You being a lawyer is as likely as me growing up to be a cop. God, I hate cops."

"How do we make it stop?" Alex asked Dilynn, whose eyes were crinkled in the corners.

"Feed me!" Evie practically yelled.

"What would you like to eat?" Dilynn asked Alex.

They can't stop the dirty thought in their head. That is until Evie interjected, "If you say you want to eat her, I swear I will scream, and everyone will think you are trying to murder me."

Dilynn patted her hand against their chest, then leaned in close. She didn't bother to whisper when she said, "I rather enjoy being dessert."

Acknowledgements

I wish to express my deepest gratitude to the remarkable individuals who have contributed to the creation of this book in various ways. Your support, insight, and understanding have been instrumental in bringing these words to life.

First and foremost, I want to extend my heartfelt thanks to my wife. You have shown incredible patience and an extraordinary capacity for forgiveness during the turbulent journey of writing. Your willingness to endure my moments of creative madness and to let me act out scenes to capture the perfect facial expressions was a priceless gift. Your unwavering support is the cornerstone of my creative endeavors.

To Tara, my friend and confidante, thank you for being a dedicated partner in this creative journey. Your willingness to sit across the lunch table and engage deeply with my characters allowed them to evolve into multifaceted, authentic individuals. Your commitment to reading each chapter after dinner has been a constant source of motivation, and I'm profoundly grateful for your friendship.

I am indebted to Robin, for reading close to several hundred versions of this story. Your constant love for these characters made it possible to bring this story of open doors to fruition.

A special thank you goes to the young women who shared their stories with me. Your willingness to open up and provide insights was instrumental in shaping the narrative. Your bravery and candidness have made this book richer and more meaningful.

To everyone who supported me, whether through sharing experiences, providing guidance, or simply believing in the value of this project, I extend my thanks. This book is as much a product of your generosity and understanding as it is of my creativity. As I send this book out into the world, I do so with gratitude in my heart. I hope that it resonates with readers and serves as a testament to the collaboration and support that brought it to life.

About the Author

Chelsey Blue Spicer is a trailblazing author with a deep commitment to amplifying the voices and experiences of the LGBTQ+ community. Born with a storytelling spirit, Chelsey embarked on her writing journey at the age of twelve, inspired by her mother's own published autobiography. From a young age, she understood the power of words to spark conversations, challenge norms, and create positive change.

Chelsey's novels stand out for their fearless exploration of post-coming out narratives within the LGBTQ+ community. Fueled by a deep-seated passion for representation, she confronts and dismantles harmful stereotypes, particularly the "bury your gays" media trope that has plagued LGBTQ+ storytelling for years. Chelsey's stories break free from the shackles of conventional narratives, showcasing everyday life and celebrating the diverse experiences of LGBTQ+ individuals without resorting to violence or relegating characters to stereotypical roles.

Infuriated by the lack of nuanced representation, Chelsey Blue Spicer writes with a mission—to provide models of life for LGBTQ+ individuals after they come out. Her narratives go beyond the struggles, offering glimpses into the joy, resilience, and triumphs that define the everyday lives of the LGBTQ+ community.

Chelsey is not just an author; she is a voice for those whose stories have often been overlooked or misrepresented. Through her work, she aims to create a literary landscape where everyone can see themselves reflected, celebrated, and understood. Chelsey Blue Spicer invites readers to join her in breaking down barriers, fostering understanding, and embracing the diverse and beautiful spectrum of human experiences within the LGBTQ+ community.

www.chelseybluespicer.com

Want to talk to others about the Collection of Colorful Choices?

Join the Discord Group

Turn the page for a preview of Chelsey Blue Spicer's new novel

Available August 2024

Meet Zoe

Zoe killed Vincent Gibson so many times, but not once did she do it correctly. The downtown lights of Phoenix cast a yellowish glow on the city below the seventh-floor prosecutor's office. Sighing at the window where the sun had long set, she admonished herself for having lost track of time.

With a deep breath, Zoe closed her eyes and tried to kill the prison guard correctly.

She pictures Gibson with his back to her near a small table. The scene is paused like a DVD, waiting for her to hit play.

"Something's wrong," she whispers, feeling her stomach trying to tie itself in a knot.

She scans the kitchen, cataloging the pans piled up in the sink and surrounding counter. A fly crawls around the edge of one filled with molding water.

Her tongue scraped against her teeth at the idea of the stench.

Mail is thrown over the table with the envelopes sliced along the tops. The small knife is under the electric bill. She steps from the back door to the knife and picks it up. Only four inches, but it would get the job done.

Zoe exhales slowly, and Vincent Gibson comes to life. He doesn't know she's there, and the laminate floor doesn't make a sound as she closes the distance between them.

She raises her arm, bringing it down on the top of his shoulder.

"Shit!"

The blade hit the wrong place on his back.

She'd imagined it wrong, again. She'd forgotten to consider she was bigger than the girl that had stabbed Gibson.

The kitchen vanished as Zoe's eyes popped open. She held her breath, adjusting to reality. The tension faded as she relaxed into the leather office chair. Her toes rubbed against the familiar rough carpet below her desk. She scanned the wall of legal texts across the room until she separated herself from the murderous teenager she'd been impersonating.

Zoe knew she had to go back to the kitchen for what felt like the one thousandth time. She knew if she tried to go home now, Gibson would show up in her dreams covered in blood. Just like he had every night since she'd been assigned this case. It didn't matter how many times it took; Zoe wouldn't be able to sleep until she got it right.

She closed her eyes again.

The off-white walls and yellow floor are waiting for her. She stands by the back door silently with the knife already in her hand when Vincent Gibson appears. She imagines him taller, then wider. She focuses on getting him right this time— cropped hair balding from the guard's cap, sweaty white shirt still tucked into his work issued khakis, and a cell phone in his hand.

She raises her arm again, bringing it down through his shoulder. First through the left trapezius, then slices the levator scapulae. The blade knicks the C6 vertebrae, and he falls into the table.

Gibson's patellas crack, fracturing under his weight, and she hears him cry out.

Zoe retreats a step towards the grotesque sink to continue this time as a spectator, instead of the murderer. The oily haired teenager, Olivia Moore pulls the blade from Gibson's flesh. His white shirt turns red with blood flowing from the first strike as she delivers another blow. This time into the top of his shoulder, stopping at the clavicle. Four inches isn't enough, or the teenager doesn't have the force to do that much damage here.

His phone falls to the floor. He can't call for help.

Moore thrusts the knife into his back for the third time.

All strikes to the left side.

Gibson tries to push himself up from the table, but the fractured patella stops him from being able to get up.

Zoe pauses the characters in her head. She moves to the other side of the room, where both the victim and the murderer face her. Moore's cold eyes glare in fury; her teeth bare like a feral cat. Gibson's scared face looks out the kitchen window.

Comfortable with all the details, Zoe breathes them back to life. Moore pulls the knife out of Gibson's back. Gibson again pushes at the table with the one good hand, trying to get up from the floor. Moore steps around him.

As soon as she's in front of him, Gibson goes for the knife. His size is his only advantage, and without the ability to just get up, he launches his body into the girl. The imaginary people travel through Zoe, leaving a blood trail that isn't in any of the crime scene photos.

Zoe opened her eyes again. She yanked at the roots of her hair. Pulled until real pain stifled the boiling in her veins.

The white board across from the office reminded her how long she'd been sitting there. She'd arranged the photos of the kitchen to show the entire room earlier, when the sun had been up, and the other Phoenix prosecutors were still working in their offices. With the halls eerily quiet, the people in the photos haunted her office.

She let out a huff of breath that turned into a yawn.

"Just get it right so you can go to bed," she told herself.

Closing her eyes, she started again.

Three strikes before Moore comes around to the front of him. He pleads with her to stop, so she kicks him back.

"Still doesn't make sense." Zoe hit her hand to the desk. "Even with one arm, he would have had the ability to block her kick. Stop making them do the same thing."

But she couldn't think of another way to explain how Gibson ended up on his back and stabbed in the groin.

Zoe's head rolled against the back of the chair, followed by another yawn. This time her whole body expelled the minimal energy she had left.

Her eyes drooped. She tried to keep them open, but her chin fell with her eyelids. That's all it took for Gibson to stand in front of her, the crotch and leg of his khakis' red with blood from the final blow Zoe can't explain.

The disgusting kitchen immediately dissipates until only Olivia Moore stands in the back doorway of Gibson's kitchen, looking down at what she'd done. Her mouth moves, telling Zoe what she needs to know, but no sound comes out.

"I can't hear you," Zoe calls to the girl.

Olivia's mouth closes as she looks once more at the man covered in blood. She turns from them both. Her fingers leave a trail across the back door as she walks away.

Zoe sat up. The fifteen-year-old with brown hair plastered to the sides of her face and vacant eyes stared at her from the mug shot on Zoe's desk. The girl wasn't sad, angry, or even smiling at what she had done. They simply looked at Zoe like she couldn't understand.

She tried to imagine the shadowed path of the girl's life before she picked up the knife. She searched the downtown alley crevices and along the dumpsters for the answer to the questions. So many questions.

Where was Moore's mother?

Did she have any brothers or sisters?

How did she just drop into Phoenix without a trace?

How did the child end up in the dilapidated apartment?

How many drugs did the girl have to take before she forgot killing a person was wrong?

When did Moore stop caring about anything at all?

"Nothing justifies murdering another person," Zoe reminded herself, just like her father would.

She closed her eyes once more. Went through the visualization strategy her father had taught her, even though he'd been a corporate lawyer, not a criminal prosecutor. It was the same tactic he'd used when working with Nia Williams, Zoe's current boss. She'd sat outside the office as a child and listened as her father coached Nia through a serial killer case when Zoe was 17.

First, she had to bring the scene to life.

The kitchen is exactly the same. Gibson leans against the table with three wounds on his back. Moore comes to the front with the knife because she's not afraid of him. She kicks him back as he tries to get up. He's down, but Moore doesn't leave. She kneels over him, twisting the blade into his groin.

"You're still here," the very real voice in the very real office said.

Zoe's eyes popped open as she held her chest. Nia Williams stood in the doorway with jacket and purse in hand. In all the years Zoe had known Nia, the woman's style had never changed. Her blouse even had shoulder pads, something Zoe didn't think came in shirts since the 80s.

The office didn't sound quiet with Zoe's brain shooting out a hundred commands at once to fix herself for Nia. Her feet immediately slid back into the Jimmy Choo heels under her desk. They pinched her toes, but she couldn't handle the idea of Nia considering her unprofessional. Not when the woman had known her since preschool and watched her grow up beside Nia's own daughter. Working under Nia's sharp eye and quick tongue left Zoe constantly worried she'd lose the woman's favor that she'd acquired when the woman's daughter, Ari had left for the army right after graduation. Nia hadn't cared that Zoe broke Ari's heart by pretending to be straight, in fact, Nia commended her for it. She'd shaken Zoe's hand that day for protecting both their families from a homosexual scandal during an election year. She'd also promised to mentor Zoe when the time came. Something she desperately needed now.

"Ms. Williams. I was... walking through the specifics. Jury selection is in two weeks."

Nia's authority pulled Zoe to her feet. She fumbled with the files, sliding Olivia's picture within one. Zoe picked up the folders and returned them to the white box on the table in front of the window. She hoped Nia didn't notice the way her ankle twisted when she stepped wrong in the high heel.

The District Attorney walked to the whiteboard and analyzed the crime scene photos. She tapped on Olivia Moore's mug shot with nail that was missing a chip of polish.

"I heard Judge Miller released the girl to Greyson Academy."

Zoe rolled her eyes in annoyance at the mention of Judge Miller. He hated her and she couldn't help but feel it was because she was a woman. Every chance he had the man would call her by that stupid nickname Nia once overheard when she was on the phone in law school. It had spread like fire through the office and courthouse, and Judge Miller used it to burn her when he said it in that condescending tone he reserved for Zoe.

"He *felt* she didn't pose a threat there. Some social worker woman named Dilynn showed up to plead the girl's case. Miller took one look at her and signed the papers."

"That wasn't some social worker. That was Dilynn Greyson." Nia turned to Zoe, shaking her head. "Myopic Miller is an old fool. He only has his seat thanks to Sylvia Winters and Dilynn Greyson, and that school for delinquents is just Greyson's project to pad their family's bank account. That family has their hands in everything. If it isn't Greyson-the-Do-Gooder, it's the Winter's Group."

Zoe hadn't considered Dilynn or the Winter's Group as a threat to her case. The thirty-something blonde in her bulky cardigan looked like a social worker, not someone with the type of money capable of buying judges. She didn't even wear nice shoes.

"I was having dinner with the mayor when they arrested the girl," Nia explained. "It surprised me Greyson intervened since Moore broke her daughter's nose trying to resist arrest. I was expecting assault on an officer to be added."

Zoe held up a hand.

"Wait, Greyson's daughter is a cop? How? The woman looks barely older than me."

"Yes. Greyson adopted the girl when she was in high school. I think there's maybe ten years between the two. She has three. All adopted as teenagers. Maybe two. I am not sure the last one was actually adopted. Do you care to guess who was the judge for each of those adoptions?"

Zoe narrowed her eyes at the yellow pad of witnesses on her desk.

"Miller."

She hadn't thought about the arresting officer, and it irked her that she'd failed to connect Officer Everleigh Greyson with the woman that came to court to speak on Moore's behalf.

Nia dismissively waved her hand in the air. "Doesn't matter honestly. This is not juvenile court, so Miller's opinion holds minimal influence on the jury."

"Landon Woods has convinced Moore to plead not guilty due to self-defense."

"Did he put Greyson's daughter on the witness list?" Nia asked.

Zoe flipped to the defense's witness list. She ran her finger down the list until it landed on Everleigh Greyson.

"He did."

"Figures."

"Why?"

"On Monday, I will send you over the file I've kept on the Greysons since the woman started collecting violent offenders. And just so you know, Evie Greyson was the first violent offender she brought home. The kid took a baseball bat to a friend of mine's car when she was fourteen. She was a drunk and a drug addict, and she ruined his name with her bullshit."

Zoe looked out the window. She'd met Evie Greyson briefly. Long enough to know the woman wasn't still a drug addict. In fact, she was a witness on a lot of Zoe's cases because the woman tended to take any call where a female was being assaulted.

"Just know when I say that family has their hands in everything, I am not joking. Woods is Greyson's personal attorney, and..." Nia lauded dramatically. "Her daughter's high school sweetheart. Then, there's the homeless one that Greyson picked up from the literal street that's a state's prosecutor for family court, and the third is related to someone in the family. That one works with the Department of Child Services."

Nia chuckled wickedly, before she added, "Woods looks like a giant fat baby, and he's gained so much notoriety so quickly because he's been fucking the cop since high school and Dilynn will do anything to keep her poisonous princess happy. But just be happy you're facing Woods and not my snake of an ex-husband who handles all Sylvia Winter's cases. Dilynn is keeping this in house it seems. Just watch out because where Dilynn is, Sylvia Winters is lurking in the shadows behind her. Pretty sure Winters owns half of the state because she funds anyone that will back her homosexual agenda. And Winters would definitely pay off a jury."

Zoe rubbed her hand over her eyes. She was too tired to process all the ways this whole thing had to breach some form of ethical code. It didn't stop her mind from trying though.

"So, what's the motive?" Nia asked, pulling Zoe back to the bigger problem in her hands.

Nia set her purse and jacket down before lowering herself into a leather armchair. This as an opportunity to work with the woman she'd known since childhood. The woman her father had worshiped her poise in the courtroom. She needed to learn everything she could to efficiently replace Nia someday as District Attorney. The only problem was Zoe's inability to effectively participate in these sorts of situations.

'Just act human,' she told herself. But she wasn't even sure what she meant.

Zoe gripped the edge of the table and supported her weight to alleviate some of the pressure on her feet. She tried to appear relaxed, but her heart drumming in her ears made it difficult to come up with anything that seemed halfway intelligent.

She could feel Nia studying her until Zoe confessed, "Without any statement from Moore, I am just playing it over and over again in my head trying to find a reason this happened."

"What do you know?"

"Last name she gave hasn't turned up any hits. No police reports about her as a runaway. Couldn't get her to say what school she went to. It's like this girl dropped to Phoenix from the sky." Zoe explained. "My best guess is homeless."

She handed Nia a photo of the scene.

"Police found evidence she had been staying in the apartment over Gibson's garage."

Nia looked over the photograph of the dilapidated dwelling. The only thing there was a mat made from old couch cushions with a tattered blanket. A bucket filled with urine and feces. And scratched into the wall, the words: Olivia was here.

"So, she's living on the street and finds the apartment vacant. Gibson finds her squatting on his property. She is a runaway, under the influence, and she snaps. Kills him so she doesn't get locked up."

Zoe holds up her hand, "Except she killed him in the kitchen of the house."

"So, she followed him to the house. Maybe tried to bargain with him. He doesn't want to deal with her. He deals with scum all day long; he shouldn't have to do it in his own home. Tells her he's calling the cops. She snaps."

Nia snapped her fingers, emphasizing the breaking point.

The older woman made the whole event sound so simple. Zoe went back to the scene, but this time started in the apartment. There's the confrontation. She tried to reason with him, but he won't listen. Gibson left to call the police and Moore followed him. She fixed Moore's face with one of paranoia, then stood her in front of Gibson. She can't get arrested, so she picks up the knife from the table and the murder took place again.

It didn't feel right, though. Running away made more sense than following someone. And Moore was just trying to get away from Gibson, one stab in the back would have been enough.

"Here's what I don't get." Zoe took a deep breath, and collected her thoughts so they would run in a straight line. "Moore's small, malnourished even. A rear attack would be safest. But she comes at him from the front, and he doesn't defend himself almost like he was holding something, but there was nothing there. And you said it, he worked with prisoners all day. But he couldn't take on a fourteen-year-old girl half his size?"

Nia clicked her tongue and waved her index finger back and forth. "Not something you should dwell on."

"But—"

Nia smiled wickedly. Her red lipstick had smeared across the front of her teeth, making her appear like the Twilight casting call reject the woman's daughter always claimed her to be.

"You have a drugged-out teenage girl found in the victim's blood. You have her blood on the victim. He fought back enough to cut her. Thanks to *CSI*, this is an easy conviction."

Zoe tried to swallow the honey coming from Nia's fly trap of a mouth, but a part of her was sickened at how easy Nia made it all sound. It was like when Nia's daughter Ari came out and Nia sent the girl to live with her father. Throwing away her daughter during an election year seemed as easy as convicting a fifteen-year-old girl in criminal court as an adult. It was just acceptable and necessary.

The vacant green eyes stared back at Zoe from a photo on the evidence board. She briefly wondered if Ari had looked at her mother the same way when she'd learned she was disposable. Zoe cast away the thoughts of her childhood friend and focused on Nia. Nia was here and important. And she was going to help Zoe be important because she'd always favored Zoe over Ari.

Nia stood up and headed to the door before commanding, "Go home, Zoe. Get some rest."

The kid's eyes challenged Zoe to figure out what was missing as Nia's presence lingered in the office. She kicked her shoes off and slouched into the leather armchair that still smelled like her boss's perfume. She hated the perfume because to her it smelled like Raid.

Vincent Gibson in his prison guard uniform stared at the camera for his ID photo. He didn't smile, and the photo had the same empty expression as Moore's. When Zoe had pinned his photo alongside Moore's, she'd meant it to help her recreate the scene. But together, their lack of emotion made everything blurry.

Zoe moved Gibson to the other side of the board. He was a victim. Olivia Moore murdered him in his home. No matter the reason, she'd stabbed the victim four times and left him lying in a pool of his own blood.

If she wanted to replace Nia someday, Zoe would have to start acting like her. Whatever happened to Moore to make her lose her sense of right and wrong didn't matter. It couldn't matter because a man was dead.